# Two Silver Crosses

Beryl Kingston was born and brought up in Tooting. After taking her degree at London University, she taught English and Drama at various London schools as well as bringing up her three children. She and her husband now live in Sussex.

Her other titles include *Hearts and Farthings, Kisses and Ha'pennies, A Time to Love, Tuppenny Times, Fourpenny Flyer, Sixpenny Stalls, London Pride*, and *War Baby*.

# TWO SILVER CROSSES

## Beryl Kingston

ARROW

First published 1993

3 5 7 9 10 8 6 4 2

Copyright 1992 Beryl Kingston

The right of Beryl Kingston to be identified as the author of this work has been asserted by her accordance with the Copyright, Designs and Patents Act 1988.

First published in Great Britain in 1993 by Century Random House UK Ltd, 20 Vauxhall Bridge Road, London SW1V 2SA

Arrow Edition 1994 Random House UK Ltd, 20 Vauxhall Bridge Road, London SW1V 2SA

Random House Australia (Pty) Limited 20 Alfred Street, Milsons Point, Sydney New South Wales 2061, Australia

Random House New Zealand Limited 18 Poland Road, Glenfield Auckland 10, New Zealand

Random House South Africa (Pty) Limited PO Box 337, Bergvlei, South Africa

Random House UK Limited Reg. No. 954009

A CIP catalogue record for this book is available from the British Library

ISBN 0 09 922871 8

Typeset by Deltatype Ltd, Ellesmere Port Printed in Great Britain by Cox & Wyman Ltd, Reading, Berkshire

For Darley Anderson

# CHAPTER ONE

'Just turn over on your side, Mrs Holborn, dear,' the midwife coaxed. 'Turn on your side, there's a good girl.'

Hortense Holborn was too far gone to understand her. She was very young and very frightened and to add confusion to fear the baby had started much too early. So instead of having her darling Edouard home on leave the way he'd planned it, he was away at the front fighting the Germans, or lying wounded somewhere or dying or blown to bits. Oh no, no, no. She mustn't think that. If only he were here, safe in her arms, and she safe in his. If only . . . Oh this awful pain and this awful war that tears people apart! '*Je'n peux pas!*' she groaned, retreating into her native language because she hadn't got the energy to speak English. She hadn't got the energy for anything, not even to lift her head from the pillow. '*Je'n peux pas!*'

'I don't think she can understand what you're saying, Mrs Bonney,' the midwife's young assistant said. 'She don't seem to hear you, not to my way a' thinking.'

'Quite right, Joan,' Mrs Bonney said. 'But I'm sure she *can* hear, poor girl. She don't understand, that's the way of it. And no wonder with all this stopping and starting. It's enough to try the patience of a saint.'

It had been a complicated labour. When it started, three exhausting days ago, it had seemed straightforward enough, although premature. But then for some unaccountable reason it had completely stopped and, despite hot baths and two enemas and three doses of castor oil, it had refused to start up again until early that morning. And now it was proceeding much too slowly for Mrs Bonney's peace of mind.

For this was no ordinary confinement. For a start the poor

girl was expecting twins, and at nineteen she was barely old enough for one baby leave alone two, and as if that weren't complication enough, the babies would be the first grandchildren of the great Mr Holborn who owned G. S. Holborn's Munitions, which was one of the biggest factories in the district, if not *the* biggest. And they were being born in his splendid house with a fine nursery waiting for them, all newly furnished and decorated, with enough toys on the shelves to stock a shop and the proverbial silver spoon ready for their mouths. So it certainly wasn't the sort of confinement that could be taken easily by anyone concerned.

'Turn on your side, Mrs Holborn, dear,' the midwife tried again. 'You'd be easier on your side.'

There was a discreet knock at the bedroom door. Mrs Bonney clicked her tongue with annoyance at being interrupted but signalled with her eyes that her assistant was to go and attend to it.

It was Miss Agnes Holborn, their patient's sister-in-law, and to Mrs Bonney's surprise she had a soldier standing beside her. It couldn't be Mr Edward, could it? Surely not. Mr Edward was at the front. Everybody knew that. But it *was*, looking very fine in his officer's uniform, polished boots, khaki cap and all.

'How is she?' he whispered, stripping off his gloves. His long face was drawn with anxiety and there were dark shadows under his eyes. 'Agnes sent me a telegram. I got here as soon as I could. Please let me see her.'

His request put Mrs Bonney into a quandary. Ordinarily husbands would never be allowed into the bedroom while a labour was going on. It wasn't hygienic. Or proper. Their place was outside pacing the carpet. But this was 1916 and they were all in the middle of a war, and he'd come all the way from the battlefield to be with this poor little French wife of his. And besides, he might be able to get her to do what they said, even if it wasn't hygienic.

And while she was dithering, Hortense made up her mind for her, calling out to her husband in her own language, her face suddenly bright with renewed vigour, her voice

8

stronger and more alive. 'Edouard! Edouard! It is you, is it not, my love. Oh come to me quickly, quickly. I'm so frightened.'

He was into the room in three strides, regardless of permission, tossing his cap on to a chair, reaching the bed, sweeping her into his arms, holding her close, kissing her damp dark hair. 'Don't be afraid, my dearest. I'm here. You're safe with me.'

'Mr Edward,' Mrs Bonney protested. 'You can't . . .'

But he could. He was. Smiling up at her with weary blue eyes, the light brown hair above his temples still pinched by the pressure of his cap, his long face tanned and more lined than she remembered it from the last time she'd seen him in the village, his expression clearly pleading with her. There was a scurry of frantic activity at the other end of the bed as Joan flung a sheet across their patient's swollen abdomen for decency's sake.

'Oh dear,' Mrs Bonney said. 'I'm not sure this is . . .'

But he went on smiling at her, hopefully.

'Very well,' she decided. 'You can stay. But just for a little while mind, because it really isn't proper. We'll rig a sheet up.'

'You're a pearl!' Edward Holborn said.

So the sheet was rigged, with two ends tied to the tops of two high-backed chairs one on each side of the bed so as to stretch a screen of white cloth between the birth and its begetter. And as if his arrival were all the medicine Hortense needed, the labour began to speed up. Soon it had settled into an encouraging rhythm.

'Now we're getting somewhere,' Mrs Bonney reported with great satisfaction from behind her screen. 'Does she need a drink, Mr Edward, could you ask her?'

Hortense lay back in her husband's arms and gave herself up to the power of the birth. When a contraction took hold there was nothing in the world except remorseless pain, squeezing and squeezing, but as it ebbed away Edouard was still there, sponging her forehead and kissing her fingers and telling her she was a dear, brave girl. And as long as he was there she knew instinctively that she could and would get through, bad though it was. Her darling, darling Edouard, who loved her to distraction and whom she loved with all her heart. 'Oh, Jesus mercy. Mary help,' she prayed clutching his hand. 'Here comes another one.'

The first baby was born as the evening began to draw in and the mirror over the mantelpiece turned rose with reflected light. A five-pound girl with a mop of thick dark hair, the skinniest legs, her father's long nose and eyes so tightly shut they looked red and swollen.

'Emilie,' her mother said in English. 'We'll call her Emilie.'

Fifteen minutes later the second baby slid into the world. At four-and-three-quarter pounds she was even skinnier than her sister, and had the same dark hair and the same matchstick limbs; but *her* eyes were open wide. They were large and round and very dark blue, and they gazed at the world in the wise, solemn way of the newly born. It was the sight of those eyes that lifted her parents to tears of wonder and happiness.

'Virginie,' her father said to her as she was placed in her mother's arms beside her sister. 'You have two names because you have two nationalities like your sister. Emily/ Emilie. Virginia/Virginie. Isn't your mother the cleverest girl to have two such beautiful babies?'

'I only hope Mr Holborn thinks so,' Mrs Bonney muttered to Joan behind the screen. Old Mr Holborn was a difficult man at the best of times and everyone knew he wanted grandsons to carry on the business.

But when he came in much later that evening to view the new arrivals the old man was quite taken with them. 'They're as like as two peas in a pod,' he said to Hortense, putting down a rough forefinger for Virginia to grasp. 'Two little funny faces, aren't you? They've got your thick hair, my dear. But the Holborn nose, poor little things. Still I suppose we had to expect that, eh, Edward? We run to noses in this family.'

'*I* think they're beautiful,' Edward said, giving his father a warning grimace.

'They'll do,' Mr Holborn said. And for him that was praise. 'How long are you staying?'

'Ten days,' Edward told him. 'I've put my leave forward.'

'You boys can wangle anything,' his father said admiringly. 'How's it going out there?'

'Oh much the same,' Edward said laconically. 'You know how it is.'

And his father agreed that he did. Although, in point of fact, like most other people back at home, he didn't have the remotest idea about life in the trenches.

But what did any of that matter now, with these two delightful babies safely delivered and a midwife on call night and day and the young assistant, Joan, to live in and take care of them all?

'I think they're the prettiest little things I've ever seen,' Agnes said. 'You are lucky, Edward.' And it wasn't just his good fortune in having two new daughters that she was talking about.

Every time Agnes saw him with Hortense, caught up in the glow of their passion for one another, she yearned for and was envious of their obvious happiness. She couldn't imagine anything better than to love like that and be loved in return. Not that it was likely to happen to her now, for she was twenty-eight, going on twenty-nine, with a plain rather pasty face, timid blue eyes, that awful Holborn nose and lank brown hair like her brother's. And although she did her best to disguise the fact with flowing blouses, tunics and dresses that were cut very full, she was already developing the dumpy figure of a middle-aged woman. But there was no unkindness in her and her envy was more vicarious tenderness than jealousy. Love was wonderful; she knew it and was happy to bask in the reflected warmth of it, even if she couldn't experience it herself. 'You're very, very lucky.'

'Yes,' her brother said. 'I know. Your turn next, eh, Sis?'

Agnes decided it was best to ignore that. 'They're so alike,' she said. 'How will you tell them apart?'

'That is easy for the moment,' Hortense said, speaking

11

English with her pretty French accent. 'Emilie does not open her eyes.'

'Shouldn't she?' Agnes said, stroking the baby's silky head.

'Oh, she'll do it in time,' Edward said. 'Won't you, poppet?'

But two days passed and the baby's eyes were still swollen and tightly shut. And when Mrs Bonney came in on the second evening to check her charges and settle them for the night both lids were decidedly sticky.

'How long's this been going on?' she said to Joan, frowning down at the child.

'There was no sign of it at her last feed. Was there, Mrs Holborn?'

'Well, it won't do!' the midwife disapproved. She held out her hand to her assistant for cotton wool and cleaned both eyes thoroughly, throwing the pads into the nursery fire afterwards. 'If they're no better by the morning we shall have to have the doctor in. You'll keep an eye on that, Joan, won't you? Are they feeding well?'

'Oh yes,' Hortense said happily. 'They are – how do you say? – *gourmandes*.'

'Greedy,' Mrs Bonney guessed. 'That's good.' But she could see how well they were being fed from the colour of their skin and the way their limbs were already beginning to round out. A good mother, this little French girl, for all her youth and her apparent fragility. And very pretty in her foreign way with that olive skin and all that thick curly hair. It was the heart-shaped face that did it, and those big brown eyes. Always a fetching combination. It was a pity the babies didn't take after her. But they'd probably grow better looking with time. Babies often did. 'Now let's have a look at you, my dear,' she said. 'Is my Joan looking after you?'

'Oh yes,' Hortense said again, smiling at Mrs Bonney's assistant. 'She is to keep me company tonight while the party is 'appening.'

'Oh!' Mrs Bonney said. 'We've got a party, have we? Well we've certainly got something to celebrate.'

12

'Ah no!' Hortense said. 'It is not for ze babies, you understand. It is for ze company. For G. S. Holborn's.'

'It's their staff do,' Joan explained. 'They have it once a year.'

Mrs Bonney changed her mind about the party. 'Well, I hope they don't make a disturbance, that's all I can say,' she warned. 'You need peace and quiet when you're lying-in, my dear, and they should see that you get it.'

But, in fact, Mr Holborn's staff parties were usually rather sober affairs because they were held in the great hall. A daunting place, built in the medieval style with oak beams and a minstrel gallery, it was two storeys high with huge windows stretching from floor to ceiling on one wall, and a fireplace on another big enough to contain two wooden settles on either side of the fire.

Mr Holborn moved among his guests, talking to each in turn and checking they all had enough to eat and drink, but except for a handful who'd been with the company for a long time and were used to it, most of the guests were ill at ease. They shuffled their feet and cleared their throats when their employer approached, and were obviously relieved when the annual ordeal was over.

Agnes Holborn was even more ill at ease than they were. She'd played the hostess at these events ever since her mother died when she was barely seventeen but she'd never found it easy because she was shy in company, and always conscious of how unattractive she was. But she felt she owed it to her father to do her best, so her best she dutifully did. At least at this party she had the babies' arrival to talk about and the wives would be interested in that.

Which they were, of course, saying how lovely it must be and how nice to have twins and asking what they were to be called. And Agnes shared her good news so happily she didn't notice that she was being watched.

She turned to move on to another table, and found one of her father's 'young men' standing in her way and smiling as though he knew her.

'Miss Holborn?' he said, giving her a little bow.

13

'Yes,' she said, returning the smile politely. 'I don't believe we've met, have we? Mr. . . ?'

'Everdale,' he said. 'Claud Everdale. I'm one of the sales team with the British Expeditionary Force.'

'You're in the army?' she asked. All the young men she met seemed to be in the army these days.

This one wasn't. 'Not yet,' he confided. 'I'm part of the Derby scheme, so you won't have to search for a white feather. I've taken the shilling and got my number and all that sort of thing but they think I'm more use to them providing your father's guns.'

'I'm sure you are,' she said, thinking what a handsome young man he was, so tall and dapper with his dark hair neatly oiled and a narrow moustache on his upper lip. And he was wearing a nice white shirt under his dark suit.

'I know you'll think this the most frightful cheek,' he said, smiling at her, 'but I suppose you wouldn't honour me with a dance, would you? To tell you the truth I've only just joined the firm so I don't know anybody and I've been looking at you for ages and you've got such a beautiful face that I wondered . . .'

'Oh come now, Mr Everdale,' Agnes protested. 'I do have a mirror you know.'

'I'm sure you have,' he said. 'But what does that show you? Features. That's all you see in a mirror. I'm talking about your expression. Believe me, Miss Holborn, you have the most beautiful expression I've ever seen. Kind and loving, if you don't mind me saying so. Really beautiful. But lots of men must have told you that . . . unless of course they were blind.'

Agnes didn't know what to say because, of course, nobody had ever told her she was beautiful. She was confused and charmed and flattered, despite her honest knowledge of her own worth, or the lack of it. And besides, he was looking at her with such open admiration, how could she doubt what he said, ridiculous though it was? After all Hortense thought Edward was handsome and they did say beauty was in the eye of the beholder. 'Well . . .' she said finally.

He assumed a rueful expression but continued to gaze into her eyes. 'I've offended you,' he said. Then he shook his head as if he was changing his mind. 'I'm so sorry. I shouldn't have spoken. It *is* cheek.'

'No. No,' Agnes said, plucking at her pearls.

But he continued. 'I withdraw my request, Miss Holborn. I've no right to ask you anything. You wouldn't want to dance with the likes of me.'

'Oh no. Not at all,' Agnes said, feeling she had to reassure him. Usually she retreated as soon as the music began because she was much too awkward to want to dance with anybody except Edward, but she could hardly say that when he'd asked her so politely, had said so many charming things and was looking at her like that. 'I mean, I should be very happy to dance with you.'

His eyes flashed such excitement that it gave her a sudden *frisson* of pleasure. 'You would?' he said. 'Oh, you don't know what this means to me. Which one? Do I have to mark a card or anything?'

She was warmed by his ignorance. 'We don't use cards on these occasions, I'm glad to say,' she explained. 'My father likes things to be informal.'

'Then may I claim the first dance you've got free?'

'You may,' Agnes said. And she was suddenly warm with hope. It was impossible, ridiculous. But she couldn't help feeling it. The hope that at long, long last she'd found a man who would love her as Edward loved Hortense. Oh wouldn't that be wonderful!

'You've made me the happiest man in the room,' he said, giving her another half bow and striding across the room to join the other salesmen who were standing against the wall.

'Well?' they asked him.

'It's in the bag,' he said. 'First dance. That's ten bob you owe me, Jack.'

'You toe-rag!' his friend Jack said with admiration. 'So now what? I suppose you'll be marrying her next.'

'Just watch me!'

'She's old enough to be your mother.'

15

'Give it a rest. I'm twenty-two.'

'And she's pushing thirty.'

But she'll inherit half the firm, Claud Everdale thought. Everybody in the company knows that. When old man Holborn goes it's to be divided between her and her brother. And that was what was important. She'll inherit half the firm and I've interested her already.

Agnes Holborn stayed at the party until the last dance was over and the guests had all departed. She had never danced so often nor enjoyed herself so much in all her life. And even after she'd kissed her father goodnight she was far too excited to sleep, so she tiptoed along the corridors to her brother's suite of rooms in the east wing to see if Hortense was still awake.

There was a glimmer of gaslight yellowing the lower edge of the bedroom door so she knocked and Edward came to let her in.

Hortense was feeding one of the twins, which lay in the crook of her arm sucking intently. The other was lying sleepily on Joan's lap, being expertly pinned into a clean napkin. The room smelled of milk and baby powder and starch and vaseline. Looking round at it all Agnes thought how good life was and how rich.

'Oh Hortense!' she said. 'I've had an amazing evening.'

'That I can see,' Hortense said, smiling at her. 'Tell me at once.'

'I've met an extraordinary young man.'

'And you are in love,' Hortense said happily, and as if it were the most natural thing in the world. 'Edouard, my dear, your sister is in love!'

'Oh no,' Agnes said, blushing. 'I mean we've only just met.'

'But you like him.'

'Oh yes. Very much. He was so kind to me. Just like Edward is to you. He made me feel so happy. As if the whole world was . . . Oh, I don't know.'

'It is perfect,' Hortense said. 'Two perfect babies and now a love affair. Tell us all about it.'

16

So Agnes did.

'One of our salesmen?' Edward said, making a grimace. 'I can't see Dad approving of *him*.'

'I don't care,' Agnes said recklessly. '*I* approve of him. He thinks I'm beautiful. He's asked me to go to the theatre with him on Friday. Isn't it ridiculous?'

'No,' Hortense said. 'It is wonderful. And you *are* beautiful. Look in ze mirror. See for yourself. Edouard, *cherie*, we should have champagne.'

'Never mind champagne,' Edward said, pretending to scold them. 'Time you were both tucked up in bed and asleep. Have you any idea what time it is?'

'Then tomorrow,' Hortense said, as they kissed good-night. 'We have ze champagne tomorrow. I am so happy for you, dear Agnes.'

But the next morning they woke to a nightmare of such proportions that all thoughts of celebration were quite forgotten.

Baby Emily was awake at five o'clock that morning calling to be fed. But when the gas was lit and Hortense and Joan saw the state she was in, they were more concerned about cleaning her up than feeding her. Both her eyes were running with pus and the lids were so swollen they appeared to be turned inside out.

'I'll ring for Mrs Bonney,' Joan said, trying to speak calmly, although her eyes showed how frightened she was.

Edward didn't agree with her. 'I think you ought to ring for Doctor Stimson,' he said abruptly.

So Joan summoned them both.

Mrs Bonney arrived quickly, but Doctor Stimson was a long time coming. Both babies had been fed and changed before they heard his car, and Virginia was back in her cot and sleeping soundly again. But Emily was awake and fretful, giving an odd, mewing cry that distressed her parents even more than the sight of her oozing eyes.

Doctor Stimson was a stolid gentleman, bearded, corpulent and firm, with unspoken reassurance. He examined his little patient very carefully, opening her lids and peering into her eyes with a narrow torch. He gave Mrs Bonney instructions about cleansing and care, and then, rather ominously, he asked the two midwives to leave the room.

'I'm afraid I have some rather bad news for you both,' he said. 'You must prepare yourselves for a shock.'

By now Hortense and Edward were so taut with anxiety they were ready for anything, but they waited, hand in hand and saying nothing.

'I'm afraid you will have to face the fact that your baby's eyes are badly damaged,' the doctor said.

With a horrified sound, Hortense put both her hands up to her mouth as her face crumpled. After a second, Edward spoke for them both, his voice gruff with emotion.

'But she'll be able to see,' he asked. 'She *will* be able to see, won't she?'

'No,' Doctor Stimson said. 'I'm sorry, Edward, I can't soften this. She's blind.'

'No, no, no,' Hortense said in soft French. 'That is not true. It cannot be. My poor little one. Oh not blind, Edouard. Not blind.'

'I'm sorry,' Doctor Stimson said, looking away from her distress.

'Can you cure her?' Edward asked him, gathering his weeping wife into his arms. Oh God, please say you can cure her.

The answer was crushing. 'No. There is no cure. The damage is too extreme. She will never see.'

'Not anything?'

'Nothing at all.'

'What about her sister?'

'The other baby's eyes are not affected, I'm very glad to say.'

Hortense began to wail with anguish. 'It is all my fault,' she wept. 'All my fault.'

'Hush, my dearest,' Edward said, smoothing the hair from her wild face. 'You mustn't.'

But she cried on. 'Why should the child be punished? It is too cruel.'

Mrs Bonney was back in the room, looming towards the bed with some medicine in a spoon. 'Drink this, Mrs Holborn, dear. It'll do you good.'

'Never to see,' Hortense wept as she took the medicine. 'My poor little one.'

'If you will just come into the other room with me for a few minutes,' Doctor Stimson suggested at Edward's elbow.

Edward was numb with shock. To be told such a dreadful thing after three such happy days! What else could possibly be said after that? But he didn't have the energy to disobey and followed the doctor meekly into the sitting room.

'I must talk to you seriously,' Doctor Stimson said. And then he stopped and appeared to be thinking deeply, pulling at his beard and scowling into the middle distance.

Edward waited. My child is blind, he thought. The anguish of it was so acute it was making his chest ache.

'I've known you for a very long time, Edward,' Dr Stimson began again. 'Childhood illnesses, broken leg.'

Edward was still silent, lost in his misery.

'Every kind of medical problem,' the doctor's voice went on. 'Thick and thin.'

Edward was silent.

'What I mean to say is. What I must tell you . . . Your daughter's blindness was caused by an infection.'

'Yes,' Edward said dully. He didn't need to be told that. It had been obvious when the pus ran out of her eyes.

'A serious infection.'

'Yes.'

'What I'm telling you is that her blindness was caused by a venereal disease. Do you understand what I'm saying, Edward? Your wife is infected with a venereal disease. It *could* be gonorrhoea, in which case there is a good possibility of cure. On the other hand, it *could* be syphilis and that is a very serious disease indeed and you must both take it seriously. I will endeavour to treat your wife, naturally, but I must have your word that you will report this to the army doctors so that you can be treated, too. Otherwise . . . Well I hardly need tell you the consequences will be severe.'

Edward was suddenly irritable. He knew all this. He'd already half suspected it and he certainly didn't want to be told any details. Not now, and not by his family doctor. Army doctors were a different matter and they'd told him all he needed to know. Young though he was he'd heard more than enough. 'I know about these things,' he said. And when the doctor looked shocked he decided to shock him even further. 'Most people do over in France. We all get a "dose" at some time or another, you know. It's one of the hazards of war.'

Dr Stimson was offended by the young man's casual air. 'This is serious, Edward,' he said. 'Venereal diseases are very serious illnesses. And preventable, I might add. You have only to abstain, you know.'

'Not in the trenches,' Edward said. 'Love is the only good thing we have when we're out there.'

'Preventable,' the doctor reminded him, heavily. 'Preventable. By clean living.'

'You've no idea, have you?' Edward said. 'You don't *live* in the trenches.' He paused. 'You wait to die.'

'Soldiers of the King,' the doctor said. 'Fighting an heroic war.'

'There's nothing heroic about this war,' Edward said bitterly. 'It's a dirty, brutish, wasteful, bloody awful nightmare, that's all.'

The doctor was affronted. 'I never thought I'd live to hear such unpatriotic talk from a British officer,' he said. 'Especially from your father's son. I must say I'm very disappointed in you, Edward. However, far be it from me to pass judgement.'

Edward was remembering the trenches full of dead and dying after an attack, the terror of a bombardment, the rats squealing out in No Man's Land when the guns fell silent, the stench of rotting flesh. They know nothing here at home, he thought, and he felt alienated from them all and full of angry pity for the men he'd left behind in all that squalor. 'Amen to that,' he said.

How did we get into this? Doctor Stimson was wondering, watching the anger on Edward's face. 'Your wife will have to undergo a full course of treatment,' he said. 'It could take some months.'

'Yes.'

'And then there is the question of whether the infection might have been transmitted to your children.'

Edward's heart gave a jolt of renewed fear. Oh God, he thought, isn't blindness enough? 'Do you mean the twins could have caught it?'

'They seem fit enough now,' the doctor said, 'but syphilis is a long-standing infection and we can't be sure that this isn't syphilis. You will have to watch them extremely carefully. See that they're not over-excited. Of course, if it *is* syphilis and they've taken it, marriage would be quite out of the question for them.'

Edward was too stunned and upset to answer. Poor little things! he thought. To be doomed to live without love. Oh please God protect them. Don't let it be syphilis.

'Well that's all right then,' the doctor said, relieved that his necessary homily was over. 'I'm glad you've understood. Still, not to worry, old man. It could be a simple case of gonorrhoea. We'll have to see if we can get you both patched up before your next leave.'

He makes us sound like horses, Edward thought. Or bedspreads. Or old socks. Patched up, indeed! But he was suddenly too weary to want to argue. 'I will do what you say,' he promised.

'Good,' Doctor Stimson said. 'Well I'll leave you now, eh. You'll want to get back to your wife. Talk things over. I must see Mrs Bonney about your wife's treatment. I'll see myself out afterwards.'

And he was gone on large squeaking feet.

Edward remained where he was in the living room, gazing vacantly out of the window at the trim lawns and the pink and white blossoms in his father's garden. It was a view from another world, a long way away from the dreadful reality of trench warfare and a child born blind. Or worse. Another world and another time and he didn't belong to either. He stood by the window until the bedroom was quiet and the doctor and the midwives were gone. Then he went in to say what he could to his poor Hortense.

She was lying on her side in their double bed with one hand under her cheek and her eyes closed as though she were asleep. Her cheeks were still stained with tears and she looked so beautiful and so vulnerable that he was very near tears himself.

'*Cherie*,' he said softly. 'Hortense.'

She opened her eyes and they were awash with tears. 'My poor baby,' she said. 'It is all my fault. I have another "dose" you see. I didn't know, Edouard. Truly. Or I would have got some permanganate of potash and taken a cure. Mrs Bonney's just told me. What are we going to do?'

'We are going to love them both with all our hearts and look after them and give them the best life we can. The very very best. They shall have a nanny and a governess to teach them both at home. They shan't want for anything. And if I come back when this ghastly war is over . . .'

She interrupted him passionately. 'Oh, Edouard. You mustn't say that. I couldn't bear . . .'

'We must be sensible my little love. We must face these things. All these things.' And yet even now he couldn't tell her that the twins could have caught the infection. That was too awful. It would have to wait until later when she was up and about and stronger. 'If I come back we will look after them together. Always. If I don't, you will have to do it on your own.'

'Yes, yes, I promise. But you will come back, won't you, Edouard? You will be careful.'

'God willing, I shall come back,' he said, kissing her fingers. But there was still the disease to face. 'Oh my dearest love.'

She lifted her head to kiss him gently and laid his hand softly under her cheek, the way she'd always done after they'd made love. The gesture unlocked his tears and he let them flow, weeping for their lost innocence, for his baby blinded and his men shattered and killed, for love that would be tarnished if the disease he carried was the one he feared.

'Love is all we have,' he said.

'Yes, my darling.'

'I'm ill, too, Hortense.'

Her grief for Emily was too strong to allow her to be surprised or upset, even by this. 'Yes,' she said. It was something they had to accept. Something they'd always accepted. This disease was passed between men and women all the time. That was something they both knew only too well.

'I think it's the "bad" disease come back.'

'Yes.' They'd always known that was possible. 'When did you find out?'

'Last month. I had a rash and a fever.'

'But it's gone now?'

'Yes. It wasn't bad. But if I've still got it and I make love to you again . . .' It was terrible to say this but it had to be said. 'Perhaps I shouldn't make love to you, my darling.'

Her face crumpled with distress. 'Oh, don't say that. Please Edouard, don't say that. We can be cured.'

'The doctor says he will cure you. But I . . .'

'Then he can cure you, too,' she insisted.

'Not if it's that.'

'But you don't know, Edouard. You said "if".'

'You must understand this, my darling,' he said seriously. 'If it is, it could kill us.'

Her answer was fatalistic but completely calm. 'Then it will kill us. We can't live at all if we don't love one another. You know that.'

Yes. He knew that. Even weighed down by grief for their innocent daughter and fear of this awful disease, he knew that.

'But nothing will happen yet,' she said. 'Will it? Not yet. You can live for years. Can't you? We both can.'

'It will happen eventually.'

'They might find a cure.'

23

He felt he had to allow her that comfort at least. 'They might.' Or I might be killed in the next campaign. There was a big one planned for high summer. Anything might happen in this world gone crazy. They had to be ready for anything. To accept anything.

'Then you will love me?'

'I shall always love you.'

'In every way?'

'Oh, my darling, in every way.'

She was quiet for a long time. Then she asked, 'Do you forgive me for my poor Emily's eyes?'

'There is nothing to forgive. How could you know? Neither of us knew. We both thought we were cured long since. If we'd known we'd have done something about it.'

She sighed and closed her eyes wearily.

'This must be our secret,' he said. 'Your illness. Mine. Whatever happens we will look after one another. But we will keep it secret from everyone.'

'The doctor knows,' she pointed out, looking at him again. 'And Mrs Bonney.'

'They are like priests, my darling. They keep secrets.'

'Then we will keep our secret, too. I promise you, Edouard.'

'All our secrets. Where we met, when we married. All of it. Not just the illnesses.'

'All of it,' she promised, looking steadfastly into his eyes.

'I love you so much,' he said. 'More at this moment than I have ever done.'

'It is the same for me,' she said. 'You are everything to me. Everything in all the world.'

And as if to remind her that she had other loves now, Virginia sneezed and whimpered.

'You and my darling babies,' she said. 'I love you all with all my heart.'

# CHAPTER TWO

It was Wednesday May nineteenth 1926. The sun was shining through the long lattice windows of the day nursery at High Holborn, the roses were in bloom beside the terrace and the Holborn twins were being dressed for their tenth birthday party.

'*Comme vous êtes belles, mes petites!*' Hortense said, speaking in French as she always did when she was doting on them. 'How pretty you are.'

She was wrong, of course, but then she was seeing them with a mother's eye. They weren't pretty children. Well dressed and well groomed, certainly, distinguished perhaps, with their long equine faces, their straight spines and their confident air, but not beautiful.

They were very much alike, small and slight with slender bones, their mother's olive skin and the same shock of thick, dark frizzy hair, cut short just below their ears in the fashionable style which bushed out as thick as a thatch on either side of their cheeks. The only differences between them were the way they walked, Ginny darting and precipitate, Emily plodding and steady, and the colour of their eyes. Emily's were pale blue disks without light or expression, while Ginny's were so dark as to be almost black, quick and lively and intelligent and the most dramatic indicators of her changing moods. Now they were flashing with pleasure.

'Do the dresses please you?' Hortense asked.

It was an unnecessary question, because she could see how pleased they were. Emily's blind eyes were flickering from side to side as she fingered the white silk, and Ginny was so excited she was squealing and pirouetting before the long mirror, twirling her lovely frilled skirt, three frills, one

25

above the other and all ruched so prettily and edged with satin in a pale lilac to match her sash.

'*Mais oui, Maman. Oui. Oui. Oui,*' she sang. And then dropping from French to English in the effortless way of the truly bilingual, 'We love them. They're so chic.'

Maman brought her clothes in Paris and was always very chic, especially when it came to putting colours together. Ginny was particularly proud of her because she looked so French, with long, elegant legs and a wide-eyed face. She was the only one in the family with an oval face and that, combined with high cheekbones and large brown eyes, gave her a striking beauty. Today she was wearing a grass-green crêpe de chine dress that set off her olive skin and her thick bobbed hair to perfection. The trimmings were marvellous. Where poor old Aunty Agnes would have chosen trimmings in a nice safe colour like beige, Maman had *her* dress pointed up with a lovely bright emerald green silk patterned all over with white polka dots. Her clothes were always exciting and the party dresses she chose for her daughters always superb. But these were the best of them all.

Nanny was trying to do up the row of tiny pearl buttons on the back of Emily's bodice. 'You're very lucky little girls,' she said. But there was reproach as well as approval in her voice.

'Yes, Nanny,' Emily said gently. 'We know we are.' And it was true. They were both comfortably aware of their good fortune, that they were loved and special, half French and half English, with two langauges to speak where everybody else only had one, and a great house to live in and a fine garden to play in and servants to wait on them and dear old Babbers, their governess, to teach them and a life of ease and comfort to look forward to. Oh very, very lucky.

'You look a picture in white, the pair of you,' Nanny said. 'Don't you think so, ma'am? Can't you just see what pretty brides they'll make.'

It was just as if she'd thrown a bowl of cold water over them, the atmosphere in the room changed so quickly.

Hortense Holborn sucked in her breath as though she'd

been stung. The excitement and pirouetting stopped at once and her daughters turned towards Hortense, instantly alert and protective. It was part of the pattern of their lives protecting Maman, especially when there was that vulnerable note in her voice or that stricken expression on her face. They all had to care for one another, Daddy said so. That was the way things were. Ginny looked after Emily because she couldn't see. Maman looked after Daddy because he was ill with a disease called *locomotor ataxia* that made him stumble as if he were drunk, and gave him sudden attacks of terrible pain. They all looked after Maman, because she could swing from happiness to misery in a second, and she needed a lot of care and consideration.

'Clear these things away, Nanny, if you please,' Maman said, and she spoke in her cold voice. 'I wish to speak to my daughters.'

Oh dear, Ginny thought, as Nanny bundled their discarded clothes together and shot out of the room, Maman *is* upset. As soon as the door had closed, she and Emily crept to their mother's side to find out what was wrong, and to put it right if they could.

'A foolish woman,' Maman said, speaking in French. 'Always talking about weddings and marriage. She reads too many romances. To be married is not the only thing for women to do these days. Women have careers now. Many, many women. It is quite the fashion. In any case not all young women want to marry, do they?'

Her daughters took their cue and responded to it at once. 'No, Maman.'

'You might not want to get married yourselves, isn't that right?'

Neither of the twins had given it much thought until then, so they didn't know what to say.

Their silence was a mistake. Maman's mood crackled into bad temper. 'Now think!' she ordered. 'Think of all the things women can do nowadays. You could go to college, or be an Olympic swimmer, or an actress, or a film star. Anything. Think of it. You could work in all sorts of places.

27

You could fly an aeroplane if you wanted to. You'd like that, wouldn't you?'

Both girls were baffled by the bombardment and alarmed by her temper. Something was badly wrong.

'Yes, Maman,' Emily said, quickly. 'We would, wouldn't we, Ginny?'

And naturally Ginny agreed, equally quickly.

Maman's voice grew softer. 'It would be so much better for you not to get married,' she said, putting her arms round them.

'Yes, Maman,' Emily said, dutifully. It was a very odd thing for Maman to say. Babbers said *everybody* got married.

'Some girls are cut out for it,' Hortense went on. 'But you are not. For you marriage would be a very serious error. For you it must be different.'

Ginny wasn't convinced. 'Why?' she asked.

It was her second mistake. 'Because it must,' Hortense said, and her voice sounded irritable again. 'I can't explain to you now. You must take my word for it. But I am telling you the truth. You must understand that. It would be much much better for you not to marry. It would be much better never even to think of it. You must promise me never to think of it.'

It seemed a peculiar request but because she was so agitated they promised. Ginny put her arms round her mother's neck and hugged her. '*I* am never going to get married,' she declared. 'Never, ever. Not if I live to be a hundred.'

'Nor am I,' Emily echoed stoutly, hugging her mother, too. That was what Maman wanted to hear. That was the way to comfort her.

And it *did* comfort her. Her voice relaxed. 'That's my sensible girls,' she said, kissing them. 'Now I must see to the table, *n'est-ce pas?* Stay here, my darlings. Stay here until Miss Babbacombe comes to fetch you. You can wait by the window.'

Arms resting on the sill, they waited at the open window, positioned so that Ginny could see and Emily could hear what was happening on the terrace below them, and tried to make sense of what they'd just been told.

'Do you think she meant it?' Ginny asked. Emily always knew when people meant what they said. She could hear it in their voices.

'Yes,' Emily said. 'I'm sure she did.'

'She made me feel quite frightened.'

'Yes. She did.'

'Still,' Ginny said, trying to cheer them up. 'I don't suppose it'll matter. I can't see the point of getting married, really. There's no fun in it.'

'Isn't there?'

'No. Most people aren't a bit happy.'

'Daddy and Maman are happy. Most of the time.'

'Well yes,' Ginny admitted. 'But look at all the others. They're always getting peeved and shouting at one another and having headaches. Look at Uncle Claud.'

Uncle Claud was always shouting about something or other, the General Strike, or the miners, or Aunty Agnes' hats. He was shouting now and charging about the terrace where the maids were setting up the trestle tables for their birthday tea.

Emily agreed with that. 'Being married makes you cry, too,' she said. 'If you're a lady.' Aunty Agnes cried ever such a lot, especially when Uncle Claud had been roaring at her. She usually did it at night, when she didn't think anyone was listening, and into her pillow, which made her sobs sound very peculiar, as if they were a long way away. But Emily always heard her, even though her bedroom was right down at the other end of the corridor in the west wing.

'What will you do instead?' Emily asked.

'Instead of what?'

'Getting married?'

'Oh I shall stay here,' Ginny said. 'I shall stay in this house for ever and ever. This is the best house in the world.'

Young though they were they both knew how extra-ordinary High Holborn was, and how privileged they were to live there. For a start it was very big. Over fifty rooms, so

Miss Babbacombe said. And the garden was enormous, with two fish ponds, a rose garden, a tennis court, a meadow big enough to graze four horses and two great avenues of trees where you could go for a walk in the shade. But it was the house they loved most because the house was like something out of a fairy tale.

It had been built by their great-grandfather nearly fifty years ago; the architect had adored the Gothic style, considered symmetry boring, and had been convinced that a plain, square room was an affront to the senses. Consequently he had designed a building that was a hodge-podge of all the styles he most enjoyed. It was part Norman castle, part Tudor manor house, part Gothic mansion, a rambling red-brick confection of battlemented towers, tile-hung gables, long-necked chimneys, half-timbered walls and leaded windows of every size and shape and design. It had an east wing, where the twins lived with Daddy and Maman, and a west wing for Uncle Claud and Aunty Agnes and the boys. Their grandfather lived in the long main house where the special rooms were, the library, the dining room and the morning room, not forgetting the great hall where grandfather held his board meetings and gave parties for the grown-ups. Oh, a wonderful house.

'But what will you *do* if you don't get married?' Emily asked.

'I shall probably help Grandfather run the firm.'

Emily was impressed but doubtful. 'Will he let you?'

'I don't see why not. Women can do things just as well as men. Babbers told me. Maman is right about *that*. And anyway it's only signing papers and stuff.'

'D'you think I could do it, too?' Emily asked, her blind eyes flickering with interest.

'Well, not signing papers,' Ginny said practically. 'You couldn't do that could you, because you have to read them first, and you couldn't do that unless they were in braille. But you could chair meetings. That's ever so easy.'

Emily wasn't sure. 'What do you have to do to chair meetings?'

30

'You sit in a chair, of course,' her sister said practically, 'and the others sit round the table and you tell them to say things.'

'What sort of things?'

Ginny didn't know the answer, but she didn't have to think one up because at that moment Emily stiffened to attention and she began to speak in French.

'*Écoute! Quelqu'un s'approche,*' she said.

'You are sure?' Ginny said, in the same language. 'I don't hear anyone.'

'Yes, yes. It is Mademoiselle Babbacombe.' And of course it was. Emily was never wrong about footsteps.

Feet splayed and hands clenched into fists as though she was going to beat the world, their governess strode into the room, wafting a smell of starch and carbolic soap before her. She was an eccentric-looking woman, tall and skinny and awkward, and her face, framed by a curly fringe and a long pageboy bob of brown hair, was bizarre. She had pale blue eyes, a very small chin, a rosebud mouth like a doll's and, sticking inappropriately out of the middle of her face, a long sharp, triangular nose like a beak. But the smile she was beaming towards the twins was all affection.

'Ah, there you are!' she said, briskly. 'Good gels! Ready for the off, are we?'

The twins answered in chorus. 'Yes, Miss Babbacombe.'

'That's the ticket,' Miss Babbacombe said. 'Your grandfather's waiting in the library. I must say you look super.'

This is better, Ginny thought, pushing all thoughts of marriage and Maman's inexplicable mood away. Now the rituals of the birthday could begin: down to the library to see Grandfather and be given his presents, out to the hall to welcome their guests and then on to the games, the prizes and the birthday tea.

'All set?' Miss Babbacombe asked, taking Emily by the hand.

'I wonder what it'll be this year,' Ginny said, as their governess escorted them down the stairs.

31

'Something lovely, I'll be bound,' Miss Babbacombe said. 'Soon see. Now are you neat and tidy?'

In his gruff and rather enigmatic way old Mr Holborn was quite fond of his granddaughters, but he was very particular about them being neat. He sat in his special armchair beside the library fireplace, looked down his long nose and examined them critically, his rough grey head cocked to one side.

'Hello, funny faces,' he said. 'How's the birthday going then?'

'Very nicely, thank you, Grandfather,' Ginny said politely. And Emily smiled towards the sound of his voice.

There were two small boxes on the table by his elbow.

'Birthday presents,' he said. 'Something special this time because you're into double figures. And that only happens once in a lifetime, eh? Hold out your hands.'

It's too small to be a toy, Emily thought, passing her intelligent fingers over the package he'd put into her hands. Perhaps it's more furniture for the doll's house. Puzzling, she unwrapped the parcel, smoothed back the paper, folded it neatly and set it down on the table she knew was behind her.

She was holding a long narrow box, with a hook-and-eye catch that she lifted with a finger nail. She raised the lid, balancing the box on the palm of her left hand, and, breathless with curiosity, felt inside with the tips of her forefinger and thumb. The box was lined with velvet and stretched across the soft nap was a delicate metal chain suspended from a tiny hook. She rolled the chain gently between finger and thumb, following it down until she encountered a small metal cross. It had rounded ends and the front of it was ridged and carved into tiny intricate patterns. There was a stone of some kind embedded in the centre, a stone that was smooth and oddly soft to the touch so that she knew at once that it was something rare and precious.

'An amethyst,' Mr Holborn said, watching her fingers and the flicker of those poor blind eyes. 'The cross is silver.

32

Virginia's got one just the same except that her amethyst is oval and yours is round, so that you can tell the difference.'

'It's beautiful!' Ginny said. 'Thank you ever so much. I shall wear it for ever and ever.'

'So shall I,' Emily said. 'Thank you very very much, Grandfather.'

'Well put them on then,' Mr Holborn said gruffly. 'Put them on.' The clock on the mantlepiece was pinging the hour. 'Three o'clock. Your guests will be arriving.' The house would soon be full of screaming children so the sooner he was out of it the better.

The twins kissed him affectionately and were led from his presence, excitement rising; now the party could begin. As they walked into the panelled twilight of the hall they heard the first car scrunching to a halt on the gravel drive outside. Now for the fun.

Because they were both being educated at home, their birthday party was the one occasion in the year when they had lots of other children to play with. It was a heterogeneous gathering, children from the village, who were very rough and lots of fun, sons and daughters of some of the people who worked in grandfather's office, who were carefully polite and rather cautious until the party really got under way, and this year their two baby cousins, George and Johnny Everdale, who were being allowed to join in, too. Ginny wasn't sure about the wisdom of that, because they were very young, only two-and-a-half and just four, and horribly naughty, so they would probably be rather a nuisance unless Aunty Agnes could keep them in order.

As it turned out, they behaved themselves surprisingly well, joining in the milder games, such as pass-the-parcel and grandmother's footsteps, and content to watch the rougher ones, like tug-of-war and rounders. When it came to tea they sat in their high chairs, bibs smothered in jelly, and cheered with the rest when the birthday cake was carried out.

All in all, it was a lovely party . . . until the moment when the twins were standing side by side at the table, with the cake knife held firmly between their hands, ready to cut the cake.

The sun felt warm on their shoulders, their new silver crosses hung importantly about their necks, their guests watched them ready to cheer again and all was right with their world. Suddenly a man's voice, shouting and swearing, erupted into the peace of the afternoon.

'Who left that bloody chair in my way? Goddamn it all. You can't walk for bloody chairs.'

It was their father, who'd come staggering round the corner of the house and crashed sideways into the stools they'd been using for musical chairs. Now he lurched towards them in his dreadful awkward way, legs straddled as if he was riding a horse and his body tipped forward and completely off balance. He was lifting his feet even higher than he usually did, so with every step his knees rose almost to the level of his waist, and he stamped his feet down with such violence that the impact spun gravel in all directions. His face was dark with bad temper. Worse than Ginny had ever seen it, even when he had one of his really bad attacks.

Maman was already running towards him along the terrace, beckoning to Nanny to follow her. And the tea party stopped in mid-giggle as all their guests turned their heads to stare at him, shocked and fascinated.

'He's going to be ill again,' Ginny whispered to her sister, speaking in French for privacy.

'I know,' Emily whispered back. 'I can hear it.'

That was all they had time to say.

He collapsed before Maman could reach him, falling in a heap as his knees gave way, and lay where he fell, still swearing, his arms thrown out like a rag doll's.

'Aren't we going to cut this cake?' Miss Babbacombe said, stepping up briskly to stand between her two worried darlings. 'Poor Mr Holborn is very ill, you know,' she explained, looking round the table at the startled children, and demanding the return of their attention by the sheer force of her gaze. 'The war, you know. We must all feel sorry for him, mustn't we? Make allowances. Christian charity. Look away, if you please.'

One or two said 'Yes Miss Babbacombe' dutifully. And a village boy asked, 'Was he wounded, Miss?'

'Terribly,' Miss Babbacombe said. 'But Mrs Holborn will look after him. Now what about this cake?'

So the cake was cut and the slices handed round. When Ginny looked up after the little ceremony the terrace was clear. Her father had been carried away into the house.

Their pleasure in the party was gone, drained away like blood from an open wound. They wanted to rush indoors, to see poor Daddy and protect Maman and find out what was happening. But, of course, they couldn't. They had a duty to their guests. And if you were a member of the Holborn family, duty had to be done, no matter how difficult.

It was past six o'clock before the last car had been waved away and Miss Babbacombe finally nodded her approval and allowed them to run off into the house. Maman was in the morning room, curled up on one of the upholstered window seats like a cat, apparently enjoying the last rays of the afternoon sun. She looked far too bright and cheerful, and there was an odd note in her voice.

'Come here my little ones,' she instructed, patting the upholstery beside her. 'Come and kiss your Maman.'

The twins sat in the sun together, worrying.

'Is Daddy very ill?'

'Oh no, no, no. A little fall.'

'Is it his illness?'

'Yes. But it is nothing, nothing.'

Emily pinched Ginny's hand to show that she knew poor Maman wasn't telling them the truth. And Ginny pinched back to show that she agreed.

'Was it lightning pains?' she asked. She knew all about lightning pains. Miss Babbacombe had explained them. They came and went like lightning.

Maman admitted that, but she was still too bright. 'Yes, your poor Papa. But you mustn't worry, my darlings.'

'May we see him?' Emily asked. Usually if they were allowed to see him, he wasn't too bad.

But her mother gave them the wrong answer. 'Not now. Doctor Stimson gave him something to make him sleep. In the morning, if you are good little girls.'

They were exemplary and stayed in the nursery all through a long sleepless night, even though they could both hear their father groaning, their mother soothing, in her soft purring French, and somebody coming and going along the corridor. But when morning arrived they didn't see their father and there was no sign of Maman either. Nanny yawned as she strode in to get them washed and dressed, but she was no help at all.

'No good asking me,' she said, as she stripped their beds. 'I'm the *last* one in this house to know what's going on. You just cut on down to the dining room like good girls and don't make a fuss.'

There was no one in the dining room at all and the twins knew things were serious. While they were eating what breakfast they could manage, Emily heard the doctor's car arrive. They'd never known him to call as early as this. Then they heard urgent footsteps up and down the stairs, and voices speaking so quietly that even Emily could only hear a word or two. '. . . for the best . . . Hurry! . . . only to be expected, poor man.'

'He's terribly ill,' Emily said.

'Yes,' Ginny said. There was no doubt about that now. 'Poor Daddy.'

'What shall we do, Ginny?' Emily asked. 'If we went up, would they let us see him?'

'Not with all this going on,' Ginny said.

'I s'pose we'd better go to the schoolroom then.'

'No,' Ginny decided. 'We'll leave Babbers a note to tell her where we are and we'll go to the library and wait there. It's the nearest we can get to the hall.' The hall was always the best place to be, because all family activity went through its central point at some time or other.

The library was quiet and musty with smoke from

Grandfather's cigars. They sat on the curly hearth rug beside his special chair and waited while anxious activity swirled and muttered on the other side of the door. Nine o'clock tinged, half-past, a quarter to.

Then there was a long ominous silence, as if the house was holding its breath. Just before ten, a strange car drew up outside the front door. Peering through the crack of the library door, Ginny saw two uniformed men carrying an odd sort of folding chair up the main staircase. The sight of it alarmed her more than anything else she'd seen or heard in the last eighteen, awful hours.

'I think it's a sort of stretcher,' she said to Emily. 'I think they're going to take him away.'

Twenty minutes later their father was eased down the stairs one step at a time, strapped into the odd-looking chair, his face grey with pain and his eyes closed. Behind him came Maman, crying so much that her face was awash with tears.

'Daddy!' Ginny cried, and rushed out of the library, pulling Emily behind her.

'Very ill,' their father explained wearily, reaching out his hands to draw them to his side. 'Got to go to . . . clinic. Be good girls. Help Maman.'

Ginny pounced forward at once to kiss him, but the doctor intervened, removing her gently with one hand and holding Emily back with the other.

'Better not, Mr Holborn,' he said.

And to the twins' horror their father agreed. 'No, I suppose not.'

The chair was carried out of the house, Maman following it, a handkerchief to her eyes. Miss Babbacombe appeared at the foot of the stairs, swished forward to catch her charges round the shoulders, and hold them firmly against her sides.

'Why have they taken him away?' Ginny said furiously.

'It's for the best my precious,' Miss Babbacombe said. 'They'll look after him.'

But Ginny couldn't see it was for the best at all. 'Why can't he be nursed at home?' she demanded. 'He's always been nursed at home before. He's worse, isn't he?'

'Coats and hats!' Miss Babbacombe commanded. 'Chop chop. Time for a nice walk. I'll take you down to the village.'

It was not possible to talk until Babbers popped into the chemist. 'He's much worse this time,' Emily said. 'You could tell by the way everyone was talking.'

Thank heavens for Em, Ginny thought. Until that moment she'd simply taken it for granted that her sister had the ability to hear what people were thinking; now she realised that it was a skill that was going to be very useful to them. 'Does Babbers know what's the matter?' she asked.

'Yes. She was embarrassed when you asked her. She changed the subject.'

'What do you think he's got, Em?'

'Well it's not just lightning pains or a stomach upset. What did he look like?'

'Very ill. Sort of grey.'

'Worse than usual?'

'Yes.'

'Perhaps Maman will tell us when she gets back.'

But she didn't. Her eyelids were red, but she was even brighter than she'd been the evening before, and so cheerful that they felt she would snap.

'What a lot we all have to do today!' she said, kissing them briefly. 'I must hurry.' And was gone from the schoolroom before they could ask her anything.

There was nothing they could do but wait for a better moment, which never came.

The days passed, became weeks, and their father remained in the clinic. Babbers told them they couldn't go and visit him there, because it wasn't that sort of place and when they asked her what sort of place it was she pretended she didn't know. Maman visited him every day but she didn't tell them anything except that he was being looked after.

Nobody at all was prepared to talk about their father's illness, and their concern for him became a perpetual nagging ache, like toothache.

They did their lessons as well as they could, ate their

38

meals, went for obedient walks with Nanny or Miss Babbacombe, and to the comfort of mass on Sundays with Maman. Clutching their new silver crosses between their fingers, they implored gentle Jesus to make their father better, concentrating with such intensity that Hortense was riven with unspoken pity for them.

The weeks worried into months and their father still didn't come back. There was no real news of him. Sometimes Emily gleaned a fragment of conversation and then they would know that he'd been sick, or that he was rallying, or that he had an ulcer on his leg. Once she heard that he'd been through a crisis of some sort.

'I think she said "bronchial",' she reported to Ginny. 'That's breathing, isn't it?'

But Ginny couldn't say, and, in any case, all they really wanted to know was when he was going to get better and come home.

One lovely warm morning in the middle of July, they came down to breakfast to be told that Maman had gone to the clinic during the night. Neither of them liked the sound of that, but when they asked Nanny for an explanation she said they were to ask no questions. So they resigned themselves to wait.

Each minute as long as an hour and fraught with prickling anxiety, the morning crept by. So inattentive were the twins that Miss Babbacombe gave up all hope of teaching them and took them out into the garden after lunch. They sat on a travelling rug under the shade of the willow beside the lily pond and did their best to listen while she read them two *Just-So Stories*. But their hearts weren't in it.

'Where is she?' Ginny fretted, when the second story was finished.

'She ought to be back by now, surely,' Emily said.

'I think he's worse,' Ginny said, 'and that's why she's staying there all the time. Don't you, Miss Babbacombe?'

'Yes, my precious, I'm afraid I do.'

'Much worse?'

They all knew where the questions were leading but Miss Babbacombe answered steadfastly, 'Yes, my darling.'

'Do you think he's going to die?'

'Oh my poor darlings,' Miss Babbacombe said, wincing with grief. 'I wish I could say no . . .'

'Shush!' Emily said, lifting her head to listen. 'There's the car coming up the hill.'

The two girls were on their feet immediately, running down the incline towards the terrace and skidding along the gravel path. They reached the front of the house just as the car rounded the bend of the drive. Ginny pulled her sister to a halt. The anxiety of that long difficult day had swollen into terror that filled her throat and made her knees tremble too much for her to walk any further.

Maman's long slim legs emerged out of the car door. They looked all wrong somehow, awkward and inelegant, like a baby kangaroo's legs poking out of its pouch. Then she got out of the car and stood in a most peculiar way, her handbag under her arm and her hat and gloves in her hand, looking as if she didn't know where she was. She seemed to fall towards them, eyes shut like Emily, her lovely face so changed that Ginny could hardly recognise her mother; all the colour had been drained from her cheeks, except for the flesh round her eyes, which was bright pink and puffy. There were streaks of dirt on her cheeks, and her dark hair was black with perspiration.

'Oh my babies!' she said, running towards them. 'My poor babies! My little *orphelines*!' She dropped her hat and her bag and her gloves as she ran, and didn't notice that Miss Babbacombe was behind her picking them up. 'Oh your poor father! I loved him so much.'

The twins fell upon her to hold and kiss her in an anguish of grief.

'He's dead,' Emily said.

'I loved him so much,' her mother choked.

As if she was a sheep dog herding them into cover, Miss Babbacombe chivied them inside and they obeyed her instinctively. Together they stumbled into the house and through the hall into the morning room, with the twins' arms wrapped protectively round their poor Maman, weeping and kissing. Here they cried for a very long time. Somebody tiptoed in with a tea tray and set it silently beside them, somebody else removed Maman's crumpled coat, but the three of them were lost in their sorrow.

'What shall we do without him?' Hortense mourned, as gathering cloud outside softened the light in the room and their first terrible grief had been wept to a halt. 'Your poor darling father.'

Emily recovered sufficiently to be practical. 'We shall go on living here, Maman,' she said, 'and Ginny and me will look after you.'

'I suppose so,' Hortense said, wearied by grief. 'Yes I suppose we will.'

'Of course, we will,' Ginny said, comforting her furiously. 'It'll be all right, Maman. You'll see. You've still got us and we've got a good home and a garden and lots of friends and lots of relations. We'll look after you always, won't we, Em? It'll be all right.'

But they were reckoning without Uncle Claud.

# CHAPTER THREE

The last ten years of Claud Everdale's life had not gone according to plan. Not that anyone who met him socially would ever have suspected it. On the face of things he appeared to have achieved all his ambitions. He'd married Agnes Holborn after a two-year courtship and, despite her father's opposition, had risen from junior salesman to assistant manager of overseas sales. He was now living in a comfortable suite of rooms in the west wing of High Holborn, having produced two sons to carry the fortunes of the family into the fourth generation. But it was all to no purpose.

In public, he was courteous and urbane, universally accepted by his many acquaintances as a charming man, generous both with his time and his attention. In private his sense of injustice rankled like poison, bubbling and seething in his brain and belly until it spilled out into irritability and violent stomach upsets. For no matter how polite he was to Mr Holborn, no matter how often he kow-towed to fools, guarding his tongue and exercising iron self-control, he was still an outsider, still the office boy made good.

The obstacle to his preferment had always been Mr Edward, of course. Despite his illness, his outbursts of foul temper and his totally unpredictable behaviour, Edward Holborn had been the apple of his father's eye. As far as Claud could see it was simply because his brother-in-law had seen service in the trenches. As if *that* were a virtue! But now he was gone and everything was changed. If he played his cards right *he*, Claud James Everdale, could be the future director of the firm. The way could be cleared. In fact, it *had* to be cleared. He knew that. There was no point in being squeamish or paying attention to sentimental nonsense about women and children. If he wanted power he would have to take it. God knew he had a right to it after all this time.

The Fates were on his side. Three days after the funeral, when the women and children were breakfasting on their own upstairs, old Mr Holborn gave him a piece of unintentionally helpful news.

'I'm off to South America,' he said, ladling marmalade on to his third slice of toast. 'Thought you ought to know.'

'When would that be?' Claud asked, at his most urbane.

'S'afternoon,' the old man said gruffly. 'Bad timing, eh? I know what Agnes'll say.'

Claud made a face to deprecate anything Agnes might say.

'Can't be helped,' Mr Holborn went on. 'I've postponed it twice because of – um – er. Can't be put back a third time or I shall lose the order.'

'Of course.'

'Business is business.'

'Of course.'

'Thought you ought to know.'

There was something about the set of the old man's jaw that gave lie to the casual tone of his words. He's running away, Claud realised. This house is wallowing in emotion, all those women weeping and carrying on, and he can't take it. He's running away. The thought gave him hope and an idea. 'Is there anything you'd like me to do while you're away?' he asked.

Mr Holborn screwed up his eyes to consider the offer. 'Don't think so,' he said. 'Keep things ticking over. Look after Hortense and the funny faces. The factory can run itself for a week or two.'

'How many weeks? If you don't mind telling me.'

'About six. Depends on the state of the market.'

It was about the right amount of time. All he needed now was the right moment.

Four days later it came, as if the gods had ordered it for him.

Since it was the middle of July lessons had stopped for the summer, so the twins had nothing to deflect them from their grief, especially as their mother stayed in bed until late morning and couldn't bear to talk to anyone until the afternoon. That morning the two little girls came downstairs after their solitary breakfast in the east wing and the sight of their bleak faces spurred Agnes into an uncharacteristically impulsive decision.

'Nanny and I are going into Wolverhampton this afternoon,' she said, 'to get the boys measured for their winter coats. How would you like to come with us? We could have tea at Reynolds' restaurant afterwards.' A trip into town might take them out of themselves, poor little things.

So it was agreed, although without much enthusiasm. And that afternoon, knowing that Hortense would be alone in the house, Claud Everdale took an hour off from his office and drove back to talk to her. She was alone in the flower garden, lethargically dead-heading the roses. She was surprised to see him, but made an effort to be polite.

'Hello, Claud,' she said. 'You are back very early.' Then, noticing the expression on his face, 'Is something the matter?'

'Yes,' he said curtly. 'You'd better come inside.'

Raw and grieving as she was, Hortense was instantly alarmed.

'What is it?' she asked, following Claud, the garden trug still over her arm. 'It is not the children. Oh please God, it is not the children. Tell me quickly. What is it? What is the matter?'

He led her inside the drawing room where none of the servants could hear them.

'I think you will find that *you* are the matter,' he said coldly. 'You and your daughters.'

For a few seconds Hortense didn't understand him. She was limp with relief that the girls hadn't been hurt, and his words made no sense to her. ' 'Ow do you mean?'

'You know perfectly well what I mean. I'm talking about Edward's illness and Emily's blindness and you.'

She flinched under his attack, and her heart constricted with a new fear. But she gathered her courage, put the trug down on the nearest table and fought back in the only way she knew, by appealing for sympathy.

'My dear Claud!' she said, giving him the full benefit of her brown eyes. 'You mus' not expect us to be at our best at a time like this. When you think what we 'ave suffered. But there is nothing the matter with us. Nothing at all. I assure you.'

'Isn't there?' he said, menacing her with his face. How hard his eyes were. Like the twin bores of a shot-gun. 'Oh I think there is, Hortense. I think there is. It wasn't just Edward who was ill, was it? It came from you.'

The colour drained from her face. 'I don't know what you mean,' she lied, and moved away from him while she still had the strength. She sat stiffly in one of the armchairs beside the fireplace, her face averted.

'Then I will explain,' he said, following her across the room. 'We are talking about Edward's illness, or your illness, or whoever's illness it really was, because I know what sort of illness it was. I made it my business to find out. We're talking about that illness and what is going to happen to you and your children now that your husband is dead.'

She looked up at him, her pretty face pleading and vulnerable. 'It is not the time,' she begged. 'Not so soon. Please, Claud. I cannot bear it.'

'It's no good looking at me like that,' he said. 'I'm proof against your wiles. They don't work on me.' Actually she was having a profound effect on him, arousing his sympathy most powerfully. He felt impatient with himself for the weakness because he would need all his anger if he was to get his own way. 'We have to make a decision.'

She continued to plead. 'But not now. Please, Claud. It is not the time.'

He ignored her pleas and supressed his own pity. 'Oh yes,' he insisted, heavy with determination and menace. 'It is

45

precisely the time. A decision has to be made. You don't expect us to go on giving you houseroom in the circumstances? I have children of my own to consider. I can't put them at risk.'

'Nobody is at risk,' she said.

He brushed that aside with a wave of his hand as if it were a fly annoying him. 'We won't tell lies,' he said. 'Or talk nonsense. We both know what we're talking about. A highly contagious disease. And it didn't die with Edward, did it? Good God, woman. Do you really think you can bring your filthy disease into this house and get away with it for ever? There *are* limits.'

'It is nearly tea time,' she tried. 'The children will be home. Could we not talk of this some other time?'

He was adamant, ruthless, lowering down upon her, black as a cannon. 'They are taking tea in town with Agnes,' he said, 'as you know very well. They won't be back for hours. I'm sorry, Hortense. This shameful business . . . oh yes it *is* a shameful business . . . this shameful business can't be hidden any longer. You will have to face it. We will *all* have to face it.'

Hortense was so frightened that her legs trembled. She spread her hands over her knees to steady them. How could she keep her secret when he was bullying her like this? Had he really found out? How could he have done? Oh if only I hadn't . . . But what was the good of wishing that now? If only there'd been a cure for . . . But there hadn't been. There wasn't. Oh, Edouard, my dearest, why did you have to die and leave me so alone?

'Very well, then,' Claud went on. 'I will tell you what I think you ought to do. I think you ought to pack your bags and leave this house on the first possible train. You're not wanted here. You realise that, don't you? We endured you while Edward was alive but it is quite different now. You should pack your bags and you and your daughters should catch the first train out of here, and take your dirty disease somewhere else.'

Hortense wanted to weep or scream or run from the room

but she made an enormous effort to keep herself under control. 'I will talk to Agnes,' she said.

'You can if you like,' he said easily. 'It won't do you any good. Agnes thinks as I do.'

The interview was becoming more and more like a nightmare. 'How could she? We are friends.'

'How many more times have I got to tell you? Things have changed. You're not wanted.'

'But where could I go?'

'That's your affair,' he said coldly. 'But I'll tell you one thing. If you don't go I shall tell everybody what I know about you. Everybody. Do you understand me?'

She could hardly avoid understanding him. 'I will do as you say,' she said. Then she got to her feet and walked as calmly as she could to the hall door, moving slowly and deliberately so that he wouldn't see that she was trembling. Holy Mary, Mother of God, she prayed as she climbed the stairs, pray for us sinners, now . . . I must keep my promise to Edouard. I must. I must. I must keep our secret and protect my little ones. If only they'd been with me, she thought illogically, none of this would be happening.

But her little ones were in Beattie's department store and they weren't thinking of her at all. They were trying to catch their cousin Johnny, who had slipped his reins and scampered off behind the counters the minute they walked into the shop. For the first time in months they were both laughing.

Since the funeral they'd been too stunned by grief and loss to respond to anything. But the trip to Wolverhampton had taken them out of themselves, just as Agnes had hoped, and that was mainly because George and Johnny had been so naughty. The two boys had spent the journey into Wolverhampton climbing all over everybody in the car, and now Johnny was causing havoc in Beattie's. Nanny declared she didn't know what was to be done with them.

'We'll take them to tea,' Aunt Agnes said. 'See what a chocolate cake will do.'

So they were taken to Reynolds' restaurant, where they

47

stood on the high-backed chairs and smeared chocolate on the tablecloths. And Nanny said she'd be jolly glad to get them home and bathed and in bed, so she would, and for the life of her she couldn't think why anyone should ever bother to measure them for nice little coats the way they went on.

Agnes took their misdemeanours with tea-sipping calm. 'Your Daddy was just the same when he was a little boy,' she said to Emily and Virginia.

'Was he?' the twins said, almost in unison.

'Oh yes. A proper little tinker. I remember once when we were little he climbed the holm oak, bird's nesting, I think; anyway he missed his footing and fell into Hodge's vegetable garden and squashed all the tomatoes. Hodge was livid.'

Oh the comfort of remembering! It brought him back, alive and well and laughing, the way he'd been before he fell ill.

'What else did he do, Aunty Agnes?' Ginny prompted.

They talked of Edward all through tea, letting memory trail them from one pleasant moment to the next, until little Johnny put his head down on to his crumb-filled plate and fell asleep. And they talked of him all the way back to High Holborn, which they reached much later than they'd intended but feeling happier than they'd been for months. Johnny and George were carried upstairs to a bath and bed and the two girls followed behind them, hand in hand, chattering in quite their old way.

Outside their nursery door Agnes stooped to kiss them. 'We must make haste and dress for dinner,' she said.

'It's been a lovely afternoon,' Emily said.

Ginny said, 'Thank you ever so much, Aunty Agnes.'

They went cheerfully through the door and found themselves in a maelstrom.

Every single drawer and cupboard in the room had been pulled open, emptied and left askew. There were clothes everywhere; heaped on chairs, flung across the beds, lying on the floor, where they were being kicked and trampled like old rags. And the person trampling them was Maman, beautiful, chic Maman, who was running round and round the room weeping and panic-stricken with dishevelled hair and staring eyes. She was in such a terrible state that both girls stopped dead. There was a huge black travelling trunk in the middle of the room with its lid open, and Hortense was throwing things into it, haphazardly, as if she didn't know what she was doing.

'Quick! Quick!' she cried, looking round at them. 'There isn't a minute to lose. We have to be out of here by morning.'

It was staggering news. '*Out* of here?' Ginny said, stupid with shock. 'What do you mean, Maman?'

'Out of here,' her mother screamed. 'Out of the house. Away. There isn't a minute to lose.' Her face and her voice were so distorted that she was barely recognisable.

'But why?' Emily asked, trying to be reasonable.

'Don't ask! Don't ask!' her mother gasped. 'I cannot tell you. It is too dreadful. You must help me pack. If we are not gone by morning 'e will tell everyone. 'E means it. Everyone. Holy Mary, Mother of God pray for us sinners now and at the hour of our deaths. I've ordered the tickets. I 'ave done that. Yes, yes, I 'ave ordered the tickets. What else is there? *Hélas*, what will become of us?'

The two girls sent pinching signals to one another. Do as she says? Yes. This is serious.

'I'll fold. You sit by the trunk and pack,' Ginny said to her sister. 'Are you taking everything, Maman?'

'Yes, yes, everything.'

Then she means it, Ginny thought, her heart throbbing with alarm, and began to untangle the nearest heap of clothes. We really are leaving. Something awful must have happened. But what? She couldn't think of anything that would account for such a panic. But she daren't ask because Maman was now kneeling on the hearth rug saying her prayers in a gabble of Latin and French and total distress.

The two girls worked methodically, without talking, although both of them were thinking hard. Occasionally they pinched one another for reassurance, and weren't reassured in the least.

49

The gong sounded but they didn't go down to dinner.

'No, no,' their mother said. 'I could not face it. We must stay here.'

Nanny didn't come to undress them that night either. They just stayed in the room and laboured on. It grew dark and the room still wasn't clear; Maman hadn't given them any explanation.

'You must get to bed,' she said. 'I will finish. It is only the linen now, I think.' There were dark shadows under her lovely brown eyes and she looked haggard.

'Is it something we've done, Maman?' Emily asked, as she undressed.

'You?' Hortense said. 'Oh no, no, no. You must not think that, either of you. *You* 'aven't done anything. It is me. I am to blame.'

'But what . . . ?' Ginny tried.

'You must not ask. Please. I cannot tell you. It is all too dreadful.'

In the privacy of the bathroom the twins tried to guess what had happened. But they couldn't.

'She's terribly scared,' Emily said. 'So it must be something really awful.'

'Perhaps things'll be better in the morning,' Ginny hoped.

They were worse. Maman woke them at seven o'clock with the news that the trunk was gone, Nanny wouldn't be coming in to dress them, and that their breakfast would be left 'outside the door'.

'It's as if we were criminals,' Ginny said, 'in prison or something.'

It was a feeling that increased when they left the house. Two hours later, they crept down the stairs, ran through the hall and out of the front door as if they were being hunted.

'Aren't we going to say goodbye to anyone?' Emily said, as they walked briskly down the drive.

'No,' Maman said, breathlessly. 'We cannot. It is not possible. Quickly or we shall miss the bus.'

*That* was another thing, Ginny thought. Why were they

going on a bus? Why couldn't they use the car? Oh, if only Maman would tell them. But her mother's face was set as if it had been frozen and she clutched her travelling bag before her like a shield.

They caught the train to London using single tickets, which Ginny was quick to notice. And although it was a very long journey Maman hardly said a word all the way. It wasn't until they were climbing out of the carriage into a huge bewildering station called Euston that she finally began to speak. Then she told them so much and so quickly that they couldn't take it all in.

'We are going to France,' she said, shouting above the noise of the crowds and the snorting engines. 'We 'ave tickets for the overnight boat to Boulogne. We shall be better in France. It is where we belong. Now we 'ave the rest of the day to see to everything, the passport, the bank, to transfer my shares, to spend our English money. It won't be any use to us after tonight. We shall live in France where we belong. It is all arranged.'

'For ever?' Ginny asked, struggling to keep up with her in the jostling throng.

'Yes, yes. For ever. Look for a taxi, *mes petites*. There must be a rank somewhere. We must 'urry. There is so much to be done.'

She rushed them about for the rest of the day, through more traffic than they'd ever seen in their lives, to offices full of people and paper and a bank built like a cathedral. They stopped briefly for an unappetising meal in a small restaurant that smelled of dust and congealed fat. And, finally, when they were feeling too exhausted to walk another step, she bundled them into yet another taxi and took them to Victoria Station.

By now it was early evening and the suburban half of the terminus was filled with office workers streaming towards the ticket barriers and home. The sight of the multitudes at the end of such a day was so daunting that Ginny was transfixed. She and Emily stood on the pavement and clung to one another for protection. Their mother paid the taxi

51

driver, tipping him generously with the last handful of English money.

'*Eh bien*!' she said, as the taxi pulled away. '*Marchons!*'

'Are we going in *there*?' Virginia said, staring at the hordes.

'No, no, no. I told you. We are going to France. This way.'

The continental half of the station was also crowded but, to the twins' relief, there was no rush. The passengers seemed well-to-do, at ease and in command: women in fur-trimmed coats and neat cloche hats followed by porters pushing their expensive luggage on trolleys like upturned bedsteads; men in well-cut suits, wearing camel-hair overcoats over their shoulders like cloaks. A group of very young men in mackintoshes and bowler hats stood in a circle and laughed at one another in an odd barking way.

Above their heads, steam rose up to the high arch of the roof where it billowed like summer clouds. The air was spiced with the smell of soot and sulphur, and the occasional trace of an expensive perfume, new clothes and new leather. There was luggage everywhere, trunks, suitcases, battered carpet bags and packing cases of every size and description. There was even a theatrical skip standing rather grandly beside the barrier next to a cluster of grubby mail sacks.

'The very thing!' Maman said, walking her daughters towards it. 'Sit there and don't move. I 'ave to get the tickets. I shall not be long.'

They sat obediently, glad to be out of the way of the crowds, and waited, perched side by side on the rough weave of the skip, their straw bonnets and yellow summer coats daffodil-bright against the grey-green of the barrier.

# CHAPTER FOUR

When Hortense and the twins didn't appear at dinner that evening, Agnes made no comment about it. A skipped meal was only to be expected when they were all so distressed. But she missed their company very much, especially as Claud was so engrossed in the evening paper that he didn't address a word to her, from the soup to the coffee.

'I hope they'll feel better tomorrow,' she said, as she and her preoccupied husband left the table.

He was already on his way out of the room and didn't appear to hear her.

The next morning when it was past eleven and the twins still hadn't come down, Agnes sent her personal maid to the east wing to find out how they were and was astonished when the girl came running back to tell her that the entire family was gone.

'They've had their breakfast, Mrs Everdale, same as usual,' she said. 'There's the dirty things still on the tray. I think they've taken the travelling trunk. Leastways there's no sign of it. An' everything's empty. All the drawers an' the wardrobes an' everything.'

'They must have gone on holiday,' Agnes said, speaking calmly to still her own anxiety, adding, so as not to lose face, 'I expect they arranged it before – all this – and it's gone out of our minds.'

As soon as she'd dismissed her maid, she put on her summer coat and her straw hat, snatched up her cotton gloves and went down to the village to see if Miss Babbacombe knew anything about it.

Which she didn't. 'Very rum!' the governess said. 'I've never known them to go off anywhere without letting us know. You'd have thought Virginia would have told us at the very least. And yet they've taken a trunk, you say.'

'Apparently.'

'Then they'll have gone a distance.'

'But where?'

'France,' Miss Babbacombe said. 'Bound to be. Back to her family. Best place when you're grieving.'

Agnes doubted it. 'I'm not even sure she's got a family,' she said. 'Edward told me once she came from a farm, I remember that, but I've never known her to speak about it. In fact, between you and me, Miss Babbacombe, I got the impression she was an orphan. Oh dear! It *is* worrying.'

'Tell you what,' Miss Babbacombe suggested. 'Why don't we go in to Wolverhampton and ask at the station. If they've caught a train, someone there might have seen them. That'd settle it.'

One of the porters remembered. 'Two young 'uns,' he said. 'Dressed in yellow. Took the London train, jest afore nine.'

'Wasn't I right?' Miss Babbacombe said. 'They'll be halfway to France by now.'

'No,' Agnes said. 'They couldn't have caught the boat train this morning. They wouldn't have got there in time. If that *is* where they're going it'll have to be tonight.'

'Then you've got time to go after them,' Miss Babbacombe said, ever practical.

'Oh I couldn't do that,' Agnes said. 'They might not . . . I mean, it might upset them. I don't know what sort of state they're in. Besides I'd be missed. It wouldn't be . . . Oh dear, Miss Babbacombe, it's all very difficult.'

'Would you like *me* to do it? I'd be very discreet.'

'*Would* you Miss Babbacombe? That *would* be kind.'

'Well as we're here,' Miss Babbacombe said.

So a day return to London was bought there and then and Miss Babbacombe set out on her errand, handbag clutched against her bosom and her doll's chin tenaciously set. During the journey she had time to doubt the wisdom of her offer, and wondered whether it would turn out to be a wild-goose chase. But when she reached Victoria and discovered that the boat train to Boulogne was due to leave in three-quarters of an hour, she strode through into the continental half of the station, determined to do what she could.

Almost the first thing that caught her eye among the sober greys and greens of the station was the bright daffodil-yellow of the twins' summer coats. And there they were sitting on a large theatrical skip right beside the ticket barrier.

'Well here's a thing!' she said, beaming with relief to see them. 'What are you doing here? Off on your hols?' And was delighted when their funny little faces lit up at the sight and sound of her.

'No,' Emily said. 'We don't think so. We really don't know. Do we, Ginny? Maman says we're going to France for ever.'

'Where is she?' Miss Babbacombe asked, looking round for her.

'She's queuing up for tickets,' Ginny said. 'She's been ages. I went round the corner to see and it's ever such a long queue.'

'Tell me where you're going,' Miss Babbacombe encouraged.

They couldn't tell her that, but the rest of their story came tumbling out; how Maman was upset and how they'd run away and how they didn't know what was going on.

'Maman says we're not to see anyone or talk to anyone,' Ginny confided, when the tale was told. 'I don't think we're even supposed to be talking to you.'

Miss Babbacombe was thinking hard. Would it be sensible to wait for Hortense and talk to her? No, she decided, better not. If she's made up her mind, it's not *my* business to try and change it. Discretion being the better part of valour. 'If that's the case,' she said, making a joke, 'I'd better cut off and catch my train before she comes back and catches me at it. Send me a letter when you get there, eh, and let me know you've arrived in good order.'

'But we don't know where you live,' Ginny said.

'The Post Office, Wittick,' Miss Babbacombe said. 'That's easy enough, isn't it? Goodbye, my dears. Take care of yourselves. I'll see you when you come home.'

'D'you think we ever will come home?' Emily asked forlornly.

' 'Course,' Miss Babbacombe said, assuming a cheerfulness she didn't feel. 'Bound to.' And she got out of the station as quickly as she could before her feelings gave her away.

Something was very wrong. There was no doubt about that. Mrs Holborn had always been given to impulsive decisions but there had always been a reason for them, and she'd never done anything quite as drastic as this. It simply didn't make sense to be leaving the country for good. Not just when they were beginning to get over Mr Edward's death and the girls were doing so well at their lessons. Oh no! she thought. There's been mischief here or my name's not Felicity Babbacombe.

By the time she got back to Wittick it was late at night and spitting with rain, but she climbed the hill to High Holborn to report to Mrs Everdale because she knew she'd be waiting up.

Too anxious to go to bed, Agnes had been sitting in the library, pretending to read. Her anxiety wasn't stilled by Miss Babbacombe's news. But she couldn't bring herself to agree that mischief had been made.

'It's grief,' she said, taking the most charitable view. 'That's what it must be. Grief. They say it makes people do all sorts of strange things. Poor Hortense. I wish she'd talked to me instead of running away. And now they're crossing the Channel and the wireless says there is going to be a storm. Oh dear, I wonder how they'll all get on. I do hope they'll be all right.'

It was a terrible crossing, dark and cold and very rough, every bit as bad as Agnes feared. Both the twins were seasick and sleep was completely impossible. By the time they stumbled down the gangplank in the grey light of a squally morning and took their first unsteady steps into the port of Boulogne, they were chilled to the bone and green with fatigue and sickness.

'We will find a café,' Hortense comforted, taking Emily by the hand. 'A good strong cup of French coffee, a little breakfast and we shall all be restored. You'll see. We are in France now, my little ones. Think of that. In France, among our own people where we belong. Now we shall have nothing to fear, I promise you. Oh, my darlings, you can't imagine how happy I am to be home at last. I shall never be a foreigner again.' She was quite girlish with relief and happiness.

'It's all very well for her,' Ginny whispered, out of earshot. '*She's* French. She belongs here. She seems to forget we're English and we don't.'

'It does smell funny,' Emily said. 'There's a lot of fish.'

'Crates of it. We're on a quay.'

'Horses,' Emily went on. 'Men sweating. Something burning, sort of sharp and bitter.'

'That's their cigarettes. I think it smells dangerous. And foreign.'

'What does it look like?'

'Beastly. Not a bit like England.'

Which was true enough, for the quay was full of hefty porters who were as unlike their quieter English counterparts as it was possible to be. They were dressed like pirates in serge trousers and dark blue jerseys made of oiled wool, with knitted skullcaps on their heads and those pungent cigarettes dangling from their lips. They shouted and swore at one another in a clipped French that neither of the girls could understand. Some of them were man-handling trunks or rolling barrels down the gangplanks, and some, grunting under the weight, were carrying cases on hooks suspended from their belts while they shouldered the larger luggage.

There was a train standing on the quayside with its engine steaming as if it were at a station and looking most peculiar because there was no platform beside it. The doors were so high above the ground that the passengers, who were mostly women dressed in old-fashioned black clothes, were forced to haul one another up into the carriage in a most undignified way, with much shrieking and giggling and protestation. Oh, a very foreign place.

'Coffee,' Maman said again, leading them across the tracks and out into the streets. 'Let us see what we can find.'

They found a café called *Boulanger de Boulogne*. A tall narrow building squashed between two rather seedy-looking tenements, but brightly lit in that dull morning, it sported a smart blue and white shop-blind and exuded a most appetising smell of freshly ground coffee.

Maman said it would do and marched them through the door into a small room crowded with furniture and large potted plants. There was a bow-fronted bar in one corner and standing behind it, resting her considerable bosom on the counter, was a plump and amiable lady shaped like a cottage loaf. She looked up at their entry and smiled at them.

'*M'dame?*' she said.

'Do you serve *petit déjeuner?*' Maman said.

To the twins' relief the woman spoke French slowly and very clearly. '*Mais oui.* For three?' She moved slowly, too, sailing through the bead curtain that hung across the open doorway beside the bar, like an ocean liner breasting the spray.

'If she's Madame Boulanger,' Ginny said to Emily, speaking in English for privacy, 'she's jolly well named. She looks like Mrs Bun the baker's wife in *Happy Families.*'

'She's got stays on,' Emily observed. 'I could hear them creaking. What's this place like?'

'It's better than the quay,' Ginny admitted. 'I think it's a sort of pub. There's a bar in the corner with a mirror behind it and lots and lots of bottles.'

'Are we the only ones here?'

'Yes.'

'I thought so. There's a cat, though, isn't there?'

'Is there?' Maman said, looking round for it.

'Yes. It was purring.'

It was lying in a furry heap on the counter with its eyes shut, a large rather shaggy-looking tabby and as fat as its owner.

'Could we go and stroke it, Maman?' Emily asked.

The cat was still being rapturously petted when Madame Boulanger reappeared through the bead curtain with a tray piled with cups and plates, a basket full of chunks of very crisp bread and a jug steaming with coffee.

'She is called Minouche,' she said to the twins. 'Lazy old thing. I brought her to catch mice, but you see how it is, she does nothing except sleep. Where are the mice, Minouche? Tell me that.'

The cat opened the slit of one eye and looked at her pityingly.

'What can one do?' Madame asked the twins as she creaked off towards their table. 'She rules the household. Such an animal. We cat-lovers are putty in their hands.'

She was so friendly that the two girls felt a bit better and the smell of the coffee made them realise that they were hungry. They followed her back to the table.

'You have just arrived, Madame?' their new friend asked, as she set the tray down on the table and began to unload it. 'Warm milk, sugar, butter. You have come from the ferry, *n'est-ce pas?*'

She was obviously the sort of woman you confided in. Within seconds she and Maman were gossiping as though they'd known one another all their lives; remembering the war, commiserating with one another on their widowhood, and comparing the merits of their dead husbands. Monsieur Boulanger had died in the trenches 'of gas gangrene, poor man'.

'Such suffering,' Madame Boulanger said, returning to her counter, 'and all for what? That's what I should like to know. Do the generals suffer in these wars? Never! Do the politicians lose their lives? Unimaginable! It is the likes of you and me, Madame, who are left to pick up the pieces.' She stretched out her hand for the dishcloth to mop a damp patch on the counter, found the cat and absent-mindedly used that instead.

Ginny watched with amazement, especially as the cat didn't seem to mind and went straight back to sleep again

59

afterwards. How extraordinary! What would this Madame Boulanger do next?

What she did was to arrange their lives for them.

It didn't take her long to discover that Hortense had come to France to look for work, that she spoke English and that she was a good cook.

'Go to Le Touquet, Madame, if that is the case,' she advised. 'The playground of the English milords. It is just the place for you. Would your daughters like more bread?'

By the time they'd drunk all her coffee, eaten a second basketful of her crusty bread and scraped the last of her delicately pale butter from its little pot, the bar was besieged by porters and fishermen and everything had been settled. They were going to rent Madame's 'nice front bedroom' until their trunk had arrived and Maman had found a job; when the porters had been served Madame would show 'les petites' upstairs and they could have a 'nice little nap'. Maman was going to Le Touquet that very instant.

They spent the next three days with Madame and Minouche. At night they felt homesick for High Holborn, but during the day they served at table to help Madame, shopped for fish at the quayside for themselves and Minouche, and were too busy to be unhappy. They grew accustomed to the dialect being spoken around them, accepting that their names would only be pronounced the French way, as Vair-gin-ee and Ai-me-lee, in short gradually learning how to be French children in a busy French town. They hung their mattresses out of the window every morning to give them an airing. They went for the baguettes and they learnt how to make coffee.

'Such good wives you will be,' Madame said.

'Will we?' Virginia asked.

'Why not ma petite?'

'Maman doesn't want us to get married,' Emily said.

'Well no, not at the moment, naturally, of course not,' Madame said. 'But later, when the time is right. There is a time for everything, you understand.'

'Do you really think there will be a time for *me* to get married?' Emily said. 'Being blind?'

Madame snorted. 'So what is being blind?' she said. 'You see as well as the next child, in your own way, *ma petite*. Such hearing! I never knew the like of it. No, no, why should you be different? Depend on it, you will both marry. Love will find you. Nothing is more certain. When the time is right and if you are prepared to catch the tide.'

That intrigued them both. 'How will we know how to do that?' Ginny asked.

'Oh you will know,' Madame assured them. 'It is like everything else in life, love, marriage, work. You simply have to catch the tide. That is the trick of it. Catch the tide and be happy while you can, that's what I say. You're a long time in the grave. Did you ever taste such shrimps? We have the best shellfish in the Pas de Calais.'

On the third afternoon they gave Minouche a garlic pill to cure her of worms and both got scratched for their pains. It was a very different life from the pampered existence they'd had in High Holborn but, foreign though it was, they enjoyed it more each day. It was a disappointment when Maman arrived back in the café that evening to tell them that she'd found a job. They were off to Le Touquet the next morning.

'From now on,' she said, as the girls undressed for bed, 'I shall revert to my maiden name and we shall all call ourselves Lisieux, not Holborn. We shall be a French family. It will be safer and more practical.'

Why will it be safer? Ginny thought. Why does she make us think we're in danger? In danger of what? But she didn't feel she could ask.

'We shall do well enough, if we work hard,' Maman was saying. 'You will help me, of course, when you're not at school. But you mustn't talk English where anyone can hear you. If people ask about your father you can say he was a soldier killed by the war. On no account tell them he was English. All that is in the past. You must promise me never to talk of it to anyone. Do you promise?'

61

They didn't understand why she should be giving them such orders but they answered dutifully. 'Yes Maman.'

'Good girls. And no talk of Wolverhampton or High Holborn, ever. You must put all that out of your minds completely.'

'Aren't we going to write home?' Emily asked. The bleakness she'd felt when they walked away from their lovely house had come back, making her ache with homesickness. It was bad enough to think they were never going to see Aunty Agnes and the boys and Grandfather again, but surely they were going to write.

'No!' Maman said crossly. 'How many more times have I got to tell you? We've left all that behind us. You are not to write any letters at all. Not to anyone. It would be far too dangerous. Nobody is to know where we are. You must forget England. That part of your lives is over.' Then with an abrupt change of mood and tone, 'Now you must get to bed. We've got a long day ahead of us tomorrow.'

So their pleasant interlude with Madame Boulanger was over.

'Poor old Babbers,' Emily said, when their mother had turned down the gaslight and left the room. 'She'll be waiting for a letter.'

'Yes.'

'And now we can't write one.'

'Well,' Ginny said into the darkness. 'I know we can't write a *letter* because we've promised not to and because of honour your father and mother and everything, but we could send a postcard.'

Emily was doubtful. 'We couldn't. Could we?'

'It's not like a letter. You don't put your address on a postcard. It's like saying hello, really. A sort of message, only she wouldn't know where we are.'

'Oh, Ginny!' Emily said, caught between admiration and a guilty conscience. 'Would you have to confess it?'

'No,' Ginny said firmly. 'Because it wouldn't be a sin. A sin would be if I wrote a letter. That would be disobedience, because Maman said we weren't to. She didn't say anything about postcards.'

'I think it's the same,' Emily worried.

But her sister was determined. 'I don't,' she said. 'We'll get one tomorrow on our way to the station. When Maman is buying the tickets. I've got enough money left over from when we bought the fish and Madame said we could keep the change.'

They chose the prettiest postcard they could find, a pastel drawing of the harbour, with the sea coloured a lovely pale blue and the harbour walls the palest yellow. While Maman was still in the ticket office, Ginny wrote on the back in her best handwriting, '*We are in Boulogne. We are all well. The weather is very good. Very much love, Virginia and Emily.*'

But when they'd committed it to the post and it was out of their hands and gone, they were both assailed by such dreadful homesickness that it made them want to cry.

Emily was very tearful. 'Why did we have to leave High Holborn?' she grieved. 'It was so lovely there. Why did we, Ginny? It doesn't make sense.'

It didn't make sense to their grandfather, either.

'Gone!' he said. 'What d'you mean "gone"? They can't have gone. Don't talk nonsense.' His trip to South America had been more fatiguing than he'd expected and what was worse it hadn't produced anywhere near enough orders. 'Where have they gone?'

'France, I believe,' Claud Everdale told him. 'Wasn't that right, Agnes?'

'Bloody ridiculous,' the old man said. 'Sorry Agnes, but really! What do they want to go and do a thing like that for?'

'I'm sure I couldn't say,' Claud said.

'Good God, boy, you ought to be able to say. I left you in charge. You should have stopped them.'

'I felt I ought to respect their grief,' his son-in-law said piously.

The expression on his face made Agnes feel irritable. He's putting this on, she thought, and she realised that she was feeling ashamed of him and angry with him. Then she was ashamed of herself for thinking ill of her husband and did her best to cover up for both of them.

'It was a terrible surprise to all of us,' she said, trying to suggest with her eyes that they ought to retire into the morning room, out of earshot of the servants. 'And then not writing . . .'

'Haven't they written?' her father said.

'Not so much as a word,' his daughter said, leading him purposefully by the arm. 'They sent a postcard to Miss Babbacombe from Boulogne, but we haven't heard a thing. I can't understand it. Bad enough leaving all of a sudden without saying anything, but then not to write . . .'

'Bloody ungrateful,' Mr Holborn said tetchily. 'After all we've done for them.'

Agnes began to fear she might have been too critical of her poor sister-in-law, too, and tried to make amends. 'Of course, it could have been grief, as Claud says. That would only be natural. I daresay that was what it was . . .'

Neither of the men were listening to her. Claud asked, 'How was the trip, Father-in-law?'

Grumbling, her father settled himself into his favourite armchair.

'Just as well I've got some good news for you then,' Claud said, sitting opposite him.

'Orders?'

'As near as, damn it. I've found a use for our spare nitrates.'

The old man was interested, narrowing his eyes, and reaching in his pocket for a cigar. 'Have you now?'

'I was talking to Catherside. Of Benbow and Richardson's. You remember him. Seems they've found a way to convert their nitrates into agricultural fertiliser. Farmers are crying out for nitrates, apparently. The land's drained of 'em. Normally they have to put 'em back by growing beans or some such, which takes a year with reduced profits. Now we can do it for 'em in a matter of hours, and make a handsome profit on the transaction.'

'Have a cigar,' Mr Holborn said. 'This sounds promising. We'll have Mr Catherside to dinner.'

Business, Agnes though sadly, as she left the room. There was no point in staying there with them. They wouldn't talk to *her* any more. They wouldn't even notice her. She realised yet again how lonely she was without Hortense and the twins, and wondered, for the hundredth time, what *could* have become of them. They will write to me soon, she thought. It wasn't natural just to disappear.

But the only one to write a letter was her husband and that was a summary dismissal to Miss Babbacombe.

'Mrs Holborn has left the country,' he wrote. 'She wished the girls to further their education in France, I believe. That being so, I'm afraid we shall have no further need of your services. Your salary will be honoured until the end of August and I shall be happy to furnish any references you might require. Can you have the schoolroom cleared by the end of this Friday afternoon?'

Agnes was very surprised to find Miss Babbacombe clearing the schoolroom on that Friday afternoon and angry when she read her husband's letter. It wasn't kind to dismiss their governess like that, neither was it wise when they didn't know when the girls were coming back. But, of course, she didn't say anything.

'When you've finished, perhaps you'll stay and take tea with me?' she suggested.

'Very kind of you, Mrs Everdale,' Miss Babbacombe said. 'Yes, I'd be glad to.'

'I suppose you haven't heard from the twins again?' Agnes asked, as she poured the tea.

'No. Afraid not.'

'Neither have we,' Agnes said sadly. 'I *don't* understand it.'

'It's a mystery,' Miss Babbacombe said, accepting her cup.

'You'll tell me if you do hear?'

'Directly. You have my word.'

'Perhaps you would like to come to tea next Friday. We might *both* have heard by then.'

But the second postcard didn't arrive until their sixth

Friday tea and, by then, Miss Babbacombe had a new job at the village school and Agnes was beginning to give up hope of ever hearing from her nieces again.

'It says they've been in Le Touquet and now they're moving on to somewhere else,' Miss Babbacombe reported, handing the postcard across the table.

'But no address,' Agnes said. 'It's as if they don't want us to know where they are.'

'I'm sure that's not true,' Miss Babbacombe tried to comfort. 'But it's a mystery, certainly. Time will tell.'

But time merely passed and didn't tell them anything very much. Certainly nothing to explain the mystery. More postcards arrived at very irregular intervals but they contained only snippets of information and they never gave an address.

*'I have started school. They are very stern. I miss you very much. It is lonely here.'*

*'Happy Christmas, Miss Babbacombe. Christmas in France isn't the same. We still have our silver crosses.'*

*'We are in Paris Plage this summer working for a doctor. Maman has been ill but is better now.'*

*'We have been to our first communion. We wore our silver crosses. It was a beautiful service but I really don't feel any different and I should, shouldn't I?'*

*'We are in Chartres. There is a beautiful cathedral here. You would like it.'*

*'This is our third Christmas in France. I am learning to use a typewriter for when I leave school in July. We are well and still wear our silver crosses. Do you remember that birthday?'*

The postmarks told a story of constant change and travel. Le Touquet, Etaples, Hardelot, Montreuil, Beauvais, back to Le Touquet again, Abbeville. Sometimes, Virginia gave a brief explanation of the latest move: *'Maman was upset'*; *'Maman saw an English lady she knew so we had to leave'*; *'Somebody said something and it gave Maman her nerves. We don't know what it was.'*

Then, in October 1932, a plain card arrived, postmarked Chartres, and containing some alarming news. *'Maman has*

66

lost all her money. She says her stocks are not worth the paper they are printed on. She has been quite ill with the worry of it, but Em and I are well and have nursed her. Now we are all working in a hotel, because we cannot afford a winter rent if we are not working. It is very hard work but perhaps it will not be for very long. We miss you very, very much and wish we could see you again, if only for a few minutes. Life is very hard here. We still have our silver crosses. Love from Virginia and Emily.'

'Now,' Miss Babbacombe said to Agnes as she put the card in her album along with all the others, 'perhaps they'll stop all this nonsense and come back to England where they belong. It's high time.'

But they didn't. And what was even worse, they didn't send any more postcards.

Christmas came and went without a word. Miss Babbacombe started a new term at the village school. The winter continued. And there was still no news.

'It'll be different come the Spring,' Miss Babbacombe said, to cheer them both up. 'Things come to life again in the Spring. They'll write then. You'll see.'

But she didn't convince Agnes. 'It's nearly seven years now since they all went away,' she said. 'I don't think we shall ever see them again.'

'Never say die, my dear,' Miss Babbacombe advised. 'They've kept their silver crosses.'

'I don't see what difference that makes,' Agnes said sadly.

'They're an omen,' Miss Babbacombe said, nodding her head wisely. 'That's what they are. That's why they write about them so often. They're a good omen. You see if I'm not right.'

# CHAPTER FIVE

Spring was a long time coming in 1933. Even when April was a mere four days away, the March winds still howled like demons round the Elizabethan chimneys of High Holborn. The gardens were as cold as the sky, the yew trees black in the wild air, the long lawns chilled colourless, the emerging daffodils like rows of wicked spikes in the clammy beds.

Old Mr Holborn, confined to his bed after an unaccountable fainting fit, shifted irritably against his pillows and glared at the sky because he was too cross to look at his old friend Doctor Stimson.

'I can't do that,' he said. 'Not with all this business in Germany. Have you seen the papers? Herr Hitler's declared a Third Reich. It's all over the front page.' He picked up the morning paper from his bedside table and shook it at the doctor. 'Look at it! Versailles has been shot to pieces. "TREATY OF VERSAILLES ATTACKED." You see? "HITLER JAILS OPPOSITION." "Thanks to the new Enabling Bill Herr Adolf Hitler, the new Chancellor of Germany may now rule by decree." He can do what he likes. There's nothing to stop him. He'll have an army before we can say "Boo!" And an air force, too. It'll mean war, Harry. Sooner or later it'll mean war. Imagine the trade it'll bring to Holborn's. We shall be working night and day like we did last time.' His eyes were bright with avarice at the thought of it.

'Then let somebody else do it,' the doctor said.

'There isn't anybody else.'

'Your son-in-law?'

Mr Holborn snorted. 'He wouldn't know where to begin.'

'You've got a weak heart, old boy,' Doctor Stimson warned. 'Stokes-Adam syndrome. Probably a result of that bout of rheumatic fever last November. It's left a weakness. I mean what I say. You ought to go abroad until the summer and give yourself a chance to recover. I told you that in November. Try the Canaries.'

'Not with a war just round the corner,' his patient insisted, thinking of the profits he could make. 'Oh come on, Harry. I can't stop now. This could be the biggest thing that's ever happened to G. S. Holborn's. That Hitler feller'll re-arm in millions. He means business. Can't you give me a bottle of jollop? That's all I need. A pick-me-up or something.'

'There's no pick-me-up for a weak heart. I'm serious, George. You don't want heart failure, do you?'

'It won't come to that,' his patient growled. 'I fell over, that's all. If I hadn't hit my head on the sideboard going down, you'd never have been called out. I could have got up, walked away, no one a penny wiser.'

'You had a fit,' the doctor told him implacably. 'You were unconscious. Another one could kill you.'

'Bosh!'

'Well, don't say I didn't warn you. If you won't go abroad I can't make you. At least try and take things easy for a week or two.'

'With all this going on?'

The doctor closed his eyes, and then his case, and made for the door, sighing his displeasure at his old friend's obstinacy.

'Oh, very well, you old bully,' George Holborn said. 'I'll stay off work till the end of the week. How will that be?'

'Insufficient.'

'I can't do more.'

'Then if I were you,' the doctor said wryly, 'I should make my will.'

It was a sobering thought for such an exciting time, but old Mr Holborn had the courage of the single-minded, so he braced himself to think it. If his heart really was weak he would have to grab as much business as he could while he still had the strength and the orders were coming. But he had to face facts. He hadn't changed his will since the one he'd had drawn up when Edward was alive. The firm was going to expand again, there was no doubt about that, so it ought to be tied up legally and left in good hands. Just in case. Whose good hands was the problem. His managers were trustworthy, but they weren't family and, annoying though it was to have to admit it, his family was useless; Claud too ambitious, Agnes too feeble, the boys too young. He was pondering the problem and a long way from a solution when Claud and Agnes arrived to see how he was.

Agnes was upset by what the doctor had just told her. 'Heart failure!' she scorned, trying to quash her alarm with righteous indignation. 'The very idea! You're as strong as an ox. You always have been. Why, Mummy used to say you were the strongest man she'd ever known.'

'I'm seventy-five,' her father said. 'And very human, let me tell you.' Her attitude was making it easier for him to face the truth. 'I'm not what I was.'

'He could be wrong,' Agnes insisted, her plain face taut with distress. 'Perhaps you ought to have a second opinion.' She couldn't bear the thought of her father dying. She'd be on her own with Claud all the time, except when the boys were home from school, and that would be really dreadful. 'He could have made a mistake.'

'No, he hasn't,' her father said. 'He's a good man. I think he's got it bang to rights.'

'Perhaps you ought to hand the business over to me,' Claud suggested, trying not to look too hopeful. 'Let me take the weight off your shoulders, eh?'

And the power, and the money, Mr Holborn thought. Oh yes. You'd like that, wouldn't you, Mr Grab-it-all. 'I'm not *that* bad Claud,' he joked. 'I'm good for a few more years yet. But I tell you what I'll do.'

'Yes,' his son-in-law encouraged, still hopeful.

'I'll make a new will. Dispose of my worldly goods, see the firm's in good hands, that sort of thing.'

'An excellent idea,' Claud said. There was only one person the old man could possibly leave the business to, and he was that person.

Agnes watched him preening himself and was so irritated by his smug expression that she stopped feeling anxious about her father and recovered her composure. It was odd how her annoyance at Claud's hypocrisy renewed her strength. She'd noticed it several times during the last few months.

'Yes,' she said, walking over to the window. 'That makes good business sense. I'll phone Hedgethorn and Crabbit, shall I?'

'I'd use a local firm, if I were you,' Claud said, on his way out of the room. 'Hedgethorn and Crabbit are all very well but they do charge London prices.' But when his father-in-law scowled at him, he added lightly, 'However, it's your will.'

'Quite right,' Mr Holborn said when the door was shut. 'It is. You phone 'em up, Agnes. Tell 'em to send old Horace Crabbit down. He's the man.'

'Have you thought who you'll leave the firm to?' Agnes asked.

He was surprised at such a direct question. 'Well, not Claud,' he said. 'You can depend on that. A seat on the board's quite enough for him. And I only gave him that because of the deal he pulled off over the nitrate fertilisers. To tell you the truth I'm not sure, really. The boys probably, when they're old enough, with you as Queen Regent meantime. How would that be?'

'Difficult,' Agnes admitted.

'Well, I can't see what else to do.'

'Have you ever thought of finding the twins?'

'Constantly. Whenever I remember Edward. Why?'

His questioning made Agnes dither. 'Well . . . It's only just that I was thinking . . . What I mean to say is it might be . . . I mean it seemed to me . . .'

'Oh come on, Aggie,' her father said. 'Spit it out.'

'Well,' she said. 'It might be an idea to leave everything to all four of your grandchildren, my boys *and* the twins. If you did that you could put an advertisement in the paper for them. "They will hear something to their advantage" sort of thing.'

71

'But we don't know where they are. They could be anywhere.'

'Actually,' Agnes said, 'they're in France. We don't know exactly where they are, but we usually know where they've been. Ginny sends postcards to Miss Babbacombe.'

'You never told me that.'

Agnes felt embarrassed. 'We didn't know whether you'd want us to,' she said. 'You never spoke about them.'

'Well, no. But that's as may be. You might have known I'd want to know about any letters.'

'They weren't letters. They were just postcards.'

'Did you write back?'

'We couldn't. We never had an address.'

'Extraordinary,' the old man said. 'And now you want me to make a will to tempt them home. Is that it?'

'I thought it would be an idea.'

'It would halve your sons' portion,' Mr Holborn pointed out.

'Yes,' she agreed seriously. 'It would. But if you were to do it, at least it would be fair, wouldn't it? After all, they *are* Edward's children. They ought to inherit.'

'You're a good woman, Agnes,' Mr Holborn said affectionately, and he wondered yet again how she'd ever come to fall for such a pip squeak as Claud. 'You've got a good heart. Better than mine, eh?'

But his joke fell flat. Now that she'd made her suggestion she was anxious to keep news of it from Claud. 'You could do it sort of privately,' she worried. 'Couldn't you, Father? I mean there wouldn't be any need to tell anyone else, would there?'

'Leave it to me,' her father said. 'It'll be our secret.'

Two days later he drew up his will. It was, as Horace Crabbit was happy to tell him, a masterpiece.

*'I leave and bequeath my estate, in toto, to my four grandchildren, my grandsons, George Norman Everdale and John Arthur Everdale of this address, and my granddaughters,*

*Virginia Holborn and Emily Holborn, late of High Holborn, presently residing at a place unknown to me somewhere in France.*

   *'Cognisant of the fact that my grandsons are not yet of age and that it may take considerable time to trace the whereabouts of my granddaughters, I hereby give instructions that the search be continued for four years after my death and its initial institution, during which time the Company is to be administered in trust by my son-in-law, Claud James Everdale, and his wife, my daughter, Agnes Everdale, in conjunction with a board of management consisting of my works manager, Mr Jack Pennyfield, my chief engineer, Mr Roger Smith, the company secretary, Mr Thomas Reinhart, and Claud and Agnes Everdale, all with equal voting rights. During this time, neither the house, nor the company, nor any part of the estate is to be sold or altered in any way. If, at the end of four years, or by the majority of my younger grandson, whichever is the later, my granddaughters are not discovered, the estate is to pass, in toto, to my grandsons.'*

   'There's only one thing I regret about this,' the old man said.
   'And what's that?' Mr Crabbit asked, wiping his pen.
   'I shan't be here to see Claud's face when it's read.'
   'Come back and haunt us just for the day,' Mr Crabbit suggested.
   'If I can find out how it's done, I will.'
   'Well, if anyone can find out how it's done,' Mr Crabbit chuckled, 'you'll be the man.'
   So the will was signed and witnessed by Agnes Everdale and Horace Crabbit and the two men parted in high good humour, Mr Holborn to the afternoon rest he swore he didn't need, and Mr Crabbit to Wolverhampton station and the journey back to town. He couldn't wait to break his good news to Mr Hedgethorn.

Crabbit and Hedgethorn, Solicitors, had their offices in Little Medlar Yard, a small dark cul-de-sac leading north out of the Strand in London. Lined by the blackened façades of three Georgian terraces that had once been the townhouses of various up-and-coming merchantmen, it didn't, at first sight, look impressive. Nowadays the houses were used in a more discreet fashion by several well-established solicitors, among whom Messrs Hedgethorn and Crabbit were two of the more prestigious. Their clients might be few in number but they were mostly wealthy industrialists who had managed to hold their own during the depression, and, in addition to the trade they provided, the rash of bankruptcies that had spread through the City during the last few years had brought the firm a great deal of extra (and delicate) work. So much, in fact, that Mr Hedgethorn was planning to expand into a second storey and had let it be known that the firm was prepared to take on another articled clerk.

That afternoon, while Mr Crabbit was in Wolverhampton, he'd been interviewing the resulting candidates and now they were sitting in a row in the outer office waiting to be told their fate. Mr Crabbit walked right past them on his way into the inner sanctum.

'Read that,' he said, tossing the will on to the mound of paper on his colleague's desk, 'and tell me if you don't think it's the prettiest piece of business I've done in a long while.'

Mr Hedgethorn was impressed. 'There's a deal of work in it,' he said, when he'd read it. 'Yes indeed. It's most satisfactory. Are we to institute the search *instanta*?'

'We can make an unofficial start as soon as we are given an address,' Mr Crabbit told him. 'The old boy's waiting for somebody to write. Officially, of course, it doesn't begin until his death. Either way we shall have plenty to keep us occupied.'

'Excellent,' Mr Hedgethorn said, patting the will. He always patted papers when he was pleased with the contents. But then he frowned. 'Now what are we to do about our new clerk?'

Mr Crabbit was lighting a cigar. 'Haven't you chosen one?' he asked, his bushy eyebrows twitching against smoke and incredulity. 'I thought the interviews were this afternoon.'

'They were,' Mr Hedgethorn said. 'In point of fact they still are. They're waiting in the inner office.'

'So they are,' Mr Crabbit remembered. 'I passed them on my way in. Well then, high time you made your mind up.'

'It's all very well for you to take that tone,' Mr Hedgethorn complained. 'I've whittled it down to two but it's a very difficult choice. Mr Bond has all the right credentials, eighteen, good school, family backing, that sort of thing, and of course he's available now, but Mr Commoner has the sharper mind. There's no gainsaying that. Grammar school, of course, and only sixteen, but they expect excellent results of him in the Lower School examinations. I can't help feeling we'd be missing an opportunity if we passed him over.'

The two men surveyed the waiting candidates in the deserted room through the frosted glass of the inner office, six young men in their best suits sitting on a row of chairs against the wall looking ill-at-ease. The gaslight had been lit, but Mr Grossman and old Mr Thomas had long since gone home and the office had been tidied for the night, all files put away, out-trays empty, covers over the typewriters.

'Poor kids,' Mr Crabbit said. 'Put 'em out of their misery. Which one's Mr Bond?'

'The dark one at the end. The one with the good suit.'

'Ah yes. And Mr Commoner?'

'The fair boy next to him.'

'He's tall enough!'

And he certainly was. For even though he was only just sixteen, Charlie Commoner was over six feet in his grey socks, his cheap business suit and his uncomfortable paper collar, skinny and pale, like a young plant deprived of sunlight. His hair was so very fair that the highlights in it shone like white water, and his skin had the translucent pallor of bone china. He looked industrious and had a text book on his lap which he was studying with an air of intense concentration that Mr Hedgethorn found pleasing.

'It's such a difficult decision,' he said. 'I don't know which of the two to choose.'

'Then take them both,' Mr Crabbit advised. His success at High Holborn had put him into an extravagant mood.

'Would we have the work to warrant it?' Mr Hedgethorn worried.

Mr Crabbit patted Mr Holborn's last will and testament. 'Yes,' he said.

He might not have made quite such a rapid decision had he known that Charlie Commoner wasn't actually studying anything at all. His eyes were simply resting on the book in front of him. Inside his head he was happily and heroically occupied in one of his daydreams.

He was much given to daydreams, which were usually the kind of thing he saw at the pictures every Saturday night. At that moment he was rescuing a damsel in distress. She was locked up in a dreadful dungeon somewhere in deepest Africa where he had been sent by her distraught father, with the passionate plea, 'Find my daughter! Bring her back to me safe and well.'

'Trust me!' he cried, buckling on his trusty sword. The villains leapt at him, rapiers at the ready, snarling and showing their teeth like Basil Rathbone, and one hand nonchalantly on his hip *à la* Douglas Fairbanks he parried their attacks. The damsel watched from the gallery, her blue eyes wide with alarm and her long blonde plaits swaying across her pretty tip-tilted breasts. (All his heroines had long blonde hair and pretty tip-tilted breasts.)

'Never fear!' he called to her, smiling encouragement. And the damsel called back . . .

'Ah – um – gentlemen. Thank you for attending this interview this afternoon. Mr Crabbit and I will be conferring together and I will let you know the result of our deliberations in due course. Thank you very much.'

It took Mr Commoner quite an effort of will to drag himself away from the delights of the rescue. He closed his book, nodded politely at Mr Hedgethorn and stood up, stretching himself to his full height.

Looking up at him Mr Hedgethorn was surprised to see what fine eyes the young man had. Large and almond-shaped, and a rich, dark, warm speckled grey that reminded the solicitor of sealskin, they were fringed by thick lashes and arched over by sleek eyebrows. He would have called them passionate eyes, if the words hadn't been totally inappropriate for an articled clerk. They were really rather disquieting. And as the young man went on looking straight at him, holding his gaze quite steadily, he realised that the most disquieting thing about those eyes was that they seemed to be smiling, even though the rest of the young man's face was politely composed. But no, that couldn't be right. No applicant would ever smile at a senior solicitor and certainly not when he'd just been interviewed. Some trick of the light, doubtless.

'That will be all,' he said. And watched with relief as they all trooped through the door.

'What a sell!' Jack Bond said, as he and Charlie walked out into Medlar Yard. 'They might have told us.'

'Perhaps they haven't made up their minds,' Charlie said.

' 'Course they have,' Jack said, adjusting his hat. 'They just like to keep you waiting that's all. It's the way they go on.'

And he was right. The decision *had* been made as they were both to hear three days later. And, as is so often the case with important decisions, it was to provoke a second. But as this one was worried about in a terraced house in Abbeville Road in Clapham, neither of the two solicitors were ever to hear anything about it. It was a far-reaching decision all the same.

# CHAPTER SIX

Charlie Commoner was an only child. Born just after Christmas in 1916, while his father was away in France fighting in the trenches, he had spent the first two years of his life alone with his mother in a two-roomed flat over a greengrocer's shop in the Balham High Road.

His father had been a carpenter before he volunteered for the army, and so when he came back to Civvy Street he was convinced there would be plenty of work for him building all those 'homes fit for heroes' that the government had promised. But, as the Commoner family discovered along with everyone else, promises are one thing, bricks and mortar another. Work in the building trade was hard to come by in the postwar years and, as their income fluctuated, the family became used to moving from flat to flat.

During the last three years trade had picked up enough for them to rent a whole house in Abbeville Road in Clapham. There among the plane trees and the privet hedges and the long stolid rows of Victorian terraces, they'd never been so comfortable nor so happy. In many ways it was more like living in a village than a London suburb for there were more than twenty shops in the road, and the church of the Holy Spirit, where they worshipped every Sunday, was just round the corner in Narbonne Road. Charlie's school was within walking distance, and it was a mere stone's throw to the Windmill pub, the two ponds and the almost rural space of Clapham Common. A first-rate place, all three of them agreed.

Charlie had worked hard at school. He might be a dreamer, especially after a Saturday night at the pictures, but he was well aware that his fantasy world was froth and that the really important and difficult thing in life was to get himself apprenticed to a dependable trade. So when Mr Hedgethorn's letter arrived, with its good news, the thrill of being accepted was so intense that he spent the rest of breakfast time leaping around the kitchen, alternately crowing like a cockerel and rapturously hugging his mother.

'Now you'll see something, Mum,' he triumphed. 'Now you'll really see something. Articled clerk! Imagine it! You an' Dad'll never need to worry about money again. Once I'm qualified we shall be real swells. My eye, there'll be some changes then!'

'Never mind changes,' his mother laughed, extricating herself from his third bear-hug. 'You'll be late for school if you go on.'

He glanced at the clock on the wall, saw how late it was and whooped off into the narrow hall, gathering raincoat and satchel on his way.

'See you, Mum!' he called, and was gone in a flurry of flapping coat and leaping excitement.

Left on her own in a silenced kitchen, Ruby Commoner picked up the letter from the table where Charlie had tossed it and read it through quietly, her face furrowed with anxiety.

Even though he'd won a scholarship to Henry Thornton and had a grant to cover the cost of his uniform, keeping Charlie on at school until he was sixteen had been a struggle. With this letter, wonderful though it was, they were going to have to face the last, and most difficult, challenge of all, because now there were fees to pay.

She and Stan had talked it over and over, naturally, ever since they agreed with the teachers that Charlie ought to train for a solicitor and decided to let him stay on. Talking was one thing, now the moment of decision had come and that was quite another.

Still, Ruby thought to herself, as she started to clear the breakfast things. Look on the bright side, Rube. It's no good getting down. They've offered him the chance. That's what really matters. We shall manage somehow or other. My Stan'll sort it out.

79

Stanley Commoner was a sensible man, the type that could be depended upon to sort out most difficulties without making a fuss. Ten stone in weight and five-and-a-half feet tall in his grey cloth cap, he was broad of shoulder, brow and opinion; a thick-set sturdy individual with close-cropped gingery hair, kindly blue eyes, a broken nose and a brindled moustache as bristly as a brush. On first acquaintance he seemed a slow man, for he took his time before venturing an opinion and spoke and worked with extreme care, but those who knew him well valued him for his dependability and were prepared to wait for his advice, knowing it would be sound when it came.

'Well,' he said that Friday evening, when Charlie and his friends had gone roaring off to the pictures and he and Ruby were on their own together, 'one thing's certain. We can't let him down now, Rube. Not when we've come so far and he's done so well.'

'I suppose we *could* move somewhere cheaper, if it come to it,' Ruby said. 'I don't want to though, Stan, an' that's a fact, what with all the decorating you've done an' the garden an' everything. I've just got those flower beds lovely. It'd be a pity to leave it all for someone else to get the benefit. It's the best house we've ever had.'

'I done some sums,' her husband said, producing a battered notebook from the inside pocket of his jacket. 'Seems to me we got two options. We could move somewhere cheaper up the old town, or . . .'

'Or?'

'We could take in a lodger.'

'Meaning Grandpa or Aunty Grace?'

'Not Aunty Grace,' Stan said, making a wry grimace. 'We're not *that* desperate.'

'Poor old Grace. She *is* awful.'

'But Grandpa's all right.' Stan prompted.

'Yes,' Ruby said, but she was acknowledging his words, not accepting necessity. At least, not yet. Grandpa Jones *was* all right. Most of the time. And ever since Gran died they'd known they would have to take him in sooner or later. Of course he would help with the rent; he'd always promised that. But all the same it would be hard, sharing their home after all these years alone together, her and Stan and Charlie.

It took her time to think about it and Stan sat silent and watched her as she thought, that round face of hers brooding and serious and those fine grey eyes hidden in the shadow of the gaslight. And it seemed to him that he had never seen her looking so warm and rounded and accommodating, not ever, and he wished it wasn't necessary to ask her to accommodate quite so much.

'It'll 'ave to be your decision, old gel,' he said, 'seeing as you'll bear the brunt a' the work.'

His concern made her decision possible. 'I daresay we shall manage,' she said, smiling at him. 'After all we can't let our Charlie down, can we? Not now, not when all's said and done. An' we've got the room.'

So the necessary burden was accepted. The next day Charlie wrote a much displayed letter to accept Mr Hedgethorn's offer and his father composed a very private one to agree to the payment of the necessary fees. Now it was simply a matter of studying hard for the School Certificate and waiting for August eighth, the day after Bank Holiday Monday, when he would embark on his chosen career.

'I'll get Dad to find me a job on the buildings as soon as the exams are over,' he promised his mother. 'You've kept me quite long enough. Time I brought in a bit of money for a change.'

He started work at eight o'clock on the morning after he'd taken his final examination, and cycled off with his father to a building site at Streatham, returning late that evening in cheerful triumph, full of jokes and stories to entertain his mother. He had grazes on his hands, a bruise on his forehead, two pints in his belly and an enormous appetite.

Ten days later, Grandpa Jones took up residence with his youngest daughter and his son-in-law. Although the old man put himself out to be as helpful as he could, diligently filling coal scuttles, chopping firewood and mending all the boots and shoes, there was no doubt that his arrival had changed the atmosphere. The trouble was that he dominated every mealtime with interminable tales of the good old days when he won every school prize that was going and passed more examinations than anyone had ever thought possible. Apparently, he was 'the best looker' in the street.

Ruby had been weaned on these stories and knew them for the fantasies they were, but Charlie, hearing them at length for the first time, was irritated and told his mother he considered Grandpa a bore. 'How can he say he was a looker with that great hooter stuck in the middle of his face and those awful piggy eyes?'

It was hard to have her Charlie criticising the old man because it implied that she shouldn't have invited him into the house, but Ruby held her peace and didn't explain why she'd done it. The essence of a good sacrifice is that it never puts the recipient at a disadvantage.

'I wouldn't shout so loud if I was you,' she said, half teasing, half rebuking. 'You could end up just the same.'

'No chance,' Charlie told her, cheerfully. 'I'm going to end up a cross between you and Dad. That's all signed, sealed and delivered. Your eyes, Dad's mouth, your hands and feet, Dad's good temper. I'm going to be perfect.'

'I don't know where you get your cheek from, I'm sure,' his mother laughed at him. 'That's not me, or your Dad.'

'Got to have something of me own,' he said. 'How long till church?'

'Twenty minutes.'

'Right then. I'm off to get some earplugs.'

'You're a bad boy.'

'No, I'm not,' he grinned at her. 'He wouldn't know the difference. You watch. When we come back and we're all sitting down to dinner I shall say, "Um" and "Yes" and "Fancy" and not listen to a word, and he'll be happy as a sandboy. He doesn't want any of us to listen. He just wants to tell us.'

'You're too clever by half,' his mother said. In the quiet

order of her kitchen, with her dinner plates warming in the rack, the Sunday roast filling the room with its lovely rich smell and her steamed pudding rising gently before her eyes, she couldn't help admiring him. He was very young to understand the old man so well. Besides he was only being saucy. Everything would work out in the end somehow or other. It always did.

She put the last of the peeled potatoes in the saucepan, comforted by the familiar pattern of her chores. Cooking for four wasn't all that different to cooking for three, not really. It wasn't so bad. And when all's said and done, you have to make a few sacrifices for your children, don't you? That's only natural. You have to help them. That's what being a parent is all about.

On that same Sunday morning in France, three kilometres west of Amiens, in a little village called Boves, Emily and Ginny Lisieux were on the verge of a quarrel as they struggled to walk and talk against a westerly wind. It was gusting so strongly that there were moments when they could hardly breathe. It tossed their hats in the air, tangled their scarves, slapped their cheeks and whipped their skirts behind them, to flap and crack like flags. Ginny revelled in it. The world was full of vibrant colour and furious energy, clouds heaped layer upon layer, grey-blue and rose-white and moving with visible speed. It was just what she needed to strengthen her resolve.

'We must find a room,' she said passionately, standing still as well as she could against the buffeting, and shouting because that was the only way to be heard. 'You *can* see that, can't you, Em?'

'No. I can't really,' Emily shouted back. 'I think we ought to wait until Maman finishes work.'

Their mother had started a new job that morning as general housekeeper to the village Advocate and his sister. And, for the first time in all their years as domestic servants, there was no live-in accommodation for them at the house.

'She'll stay there all hours,' Ginny said. 'You know how

hard she works. If he's said half-past six, she won't be out until at least a quarter to seven.'

'But what if we find somewhere and she doesn't like it?' Emily worried.

'If we don't find somewhere,' her sister said forcefully, 'we shall be sleeping in the fields.'

In the seven years since they'd left High Holborn the two identical little girls had grown into two highly individual young women. Their colouring was still the same and, at five foot two, they were the same height, although few people realised it, for Ginny was slimmer than her sister and consequently seemed taller. Certainly she was a great deal more fashionable. She wore her dark hair cut short in the latest bob and did her best to make clothes for herself that were as modish as she could get them, which was difficult because none of the houses they'd worked in ever possessed a sewing machine and everything had to be done by hand.

Emily on the other hand, was content to wear whatever her mother provided for her which was, usually, an old-fashioned full skirt, a cotton blouse and a heavy apron. Clothes didn't concern her. It was enough that they were cool in summer and warm in winter, and that she had a piece of wide ribbon with which to tie back her long hair. Over the years she had become an excessively devout Catholic and her concerns were inner and other: that she should be patient and gentle, help her mother, obey the commandments and avoid sin whenever she could. Her life was less active than her sister's and consequently she had put on more weight so that her arms were rounded, and her face full-cheeked. And long periods of contemplation locked in her dark world had given her a peculiar serenity, like a nun, and the same soft speech and gentle movements.

Ginny was still sharp-featured and angular. There was a sense of energetic bustle about her, even when she was still. Her dark eyes were watchful, her spine and shoulders perpetually straight, as though her entire body were flexed, ready to bound away at a word.

84

'I shall go to Amiens,' she declared. 'That's what I'll do. I'm sure to find somewhere there.'

'Why Amiens?' Emily shouted, clutching her hat to her head.

'Because there's nothing here,' Ginny shouted back.

It was true. Boves was a small place and a very quiet one, smelling of horses and dung heaps, with vegetable gardens behind every house. There were plenty of stables and several smithies on the outskirts, but the village itself was nothing more than two streets, one straggling beside the river Avres, the other running uphill to the church. The church had been built in an imposing position in the shelter of a very tall escarpment and it overlooked the village square, which was where the two girls were now standing. Naturally, it was made of stone, with Doric columns in front of the entrance and a belfry as tall as the hill; it was a handsome sight, framed by the wild sky. The houses below it stood in shadow and were humble affairs, mostly single-storey cottages made of lathe and plaster and badly in need of repair. In fact, as far as Ginny could see there were only two in the entire village that could be termed well built, one was the town hall, which was almost as imposing as the church, and the other was the house of the village Advocate, where their mother now worked.

'But why Amiens?' Emily insisted. 'If we live there Maman will have to travel to work every day.'

'At least we'd be in a place where there's some life. We could go out in the evenings. There are cafés and cinemas and all sorts of things there.'

'What do we want with cafés?' Emily said. 'As long as we've got enough money for food and a roof over our heads I don't see that it matters where we are.'

'And is that all there is to life?' Ginny asked furiously. 'Food? A roof over our heads? I want more than that. Don't you?'

Emily looked doubtful. 'Well . . .'

'Be honest.'

'Perhaps.'

'There's no perhaps with me,' Ginny said. 'I want a lot more. I tell you, Em, I felt ashamed to be working in some of the places we've been. That last kitchen was crawling with cockroaches. I can't think why Maman always takes such foul jobs. We ought to be aiming higher. Why should we be skivvies for the rest of our lives? We didn't start out as skivvies. I ought to be a typist, earning a proper wage. I spent enough time learning how to type and I've only ever had one job as a typist. One job! Do you realise that? It's ridiculous.'

'But you can't be a typist here, can you?' Emily said reasonably. 'There wouldn't be any work for typists in a village.'

'But there would in Amiens.'

'Ah!' Emily said, and in that one gentle sound she told her sister how much she understood. 'So that's how it is. This is all so that you can get yourself a job.'

Ginny's irritation swelled alarmingly. Sometimes Em's ability to hear what you were thinking was a real nuisance. 'Yes,' she admitted. 'It is. And why not?'

'Because it's selfish,' Emily said, her eyes flickering. 'You ought to wait until you know whether Maman wants you to help her at Monsieur the Advocate's. I don't think you should do it.'

'Well, I do,' Ginny said. Out here in the tempestuous air she was certain of it, selfish or not. 'I want to get a good job, a job that'll last. I want to go out of an evening. Meet people. Make friends. Stay in a place I like instead of running away. I'm sick of running away and we do it every time Maman gets upset.'

'Oh, be fair,' Emily pleaded. 'She doesn't have a choice. She can't help it if she gets driven out of places. Remember how horrid the pharmacist was that time. He called her the most terrible names.'

'And she ran away. She got hysterical and ran away. If she'd only stayed calm it would all have been different. But she never stays calm.'

'It's because she's frightened.'

'Well, I'm not. I'm sick of this sort of life. I want to do

things. See a bit of the world. All I ever get to see is the inside of a stinking kitchen.'

'I'd be glad of a chance to see *that*,' Emily said, stung to remonstrance.

Ginny turned on her in guilty fury. 'That's a beastly thing to say.'

'It's not.'

'It is. Absolutely beastly. It's not my fault you can't see.'

'Nobody said it was.'

'Yes, they did,' Ginny shouted into the wind. 'You did.' An outright quarrel was the very thing she'd wanted to avoid, but she couldn't hold back.

Emily withdrew her hand from her sister's arm and stood alone with the wind buffeting her so strongly that she tottered sideways. 'How shall I manage if you go away?' she asked miserably. 'You don't think of me.'

'Now who's being selfish?'

'Yes,' Emily agreed, accepting her sinfulness miserably. 'It's true. I am. I'm a wicked sinner.'

'Oh!' Ginny said in fury. 'There's no talking to you. You turn everything into a sin. I'm going to Amiens. Are you coming or not?'

'I suppose so. I can't stay here on my own.'

'Then you'd better hold my arm.' That was the trouble about quarrelling with Em. You had to lead her no matter what you might be feeling. You couldn't leave her on her own in the dark. 'Pick up your case. Come on.'

But just as they'd picked up their travelling cases and were walking out of the square they heard someone calling to them over the wind.

'*Mesdemoiselles!*'

There was a woman walking briskly across the square towards them.

'Madame Gambetta,' she said, introducing herself as she approached. 'I understand you are looking for somewhere to stay. Is that right?'

She was a surprisingly fashionable woman for such a sleepy village. She was wearing a long checked coat, and a little felt hat perched on the side of her head in quite the Parisian style. She even had high-heeled shoes on her feet.

'What good fortune I was passing,' she said. 'I have just the place for you. Two of the prettiest rooms. Would you care to come and see them? How many of you are there?'

'Three,' Ginny said. 'Our mother is Monsieur the Advocate's new housekeeper.'

'Then, if that is the case,' the woman said, 'you must follow me.' And she led them into one of the houses that fronted the square, up the stairs and into a large sitting room with an equally large bedroom through an archway beyond it. They *were* pretty rooms, just as she had claimed, their windows which overlooked the square were framed by ruched curtains, and the paintwork was grass green to match the pattern on the bedspreads. There were wash-stands and towel-rails in the bedroom, and a table set under the living-room window where they could eat their meals and look out over the square. In fact, they were just the sort of rooms to appeal to Ginny in her present mood.

'You are tempted,' Madame Gambetta said. 'I can see it. Wasn't I right? Aren't they just perfect for you?'

'Yes,' Ginny had to admit. 'But . . .'

'You are worried about the price,' Madame Gambetta said. 'Things are so expensive in Amiens, but here it is quite different. Here we are more amenable. For you, my dear, I am prepared to make a special concession. I've quite taken to you, you see, especially as your mother is working for Monsieur the Advocate. I'll tell you what I'll do. In the ordinary way of business, you understand, I charge twenty francs per week, per person. Because I've taken to you, I'll make it fifty for the three of you as a special concession. How would that be?'

It *was* a temptation, even though Ginny didn't have much more than five francs to her name, leave alone in her purse. She stood by the window looking down into the square, thinking about it.

'When would you wish to take up residence?' Madame Gambetta was saying.

'Tonight,' Ginny said, pulling her attention away from her thoughts. 'As soon as possible, really.'

'Then I tell you what I'll do, my dear, because I've taken such a fancy to you. Ordinarily I charge my customers a full week for the first week no matter how short it is, if you get my meaning. One has to live. My weeks run from Saturday to Friday, payment Saturday morning, you understand. But for you . . . how 'bout if we say thirty-five francs from tonight until Friday? Taking up residence straightaway of course.'

The tumbling price and the instant accommodation were too great a temptation to be resisted. I could do it, Ginny thought. Even if Maman hasn't got the money, I could earn it. Somehow. It *was* possible. She would make it possible.

'I'll take them,' she said to Madame Gambetta. 'Can I pay you tomorrow?'

'Tomorrow will be perfect,' her new landlady told her.

'I do hope Maman will like them,' Emily said, as they unpacked their cases and made up the beds.

And when they met her outside the Advocate's house at a quarter to seven that evening, Maman said they were the dearest girls alive to have taken the trouble.

'Just so long as they're not too expensive, these rooms of yours,' she said. 'I've only got ten francs until pay day. I'm afraid I couldn't get a job for you, Ginny, although Monsieur *did* say I could take Emily with me to help with the cooking.'

'In that case I'll go to Amiens tomorrow and get a job there,' Ginny said, and was shamed to realise that she was feeling noble and fraudulent at one and the same time. 'Don't worry about the rent. I'll manage the first week.'

'You are such good children,' Hortense said. 'I don't know what I would do without you. I've been such a bad mother, making you work, depending on those worthless shares, dragging you about all over France. And you repay me with love. I don't deserve it.'

It would be a lot easier for us, Ginny thought, if you hadn't run away from your last job without being paid, but she didn't say anything. Maman was looking too worn to be criticised, her greying hair straggling over her ears and her wide forehead even more deeply lined than usual. Poor Maman.

The next morning the family woke soon after dawn and after a filling breakfast of strong coffee and warm baguettes, Ginny kissed her mother and sister goodbye and set off on her own to catch the train to Amiens.

There were already people waiting on the platform, early though it was, and they smiled at one another and said, '*Bonjour.*' And after a few minutes, a young woman of about Ginny's own age arrived in a great hurry and stood beside her catching her breath. She was a rather chubby girl, with grey-blue eyes and untidy fair hair bushing out from beneath her knitted beret, and she looked as hard up as Ginny felt. Her shoes were down-at-heel and she seemed to be dressed in some sort of regulation black and white under her raincoat.

But she was friendly. 'You're new in Boves, aren't you?' she said to Ginny, as the train arrived.

Ginny opened the door and climbed in, agreeing that she was.

'Village gossip,' the girl said, settling into the seat beside her. 'My name's Mauricette. What's yours?'

'Virginie, but my family call me Ginny. Are you going to work?'

'Don't remind me,' Mauricette grimaced. 'Are you?'

'I'm going to find a job.'

'What as?'

'A typist.'

'There's a job vacant at my place,' Mauricette said. 'You could try for that.'

'Where is it?'

'I'll show you, if you like.'

'You're very kind,' Ginny said, smiling at her new friend. What a bit of luck!

The train reached Amiens quickly, slowing past a muddle of warehouses and factories and long streets full of identical sooty houses and long chimneys smoking dirt-black columns straight up into the sky. This is better, Ginny thought. This was the sort of place where she belonged, a place with some life, and people at work making things. It reminded her of somewhere else, but for the moment she couldn't remember where.

'Now where's this place of yours?' she said to Mauricette.

It turned out to be in the old town just across the river from the Cathedral of Notre Dame, and from the outside it was rather a disappointment, being little more than a long wooden shed with windows. But there were two horse-drawn delivery vans waiting beside it and the sign above the entrance was encouragingly grand, 'QUALITY VELVETS,' it declared in red and gold lettering 'AS SUPPLIED TO THE COUTURIERS OF PARIS'.

Mauricette gave the door a push and in they walked.

The space inside the shed was full of looms. There were more than Ginny could count and every one of them was weaving a different kind of velvet, figured and patterned, shot and plain, in deep black and creamy white and the rich glowing colours of jewels, ruby, amethyst, emerald, sapphire, roll after sumptuous roll. The air was full of the luxurious smell of new cloth and the click and rattle of the looms. Oh yes, she would certainly like to work here.

'Come on,' Mauricette said. 'It's up the stairs.'

There was a gallery at one end of the shed, spiral staircases at either end of it and doors all along its length. The second door on the left was labelled 'M. GUERIN – MANAGER' in the same important red and gold lettering as the front door. It was firmly closed, but once again Mauricette walked straight in.

There was only one person in the room, a short, thin, dark-haired man, expensively dressed and sporting a very small pince-nez, a pencil-slim moustache and an irritable expression. He was rummaging through a heap of folders that were strewn all over his desk and there were ink stains on his white shirt cuff. 'Mam'selle?' he said, looking up.

Ginny introduced herself. 'Virginie Lisieux,' she said. 'I am a typist. I'm told you have a vacancy here.'

91

He put both hands on the desk and looked at her with such obvious relief that she was quite taken aback. 'Saved!' he said. 'Do you see that, Mam'selle Lalange? Reinforcements have arrived. I assume you can type, file, that sort of thing.'

Ginny took her certificates and her one and only precious reference out of her bag and held them out towards him. But he barely glanced at them.

'When can you start?' he said. 'I lost my other girl last week and we can't find *anything*. You see how it is. Mam'selle Lalange will show you the ropes. Usual rates of pay.' He was walking across the room, obviously on his way out. 'Oh what a blessing!' he said. And left.

'Does he mean me to start work now?' Ginny asked her new friend.

'Evidently,' Mauricette said, speaking in a whisper. 'He's a funny bloke, but he treats you fair if you work hard. Only we mustn't talk. He hates that.'

'Would he hear us from down there? With all those looms going?'

'Yes. He has ears like a bat.'

So Ginny kept quiet and started work.

It didn't take her long to discover that Monsieur Guerin's office was in chaos because there were no systems in it, so while Mauricette typed letters, she began to organise the files into alphabetical order and mark them with tags. And she started with letters and information from the Paris fashion houses.

It was a wise decision. Half an hour later, when Monsieur Guerin came roaring up the stairs to demand the latest letter from Monsieur Worth, the Worth file was on the desk in front of him and the letter retrieved in seconds.

He was impressed. 'You are formidable,' he said, grabbed the letter, beamed hugely and went clattering off down the stairs again.

The two girls followed him to the door and watched as he raced through the shed waving the letter and ran out of the double doors at the far end.

'He's gone to the goods yard,' Mauricette said. 'He always does that. To supervise the loading. He makes such a fuss about his wretched velvets. Now we can talk.'

It wasn't long before they were confiding in one another. Ginny told her new friend about Emily and her blindness and how patient she was, and Mauricette told *her* new friend that she had seven brothers and sisters and she wasn't going to work as a typist for ever.

'Nor me,' Ginny said. 'Although I'm not sure what I shall do next.'

'Will you stay here, d'you think?'

What a question. 'Yes. Of course.'

'I'd better warn you. Nobody else has.'

'I'm different.'

'Well, you're not like Madame. I'll say that for you. At least you arrange things. She never arranged anything. She said she didn't believe in it.'

'Was she the other girl?' Ginny asked, as she went back to her filing. 'The one he said he'd lost?'

'They had such a row, you'd never believe it. She threw all the files at him and walked out.'

'No wonder he was glad to see *me*. What's he like to work for?'

'Awful. He's always running about saying, "I haven't got time! I haven't got time!" That puts you off. And he throws fits.'

'Fits?'

'He screams and roars and runs up and down the stairs and shouts at everybody.'

'What's he like when it comes to wages? Do you think he'd give me an advance as it's my first week?'

'No. He wouldn't. I can tell you that for certain. Why? Are you skint?'

Ginny explained about the rent, fiddling with her silver cross as she spoke because she was feeling so worried.

'You'll have to pawn something then,' Mauricette said.

'I haven't got anything worth pawning,' Ginny said.

'What about that cross?'

My silver cross, Ginny thought, clutching it in her hand. Have I really got to sacrifice that? But she knew she had no other choice. The rent had to be found. She made up her mind at once, quickly, while her courage was high.

'Is there a pawn shop anywhere near?'

Mauricette said she knew just the man. 'He'll take anything,' she said. 'When we have our lunch break I'll show you where to go.' And she did.

The pawnbroker was a huge man with a belly like a barrel and hands like spades. Ginny's little cross looked pathetic lying in his palm. But he paid up forty-five francs, with fifty centimes deducted for the first week's interest and although she was torn to be parting from her one and only treasure, at least the rent was secured and she could redeem her little cross once she got her first week's wages.

Parents were a terrible responsibility, she thought. But you had to look after them, even if it meant pawning your most valuable possession. What else could you do?

# CHAPTER SEVEN

Supper that evening was a cheerful meal. The rent was paid, the bags unpacked and all three members of the Lisieux family were gainfully employed. They kept one another entertained with stories of their day and vowed that they were now well and truly at home. Then, because they were all tired and because Maman said that until they'd got their first week's wages she really thought they ought to save the gaslight, they went to bed early.

But not to sleep. Despite their long hours of unfamiliar work the two girls were restless and wakeful, tossing and turning . . . and scratching. But it wasn't until Maman came to their bedside to wake them in the morning that they discovered why.

They were covered in insect bites, large, red, angry mounds, under their armpits, round their waists, on their arms and legs. There was even one on Emily's cheek.

'By all the saints!' Maman said. 'What's done that to you?'

'Mosquitos?' Ginny suggested.

'I don't think so. They look more like flea bites to me, and big ones at that. Sponge them with cold water and give all your clothes a really good shake.'

But although the girls shook all their clothes so vigorously it was a wonder they didn't fall to pieces, no insects of any kind fell out and the mystery remained.

On Tuesday night there were no new bites and although the old ones itched unbearably the twins were satisfied that their shaking must have done the trick. But on Wednesday night they were bitten again, and so was Hortense.

'I begin to have grave suspicions about these insects,' she said, examining the bumps on her arms. 'Tonight I shall buy a big cake of soap from the chandlers and then we shall see.'

She looked and sounded so grim that neither of her daughters dared to ask what she was planning. They would see soon enough. Once Maman had made up her mind to do something she always acted quickly.

Ginny's train was late that evening and when she got back to the *pension*, Maman was already home, soaking a large cake of soft soap in a dish full of water.

'Lie down on the bed and keep quite still,' she ordered. 'Pretend you're asleep.'

Emily was already lying under the covers. Obediently, Ginny took off her coat, hat and shoes and lay down, too, giving her sister a pinch to show how puzzled she was.

They didn't have long to wait.

'I knew it!' Maman shrieked, striking the wallpaper with her cake of soap. 'Up! Up! Strip the bed! Quick! Oh, the filthy things.'

There was a flailing of activity. The two girls leapt from the bed flinging the sheets and blankets back as they rose and Maman beat the mattress and the pillows and the wallpaper with her soap, moving so quickly that she looked as though she had half a dozen arms all whirling at once.

It was all over in seconds.

'There!' Maman said, glaring at the soap. 'I knew it.'

There were half a dozen brown insects stuck in the tacky side of the soap, round brown insects with little dark legs wriggling frantically.

'What are they?' Ginny asked, gazing at them in horror.

'Bed-bugs, that's what they are. Filthy things,' Maman said. 'So now we'll see what our painted Madame has to say about it. And she had the gall to charge us fifty francs.'

She was down the stairs and shouting at Madame Gambetta before Ginny and Emily had time to put on their shoes. But they could hear her voice, sharp with fury, berating their landlady. 'Fifty francs for bed-bugs. You should be ashamed of yourself.'

'There were no bugs in my beds before you came,' Madame Gambetta answered coolly. 'If there are bugs now then you must have brought them with you.'

The effrontery of such an answer took Hortense's breath away. 'How dare you say such a thing!' she roared, as her daughters clattered down the stairs to join her.

'Ah, you see, the truth hurts.'

'I've never been so insulted,' Hortense roared on. 'That you . . . you . . . a dirty painted slut . . .'

'Mind your mouth,' Madame Gambetta roared back, raising her comb as though she was going to attack with it. 'You bring bed-bugs to my house and you dare to call me names. I'll call the gendarme.'

'Call away. I'll show him this.' Waving the soap. 'He'll like to see the evidence.'

'Evidence! Pooh! I don't give that for your evidence.'

They were standing face to face, glaring at one another like fighting cats.

I must stop them, Ginny thought, her anxiety gathering into fear. I can't let this go on. Maman could get hurt. And she put her free hand on her mother's arm and begged, 'Maman. Please don't.' To her horror her mother rounded on her.

'And you can shut up,' she shouted. 'This is all your fault. You arranged it. I hold you responsible.'

The unexpectedness and ingratitude of her attack was such a shock that tears welled in Ginny's eyes.

'How can you say such a thing?' she cried. 'I was trying to help you.' And then because she felt so guilty and because she couldn't bear the gloating expression on Madame Gambetta's face or the fury on her mother's, she dropped Emily's hand, turned her back on them all and ran. This was awful! Awful! Everything was going wrong.

The square was empty except for a horse and cart driven by a boy, who wasn't taking any notice of anything, and three old women who were standing in the doorway of the chandler's and were out to notice everything and everybody. Ginny didn't give them time to greet her. She ran across the square like a rabbit bolting for its hole, and made for the nearest cover, a dark pathway overhung with trees.

She discovered it wasn't a pathway at all, three strides into its welcoming darkness. It was a flight of earth steps cut into

97

the side of the escarpment which led up and up to the top of the hill. Lungs straining with effort, she took them at a run, only stopping when she was at the top and beyond the trees. She found herself beside the gate to the village cemetery. The sight of the cemetery comforted her. It was the perfect place for misery. Quiet, deserted and shielded by sympathetic shrubs and trees.

She flung herself across the nearest basalt slab, face down and with her arms across her eyes, and cried as though her heart were breaking. It was such a relief to cry it was almost a pleasure, although a decidedly painful one. She wept on freely, full of self-pity, letting her tears soak into the sleeve of her cotton blouse, conscious of the chill basalt against breast and belly, and of the evening breeze stroking the hairs on the nape of her neck this way and that. Oh how unfair Maman was! How horribly unfair!

She was making such a noise she didn't hear Emily and Mauricette scrambling across the tombstones to join her. It wasn't until Emily sat down beside the weeping figure and put her arms most lovingly about her neck that she knew they were there. Then she sat up and cried all over again in her sister's arms. 'It's so unfair, Em. So unfair.'

'Yes,' Emily murmured, stroking her sister's tear-damp hair. 'My poor Ginny.' She'd forgotten how she'd warned poor Ginny and how worried she'd been. Now she was all sympathy. 'My poor darling Ginny.'

'I did it for the best,' Ginny said, looking at Mauricette.

'I know,' her friend said loyally. 'I know you did.'

With loving fingers, Emily wiped away Ginny's tears, smoothed the hair out of her eyes, and straightened the crumpled collar of her blouse.

'Where's your cross?' she said. 'Oh dear! You haven't lost it, have you?'

Her question cast Ginny back into renewed misery. 'I pawned it,' she wailed. 'I pawned it to get the rent. Oh! Oh!'

'Oh Ginny,' Emily said, and now she was weeping, too. 'You didn't. What a sacrifice to make. It's terrible! Noble! Your lovely silver cross.'

And then all three girls were weeping together, holding one another and rocking to and fro, wallowing in misery and urging one another on to louder and louder howls. How noble! How awful! How unfair!

And a man's voice roared across their misery, rough as thunder. 'Stop that racket at once!' he commanded. 'You'll upset my boys.'

They were so surprised they stopped in mid-sob. Boys? Ginny thought. What boys? There was no one else in the cemetery except themselves and this man. He was so large and so extraordinary that he put everything else out of her mind.

He was as dark as a gypsy, with skin so weatherbeaten that it was as brown and wrinkled as old leather, and he was dressed like a farm labourer, in coarse blue shirt, grimy sweat-band, moleskin trousers and earth-caked boots. But, large though he was, it wasn't his general appearance that alarmed her, as much as the peculiar disarrangement of his features. He looked as though his face had been cut into jagged pieces and re-assembled. One eye was lower than the other, his nose had been broken in two places and bore a long blue scar between the breaks, his upper lip appeared to have been cut in two and stitched together at a new ugly angle to reveal how very few teeth he possessed and how cracked and brown they were. In addition, his eyebrows, which should have been thick and black and straight, were chopped into a series of sudden fault lines like a diagram from a geographical text-book. In short, he looked like a monster, and a monster, what's more, holding a sharp fag-hook in his left hand.

'That's better,' he said, nodding at them. 'That's more the ticket. No need for all that rumpus, now was there.'

'We're ever so sorry, Monsieur Joliot,' Mauricette said, wiping her tears away on the back of her hand. And she whispered to Ginny. 'It's old Joliot. It's all right, he lives with Cousin Berthe. Just say sorry. She's sorry, Monsieur Joliot.'

'So I should think,' Old Joliot said. 'Only one reason I allow people to cry in my cemetery. You should know that,

Mauricette. One reason an' that's if you've suffered a bereavement, which is not the case, as I know on account of nobody's died. So what's the problem? Why were you yowling?'

The twins were still so stunned by his arrival they couldn't say a word and Mauricette didn't know what to answer without embarrassing her new friends.

'*Alors*!' Old Joliot boomed. 'Follow me.'

They followed, mesmerised by his ferocity, trailing behind him as he strode through the graves, into the centre of the cemetery.

'There!' he said, pointing with the fag-hook. 'Look at that.'

They had come to a halt beside four neat rows of identical headstones, plain and white and standing in line like dominoes on the green cloth of a very well-kept lawn. Ginny and Mauricette looked at them obediently.

But looking wasn't enough. 'Read them!' he ordered. 'Read their ages. My poor boys. Consider the day they died. Read them.'

So they walked along the mute rows and read the inscriptions, as the light thickened towards dusk in the empty fields below them and a robin sang with piercing sweetness from the topmost branches of a nearby hawthorn.

The hair stood up on the nape of Ginny's neck at the horror of what was hidden in that docile earth. 'But they're English,' she said to Emily. 'They're all English. Smith, Robinson, Harris. Look. And they all died on the same day. How dreadful.' And she began to read their ages aloud, her voice trembling with pity. 'Eighteen, nineteen, twenty-one, eighteen, seventeen, twenty-one. Oh Em. Seventeen. They were the same age as us.'

'Cut down in their prime, my poor boys,' Old Joliot said, shaking his ugly head. 'The valley of our river Somme is full of mutilated men. Dead bones crying for justice. I hear them every day of my life. Look out there little ones. Look at the fields. D'you see 'em? I can remember days when that hill was brown all over. Imagine that. An' d'you know what

100

turned it brown? Horses, that's what. Thousands of horses being led down to the river to be watered. Imagine that. Horses from all over the world. All blown to bits, poor animals. And the men! You could never imagine how many men there were an' their guns an' rifles an' bayonets an' backpacks an' all. Millions and millions of 'em. Brave young men. They come from all over the world as well. Never should ha' been sent here, never should ha' died. All blown to bits. Slaughtered they were, hundreds and hundreds of 'em all in a second. I tell you *mes filles*, this ground is full of grief, groaning with it. You must never add to it. No matter what. There's enough sorrow in this place without you adding to it.'

After such a story, what could they say? Their tears looked hysterical and unnecessary beside those dreadful silent graves. They shuffled their feet and looked ashamed of themselves and after a pause Old Joliot was appeased.

'So, now tell me,' he said. 'What was it all about? Why were you yowling? You're the newcomers, *n'est-ce pas?*'

'We've got rooms with Madame Gambetta,' Ginny explained, trying to start at the beginning. 'And they're – well – they're not very clean.'

'Bug-ridden,' Old Joliot said. 'Naturally. *Alors*. Find somewhere else.'

'But where?' Ginny asked. 'Who . . .'

He was cleaning his fag-hook with a handful of grass, peering at the blade in the poor light. 'We will ask Cousin Berthe,' he said.

Ginny was so drained by the emotions of the last few days that she obeyed almost mechanically. She took Emily by the hand and followed their new friend down into the square, with Mauricette bringing up the rear. The entrance hall of the *pension* was empty. There was no sign of Maman or Madame Gambetta.

Old Joliot paid no attention to the *pension*. 'This way,' he said, striding off down the Rue Jeanne D'Arc. 'Follow me.'

And there was Maman sitting on the wall of the Advocate's house, looking as though she were lost.

'*Madame,*' Old Joliot said, looming upon her. 'We have come to find you somewhere else to live. We are going to ask Cousin Berthe. You cannot possibly stay with Madame Gambetta, *n'est-ce pas.*' It was a statement, not a question.

For a few seconds Ginny pinched Emily's hand and watched her mother, wondering how she was going to take it and fearing another outburst. But to her relief Maman smiled her sweetest smile, stood up and said that Monsieur Joliot was '*très gentil*'. And it seemed to be agreed.

They trooped downhill together and arrived at number twenty-six, which, it appeared, was Old Joliot's house. It was one of a terrace of dusty cottages, with long green shutters at the windows and a front door so thoroughly out of alignment that they had to lean sideways to get through it. But inside it was a comfortable home, lit by gaslight and surprisingly well furnished, with a heavy dining table and six high-backed chairs, a dresser loaded with brown china, a canary whistling in one corner and a jardinière sprouting a magnificent aspidistra in the other.

And waddling about the room setting the table with a red-and-white-checked cloth and a very large quantity of the brown china was a little fat woman dressed entirely in black. She had the oddest, roundest face that Ginny had ever seen, and a childlike brightness of expression that was disconcerting above such a middle-aged body. She looked up when they all crowded into the room and smiled inanely at them.

She's not all there, Ginny thought; she'll never know what to do. We're wasting our time. We shouldn't have come here.

But Cousin Berthe was one of those innocent creatures who have the knack of going straight to the root of a problem without the need to think about it.

When the tale of bugs and Madame Gambetta had been told she had her answer ready before Old Joliot had finished speaking. 'But it is Madame Lisieux!' she said, beaming at Hortense. 'She is my friend. She works for Monsieur the Advocate, same as me. She must stay here with us, Joliot.

She shall have the front bedroom. Come with me, my dears. I will show you.'

And, as Old Joliot was nodding his approval, they followed her. She led them out of the room into a narrow corridor and up a flight of impossibly steep stairs to the room above the living room. It was dark and low-ceilinged and there was nothing in it except an iron bedstead and a double mattress full of straw. But Maman accepted it gladly.

'You are so kind, Cousin Berthe,' she said. 'Without you I dread to think what would have become of us. We should have slept on the street.'

Cousin Berthe clicked her teeth to show that thanks were superfluous. 'That ol' Madame Gambetta!' she said. 'She's no better than she should be, that one. You don't want to stay with her. You'll be lovely and comfortable here. I got some vegetable soup on the hob. How will that be? Good, eh?'

On the way back down the stairs the twins pinched one another in warning. And they were right. It was the most unappetising hotch-potch they'd ever tasted. But they ate it with as much enjoyment as they could feign because she was a funny old thing and she meant well.

And then Maman played chess with Old Joliot, which was rather a surprise, and at long last they took a candle and went up to their empty room to settle for the night, the girls at one end of the bed and Hortense at the other.

Ginny didn't know whether to laugh or cry.

'After all my efforts,' she whispered to Emily when Maman was asleep, 'we end up on straw in an empty room. First cockroaches, then bed-bugs and now this.'

'At least it's clean,' Emily whispered back.

'And that awful stew.'

'And the earth closet in the garden.'

'Didn't it just *stink*.'

'Still, you've got the job you wanted,' Emily said, trying to be positive, 'and Monsieur the Advocate says Maman is an excellent housekeeper.'

'Yes,' Ginny said. But she wasn't comforted. She'd

pawned her precious cross and she didn't know how she'd ever earn enough money to redeem it, all for what? A straw pallet, a foul stew and that dreadful earth closet. 'We've come a jolly long way from High Holborn,' she sighed.

'I can hardly remember it,' Emily whispered.

'I used to say we'd go back. Do you remember that?'

'We won't, though, will we? Not now.'

'No,' Ginny said sadly. 'We won't. We've been French for too long. And we've sunk too low. You imagine what old Babbers would think if she knew where we were?'

'You won't write to her now, I suppose.'

'No. How could I? I'd be ashamed.'

'I wonder where we'll go next?'

'Well we can't stay here, that's for sure,' Ginny said and tried to settle to sleep.

But when she got home from work on Saturday afternoon Emily met her at the door to say that Maman had come straight home with her wages, agreed on a rent with Old Joliot and gone straight out again with Cousin Berthe to buy some furniture.

'They've been giggling and laughing ever since they came back from the Advocate's,' she said. 'He's given us some curtains and Old Joliot's found a bench and Mauricette's maman has made us three lovely pillows.'

Ginny's heart sank. 'I don't want to live here with that awful old man or that stupid old woman,' she said. 'Why can't we find a place of our own? Oh Em! This is awful!'

But there was worse to come.

Half an hour later Maman and Cousin Berthe came rattling up the street pushing a hand cart stacked with furniture. It took all four of them to carry the things all up the narrow stairs and reassemble them in the bedroom, a single bedstead, two flock mattresses, a washstand and a wicker chair.

'Isn't it grand?' Maman said, when Cousin Berthe had gone downstairs to attend to the supper. Ginny was cleaning the washstand with a damp cloth and Emily was helping to hang the curtains. 'We shall have to spend all our wages to get it as it should be, but when we've finished we shall have a little palace.'

'*Our* wages?' Ginny said.

'Why yes. Of course,' Maman said gaily. 'Every centime. But it will be worth it. You'll see.'

'But Maman,' Ginny said, putting down the cloth and moving her right hand instinctively to the empty space where her cross used to hang. 'It's not . . . I mean, I've got . . . I can't . . .'

Both Emily and Hortense were alerted by the change in her voice and expression.

'What is it, my little one?' Hortense asked. And her voice was full of affection.

But Ginny's throat was choked with tears and she couldn't answer.

'She pawned her cross, Maman,' Emily explained into the silence. 'To get the rent for Madame Gambetta.'

Hortense threw the curtain down on to the nearest bed and leapt across the room to take her poor dear brave daughter in her arms.

'My dearest girl!' she said. 'Your lovely cross. And here I've been shouting at you and telling you what to do and what not to do and how to spend your money. And all the time you've given up your lovely cross to help us. Why didn't you tell me? You are the dearest daughter anyone could ever wish for. The dearest. What a beautiful, brave, lovely thing to do.'

And at that they all cried, Hortense with joy and shame and pride in her daughter, Emily with passionate affection and Ginny with the sheer uplifting pleasure of being loved and valued. And they sat on the bed with their arms round each other, kissed one another and wept again as the full story of the cross was told and re-told and praised.

'Put your hats on,' Maman said, when they were recovered sufficiently. 'We're off to Amiens. Never mind any more furniture. We will buy that by degrees. First we will redeem our cross.'

'Now?' Emily asked, pleased but surprised.

'But of course. Pawn shops stay open all hours on a Saturday night. It's their busiest time. And besides, the sooner we get it back the less we shall have to pay. They add on interest day by day. Such sharks! Come along.'

She was right about the time it would take. They had to stand in a queue outside the pawn shop for nearly an hour. But at last the cross was redeemed and hanging in its rightful place.

'Never let it out of your sight again,' Maman ordered, kissing her daughter's cheek as she fastened the clasp.

And Ginny promised most ardently. 'No, Maman. I never will.'

The return of the cross marked a change in all of them. In that moment it had become a symbol of the sacrifices they were prepared to make for one another and a visible sign of their mutual affection. They went back to Boves in the smoky darkness of the evening, strong enough for anything.

And so they settled down to their new life among the ancient battlefields and found rather to their surprise that they were peacefully happy there. There were difficulties, of course. Thanks to Cousin Berthe, and to Hortense's embarrassment, the filthy state of Madame Gambetta's *pension* occupied the village gossips for nearly a fortnight. It was superseded by an illegitimate pregnancy on a neighbouring farm, but the rift it had caused was slow to heal. They were perpetually short of cash, the weather was appalling and it took six months and every centime they could spare to furnish their room to Hortense's satisfaction.

But there were pleasures, too.

Despite Ginny's misgivings, Cousin Berthe turned out to be extremely easy to live with. As the twins soon discovered, she existed from moment to moment, and rarely looked back into the past and never forward. There had been too much sorrow and too much manual labour in Cousin Berthe's life for her to waste any time on memory or speculation. Or on anger.

She was a terrible cook, but it didn't worry her. After their third, indigestible supper, Maman suggested tentatively that perhaps Monsieur Joliot might like *her* to cook Sunday dinner for them all. Cousin Berthe said she thought that was a lovely idea and could she help? From then on Maman was in charge of the kitchen and the meals were much improved, Cousin Berthe didn't seem to mind her change of status at all, or even to notice it.

'Company!' she would declare, clapping her hands with delight every time they sat at the dining table ready to say grace. 'I like a bit of company. You don't want to live with that ol' Madame Gambetta. She won't do you no good. You're better off with us.'

And Old Joliot would say, 'Hush now, Berthe,' in the gentlest way. 'Time to say grace, my friend.'

At that she would beam at him rapturously and take up her spoon ready to beat time to the familiar words. The twins couldn't help feeling fond of her, with her great, round, simple face and her honest affection. There was, as their neighbours often said, 'simply no harm in Berthe'.

She was good company in the garden, too, for she was a dogged labourer, and loved her plants as if they were her children. The garden was a long, fertile strip of land which led down to the river, and she and Old Joliot cultivated every inch of it. That autumn there were five pairs of willing hands to dig, plant and spread manure, and later on there were five willing and eager to pick the ripened crops. They ate raspberries straight from the cane, peas sweet from the pod, new potatoes, spinach and beans. Only the carrots were a disappointment, eaten away by the fly and horribly soapy.

'Dratted fly!' Cousin Berthe said, throwing the discarded vegetables at the compost heap. 'What we done to deserve them? That's what I say. Oh I'd give 'em what-for, dratted ol' flies. Never mind, eh. We got plenty of other good things. It's a good ol' life.'

And it was. Hortense was happier and more settled in her job with the Advocate than she'd been since they came to France and Ginny and Emily had a bosom friend in Mauricette. The three of them spent many happy and secret hours walking in the fields, talking about life and love and

107

speculating as to what sort of men they would marry. The twins were careful not to let Maman know what they were thinking because she was still determined they would never marry anyone and, from time to time, made it her business to tell them so.

But they were young, full of life and beginning to learn how to ignore the things they didn't like. In February, there was a riot in Paris and a gang of right-wing demonstrators tried to storm the Chamber of Deputies, but they were too busy preparing a birthday treat for Mauricette to read about something so nasty.

In the summer, French prime ministers came and went, but the girls were more concerned with their hair. Emily's had grown to waist length, which was how she liked it. Mauricette favoured short hair, like Ginny's fashionable bob, and Ginny persuaded her friend to cut *hers* into a bob, too, and to re-sew one of her dresses into the latest style, or at least an approximation of the latest style. They all thought it was extremely chic, but it made their mothers rather cross at the thought of all the material they'd wasted.

In October, when news came from Marseilles that a Croat terrorist had assassinated the French foreign minister and the visiting king of Yugoslavia, the three girls were busy planning the Christmas presents they were going to make with off-cuts of Monsieur Guerin's velvets – smoking caps for Old Joliot and Mauricette's papa, and purses for their two mothers and dear old Cousin Berthe.

And even when the new year of 1935 began and the papers were shrill with the news that the people of Saar had voted to throw in their lot with Herr Hitler's Germany, the three friends did no more than glance at them. They were fully occupied planning yet another birthday celebration. Mauricette was going to be eighteen and she was quite sure that this was the year that they would all fall in love.

# CHAPTER EIGHT

'Seen the news, fellers?' Horace Crabbit said, striding into the outer office in a cloud of blue cigar smoke.

'What news was that, Mr C?' Jack Bond teased. He and Charlie had been with the firm long enough to know that they had to keep abreast of current affairs, and to be prepared to be quizzed on them at any time. They also knew that Mr Crabbit enjoyed being ribbed when he was in the mood for it. Plainly, he was in the mood for it that morning.

Charlie took his copy of the *Daily Mirror* out of his pocket and spread it across the desk they shared. ' "JACK HOBBS TO RETIRE"?' he suggested, grinning at Mr Crabbit. ' "OUR GRACIE LANDS FILM CONTRACT FOR £150,000"? Nice work, if you can get it.'

'No, I know what it is,' Jack Bond said, reading the paper over his shoulder. ' "NUDE MODEL FOUND DEAD IN BATH." '

'Dunderheads!' Mr Crabbit roared at them happily. 'Read the bloody thing. Front page. Nude model! For crying out loud! Good God boy, where are your brains? I said news not titillation.'

' "HITLER RENOUNCES TREATY OF VERSAILLES",' Jack read from the front page. 'Oh! Was *that* what you meant? "Herr Adolf Hitler plans to recruit an army of half a million men." That'll put work our way, Charlie. I suppose he's one of our clients, is he Mr C?'

'G. S. Holborn's, you over-educated moron,' Mr Crabbit said, flicking his fedora neatly on to the hatstand. 'Old man Holborn'll have a field day.' He strode into the inner office snorting with satisfaction.

'Lucky him!' Charlie Commoner said. 'I wish we could.' He and Jack were studying hard for their second law examinations and finding endless academic application very trying.

'Wouldn't hurt him to send us out on a real case once in a while,' Jack said.

'Where would you go, if he gave you the chance?'

'America. Where would you?'

'Paris.'

'They have riots in Paris.'

'Just the ticket. I like a good riot.'

'You're a bloody idiot.'

'I know,' Charlie said, cuffing his friend's head with the rolled-up newspaper. 'More brains than sense, that's me.'

Mr Grossman looked up from his desk in the corner of the room and gave them his dour look. 'He only wants to go to Paris to get after the girls,' he said.

'Chance'd be a fine thing,' Charlie said, grimacing. Getting after the girls was easier said than done. He spent all day in the office, where the only female company was Mr Crabbit's secretary who was a hundred and five if she was a day, and all his spare time with his old school mates either at the pictures or the dogs, or mooching about Clapham Common on the look-out for the meeting that would change his life. They talked about girls all the time, but none of them had the least idea how to get to know one.

'There you are!' Mr Crabbit said, putting a triumphant head round the door of the inner office. 'What did I tell you? Holborn's are extending.'

'It's all right for some!' Mr Grossman said sourly. 'I'll have to do all the work, you see if I don't. All Mr G. S. Holborn's got to do is put his hand in his pocket.'

Actually, it was rather more difficult for Mr G. S. Holborn than Mr Grossman imagined. And the difficulties were all coming from the same direction.

At that very moment, in the boardroom at High Holborn, Claud Everdale was expounding his latest proposition.

'It's the very latest in weaponry,' he was urging. 'Tanks are the coming thing. You said so yourself, Father-in-law. Well then, why not an anti-tank rifle?'

The prototype lay on the table between them. It was a heavy, ugly weapon and Old Mr Holborn obviously didn't approve of it. But he wasn't speaking against it. He was doing his best to keep his temper and spare his heart. It wasn't easy. Claud could get him into a state quicker than anyone else he knew. He'd done himself no favours by giving the wretched man a seat on the board.

'Mr Pennyfield?' he asked his works manager.

'Well sir,' Jack Pennyfield said, 'we could make 'em right enough, but I wouldn't advise it.'

'Why not?'

'It's not a good weapon.'

'In what way?'

'It's cumbersome and it's heavy. Wouldn't be the easiest thing to cart about, especially under fire. I could see it being thrown away when push came to shove.'

'How does it compare to the Lee Enfield?'

'No comparison, sir. The Lee Enfield's a bloody good rifle.'

'How about the plant?' Mr Holborn asked his chief engineer.

'Difficult, but not impossible,' Roger Smith said. 'I've drawn up a blueprint.'

'Would you advise it?'

'No, sir. Not really. I'd rather step up production of the Lee Enfield. We've got the concession.'

'Mr Reinhart?'

The company secretary, who was the smallest man at the table, gave them all a deprecating smile. 'I would rather be advised by you,' he said. 'I have very little knowledge of this side of things. We can certainly afford the expansion you propose. That I can say.'

'This thing can shoot through armour plating twenty millimetres thick,' Claude Everdale urged, glaring at them. What was the matter with the fools? With re-armament just round the corner it was a sure-fire money spinner.

'The minute the Germans know it's going into production they'll strengthen their armour,' his father-in-law said, arguing back at last and with authority. 'It'll be obsolete before we can get it off the assembly line.'

'If we're going to expand production,' Claud insisted, 'why not give it a chance?'

'Because the general feeling is against it,' Mr Holborn said brusquely. And that was the end of the matter.

'He never listens,' Claud complained to his wife later that day as they dressed for dinner. 'We could have made a fortune and he wouldn't entertain it. He's nothing but a dyed-in-the-wool reactionary. And Pennyfield's no better. He kept wittering on about how cumbersome it was. Namby pamby nonsense. What are infantry for, if not to carry guns about? There wasn't any of that nonsense in the war.'

'How do you know?' Agnes said, stinging him because she was annoyed by the arrogance in his voice. 'You weren't in it.'

'Oh, throw that in my face, I should.'

'Mr Pennyfield was three years in the trenches.'

'Like your precious brother,' he sneered. 'Go on! Say it!'

'I don't need to. You've said it for me. And you needn't take that tone. He *was* precious. He died for his country.'

The words hung in the air between them as Claud turned from the mirror and looked straight at his wife for what felt like a very long time. He had an expression on his face that made her feel afraid, a hard, calculating, hateful expression.

'You don't want to be so sure,' he said at last, 'or one of these days I might just tell you what your precious brother did die of.'

'I know what he died of,' Agnes said, but now her heart was drumming with alarm. Claud did this to her frequently these days, throwing out hints that there was something dreadful about poor Edward's illness. It was very cruel. 'We all know.'

He was fastening his tie, looking at her in the mirror with another hateful expression on his face, sneering and superior – as if he knew something she didn't, as if he was going to defeat her. 'You all think you know,' he said. 'But you don't.'

112

'And you do, I suppose,' she said, trying to sneer back.

'Yes,' he said, watching her distress. 'I do. And one day I might just tell you.'

She didn't want to hear this or talk about it. She didn't even want to think about it.

'Ready?' Claud said, not looking at her.

He'd upset her so much she pushed ahead of him down the stairs without saying another word. Halfway down, he started to talk to her as though nothing was the matter. The mocking note had vanished from his voice and he was his urbane self again, preparing to greet her father's guests.

'Your father's a brute, you know,' he said jovially. 'He's sending me to Paris next week to negotiate another deal for those wretched Lee Enfields of his. As if we haven't got enough orders for them.'

'Paris?' Agnes said, turning her head. Oh how wonderful to be going to Paris.

'Yes. Damn nuisance.'

'I suppose I couldn't come with you, could I?'

'Whatever for?' he said. 'You'd hate it. All that traffic and garlic all over the food and people talking French all the time. Bad enough I've got to go without dragging you there.'

'I might like it,' Agnes said. She didn't have the energy for a second argument, especially after the worrying inferences of the first. Paris, she thought longingly. Paris in the Spring. Edward had told her all about it. The most beautiful city in the world, he'd said, and at its very best in springtime. Oh yes. I wouldn't just *like* it, I'd adore it. Right away from Claud and his hints and that nasty way of his. I'd give anything to go there.

'I've got to go to Paris!' Mauricette wailed, running through the garden towards her bosom friends. 'Isn't that just foul!'

It was that easy time on a Saturday when the week's work is done, and afternoon is drifting gently into evening. Cousin Berthe, Hortense and the twins were in the vegetable garden, weeding rows of spring onions and cabbages. From a distance they resembled figures from a

Renoir painting, for all four of them wore wide-brimmed hats made of straw, gardening clogs and sackcloth aprons to protect their skirts from the mud in the well-watered rows. It might be 1935 in fashionable Paris, but here, in Boves, among the rolling wheatfields of the Somme Valley, working women wore the sort of clothes their mothers and grand-mothers had always worn. Sometimes the very same ones.

'What's the matter?' Ginny called back, as Mauricette hurtled towards them.

'We're moving,' Mauricette wept. 'Papa's been fired. We've got to go to Paris and help Uncle Felix with his flower stall.'

'Oh, Mauricette!' Emily said, all sympathy. 'That's awful. When?'

'In ten days,' Mauricette said, and wiped her nose with the back of her hand. 'I've got to give in my notice on Monday.'

'So soon!' Ginny wailed, flinging her arms round her friend's neck.

'So soon. I shan't have time to say goodbye. Oh Ginny, Emilie, I can't bear it. We shall never see one another again. I shall die.'

'No, you won't,' Hortense said, intervening to prevent any further hysterics. 'You can come here and stay with us. Paris is no distance.'

Mauricette was comforted. 'Just as I was going to fall in love too,' she wept.

'Who with?' Cousin Berthe wanted to know.

'How do I know?' Mauricette wailed. 'I haven't done it yet. Oh isn't it foul, Ginny! To have to live in a city. I'm a country girl. I shall hate it in the city. What am I going to do?'

Cousin Berthe knew the answer to that. She gave Mauricette her widest smile. 'Get a hoe,' she advised, 'and help us shift some of these weeds, eh?'

It was sound advice. It's difficult to cry when you are working hard, and wielding a hoe in the gentle evening sunshine soothed poor Mauricette, whether she would or no.

114

The parting hung over all three girls like an impending storm, growing more and more oppressive through the next ten days. And when the awful moment came and they kissed goodbye at the little station, Mauricette cried so much she couldn't speak.

'Poor Mauricette,' Emily said, as she and Ginny walked home. 'At least we've got one another. She hasn't got anyone. She'll be terribly lonely.'

And so Mauricette was. She wrote to her old friends nearly every day all through March, repeating the same things over and over again – that she knew no one, that the work on the flower stall was hateful, that her brothers and sisters were being vile, that the weather was foul, that she missed them more than she could say.

'You are to come and stay with us at Easter,' Ginny wrote back. 'Nothing has changed here. We can't wait to see you again.'

But when Easter came, Mauricette wrote postponing the visit. The letter was short and to the point. Because the tourists had started to arrive, the stall was too busy to be left, but she would see them soon. They would plan another time.

Then there was a long silence into which the twins sent four letters which both signed – Ginny guiding her sister's hand. April passed. They were two weeks into May and there was still no reply. Having roared three new secretaries out of the office, Monsieur Guerin hired a fourth called Veronique Tilliette who could cope with his rages. Ginny was just debating whether it would be politic to write and tell her old friend all about it, when a letter from Paris finally arrived.

It was written in a new, controlled handwriting that was only just recognisable as Mauricette's.

'*I can't come and stay with you this year, after all,*' she wrote, '*but you must come here and stay with me. You first, Virginie, as soon as M. Guerin will let you off, and Emilie the next time. I am so happy. I have found a cause.*'

'That's nice,' Cousin Berthe said. 'Where d'you think she

115

found it, eh?' She seemed to be under the impression that a cause was some kind of pet. 'Nice to have a cause to look after. It'll give her something to do.'

Monsieur Joliot had a very different opinion. 'I don't hold with causes,' he growled. 'We were supposed to be fighting for a cause back in the Great War, an' a fat lot of good it ever did us.'

But the twins were thrilled and Ginny began making plans for her visit straightaway. 'I'll ask Monsieur Guerin this morning,' she said. 'Three days wouldn't hurt, I know. I'll persuade him.'

'How?' Emily wanted to know.

'I'll offer to stay late when there's a rush. Something like that.'

'Be prepared for disappointment, then,' her mother said drily. 'I've never met an employer yet who saw things the same way as his workers.'

That evening, after a day in which Ginny had thrown out her first hint to Monsieur Guerin and been ignored, the sisters took a stroll out of the village. They usually did this when they wanted to talk to one another in private.

'Maman doesn't want you to go to Paris,' Emily said, as they rustled through the corn.

'How do you know?' Ginny asked, pulling her sister closer to her side to keep her on the footpath.

'I could hear it.'

'She was surprised, that's all. She'll come round to it.'

'You sound like Babbers,' Emily said. 'Do you remember how she used to say – what was it in English? – "They'll come round to it"?'

'Dear old Babbers. I ought to write to her. Perhaps I'll send her a postcard when I get to Paris.'

'*If* you get to Paris.'

'*If* I can remember enough English to write it properly.' The twins still spoke English together as a secret language, but they hadn't written it for years.

A skylark rose out of the corn beside them and spiralled into the air, trilling its sharp, sweet song as it climbed. It was

116

such an optimistic sound that Ginny was heartened. 'She'll change her mind, you'll see.'

'I hope you're right,' Emily said, giving her sister's arm a squeeze. Still she felt she had to warn Ginny. 'She *did* sound hard.'

'I'll get there,' Ginny said. 'You'll see.'

Due to Monsieur Guerin's intransigence, it took a very long time. At first, he declared a holiday was out of the question because they were too busy. Then, as Ginny continued to wear him down, he said it *might* be possible but not until the middle of June. When June drew to a close, he said it had been an impossible month and Ginny would have to wait until July.

This could go on for ever, Ginny fumed, and decided it was time for a really determined stand.

'*Le Quatorze* is on a Sunday this year, Monsieur Geurin,' she said. 'Since you are renowned for your sense of fair play, may I ask, are we to have some other day off in lieu?'

It was a daring question. She was running the risk of triggering off a Guerin rage.

Monsieur Guerin bristled. 'That is my affair, Mam'selle Lisieux,' he said, giving her a warning look.

Ginny hung on to her courage. 'But you will tell us, being a man of honour?'

The mention of honour made him draw himself up to his limited height. But he gave her a fair answer. 'Assuredly.'

'Then perhaps I could take two or three days off at around the same time?'

He went quiet. 'You would lose pay.'

'That is understood.'

'I will think about it,' he said. 'Now, find the Lanvin file, if you please, and don't waste any more of my time.'

Monsieur Guerin thought about it for three days. But, at last, permission was given and Ginny could write to Mauricette to say that she would be coming to Paris on Wednesday 11th July and would stay until Sunday if the family could endure her for so long. It was a little triumph.

It didn't please Maman.

Hortense brooded on it and frowned whenever the trip was mentioned, and, the more she thought about it, the more distressed she became. It was the moment she'd been dreading all these years; the awful, awful moment when she would have to tell the twins the truth about their health – and love and marriage and everything else. Now that it had come she didn't know how she could bear it.

Sweating with a combination of guilt and fear, she lay awake at night, remembering the promise she'd given to Edouard all those years ago and his anguish when he'd told her that they might have passed on the 'bad' disease to their two innocent babies. The terror of the illness had never left her and now it loomed, ever blacker and more horrible.

On Wednesday morning when Ginny was packed and ready to leave, she suddenly told the twins to put on their hats and come out 'for a breath of fresh air'. Pinching warnings to one another they followed Hortense into the village square and up the hillside steps of the Chemin de la Montagne into the cemetery, neat and empty in the cool sunshine of early morning. It must be something very private, Ginny thought. I hope she'll hurry up or I shall miss my train.

'Sit here,' Hortense said, settling her daughters on the low brick wall beside the hawthorn. She remained standing, with her back to the tombstones, frowning and distressed, rubbing her left hand with the roughened palm of her right.

'What is it, Maman?' Emily prompted.

'I have something to tell you,' Hortense said, and then she stopped, sighed, looked out over the peaceful countryside and sighed again.

'Yes?' Emily said.

'What I have to tell,' Hortense said at last, 'is that you are not like other young women.'

'No,' Emily said easily. 'I'm blind.' How odd of Maman to be talking about that now, after all these years.

'No,' Hortense said, speaking with difficulty. 'It is not that, Emilie, although I suppose that is part of it. Oh dear, this is dreadful. How can I tell you?' But she had to tell them.

She had to warn her poor Virginie. 'You are not like other women. Neither of you.'

They waited in silence, puzzled and rather alarmed.

'I think,' Hortense said, struggling to find something that could be said, something they could understand, 'I think you should change your mind about this visit, Virginie.'

Rage and incomprehension flared in Ginny like new-fired tinder. Why was Maman putting difficulties in her way now, just when she was going to catch the train, and after all the effort she'd made to get Monsieur Guerin's permission. 'Not go, do you mean?' she said. When her mother nodded she added, 'Why not?'

'Cities are dangerous,' Hortense replied, looking dogged. 'You never know who you might meet.'

'I'm going to meet Mauricette.'

'You know perfectly well what I mean. There are criminals in big cities, thieves, pick-pockets, seducers. No, no, it's far too dangerous.'

'I'm nineteen, Maman,' Ginny protested. 'I'm not a child. I can look after myself.'

'You *think* you can look after yourself, but in reality ... You don't know what a big city is like. No, no, no, you're too young.'

'But you were the same age as me when you left home, Maman. You must have been.'

'Yes,' Hortense said bitterly, 'and look what happened to me.'

'You married Daddy,' Ginny said.

'Ah,' her mother sighed. 'If only that were all. You don't know the half of it.'

Emily had been listening to the emotion as well as the words. 'Why don't you want her to go, Maman?' she asked. 'Is it because of what you wanted to tell us?'

Hortense looked bleakly at her daughters. 'You are not like other young women,' she said again. 'You have an illness. A terrible illness. It ... It is ... It sets you apart.'

This time, the shock and hurt was visible in their faces: Ginny's flushed and angry, Em's pinched and pale.

119

Ginny fought back at once. 'We're as fit as fleas,' she said. 'How can you say such a thing? We're both very well. Fit and strong. Look at us.'

Emily had digested the information quietly, and was considering it. 'What sort of illness?' she asked. What sort of illness could you have that didn't make you feel ill, and set you apart from other people? The very idea of it was making her feel chilled and afraid.

'You've got bad blood,' Hortense confessed. 'It's a – what can I call it? – there isn't a word for it. I suppose it's a sort of – well, a sort of taint. Yes, that's what it is, a taint. While you are virgin you are safe, but if you fall in love, marry, love a man, you understand what I mean, then you will suffer, you will be ill.'

'It's not true,' Ginny said, still fighting. 'There aren't diseases like that.'

'There are,' Maman said, twisting her fingers together in her anguish. 'I wish there weren't, but there are. Nobody talks about them, but they exist. Remember your father. You would end up like him.'

'But he was wounded,' Ginny said. 'He died of war wounds.'

'Yes,' Maman said. 'He was wounded, but he was ill, too. He had this illness. Now do you see why you must be careful, both of you? You must never get married. Do you understand that? You mustn't even think of it.'

'Very well, then,' Ginny said crossly, 'if that's how it is, I'll give you my word here and now, Maman. I won't fall in love, I won't get married, I won't talk to any young men, I won't even look at them, I won't go anywhere near them. Will that satisfy you?'

'It's serious, Virginie,' Maman said, and her voice was riven with pity and misery. 'I only tell you for your own good.'

'Well, then, I've given you my word so you don't need to worry. Now may I go?' And when Maman hesitated. 'I'll stay with Mauricette and her family and I won't see anyone else, if that's what you want.'

120

'It's not what I want,' Maman said. 'I don't say any of this to hurt you. I had to warn you. You must see that.'

'I've seen it. Now may I go?'

But, one hand clenched against the side of her face, Hortense shook her head in agony. 'You mustn't marry,' she said. 'I *have* to tell you.'

There really is an illness, Emily thought. She is telling the truth. And dread clenched her belly as all sorts of questions crowded out of the darkness into her mind. Did we catch it from Daddy? And if we did, how did we catch it? Was it from sneezing or from skin or what? Could we give it to someone else in the same way? Has Maman got it, too? But she couldn't ask any of them because Ginny was fighting back, her words quick and angry and slightly hysterical.

'You're always saying that. You do it all the time. Well, I don't believe you. There's no such illness.' Maman was being over-dramatic. It couldn't be true. There couldn't be an illness like that.

'I wish there weren't,' her mother said, 'but there is.'

'Then name it. Tell us what it is and we'll go to *Monsieur le Medicin* and see what *he* has to say.'

'You can't do that,' Hortense said. 'It's too shameful.'

'Rubbish!' Ginny said. 'If it's an illness, it's got a name, hasn't it?'

'Yes,' Hortense said, but the word was little more than a whisper. 'A terrible name. A frightening name. You must believe me.'

Ginny was feeling so frightened her stomach was churning, but she went on fighting. 'Tell us what it is,' she insisted.

Hortense closed her eyes in anguish and groaned, backing away from them. 'I can't. I can't.'

All this time Emily had remained quiet, but now she *had* to intervene. 'Please Ginny, don't shout at her,' she begged, reaching out a hand to find her sister's arm. 'You're upsetting her.'

'She's upsetting me!' Ginny said angrily, standing up

121

and shaking the hand away. 'I think it's disgusting to tell us such nonsense. Do you hear that Maman? Disgusting.'

'Yes,' Hortense blazed back, snatching strength from her daughter's anger, and turned to face her. 'It *is* disgusting. But it's true. It's all true. And I've *got* to warn you. I promised your father.'

For a few seconds neither of them knew what to say next. They stood glaring at one another, their faces distorted. Among the spikes of the hawthorn hidden sparrows were quarreling and the sun was making the grass blades shine like steel.

'Perhaps we should never have been born,' Ginny said bitterly. 'If this illness is as disgusting as all that perhaps you and Daddy should never have had any children. It's your bad blood you've passed on, isn't it? Perhaps *you* should never have married.'

'How dare you say such a thing!' Hortense shouted. 'How dare you! You wicked girl.'

Now Emily was on her feet, too, reaching out to find them and placate them. 'Please! Please! Oh, please don't quarrel. Maman! Ginny!' Her hands swam like starfish through the empty air and her eyes rolled in agitation.

'Your father was a fine man,' Hortense said, and now she was weeping. 'A good man. I loved him more than all the world. More than all the world. My dear, dear Edouard. And he loved me. We were everything to one another. He couldn't help being ill. We didn't know about it then. It wasn't his fault. He was a fine good man. A good father. You should be proud of him.'

'We are!' Emily said, still searching for them. 'We are, Maman. We love you both. You must know that. We always have.'

Hortense caught her hands, pulled her into her arms, holding her tight, and wept into her long hair. 'You mustn't say things about your father,' she whispered. 'I can't bear it.'

'No, no,' Emily soothed, rubbing her mother's spine. 'We won't. Will we, Ginny? We loved him, too.'

Isolated on the other side of a tombstone Ginny put her

122

face in her hands and struggled to fight back her own tears. 'Yes, yes, yes,' she said, and the struggle made her voice sound cross. 'We loved him, too. You know that, Maman.'

Hortense looked up through her tears and held out her free hand towards her other daughter, begging for the forgiveness of an embrace. 'Oh, my dear Virginie,' she said. 'We must help one another, you and I. I only told you for the best.'

But Ginny stayed where she was, knowing that if she hugged her mother she would be weeping, too.

'I *am* going to Paris, Maman,' she said.

'Oh, Virginie!'

'I've given my word to Mauricette.'

After all this, Hortense thought, catching her breath. After all this I'm defeated. But she was too spent to argue any further. 'If I say yes, you will be careful.'

'Yes,' Ginny said. 'I will. I promise. I won't have anything to do with any men at all.' And she walked round the tombstone to kiss her mother's tear-stained cheek. It was the merest touch and stiffly given but it was all she could manage. The church bell was tolling the hour. If they didn't leave soon Maman and Emily would be late for work and Ginny's train would leave without her. 'Now, may I go?'

So permission was given at last with sighs deeper than any Emily had ever heard and they dried their eyes and set off down the hillside to work and to the station.

'Don't worry,' Ginny whispered as she kissed her sister goodbye outside the Advocate's house. 'I shan't come to any harm. She's exaggerating.'

Emily didn't argue because there wasn't time, and because Maman might hear and, in any case, she was too drained by the emotion of the last few minutes to want to provoke any more outbursts. She simply kissed Ginny's cheek and said a private prayer for her safety. But she was still cold with dread and she went on feeling afraid for the rest of the day; when she finally got to bed, she carried her unspoken fears into nightmares.

Lacerated with rage, Ginny ran to the station. To say

such things just at the very moment when she was packed and ready to go! It was hateful. And unnecessary. She felt upset all the way to Paris, justifying her anger with her mother and pushing pity to one side, concentrating on feeling aggrieved and hurt so that she didn't have to face the possible truth of what had been said. Because it couldn't be true. She wouldn't let it be true. It was too horrible.

# CHAPTER NINE

By the time Ginny stepped off the train into the noise and bustle of the Gare du Nord, her natural ebullience had reasserted itself. There was no sense in dwelling on the quarrel or prolonging her anger. She was in Paris now, all on her own, with no work to do for five whole days and a holiday to enjoy. *That* was what was important. Now where was Mauricette?

She was waiting at the barrier, as she'd promised, but in the four months since they'd last seen one another she'd changed so much that Ginny hardly recognised her. She'd lost a lot of weight, cut her hair in a new gamine style with a kiss curl on one cheek and she was wearing really stylish clothes, a short straight skirt, a red blouson shirt, high-heeled shoes and a little blue beret perched on the side of her head. But she leapt at Ginny and kissed her on both cheeks, as affectionately as ever, before pirouetting her new appearance for her friend's opinion.

'What do you think? Chic, eh?'

'Very, very chic. Oh, it is good to see you.'

'We're going to have five days' absolute holiday together,' Mauricette said happily, as they linked arms and walked out of the station. 'I'm going to show you all the sights and in the evenings . . .' There was a daring, triumphant expression on her new slim face.

'In the evenings?' Ginny prompted, grinning at her.

'You'll see. But now I shall take you home and settle you into the apartment and then you must tell me where you'd like to go first.'

The apartment was on the south bank of the Seine in an old rooming house, down one of the narrow alleys. On the fifth floor just under the eaves, Mauricette's room gave out on to the cobbled courtyard below where pigeons strutted and pecked and the concierge was beating rugs against the wall. Clouds of dust rose into the air. They could hear a car hooting in the alley and sharp Parisian voices raised in argument somewhere beyond the gateway.

'Do you like it?' Mauricette asked.

'Yes. It's wonderful.'

'Now. Where shall we go?'

'Montmartre?'

So Montmartre it was, to watch flamboyant artists at work in the Place du Theatre, and to climb the long flights of narrow steps up to the cathedral, high and white on its mount like a castle from a fairy tale. The huddled roofs of Paris below it stretched as far as they could see, and all the familiar landmarks were clear under the open blue of the sky – the Eiffel Tower, the Arc de Triomphe, Notre Dame, the long, straight, tree-lined boulevards bisecting the city like the green spokes of a wheel.

'It's beautiful,' Ginny said. 'And you're happy here, aren't you?'

'Oh yes. I am now. You'll see why this evening.'

'Where are we going this evening, then?'

But Mauricette wouldn't tell. 'You'll see,' she said mysteriously.

'Is this the cause you've found?'

'Yes. Yes. You'll see.'

That evening after dinner they put on their berets, made sure they had small change in their pockets and went to a café on the Boulevard Saint Michele.

It was crowded with people, most of them young and most of them deep in argument. Mauricette pushed her way through the throng on the pavement to a table where a tall young man in an open-necked shirt was sitting, cigarette in hand, haranguing the crowd.

'Gérard,' she said to him. 'This is my friend from Boves.'

He gave a quick formal bow in Ginny's direction, said, '*Enchanté*', smiled at her briefly and continued his discourse.

'All that we on the left have to do,' he said, 'to allow the right wing to bully their way to political power is to continue in our usual short-sighted way, bickering amongst ourselves, fighting one another instead of attacking the real enemy. No doubt about it, the Leagues are the enemy. Of the working class, of Jews, of independent minds, of books, of us. And make no mistake about it, they mean to take power, legally or illegally, it doesn't matter to them. The object is to take power and never let go. Once that's done we are finished. They'll only need to be elected once and that will be the end of democracy in this country. They won't allow any opposition. There'll be no more elections. No more political parties except theirs. They'll do what Herr Hitler is doing in Germany now. We shall end up in concentration camps or exiled abroad in fear of our lives. Or dead.'

It sounded exciting and dangerous. 'What are the Leagues?' Ginny whispered to Mauricette.

But the young man heard her and answered. 'Right-wing activists,' he said. 'Street thugs. Fascists. The men who came out on to the streets last February and tried to take the National Assembly by force, the *Camelots du Roi*, *Solidarité Française*, the *Croix de Feu*, the storm troopers of Colonel Casimir de la Rocque.'

'And who's he?'

'He, Mademoiselle, is the man who would like to be the French Adolf Hitler and rule this country without opposition for the rest of his life. And we are the men and women who will stop him. As we stopped him in February.'

Her interest was now thoroughly roused. 'Were you there?'

'Show her your battle scars, Alphonse,' Gérard said to a fair-haired young man on the other side of the table.

The young man lifted his hair from his forehead to reveal a long red scar.

My God, Ginny thought, he's actually been in a fight, out here in the streets. She looked round the table at the ardent faces turned towards her. No wonder they're so full of life and so proud. They've seen history being made. They've fought for the things they believe in. How wonderful.

127

'Tell me more,' she said.

So they told her. How the Leagues had grown, how they were supported by powerful businessmen, 'Monsieur Coty pays for the *Croix de Feu*, perfume and talcum powder Coty, you know,' and how they would run the country if they seized power. 'There would be no newspapers or radio stations to put the opposition point of view as there are now. We would be silenced. Then God help the Jews.'

'Why?' she asked. 'What would happen to the Jews?'

'They are the scapegoats for everything that is wrong in Germany,' Gérard explained, 'and the Leagues would make them the scapegoats here, too. Hitler hates them.' He was fishing a battered booklet out of his pocket. 'There you are,' he said, pushing it across the table at her. 'See for yourself. This is what he says. See. Read that.'

Ginny read the quotation he was pointing at. ' "The Jew is the ferment of decomposition in people. Adolf Hitler." And is that what the *Croix de Feu* think too?'

'Now you begin to understand,' he said, eyes blazing. 'These men are evil. They want power for its own sake and they'll do anything to get it. They'll cheat. They'll beat people up. They'll lie. And if anything goes wrong they'll blame the Jews.' He turned the pages as he spoke. 'They've got a twisted little creep called Goëbbels in the Nazi Party who says the best way to get elected is to tell lies, and if you're going to tell a lie you'd better tell a big one. And why? Because you're more likely to be believed if you tell a big lie. He calls it propaganda. Totally dishonest. And the damn fool Germans believe him. Just as the French will believe de la Roche if we don't stop him. There you are. I've found it. Read that.'

She read again, holding the page down with her fingers. Mauricette watched her proudly, like a mother watching a favoured child doing well at her lessons. 'The election is upon us but the struggle is a light one now, since we are to employ all the means of the State. Radio and Press are at our disposal. We shall achieve a masterpiece of propaganda. Even money is not lacking at this time. Goëbbels.'

128

'And they won,' she said.

'They won and they've already turned the Jews into second-class citizens. No German is allowed to marry a Jew. No Jew is allowed to hire a German servant. And if you're a German with Jewish blood you lose your citizenship altogether. If you're Jewish you're inferior, worthless. You can be beaten up in the streets and nobody will help you and you can't do anything about it.'

She was shocked. 'That's horrible.'

'Yes,' Gérard said grimly. 'It is. But they won't win here.'

When the two friends finally walked back to the apartment in the early hours of the morning, Ginny was still stunned and uplifted by what she'd heard. 'When do they meet again?' she asked.

'Every night,' Mauricette said happily. 'We'll go again tomorrow, eh? What do you think of Gérard?'

'You love him.'

'Oh yes, passionately.'

'And does he love you?'

'No,' Mauricette admitted. 'He doesn't think of me in that way. I'm a comrade.'

'Is that enough?' Ginny asked. 'It wouldn't be enough for me.'

Mauricette shrugged. 'It has to be for the moment, while they're all so busy with the cause. Later, perhaps . . . Who knows? But what do you think of him?'

'He's very passionate.'

'That's because he's Jewish. I think he's wonderful.'

'They all are,' Ginny said. 'They're like warriors.'

'Yes,' Mauricette agreed, sighing rapturously. 'That's just what he is. A warrior. Isn't it noble!'

From then on the holiday fell neatly into a pattern, sightseeing by day and politics by night, and Ginny felt as though she was suddenly living two lives.

On the second day, they visited Fauborg St Honoré, where they found an evening coat in Lanvin's window made from Monsieur Guerin's amber velvet. It had a great red fox fur collar spreading like a cape over its shoulders, and

Mauricette said it wasn't right for the rich to buy such extravagant clothes when the poor were in rags. They walked the length of the Champs Elysées under the summer shade of the chestnut trees, sat in the Tuileries Gardens and took a trip to the top of the Eiffel Tower. They went to the great market of Les Halles where they bought more fruit than they could eat and to the great cathedral of Notre Dame where they said happy prayers. They even went window shopping in a huge store called Samaritain, which was decorated inside and out with beautiful blue and amber tiles patterned with fruit and flowers. There was a huge wrought-iron staircase rising four storeys without any apparent support to a domed roof, painted amber and duck-egg blue to match the tiles. The prices were so far beyond them that they didn't even bother to look, but it didn't matter when there was so much else to see. And Mauricette said that when the socialists were in power shops like that would be turned into palaces of culture for all the people.

But the evenings were the best times back at the Boule' Miche, at 'their' table on the pavement in the heat and passion of politics.

On Saturday evening Gérard announced that they would all meet at the Place de la Bastille at three o'clock the following afternoon.

'Will you join us?' he asked Ginny. 'It will be the biggest gathering of the Left this city has ever seen. If it goes well we might see the beginning of a popular front against the fascists.'

'They're on the march tomorrow, too,' Mauricette said. 'We'll go and see them first, if you like.'

It took a long time for all the left-wing groups to gather in the Place de la Bastille the following afternoon.

'Take a good look at them,' Mauricette commanded. She and Ginny stood on the cobbles among their friends, as the crowds of demonstrators jostled into position around their various banners. 'I want you to pay particular attention to what they look like.'

'They all look quite ordinary,' Ginny said. And so they did, old men in the ubiquitous blue beret, middle-aged women in little flat hats, young men in cheap crumpled suits and young women in cheap cotton frocks. 'Very ordinary.'

'Good!' Mauricette said. 'Now come with me.' And when Ginny looked puzzled. 'We've plenty of time to see the other lot. We won't be marching out of here for another hour.'

They took the Métro to the Champs Elysées and emerged into the summer sunshine to the sound of drums and a military band.

'That'll be them,' Mauricette said and, seizing Ginny's hand, she ran towards the sound, pushing through the crowds who were waiting on the pavements for the march to pass. 'Up here!' she said. 'Now! Look! There they are.'

There was a column of dark-suited men marching towards them up the Champs Elysées. They were preceded by a military band and a line of flag bearers carrying long black, red and white pennants and they all marched in step with perfect discipline, like an army. For a few crazy seconds Ginny had the impression that they were robots – there was something so mechanical and menacing about them. But then she realised that it was because they were all men and so alike. Dressed in dark uniforms with medals on their chests and red, black and white armbands on their left arms, they had the same hair-cut, short, severe and glued to their skulls with pomade, and what was worse, oh much much worse, the same terrible expression on their faces, a hard, set, hating expression. They made her blood run cold.

'Now do you see?' Mauricette asked at her elbow.

'Oh yes,' she said. 'They are men capable of cruelty, Mauricette. You're right. We've got to stop them.'

Mauricette kissed her with pride and affection. 'I knew you'd see it,' she said. 'And you'll join us?'

There was no doubt about that now. 'Yes. I'll join you.'

On the first floor at the Hôtel Royaume D'or, just behind the pavement where the two girls were standing, somebody else was watching the demonstration from the windows of the banqueting rooms. Claud Everdale and his new military friends were meeting for the second time that year and they'd been enjoying their aperitifs when the thud of the drums called their curiosity to the window.

'Human nature,' a French major said in sing-song English that made Claud think of Maurice Chevalier. 'You see 'ow it is. We march in *battaillons*. We sing ze hymns of war. Always we 'ave to fight one anozer.'

'Which is just as well,' Claud said, 'or *we* should be out of business, *tous les deux*.' He was rather proud of his ability to throw oddments of French into the conversation, and the military men seemed to like it.

' 'eads will be broken before ze end of ze day,' the major said, stroking the rim of his glass. 'Ze communists, zey march today also. Zey will fight unless the *gendarmerie* can prevent it.'

Good, Claud thought happily. Let them. First on the street with fists and staves, then on the field of battle with G. S. Holborn's rifles. We shall make a fortune.

Left alone in the permanent darkness that was her world, Emily Lisieux was thinking most unhappily. For the first time in her life she had no daily companion to act as interpreter; no bedmate to gossip with, either, and it was making her feel very lonely.

Maman got on with her work and sounded cheerful and Cousin Berthe and Old Joliot were the same as always, but Emily knew that she herself had suffered a change. Her mother's warning was constantly in her thoughts, the words echoing and re-echoing, 'You are different from other young women. You have an illness. A taint. You could end up like your father.' She couldn't make any sense of it. She could only feel afraid. And remember.

It was now that she realised there had been frequent clues to all this, things she'd heard and stored away even though she hadn't understood them at the time, now, she enumerated them and turned them over in her mind: the secrecy that surrounded Daddy's illness, Maman's hysteria when they left High Holborn, her insistence that they shouldn't let anyone in England know where they were, the way she panicked for no apparent reason and rushed off without references or pay to get a worse job than the last. The more she thought about it the more anxious Emily became.

Eventually on Thursday evening when she and Maman were weeding in the garden – Cousin Berthe had gone stomping off down the cinder path to the earth closet *pour faire pipi* – she tried to ask a careful question.

'Maman,' she said, resting on her hoe, 'I've been thinking about this illness you told us about . . .'

Her mother's reaction was so quick and extreme it made her heart skid with fear.

'Be quiet!' she ordered, laying her hand across Emily's mouth. 'You foolish child. What are you thinking about to speak of it out here? Don't you understand? You must never mention it. Never, never, never. Someone might hear. Holy Mary, Mother of God pray for us sinners. Where's your sense? She could be back at any moment.'

Emily mumbled an apology, her heart thumping.

'I've told you about it,' Maman said. 'That should be enough. Now speak of something else. She's coming back.' She turned to say something about the beans to Cousin Berthe in a voice that was so artificially cheerful that Emily felt quite ashamed for her.

There was no doubt now in Emily's mind. She stood with the warmth of the easy sunshine on her upturned face, and the summer sounds of the village all about her; horses whinnying and scraping their hooves in the stables, Old Joliot's hens crooning in that odd plaintive way they had, cart wheels creaking under some great weight, the Advocate's little dog yapping as he trotted off for his evening walk, and she was afraid. This illness was serious and shameful and threatening. She had reason to be afraid. Oh, if only Ginny hadn't gone off to Paris.

The days passed slowly. Being unable to share her thoughts increased Emily's fears and diminished her pleasures. Even Mass was lessened without Ginny's hand to pinch at high moments, although she was soothed by the ritual, the heady scent of the incense, the clink of the swinging censor, the hymns echoing into the high roof and the steady, familiar chant of the responses.

But when she and Maman walked out of the church into the sunshine she heard something that sharpened her fear to such a pitch of intensity it gave her a hard, heavy pain in her chest.

Father André was speaking to Maman, but not in the usual way he spoke to parishioners as they left his church. His voice was lower than usual, and confidential, and there was an insistent tone to it, too. And when Maman answered him she spoke very quietly, as if she didn't want anyone else to hear.

'I hope I shall see you take communion soon, my daughter,' the Father said.

'Oh yes, Father. Very soon.' But her listening daughter knew she didn't mean it.

'It's been many a long month.'

'Yes, Father. I will put it right.'

'Soon?' Father André was insistent.

'Yes, Father. Very soon.'

'The confessional is always open to a contrite heart.'

'Yes, Father.'

'Pray for grace, my daughter.'

Holding her mother's arm, Emily walked back to Cousin Berthe's house deep in the most painful thoughts. Maman didn't take communion. She didn't take communion because she hadn't been to confession. And the reason why she hadn't been to confession must be because she'd committed a sin too dreadful to be spoken about, even to a priest. The pattern was clear, the reasons obvious. It was only the sin that was unknown. A sin so dreadful it couldn't be mentioned. A mortal sin. It must be. Oh, poor Maman. How dreadful to have such a secret. How awful not to be able to confess it and to be cleansed of it. How terrible to be so unhappy and to have to keep her unhappiness hidden.

Underneath Emily's thoughts fear of that unknown illness crept like a snake, subtle and full of poison. If only Ginny were home, she yearned. If only I could talk to my Ginny. The evening, and her sister's return, seemed impossibly distant. Once we can talk about it everything will be better.

But Ginny returned to Boves a changed woman, happy and excited, with a copy of the left-wing paper *Le Populaire* under her arm and leaflets in her bag, bubbling with the news that she'd been on a demonstration. She was not in a fit state to listen to anything.

'You should have been there, Em,' she said, kissing her sister. 'It was really exciting. I've got such a lot to tell you.'

She seemed charged with energy. Cousin Berthe and Maman watched in amazement as she rushed precipitately up the stairs, returned with her box of talcum powder from the washstand, flung open the back door and emptied the contents on to the cinder path.

'That's that!' she said triumphantly. Then she crumpled the empty box to pieces and burnt the pieces in the stove.

'This is what comes of visiting the capital,' Maman remarked, in her teasing voice. 'Now she has money to burn, you see.'

'No, no, my dear,' Cousin Berthe contradicted. 'It's only an old box, that's all.'

'I've joined the socialists,' Ginny told them.

'So you burn boxes?' her mother said.

'Monsieur Coty's boxes, certainly. He uses his money to support the *Croix de Feu*.'

'Oh well,' Hortense said with mocking sarcasm, 'that explains everything. What else do you intend to burn?'

'Nothing else,' Ginny laughed back. 'I've scorched enough for one day. You're quite safe. I'm a socialist not an arsonist. You should be pleased, Maman. I didn't fall in love or get married or anything like that. I went to a political meeting instead.'

Hortense *was* relieved to hear it, but she didn't say so. Partly because Cousin Berthe was in the room, partly because their easy teasing was so pleasant she didn't want to

135

bring it to an end, and partly because she was trying to forget the other reminders: the painful scene in the cemetery, Emily's unwonted questioning in the garden and Father André's prodding reminder that morning. But whatever else might be hard in her life, at least the warning had been given. She'd done her duty by these two, dear daughters of hers. There was no need to talk about it any further. Providing her girls were sensible they could all go along the way they had before this visit to Paris. They could be happy. She could watch over them and remind them from time to time. There needn't be any changes.

But her newly political daughter had other ideas. The very next day, she stayed in Amiens after work to meet the local socialists. On Tuesday, she was again late home because she'd been addressing envelopes. By Friday, she was the secretary of the group.

Hortense declared she couldn't keep up with her.

'She's like a greyhound at full pelt,' she said, and her voice was warm with admiration. Because she felt such relief, it was easy to admire this headstrong daughter of hers. This plunge into politics was turning out to be a good thing. It might put Virginie in the path of rather too many young men but, at the moment at least, she was so fully occupied she didn't seem to be interested in any of them. Not in that way. So, thank Heaven for it. Perhaps there was truth in the English proverb that there was safety in numbers.

Emily tried to take an interest in what her sister was doing, too, but with anxiety nipping at her thoughts all the time it was very difficult. Ginny will listen to me soon, she thought. But it wasn't until the second Sunday after her return that Ginny found a moment for conversation. Walking home from church after mass she suddenly noticed how pale and quiet Em was, and asked what was the matter.

'Come for a walk,' Emily said, 'and I'll tell you.'

Ginny listened until the entire garbled story was unravelled, fears, suspicions, ancient clues, nightmares and all.

'Oh, Em, my darling,' she said, 'you mustn't worry about it. You really mustn't. I'm sure it was just Maman's way of putting me off.'

'Well, I don't,' her sister said. 'She doesn't take communion, Ginny.'

'I know,' Ginny said. 'But that could be for a hundred different reasons. Trust you to think of all the sins there are.'

'This one's so bad she can't confess it.'

'It could be something she did during the war. Lots of people did wicked things during the war. I've been hearing about some of the atrocities. Gérard said . . .'

Em didn't want to hear about atrocities. 'This illness,' she insisted, 'Maman wouldn't let me talk about it.'

'Because there's no such thing,' Ginny said trenchantly. 'We'd have heard of it if there had been. It was just her way of telling us she doesn't want us to get married. She's always been on at us about that, hasn't she?' Ginny had to believe her own conclusion, it was the only way to still her own fears. 'Look at us. We're not ill. We don't have fevers or coughs. We can both walk and talk and do everything we're supposed to.'

'I can't see,' Emily pointed out.

'But that's because you were born blind.'

'Yes,' Emily said sadly but doggedly. 'But *why* was I born blind? That's the point.'

'Because you were. Some people are. Some people are born with club feet or a harelip. It's the way things are.'

But Emily insisted. 'What if it was something to do with the illness?'

Ginny simply wouldn't allow it. That would have been too terrifying. 'Well, it's not,' she said, 'so you can stop worrying. Listen, why don't you come to the meeting with me on Wednesday? You'd love it. You should hear what we've got planned for after the election. Nobody's going to work more than forty hours a week. We're planning a national fund to pay people a wage when they're out of work. We're going to nationalise the armaments industry.'

137

That intrigued Emily despite her fears. 'Why?'

'Because it's immoral for a rich man to grow richer making weapons. Leon Blum says, "Socialism has to be moral or it will not be at all." '

'Who is Leon Blum?'

Relieved that their conversation was on safer ground, Ginny clicked her teeth in mock exasperation at her sister's ignorance. She'd never heard of him either before she went to Paris. 'Who's Leon Blum! Shame on you, Em! He's the man who will be prime minister when the Popular Front have won the election.'

'Do you think they *will* win, Ginny?'

'Yes,' Ginny said stoutly. 'The way I'm working, yes they will.'

'I love you when you're fierce,' Emily said, and kissed her.

'So you'll come to the meeting.'

'Yes, I suppose so.' It would be better than sitting at home worrying about an illness.

But as the weeks passed she worried about it anyway.

They were frightening times. That autumn the news was almost invariably bad and the papers were full of articles analysing the likelihood of another war. It came on October third when Mussolini marched a hundred thousand Italian troops into Ethiopia while his new war planes roared off to bomb the border town of Adowa.

'Now,' Ginny said to Emily, 'we shall see whether the League of Nations can stop them.'

'How can they?'

Her political sister knew the answer. 'By imposing sanctions against Italy, refusing to trade with her, refusing to send supplies, cutting her off from the things she needs. That's what they're going to do.'

'Will it work?'

'If every single nation joins in,' Ginny said.

But every single nation didn't. Austria and Hungary voted not to apply sanctions. Trainloads of arms were sent to Italy from Czechoslovakia. The League dithered. The British Cabinet met in London. And dithered. The war continued and escalated. Adowa was captured. Mustard gas was dropped on the Ethiopian troops with appalling effect. Mussolini bragged to his people that Italy would soon have her own empire to rival the other great imperial powers. And Adolf Hitler observed it all.

On March seventh he opened his own campaign. That morning, just before dawn German troops marched into the Rhineland. The shock of it reverberated along the Somme Valley like the echo of remembered guns. The French government was thrown into confusion, some deputies called for immediate military action, others urged restraint. The British government still dithered, sent messages to France that no action should be taken until the matter had been given full consideration, and then decided, considerately, that nothing should be done about it anyway. As one newspaper commented, 'Hitler had merely re-occupied his own backyard.'

The French newspapers took a different view.

'The Shadow of war draws closer to us,' *Le Populaire* declared. 'Does London imagine that Hitler has renounced any of the projects indicated in his book *Mein Kampf*? If so, the illusion of our friends across the Channel is complete. We are at risk and we know it.'

'Will there be a war here?' Emily asked anxiously that evening.

She and Ginny were out in the garden feeding the hens their evening mash. The Advocate was giving a dinner party that night so Maman was still at work.

'All this talk of war,' Old Joliot said, 'makes me spit.' He spat to prove it. 'War's an obscenity. We must never go to war again.'

He was hard at work forking his good, black compost into the vegetable patch, his ugly face scowling and intense.

'But if the Germans invade and we don't fight them,' Ginny protested, 'they'll defeat us.'

'Then let them.'

'You don't mean that,' Ginny said. 'Nobody could mean that.'

139

'Oh yes,' Old Joliot said, digging furiously. 'I do. Anything is better than a massacre. Surrender, run away, admit defeat but never go to war. Never. War isn't noble. It's slaughter. Chaos. Obscenity.' And he spat again, spewing forth a long straight stream of saliva that landed on the back of one of his brown hens. Most aggrieved by such an attack, she jumped into the air, ruffling her feathers and squawking protest.

Pinching messages to one another, the twins carried the empty bowl into the house. Would it really be better to give in without a struggle? Was he right? Holy Mary, Mother of God, what would happen if Hitler invaded?

'Perhaps the Rhineland will be enough,' Emily hoped. 'Perhaps . . .'

'It won't,' Ginny said grimly. 'He wants Poland and Czechoslovakia, too. He's never made any secret of it.'

'Who does?' Cousin Berthe asked, smiling at them. 'Who does, what you said?'

Ginny could see the dear old thing was only trying to make conversation, but she answered her just the same. 'The Germans,' she said.

The response was a surprise.

'Don't talk to me about *les Boches*,' Cousin Berthe said. 'They're bad old boys, *les Boches*. They knock things down.'

The twins pinched hands, ready to be amused.

'Do they?' Emily encouraged.

'Oh yes,' Cousin Berthe nodded, smiling her empty smile at them. 'They knock everything down. They got great big guns. Boom! Boom! And then down it all goes. Oh yes. They knocked my convent down. There was a great big hole. You could walk in and out. We all walked in and out you know. Of the hole. Oh yes. Mind you don't drop that bowl, little Emilie.'

'I didn't know you were in a convent, Cousin Berthe,' Ginny said, starting to cut the onions for their supper.

'The Little Sisters of Divine Mercy,' Cousin Berthe said. 'You see, I remember it.'

'Were you there long?'

But the memory was already gone and another had taken its place. 'They shot Joliot's face,' Cousin Berthe said. 'They're bad old boys. All full of shrapnel it was, bits of it sticking up everywhere, when they brought him in. And Sister Sebastian said, "He'll die that one." And Sister Dominique said, "No. We'll save him." And we saved him.'

The twins were listening to her now with all their attention. What a story. No wonder old Joliot's face looked so peculiar. Poor man!

'Of course,' Cousin Berthe went on, almost to herself, 'there's all bits still wandering about.'

'All bits of what?' Ginny asked at the same time as Emily was saying, 'Wandering about where?'

'Wandering about all over him,' Cousin Berthe said, smiling her empty smile. 'In his veins, wandering about. One day a little bit'll get into his heart, so they say, an' then he'll die. "Pouf!" just like that.' She smiled again.

'Does he know?' Emily asked, in an awed voice.

'But of course,' Cousin Berthe said easily. 'Oh yes, he knows, my Joliot. He said, "You come home and look after me, Cousin Berthe." When the wall fell down. That's what he said. And Mother Superior said, you go and look after the soldier. So I look after him and he looks after his poor dead boys, and when he dies they will look after him. That's a good thing, n'est-ce pas? He'll go straight to Heaven, my Joliot. He's been a good man.'

'What an amazing thing!' Ginny said, when she and Em were getting ready for bed that night. 'No wonder he's bad tempered sometimes.'

'I think he's remarkably good tempered, considering,' Emily said, carefully hanging up her skirt. 'What courage! To go on with your life knowing you might die at any moment. And never saying anything about it.'

'It's a lot worse than our "illness",' Ginny said, glad of the chance to put their fears in perspective. 'He knows what's going to happen to him. It's a certainty. We've been afraid of a shadow.'

Emily decided to think about that later. 'No wonder he's

141

so devoted to his boys,' she said. 'I'll tell you one thing, though, Ginny. I think he's right about war. It *is* an obscenity. We should never allow it to happen again.'

'All the more reason to get the right government elected in this country,' Ginny said, and her face was grim. 'I shall work twice as hard. I wish they'd give women the vote. That would make all the difference.'

It was a bitter election campaign. Leon Blum was abused by the right-wing press as *the worst kind of Jew*, Colonel de la Rocque's leather-jacketed troops were constantly on the streets, one deputy had an eye knocked out at a political meeting and another had acid thrown in his face. But at long, long last, on May third, France went to the polls, and, to Ginny's total, exhausted and justified delight, the Popular Front won a conclusive victory.

'What will you do now?' Emily asked, when the two of them got back to Boves after a celebratory party that had lasted into the small hours.

'I shall write to old Miss Babbacombe,' Ginny said. All through the party, the memory of their governess had drifted in and out of her mind. 'I meant to do it when I was in Paris but I was too busy. She'll be really pleased to know what I've been doing.'

'I don't know about pleased,' Emily said. 'If you ask me she'll be jolly surprised if you write after all this time.'

'But she'll be pleased, too,' Ginny said. 'She used to say, "Women have to take their place in the world." And now I have, haven't I? I ought to tell her I haven't forgotten.'

The postcard was written the very next day – in very stilted English, because they'd forgotten so much over the years, but more or less to their satisfaction. They posted it in Amiens so as to obey Maman, and not let anyone know exactly where they were. Despite subterfuge and shaky English, it seemed a fitting conclusion to all those months of effort.

# CHAPTER TEN

Miss Babbacombe wasn't a bit surprised to receive a postcard from Ginny, even after all this time.

'Always knew it,' she said to her cat. 'Didn't I tell you, Sam? You can't be that fond of a person and cut them out of your lives altogether. Wouldn't be natural. Won't our Mrs Everdale be pleased. I think I'll just pop up to the house and tell her. This won't keep till Friday. And it's a lovely afternoon. Just the thing for a little walk.'

It was very quiet in the grounds of High Holborn. A blackbird was singing in one of the elms, and somewhere in the formal garden she could hear the sound of hedge clippers, but there were no cars in the drive and the terrace was empty.

I hope they're not away, she thought, as she rang the bell and waited. That would be a real pest when I've got such good news.

But the butler was there and happy to recognise her.

'Come to see Mrs Everdale,' she said cheerfully.

'Oh dear,' the butler said, his face dropping. 'Haven't you heard? Well no, obviously not.'

'Heard what?' Miss Babbacombe asked, feeling rather alarmed.

'Mr Holborn's dead.'

'When?'

'Monday afternoon.'

Miss Babbacombe was so cross she forgot to be discreet. 'Oh!' she said. 'How could he? How could he go and die now? Just when we've had another postcard. How inconsiderate!' Then she realised what an awful thing she'd said and blushed. And then she looked stricken.

Her reaction put the butler into something of a panic. It

143

wouldn't do for any of the family to come out and hear her saying things like that.

'You'd better come in,' he said. 'You can go down to the kitchen if you like. They'll be able to tell you more about it.' And he hustled her out of the hall as quickly as he could.

The kitchen staff had all the details and were happy to pass them on.

'Dropped like a stone, he did,' the parlour maid said. 'One minute shoutin' for his evening newspaper and the next minute dead as a door nail.'

'Heart failure,' Cook explained. 'We all knew it was coming. Had you come up to see Mrs Everdale?'

'Yes, I had,' Miss Babbacombe said ruefully. 'How's she taking it?'

'Ever so bad, poor lady,' the parlour maid said. 'She's been in a proper state.'

'And just when I've got some good news for her,' Miss Babbacombe said, and told them about the postcard.

'You can leave it with me, if you like,' the parlour maid said. 'They're all in the library readin' the will, but I could take it in after. Might cheer her poor soul.'

'Very good of you,' Miss Babbacombe said. 'If you've got an envelope I'll write a little message of condolence to go in with it.' Which she did.

'If you ask me, this will's proving a bit sticky,' Cook said. 'They've been at it for ages and Mr Everdale's been shouting fit to bust.'

'Well, that's the way he goes on, isn't it?' Miss Babbacombe said. 'It wouldn't hurt him to think of his poor wife now and then.'

But Claud Everdale wasn't thinking of anybody except himself. He was dark with rage at the way his father-in-law had bequeathed the estate.

'He must have been out of his mind,' he roared. 'I shall dispute it.'

'On what grounds? If I may be permitted to ask,' Mr Crabbit said with superlative courtesy. He glanced at the late Mr Holborn's special chair beside the fireplace and

144

wondered if he'd managed to take a few minutes off from eternity to enjoy the rumpus he'd caused.

'On the grounds that it's ridiculous. Nonsensical. On the grounds that he was off his head. Must have been.'

'You are perfectly entitled to take such action, should you so wish,' Mr Crabbit said, 'however I should point out that Mr Holborn was in full command of his faculties when the will was signed and I should have to testify to that effect.'

Claud Everdale looked at the signatures. H. L. Crabbit and Agnes Everdale.

'Good God, woman,' he roared at his wife, 'what were you thinking of? Why didn't you stop him?'

Agnes was too grieved to be able to answer him diplomatically. 'Perhaps I didn't want to.'

'You mean you couldn't,' Claud disparaged. 'Goddamn it, you should have told *me* what he was doing. I'd have stopped him. Now look at the mess we're in. You've pushed me right out of the driver's seat. *And* you've halved your sons' inheritance, I hope you realise. They won't thank you for that.'

Agnes turned her eyes away from him and let him rage on. What did it matter? she thought. What was done was done and he would just have to accept it. For once in his life he wasn't going to get everything his own way.

'To leave half his inheritance to two girls,' Claud complained to Mr Crabbit. 'That's what gets me. Two girls! If he'd left it to Agnes there might have been some sense in it, but two girls! That *can't* be legal. What could they possibly know about running a business?'

'Since the Married Woman's Property Act,' Mr Crabbit said, 'it is perfectly legal for a woman to own property and run estates. There are several to my knowledge who have large holdings in industry *and* commerce. The world is changing.'

'The world, Mr Crabbit, is going to the dogs.'

'Quite possibly,' Mr Crabbit said smoothly. 'However, it is going there entirely legally. Now concerning this advertisement the late Mr Holborn wanted, I assume you would wish to draw one up.'

'Of course,' Agnes said.

And Claud said, 'I suppose so. If you must. Damn load of rubbish, if you ask me.'

'I will make it my first priority,' Mr Crabbit said. 'And now if there's nothing further, I must be on my way. Thank you for your kind hospitality, Mrs Everdale. The tea was delicious.'

The first priority didn't actually get attended to until the beginning of the next week, as is the custom in solicitors' offices. But it was neatly put together and even Mr Hedgethorn was pleased with it.

'*HOLBORN,*' it read, '*for the attention of twin sisters Virginia and Emily Holborn, late of "High Holborn" near Wolverhampton, last seen ten years ago, in July 1926, at Victoria Station, London, boarding the boat train to Boulogne, each wearing about her neck a silver cross. Should the above mentioned care to contact Messrs Hedgethorn and Crabbit, solicitors, of Little Medlar Yard, London WC1, they would hear something to their advantage.*'

'That should satisfy,' Mr Hedgethorn said, patting the paper happily. 'Now, Horace, all that remains to be done is to send someone up to Wolverhampton with a copy for clearance before we submit it irrevocably to the press. I would go myself if I had the time.'

Mr Hedgethorn never had the time for anything other than signing letters and the occasional well-prepared interview with a prestigious client. He waved a pale hand at the pile of documents that had been accumulating dust on his desk for the last three months. 'You see how it is. It's a pity he won't let you deal with it.'

Two days after Mr Crabbit's visit to High Holborn a furious letter had arrived from Mr Claud Everdale, addressed to Mr Hedgethorn, *Senior Partner*, Hedgethorn and Crabbit, Solicitors. Now it lay on the desk under Mr Hedgethorn's left hand.

'Mr Crabbit is to have *no further hand* in these proceedings,' Mr Everdale had written. 'The matter is *not* to be discussed. It is to be handled by you and *one other* who should be a man of the utmost *discretion* and *delicacy*.'

'That's what comes of setting the cat among the pigeons,' Horace Crabbit said easily. 'I told you he wasn't happy. He'll complicate things very nicely for us, will our Mr Everdale. Who will you send?'

'I thought Mr Commoner,' Mr Hedgethorn said. 'Mr Thomas would be ideal, but he's too old to travel any very great distance, Mr Bond is too garrulous by half, Mr Grossman has too many bankruptcies on his plate, you're forbidden, so it only leaves Mr Commoner.'

'He'd do it well,' Mr Crabbit said. 'He handled the Ferguson affair very neatly.'

'He was working with you on the Ferguson affair,' Mr Hedgethorn pointed out.

'Give him the chance,' Mr Crabbit said. 'See what he makes of it.'

So Mr Commoner was sent for and given his instructions.

'You will travel tomorrow,' Mr Hedgethorn told him. 'We will telephone Mr Everdale to advise him when to expect you. You are to acquaint yourself with the contents of this file, read the correspondence and the relevant passages in the will, which I have marked for you, and pay particular attention to this advertisement. You will need to proceed with discretion in this matter. I trust that is understood.'

'Yes sir,' Charlie said.

'You must be *entirely* discreet,' Mr Hedgethorn warned. 'Not a word to anyone. People are highly inquisitive when it comes to inherited fortunes, as I'm sure you understand. So you must be extremely careful not to divulge any information. In fact, I would go so far as to instruct you not to discuss this with anybody outside the office.'

'Of course not, Mr Hedgethorn,' Charlie assured him. 'You can depend on me. I shall be the soul of discretion.'

'I hope so,' Mr Hedgethorn said. 'A great deal depends on it, for your career as well as the firm, as I need hardly point out to you. We shall all be watching very closely to see how you shape up. Well, Bon Voyage, as the saying goes.'

'Thank you sir,' Charlie said politely. But he was keeping

calm with an effort, thinking, My first case. My very first case. And what a case! For he'd heard a lot about it back in the outer office. It had been the gossip there ever since Mr Holborn died.

'So?' Jack Bond asked, when Charlie got back to his desk.

'Oh, nothing much,' Charlie said airily. 'I've only got to be a messenger boy, that's all. To Wolverhampton. All day tomorrow.'

'Not to High Holborn?'

'Well, yes, actually.'

'You mean they've given you the munition king and his long-lost heiresses?'

'Yes.'

There were groans of envy all round the office.

'Jammy beggar!' Jack said. 'I wish it was me.'

It was *jammy*, Charlie thought. A day's idleness on a journey he hadn't paid for *and* an important client to interview. He might even get a chance to find out what all the mystery was about and why the heiresses had been 'last seen ten years ago'. You never knew. It was certainly a lot more exciting than the small bankruptcies and general conveyancing he'd handled up to now. He couldn't wait to get started. He opened the file with real pleasure and began to read.

He was still reading late that afternoon, when Mr Hedgethorn's secretary phoned High Holborn with a message for Mr Everdale that the advertisement had been prepared and that they were sending one of their clerks down with a copy for his approval.

Claud took the call himself. 'I shall be here,' he said into the mouthpiece. And the look he gave his wife as he put the receiver back in its cradle was too triumphant to be avoided. 'I'll deal with this,' he said. 'No need for you to worry yourself about it.'

Agnes agreed with him meekly. She could hardly argue with him out there in the hall where the servants might hear. But inside her head she was making secret plans to keep him under surveillance.

If it was wet she would sit in the hall after the clerk arrived and hope they'd leave the door sufficiently ajar for her to eavesdrop. If anyone came out she could pretend to be arranging flowers in the hall. If it was fine she would open one of the south-facing windows in the morning room just before the clerk was due and take her deckchair out on to the terrace. She could tuck it behind the wisteria. Nobody would see it there from inside the room but she would be able to hear everything that was being said and hear it in comfort. Either way and whatever happened she was determined to know what was going on.

And so all the preparations were made. That evening Charlie Commoner spruced up his business suit, steamed his trilby hat and decided to wear his new white shirt. And the next morning he set off for High Holborn.

He was in a state of suppressed excitement throughout the journey, and when he emerged from the station at Wolverhampton he knew beyond any doubt that he was on to something really special. He could feel it.

What a place it is, he thought. Not a bit like London. Anything could happen here. The air was hot with strange smells, grease, burning coke, hot steel, long-settled soot, and the curving street in which he found himself was as exciting as the air. It was lined by hoardings advertising Whitbread's London stout, Bass pale ales, and Bile Beans for Biliousness, and it was full of impatient travellers, bustling in and out of the station or climbing aboard the local buses – odd-looking snub-nosed vehicles that snorted and chuntered and shuddered their sides as if they too were impatient to be off. They travelled fast, too. His rattled him to the Mermaid pub in no time at all.

'Follow the road,' the conductor advised pointing to a footpath which ran uphill alongside the pub between steep banks of brick red sandstone and heavily overhanging trees.

Charlie climbed eagerly, passing under a flimsy wooden foot-bridge, rounding a slight bend towards the top of the hill, and found himself entering the grounds of a very great house. Wow! he thought, gazing up at it. This is going to be a *very* special assignment. Fancy living in a house like this. He straightened his tie, adjusted the angle of his trilby and knocked at the oak door.

A butler, correct in black morning suit and bland expression, ushered him into a panelled hall, received his cheap trilby into gloved hands and asked him if he would be so good as to wait in the morning room, which he did, awe-struck by the rich furnishings, ornate fireplace, real paintings, stained-glass windows, and the grandest of grand pianos, all made of inlaid wood. What a place!

He was just beginning to wonder how much longer he would have to wait when a hidden door cracked open in the wall beside the fireplace with a noise like a gunshot. It was so sudden it made him jump to attention. And just as well because the man entering the room had to be Mr Everdale.

He certainly looks the part, Charlie thought, assessing him quickly; tall, dapper, oiled hair, sharp eyes, narrow moustache, wary expression. A man used to making hard bargains and getting his own way. He was dressed in a black suit, of course, being in mourning, but it was from Savile Row and worn with a gold wrist watch and a shirt that was a dazzle of whiteness with immaculate cuffs and a perfectly fitting collar. He made Charlie feel instantly and uncomfortably aware of his own humble origins.

He came straight to the point. 'You have the document?' His voice was as sharp as his eyes.

Charlie handed him the folder. 'Yes, sir.'

The advertisement was perused. 'It meets the legal requirements?'

'So I understand, sir.'

'Mr Holborn was very old, of course,' Mr Everdale said. 'A sick man or he would never have complicated our lives in this ridiculous way.'

No answer seemed to be required so Charlie simply waited.

'However, providing we keep within the letter of the law there is no reason why this matter should trouble us overmuch, I think. If the advertisement is displayed, shall we say discreetly, in *The Times* for example? And *The Telegraph*, should Mr Hedgethorn feel a plurality is advisable. I leave it entirely in your hands. The less fuss the better, if you understand.'

'Um . . .' Charlie wondered.

His host paused. 'Yes?'

'Would you require a similar advertisement to be inserted in a French newspaper, perhaps?

'Does the law require it?' Mr Everdale said. His voice sounded calm, but there was an increased sharpness about it and a suspicious tilt to his well-groomed head.

'No sir, not as far as I know.'

'Then we need not consider it.'

'No, sir.'

'They left of their own accord,' Mr Everdale explained. 'It was what they wished. We have had no correspondence with them in ten years, you understand. Had they wished to continue as members of this family they would have written. As they have *not* written we must assume that they do not wish to continue as members of the family. It is sad, of course, but we must accept it. There is no necessity to make strenuous efforts to find them.'

'No, sir.'

'I'm glad we understand one another,' Mr Everdale said, allowing his visitor one neat smile. 'Sleeping dogs, you know. I mustn't detain you.' And that was that. He was turning away, his hand already on the bell. Such a hard white commanding hand.

The bell buzzed softly and the butler arrived smooth-footed; the interview was over. As he left the room Charlie was aware that the sun was dappling the parquet surround with lozenges of brightness, sky-blue and rose-pink and buttercup-yellow, and he felt aggrieved that such a hard man should live in such a softly beautiful house.

And out on the terrace, crouched among the foliage, dowdy and brown and quiet as a nightingale, Agnes Everdale was aggrieved, too. What she had just heard had put her into one of her rare, icy tempers.

151

'*Providing we keep within the letter of the law . . . no reason why the matter should trouble us overmuch . . . they do not wish to continue as members of this family . . . there is no necessity to make strenuous efforts to find them.*'

Oh, isn't there? she thought, appalled by his dishonesty. We'll see about that, my lad. As soon as Claud had gone back upstairs she emerged from her hiding place and ran round the side of the house to catch the clerk before he could get out of the gate and she lost her courage. It was the most positive and daring thing she'd ever done in her life.

As he walked back down the gravel path towards the gates, Charlie was doing his best to be professional and to assess the situation according to his training. Mr Everdale was a businessman, so naturally he was protecting the interests of his two sons. It was a reasonable position to take when you saw it his way, in the world of money and property and hard-headed business deals. All the same he couldn't help feeling cast down to have come so far and for so little.

He was thinking so hard that at first he didn't hear the voice calling to him.

'Young man! Young man! Just a minute!'

He stopped and looked back. A middle-aged woman wearing a tweed skirt and a buff twin set and pearls, ran flat-footedly along the path towards him, a dumpy-looking woman with mouse-coloured hair and a long nose and an anxious expression.

'You are Mr Hedgethorn's clerk, aren't you?' she said, out of breath from her exertions.

'Yes, ma'am.'

'I'm Mrs Everdale,' she said, holding out her hand towards him so that he could shake it. 'We must talk. Would you follow me into the garden.' She led him off the path and through a gap in the hedge that bordered it, a formidable hedge of tightly cropped yew, ten-feet high and three-feet thick, if it were an inch. Where were they going?

'I would rather we weren't seen from the house,' Mrs Everdale explained. 'It's more private here.'

Charlie found himself in a formal garden surrounded by clipped hedges, well away from everybody.

'Do sit down,' Agnes said. And they sat side by side on the garden seat.

'I want you to tell Mr Crabbit that you have my full support,' she said, 'in everything that has to be done in the search for my nieces. My father wanted his granddaughters found as soon as possible, you know. And so do I. Please feel free to put our advertisement in any paper you think fit, here and in France. You must do everything you can to find them. That is what my father would have wished.'

'Of course,' Charlie said. 'You shall have our very best endeavours.'

'I'm sure of that,' she said, smiling at him. 'Do you know where to look for them?'

'No, ma'am,' Charlie said smoothly. But he was thinking, Now what? Does she know more than her husband? What a lark!

'If I were you I should start your search in Amiens.'

'Amiens?'

'Yes.'

'You mean they've been writing to you?' Charlie asked, very much surprised.

'Virginia has. Not regularly, you understand. Now and then. The last was from Amiens, just before my father died.'

'Do you have an address, ma'am?'

'I'm afraid not. She only sends postcards, you see and she never gives an address. We work it out from the postmark.'

'We?'

'She writes to her governess, Miss Babbacombe. Miss Babbacombe shows the cards to me.'

But not to your husband, Charlie thought. Well, well.

'You will find them for me, won't you?' Agnes asked.

'I will do my very best,' Charlie promised.

'I should be so grateful,' she said. 'They're my brother's children, you see.'

And he did see. Her affection for them was obvious.

It wasn't until he was halfway back to London that Charlie realised that there were all sorts of questions he ought to have asked Mrs Everdale. He'd agreed to look for the girls, no, more than that, he'd agreed to find them, and he didn't know anything about them apart from their names. He didn't know what they looked like, why they'd left, anything. He didn't even know how old they were. I shall have to ask Mr Crabbit, he thought. He's a good old boy. He'll tell me.

The good old boy was lounging in Mr Hedgethorn's chair, smoking a cheroot and flicking through the pages of a brief. 'Ah, there you are,' he said, glancing up as Charlie came in. 'How did you get on with our Mr Everdale?'

'Well, sir,' Charlie said, choosing his words with caution. 'This is only my opinion, but I don't think Mr Everdale actually wants us to find these girls.'

'Quite right,' Mr Crabbit said, grinning at him. 'No more he does. But their grandfather did. He made a most particular point of telling me so. So does their aunt, if I'm any judge.'

'Yes, sir,' Charlie said happily, sensing a moment of triumph. 'I know. She spoke to me, too. She knows where they are.'

The bushy eyebrows were raised in query.

Charlie explained.

'And Mr Everdale doesn't know this, you say?'

'No, sir. I'm sure he doesn't.'

'Um,' Mr Crabbit said, flicking ash from his cheroot. 'Then that's the way we'll keep it, for the time being at any rate. We'll put the advertisements in hand tomorrow morning, starting with the national newspapers in London and Paris. You can attend to it.'

'Yes, sir.'

'And if anything comes of it we'll send you over to investigate, eh? I'm told you have a yen to see the capital of France. How would that be?'

Charlie gave him an entirely honest answer. 'Smashing,' he said, thinking, wait till Mum and Dad hear this. I'll tell them the minute I get in. Won't they be bucked!

But when he finally got home to Clapham, much later that afternoon, it didn't work out quite the way he intended because his Aunt Grace had arrived. And when Aunt Grace arrived in any house everything instantly became different and difficult.

# CHAPTER ELEVEN

Grace Allicott was the bane of her relations' lives. She was actually Stanley Commoner's first cousin, but they weren't the least bit alike. He had grown up in a large, hardworking, noisy family, and his mother and father had always been poor but loving. She had been the only child of elderly parents who were comfortably off, but dour and disapproving. Consequently, she'd been spoilt and querulous as a child, had never found anyone she liked enough to marry and, now in her late sixties, was sliding gracelessly into her second childhood, lonely and dissatisfied.

Her miserable outlook on life had left its mark on her features, pinching her nose to sharpness, scoring her cheeks and forehead with deep lines, and reducing her greying hair to a greasy limpness, despite two 'permanent' waves a year. Her eyes were hooded and her mouth perpetually downturned.

She spent a great deal of her time visiting with one of her cousins after another, knowing that she was being endured rather than welcomed, but arguing with herself, as well as her relations, that she was owed a little consideration now that she was getting on.

'After all,' she would say, 'you lot've had husbands an' wives an' children an' all sorts, an' what've *I* had. Sweet bugger all.'

Half an hour after Charlie left for work and Wolverhampton, she descended on Abbeville Road for the second time that year. She was six days earlier than expected and weeping because her cousin Maud had been 'a pig'.

'The things she said to me, Ruby,' she wept, 'you'd never believe. I never thought I'd ever live to hear such things.' Which was true enough, as Maud had told her she was being a nuisance.

'Well, never mind,' Ruby said, speaking kindly although she was a bit put out to be visited without warning. 'You're with us now. Come an' have a nice cup a' tea.' But how would she explain to Stan and Charlie? And what would Grandpa say when he came down for his dinner? Oh dear!

Grandpa Jones was furious. He stood on the stairs glaring at the luggage Aunt Grace had left piled all over the hall, narrowed his eyes until they almost disappeared and made snorting noises through his nose.

'Damn woman!' he said. 'What's she doing here? She's not due for another six days.'

Ruby rushed out of the kitchen to placate him. 'She was upset,' she tried to explain. 'Maud upset her.'

'Oh, that's lovely,' the old man said. 'So now she can come barging in here an' upset all of us. Come to something when you can't take a bloody nap without her barging in. She's not due till Thursday. I've got it in me diary. Oh fer crying out loud, Rube, how can I get to me dinner wiv all this junk in the way. She'll have me arse over tit. Bloody woman!'

'Yes, well,' poor Ruby said ineffectually, hauling Aunt Grace's bulky portmanteau out of his way.

The lady herself had retired to the front room and was asleep on the put-u-up with a rug over her legs and her mouth wide open, snoring rhythmically. Now she gave a splutter, woke up instantly and waved at her adversary.

'Coo-ee, Grandpa,' she said. 'Still got yer gammy leg, I see.'

'I'm not your bloody Grandpa,' the old man said. 'And there's nothing the matter with me leg,' kicking her hat box to prove it.

We shall have ructions all day, Ruby thought. And she was right.

They quarrelled through dinner and bickered all through the afternoon, sitting, scowling and scoring points, on either side of the empty fireplace in the front room.

When Charlie came home flushed with his success at High Holborn they took no notice of him whatever, and even Stan had a hard time getting a civil word out of them.

They took their places at the tea table like boxers returning to their opposing corners at the end of a bruising round.

Ruby looked as harassed as she felt.

'It's only for a couple a' weeks,' Stan comforted, as he helped her to ease her meat pie out of the oven. 'It'll pass. That smells good.'

Once they were all at the table, Charlie tried to keep the peace between his two cantankerous relations by telling them about the heiresses and his mission to Paris. But they were too disgruntled to listen and far more interested in continuing their quarrel.

'You don't wanna go to France,' Aunt Grace grumbled. 'They're a horrible lot the Froggies. They don't 'ave lavvies, you know. They just do it anywhere.'

'You do talk a load of old guff an' gubbins, Grace,' Grandpa said. 'You leave 'em be. They're all right, the old *parlez-vous*.'

'How do *you* know?' Aunt Grace said aggressively. 'Been there 'ave yer? No 'course you ain't.'

'You got no memory, Grace Allicott,' the old man said, squinting at her. 'Where d'you think I was during the war?'

'Well *I* think it's a real step up being sent to Paris,' Stan said, putting the pie on the table. 'They must think well of you, Charlie. Don't you think so, Ruby?'

Aunt Grace was looking thoughtful. 'Will you be away long then, Charlie?' she said.

'A day or two,' Charlie said. 'I don't know. It depends.'

'A week, maybe?' Grace asked, and her eyes were sharp with interest.

'It could be a week,' Charlie said.

'Tell us what happened,' Stan said. 'Tuck in, Grace, it's a smashing pie.'

So Charlie told his story at last and Grace ate her pie and none of them noticed how quiet she was being. And when the meal was over, the dishes were all washed and the white tablecloth had been swept, folded, put in its drawer and replaced by the yellow chenille and the table lamp, she was still thinking.

Even when her four relations passed the cigarettes round and lit up, she still didn't say anything. She didn't even complain about the smoke. So the story continued and Stan and Ruby smiled encouragement at their clever son as he told them about the great garden at High Holborn and how Mr Everdale had said one thing and Mrs Everdale another.

'We 'ad a great big garden at my old school, you know,' Grandpa said. 'Must ha' been quite four acres. Five even. Rose arbour we 'ad. Fountains. Best school in the 'ole a' South London that was. They used ter say . . .'

The Commoners let him run on and didn't listen. Grace was still sitting quietly in her chair and didn't look like interrupting. It was peaceful at last.

The room softened into blue shadow as a slow sunset stained the sky in the window flamingo pink and streaked it with orange and scarlet and smokey lilac. Gradually its reflected light transformed the everyday objects all around them into things mysterious and magical. Ruby's two cherished horse brasses glowed like gold beneath the dark red fringe of the mantel cover, the toasting fork turned into a barley sugar stick, the fire irons were silver horseshoes, the clock face gleamed like mother-of-pearl.

Wherever I may go, Charlie thought, whatever happens in France, I shall always remember being here in this room and feeling happy. Because he was happy, entirely happy, with a good meal warming his belly, Mum and Dad beaming at him, and his first case about to begin so promisingly.

And as if to set the seal on his contentment Aunt Grace suddenly made an announcement.

'I think I'll go back to me flat termorrow,' she said. 'I oughter see how things are. Have a bit of a tidy-up. I could come an' see you another time, couldn't I, Stan? When your Charlie's in France. You'd 'ave more room then. Wouldn't be such a squash.'

'We don't know when it'll be yet,' Stan told her. 'Do we Charlie?'

'No,' Charlie said happily. 'We've got to run the advertisement first. But pretty soon, I expect.' The

159

excitement he felt to be saying such a thing. Pretty soon. By this time next week, he thought, I could be in France.

The advertisements were run for three weeks in *The Times*, *The Telegraph* and *Le Temps* in Paris, and there was no response at all.

After the drama of his visit to High Holborn, Charlie was disappointed. But Mr Crabbit said it didn't surprise him.

'It all takes time,' he explained to his impatient clerk. 'You need patience in this sort of case.'

Patience was a quality Charlie Commoner had yet to acquire. He chaffed and fretted, watched the post and got snappy with his mother when she asked how things were 'going along'.

But, at last, at last, when they were into July and he'd almost given up hope, a letter arrived from the offices of *Le Temps* to say that two sisters had written in to lay claim to the inheritance and could Messrs Hedgethorn and Crabbit kindly send a person to Paris to verify the claim.

The person caught the nine o'clock boat train to Paris from Victoria the very next morning, after another pep talk from Mr Hedgethorn. He was full of happy excitement. To be hurtling through Kent in a great train labelled Pullman, to be one of a huge cosmopolitan crowd filing through the echoing barn of the customs shed at Folkestone, to be actually walking up a gangplank, actually on board ship and heading out to sea. It was smashing.

His cheerfulness diminished a little when some of his fellow passengers in the third-class lounge began to turn green and a little boy was sick all over the floor, but he didn't have to stay with them. There were seats up on the deck. He picked up his travelling bag, slung his mackintosh over his arm and climbed into the fresh air.

The long rows of slatted benches he'd noticed on his way on to the ship were now occupied by a troop of uniformed boy scouts and the heaped mounds of their luggage. It was surprisingly cold out at sea. Cold and damp, for the Channel was choppy and showers of spray were being blown back from the plunging bows. Charlie put on his mackintosh and turned up the collar, feeling dashing. Then he set off along the swaying decks to look for somewhere to sit.

The only space available was on a bench, set in an alcove opposite one of the life boats, and that wasn't really a space because it was occupied by a man who was stretched out at full length with his head on his knapsack and his eyes tightly closed. He was a large man, bulky and awkward in a Norfolk jacket and knickerbockers, and a very ugly one, with balding hair, a narrow forehead and a pear-shaped face dominated by a big fleshy nose.

Jolly selfish, Charlie thought looking down at him with disapproval. Well, he can jolly well make room for me, that's all.

'Mind if I sit down?' he said.

The man opened brown eyes and smiled at him. The smile transformed his ugliness, revealing a well-shaped mouth, good teeth and a kindly expression. 'Not a bit,' he said, lifting his knees and sitting up. 'If you don't mind talking to me.'

Charlie concealed his surprise, and sat down in the space provided. 'That's all right,' he said, wondering what he was letting himself in for, but feeling adventurous. 'I don't mind at all.'

'I know two cures for seasickness,' the ugly man said. 'One is to lie perfectly still all the way across and not move a muscle, the other is to talk to someone.'

'Does it work?'

'It has up to now.'

'What shall we talk about then?'

'Tell me where you're going. That'll do for a start. I'm off on a cycling tour of the Loire. To see the chateaux. Are you on holiday, too?'

'No,' Charlie said, adding importantly, 'I'm going to Paris. On business.'

'What business?'

Charlie knew he was supposed to be discreet and he remembered his promises to Mr Hedgethorn, but the temptation to show off, just this once, was too strong. It wouldn't hurt to tell this man. He was a perfect stranger and they were not likely to meet one another again. 'Well,' he said. 'I'm on the track of two heiresses, actually.'

'Good Lord!' the ugly man said. 'Are you! Tell me all about it. My name's Ken, by the way. Ken Hopkirk.'

'Charlie Commoner.'

'Pleased to meet you. Tell on.'

So Charlie's tale was told, without giving names, naturally, because that would have been *really* unprofessional, but with plenty of embellishments to show how resourceful and intelligent he'd been.

'Of course,' he said, 'they know they can trust me. I've got their confidence. You often find that with solicitors.'

'And they're millionaires, you said?'

'Oh yes. Stinking rich. You should see the house they live in.'

'I wonder they didn't send you first class.'

That gave Charlie pause. But not for long. 'Didn't want me to be too conspicuous,' he said airily. 'Mustn't frighten 'em. I mean they're bound to be a bit timid being out of England all this time. I expect we'll come back first class, though.'

'You think they'll be timid.'

'Oh yes,' Charlie said, without thinking about it. 'Bound to be, all on their own in a foreign country.'

'So it'll be quite a relief to see you galloping to the rescue.'

Charlie preened himself. 'Yes,' he said trying to look modest, 'I suppose it will. Bringing the good news and all that kind of thing.'

'Like something at the pictures,' the ugly man said.

There was a slightly mocking note in his voice that brought Charlie up short. Had he laid it on a bit too thick? Made himself look silly? 'Well, I don't know about that,' he said.

But his new friend wasn't mocking. In fact, he seemed impressed. 'Amazing,' he said. 'Makes my life look pretty dull, I can tell you. But then I'm a pretty dull dog when all's said and done.'

'What do you do?' Charlie felt obliged to ask.

'I run a factory.'

Now it was Charlie's turn to be impressed. 'Gosh!' he said. 'Do you mean you own it?'

There was no side to this ugly man. 'Yes,' he said simply. 'It's only a little place. Not much more than a shed really. Me and three men. We make gas meters. I'm building it up.'

'No wonder you holiday abroad.'

'Ah, but think of all the holidays you'll have when you've found your heiresses and claimed your reward.'

'Whereabouts is it, your factory?'

'Merton. Out in the sticks. Near Wimbledon.'

'That's not far from where I live.'

'Which is?'

'Clapham.'

'I know Clapham. I was born in Stockwell.'

So they talked about the places they knew in South London, sharing their knowledge of pubs and ale, cinemas and films, dirt-track racing and the dogs, and grew warm with affection for their native city – which was just as well, considering how cold they were getting out in the wet. And having reached safe factual ground, there they stayed.

For Charlie Commoner wasn't the only one to indulge in a fantasy now and then.

Ken Hopkirk took a bicycling holiday in France every year and told his friends he was off to see Lourdes, or get as far south as he could, or, as he'd told them this time, explore the chateaux of the Loire. But there was another and totally private reason for his travels.

Despite his own logical nature and the image he saw in the shaving mirror every morning he nurtured a secret, impossible hope that somewhere in this other, unpredictable country he would find a woman who would see through his ugliness and love him for himself. He was twenty-four, but as far as love was concerned he might as well have been sixty. None of the women he'd met had ever considered him marriageable. In England he was simply 'old Ken', a confirmed bachelor, a man outside the marriage stakes; to be teased and taken on outings as an extra, but beyond the pale when it came to women. In France, things could be different. Although he would never have admitted it to anyone, and only dared to face it himself in the most private of his thoughts, he wanted to be loved more than anything else. Even the success of his factory came second to that. In fact, there were times when his dream of love consumed him. And never more powerfully than when he was on his way across the Channel. That was how he'd recognised that Charlie was dreaming, too, and knew how to tease him.

The sea heaved past them, rolling glass-green and tipped with white spume, and there on the horizon was the long, blue smudge of the distant coast.

'There it is,' he said to his companion. 'That's France.' Beautiful, fast-talking, sensuous, exciting, highly cultured France. The land of dreams.

'Gosh!' Charlie said, gazing at it. 'France! I can't wait.'

Back in Clapham, Grace Allicott was full of urgency, too. She and her luggage arrived in Abbeville Road just after midday. She'd timed her visit most carefully, turning up during Grandpa Jones's afternoon nap and just as Ruby was on her way out to work.

'I won't be no trouble,' she promised. 'I'll jest get settled in. Take me time. No need to rush. Then I can have a nice cup a' tea ready for yer when you get back. How about that?'

Ruby set off for her job at the newsagents feeling quite heartened by her cousin's helpfulness. If they could keep Grandpa sweet perhaps this visit would go off well. Charlie would be away for part of it, too, which was all to the good. Maybe old Gracie's turning over a new leaf, she thought. Sure enough, when the evening papers had been dispatched and she got back to the house again, Grace was waiting in the kitchen with the kettle actually on the boil. Wonders would never cease!

'I been thinking while you been out,' she said.

'Oh yes,' Ruby said, taking off her hat and coat.

'About me bed,' Grace said, wetting the pot. 'Wouldn't 'alf be nice to 'ave me own bed.'

'But you've got a bed,' Ruby said, setting out the cups.

'In me flat, yes,' Grace said, measuring the tea. 'I was thinking of here. Might be an idea to move me bed in here. What d'yer think?'

'Can't see the point,' Ruby said, trying to deter her. 'You'll only have to move it out again when you go home.'

'I don't mind,' Grace said, waving the idea aside as if she was being generous.

Ruby knew she was being put under pressure but she didn't know how to cope with it. 'You've got the put-u-up,' she said, pouring the tea. 'What's wrong with that?'

'It's goin' home,' Grace said decidedly, 'that's what's wrong with it. It's been givin' me gyp fer ages. No. Me own bed. That's what I want.'

Ruby felt trapped. 'Well,' she said, doubtfully, 'I don't know. It'll be a bit of a palaver moving it in an' out all the time.'

'It could stay here, if you like,' Grace offered. 'I could 'ave a cover made for it. Like a divan. An' cushions. Look lovely that would. You could 'ave the use of it when I'm not here.'

'But won't you want it when you're at home?'

'That place,' Grace said with feeling. 'Don't remind me. That's just a rotten 'ole, that's all that is. Don't talk to me about that. I can't bear it.' And she managed to squeeze out a tear.

There was a shuffle at the kitchen door and there was Grandpa Jones, blinking the sleep out of his eyes.

He scowled. 'What's *she* doin' here?'

'She's come to stay,' Ruby tried to placate him. 'You know. I told you.'

'Oh 'as she? When's she going?'

It was just the sort of attack Grace needed to set her off. She put down her cup and burst into extravagant tears, taking off her glasses to display the flow and make herself look pathetic. 'Oh!' she howled. 'It's always the same.

165

Everywhere I go. Nobody loves me. Nobody. What've I ever done to deserve it, eh? I don't know I'm sure. I offered you the bed, didn't I? I said you could 'ave it all done up like a divan wiv cushions an' everything. I try ter do me best. Can't do no more, can I Rube?'

'Don't take on so,' Ruby begged. 'You'll make yerself ill.'

'What's it matter?' Grace wept, sensing her advantage. 'Don't mind me, Rube. Never did count fer much. Can't last for ever. Soon be turning up the daisies. Then you won't have to worry about me no more, will yer?'

'If she's goin' on like that, I'll 'ave me tea upstairs,' Grandpa said. And he took his cup and shuffled out.

'See!' Grace cried. 'See what I have to put up with. It's always the same. I wish I was dead.'

'Oh, come on, Grace,' Ruby said. 'You mustn't say things like that. Drink up yer tea. That'll make you feel better.'

Grace ignored her and the tea. 'An' now,' she complained, 'I suppose you'll say I can't even 'ave me bed.'

'No, I shan't,' Ruby tried to comfort.

'Then I can?' Grace said, looking up at her with surprisingly clear eyes. 'I can have it, d'you mean?'

'Well,' Ruby said helplessly. 'For the time being, maybe.'

The bed arrived the very next morning, along with a dressing table, a stool, a huge chest of drawers and an aspidistra in a pink and green pot.

'She's moved in, then,' Grandpa Jones said to his son-in-law, when they met outside the lavvy on the landing later that evening.

'Looks like it,' Stan admitted.

'You'll never get rid of her now,' Grandpa warned. 'You mark my words.'

'It's Charlie I feel sorry for,' Ruby said, when she and Stan were in bed that night and Grace was still hauling furniture about in the room below them. 'Poor kid. What'll he say when he comes home and finds what she's done. I never saw such a mess as that front room.'

'Try charging her rent,' Stan suggested, half in jest. 'Perhaps that'll shift her.'

But Grace had thought of rent and offered it at breakfast the next morning. 'Now me furniture's in I ought ter pay me way. What does *he* pay?'

Grandpa bristled. 'Mind yer own business,' he warned.

'I'll pay the same as 'im,' Grace decided. 'Or a bit more, if yer like, Stan. *I'm* not a skinflint.'

'No,' Grandpa said, 'you're a bloody nuisance.'

But Grace had got her way and could endure any insults now. 'Water off a duck's back,' she said smugly. 'I'll go up the market this morning, Rube, and get the material fer the divan.'

Ruby was staring into the middle distance wondering, yet again, how on earth she'd managed to get herself tricked into all this and thinking about her son. Poor Charlie. What *will* he think when he comes home? I hope to goodness he finds those heiresses of his. At least that'd be something to cheer him up, poor kid. Oh dear, oh dear.

# CHAPTER TWELVE

'Today's the day,' Mauricette Lalange said. 'Are you ready Emilie?'

Emilie Lisieux was in two minds about her visit to Paris. It was all very well everybody saying it was her turn now and telling her how much she'd enjoy it. They didn't seem to realise how very alone she was going to be, in a strange house in a strange place with people who wouldn't know how to help her. The thought of being dependent on someone other than Ginny was daunting. Of course, it would be nice to meet new friends and to be taken to famous places like the Place de la Bastille and the Champs Elysées, but it was daunting just the same. Mauricette was a dear, dear friend, but would she be prepared to do all the intimate things that Ginny did without thinking, like checking her teeth were properly cleaned and taking her to the w.c. and that sort of thing? Could she be trusted not to walk off and leave her when they were in some crowded place?

After Ginny's trip to Paris, Maman said she wasn't worried about it at all. 'I know I can trust you to be sensible, my darling,' she said. 'You know what I mean by sensible, don't you? That is really all that matters, *n'est-ce pas?*'

And Ginny was full of enthusiasm for it. 'You'll love it, Em,' she promised. 'There's something new there every minute of the day.'

But Em preferred her minutes to be spent with the loved and familiar. The last three days had been just like old times, with Mauricette in Boves again and the three of them visiting old haunts. That was holiday enough, wasn't it? There wasn't really any need for her to go to Paris.

But nobody seemed to understand, and it would have been impolite to refuse Madame Lalange's invitation. So what could she do?

She was in such a nervous state when she finally set off for the station, with Mauricette holding one arm and Ginny the other, that she could barely summon up enough voice to say goodbye.

Fortunately, Mauricette was in a bubbling mood and chatted all the way to Paris, describing the places they were passing and talking endlessly about 'My Gérard'. 'He knows about everything, Emilie. You wait till you hear him talk. And he's so handsome. I can't tell you how handsome he is.'

When they got to Paris all seven of Mauricette's brothers and sisters were there to welcome them in a babble of remembered voices and ready kisses.

Smelly, rough and horribly noisy, Paris was even more difficult than Emily had feared. There were so many sounds they battered her ears; car engines growling and throbbing, horns hooting, wheels squealing, people shrilling whistles everywhere and so many voices all talking at once that she couldn't distinguish one from another. If that wasn't bad enough, there was such a crowd of bodies all around her that it made her feel dizzy.

'We're going down the Métro,' Mauricette said, taking her arm. 'There's steps just here.'

'Underground?' Emily asked fearfully.

'Yes. It's all right.'

But it wasn't. It was hideous, claustrophobic and smelling of hot tin and sulphur and Gauloises, and the sweat of a thousand bodies packed in close together. By the time they reached their stop, which Mauricette said was called the Odeon, and the family had bustled her out into the air again and jostled her to their apartment, she was pale and distressed.

'Was it a very bad journey?' Madame Lalange asked, alarmed by her appearance.

'No, no,' Emily told her politely. 'It's just that I'm not used to crowds, that's all.'

'I was just the same when I came here,' Mauricette said carelessly. 'You'll get used to it in a day or two. You'll see. Now then. Let's get you unpacked and then we can take you off to see the sights.'

So despite Madame Lalange's concern and Emily's anxiety, the sights were seen. The Eiffel Tower, the Arc de Triomphe, the Rue de Rivoli, one famous name after another. But to Emily they were all the same, merely noise and confusion and an all-pervading fear of being lost in the crowd, or knocked off her feet, or pushed under one of those awful, aggressive cars. She didn't want to be a difficult guest, and tried to feign interest in what she was being shown, but it became more impossible by the minute. The evenings were the worst, crushed against a table on the pavement, with endless political arguments swirling over her head.

Fortunately, the third day of the holiday was Sunday and Sunday brought the lovely familiar peace of the Mass. Holding her silver cross, Emily sat between Madame Lalange and Mauricette, breathing in the incense, keeping very still, and praying most earnestly for the grace to endure the next eleven days of her holiday. Eleven days! It was a lifetime.

Glancing sideways at her quiet guest, Madame Lalange was upset to see how distressed Emily looked, with her forehead creased into anxious lines and pale mouth working.

'No more sights today,' she said, as they all walked back to the apartment. 'It's too hot.'

Mauricette was annoyed. 'You surely don't mean we've got to sit at home all afternoon,' she said.

Monsieur Lalange knew the answer to that. 'We'll go to Versailles,' he said.

'Excellent!' his wife agreed. 'You'll like it there, Emilie. The gardens are enormous. It's like being in the country-side.

It was blisteringly hot and the train to Versailles was slow and crowded. Jean Paul and Zabette, who were six and seven and vociferous, complained all the way; they were hot and thirsty, they felt sick, they wanted to do '*pipi*'. So the first thing Emily's hosts had to do when they'd reached the palace, after they'd walked up a long avenue and crossed a noisy road and struggled across a vast expanse of cobbled courtyard, was to find a w.c. for their complaining infants.

'You are a great nuisance,' Madame Lalange scolded. 'Wait here the rest of you. We shan't be long.'

Emily, Mauricette, Marie Claire and their two brothers stood on the uncomfortable cobbles in the broiling sunshine and waited.

Suddenly, without any warning at all, Emily's fears became a painful reality. She was struck such a blow in the small of her back that she fell forward on to her hands and knees on the cobbles, crying out in alarm.

There was confusion all around her, feet trampling so close to her fingers she could feel the eddy of the air they made, a rush of heat and fury, voices shouting, 'Fool! Idiot! Imbecile! Why don't you look where you're going? Can't you see she's blind? You should be ashamed of yourself.' And a man's voice stuttering in halting French that he was '*triste*'.

For several long seconds Emily stayed perfectly still where she was, too stunned and afraid to move. Then her fear began to recede and she realised that she wasn't hurt. It was only her hands that were stinging. She found herself thinking what an odd thing it was for a man to be saying he was '*triste*'. She steadied her hand against the cobbles and sat up, gently exploring the graze on her right palm. No blood flowing. Just a graze.

There was a rush of skirts, hands on her arms, and Mauricette's voice sharp with fury, saying, 'Are you hurt? Look how you've hurt her, you clumsy ape.'

The man spoke again, this time in English. 'Look, I'm terribly sorry. I didn't mean to hit her. Oh God, this is awful. I don't know how to tell you in French. Don't any of you speak English?'

He sounded so distraught that Emily turned her body towards his voice and spoke to him in his own language, finding it odd and unfamiliar. 'Yes,' she said awkwardly. 'I do. It is all right. I am not hurt.'

A strange hand was under her elbow lifting her to her feet, a large body, warm and very close to her, the voice again, richer and deeper. A good voice. 'Are you sure?'

She held out her right hand, palm upwards. 'Yes. Look. It is only – um – *une éraflure.*'

He was still standing beside her, steadying her with a hand under her elbow. A kind man. 'I'm awfully sorry,' he said. 'Believe me. I'm not usually so careless. I mean, I don't go round pushing people over all the time. I wasn't paying attention. I was looking for somewhere to put my bike, you see. I really didn't see you.'

'I didn't see you either,' she said, trying to make a joke of it.

'I didn't know you could speak English,' Mauricette said. She sounded surprised and a bit cross.

'I learnt it when I was little,' Emily explained, sorry that the hand had vanished from her elbow. She remembered her promise to Maman and blushed to realise that she'd disobeyed her, and broken the fourth commandment, too, although she hadn't meant to. But there wasn't time to think about it properly because the man was speaking again.

'I'm glad you did,' he said in English. 'You speak it very well.'

'Like a . . . a native,' she said, searching for the word. There was something about his voice that made her want to joke, even now when it wasn't really appropriate, when she'd just been knocked off her feet and disobeyed her mother and committed a sin.

'Should you bathe them?' he asked. And she realised he was referring to her grazes.

'I don't know,' she said. 'Is there water?'

That made him laugh. She liked his laugh very much. There was so much warmth in it, 'Good God, yes. The gardens are full of the stuff, lakes and ponds and fountains all over the place.'

Monsieur and Madame Lalange were approaching with

172

Zabette and Jean Paul. '*Dieu! Dieu!*,' Madame called. '*Qu'est-ce qui se passe?*'

The family were all speaking at once explaining and complaining.

'I'm not hurt,' Emily said into the bedlam. 'It was an accident.'

'Who are you?' Madame Lalange said furiously. 'What are you doing here?'

'*Je m'appelle Hopkirk*,' the man said. 'Ken Hopkirk. *Je fais un vacance ici.*'

'It was an accident,' Emily said again. To have anger bristling all round her, just when she'd thought the worst was all over, was upsetting. 'He was looking for somewhere to park his bicycle.'

'Such clumsiness,' Madame Lalange grumbled.

Her husband was more sensible. 'No harm is done,' he said. 'Why make a fuss? We are wasting the afternoon. Now then, who wants to see the palace?'

There was a clamour of applicants.

But Emily stayed silent. She didn't really want to go indoors, especially among crowds of people, but she couldn't say so, not when she was a guest and they were all being so kind.

Observing the way she was biting her pretty lip and those sightless eyes flicking from side to side, Ken Hopkirk understood the dilemma. She's too soft and gentle, he thought. She doesn't want to upset them by refusing, but she doesn't relish the idea of walking round the palace.

'Excuse me,' he said, struggling to try to help her. 'We thought, Mademoiselle and I, her hands ought to be – um – in the water –um – cleaned.'

Madame Lalange bristled at him. 'Then we will clean them, Monsieur.'

'I wish to make reparations,' he said.

Madame snorted. But her husband found a compromise. 'We will all take a turn in the gardens,' he said. 'The palace can wait. No, no, my little ones. We must attend to Emily's wounds, must we not? They shall be bathed. This young

173

man shall make his reparations.' And, his expression to his wife inferred, we can keep an eye on him.

It was agreed. Ken Hopkirk parked his cycle and he and the family walked into the gardens.

Afterwards, Emily was shocked to realise how readily she'd accepted a stranger's help. But, at the time, it seemed natural, somehow, as though he were an old friend or a relative. She held on to his arm as he talked her down the steps towards the nearest pond, sat obediently on the narrow grass verge beside the water and held out one hand after another so that he could bathe her grazes, touched and impressed that he knew exactly what she needed to be told. It was almost as if he was blind himself.

'There's a little bit of grit in here,' he said. 'I'm going to ease it out with the corner of this handkerchief. Tell me if it hurts. I'll be as gentle as I can.'

He *was* very gentle. 'Are you a doctor?' she said.

That made him laugh. 'Good Lord, no. No such luck. I'm just an ordinary bloke. I make gas meters.'

She was surprised. 'Do you?'

'I do. Very good ones, mind you.' And because her expression was encouraging him and it diverted her attention while he was cleaning her hands, he told her about his factory and how he planned to build up the business.

She listened seriously. 'It must be very good to be able to plan your life,' she said, choosing easy words because they were the only ones she could remember. 'To make things happen.'

'We all do it to a greater or lesser degree,' he said, and she heard him dip the handkerchief in the water again.

'I don't,' she said, when he'd walked back to her. 'I live – um – from day to day. I don't think I have ever said, I want this to happen.'

'You think it, though.'

'Well, sometimes,' she admitted. And then because he'd sounded so sure, 'How did you know?'

'When your – uncle, is it?'

'Mauricette's father.'

174

'When he said you were all going to see the palace you didn't want to go, did you?'

'No, I didn't. It is true. How did you know?'

'I could see it on your face.'

It had never occurred to her that other people could read her face in the same way as she read their voices. 'Oh dear,' she said. 'Do you think he saw it, too?'

'No,' he said, and he sounded sure of that, too. 'He was too busy looking at his children.'

It was so comfortable being reassured and cared for. 'I would like to sit here in the sun like this all afternoon,' she said. 'To be away from the crowds. I don't really like crowds.'

Mauricette was crunching across the gravel, calling as she came, 'We're going for our walk now, Emilie. Are you ready?'

He was still holding her hand, still comfortably close, and the thought of being parted from him made her feel bleak, as though she'd be losing an old friend. She made the first deliberate move into a life of her own. 'Will you come with us?' she said to him.

'I'd love to,' he said. And she could hear how honestly he meant it.

So he became her escort.

'Emilie,' he said. 'That's a nice name.'

'It is Emily in English.'

'That's even nicer. Would you like to walk in the shade? There's an avenue of trees just here.'

He guided her into the shade. There were smaller ornamental gardens on either side of the long central avenue and they took occasional detours to explore them, talking to one another in a mixture of struggling French and English. Monsieur and Madame Lalange let them go and told their ebullient children to leave them alone.

'These are delicate moments,' Monsieur Lalange said, 'these first moments.'

'But they don't know one another,' Mauricette said, 'You surely don't mean . . .'

175

Her mother had been watching the couple as closely as her husband. 'Not yet,' she said. 'But who can tell?'

After an hour in the garden the younger children were restless. 'When are we going in the palace?' Zabette demanded. 'You did promise, Papa.'

So Mauricette was sent with a message. 'Papa says we're going into the palace, now; but you can stay in the gardens, if you like. You can meet us outside the Petit Trianon at half-past five.'

'I will guard her,' Ken Hopkirk said in his laboured French.

'Half-past five,' Mauricette warned him, giving him a glare to show that *she* didn't approve, even though her father was aiding and abetting.

So now, Emily thought, we're on our own. It occurred to her that she ought to be feeling alarmed or worried at the very least. But she didn't. She felt secure.

He walked her past elaborate fountains, describing the shapes he saw. 'This one's a golden goddess with purple grapes in her hair and there are grapes all over the mound she's sitting on.' 'This one's Apollo driving his chariot. The horses are pulling in four different directions. They're marvellous horses. You can see the muscles straining under the skin. You'd think they were flesh and blood, not stone.'

'Now we're in a sort of summer house, perfectly round, made of marble, only the walls are more gap than wall, if you can imagine it. It's like a kind of marble trellis.' And he raised her hand to put it on one of the marble columns. 'Feel that. Isn't it lovely and cool? What a place! There are fountains in all the gaps.'

'Are they playing?' she asked, as they walked out of the summer house. 'I can't hear falling water.'

'No. They're not. Fact, I've been here three times now and I've never seen them play.'

'*Quel dommage!* That is a pity.'

'I don't mind if you don't mind.'

It was a pretty compliment, but she thought perhaps she

shouldn't respond to it. It sounded too intimate and they'd only just met – even though it didn't feel like it, they had only just met.

'Now we're standing at a crossroads,' he told her. 'You must tell me which way you want to go.'

'Is there another – um – *un étang, un lac*?'

'A pond, you mean? Yes.'

'Then we'll go to the pond. It is cooler by the water.'

They walked on together and this time he put his arm round Emily's shoulders to steer her through the trees. Dead leaves crunched under her feet, a bird piped in the branches over her head and she could feel shadows flickering across her face, now warm, now cool.

'Oh,' she said, 'this is a lovely place.'

'There's a bench here,' he said. 'Would you like to sit down?'

So they sat down together and were companionably silent for quite a long time. When he finally spoke it was hesitantly and his voice had quite a different note.

'Emily?'

'Yes,' she encouraged.

There was another pause, while he pondered and she waited.

'What is it?' she said.

He answered her, but dubiously. 'No,' he said. 'It's silly. It'll sound silly.'

'You have started to say this,' she told him. '*Alors*. Say it all, whatever it is. I shan't mind.' All the same, she felt anxious in case it was something she didn't want to hear.

His answer when it came was so warm and affectionate it made her blush. 'I feel I've known you all my life.'

Lost for words, she put her hands up to her hot cheeks to hide their colour.

'I've upset you,' he said, full of remorse. 'I shouldn't have said it. I'm sorry.'

She felt she had to reassure him. 'No,' she said, speaking quickly. 'It is not silly. I feel the same thing.' Then she was really worried. To have said so much so soon. It wasn't

177

decorous or proper, or Maman's word, 'sensible'. What was the matter with her to be behaving so. . . ?

He took hold of her hand again. 'Do you. Really?'

'Yes, I do.'

The moment was charged with emotion, almost as if they were exchanging vows.

'You won't laugh if I tell you something else?' he asked.

'No.'

'I've never spent an afternoon on my own with a young lady before.'

Her respose was too direct for comfort. 'Why not?'

He was embarrassed. 'I don't know.'

'Are you so young?'

'I'm twenty-four. *Vingt-quatre.*'

'*Ah bon.*'

'I suppose,' he said, feeling he ought to offer her some explanation, 'I mean, what I really ought to have said is I've never met a young lady who wanted to spend an afternoon on her own with *me.*' That was nearer the truth and it hadn't required him to confess how ugly he was.

She gave him a very French answer and a delicious smile. 'That was their loss, I think.'

'You'll make me conceited if you say things like that.'

She had to think for a second to remember what the word 'conceited' meant. 'I don't think so,' she said. 'You don't sound conceited.'

'How do I sound?'

'Kind. Sympathetic. And . . .'

He waited while she considered whether she ought to go on and decided that she could. 'Sometimes as if you are not quite sure of yourself.' Then she worried in case she'd been too daring. What if she'd upset him?

But his voice remained steady. 'Yes,' he said. 'That's true. How did you know?'

'I heard it in your voice.'

'Amazing!'

'No,' she said. 'It is because I can't see. I use my ears instead.'

178

They were on very delicate ground but he felt he could ask her. 'How long have you been blind?'

'Since I was born.'

'So you've never seen anything?'

'Well, not the way you do. I don't know what colours are. But I can see *les formes*, you understand? And – um – *les textures*. I see with my hands.'

He was stroking her hand with his thumb, very gently, making her skin prickle with pleasure. Should he be doing this? she worried. Should I be allowing it? But she couldn't stop him. It was too delicious. 'Shapes and textures,' he said, translating for her.

Suddenly the hot air was full of rushing sound.

'They've turned on the fountains,' he said, springing to his feet. 'Come on. We must see this. Apollo first.'

They ran together, holding hands like children. And there was Apollo driving his chariot through billowing white clouds with the waves of the sea tumbling and foaming around his horses' hooves.

'It's magical,' he told her, full of excitement at what he was seeing and aching to share it with her. 'It's sculpture with water. It looks exactly as though he's driving straight at us through a high sea. I've never seen anything so clever.'

'I wonder what the summer house is like?' Emily said. 'You said there were fountains there, didn't you?'

The summer house was transformed, too. Now, it had walls all around it but they were walls of falling water, cool, musical and shimmering with rainbows.

They stood beside the walls for a long time so that Emily could enjoy the cool water spraying against her face.

Then they went to the waterfalls and the goddess with the grapes and all the other fountains they'd found on their first walk. By degrees, they made their way back to the terraced steps and the pool where he'd bathed her hand, which turned out to be the most beautiful water sculpture of them all.

'I thought this one was ordinary,' he said. 'It didn't look much without the water. Just a lot of funny little fat frogs sitting in circles, sort of squatting in the water and a goddess standing on a sort of plinth, but now . . . now it's terrific. The frogs are part of the design you see.' And he seized both her hands to show her what he was talking about. 'The water comes out of their mouths and rises up and up, like that, and then it curves over and falls down the other side, like that, and all the sprays are sort of woven into one another in mid air, like a wickerwork basket.' Entwining their fingers. 'And the frogs at the very top spout their water out so high it makes a bower over her head.' Lifting her hands so that they moved through a long slow upward curve and came to rest, clasped between his own hands as high as he could make her reach above her head. 'The water looks like white silk,' he said. 'It's magic.'

They were both breathless, standing close together in the cool, hissing air. He lowered her hands very gently and held on to them.

'I would like to know what you look like,' she said.

'I'm hideous,' he joked, glad she couldn't see him. It would be dreadful if it all went wrong now. Oh, God, please don't let it all go wrong now.

'May I see for myself?' she said. 'Would you mind?'

How could he say no? It would be unkind, like a sort of insult. 'OK,' he said and stood still and apprehensive while she explored his face with her finger tips. And despite his apprehension, was aroused most powerfully.

'Well?' he said fearfully.

'You have a good face,' she said. 'Strong. A kind mouth.'

Oh, those soft fingers on his lips! 'I'm going bald,' he felt he ought to warn her. *Pas de cheveux.*

'I know,' she said. 'Lots of men do, don't they? You smile a lot. You have a temper.'

'Yes,' he admitted.

'A good face,' she said, tracing the line of his chin.

'Not hideous?'

'No. A good face. A face I could – um (*Oh, what was the word?*) – A face I could trust.'

The sun came out from behind the small cloud that had

been shielding it while she explored his features and, suddenly, they were standing in a rainbow. The shining colours arched in the spray above her head, and there was no need for words anymore. He bent his head, lifting her chin with his finger tips and kissed her, very gently and tenderly.

She gave herself up to the magic of it, amazed that her lips could be feeling so much pleasure, caught in the magic of sunshine and birdsong and tumbling water.

'You are the dearest, dearest girl,' he said. 'I think I love you.'

He was to say the same thing over and over again in the days that followed, with more and more certainty. For, of course, he abandoned his tour of the chateaux, found lodgings on the Left Bank and saw her every day for the rest of his holiday. Now that he'd found her he had no intention of ever losing her. She was much, much too precious. Having arranged for her to stay in Paris until his holiday was over, the Lalange family encouraged the romance, warmed and delighted by it. It was the prime topic of conversation when she was out of the apartment. Even Mauricette approved.

To keep her away from the crowds, Ken took his new love to the Luxembourg gardens, and the Jardin des Plantes and the Bois de Boulogne. On Sunday they discovered to their mutual delight that they were both Catholics and went to mass together. Every evening they ate in a local café, walked arm in arm beside the Seine in the cool dusk, and talked and kissed, and talked and kissed again. Emily remembered more and more English and grew more and more happy.

She introduced him to French cooking and told him what a good cook Hortense was. He told her his mother had been dead for nearly twelve years.

'Dad walked out on us when we were little,' he said. 'We had quite a struggle. When she died the family sort of split up. My sisters went to Australia, one brother went to Canada and another to America and the little one to New Zealand. I'm the only one left in England.'

181

She was drawn with pity for him. 'Never mind,' she said. 'Life is better now, isn't it?'

'Life is perfect now,' he said. 'I love you so much.'

'And I love you,' she said. She could hardly believe she was saying such a thing but it was true. 'Oh my dear, dear Ken.'

By the end of his holiday he was so immersed in this new, perfect life he'd forgotten all about his old one. It was as if he'd never had a family, never been to school, never made any other friends, never lived or experienced anything until that moment. He'd almost forgotten his factory.

'I shall write to you every day,' he said on that last morning when he came to say goodbye, 'and I shall return to France the minute I can.'

# CHAPTER THIRTEEN

Despite the bravado displayed to Ken Hopkirk, Charlie Commoner was nervous about being abroad. He had learnt French at school but had never been happy about speaking it, and he wasn't at all sure how well he'd be able to cope with finding a room, or ordering meals, or travelling on the Métro. So he was pleased when his first taxi driver not only understood where he wanted to go, but advised him on the right amount for the tip. He was even more pleased when he arrived at the offices of *Le Temps* to find an elderly man waiting for him who actually spoke English and welcomed him most helpfully.

'There is, 'owever, one little *problème*,' the gentleman said. 'Ze young ladies have cancel' their appointment. Zey will not be to ze office until next Friday morning. 'Owever I am certain you will not mind to wait for ze few days 'ere in Paris. Zere is plenty to amuse oneself in Paris, *n'est-ce pas?*'

Charlie agreed to wait, happily enough. Mr Crabbit had told him he could stay a day or so, if the need arose, and Paris looked like a thrilling place. Full of smartly dressed men and fashionable women wearing tiny hats and elegant suits and the highest heels he'd ever seen, it certainly seemed very different from London. The roads were lined with chestnut trees, cars were being driven at amazing speeds, and there were cafés with coloured awnings over the pavements, where tables were set out in the open air, and waiters danced between them carrying their trays balanced on outspread hands above their heads. As he set off along the boulevard, Charlie was more than ready to enjoy himself.

But foreign cities rarely turn out to be exactly what imagination or first sight leads you to expect. The capital held rather a lot of surprises for Charlie Commoner and some of them were embarrassing.

That evening he decided to visit the Moulin Rouge, but the tickets were so prohibitively expensive and the clientèle so obviously wealthy that he changed his mind and went to the cinema instead, to see Franchot Tone in *Mutiny on the Bounty*. But even going to the pictures was different in Paris. The usherette wanted a tip for showing him to his seat and the couples on either side of him spent the entire film smooching in a really – well –unbridled way. Afterwards lying in an uncomfortable bed, it made him hot even to think about it, and he thought about it most of the night.

However, there were consolations, most of them edible. The food in the local cafés was delicious and not as expensive as he'd feared, and breakfast of coffee and hot bread was a revelation. The trouble was that after eating came the pressing need to find a public lavatory and the public lavatories were nightmares.

The first one he ventured into was used by men and women, which sent him scuttling out again, unrelieved and suffused with embarrassment. The second was presided over by an enormous woman dressed entirely in black who was feeding her family at a table in the space between cubicles. She paused, ladle in hand, to greet him as he came down the steps, and horror of horrors, when he emerged from his cubicle, blushing furiously, she advanced upon him, ladle still in hand, and demanded '*Service, M'sieur*', holding out her free hand for a tip.

'*Non. Non*,' he said backing away. Surely you didn't have to pay a tip to pee.

But she insisted. '*Mais oui, M'sieur. Service.*'

Charlie fished in his pocket for a coin and found one that seemed to please her. Then he fled.

At last it was Friday and time to identify his heiresses.

He was careful to arrive ten minutes before the appointment, which was just as well because it was some time before he was creaked upstairs in the lift and ushered into his interpreter's office. But he was welcomed as courteously as he had been the first time and, now that he had someone to talk to again, it struck him that he'd been quite lonely during his 'little holiday'.

Coffee was steamed into the room to refresh him, and he and the interpreter made careful small talk. Charlie revealed as much of the story as he thought prudent, and his host checked that 'the necessary documentation' was to hand.

'Are zere other arrangements we should make, Monsieur Commonaire?' the latter asked politely.

'None that I can think of,' Charlie replied, drinking his coffee, and feeling much more at ease now he was back at work. And suddenly, because the moment of meeting was so close, his imagination ran riot. A string of young and beautiful heiresses, paraded before him, blonde-haired and blue-eyed, dark-haired and brown-eyed, lissom and shy, all breathlessly waiting to hear his good news. It was the stuff of his sixteen-year-old dreams, and he knew it. But he enjoyed it just the same.

The door was opening. The real heiresses had arrived. Charlie started and went red. He put down his cup and stood up to welcome them, annoyed to be caught blushing.

Flat-footed, flat-faced, with straight, mouse-brown hair and rough complexions and awful, dumpy, middle-aged bodies, they were a horrible disappointment.

And they giggled when they were introduced.

'No,' the taller of the two said in French, 'we don't speak English.'

Their host assured them that this would present no problem. 'I will translate, Madame and Mademoiselle.'

So one's married, Charlie noted, as he settled to the business that had brought him to Paris. There was no need to look at his papers; he knew the salient facts by heart. But could this pair really be the heiresses? He hoped not. They didn't look like heiresses. Or twins. If it came to that, they didn't look twenty. If he was any judge, he'd put them nearer thirty.

At first they got their answers right. They had come to

France in May 1926. With their mother? Oh yes, Monsieur. Assuredly. They had lived here ever since. *Malheureusement*, they had forgotten how to speak English but they still had the crosses. You see? And sure enough there was a plain silver cross hung about each plump neck. They had been born in England. Yes, yes. Assuredly. At a place called 'Igg Ollborne'.

The mispronouncement encouraged him. 'Would you tell me the date of your birthday?' he asked.

To his delight he got two different dates and both of them were wrong. They *were* thirty. Thirty-one and thirty-four, to be precise.

'I'm afraid,' he said, striving to maintain a serious expression and finding it difficult, 'you are not the young ladies we are looking for.' He felt almost light-hearted with relief.

The sisters protested volubly. They had the crosses. See! Here they were. They were called Ollborne.

'Ho'bun,' he said, pronouncing the name in its correct, idiosyncratic English way. And he turned to his host. 'The ladies in question are twins,' he said. 'The advertisement should have made that clear.'

But apparently the advertisement had only mentioned sisters.

The two imposters were aggrieved, but eventually they were talked out of their bad temper and persuaded to leave.

'I'm sorry about that,' Charlie said. 'Wasting your time, I mean.'

His host shrugged. 'It 'appens, Monsieur. Always where zere is money zere are imposters.'

'I suppose so.'

'*Alors*,' his host said, 'Shall we put ze correct advertisement in our paper? Tomorrow perhaps, for ze weekend. You could remain 'ere to see what will 'appen. Other ladies could appear, *n'est-ce pas?*'

'Well,' Charlie wondered. 'I'd have to write to Mr Crabbit and get his instructions. I was only expecting to stay a few days you see, but I suppose . . .'

'We will telephone Mr Crabbit.'

'To England?'

'*Mais oui*.'

What next? Charlie thought. First a holiday I didn't expect and now a phone call to London. I'm living like a toff.

He agreed just the same.

So the continental exchange was called. After a surprisingly short wait, the telephone was handed to Charlie and there was Mr Crabbit on the line, faint, far away and disembodied but undeniably Mr Crabbit, saying, 'Any luck lad?'

Charlie told him what had happened. 'Should I stay here any longer, sir?'

'Why not?' Mr Crabbit said from his great distance. 'Stay till Wednesday. That should give enough time. Cut off to Amiens first, though, and put our advertisement in the papers there. Then we can tell the old dear we're working according to plan. Have you got sufficient cash to cover?'

'Well no, actually, sir. It's rather expensive here.'

'I'll send you a cheque. To *Le Temps*. They'll cash it for you. Don't spend it all at once.'

'No, sir. I won't. Thank you.'

'Good luck.'

And that was that. He'd been given another five days to kick his heels in France, expenses paid. The trouble was, Paris had lost its appeal for him. It was too big, too impersonal and he was too isolated there. As he left the office, he decided to go straight to Amiens. He'd catch the very first train.

Whenever Charlie thought about Amiens he imagined a small market town, a place where everyone knew everyone else, where it would be more than likely that he could ask for the Holborn twins at a shop or kiosk and be directed, if not to their house, then at least to someone who would know them. So when he walked out of the station into a huge industrial town, it came as something of a shock. There were trams rattling and clanking in every direction across a wide cobbled square and the air smelt of factory chimneys and horse manure. And although there were lots of people about, they were far too busy with their own affairs to pay any attention to *him*.

At least there were newspaper sellers though, standing inside their little kiosks surrounded by papers. That was something. Charlie approached the nearest one gingerly, endeavouring to put together a grammatical request and to get his mouth into the right shape to pronounce it properly.

'*Excusez-moi,*' he said. '*Avez-vous des papiers?*'

The news seller looked baffled. '*M'sieur?*'

Charlie tried another tack. '*Avez-vous* – um – *quelles* – um – "*Temps*"?'

'*Fait beau,*' the news seller said, shrugging his shoulders and looking at Charlie in disbelief. What sort of a fool was this to be asking about the weather?

What is he talking about? Charlie thought, gazing at the rows of papers with their unfamiliar titles. *Beau* means beautiful, doesn't it? Why is he talking about something beautiful? There was no sign of *Le Temps* in the racks, nor of any of the other papers he had noted in Paris.

'Are these all local papers?' he said, retreating into English. Amiens was as bad as Paris. Was there really only *one* man in the whole of France who spoke English?

But the news seller had already turned away from Charlie to give his attention to a customer who knew what he wanted.

Now what? Charlie thought as he wandered out into the square. He tried to be practical. First, he needed to find somewhere to stay, after that he would look for the newspaper offices. What were they called? *Maison de la presse*. Yes, that was it. *Maison de la presse*. He would soon find that, and this time he would use the phrase book.

It took him the rest of the morning to discover a room he could afford, and by the evening he'd walked from one end of the town to the other and failed to find a *maison de la presse* anywhere. Tired and foot sore, he tried not to be dispirited. At least he had learned the layout of the place. He knew where the old town was and could probably retrace his steps to the cathedral square at the heart of it. That sort of thing. Tomorrow would be different.

The next day it was drizzling with rain. By late afternoon he had worked out that there were five local papers on sale in the kiosks but, as there was no sign of any *maison de la presse*, he concluded that they must be printed somewhere else. But he was baffled in all his attempts to find out where. He tried to strike up conversations with all sorts of people during the day – like the waiters at the café, or the concierge at his boarding house – but none of them could understand what he was saying. He was locked in silence and incomprehension by his own awful ignorance. On top of that, his jacket was like a damp rag. It was demoralising.

It was wet on Sunday, too. Feeling a fool, he pressed on with his search. It yielded nothing.

That night, after his evening meal, he left his jacket steaming over the back of a chair, put on his fairisle jersey and mooched off into the centre of the town to take stock of his difficulties. The rain had gathered itself while he was eating and become a proper shower, pattering against the windows and darkening the sky. Now that the downpour was over, the air was fresh and clear, and the bells of the cathedral were ringing into a sky crazed with green and gold.

There was a racket of some kind going on near the cathedral, a band playing and lots of voices shouting and laughing. The nearer he got to it the more attractive it sounded and as everybody else seemed to be heading that way, he followed.

It was a celebration. The band was playing on the cathedral steps and the square was packed with people in a voluble state of excitement, most of them dancing. The street lights were lit like a blossoming of summer flowers, and there was red, white and blue bunting draped over all the houses. The two cafés on the square were so crowded that every seat was taken and groups of people stood round tables on the pavement. What a lark!

Tapping his foot in time to the music, he drifted to the

edge of the dancing crowd, and wished he could find an excuse to join in.

'Who's that?' Veronique Tilliette said to her friend Ginny Lisieux.

'Who's who?' Ginny said, glancing over her shoulder as she spun past.

Veronique's partner was her cousin, so he got pushed about so that she could carry on her conversation. 'That blond feller on the edge of the crowd. See? Tall. Gorgeous blond hair. I could fancy him.'

'He's not French,' Ginny warned.

'How do you know?'

'That jersey.'

'Scandinavian? D'you think he's Scandinavian?'

Ginny was enjoying the dance too much to be interested. 'Maybe,' she said, and she and her partner spun like tops and were lost to Veronique in the mass of twirling bodies.

'He's a handsome beast, whatever he is,' Veronique called after her. 'Let's go and chat him up.' But Ginny was out of earshot. 'Mind your feet, you clumsy thing,' Veronique said to her cousin. 'You nearly had me over.'

'Well, I like that,' her partner said indignantly. 'You weren't looking. You can dance by yourself if that's the way you're going to talk.'

The waltz was over and a round dance was beginning. Veronique plunged into the crowd to find her friend, catching her by the hand and holding on tight. The circle went stamping off in time to the music. They were moving faster and faster, running and tripping, reckless with excitement.

'After this,' Veronique yelled. Her dash through the crowd and the speed of this new dance were making her pant, and she had to yell because there was so much noise.

'What?' Ginny yelled back.

'*Le blond*!' Veronique said, jerking her head in the direction of the handsome man.

The movement was so violent that she lost her grip on

190

Ginny's outstretched hand and, in a second, she was gone, hurled backwards by the dangerous impetus of the dance, out of the circle, through the crowd, to the edge of the square – where she would have fallen, had it not been for the fact that somebody's chest had cushioned her impact.

She turned, apologising profusely, and found she was gazing up into the surprised grey eyes of her *blond*. She blinked and caught her breath. Apology rapidly became flirtation.

'What good luck you were there,' she said, opening her eyes wide, knowing they were her best feature. 'Waiting to catch me, *n'est-ce pas?*'

Charlie Commoner was monstrously embarrassed. To have this strange plump woman hurtling into his chest was bad enough, but now she was making calf's eyes at him and saying things that, even though he couldn't understand them, were making him blush.

'*Ça ne fait rien,*' he said carefully. 'It doesn't matter.'

But she continued to talk to him, making ferocious eyes. Oh God! he thought, backing away. How could he make her stop? He wasn't the least bit interested in her. Couldn't she see he wasn't? Frantically he looked around for someone else to talk to, and saw a slim dark-haired girl pushing her way towards them through the crowd. There was something so determined and forceful about her expression that he cast around in his mind for the French words to explain that no harm was done.

'*Nous ne sommes pas*' – What was the word for hurt? – '*blessés Mademoiselle,*' he said.

'Good heavens!' she said answering him in his own language. 'You're English.'

He was so relieved that it made him babble. 'Yes, yes, I am. How did you know? My awful French, I expect. Are you English, too? Or do you just speak the language, I mean? Not that it's any of my business . . . What I mean is, I haven't found anyone who could speak English, not since I got here. I've been trying to . . . What I mean is . . . Gosh, you don't know what a relief this is.'

What a foolish young man, Ginny thought, listening to the babble. 'Yes,' she said. 'I see it is.' She turned to Veronique ready to walk away and jerked her head as if to say 'Let's go!'

But after being thrown into the blond stranger's arms Veronique intended to make the most of it.

'*Alors!*' she said. 'What nationality is he?'

'English,' Ginny explained.

'Is that what you were speaking?'

'Yes.'

'Ask him what he's doing here.'

'We don't want to waste time on him. He's an idiot. Come away.'

'Oh, go on, Ginny. It wouldn't hurt. Just ask him. For me. I really fancy him.'

'You fancy a new man every week.'

'This is different. Oh, go on! Please.'

'Oh, very well,' Ginny said. 'But I warn you, he'll be a waste of time.' And she turned back to the young man and licked her lips ready to speak English again.

'My friend wants to know,' she said, in her accented English. 'What are you doing in Amiens?'

'I'm on business,' Charlie said, delighted to be spoken to again.

'Cloth?'

'Pardon?'

'It is cloth, your business? Velours?'

'Oh no. Nothing like that.' What amazing eyes she has. Great big, beautiful, brown eyes, shining like . . .

'He's on business,' Ginny translated.

'Ask him if he'd like to dance.'

'No fear. He might say yes.'

'Very well. I'll do it myself then,' Veronique said. And she turned to the young man. '*Dansez!*' she commanded, putting out her right hand to tempt him.

He took it eagerly, offering his own right hand to the dark-eyed girl at the same time.

She ignored it, and scolded her friend, 'What folly! Now

you'll be stuck with him, I hope you realise, and he's an absolute idiot. Look at him!' But the dance had already swept them up and was carrying them along. She was hand in hand with the idiot whether she would or no, and after a few steps, because she was excited and happy, she gave herself up to the rhythm and returned to enjoying herself. The idiot could dance beside her if he wanted.

Beaming with pleasure, Charlie bounced to the music. All his difficulties appeared to have been swept away in an instant. He couldn't believe his luck to have found a girl who could speak English. Such a gorgeous girl, too, so small and dark and full of life. The dancers turned and began to leap and cavort in the opposite direction, dragging him along with them.

'Do you always dance in the streets?' he shouted, holding on to her hand for dear life, 'or is this a celebration or something?'

'Often,' she shouted back, giving him the benefit of those shining eyes. 'We like it. But you're right. It *is* a celebration. *Le Quatorze*. We've got a new government. The Popular Front.'

'Bastille day,' he said. ' 'Course!'

The dance spun them apart, together, apart again. And then as the final figure began it became a whirling twosome in which the couples held hands and spun like dervishes, round and round in the same direction at an impossible speed. And this extraordinary dark-eyed, happy girl was Charlie Commoner's partner. He was actually holding both her hands, as tightly as he dared, and she was throwing back her head and squealing with enjoyment as they whirled. When the dance finally spun to a standstill, she stood before him panting and laughing, white teeth gleaming in the torchlight, eyes glimmering, and he was so overwhelmed by the sight that he didn't know what to say.

'I love dancing,' she said matter-of-factly. And was off into the crowds before he could catch his breath.

The plump girl was still lurking, making eyes at him.

Oh, go away, he thought. You're not the one I want. But at this point, it occurred to him that these two girls were friends and that if he wanted to find out about the dark-eyed one, this one . . .

'*Comment vous appellez-vous?*' the plump girl was saying.

He could cope with that. 'Charlie,' he said. '*Et vous?*'

'Veronique.'

'Ah!' he said. There was something you were supposed to say when you were introduced. What was it? '*Enchanté.*' He experimented.

The result was alarming. She bridled at him and launched into a babble of French, speaking quickly and with great animation. He couldn't understand a word.

'Yes,' he said. 'Yes. I see.' But what he really wanted to see were those brown eyes, and they had disappeared into the crowd.

'*Votre amie,*' he said. '*Elle s'appelle?*'

'Ginny.'

'Jeannie,' he repeated, thinking what a lovely name it was and that he would never forget it, ever. And, then, trying some more badly pronounced French. 'Where is she?'

'Over there,' Veronique told him. 'She's dancing.'

'Ah, yes. Would you like a cup of coffee? You and your friend.'

'*Vous êtes très gentil,*' Veronique said. '*Allons.*' And she led him through the dancers until she and Ginny were side by side.

'He wants to treat us all to coffee,' she said.

'All?' Ginny said, and she looked and sounded quite cross. But then she grinned because an idea had formed in her mind. 'How many is all?'

'You and your friends, he said.'

'Oh, did he? Well then . . .'

She made a grab at a tousle-headed girl who was skipping past with two skinny young men beside her. '*Ça va, Marie?*'

Charlie's heart contracted with disappointment. He could feel it quite distinctly, shrinking in his chest. No! he thought. Please don't talk to someone else, and especially not in French. Not when I've just asked you to come and have a cup of coffee with me.

To his horror it appeared that he'd asked no fewer than five people to take coffee with him. They were all thanking him and shaking his hand and introducing themselves. Oh Lord! Now what was he going to do? He'd be well out of pocket if he had to buy coffee for all that lot. But he couldn't leave her now, and he couldn't say he hadn't invited them. His French wasn't up to it. Besides, it would look boorish. There was nothing for it. He had to stay with her and treat them, no matter what it cost. In any case, they were already on their way to a café; the girls deep in an animated conversation and the young men part of it, too, laughing and teasing. He made frantic and probably inaccurate calculations in his head. Coffee wasn't so expensive here so perhaps it would be . . . perhaps he could . . .

The café Ginny took them to was quite a distance away from the square, and quiet enough to allow conversation. While the coffee was being served and Charlie was still fretting about whether he'd have enough money to pay for it, the talk was all in French.

It wasn't until they embarked on a jokey conversation about work that he got the chance to chip in and ask them what they did. Amongst a rush of information that he didn't want, he found out that Jeannie was a typist in a velvet factory and that the fat girl was her workmate. So far so good.

'What do you do?' Veronique asked in return.

'I am looking for a *maison de la presse*.'

'Why? Are you a journalist?'

His French wasn't up to answering that. 'I've got to put an advertisement in one of the local papers,' he said in English and, naturally, he addressed the remark to Jeannie.

'Why?' she asked him.

'I'm looking for two heiresses,' he told her, feeling rather proud to be able to say such a thing, and was cock-a-hoop when she looked impressed.

'Truly?'

'Yes.'

'English ones.'

'Yes.'

'Are you – um – *un détective?*'

'No, a solicitor.' And when he saw she didn't understand him. 'A lawyer.' What were they called in France? '*Un Advocat.*'

That didn't impress her at all. He wasn't old enough to be an Advocate. '*Un avoué,*' she said, and shrugged.

'I believe there are five local papers,' he persisted. 'That's right, isn't it?'

'Yes,' she said casually. 'I suppose there are.'

'I have to put an advertisement in one of them. Which would you recommend?'

'The *Chroniquer,*' she said at once. 'That's the paper the rich people read. They are rich these heiresses?'

'Stinking,' he said. 'You should see where they live in England.'

'Stinking' made her laugh. 'Is that what you say?' she said. 'Stinking.'

'Stinking rich. Yes. Smelling of money I suppose. So you recommend the *Chroniquer.*'

'Yes.'

'The trouble is,' he said, 'I know it sounds silly, but I can't find the newspaper offices. I've looked everywhere. Maybe they're not here. Not in the town, I mean.'

'Of course they're in town. Where have you looked?'

He tried to tell her but she grew impatient.

'You should use a map,' she said. He was more of a fool than she'd thought.

He produced his copy of the town map from his trouser pocket. 'Perhaps you could show me,' he coaxed.

She passed it across the table to her friends, explaining what he wanted. Within seconds it was back in his hands, marked with crosses to indicate where the newspaper offices were, with a circled cross beside one labelled '*Chroniquer*' and the words '*Cherchez l'Imprimateur*' written across the top margin.

While he was thanking them all, they were suddenly on their feet and preparing to leave. And the waiter was heading towards him with the bill.

196

'Just a minute,' he said, struggling to get his change out of his pocket, desperately hoping there would be enough of it. 'Jeannie! Veronique! When can I see you again?'

Ginny took no notice of him, but Veronique was back at the table like a shot. 'I will write you my address,' she said. 'Do you have *un carnet*?'

He guessed that she meant a notebook but he couldn't provide one. The only thing that was suitable was his pocket diary and he'd left that in his jacket back at the boarding house. And now the bill was being shoved towards him on the paper tablecloth. The paper tablecloth!

'*Attendez un peu!*' he begged, addressing the waiter *and* Veronique as he scrabbled sufficient coins together to pay the bill. There *were* sufficient. Thank God for that! As soon as the waiter had turned away he ripped off a corner of the cloth and gave it to her.

She rummaged in her coat pocket and found a pencil and wrote her name and address in curly French script.

'And where you work also,' he said, hoping she would understand his awkward French.

She wrote down something else and gave him the paper with an encouraging smile.

He was full of excitement at his cunning and the success of it. 'I see you tomorrow, *n'est-ce pas*?' he said to her. 'At Monsieur Guerin, Quality Velvets. *Merci beaucoup*.' And escorted her most happily out of the café.

Out on the pavement there was a moment's awkwardness while she waited, hoping he would see her home to her door. Charlie managed to extricate himself from this predicament by playing English and saying '*Au revoir*.' He watched with relief as she ran off along the road after her friends. What an evening! What an absolutely amazing evening! He was flat broke but what did that matter when he'd met a girl like Jeannie, and danced with her and taken her to a café and spent nearly three hours in her company? Financial problems paled to insignificance next to that.

The following morning, sitting soberly over breakfast, he had to face the fact that he had so little money left that he would have to return to Paris to request replenishment. There was barely enough to buy a third-class fare and taking Jeannie out to lunch was out of the question.

Still, he told himself cheerfully, if he hurried he could be there and back before lunchtime – and still have two whole days before he had to catch the boat train.

Unfortunately, his interpreter was in a meeting which went on for so long that it was mid-afternoon before he finally obtained the money. By the time he got back to Amiens it was too late to meet the two girls when they came out of work. It was a disappointment, but he would just have to make the most of Tuesday and Wednesday.

On Tuesday morning, he found the newspaper office and paid for the advertisement, issuing careful instructions (with the help of his phrase book), that it was to be printed in the personal column of the weekend editions and all enquiries were to be sent to Hedgethorn and Crabbit. Then, and at last, he was free to go down to the old town and find the place where Jeannie worked. After so much time and effort, he felt he'd earned the right to see her again.

She didn't even look at him. Veronique did, and was very happy to accept his invitation to lunch. It was a difficult meal because Charlie couldn't understand half the things she was chattering about, and he was thinking about Jeannie all the time.

Afterwards, he walked her back to the factory, hoping to meet up with Jeannie there. But there was no sign of her.

'Tomorrow,' he said in careful French, 'we dine again?'
'*Mais oui.*'

'You and your friend Jeannie? If you please.'

She was disappointed and showed it, but promised to pass on his invitation.

'He's very handsome,' she said to Ginny, when they were both back at work and Monsieur Guerin was out of earshot, 'but he isn't interested in me. It's you he wants.'

'That's nonsense.'

'No. It's true. He talks about you all the time and now he wants you to have lunch with him tomorrow.'

'I told you he was an idiot,' Ginny said. Even so, there was something about the young man's persistence that was rather flattering.

'Shall you go?'

'I might. I'll think about it.'

She didn't think about it at all. But when they stopped work that evening and put on their hats and coats, she saw the *idiot anglais* standing by the gate.

'I was wondering whether we might not have coffee again tonight,' he said as they came face to face.

'I'm going to the cinema,' she said.

His face fell so visibly she felt sorry for him despite herself. 'We could all meet up at the café afterwards, if you'd like,' she said. That was kind and it wouldn't commit her to anything.

So they met at the café. This time she allowed him to talk to her and discovered that he had a sense of humour, which surprised her.

'Tomorrow?' he hoped as they parted. 'It's my last day. I go back to London tomorrow evening.'

'All right, then,' she said. There'd be no risk in it. If he was going back to England she wouldn't be likely to see him again afterwards.

So on that warm Wednesday afternoon, Charlie Commoner had lunch with his bewitching girl. Their conversation was exploratory and happy, but guarded. They told one another about their lives; about Monsieur Guerin and his velvets and Mr Crabbit and his cigars, about London and Amiens and the boredom of paperwork. He was careful not to say anything about his mission, in order to keep his promise to Mr Hedgethorn, and she was careful to conceal her English origins to keep her promise to Maman. They got on so well that, by the end of the meal, Ginny had revised her original opinion of him, and Charlie was so happy he felt light-headed.

He knew he would have to travel back overnight, and wasn't at all sure whether he'd have time to get to Clapham first thing in the morning to change into his office clothes for work, but he didn't care. He was in France, and he was in love, and so full of hope and apprehension that everything else in his life seemed insignificant by contrast.

# CHAPTER FOURTEEN

Oh, the pain of being parted from your very first love! Nothing is so exquisite, so unendurable, so all-absorbing.

On that fateful Wednesday, Charlie Commoner and Ken Hopkirk travelled back to England on the same overnight boat. This time they didn't meet up with one another. They didn't even see one another. Neither of them was aware of anything except their thoughts.

They stood by the rail, one to port and one to starboard, and gazed out to sea, seeing nothing. The Channel was calm and so inky black that the sky looked denim blue by comparison and the moon was a yellow magnet shimmering a pathway of white light across the water. But what was that to them? Charlie was reliving the trials and delights of the past three days, remembering Jeannie's beautiful eyes, her wild springy hair and the delicious smell of her skin when he'd danced with her, and aching with anguish because he didn't know whether she was interested in him or not and the boat was taking him in the wrong direction.

Ken was doing complicated mental arithmetic.

When he left his workshop fourteen days ago – was it really only fourteen days? – he had just completed the design of an entirely new gas meter. At the time, he'd been pleased by his skill and calculated that the gas boards might be interested in what he was doing. Now, he was determined that they shouldn't just be interested, they should buy his design *and* commission his workforce to produce it in large quantities. He would badger them until they did. He'd write every day, he'd have a telephone installed and phone them constantly, he'd haunt their offices, work all hours, do anything. If the design needed adapting, he'd adapt it. If capital had to be raised, he'd raise it. In a year's time he needed to have enough money to buy a bungalow near the factory where he and his darling Emily could live – it had to be a bungalow so that Emily wouldn't have to manage stairs. It should have a garden he could fill with scented flowers for her to smell, and a bird-table to encourage the birds for her, and a hammock so that she could sit in the sun. In a year's time.

As soon as the boat train sighed in to Victoria Station, Ken set off at a brisk pace for the Underground to South Wimbledon, and the work that had to be done. There was no point in going back to his flat to change his clothes. The sooner he got started the better. If he hurried he could get in half an hour's peaceful effort before the machines were started up.

If his workmen were surprised to see him wearing plus fours, they were far too wary of his temper to say so. It was normal for Mr Hopkirk to be in the drawing office by the time they arrived and being the boss he could wear whatever he fancied. Later, he would emerge to check how the work was going, and tell them how he'd fared in France, like he usually did. But this morning the boss didn't stop and soon there was a stack of letters by his elbow.

'*Dear Sir,*' his pen scratched over and over again.

'*You will be interested to know. . .*' You may not think it yet but you *will* be interested.


Charlie Commoner had to go straight from the train to his office, too. But to a rather different reception.

Mr Hedgethorn's eyebrows rose into curves of grey amazement at the sight of him. 'My dear young man!' he said. 'What is the meaning of this outlandish attire?'

His disapproval was so marked that Charlie was reduced to stuttering. It brought him down to earth and made him realise that, despite the excitement of the last four days, his mission had actually been a failure. He did his best to explain and tried hard not to blush. Fortunately, after a few stumbling seconds, he was rescued by the arrival of Mr Crabbit, all cigar smoke, flapping raincoat and booming cheerfulness.

'Not to worry,' he said, when Charlie had apologised to them all for his travelling clothes and told them about the imposters, confessing his failure to find anyone else. 'Good work never gets done in a rush. We'll find 'em in the end. I've got a hunch about it. Now if I were you, young shaver, I'd cut off home and get changed. Back after lunch. That would suit, wouldn't it, Mr Hedgethorn?'

The young shaver cut off at once, but his sense of failure travelled home alongside him. He couldn't help feeling that he hadn't behaved at all well while he was in France. He had never checked back with the *maison de la presse* after putting in the advertisement, neither had he gone back to *Le Temps*. Mrs Everdale would be waiting to hear about his progress, and he couldn't tell her anything. I'll write to her anyway, he decided, as his tube train pulled out of Stockwell station. But it was Jeannie he really wanted to write to.

Oh Jeannie, Jeannie! he thought. I love you. I *know* I love you. How can I bear to be in England and not see you? And it seemed to him that everything around him was dull and grey and covered in dust; platform, escalator, pavements, plane trees, privet hedges, everything.

He was sighing as he slid his key into the lock at Abbeville Road. It was all too miserable for words.

Grandpa Jones was hobbling down the stairs, puffing and grunting, his body turned sideways to ease his descent. 'Oh, you've come 'ome 'ave yer,' he said. 'You won't like it back 'ere, I can tell you.' His eyes were smaller than Charlie remembered, narrowed into red-rimmed slits of rheumy bad temper, and his jowls bristled with at least three days' unshaven stubble; harsh, grey, dirty-looking stubble.

'Hello Grandpa,' Charlie said. 'See you're still the handsomest man in the street.'

'You don't wanna be so quick,' Grandpa scowled. 'It's all very well you standin' there grinning. You won't grin so much when I tell you what's been goin' on.'

Oh lord, Charlie thought. He's in a mood. Better let him get it off his chest. He'll only belly-ache about it otherwise. 'OK.' he said. 'What's been going on?'

'*She's* moved in. That's what. While you was away. Merry hell we've 'ad.'

'Who's moved in?'

'That Grace. Who d'yer think? There y'are. That's wiped the smile off a' yer face. Knew it would. Took over the front room she 'as, bloody woman.'

She can't have, Charlie thought. Dad wouldn't let her. 'Where's Mum?' he asked.

The old man had reached the bottom of the stairs. 'Out shopping,' he said. 'The pair of 'em. She'll get the pick 'a the meat come dinnertime, you bet yer life. I shan't get a look in, you mark my words, an' nor will you. I dunno what the world's coming to.'

Since there was evidence of Aunt Grace's occupation in every room in the house except the kitchen, it felt as though it had been stood on its head. Their nice tidy parlour was now an untidy bedsitter, crammed with her unfamiliar furniture and littered with her discarded clothes. The cupboard under the stairs was stuffed with travelling cases and cardboard boxes labelled Grace Allicott. Even the bathroom was affected. It now sported two new shelves on the wall, both crammed with her medicines; Carter's Little Liver Pills, Milk of Magnesia, syrup of figs, a bottle of Sanatogen, Vick's Vapour Rub, lozenges and embrocations and two blue eye baths.

Why two? Charlie shuddered, looking at them and imagining her with a bath to each eye like a pirate with two patches. Or was one for those awful false teeth of hers? Her towels were spread flamboyantly along the side of the bath and her scented soap had pride of place on the soap dish. He used it to wash his hands. Even a small revenge is sweet when your territory has been occupied by a foreign power.

But it was when he walked into his bedroom that he felt most upset. It was full of furniture from the front room that had obviously been thrown out to make way for hers. A heavy chest of drawers bulged in one corner, two chairs jostled edge to edge in another, and the chiffonnier was wedged beside his bed, still full of curios and old calendars and presents from Brighton and Margate and Weston super Mare.

How am I supposed to get into bed? he thought, assessing the crush. There isn't room to swing a cat. There was barely room to change his clothes, and it was impossible to hang his holiday jacket in the wardrobe because the door would only open about six inches before it was wedged against the side of the bed.

While he was still struggling to unpack, Mum and Aunt Grace came in through the front door.

'That you, Charlie?' Mum called up the stairs.

'No,' he called back crossly. 'It's a contortionist.'

'What?'

He walked to the turn of the stairs and looked down at his mother. 'What've you done to my bedroom?'

'Oh,' she said, looking sheepish. 'I was going to tell you. Sort of break it to you.'

Aunt Grace started to flirt with him. 'Oh, come on, sweetie,' she wheedled, 'you don't mind a few bits a' furniture, do yer, not fer yer old Aunty?'

'Yes,' he said, 'as it happens, I do.'

Aunt Grace wasn't in the least abashed. 'Naughty!' she said, and taking firm hold of Mum's elbow she skipped off into the kitchen.

Charlie returned to the Strand considerably earlier than he'd planned. Grandpa Jones was right. He didn't like it a bit back home.

That evening he took himself off to his room after supper, and sat on the edge of the bed to write a long impassioned love letter, in which he remembered the celebration in the square and the evenings in the café, recalled his feelings when he was waiting outside Monsieur Guerin's factory, and enthused about how marvellous their meal together had been.

'*I know I have no right to write to you like this,*' he confessed, '*but it is the truth and I have to say it. I love you. I loved you the first moment I set eyes on you and each time after that I loved you more and more. Being back in England hasn't made* me forget you. I just love you more than ever. I miss you every minute of the day. I can't bear to think of what the night will be like knowing I can't see you tomorrow. This evening has been absolutely lousy. It is absolutely lousy all the time without you. I don't want to be here. I want to be in France with you even if you walk away from me and refuse to speak. I shall come back to Amiens just as soon as I can save up the fare.

'Please write back and say I may write to you again unless there is someone else you love or you are engaged, or something like that. Then I shall understand and I won't write again, although I shall always love you.

Always,
Charlie Commoner.'

In his spartan bedsit in Merton, Ken Hopkirk was writing his last letter of the day, with only the wireless for company. The letter was as sober as he could make it because he was mindful of the fact that it would have to be read aloud to his darling and so someone else would hear it.

'My dear Emily,' he wrote, 'Calm crossing. Good weather. No problems. Factory in good order.

'I have sent out letters to all the local gas companies offering them the new meter I told you about. If all goes according to plan I could put them into production in approximately two months and be in full production before Christmas.

'I shall begin house-hunting as soon as I have amassed enough capital. I think a bungalow would be the best, all on one floor with no necessity for stairs. What do you think? I should value your opinion. It would have a garden, naturally, and a bird-table to encourage the songbirds. A hammock, too, but I might have to wait until the summer for that. Nevertheless, you will be pleased to know plans are all in hand. I am determined to succeed. The events of the last fortnight have made me determined.

'I would be grateful if you could write back fairly soon. I often think of Versailles and the way the fountains played and the frogs spewed water out of their mouths to make a bower for the goddess. If I were a frog I would make a bower for my goddess.

*'With very best wishes from your friend and admirer,*
*Kenneth Hopkirk.*
*P.S. I should perhaps mention that it is only fair to tell you that I am ugly enough to be a frog. K.P.H.'*

Please write soon, he urged his beloved as he sealed the envelope. Please write very, very soon.

He would have been surprised to know that, at that very moment, down in the hold of the cross-channel ferry among the freight and the bicycles and an awkwardness of mailbags, a postcard from Emily was already on its way to England.

On that awful Wednesday afternoon when she'd said goodbye to her dear Ken and he'd handed her gently back into Mauricette's care, his lips so soft kissing her goodbye, Emily had stood beside her friend in the noise and stench of the Gare du Nord and listened to the gathering speed of the train that was taking him away from her – and wept with loss.

'I miss him so much,' she cried, as Mauricette led her to the Métro. 'You can't imagine how much. Oh, Mauricette, perhaps I should never have met him. Do you think I should never have met him? We've had such a very short time together. Hardly any time at all. A few days. Not even a fortnight. So little. Perhaps Maman was right. She said . . .' But no, she thought, stopping herself just in time, that wasn't something she could tell Mauricette. Being unhappy was making her careless. 'Oh why does he have to be English?' she wailed, fingering her cross for comfort. 'If he was French he wouldn't be going away. We were so happy, Mauricette. And now he's gone. Shall I ever see him again?'

'Of course you will, *ma cherie,*' Mauricette comforted. 'He promised to write, *n'est-ce pas?* He promised to return. Very well then. He will write. He will return. You will see him again. Dry your eyes and hold on to my arm. We are going down the stairs.'

'If I knew where to address the letter I could write to him,' Emily wept. 'You'd write for me, wouldn't you, Mauricette?'

'Of course,' Mauricette said. 'You know I would. But let

me tell you it's better for a woman to wait for her lover to write to her first. I wrote to Gérard, right at the very beginning when we first met and between you and me I'm sure that's why he keeps me at arm's length now. You wait for your Englishman to write to you, Emilie, and then write back. That's much the best way. Here's our train.'

But Emily was in an unsettled mood that afternoon and her thoughts were never far away from the letter she wanted to write.

'Perhaps we could start on it,' she said to Mauricette. They'd spent most of the afternoon walking in the Tuileries Gardens and now they were outside a café, sitting at one of the pavement tables enjoying a *café filtre*. 'That wouldn't hurt, would it?'

Mauricette's patience was wearing thin. 'I'll tell you what,' she said. 'If you must write a letter, write it to somebody else.'

'There's nobody else I want to write to.'

'Oh, come on, there must be someone. Who do you write to when you're at home?'

'Nobody. Truly.'

'You write to me. You put messages at the bottom of Ginny's letters.'

That was true. 'But I don't write to anyone else.'

'Who does Ginny write to?'

'She sends postcards to Miss Babbacombe but apart from that . . .'

'*Voilà*!' Mauricette said, as though the problem had been solved. 'So you write a postcard to Miss Babbacombe, whoever she is. She's got a peculiar name.'

'She's English.'

'That explains it. There's a tobacconist just along the road. Stay there and I'll get you a card.'

So the little message was written, in French, of course, because Mauricette couldn't have managed English. Spelling out the English address to her was trouble enough. But the message was simple.

'Tell her I'm here in Paris with you,' Emily said. 'Say I'm

208

well and happy. Say I remember her and the house. Say I would love to visit England again.'

'I never knew you'd been to England,' Mauricette said. 'You're one surprise after another. Was that where you learned English?'

'Yes,' Emily said, remembering the warmth of the sun in the morning room at High Holborn, the settled smell of polish on old furniture, the sharp scent of cut flowers, the intricacies of the carvings along the edge of the mantelpiece. 'When I was little.'

Mauricette didn't notice the yearning in her friend's voice. '*Alors*,' she said briskly, 'what else shall I write? You've got room for another sentence.'

Emily thought about it. 'Tell her we live on the south bank of the river near the Sorbonne,' she said. 'She'll like that. She used to be a teacher.'

So the last words were written and Emily's hand guided so that she could sign her name and the card was posted.

'Time to go home,' Mauricette said.

'He will write, won't he?' Emily asked. 'You do think he'll write.'

'Hold on to my arm,' her friend said, suppressing a sigh. 'We're going to cross the road.'

The following afternoon Emily's first holiday away from home came to a tearful end.

'I shall remember it always,' she told Madame Lalange, as they kissed goodbye. 'I can't thank you enough. You've been so good to me. All of you.'

'You must come again,' Madame Lalange said. 'Now, be sure to sit by the window where Virginie can see you.' For the poor child was travelling back to Boves on her own and Ginny was to meet her at the station.

'I'll find someone to look after her in the carriage.' Mauricette promised. 'Don't you worry.'

The person she found was an elderly woman with a kind smile and a need for conversation, who told her unexpected travelling companion all about her husband and his bunions (how he suffers, poor man) and the foibles of her son and daughter (delicacy of the temperament, my dear, but how they suffer, too) and the name of every station they stopped at. Emily answered politely and was secretly very glad when Boves was announced.

'There's your sister!' the woman said. 'I can see the resemblance. It's quite remarkable. The door is open for you, my dear.'

It was such a relief to be folded in Ginny's arms and to hear her lovely warm voice. 'Em! My darling! Did you have a good time?' And then with a complete change of tone. 'What is it? What's the matter? Something's happened.'

'Oh Ginny!' Emily said. 'I think I've fallen in love.' And tears began to roll from the corners of her sightless eyes.

'What!' Ginny was completely taken aback. 'You can't have.'

'But I have. Truly.'

'How? Who is he? Oh Em!'

'I didn't mean to,' Emily said. 'It was the last thing . . . After what Maman said about the illness. Oh Ginny, what *am* I going to do?'

'First,' Ginny said, taking her case and her arm, 'we'll go for a nice long walk and you can tell me all about it.'

'But what about Maman? She'll be expecting us.'

'No, she won't. We'll tell her the train was late. Come on. I want to hear all about him.'

They walked into the cornfields where the wheat looked brown in the evening sunlight and rustled like starched cotton, and strolled until they were out of sight of the village and the station. Ginny found a comfortable spot for them to sit underneath an oak tree, and Emily told her everything she could remember.

'It's all happened so quickly,' she said. 'That's what amazes me. Just a few days. I still can't believe it. But I *do* love him, Ginny. I'm quite sure of that.'

'Yes,' Ginny said. 'I can see you do.' She watched the rapturous expression on her sister's face and remembered Mauricette saying, 'This is the year we shall all fall in love.' And now Em was in love with Ken and Mauricette was in love with Gérard, and she, Ginny, was the only one left out. It made her feel lonely and almost – well, unwanted. 'I'm quite jealous of you,' she said.

'Oh Ginny! You mustn't be jealous. It'll happen to you, too. Don't you remember what Madame Boulanger said?'

'Who?'

'Our landlady at Boulogne. Boulanger of Boulogne.'

'Oh yes. I remember.'

'She said we would fall in love when the tide came in. All we had to do was catch the tide.'

'Yes. That's right. So she did. Well you've caught the tide, haven't you, even if you didn't mean to. Oh Em, my dear lovely Em, I think it's wonderful.' And she threw her arms round her sister's neck and kissed her.

'Will it be all right?' Em said, kissing her back.

'Yes, of course. If you love one another.'

Emily hesitated and then brought up the subject that had been troubling her all the way home. 'But what about the illness? What if I catch the illness? You know what Maman said. She said it would come out if we fell in love.'

'Well, it won't,' Ginny said fiercely. 'That's all nonsense, so you mustn't even think it.'

'But she said it. If it's nonsense why did she say it?'

'Because she doesn't want us to get married. It was a sort of warning. She didn't mean it.'

Emily wasn't comforted. 'And that's another thing,' she worried. 'What shall I tell her?'

'Nothing,' Ginny said, with a determined expression. 'Not yet anyway. There's no need. It would only get her in a state. You know how she goes on.'

'But that's dishonest,' Emily worried. 'If I don't tell her it'll be a sin of omission.'

'No, it won't,' Ginny said. 'It'll be a kindness because you don't want to upset her. It's not as if you're engaged to be married or anything like that now, is it?'

The very idea of being engaged made Emily's face glow. But she tried to be sensible. 'Well, no,' she said. *Not yet*, she added silently.

211

'Well there you are then. You might be getting her upset for nothing. If you'll take my advice you'll wait till he's written.'

'Do you think he will?' Emily asked quietly.

Ginny thought of another hazard. 'What address did you give him?' she asked. If the letter was delivered to their house then Maman would certainly get to know about it.

Emily blushed at her own duplicity. 'Mauricette's,' she said, in a shamed voice.

'You see!' Ginny said in some triumph. 'You can't tell her. Not yet. You *do* have to wait. You know you do. You knew it then.'

'Yes,' Emily said, but her face was miserable. 'I wish I could though.'

'It's getting cold,' Ginny said. The setting sun cast long blue shadows across the fields and the cooling air was making them both shiver. 'We'd better go home. Old Joliot'll be back for supper. If we don't go now we shall keep them waiting and then there *will* be trouble.' As Emily still looked unhappy, she added, 'We'll find a moment to tell her sooner or later, you'll see. And then it'll be the right moment and we shan't hurt her.'

'I hope you're right,' Emily said, brushing down her skirt as she stood up.

'You'll see,' Ginny comforted. 'I wonder when your first letter will come. Just think of it, Em, a letter from England after all this time.'

But the first letter from England was addressed to '*Jeannie, care of Veronique Tilliette*'.

Ginny didn't know whether to be cross or flattered.

'The idiot!' she said to Veronique. 'It's a love letter.'

Veronique made a grimace. 'Told you so,' she said. 'Will you answer it?'

'No fear. If he wants to be stupid, let him.'

But the next day Ken's letter arrived, forwarded on by Mauricette, and when Ginny read it aloud to her sister she began to have second thoughts. For a love letter Ken's epistle wasn't a patch on the sort of things Charlie had written, foolish though he was. And while Emily was quietly thinking out her reply, she took her own love letter out of her handbag and read it through again.

'*It is the truth and I have to say it. I loved you the first moment I saw you . . . I shall always love you, Always, Charlie Commoner.*'

Even though Ginny felt nothing towards this ridiculous creature, or at any rate nothing very much, she was moved by an extraordinary feeling of warmth when she re-read his words.

For all that, she didn't answer them. There were too many other things to do. First there was a letter to be written at Emily's dictation, addressed to her 'Frog Prince', saying she was glad his business was doing so well and she thought a bungalow was a lovely idea. Then there was Mauricette's letter to reply to. She had written from Paris in great excitement to urge her friend to be sure to follow the news from Spain.

'*This is going to be a serious war,*' she'd declared, in her new political vocabulary, '*if we don't do something about it. The rebel armies mean business. General Franco is already at Cadiz. Did you know that? Now that the Spanish government has appealed for assistance we should see some action taken to support them. We cannot allow a fascist uprising to defeat a democratically elected government. There will be a demonstration here in Paris to show our solidarity. I will let you know the date. What terrible times we live in!*'

Terrible, indeed, Ginny thought, as she settled down to write her reply. Certainly not the right ones for embarking on a love affair, even if she wanted to. Falling in love was all very well for Emily and Mauricette. *She* had more important things to attend to.

# CHAPTER FIFTEEN

Agnes Everdale was concerned about the Spanish rebellion, too. And she'd had the gall to express her concerns to her husband while they were sitting at breakfast. He was so cross he could barely swallow his tea.

'It's no business of yours what I do,' he said, setting down his cup.

'I'm a director,' Agnes said, breathing deeply in a vain attempt to stay calm. 'I should have thought . . .'

'This is all the fault of that damn will, giving you ideas,' Claud said, his handsome face dark with anger. 'You're no good at business. You know that. Women never are. You take my advice and keep out of it.'

'It isn't business,' Agnes said stubbornly. The sneer in his voice made her feel insulted.

'Oh, for crying out loud!' Claud said. 'I'm going to Spain to sell guns. Guns and ammunition. If that's not business I'd like to know what is.'

'To both sides,' Agnes insisted. Her heart was beating painfully and she knew she was going to lose, but she had to make a stand. 'That's not moral.'

'It's profitable,' her husband said, delicately dabbing his lips with his table napkin, first at one corner of his mouth and then at the other. 'It makes money. That's what it's about. That's business. In case you didn't know.'

'But this is a rebellion,' Agnes protested. 'An armed rebellion. General Franco is a fascist. Don't you honestly think we should be supporting the government?'

'No, I don't,' her husband said. 'They're both as bad as one another. The government's red. Or don't you know that? Communists every man Jack of 'em.'

'Yes, I know that,' Agnes said, flushing. 'But they were

properly elected. You must allow that. Democratically elected.'

'Perhaps you'd like to go to Spain instead of me,' her husband said acidly. 'Perhaps you'd pull off a better deal, seeing you know all about it.'

'I never said I knew all about it,' Agnes said. 'I just don't think it's moral, that's all.'

'Morals for breakfast!' Claud Everdale mocked. 'That's all I need. While I'm away I suggest you turn your moral sense to the way this house is run. The eggs were stone cold again this morning.'

'Must you go today?' Agnes said, making a last attempt to persuade him to stay. 'It could wait twenty-four hours, surely. Then you could see the boys . . .'

'And that's what this is really about, isn't it?' Claud sneered. 'Your precious boys.'

'They're yours, too. After all this time, I should have thought you'd want to see them.'

'All this time!' he mocked. 'You'd think they'd been away for years. It's half-term for crying out loud. A few weeks.'

'It's the longest half term in the year,' Agnes said stubbornly. He'd wrong-footed her again, the way he always did. Made her look foolish. 'I'd have thought . . .'

'You think too much,' Claud said, folding his newspaper and setting it beside his plate. 'That's your trouble. You should try to check it. Time I was off. I've got a plane to catch.'

Agnes poured herself another cup of coffee and sipped it slowly as she set herself to enjoy the pleasure of her beautiful room; pink rosebuds in a green glass vase on the table, the lingering smell of toast, the well-ironed crispness of the tablecloth, the patterned china on the dresser, the ornate ceiling over her head. It was her customary way to calm down after a row and it worked, but gradually, of course. Claud put her into such a state it always took time to recover. The early morning sun beamed through the latticed windows and threw long pale stripes on to the panelled walls, edging her rosebuds with gold. It was going to be a beautiful summer day.

Ah well, she thought, setting down her empty cup in the saucer, if that's the way he's going to go on perhaps it's just as well he's off to Spain. Perhaps I ought to say good riddance to him. Anyway I've got my boys coming home tomorrow. Dear boys. And Babbers for tea on Friday. She'll be pleased to see them. That I *do* know.

Miss Babbacombe always arrived for Friday tea exactly on the stroke of four-fifteen, neither early nor late – no matter how tired or excited she might be – and she was very excited that afternoon. Emily's postcard had arrived. She'd been horribly frustrated when she'd first read it, seeing that sad little signature, 'Emilie' above a full page of words she couldn't understand. But now it was a joy to hand it over and to see the pleasure on Mrs Everdale's face.

'Good, eh?' she said.

'Marvellous!' Agnes said. 'Now we've heard from both of them. I always thought Emily would write in the end, dear little thing. If only they'd send an address we could have them home in no time at all. What does she say?'

Miss Babbacombe made a rueful face. 'I rather hoped you'd be able to tell me. French isn't my strong suit.'

'Nor mine,' Agnes confessed. 'I was never any good at it, I'm afraid. Not really. In fact, I was never any good at anything very much, if the truth be told. Johnny will know.'

'Are they home?' Miss Babbacombe asked. But of course they were, that would account for the pretty dress, the softness and contentment.

'Came on Wednesday,' Agnes said happily. 'They're on the tennis court at the moment but they'll be up presently wanting lemonade.'

The two friends were taking their tea on the terrace and Miss Babbacombe had heard the ping of tennis balls but paid no attention to it. Now she looked up to see the two boys walking across the lawn towards them.

'Ah, there you are, my darlings,' Agnes said leaning back in her wicker chair to admire her offspring. 'Was it a good game?'

'Putrid,' George said cheerfully, throwing himself down on the grass. He was a big lad for fourteen-and-a-half and seemed even bigger in his tennis whites, his eyes very blue in a tanned face. 'He can't serve for toffee nuts. Hello, Babbers.'

'How's school?' Miss Babbacombe asked.

Agnes poured more tea and smiled. Miss Babbacombe always had exactly the right approach to returned schoolboys.

'Pretty putrid,' George said. 'I've joined the flying corps, actually.'

'Good for you,' Miss Babbacombe said, responding to the pride in his voice. 'Have you been up yet?'

'Next term,' George said, taking a glass of lemonade from his mother. 'Thanks Mater.'

'What in?'

'A Tiger Moth. It's a bit of a crate, but it'll do for starters.'

'Stout lad,' Miss Babbacombe approved. 'You mark my words, Mrs Everdale, we shall see him a pilot one of these days.'

George grinned at her. 'Damn right, Babbers,' he said. 'If there's going to be another war I'm going to fly in it.'

'There isn't going to be another war,' Agnes said, quite crossly. 'We couldn't be so silly so don't let's think about it. We've got something for you to translate. Something in French.'

'Little brother can do it,' George said. 'He's the brains of the family.'

'Give it here, then,' Johnny said brusquely. His impoliteness wasn't intentional, even though George had been putting him down. Now that his thirteenth birthday was approaching he was in the gawky stage of adolescence with a pimply face, lank brown hair and limbs that had suddenly grown too big for him and were usually out of control. His voice was hard to control too, and he blushed as he took the postcard.

But he understood the French. 'She's staying with a very good friend,' he translated. 'She is well. She is happy. She doesn't forget you nor the house. Which house?'

217

'This one, you clot,' his brother said. 'They used to live here, didn't they, Babbers?'

'Anything else?' Miss Babbacombe said, hoping for a clue.

'Something about the Sorbonne,' Johnny said after re-reading the card, squinting with effort.

'What's that?' Agnes wanted to know.

'University of Paris,' her son said nonchalantly. 'Tell you what Babbers, I reckon she's a student.'

'She could well be,' Agnes said. 'She's the right age for it.'

'Twenty,' Miss Babbacombe agreed, nibbling at a bourbon biscuit. 'Always thought they'd be bright. Didn't I tell you? Now this *is* something to tell your Mr Crabbit.'

Which was how Charlie found himself summoned to 'the presence' again.

'How d'you fancy another trip to France?' Mr Crabbit said, trimming his cigar.

Charlie endeavoured to be polite and sensible, but his heart was racing. 'Very much, sir. When?' Next week? The week after? Ever since his return he'd been racking his brains to find a way to get across the Channel and see Jeannie again. Another commission from the Holborns had seemed the only solution. Now here it was.

The answer was a disappointment. 'Middle of October. Apparently they've had a card from the other twin. Emily. Mrs Everdale thinks she's studying at the Sorbonne. Wants us to make enquiries. We could write, of course, but it'll be probably be quicker to send you courier.'

Charlie swallowed his impatience and looked obedient. 'Yes, sir.' But he was thinking, October's eight weeks away. How can I wait that long? I'll write her another letter and tell her I'm coming back. She might answer *that*. And, if she doesn't, I'll write another one. And another one after that, if I have to. Faint heart never won fair lady.

He was busy composing the letter in his head when he got back to Abbeville Road that evening.

Grandpa Jones had been reading a copy of a magazine with pictures of the Spanish revolt on the centre pages, and sat in Dad's chair in the chimney corner, holding forth about the Republicans and the Civil Guard.

'Look a' this Charlie,' he said. 'Says 'ere they're ferrying troops over from Morocco. The army of Africa in Spanish Morocco. See? Hitler's been sending 'em planes. Planes from Germany and Italy. See.'

'You don't wanna hear a load of ol' rubbish about some stupid ol' war, do yer darling?' Aunt Grace said from her opposing chair.

'No,' Charlie said. 'Not much. I'd rather clear the table for supper.'

'I think it's awful,' Mum said from the scullery. 'All those poor people getting killed. I though we 'ad enough a' that the last time. 'Lo Charlie. Have a good day?'

'What's for supper?' Charlie said, sniffing his way into the scullery. Fried onions! Smashing!

'Liver an' bacon.'

'Lovely grub!' Dad's voice called from the hall. 'Smells a treat. You taken out a lease on that chair, Grandpa?'

'Keeping it warm for yer,' Grandpa said unabashed. But he removed himself from the chair and Dad sat in it and eased off his boots.

'Got a bit a' news for you lot,' he said.

'What's that?' Mum called above the hiss of frying.

'How d'yer like a seaside holiday?'

'Be lovely,' Mum said. 'When?'

'Week after next. Job's due to finish Friday. Me an' the boys got to talking. Might be an idea to hire a charabanc and all cut off to Margate for a few days. We could take bed an' breakfast somewhere. What d'yer think? He'd let you off, wouldn't he, ol' Mr Thing-a-me?'

' 'Spect so,' Mum said. 'Wouldn't half be nice.'

But Grace was scowling. 'Oh, not bed an' breakfast, Stan,' she protested. 'I couldn't be doing with that.'

'Stay here then,' Stan said, putting on his slippers. 'You don't 'ave to come with us.'

219

'I can't do that,' Grace wailed. 'Who'd cook me meals?'

'Do it yourself,' Stan said, grinning at her. 'Make a nice change. Change is as good as a rest.'

'You're the most selfish man I ever come across,' Grace complained. 'Don'tcher never think a' no one but yerself? How am I supposed to cook meals? I shall go an' stay with our Maud. She'll 'ave me. I can't be doing with bed an' breakfast.'

Stan ignored her. 'Whatcher think Rube?' he asked.

'It'd be lovely,' Ruby said. 'Yes, please. Set the table for me, Charlie, there's a dear. I shall be dishing up directly.'

'Grandpa?'

'Count me in,' the old man said, flushing with pleasure. 'Yes. Be lovely. I'll pay me way a' course.'

'Four of us, then,' Stan said. 'You an' me an' Rube an' Charlie.'

'No,' Charlie said, making his mind up as he spoke. 'Not me. I couldn't get time off. Not with this war in Spain. One of our best clients is out there selling arms. And, in any case, I've got to go to France again. If you don't mind I'd rather save up for that.'

Well, well, Stan thought, so we're there are we? Well it's only natural, when all's said an' done. Off on your own, trying your wings. You'll be leaving the nest before we know it. He wondered how Ruby would take *that*. But he had too much natural tact to comment or argue. 'Three then,' he said amiably.

'You don't wanna go to France,' Grace protested. 'It's all Froggies in France. Dirty mucky lot, the Froggies. They don't have lavvies, you know. You'll wanna go to the seaside with yer mum an' dad. Breath a' fresh air. Plate a' whelks.' And she sang in her awful cracked voice, '*Oh, I do like ter stroll along the prom, prom, prom, while the brass bands play tiddley om pom pom*.'

'Leave the boy be,' Stan said. 'He knows what he wants. Don't yer son?' And he gave Charlie a wink with the eye that Grace couldn't see.

It's true, Charlie thought, as he cut into his first slice of liver. I know exactly what I want. It's whether I shall get it that's open to doubt.

That night he wrote a cheerful letter to Jeannie explaining about his commission and asking whether she would allow him to come to Amiens and take her out to dinner. '*Or to the pictures or anywhere else you might fancy. Just say the word.*'

But no word was forthcoming. So he wrote again. '*I shan't give up unless you write back to me to tell me you're engaged to someone else. If I don't hear from you I shall write again in three days' time.*'

Which he did.

'What am I going to do about him?' Ginny said to her sister, half flattered and half exasperated.

Emily could hear the confusion in her voice. 'What do you want to do?' she asked.

'I don't know.'

Emily could see the choices quite clearly. 'Would you like to see him again? Or do you wish he'd stop writing and leave you alone?'

Ginny thought about it. She was growing accustomed to receiving letters from him now and she had to admit she enjoyed them. 'Of the two,' she admitted, 'I think I'd probably rather see him.'

'Then write and say so.'

It was a difficult letter to write because she didn't want to hurt his feelings but on the other hand she didn't want to encourage him too much.

'*If you come to Paris in October,*' she wrote, '*and you have a reason to visit Amiens which will not take you out of your way, I should be happy to have a meal with you,*

*Mes amities,*

*Jeannie Lisieux.*'

'I've kept it short,' she said to Emily, 'and I've written it under Veronique's address because of Maman, and I haven't signed my real name either because there's no need for him to know that.'

'So now we'll see,' Emily said, grinning impishly. 'Can

we answer Ken's letter now? I want to tell him what sort of bird-table to build.'

How unromantic, Ginny thought, as she took up her pen again. It's all furnishings and factories with these two.

And they still hadn't said a word to Maman.

# CHAPTER SIXTEEN

It is remarkable how a change of mood can alter the appearance of a place. Paris in October was very different from the summertime city that had daunted Charlie Commoner. Now, with Jeannie's letter in his pocket, the place looked richly coloured and welcoming. Along the boulevards the chestnut trees were in their autumn glory, their amber leaves edged with wine red, and the buildings were a warmer colour, too, under a sky smudged by the smoke spiralling up from every chimney.

It wasn't just the buildings, either. People looked different as well, from the businessmen striding purposefully across the roads in their stylish suits to the poor kids in shapeless coats and grubby anklesocks quarrelling like sparrows on their way to school. He looked at them with affection, voluble newspaper vendors in their kiosks, workmen in their inevitable blue, sharp-eyed and unshaven, with cigarettes stuck to their lower lips, plump, black-clad women carrying home bundles of long loaves. There were even a couple of fashionable ladies strolling down the boulevard in that film-star way of theirs, furs slung elegantly across their suited shoulders, smart hats worn at an angle, high-heeled shoes clicking on the pavements. As he ran down the steps into the mustiness of the Métro he felt as if he'd come home.

Work first, he told himself, and then Amiens in the evening. He had two full days in which to find his heiresses. Or his heiress. Because there might only be one at the university. He'd written to all the colleges to advise them of his visit so it shouldn't take too long. Now that he knew the place he felt he could cope with anything.

There was plenty to cope with, even for a young man

who'd spent the last four years in a solicitor's office and knew from experience that bureaucracy thrives on delay.

For a start, there were more colleges than he'd been given on his original list and each one had its own registration system. To make matters worse, even though he'd arrived fully prepared with all the necessary credentials and copies of the correspondence, it was almost impossible to get hold of anybody in charge of the records.

All through that Thursday he was passed from office to office, kept hanging about in draughty corridors and on one occasion forgotten about altogether. By the end of the afternoon he'd only got a clear answer from the Sorbonne itself and it wasn't the answer he wanted. There was no student on the records called Holborn, neither for this academic year nor for the three preceding years. Plainly this search was going to take a lot of effort.

But for the moment he didn't have to think about it. He'd done what he could for one day. Now he had a date in Amiens with Jeannie. He went galloping down the steps of the nearest Métro, too eager and excited to walk.

In their last exchange of letters Charlie and Ginny had arranged to meet on the cathedral steps at eight o'clock but, propelled by excitement, he caught an earlier train and arrived with more than half an hour to spare. Never a young man to wait with patience, he prowled and fidgeted, round and round the square, up and down the steps, smoking one cigarette after another and so tense that his neck and shoulders were aching. Oh come on! he urged. Come on! Where are you?

Ginny *was* on her way to their tryst, but unlike Charlie she was walking slowly, held back by uncertainty and a guilty conscience. Even now, after thinking about it for weeks, she wasn't at all sure she was doing the right thing. It was a temptation to be spending an evening with a young man who'd declared his love for her so passionately and openly, and besieged her with such wonderful letters, but she wasn't sure it was wise, given all this business about the illness. Worse, it was certainly deceitful. She hadn't said anything to

Maman and she ought to have done. It was a sin not to. Which was why she was feeling guilty. She'd discussed it with Emily over and over again but failed to come to any conclusion. Wouldn't she have been more sensible to refuse him? Wasn't hiding it from Maman a sure sign that things weren't as they should be? On top of all that there was still the illness to be considered –and what Maman would say when she finally had to be told. *If* she finally had to be told. It was all very troubling.

But when she turned into the square and saw him standing on the cathedral steps, so tall and blond and English, she realised how much she'd wanted to see him again. He's very handsome, she thought. Vron's right about that. And she suddenly remembered how tender his eyes were, lovely grey-brown eyes with long straight eyelashes.

Before she had time to think of anything else, he looked up and saw her and ran down the steps to greet her. He caught her by both hands almost as if he was going to kiss her, making her heart give a sudden leap. His face was shining with pleasure at the sight of her and his eyes were as tender as she remembered them, and as full of love.

'It *is* good to see you again,' he said. 'How are you?'

'Cold,' she said, answering him in English. A mist was rising from the river and the air in the cathedral square was dank.

'We'll get inside in the warm,' he said at once. 'Where would you like to go?'

'For dinner?'

'Yes, of course. That's what we said.'

It was a great treat to dine out. She was used to eating sandwiches and coffee in her lunch break in the café round the corner, but a three-course meal in the evening was quite another thing. And an expensive one. Mindful of his pocket, and not wanting to be seen, she chose one of the cheaper restaurants in the old quarter.

It was a bad choice. The room was dark and greasy, the food poorly cooked and there were only three other customers, so even though they talked to one another in English their conversation was self-conscious and stilted.

225

They talked about 'safe' things, like his journey to France and what they'd been doing at work since they last saw one another.

'What job are you doing now?' she asked.

'Here in France do you mean?'

'Yes.'

'Oh, still the heiresses. They're at the Sorbonne. Or at least one of them is. Or might be. I've got to find out.'

'You've been looking for them for ages,' she said. 'Don't you get bored with it?'

'No. I've made up my mind to find them, you see.'

'I'd have given up long ago.'

'Patience is a virtue.'

She dimly remembered Miss Babbacombe saying something like that and the memory made her smile. 'Are you patient?' she asked.

'No,' he said honestly. 'Not really. I am when I'm at work, but waiting to see you again was hideous. I don't know how I managed it.'

The tone of their conversation was getting too intimate for comfort. Glancing behind her at the other diners, Ginny shifted in her seat and bit her underlip.

'You'll have to translate this menu for me,' Charlie said, deftly rescuing her.

They chose steak *au poivre*. But that wasn't a wise choice either, as Ginny discovered after the first leathery mouthful.

Charlie struggled with his meat until he'd eaten half of it, but even he was defeated.

'It's like an old saddle,' he confided. 'What have they done to it?'

She was embarrassed to have chosen so badly. 'I've never been here before,' she said apologetically. 'I *am* sorry.'

'It's not your fault,' he said cheerfully. 'Never mind. We'll find somewhere else tomorrow.'

'Tomorrow,' she said, and the thought of seeing him two evenings in a row made her panic. She would never be able to explain two evenings to Maman. 'No, no. I'm sorry. I can't see you tomorrow.'

226

He swallowed his disappointment with the last mouthful of half-chewed steak. 'Saturday then?'

'Here? In Amiens?'

'Unless you could get to Paris? Could you? We could go to the pictures or the theatre or something.'

Paris was possible, and a lot more sensible than meeting here, where they could be seen. 'Yes,' she said. 'I have to work in the morning but I could go there afterwards.'

'I'll get all my work finished tomorrow,' he promised, 'or first thing Saturday morning at the latest and then we can have the rest of the weekend to enjoy ourselves.' And he was thinking, it'll be better in Paris. It's more lively there.

It was late by the time they finished their meal, but she wouldn't let him see her home.

'I'll catch a train,' she said.

'Do you live so far away?' he said, hoping she would tell him where.

'No, no. It isn't far. I shall soon be there.'

'Then I'll walk with you to the station.' If he could see what train she got on he'd know which direction she was going in.

But she said goodbye to him in the station entrance. Much too formally. 'Thank you for the dinner.'

'Such as it was,' he said. 'I'll do better next time. See you on Saturday then. What train will you catch? If you can tell me what time you'll get in, I'll meet you at the Gare du Nord.'

She told him and was gone, leaving him to his disappointment and carrying her own back to Boves, chilled in a very chill night. It hadn't been the sort of evening either of them had hoped for.

But the weekend will be different, Charlie vowed, his optimism returning as he boarded the train back to Paris. We were bound to be a bit awkward with one another after all this time. Now we've broken the ice it'll be quite different on Saturday.

First it was necessary to get through Friday, and Friday brought more difficulties. There was no record of anyone called Emily Holborn at any of the remaining colleges he visited, and the records at the college of medicine weren't available until Saturday morning.

'That is a problem,' he said to the registrar in his careful French.

'*Alors!*' the registrar shrugged. 'If Monsieur wishes, another appointment can be made. Tuesday morning perhaps.'

'Monday I return to London,' Charlie struggled.

Again the shrug. '*Alors!*'

There was nothing for it. He had to agree to the Saturday morning appointment.

I hope they're punctual, he worried, as he walked away from the college. I don't want to be hanging about in there just when Ginny's coming.

Twenty minutes before Ginny's train was due at the Gare du Nord, he was still fidgeting in the foyer of the college. At that point impatience got the better of politeness.

'*Regardez,*' he said to the hall porter, showing his letter from the registrar. 'An appointment with Monsieur the Registrar. This morning. He is late.'

'Always,' the hall porter agreed laconically. 'Always he is late, that one.'

'I have another appointment,' Charlie said. '*Comprenez-vous?* Another appointment. I shall return in an hour and a half. Inform him, if you please.' And as the porter seemed to have understood, he made a dash for the exit, yelling for a taxi as he emerged. It would take far too long to use the Métro and he was on tenterhooks in case he missed her arrival.

It took an agonisingly long time to get to the station. Even biting his thumbnail to the quick didn't speed the journey up by a minute. When he galloped into the station concourse, hat in hand and eyes bolting, she was already there, sitting on her case with her blue coat huddled around her shoulders and a woolly hat pulled down over her ears.

'I thought you weren't coming,' she said, and she sounded cross.

Her tone alarmed him, although, had he known it, she was actually cross with herself. All through the journey she'd been plagued by disquieting thoughts, reliving their disastrous evening together, wondering whether Maman was right to issue warnings, fearing that she might be making herself look cheap coming to him instead of making him come to her, feeling less and less sure about what she was doing.

'I'm so sorry,' he apologised standing awkwardly before her. 'It's the heiresses, I was held up – um – I was waiting for someone to tell me . . .'

His awkwardness irritated her.

'Well,' she said, standing up and rearranging her coat. 'I'm here now. So where are we going?'

'Would you like a cup of coffee?'

They went to Mauricette's café on the *Boule' Miche*. But she was distant with him. She drank her coffee slowly, cradling the cup in both hands to show how cold she was. He tried to ease the atmosphere by asking where she would like to go, offering 'anywhere within reason'.

'To the *Comedie Français*,' she decided. 'I've always wanted to go there.'

'I'll get the tickets on my way back.'

Her eyebrows shot up. 'Way back from where? Aren't we going straightaway?'

Her obvious annoyance made him nervous. 'Well no,' he said. 'The thing is . . . I mean, I've got to go to the college of medicine. They're waiting for me. It's only for a little while, to look through the registers. I'll be right back.' He knew it was an awful thing to leave her the minute she arrived, but what else could he do?

Now she really was cross with him, and showed it. 'You're not still working,' she said. 'You said everything was – would be finished by Saturday afternoon.'

Her rebuke released him from guilt into annoyance.

'Yes, I'm working,' he said stiffly. 'I have to work. You know that. I told you. It's what I'm paid for.' Surely she could understand *that*.

229

She looked at him angrily, a scowl etching two lines between her eyes, her long nose pulled sharp, her lips narrowed. 'If you had work to do you shouldn't . . .' Oh how could she express herself properly in her rusty English? 'You should not tell me to come here.'

The truth of that stung him sharply. 'There're more colleges than I thought there were,' he said. 'More people to see. It took longer. Look, I'm sorry but I've got to attend to it.'

'Can't you see them on Monday?' she said. 'They would wait for you, wouldn't they?'

'No. They won't,' he said, struggling to be reasonable. 'They're doing me a favour by seeing me at all. It's no good talking about it. I gave them my word. I've got to go . . .'

She was so cross she couldn't cope with English any longer. '*Je m'en fou!*' she said, turning her face away from him and erupting into rapid, angry French. 'I'm sick of all this. I come all this way to see you and what do you do? You go rushing off the minute I get here and leave me on my own. I've been a fool. An incredible fool. I shouldn't have come. I knew that on the train. I was thinking about it all the way here, knowing it was a mistake. I've made myself cheap. And after all the things you said to me, all the things you wrote. You didn't mean a single word of any of them. You don't love me.'

Most of what she'd said was beyond him but he understood the last sentence. 'I do,' he said, answering her in English. 'You know I do.' But he, too, was speaking angrily and there was no tenderness in his face at all. Even his eyes looked hard.

'No, you don't,' she said, still speaking French.

'I do.'

The argument continued, each of them using the language that was most natural to them. And the more passionately French she became, the more he retreated into English correctness.

'It's *les héritières*,' she said, 'those stupid heiresses of yours. That's what it is. Those silly rich kids with all their money. They mean more to you than I do.'

230

'That isn't true.'

'It is true. It is true. You think I don't understand but I see precisely how it is. I understand completely. You wouldn't go rushing about looking for me if I got lost.' And to make sure he understood her she translated into English. 'You wouldn't look for me like this.'

'Well, of course I would.'

'*Non, non, non.* You wouldn't. And I will tell you why you wouldn't. I'm not rich. If I got lost nobody would lift a finger to find me.'

Why are we quarrelling about the Holborns? Charlie thought, confused and irritated by the speed with which their argument had slithered into an irrelevant direction. 'That has nothing to do with it,' he said, stiffly.

She blazed at him. 'It's got everything to do with it. Everything.'

It was getting later and later and they were pulling further and further apart the longer they argued. There's no point going on with this, Charlie thought. We're just making things worse.

'I'm going,' he said, pulling on his hat, his face set.

'Go then,' she said, tossing her head at him. 'I don't care. I shall wait ten minutes, that's all and then I'm off.'

And on that dramatic and ridiculous note they parted, she to brood about the man she'd already fallen in love with, he to look for the heiress he'd already found.

And after all that, it only took him a quarter of an hour to discover that there were no students called Holborn at the school of medicine. The news should have disappointed him because it meant that he would have to report yet another failure to Mr Crabbit, but he took it as a release. Charged with happy energy and determined to make amends for their stupid quarrel, he went hurtling back to the café.

Their table had been cleared and now stood empty of everything except an ashtray. Jeannie was gone. For a few seconds he was too cross and too disappointed to take it in.

Then he saw that a waiter was dodging between the tables with a paper in his hand.

'Monsieur Commonay?'

It's the bill, Charlie thought, and he held out his hand to receive it. '*Oui.*'

But it wasn't the bill. It was a letter from Jeannie.

'I have gone to stay with my friend,' it said. 'I realise now that I should not have come. Perhaps it is a mistake for us to see one another. Your work is more important to you than I am. I have paid for the coffee. I am sorry I annoyed you. Jeannie.'

His first reaction was fury. She didn't have to go rushing off like that nor to say such hateful things. She could have waited a *little* bit longer, for Heaven's sake. And there wasn't any need for her to go paying the bill, either. That was humiliating. His second reaction was a momentary panic as he realised that he had no idea where she lived and that, if she wanted to walk out of his life and was determined to stay hidden, he wouldn't be able to find her. His third, and most useful reaction, was to remember his training and start to think logically.

If she was going to stay with a friend it might be that girl Veronique. If it *was* Veronique he knew where she lived. If it wasn't she might give him another address he could try. Either way Veronique was the one to contact. He consulted his railway timetable and worked out that if he hurried he could catch the next train to Amiens. It wasn't quite the way he'd imagined spending this particular Saturday afternoon, but he certainly wasn't going to let this crazy girl run out on him like that. Not without argument anyway.

Fortunately, one of the good things about a train journey is that it provides an uninterrupted stretch of time in which anger can cool. By the time he emerged from Amiens station into the clanging bustle of the Place Alphonse Fiquet, Charlie Commoner was almost himself again. Now that he was energetically trying to correct his mistake, he could admit that Jeannie had a right to be annoyed at being left alone in a great city like Paris. He shouldn't have done it, job or no job. He should have looked after her, not left her in the lurch. Now he would have to make amends.

232

It took him four minutes to find the right tram and six to travel to Veronique Tilliette's home, which turned out to be a three-storeyed brick-built tenement on the outskirts of the town. It was just sufficient time to think out what he was going to say, whoever might open the door.

It was Veronique herself. And she looked very surprised to see him.

He was prepared and word perfect. '*Bonjour Mademoiselle*,' he said. 'I am here to visit Jeannie Lisieux. Is she with you, *s'il vous plait*?'

Veronique put her hands over her lips, beamed at him and then began to laugh. Then she spoke to him in a tangle of incomprehensible French. And then, seeing he didn't understand a word she was saying, she spoke again, very, very slowly. 'She is not here. She is in Paris.'

'Where?' he asked. 'You have an address?'

'*Entrez*,' she said, allowing him into the hall. Then she trotted off through the door behind her to return a few minutes later with an address written in her curly handwriting on a sheet of pink notepaper.

He thanked her, gave her a little bow and was out of the door in a bound. Back to the tram stop, back to the station, an irritating wait for the *rapide*, back to Paris, which was already lit up for the evening, down to the Métro, feeling hungry and aware that he hadn't eaten since breakfast, standing in the slowest of all slow trains, listening to the clanking and shuffling, out into the smoky air of the Latin Quarter, still hungry but too hot on the quest to stop for food, running along the cobbles, peering at house numbers, into a dark courtyard, crashing up the stairs, knocking before he'd stopped running, thump thump thump, and then the last breathless wait, feeling ashamed to be making such a clamour, aware that his heart was racing. And the door opening.

A plump woman stood before him with a question on her face.

He plunged into his prepared speech. '*Bonjour Madame*. I am looking for Jeannie Lisieux. Is she here with you, *s'il vous plait*?'

233

The woman turned her head and called to someone over her shoulder, singing through her nose as though she were chanting the words of a song, '*Virginie! Viens ici!*'

And Jeannie appeared in the hall behind her. She looked ghost pale in the darkness but it was Jeannie, his own darling Jeannie. He hadn't lost her. The impulse to leap into the hall and lift her off her feet and kiss her was so strong it was all he could do to control it.

For a few seconds none of them moved or spoke, Madame Lalange because she knew when to keep quiet, Charlie because he didn't know what to do or say, Ginny because she was in thrall to the most exquisite surprise.

Less than an hour ago she'd been sitting in the bedroom with Mauricette and her sisters, telling them her story and weeping because her first love affair was over before it had begun. And now here he was, standing in the doorway, looking at her in the most loving way, as if nothing had happened.

'How did you know I was here?' she said, wide-eyed with amazement. '*C'est Charlie, Madame.*'

Madame Lalange welcomed him into the apartment at once. 'Come in. Come in.'

He explained. Ginny translated. The Lalange family gathered around him and were introduced.

'We were just on the point of going out,' Mauricette said to him in French. 'Two more minutes and you would have missed us.'

'Where are you going?' he asked Jeannie in English.

Ginny began to laugh. 'To the café.'

'The same café?'

'Yes.'

The humour of it struck him, too, and soon they were all laughing. 'I could have sat there and waited for you,' he said, 'instead of charging about all over the country.'

'Would you like to come with us?' Ginny asked.

'No,' he said, emboldened by his welcome. 'I'd rather go somewhere with you. On our own. To have dinner.'

And so at last they were on their own together, away from

her friends, away from the curious eyes of Amiens, in a restaurant where the other diners didn't pay the slightest attention to them, eating a good French meal with a carafe of *vin rouge* because Charlie said they were celebrating, and talking in the privacy of their nice quiet English. There were so many necessary reassuring things to be said, apologies to be made and accepted, explanations to be given, the story of his search to be told and appreciated. And it *was* appreciated.

'All the way to Amiens just to find me,' Ginny said.

'I love you.'

'Yes,' she said. 'You must do.' Wasn't this proof? It made her feel loved and warm simply to think about it.

'I'll never leave you on your own like that ever again,' he promised. 'I shouldn't have done it.'

She was generous with good food and the warmth of being loved. 'You're forgiven,' she said. And meant it.

'I'll never do it again,' he promised. 'Ever.'

'No,' she teased, 'or I shall run right away and you'll *never* find me.'

'Oh, Jeannie!' he said. 'You don't know how marvellous it is to be with you. I shall love you for ever.' And for a wild second he wondered whether French people kissed one another in restaurants.

They talked and talked and talked. She told him about the Popular Front and all the glorious things they were going to do now they'd won the election and he admired her enthusiasm and thought how beautiful she looked in the candlelight. He told her about the peculiar cases they had to deal with at Hedgethorn and Crabbit, although he took care not to give names or family details, particularly about the heiresses, because that would have been unprofessional.

'You speak marvellous English,' he said. 'Did you learn it at school?'

'When I was very young,' she said. Then, deliberately parrying question with question, she asked, 'Where did you learn French?'

'At school. We never spoke it much, though. It was all

writing exercises, filling in plurals and learning tenses and vocab and things. I've got an awful accent, haven't I?'

'*Pas mal*,' she said, diplomatically.

He grinned at that. 'Not good either.'

'No. But it doesn't matter. We understand one another.'

'Yes,' he said earnestly. 'We do now, don't we?'

Yes, she thought, we do now. I know how very much he loves me now.

'We've had our first row,' he said, cheerfully. 'Do you realise that? Our very first row. And we've survived it.'

'Yes,' she said, holding her wine glass to her lips and smiling at him across the rim. In the street outside the café someone was playing an accordion. 'I suppose we have.' Was it a lover's quarrel? And was that why they were so happy now they'd made up? And did that mean she was falling in love with him? It was easy to accept such an idea, here in this warm café with good food in her belly, the gaslights turned down low, and Charlie looking at her so lovingly. He seemed to have grown taller since the afternoon, taller and more handsome. Am I falling in love? she wondered. And the thought spun her into an exquisite state of hope and apprehension and excitement.

'You'll give me your address now,' he said. 'Won't you?'

She agreed to that, too, although diffidently. 'Yes, if you promise not to write to me there.'

'I won't, if you don't want me to.'

She felt she had to explain. 'It's Maman,' she said. 'She doesn't know about you. She's . . . she's *severe*, you see. She thinks I shouldn't . . .'

'Have a boyfriend,' he finished for her. 'But you have now, haven't you?' It was an appeal more than a question.

'Yes,' she told him. 'I have.' And was rewarded with a smile so loving it could have been a kiss.

'Don't worry,' he said. 'I won't write to you there. Not till you tell me I can. I won't ever do anything to upset you ever again. You know that, don't you?'

So she wrote her address in his diary. '*Jeannie Lisieux*', because it made her feel special to be 'Jeannie' to this young man, and because this wasn't the time to tell him he'd made a mistake over her name. '*26, Rue Jeanne D'Arc, Boves.*' And he put it away in his pocket like the treasure it was.

'Let's go,' he said. Their meal was over, the coffee drunk to the dregs. 'We could take a stroll down by the river. We've got time, haven't we? I mean, if you'd like to.'

She was suddenly and unaccountably shy, ducking her head to avoid his eyes. A walk by the river would be . . . Would mean . . . Oh it was too soon. She wasn't sure. Even now, she wasn't sure.

'No,' she said, in something of a panic. 'I must go back. They'll be expecting me.'

'Anything you say,' he reassured her. And escorted her back to the apartment like a gentleman.

'We'll meet again tomorrow?' he said, as they waited for Madame Lalange to open the door.

She was touched by his eagerness, by those dark eyes and that tender mouth and that awkward, vulnerable air. 'Yes,' she said.

'When shall I call for you?'

'When would you like to call for me?'

'As soon as I wake up in the morning.'

They compromised on ten o'clock and he was there as the hour began to strike.

Afterwards, when they were apart and wakeful and re-living their eventful weekend, neither of them could remember what they'd talked about all through that special Sunday. Naturally enough, because it was more than mere conversation. They were taking the taste of each other, sip by delicious sip, learning each other by heart.

They walked in the Bois du Boulogne and it was as if they were entirely on their own; they went to the cinema and paid no attention to the film; they dined in the same restaurant on exactly the same food; and finally, with a great sense of daring, they took their walk beside the Seine, among all the other murmuring lovers.

It was magical down there on the quayside and so quiet they could hear the rush of the river. Above their heads, the moon was full and perfect, a great patterned circle among the tiny glitter of all those distant stars.

'It looks so close,' Ginny said, gazing up at it. 'I've never seen it look as close as that.'

They were close, too, Charlie thought. Very very close, strolling side by side. If he put his arm round her would she tell him off? Greatly daring, he tried it. And was allowed.

'I can see the face,' he said. 'It's really rather beautiful, don't you think so?' But not as beautiful as you are, with your eyes as dark as water and shining so much it makes me ache to see them.

'It's so peaceful,' she said. 'I wish . . .' But then she hesitated.

'What do you wish?' he said, cuddling her closer.

She put her head on his shoulder. This was too rich a moment to waste with dishonesty. 'I wish we could stay here for ever and ever.'

'So do I,' he said, breathless with pleasure. 'I don't ever want to leave you. You know that, don't you?'

She *did* know it, and far from alarming her it seemed perfectly natural, there by the quiet Seine with the warmth of his arm round her waist. 'I suppose I'd better be getting back for my luggage,' she said. But she didn't move away from him.

'We both had,' he said. But he didn't move either. It was so quiet he could hear the water flowing. 'Oh Jeannie!' he said. 'I do love you.'

And she turned and was in his arms at last, really in his arms. As he bent his head towards her, her mouth was so close to his that he could taste her breath, and he thought of peaches and nectarines, and in the second before he kissed her he knew with triumph roaring in his blood that she wanted the embrace as much as he did. Then they were mouth-to-mouth, and their kiss was warm and delicious and gave them such pleasure that they wanted to go on kissing forever.

'Oh!' she said, when he finally raised his head to look at her. 'I never thought . . . Oh Charlie! My dear Charlie!' Their lips were only inches apart and there was nothing in the world except this lovely, lovely sensation.

He kissed her again. And again.

'You're magnificent!' he said. 'D'you know that? Magnificent. And I love you.'

'Do you?' she asked unnecessarily. 'Really?' Oh the joy of hearing him say it after such kisses.

'Yes. I do.'

She closed her eyes, still smiling. She was committed to him now. There was no going back.

'Do you love me?' he asked. In their triumph he was almost sure she did, but he wanted to hear her say it. Now, for the first time.

'Yes,' she said and her face was blazing love, bright as the moon and much much more beautiful.

'Magnificent,' he said. And kissed her again.

They stayed on the quayside for as long as they dared, only returning to the apartment at the last possible moment to collect her luggage before they rushed to the Gare du Nord to retrieve his. They'd cut it so fine that as they ran on to the platform, the train to Boves was preparing to leave in a drama of whistles and screaming steam. He wondered whether he could kiss her again in such a public place and wondered too long. She was on the step, moving away from him.

'I'll see you soon,' he said, as she stood at the window.

'Yes.'

'Write to me.'

'I will,' she said holding out her hand to him.

They held hands until the train started to move, until its increasing speed finally pulled them away from each other. It was a bitter-sweet parting, for neither of them knew when they would meet again.

But they *would* meet again, Ginny thought, as she settled into her seat and pulled up her coat collar to hide from the knowing glances of her fellow travellers. No matter what Maman might say to her, no matter how many warnings she might be given, no matter whether there really was a disease, she knew there was no stopping now. No stopping either of them. This was what she'd been waiting for all her life. Wonderful, exciting, magical, undeniable. This *was* love.

# CHAPTER SEVENTEEN

After such an emotional weekend it was hard to return to the mundane world of Monsieur Guerin and his velvets, especially as the gentlemen arrived in the office roaring with bad temper because a consignment of figured black had gone astray.

'Imbecile!' he shrieked into the phone. 'What were you doing?' And he rushed into the factory tearing at his hair. 'I despair of humanity!'

'Did he find you, *cherie*?' Veronique said, when their boss had gone. 'Your Charlie?'

'Yes. I'm sorry he came bothering you.'

Veronique clicked her teeth. 'It was no bother,' she said. '*Rien du tout*. I gave up hope of that young man weeks and weeks ago. I knew he was after you. So, tell me, was it a good weekend?'

'Yes,' Ginny said, but she turned her head away from her friend in an attempt to deflect her interest. It was all too recent, too private and too full of emotion to be reduced to a confidence. She was glad when the phone interrupted them before Veronique could ask any more questions.

Despite a rush of work and her own determined efforts to keep busy, questions and memories seeped into her mind all day long. How could she tell Maman? Would being in love make her ill? *Was* there such an illness? And over and above everything else, when would she see him again? Soon, oh soon, she yearned. Let it be soon. To love him and not be able to see him filled her with impatient anguish and an undeniable sense of loneliness. I'm not like Em, she thought, I shan't be able to wait for months like her. And she wondered whether her sister really *was* in love after all. I'll see if I can talk to her tonight, she decided. It might be easier to tell Em. Then I'll drop a hint to Maman, something subtle so as not to alarm her too much.

But Hortense was in a bad temper that evening. She stood at the kitchen table preparing the evening meal and every angle of her body proclaimed how cross she was.

'I can't see why you had to stay so late with that Mauricette,' she complained. 'It was after midnight when you got in last night, I hope you realise. It won't do you any good staying out all hours like that. You could have been back here at a decent time, if you'd made the effort, and don't tell me you couldn't.'

'Very well then,' Ginny said rather wearily. 'I won't.'

'And you see the sort of mood you're in,' Hortense said, slicing tomatoes with angry strokes of her long knife. 'This is what comes of sitting up half the night talking politics. And don't tell me you haven't been doing that, either. You've got dark shadows under your eyes.'

'It's been a difficult day.'

'You make it worse for yourself with all this traipsing about. Your precious party should learn to manage without you.'

Ginny sat down in the nearest chair and closed her eyes. The thought of her 'precious party', with those handsome grey-brown eyes and that long narrow mouth that looked so stern and felt so gentle, made her face soften into reverie, so that Hortense, glancing up as she picked out another tomato to attack, was alerted and alarmed.

Oh no! she thought. Not that! Please protect her, dear Lord, don't let it be that. But the signs were there, the softness and tenderness and drifting inattention. Holy Mary, Mother of God, she prayed, and her heart contracted at the thought of the pain and misery that love would inevitably bring to this dear daughter of hers. *She'll be ill and it's all my fault.* Yet even while she anguished, Hortense knew how unreasonable it was to deny love to a girl so worthy of it, remembering how *she*'d felt when she first loved Edouard, how headstrong and passionate *she*'d been. To stop it was to fly in the face of nature. Yet she had to try. Why must this happen today? she thought. Today, of all days, when she felt so tired and was so afraid of being ill herself. Pity and anxiety rose beyond their limits and toppled over into irritation.

'I suppose,' she said crossly, 'you're going to sit there in a dream all evening while the rest of us work.' It was an unfair thing to say because Ginny never shirked the housework, but the words were out before she could check them.

There was no hope of talking to Maman when she was in this mood, let alone dropping any hints. She might as well get on with some work. 'Where's Emily?' Ginny asked, hauling herself out of the chair.

'Out in the garden, bringing in the clothes.'

'At this time?' Ginny said, on her way to the kitchen door.

'It's been a bad day for us, too,' Hortense explained to her daughter's departing back. And she tried to justify her irritation. 'I couldn't get home at midday and neither could Cousin Berthe.'

But Ginny was already out of the house. Oh Ginny, *cherie*, Hortense thought, grieving because they'd lost contact with one another, how can I help you if you walk away?

Emily was unpegging the dry washing from the line, feeling her way from garment to garment in the dusk, the peg-bag hung over her left arm and the clothes basket shuffled between her feet. She worked methodically, unpegging, folding, stooping to add to the pile in the basket. When she heard Ginny's approach she stopped, balanced two fingers delicately on the line so as to mark her place, and turned to greet her sister.

'Did you see him?' she asked, in a very quiet voice so that Maman couldn't hear.

'Yes' Ginny whispered, throwing her arms round her sister's neck. 'We spent most of the weekend together.' And she knew she was steeling herself for questions she didn't want to answer.

Emily was concerned with a more pressing problem. 'What are you going to tell Maman?'

'Nothing yet,' Ginny said, her voice begging Em to keep

242

their confidence. 'Not tonight, anyway. She's cross enough without me making her worse.'

'It's the washing,' Em said, returning to it. 'She did it this morning before she came to work, and it's worn her out. Cousin Berthe's been scolding about it all day.'

Ginny folded as her sister unpegged. 'I wish she wouldn't work so hard,' she said, looking back at their mother, still stooped over the table, silhouetted against the light from the kitchen. Even from that distance Ginny could see how tired she looked. Her long hair had escaped from its pleat and hung about her face in greasy clusters, her cheeks were gaunt, her lips pale and her hands reddened by housework. Ginny remembered when she and Em were little girls, how chic Maman had been then, in her fashionable frocks and her pretty shoes, with her bobbed hair and her face so young and beautiful. Poor Maman.

'I think she does it because she's frightened,' Emily said, sliding the basket along the rough grass.

Fear touched Ginny's own heart with sharp fingers. 'Frightened? What of?'

'Being ill. She feels guilty about being ill.'

'But that's silly,' Ginny said, trying to reassure them both. 'You can't help being ill.'

'I know that, in the ordinary way of things. But it's this special illness. The awful illness. She feels guilty about it and then she gets frightened. It's been very difficult looking after her this weekend. She's been cross most of the time.'

'Sometimes,' Ginny sighed, 'I wonder why we try.'

'Don't say that, Ginny,' Emily whispered. 'It doesn't matter how difficult it is, we've got to look after her, haven't we?'

It's true, Ginny thought, as she folded the last garment. We don't have a choice. We are so tied to each other, bound by love and duty and responsibility and gratitude and Heaven only knows what else. Bound and hemmed in and constrained. For the first time in her life she ached to be free of it all, just for once – to be back in Paris with Charlie, with nothing to worry her, no one to hinder her and no one to consider except herself. Then she felt guilty for thinking selfish thoughts.

There was a squawk and a clatter of wings as Cousin Berthe bundled out of the earth closet at the end of the garden and waddled up the cinder path, dispersing hens right and left.

'Hello, my pretty one,' she called to Ginny. 'How was Amiens?'

'It was Paris,' both girls called in unison.

She smiled at them emptily. 'Paris. Amiens. It's all the same to me. Give your ol' Cousin Berthe a great big kiss.'

That evening a wind sprang up and, although Hortense stoked the fire halfway up the chimney, cold air rushed through every cranny into the house. Soon after supper, one of Old Joliot's cronies arrived to play cards but the twins decided on an early night and, after a wind-whipped dash to the bottom of the garden, they took their stone hot water bottles to bed with them for the first time that season.

It was very cold indeed in their unheated bedroom. Ginny sighed and shivered as she hung up her clothes.

'Wasn't it a success?' Emily asked from her wigwam of bedclothes.

'What?'

'Your weekend.'

'Oh. Yes. I think it was.'

Emily understood her sister's reticence. 'But you'd rather not talk about it.'

'No. Not yet, anyway. If you don't mind.'

'I don't mind,' Emily said easily. 'I realised that when we were in the garden. Hurry up and get into bed.'

'I'll tell you what, though,' Ginny said, pulling her night-gown over her head. 'Love is very complicated sometimes.'

There was such an odd blend of exasperation and satisfaction in her voice that Emily smiled. 'Is it?' she said.

'Very complicated. Sometimes I envy you your nice steady Kenneth.'

'Was there a letter?' Emily said, trying not to sound too eager.

'Oh Em! I *am* sorry. I forgot. One came on Saturday morning. It's in my bag.'

'Can you read it? Is it safe?'

They listened to the voices in the room below them. 'Yes,' Ginny said. 'I think so. They're still playing.'

So Ginny set the candle on the bedside table and they snuggled under the covers for warmth and the letter was read. It was all about business. As usual.

'*I have obtained the contract I wanted at last, and have found a new factory that will be plenty big enough for my present purposes and allow room for expansion when the time comes. There is a lot of work to do. I will tell you how it is going day by day . . .*'

How boring, Ginny thought as she read. But she tried to give credit where it was due.

'I'll say this for your Kenneth,' she said. 'He may not be the most romantic man alive but he's certainly a worker.'

'Yes, he is.'

'I wonder what this factory's like . . .'

It was a concrete and asbestos shed. A very large one, covering four acres of rough ground just south of Streatham between two cemeteries and a gravel pit in a scrubby wilderness that was known locally and with justification as the 'Lonesome'. It had been built with concrete flooring and a glass-panelled roof angled to provide strong north lighting and, despite its apparent isolation, was conveniently close to the railway. A cart track ran from the factory entrance to the goods yard at Streatham Common station, and above the trees and hedges to the north, the grey church spires, slate roofs and sooty chimneys of Streatham itself were clearly visible.

'It might not add up to much at the moment,' Ken Hopkirk remarked to his foreman, as they walked the empty sheds, plans in hand, 'but just wait a month or two.'

The concrete floor was marked and stained by the machinery from its last occupation; there were piles of wood shavings and oily rags in every corner and the gaslamps suspended from the rafters on long metal chains were festooned with cobwebs. But Ken could see what it was going to be. 'We'll have the pressroom here.'

'How long d'you reckon it'll take, sir?' the foreman asked. He was a stocky young man called Bill Murgatroyd, the sort who took things comfortably in his stride.

'Six weeks with a bit of luck,' Ken told him. 'Two months at the outside, I want to be up and running before Christmas.'

But the next six weeks were an aggravation of delay. A month passed and they were still struggling on in their old cramped premises. Ken wrote to Emily every night with the latest news, assuring her that everything was going according to plan, but privately he was tense with irritation.

His irritation, however, was nothing to the roaring impatience that was propelling Charlie Commoner.

'*I can't wait to see you again,*' he wrote to Jeannie, over and over again. '*It's ridiculous to be miles apart just when we were beginning to get to know one another. We should be seeing one another every day. I am saving hard, though. I shall soon have enough for the fare. I shall be in Amiens again before you know it. You'll see!*'

He was comforting himself as much as her, because it was proving extremely difficult to amass the necessary cash. Meanwhile, the weather in the Channel was getting worse and worse, which he knew only too well because he checked the forecast every day.

As the days passed and their separation extended, he was in fidgets of frustration. Grace was too caught up in her own affairs to be aware of it; Stan and Ruby noticed but kept their own counsel. It was Grandpa who spoke out.

'Time you was back in France,' he said, when he and Charlie were on their own in the kitchen one evening.

Charlie sighed wearily. 'Chance'd be a fine thing,' he said.

'Why?' Grandpa asked. 'Ain't got the sack 'ave yer?'

'No, no, nothing like that.'

'Well then, why can't you go?'

'Because I haven't got the fare,' Charlie confessed. 'I've

been saving up for it, but I'm short.' He sighed again.

'It's important, this trip a' yours, ain't it, son?'

'Yes,' Charlie said. 'It is.'

Grandpa put down his pipe and considered. 'How much you short?' he said.

'Too much.'

'Put a price on it.'

'Rather a lot.'

'*How much?*'

Charlie thought about it. 'You won't tell Mum if I tell you?'

'You know me better'n that.'

'Well then, the fare's three pounds five shillings. I've got three pounds and six saved up, but the trip'll cost nearer five pounds, with lodgings and food and everything. I've been wondering if there was something I could pawn.'

Grandpa looked at him for a long second. Then he gave his wickedest grin. 'What you're saying is you need another two pounds. That right?'

'Yes. I'm afraid so.'

'I'll give you a lend of it, if you like.'

Charlie was shocked. 'I couldn't do that. You're on a pension.'

'Wouldn't be a gift, mind,' Grandpa warned. 'You'd 'aveter pay it back. But you could do it bit by bit, couldn't yer? Ten bob a week fer four weeks.'

Put like that the transaction was possible. 'Well, it's ever so good of you,' Charlie said. 'I don't know though. I don't think I ought to.'

Granpa grinned at him. 'We can't 'ave your young lady pining away in France and you stuck 'ere, now can we?'

That was rather alarming. 'How did you know I'd got a young lady?'

'Got eyes in me 'ead,' the old man said. 'All them letters with French stamps. Don't worry. We won't tell yer Ma.'

'You're a good old boy, Grandpa,' Charlie said. 'Thanks.'

So the money was provided and a rapturous letter was sent to Jeannie that very evening. It was answered by return of post.

'*Shall we meet in Boulogne?*' she asked. '*I could travel there on Saturday morning. There is a milk train that gets in at half-past six. What do you think?*'

The milk train was agreed upon. And that Friday evening, at long long last, Charlie crossed the Channel.

He was so taut with impatience and suppressed energy that he hardly noticed what a bad crossing it was, nor how persistently it was raining. To be so near to his lovely Jeannie and getting closer by the minute! It was happiness so intense it was actually painful.

Knapsack over his shoulder, he strode off the gangplank in the early morning, walking tall like a conquering hero. It was such a pleasure to hear French voices, to recognise this familiar, foreign place with its cobbled streets and shuttered windows – to peer through the rain for the first sight of his sweetheart. Where was she? Was that her train? She'd said six-thirty in her letter and it must be that by now. Oh come on! Come on! Where are you?

She was on the milk train from Amiens, heading north through the gusting rain. And she was in turmoil, too. When Charlie's letter arrived, she'd been so happy because she was going to see him again that she hadn't thought any further than their meeting. Since then, she'd been too busy to pay attention to her conscience. But an early morning journey on a half-empty train had given her the time and opportunity to feel guilty again. She still hadn't said anything to her mother and she knew she ought to have done. At the very least she should have told her where she was going and whom she was going to meet, even if it did lead to a row. Allowing everyone to think she was off to a political meeting with Veronique was a sin of omission, and she couldn't pretend it wasn't. She should have told the truth and taken the consequences. But the consequences might have been dreadful. She could have been forbidden to come to Boulogne, forbidden to see him.

I'm thinking like Emily, she thought. Imagine me worrying about sin and confession. But it was only a small portion of her mind that was occupied with guilt, the rest of it was leaping to follow her senses . . . straight into his arms, to be held and kissed and told how much she was loved. How could she resist that? Even if it meant years in purgatory.

Oh, what a slow train it was! But at long, impatient last it was creaking into Boulogne. Ginny had the door open and had jumped down from the step before it could stop.

Which was how Charlie first saw her, leaping through the wild air with the wind pinning her blue coat against her body and her hat flying behind her like a one-winged bird. 'Jeannie! Jeannie! You're here!'

A madness of movement, running, throwing luggage aside, treading her umbrella underfoot, leaping into one another's arms, and kissing, kissing, kissing, in a breathless, exquisite, passionate hunger. 'Sweetheart! Sweetheart! Sweetheart!' The rest of the world could do what it pleased. They were back with one another again.

'Oh Charlie!' she said, when they'd kissed to a temporary halt and stood back to look at one another. 'It is good to see you.' There was no doubt how much she loved him now.

He was drinking in the sight of her, lovely olive skin glowing in the rainy air, brown eyes luminous with love, chin determined, mouth red with kisses, breasts taut under her cotton shirt. 'You're so beautiful,' he said. 'Do you know that? So beautiful!'

So, naturally, they had to kiss again, just once, before they became sensible and picked up their luggage and retrieved her hat. Then they walked with their arms round one another, her breast warm against his side, his long stride tempered to fit her shorter one, thigh brushing thigh, in a trance of desire.

'Where are we going?'

'To breakfast,' she said. 'I caught the first train, you know. The milk train. I haven't had anything to eat.'

'You starved yourself for me!' he said, teasing her. 'What can I say?'

'I'm noble!' she joked. 'Another *Jeanne d'Arc*!'

'I'll buy you the best breakfast in Boulogne to make amends.'

'Come on then,' she said, leading him across the square. 'I know just the place.'

Talk of breakfast had given her a lovely superstitious idea. She would take Charlie to Madame Boulanger's, where she and Emily and Maman had stayed when they first came to France. If the café was still there it would mean that this was supposed to happen. It would be a good omen, a sign. If it wasn't . . .

But it was. Standing in the remembered street in its remembered place between those two remembered tenements, *Boulanger de Boulogne*. It had the same blue and white awnings, the same small crowded interior, wicker chairs, house plants, bead curtain and all. There was even a tabby cat asleep on the counter. Madame looked older, with white hair and fewer teeth, but she was still cosily plump and her automatic greeting hadn't changed at all. '*M'sieur, M'dame.*'

Ginny ordered breakfast and smiled at the old lady.

'Madame,' she said, 'You are Madame Boulanger, *n'est-ce pas?*'

Madame acknowledged her name, patting the cat. 'That's me. *Boulanger of Boulogne.*'

'I stayed here once, Madame,' Ginny said. 'Years ago, when I was a little girl, when I first came to France. We had the front bedroom, Maman and me and my sister. I wonder if you remember.'

Madame narrowed her eyes and looked at her customer for a long time, still patting the cat which was beginning to grunt under the weight of her hand. '*Mais oui,*' she said at last. 'I do believe I do. Twins, weren't you? And your mother a war widow. She went to work in Le Touquet.'

It was wonderful to be remembered. 'Yes, yes. That's right.'

'And now you return,' Madame, keeping a wary eye on her next three customers who were walking towards the bar. 'Breakfast for two, you said.'

They found a table in a corner and settled to enjoy their meal, sitting as close to one another as they could get.

'Good?' Ginny asked him.

'Super,' he said, kissing her nose. 'I didn't know you had a sister.'

'You never asked me.'

'Older or younger?'

'Older. Just. Did you understand what we were saying then?'

'Bits of it. You said you stayed here once. You said "*Maman et ma soeur.*" And somebody worked in Le Touquet.'

'We all did. Maman is a housekeeper. I used to help her when I was younger. How long are you staying?'

'Till Sunday night. Back to work Monday.'

'It's such a little time.'

'Then we won't waste a minute of it,' he said, taking her hand so that he could kiss her fingertips. Oh, the delicious smell of her skin!

The kiss stirred her so strongly she was afraid that everyone in the café would notice. 'Where are you staying?' she said.

'Don't know yet,' he said, holding her hand against his cheek, the way they did in the films. 'Somewhere quiet so I can kiss you.'

She was excited, and afraid, and tremulously happy. What they were doing was very daring. Almost illicit.

'You could stay here,' she said, returning his gaze as steadily as she could. 'Madame has nice rooms and they are not expensive. If they're available.'

'Yes,' he agreed. 'I could. What will you do?'

'I ought to go home,' Ginny said breathlessly. 'But I suppose I could stay, too, if Madame has two rooms.' Now what would he say. Would he . . . ?

He swallowed. Bit his lip. Dared. 'Would you stay here? I mean . . .'

'Do you want me to?'

So much it was making it hard to breathe. 'Yes.'

How could she deny him when he looked at her like that? Tense and hopeful and so full of affection, not saying anything, not even moving he was hoping so hard, those fine

251

grey eyes huge in his pale face. Madame was edging her way through the tables towards them with an empty tray.

'Do you have any single rooms?' she said to her landlady, speaking French and delighted to hear how calm she sounded.

'You are in luck, Mademoiselle,' Madame Boulanger said. 'I have two and both are empty until Tuesday.'

'*Alors*. We will take them,' Ginny decided.

'I will show you up when you have finished your *petit déjeuner*,' Madame said. 'But you cannot occupy them until midday, you understand.'

They were two narrow rooms, side by side, with the flimsiest wall between them; neat, impersonal rooms with faded bedspreads and fawn wallpaper and identical washbowls.

'*Tiens!* Such rain,' Madame said from the window. 'You will need your umbrella if you are sightseeing this morning.'

But the weather was irrelevant. They were warm with love, walking the rain-washed town with their arms about each other and the umbrella held with such lack of attention that their heads and shoulders were soon as wet as if they'd been swimming. Rain streamed from the wet curls on Ginny's forehead, to run down her cheeks, along the ridge of her nose and even into her mouth, whence it had to be kissed away. Charlie's summer trilby became a conduit for the shower, spattering raindrops as he moved. But what of it? It was talk that was important, talk and kisses, and the unspoken, daring, certain promise of the afternoon.

They wandered through the market stalls in the Place Dalton, watched the morning catch being brought ashore at the quayside, climbed the hill and dripped through the medieval gateway to explore the old town – and when Ginny stumbled on the rough cobbles he had to hold her very close indeed, in case she fell. They ate fresh fish for lunch and watched the rain cascade down the windows of the café. And they both knew they were simply passing the time until they could be on their own together.

That afternoon the sun came out, but they didn't notice it.

By then they were lying together on the narrow bed in Ginny's room, entirely given over to the joys of kissing, rousing each other more and more strongly – but safe in the knowledge that Charlie could control himself no matter what.

'I won't do anything more than kiss you,' he promised, 'not unless you want me to.'

She lay trustingly in his arms, saying, 'Yes. I know.' For a Catholic girl, kissing was daring enough without going any further.

That evening they went to the cinema and sat thigh to thigh in the back row, returning to eat what little supper they could before retreating to their magic world upstairs. It was three in the morning when they finally decided they ought to part. They spent the rest of the night virtuously alone in the propriety of their own beds, but they were both in such an acute state of ungratified desire that neither of them slept very much.

It was, as they told one another late on Sunday night, a blissful weekend.

It was followed by three more, each happier and more tantalising than the last. Each just a little more daring, as other embraces were discovered, permitted, and enjoyed.

When they weren't kissing, they talked of the life they would live together once Charlie was qualified.

'It won't be long now,' he assured Ginny. 'I sit my final exams in June and then I shall be articled.'

'When will you know the results?'

'End of August. I can get taken on then, and we can make plans.'

She didn't understand. 'What is "taken on"?'

'Given a job. As a solicitor. I shall be a proper solicitor then, you see, when I've passed the exams. I shall start earning money. It'll make all the difference.'

'Ah!' she said. 'I see. Don't let's talk about money, Charlie. Kiss me again.'

It was after the third weekend that Ginny finally told Emily how much in love she was, and was kissed and hugged and congratulated.

'I've known it all along,' Emily said.

'You and your ears.'

'I'm *so* happy for you. Whatever will Maman say when she knows we both have lovers?'

'We won't tell her yet,' Ginny urged. 'After all, it's early days. It's not as if we're engaged or anything like that.'

Emily decided not to think about the problem for the time being. 'When are you going to see him again?' she asked.

Charlie's fourth trip to Boulogne was made in very bad weather indeed. There was such a storm that the ship stood to in mid-Channel for nearly two and a half hours and he was green with seasickness when he arrived.

'Oh Charlie!' Ginny said, torn with pity for his sickness and admiration for his steadfastness. 'You are the dearest man to come all this way in weather like this.'

'Quite right!' he joked. 'Glad you appreciate me.'

But joking apart, they agreed that the next trip would have to wait for rather better weather.

The weather got worse. Even the mail was delayed, sometimes for several days, and very difficult life in Boves was then.

The two young men wrote regularly to their loved ones all through the winter. Charlie's letters were long and passionate. Ken's short and informative.

At the end of November Ken wrote to tell Emily that the old Crystal Palace had burnt down in a blaze that lit up the whole of London and could be seen as far away as the south coast. '*I wonder you didn't see it in France,*' he added.

In early December, the papers were full of astonishing rumours that King Edward was going to abdicate, and Ken wrote about that, too. '*Everybody is talking about it. Perhaps it is all only a rumour. I can't believe it is true.*'

'*It is all perfectly true,*' Emily dictated back. '*We have known about it for ages here in France. There have been lots of pictures of them in our newspapers, going swimming and on a yacht in the Mediterranean. She is very chic, so I'm told, but has an ugly face. They say Queen Mary doesn't approve of her and that Mr Baldwin had been trying to persuade the King to give her up. It's* been going on for months. I'm surprised you haven't heard about it before now.'

But what they both really wanted to write about was the success of the factory.

It was opened on December twentieth, a day that Ken Hopkirk told Emily he would remember all his life. '*This is the first step*,' he wrote. '*The second will be the bungalow. The third I will tell you about when I next see you.*'

'Ask him when that is likely to be,' Emily said to Ginny. 'No. On second thought, first say how glad I am to hear about the factory. Then I'll ask him. Are you ready Ginny? Right then. "*Dear Kenneth*" . . .'

Ken Hopkirk carried her letter about with him all through those first satisfying days at the new works. It was talisman, love token and Christmas card all rolled into one – and a reminder that he shouldn't get too swollen-headed.

It was hard not to feel proud. The sheer size and noise of the place were enough to lift his spirits into the clouds. And when he walked out of his office to tour the works he felt like a general inspecting his army. He had created it: the corridors roofed with silver pipes, the auto shop buzzing, the well-organised drawing office, the tinsmith shop, the pressroom where the air resounded to the steady thump of his new power presses hitting old metal, and the new water pumps roared, the quiet well-lit room where a dozen women sat at benches mounting the indexes and testing them . . .

My work force, he thought proudly, smiling at the assembled faces. My work force in my uniform.

They chorused back above the din. 'Morning, sir!'

That night he wrote to Emily to wish her a happy Christmas and to tell her that he would try to get to France in the spring. '*But failing that I shall certainly be there in the summer. I dream of the fountains in Versailles. We shall see them together, very soon.*'

'Not before time,' Ginny said, 'I've seen Charlie four times since the summer.'

'But he gets his fare paid,' Emily pointed out.

255

'Not every time,' Ginny bristled. 'He pays his own way, too.' The bad weather in the Channel hadn't let up for weeks, and in his last letter Charlie had confessed that he probably wouldn't be able to see her again until the spring, ' . . .*what with work and the storms.*'

'Don't let's quarrel about it,' Emily placated her sister. 'Not when it's Christmas tomorrow.'

'Oh Em!' Ginny sighed. 'I'd rather it was midsummer's day.'

'Me, too,' Emily said, sighing as profoundly as her sister. And they still hadn't told Maman.

# CHAPTER EIGHTEEN

'We must face facts, gentlemen,' Claud Everdale told his management board, using his magisterial voice. 'The Holborn twins are not going to be found. That is the truth of it. It is now two years – a good two years – since poor Mr Holborn passed away and I have to tell you we're no nearer finding them now than we were at the beginning.'

'But the search will continue,' the secretary hastened to intervene, alerted by the disapproval on Mr Pennyfield's face. 'That is so, is it not, Mr Everdale?'

'Oh indubitably, Mr Reinhart,' Claud said smoothly, giving them all his most urbane smile. 'Letter of the law and all that.'

'Glad to hear it,' Jack Pennyfield said. 'I wouldn't like to think we was letting the old man down.'

These days, board meetings were held at the works, in a long attic converted for the purpose. It was an uncomfortable room; unheated, poorly lit, full of drifting dust that spun into the musty air with every thump of the power presses below, obstructed by metal roof beams that were too low to allow any of them to stand upright unless they were in the middle of the room. Jack Pennyfield hated it and mourned for the old days when they used to meet in comfort at the house, with drinks at the end of the afternoon and a real chance to speak their minds. This place was designed to make them keep their heads down, in every sense of the words.

'On to business then,' Mr Everdale was saying. 'Item one. The anti-tank rifle.'

Not that old thing again, Jack Pennyfield thought, as the prototype was lifted out of its box and laid on the table before them. 'Modified, is it?' he asked.

'Naturally,' Mr Everdale said, handing round the latest specifications.

Mr Pennyfield lifted the rifle from the table and held it in the firing position. 'It's no lighter,' he said. 'That's for starters. It's still cumbersome.'

Mr Everdale parried the criticism. 'So you always say, Jack. It's a good weapon notwithstanding. Tremendous fire power. With the present modifications it'll be a winner. Don't you think so, Fred?'

Fred Manners was a newcomer to the board and much in awe of his boss. He had replaced Roger Smith, the old chief engineer, after Christmas and he still felt he was working his passage. 'Yes, sir,' he said.

'We could put it into production.' It was a command, not a question, and Mr Manners responded to it correctly.

'Yes, sir,' he said. 'That would be no problem.' Then just to be on the safe side, he added. 'It's a good weapon.'

'It's a lousy weapon,' Mr Pennyfield said. 'But we'll let that pass.' With old Roger gone he felt vulnerable on this board. 'You all know my opinion, anyway.'

'And a valued opinion,' Claud said with flawless dishonesty, 'if I may say so, Jack. However, we have to consider the facts. There is another war coming. This business in Spain is a curtain raiser. There's not much doubt about that. When it comes it won't be another war of attrition. I can tell you that. We shan't get bogged down in trenches this time. Oh no. It'll be tanks and armoured cars with air support from bombers. And anti-tank guns. *This* anti-tank gun unless some other company pips us to the post. Which in my view would be a total disaster. Are there any other comments? No. Questions? Then I propose we put it to the vote. Those in favour of putting this gun into production, please show.'

Mr Manner's hand was instantly in the air.

'Hang on a jiffy,' Jack Pennyfield protested. 'With respect sir, we can't go votin' yet. Not without Mrs Everdale.'

'Didn't I tell you?' Claud said. 'Mrs Everdale sends her apologies for absence. She's taken the boys to Birkenhead to see the Ark Royal being launched or some such. Now where were we? Those in favour.'

Jack Pennyfield endeavoured not to show his annoyance. It wasn't right to take a vote without Mrs Everdale, and they knew it, but it wouldn't matter in the long run. It was bound to be a draw.

'Two in favour,' Mr Everdale said. 'And against? Two against.'

Jack Pennyfield was lighting his next cigarette from the stub of the last one, sucking hard. 'Stalemate,' he said, between puffs.

'Not exactly,' Mr Everdale said smoothly. 'There's still my wife's vote, don't forget.'

'So we wait.'

'No. There's no need for that. My wife would have voted for the motion. It's a sure-fire money spinner.'

'Got her proxy, have you, sir?' Mr Pennyfield said, pretending to be joking. 'Can we see it?' It was dangerous to challenge this man so directly, but he was too annoyed by such flagrant double-dealing to keep quiet.

Mr Everdale actually looked embarrassed, just for a second. The expression wasn't lost on his works manager. 'Well, not exactly,' he said. 'More word of mouth. However if you'd rather we disregarded it there are other ways of settling this. I still have my casting vote as chairman.'

Crafty bugger, Jack Pennyfield thought, caught between increased annoyance and a grudging admiration. I'd forgotten about the casting vote. He's done us whichever way we turn. Crafty old bugger.

'Now we know why this was all brought forward,' he said to Mr Reinhart, when the meeting was over and the two of them were walking back through the works. 'I knew he was up to somethin'. I just didn't think it would be that bloody rifle again.'

'It's an obsession with him,' the secretary said, speaking above the noise of the machines.

'Always has been.'

'He's right about one thing, though,' Mr Reinhart said. 'Another war does look likely.'

'Then we ought to make the best guns we can. That one's just a load of ol' junk, I'm tellin' you. Won't last five minutes in a runnin' battle.'

'I wonder how he got Mrs Everdale to go to Birkenhead,' the secretary said.

'Guile,' Jack Pennyfield grunted. 'It's always guile with that one.'

He was wrong. Agnes had made her decision entirely of her own free will and – almost – entirely for her own purposes. The initial idea had come from Johnny, who was enthralled by warships. He had been supported by George who preferred fighter planes but saw no reason why he should be left out of any family expedition. In ordinary circumstances, Agnes would have resisted. Standing about in the open air in the middle of April was not her idea of a pleasurable outing. But this was different. This time she had a good reason to give them what they wanted. And the good reason was Charlie Commoner.

The last time she'd gone up to London to visit Hedgethorn and Crabbit, Claud had made such a fuss about it afterwards that she had been upset for days. She and Miss Babbacombe had discussed it at length and, in the end, Agnes had phoned Mr Crabbit while Claud was at work to tell him that she wasn't at all sure whether she could send him any further instructions, 'at least not just at present.'

Mr Crabbit was pleasantly solicitous. 'Would it be more convenient if we were to send someone down to you at High Holborn?'

The very idea was horrifying. 'Oh no,' she said. 'That wouldn't do at all.'

'I see,' Mr Crabbit's voice said soothingly. 'Then we must find some other venue, must we not. A neutral ground so to speak. Are you likely to be travelling at all in the near future?'

'I might go to Birkenhead on April thirteenth. It's the Easter holidays and the boys want to see the Ark Royal being launched.'

'Singular good fortune,' Mr Crabbit said. 'Our Mr Commoner has to be in Birkenhead on that very day. How would it be if I were to arrange a meeting place?'

'It would be excellent,' Agnes said.

So here she was, between her two large sons and a very fat man waving a ridiculous little Union Jack. There was so much noise she could hardly hear herself think and they were perilously close to the edge of the quay. The great, grey side of the new aircraft carrier was little more than an arm's length from her nose, and loomed above her so far and so high that she couldn't see the sky. And the boys were arguing.

'If you're going to quarrel,' Agnes said. 'I shall take you straight back home and you won't see the launch or anything else.'

'No, you won't,' George said laconically. 'You can't. You're going to meet someone from Hedgethorn and Crabbit.'

Agnes was astonished. How on earth did he know that? she wondered, staring at him.

'Heard you on the blower, old fruit,' her son said, answering her expression. 'Don't fret. I shan't tell the old man. Your secret is safe with me.'

Agnes was so surprised she didn't rebuke him for calling her old fruit. Really! she thought. The young things of today know far too much. Altogether too much.

'I suppose it's about the cousins,' Johnny said, still gazing at the ship.

'Well, yes,' Agnes admitted. 'It's to do with your grandfather's will. Yes.'

'Pater says they'll do us out of our inheritance,' George said. 'Personally, I don't care.'

This *was* a revelation. 'Don't you?' Agnes said.

'Not particularly,' George said. 'It's only an old factory, when all's said and done. They're welcome to it. Anyway

261

you won't find them. Pater says they don't want to be found. That's why they've never given old Babbers an address.'

Agnes turned to her younger son. 'And what do you think, Johnny?'

'I don't care either way,' Johnny said. 'It don't concern me. I'm going to be an art collector.'

'Not when the war starts, you won't,' George mocked.

'There isn't going to be a war.'

' 'Course there's going to be a war, Blockhead. This is a *war* ship. That's what it's been built for. There's going to be a war and I'm going to fly in it.'

Agnes had a sudden, searing vision of her poor brother falling, arms outstretched under a hail of bullets. 'Oh, don't say things like that,' she begged.

But the tannoy was coughing and ringing and the crowds were shushing to a respectful silence.

'I call this ship,' a metallic voice intoned, 'a Wah Way-oh. And may God wah wer a wah wah wail wah.' The great cables crashed to the quay, one after the other, with a long crunching sound that made Agnes think of a house falling down. And the warship began to inch past them, sliding slowly, slowly, sticking, then gathering a little speed, grinding, slipping. A cheer swelled up from every throat and Agnes found that she was cheering too and that there were tears in her eyes. 'May God bless her and all who sail in her, especially if there's going to be another war. Oh, God, please don't let there be another war.'

The anguish she felt at that moment was so acute she couldn't shake it off. It was still plaguing her when she arrived at the restaurant Mr Crabbit had selected for her meeting with Mr Commoner. She entered the foyer nervously, clutching her handbag like an inadequate shield and peering to right and left as if she expected to be attacked. He was waiting beside the aspidistra, exactly where Mr Crabbit had promised he would be, and he continued to wait while she settled the boys at a table of their own. Then, he escorted her to the table he'd booked in her name.

262

'You're very kind,' she said. 'Shall I order?'

The restaurant was an old-fashioned place, but the owner obviously appreciated flowers as much as Agnes did. There was a bowl full of primroses on the table and the window boxes were a riot of daffodils swaying in unison like a yellow chorusline between the quiet blue of the curtains.

'Almost Spring,' she said. 'I do love daffodils. They're such jolly flowers, don't you think?'

'They certainly cheer you up,' he said, smiling at her.

What splendid eyes he has, she thought and returned the smile. She'd forgotten how good looking he was. But grown-up now, of course. The young man she'd talked to in the garden at High Holborn had been little more than a youth. This one was far more self-assured.

'It's all this talk of war,' she said. 'Battleships being launched. Everyone re-arming. That sort of thing. It's rather depressing.'

'Yes,' he agreed. 'It is.'

'My husband's convinced there's going to be another war with Germany,' she said. 'I keep hoping he's wrong. What do you think, Mr Commoner?'

'I don't know, Mrs Everdale,' Charlie said. 'My girlfriend thinks so. But she's French so she sees things differently.' And then to his horror he could feel himself blushing, the heat rising out of his collar and up his neck into his cheeks. How could he have betrayed himself to such a confession? How unprofessional! He had to turn aside and pretend to be admiring the daffodils.

Agnes was touched. By the indiscretion and the blush. Ever tactful, she busied herself so as to give him space to regain his composure. 'These little flowers are so nice,' she said, stroking the petals of the primroses with the tips of her fingers. 'Such soft petals. Like silk.' Then she tried to comfort him. 'You know Mr Commoner, your Mr Crabbit sends people across to France on my behalf from time to time. I must ask him to send you next time, since you have a girlfriend there.'

Charlie didn't enlighten her to the truth. That would have

263

taken the bloom from her gift. And it *was* a gift. That was obvious. 'Thank you,' he said.

'The trouble *is*,' she went on, 'there doesn't seem to be a reason for sending anyone just at present. I don't suppose there's been any response to our latest advertisement.'

'No. I'm afraid not.'

'I can't think what to do next. I want to find them so much, you know. My brother's children.'

'Then we must put on our thinking caps,' he said, eager to help. 'I suppose it's just possible we could have been looking in the wrong town. Do you think *that*'s likely? They might have moved away from Amiens.'

She sighed again. 'There's no knowing where they'll be,' she said. 'They've always been wanderers.'

'Wanderers?' Charlie asked. This was new.

'Oh yes,' Agnes said. 'Always on the move. We've had cards from all sorts of places. Well, Miss Babbacombe has. I'm afraid they don't write to me.'

'I thought – um – I mean, we thought there had only been correspondence from Paris and Amiens.'

'Oh no,' Agnes said. 'Oh dear me, no. They've been to lots of other places.'

A plan was forming in Charlie's sharp brain. 'Could you let me have a list of them?' he asked.

'Of course. Would it do any good?'

'It might,' he said, smiling encouragement. He had liked Agnes in the garden that time and now he liked her more than ever, despite the dowdy clothes, the plain freckled face and the earnest expression. 'They'd be worth a visit at any rate, wouldn't they? I could take them one at a time. Put advertisements in all the local papers. You'd never believe how many papers there are in France. Hundreds and hundreds. It might work. I think it would be worth a try. They could have been visiting relations in some of the places. That's possible, isn't it? And if they saw the advertisements, the relations might get in touch. What do you think?' He was warm with enthusiasm, and, in his excitement, leant across the table towards her.

'I think we should try it,' Agnes said, relaxing for the first time that day. Claud would be cross when he heard about the plan, but she'd face that when the time came. 'I will send you a list of all the places we've heard from as soon as I get home. Miss Babbacombe will help me. How often could you travel?'

'Once a fortnight,' Charlie hoped, thinking, Once a fortnight in France with Jeannie, all expenses paid. Just wait till I tell her.

Mr Crabbit said every three weeks would be *quite* adequate. 'You do have one or two other cases to attend to,' he pointed out. 'A little matter of conveyancing, if you remember. To say nothing of your final examinations in the summer. How did you get on with the Messrs Grimshaw?'

So Charlie had to feed their client's hope and satisfy his own impatience with a series of three-weekly visits. As soon as Mrs Everdale had sent him her list, he drew up a plan of campaign and wrote to her at length explaining what he was going to do. '*I shall visit Chartres first because it is the furthest from Paris,*' he concluded. '*I feel very hopeful of this endeavour. Yours very sincerely, C. S. Commoner.*'

His letter to Jeannie was more detailed and gave dates and places. '*I shall be with you every three weeks all through the summer,*' he said. '*Imagine it! I'll do the work first and then head straight back to Boulogne and Madame's for the weekends. Can you wangle it? See you soon, sweetheart. Didn't I tell you I'd get something organised?*'

But before he could take his first trip across the Channel, alarming news came out of Spain.

On April twenty-seventh 1937, German bombers, Heinkel 1-11s and Junker 52s, escorted by fighters, attacked a market town called Guernica, first dropping high explosive bombs, then incendiaries, and then strafing it with machine-gun fire. The town was crowded because it was market day but, what was worse, it was completely un-defended. Even in the most hideous days of the Great War

265

neither side had ever deliberately gone out to bomb civilians.

The shock of the news affected everyone and people pored over the newspapers. Even Aunt Grace took an interest and read out the details at the supper table, her eyes round with horror behind her glasses.

'Hark at this, Ruby,' she said, folding the paper so that she could lift it up into the light. ' *"They bombed and bombed and bombed," said the mayor. One reporter, who arrived in the city soon after the planes had left, said, "As we drew nearer, on both sides of the road, men, women and children were sitting dazed."* Dreadful! *"I saw a priest in one group, his clothes in tatters. He couldn't talk. He just pointed to the flames, still about four miles away, then whispered* . . ."* Something in Spanish. Can't make it out. *"In the city soldiers were collecting charred bodies."* Imagine that. Poor devils! *"They were sobbing like children. There were flames and smoke and grit, and the smell of burning human flesh was nauseating. Houses were collapsing into the inferno. It was impossible to go down many of the streets, because they were walls of flame. Debris was piled high. The shocked survivors all had the same story to tell: aeroplanes, bullets, bombs, fire."* I don't know what the world's coming to an' that's a fact.'

'Same as it was coming to last time,' Stan said morosely, laying his own newspaper beside his plate. 'You'd a' thought we'd all've had enough of it.'

'That's the Jerries for yer.' Grandpa Jones said, taking a moon-shaped bite out of his bread and marge. 'Never could trust the Jerries. Bomb you soon as look at you, they would.'

'Those poor people!' Ruby said. 'You imagine it.'

Charlie said nothing. He was facing the fact that another war was possible and that, if it came, they would all be in it. If bombers could attack this Guernica place what was to stop them dropping bombs on London? Or Paris? Or Amiens? Or anywhere else they wanted?

'It's a bad business,' his father said, mopping the last of the gravy from his plate with a chunk of bread. No good dwellin' on it, though. Only makes you morbid. I'm off up the pub for a quick one. You comin', Charlie?'

Best place, Charlie thought, and followed his father.

There was something unreal about their stroll to The Windmill that evening. As they crossed the road, sunset dropped grey-blue shadows across the familiar green and stained the sky pink above the chestnut trees – but the gentle colour made Charlie think of fires. There was a cheerful whirr of trams along Southside and the chirrup of small boys sailing their boats on the pond, but he was thinking; this could be destroyed – '*houses collapsing*', '*the smell of burning human flesh*', '*they bombed and bombed and bombed*'. As he walked into the pub, he found himself praying, Please God, don't let it happen here. Not in London. And certainly not in France.

In his kitchen in Boves, Old Joliot was holding forth about the Maginot Line. He had spread a map of Europe across the table and, using a broken bean stick as a pointer, he was lecturing his women.

'*Regardez*,' he commanded. 'Look at it, *mes petites. Formidable, n'est-ce-pas?*'

The three women looked at the map obediently, but they weren't paying attention. Ginny and Emily were thinking about the letters that had arrived for them that morning, Hortense was planning the next day's spring cleaning and although Cousin Berthe was hanging on his every word, her normally bland face ecstatic, she didn't understand what he was saying at all.

'If we've got to face the German army,' Old Joliot said, 'this is the way to do it. Underground, d'you see, in a series of forts. Impregnable. When I think of the trenches, how exposed we were. Terrible. All those poor boys. Two metres they'd go and then rat-a-tat-tat, blown to bits. Hands, legs, bits of bodies everywhere. Now look at this.' He traced the length of the line with his stick. 'Three hundred kilometres from end to end they say. D'you see? And now I show you pictures taken inside one of the forts. *Voilà!*'

Ginny examined the pictures – the rows of neat soldiers sitting bolt upright in trains no bigger than toys, the bright electric light, clean, concrete tunnels. But she was thinking, this isn't war. War was what was happening in Spain.

Mauricette had written to her that very morning with the news that it wasn't just Guernica that had been under attack. Madrid was being shelled, too. *'And still we won't help the Spanish government,'* she'd written angrily. *'It is an abomination.'* A demonstration was being organised. Her group was enraged, she said, absolutely enraged. As to herself . . . *'Oh, my dear friend, I am desolated. My dear fine Gérard is threatening to go to Spain to fight for the government. What if he were killed? I couldn't bear it. How can I persuade him against such idiocy? We've told him the group won't be able to function without him. He takes no notice.'*

Ginny wrote back by return to comfort her friend, but she couldn't think of anything to say to dissuade Gérard. *'Don't stop him, Mauricette,'* she wrote. *'If he wants to go, he will.'* Ten days later she was proved right.

Despite the war in Spain, it was a wonderful summer for the Holborn twins. At the beginning of May, Emily went to stay with Mauricette for a fortnight and, as he'd promised, Charlie came over for a long weekend every three weeks, throughout May and June (when he wasn't taking examinations) and, then, in July and August. The weather was miraculous. He and Ginny spent Saturday and Sunday in Boulogne, eating well, kissing whenever they wanted, which was very often indeed, and sleeping inches away from one another on either side of their chaste wall.

The strain this arrangement put on Charlie Commoner was formidable, but despite his frustration, he was proud of his ability to resist the ultimate temptation. At the end of August they planned to spend an entire holiday together. Fourteen whole days and nights! The thought of it made him ache with an exquisite combination of desire and hope.

Apart from his exams (and he really hadn't paid much attention to them) the only *real* snag that summer was that he never got any answers to his advertisements. He put one into every single local paper in every town he visited, and left stamped and addressed envelopes for the return of information. None ever came back. Every week he wrote to Mrs Everdale to report his lack of progress and her answers were always so patient and hopeful that he felt ashamed to be achieving nothing. Eventually it was the beginning of August and he had to confess to her that there was only Amiens left to visit.

'*I have been there before, as you know,*' he wrote, trying to be positive, '*but on that occasion I only advertised in two of the local papers and there are actually five of them. This time, I will place advertisements in every paper that is on sale. I have very good hopes of success in Amiens, considering that so many of Miss Babbacombe's postcards were posted there and I trust I shall be sending you good news very soon. I shall be away in France for two weeks on my summer holiday at the end of August but I will write to you from there should anything happen.*'

What actually happened was something he hadn't expected at all. In the first week of August the examination results were posted and he learned to his horror that he had failed two of the papers.

For the first time ever, Jack Bond had passed all his.

'Can't understand it, old thing,' he said. 'I thought it was a doddle. It must have been, for me to pass.'

'What will happen now?' Charlie said.

'Nothing much,' his friend reassured him. 'You'll probably have to re-sit. In November. That's what I've always done. Go and see Mr C. He'll tell you.'

Mr Crabbit was surprisingly sanguine. 'You made a right pig's ear of *that*,' he said cheerfully.

Charlie was still feeling pretty demoralised. 'Yes, sir. I know.'

'Happens to all of us at one time or another. Just make sure you pass the re-sits. That's all. Now how's the search for the Holborn twins coming along?'

'Not good,' Charlie said ruefully. 'There's only Amiens left.'

'Ah well, you'd better find them there, hadn't you?'

'Yes sir. I hope so.'

That night he wrote a long, miserable letter to Jeannie

269

telling her that he'd failed his exams, promising to pass them next time and assuring her that it wouldn't make all that much difference to the time they had to wait before they could get married. 'A few more months, that's all.'

He was very relieved when she wrote back to say how sorry she was to hear his news and that she was sure he'd pass the second time round – and, anyway, their holiday was the important thing. 'Fourteen whole days together. I can't wait.'

Ginny hadn't mentioned anything about his search for the heiresses, but that didn't concern him, because she rarely showed any interest in it. The holiday loomed so large in his dreams and his plans that it wasn't long before he'd forgotten about everything else, even the re-sits.

Actually Ginny was deliberately ignoring his search. After their silly row in Paris she'd decided to let him get on with it and meet him when the week's work was done and finished with. What were two stupid heiresses to her? They gave him the opportunity to travel to France at regular intervals and for that she was grateful to them. Otherwise they weren't important. What was worrying her was that she had told Maman that she was going to spend her summer holiday with Mauricette.

'It's terrible to be telling her lies,' she said to Emily. 'But what else could I do?'

'I wish we'd told her all about it at the beginning,' Emily said sadly.

'It's no good wishing that now,' Ginny said. 'We didn't. So we've got to find some way to break it to her gently.'

What could they say? They'd rehearsed all the alternatives over and over again that summer and none of them would do. One possibility was to tell Maman they had made friends with some English people – but they weren't supposed to talk or write to anyone from England. What if they said they had met some friends of Mauricette's? No, that would be a lie and it was no good starting a confession with a lie. And if they hinted that they thought they might be falling in love, that would provoke such a row it didn't bear thinking about.

In the end, they said nothing because Maman seemed determined not to give them the chance.

She agreed with Ginny, at once, that a holiday with Mauricette would be a very good thing. 'You go, *ma chérie*,' she said. 'You are twenty-one now. Years of discretion, *n'est-ce pas*? Even among your political friends I can trust you to behave well. *Eh bien*, we will all take a holiday this year. It will do us all good. Berthe and Emily and I will crop our little harvest in the early morning and then we'll rush through the housework, and after that we can sit in the sun all afternoon and be thoroughly idle. We won't listen to the radio and we won't read any newspapers. All they ever talk about is this wretched war, which is altogether too disagreeable. We'll sit in the sun and be peaceful.'

So it was all arranged. Ginny said goodbye to her family early on Saturday morning and half an hour later she and Charlie were travelling to Boulogne – and freedom.

Charlie had recovered his good spirits and was feeling very pleased with himself that morning. He'd been in Amiens all day Friday and hard at work. The advertisement was placed in every single local paper and would run in the weekend editions for the following two weeks. Stamped addressed envelopes had been left for the answers. He had done his very best for Mrs Everdale. Now, he thought, as he and Jeannie settled themselves as comfortably as they could on their wooden seats, there *must* be some answers. Somebody somewhere must see the name.

But the person who might have seen the name wasn't looking. A newspaper did infiltrate Old Joliot's cottage later that week, but it was wrapped around a bundle of rhubarb from the Advocate's garden – and Hortense was much too busy cutting the long red sticks into cubes to bother about reading advertisements.

# CHAPTER NINETEEN

The port of Boulogne was riding out a summer storm, the grey houses round the harbour stolid against a fury of green seas and white spume, their windows stabbed by needles of wind-hurled rain. On the hill above the town the black dome of Notre Dame basilica shone in the wet and the roofs of the old Ville Haute seemed to huddle under the menace of a sky heavy with cloud, which uncurled at visible speed and trailed long dark fringes whipped to tatters by the wind. Battling in to harbour with the morning's catch, the boats of the fishing fleet were tossed like corks on the heavy swell and the herring gulls, which usually followed them wheeling and screaming for fish, now rode the choppy water like battered flotsam. There was a pulse of elemental energy about the place, a sense that anything could happen, at any moment.

'Come on,' Charlie said, charging from the station. 'I don't know about you, but I could do with some breakfast. I'm starving.'

Cracking their coats like whips, the wind blew them straight to Madame Boulanger's. Madame was standing behind the counter chatting to the concierge from the tenement next door.

'Your lovers are returned, I see,' the concierge observed.

'For two weeks this time,' Madame said, watching them as they settled into their favourite corner.

'They love one another to distraction,' the concierge said. 'You have only to look at them to know that.'

'And yet they still sleep in separate rooms. Poor fools.'

'He is English, is he not?'

'More's the pity.'

'I understand you, Madame. If he were French there would be no such nonsense.'

'Indeed not.'

'The folly of love!' the concierge sighed. 'But who are we to argue with idealism?'

'They are ready to order,' Madame said, and eased her bulk from behind the counter. *'Bonjour M'sieur, Ma'moiselle.'*

*'Bonjour,'* Ginny said happily. 'Here we are again. At the same table.'

*'En vacances,'* Charlie said, trying out his French.

'The same table and the same rooms,' Ginny said.

*'Alors!'* Madame said. 'The same table. That is no problem. But as to the rooms, I am afraid they are not available. You may have them for the weekend, *comme d'habitude*, but during the week, they are reserved for my regulars.'

Ginny was so upset by the news that she could only echo Madame's words. 'Your regulars?'

'Commercial travellers, my dear,' Madame explained. 'They come to me month after month, you understand. There was a change of plan at the last minute, in consequence the rooms are needed this week. It is a great pity for you, I understand that. However all is not lost. There is still the front room, the one you and your mother rented. That is vacant for the next two weeks. You are more than welcome there.'

'What is it?' Charlie asked. Madame's French was too rapid for him to understand and he could see that Ginny was upset by what was being said.

Ginny explained in English. 'We can't have our usual rooms. She's offering us another one instead.'

'One?' Charlie said, thinking, My God! Are we going to share a room at last?

'It's got two beds,' Ginny hastened to explain. 'We could . . . I mean we needn't . . . What I mean is . . .'

'We'll see it,' Charlie said to Madame in French.

'Of course. When you are ready I will take you up. Enjoy your breakfast, Monsieur, Mademoiselle.'

Nothing had changed in the room. Even the wallpaper

273

was the same. Ginny remembered the pattern so well, the sharp pink rosebuds and those ghostly blue leaves. There were the same old sun-faded curtains, the same pink washbowl and ewer, the soap dish that didn't match, the single bed tucked into its corner, the double bed dominating the room, dominating her thoughts, paralysing her tongue.

Charlie was cheerfully in command. 'We will take it, Madame,' he said. And, feeling he ought to try to make the situation look respectable, '*Nous nous sommes fiancé.*'

'But of course,' Madame said, answering both his observations at the same time. 'There is no need to wait until midday. Not with this room. You may take occupation at once, if you wish.' And left them.

Ginny was still looking anxious.

'I can sleep in the single bed,' Charlie said, 'if you'd rather . . .'

'Yes,' she said, biting her lip. 'That would look better, wouldn't it.'

'Not that anyone's going to see,' he said, putting his arms round her.

'It's not that,' she said. 'It's just . . .'

'It's all right,' he said. 'I know what it is. Look you're quite safe with me.' And he kissed her to prove it.

'I wouldn't want anything to get back to Maman,' she said, between kisses.

'Well, it won't, so you can stop worrying. We're all on our own and we're going to be well behaved and sleep in separate beds. Yours is rather splendid, don't you think? Bit religious, though.'

She followed the direction of his gaze. 'It's only a crucifix.'

'Over the bed?'

'Yes. Why not? Lots of people have them there.'

'They don't in England. And what's this?' He was looking at the headboard.

'That's a stoup,' she explained, opening her case. 'For holy water. There's one on each side. Do you see?' And as he still looked puzzled. 'For when you say your prayers.'

He suddenly realised. 'You're a Catholic.'

She was hanging up her clothes in the wardrobe. 'Yes,' she said. 'Most people are. France is a Catholic country.'

'That's why you wear a cross.'

'Of course,' she said, touching her cross with her finger tips. 'Lots of women wear them.'

'So I've noticed,' he said wryly. 'My heiresses wear crosses, too. It's about the only thing we know about them. When I first started looking for them, I thought it would make them easier to find.'

'Not in a Catholic country.'

'No. Obviously.'

'You're *not* a Catholic, are you?' she said, walking back to the bed to put her arms about his neck.

'No,' he told her. 'Do you mind? Does it matter?'

The question felt dangerous, pulling them away from love and into problems she didn't want to think about. It would matter at some time. But not now. Not when they were so happy with each other. 'No,' she said.

'I suppose when we get married . . .' he said.

Remembering her mother's awful warning, '*You must never marry, you must never let a man love you . . .*' she interrupted him, knowing it would be risky to talk about marriage. There were problems enough without that. 'You've got extraordinary eyelashes,' she said, 'd'you know that? Like a horse.'

He pretended to be insulted. 'Well, thanks very much!'

'No really. They're so thick and long and absolutely straight.'

'Yours curl. Like your hair.'

So they were quickly and safely back into the delicious occupation of bestowing their entire attention on one another. After an hour or so, the storm abated and the sun came out from behind the clouds to remind them that it was August and a summer's day, so they went out to quench their thirst and to see what was on at the pictures. And the problems of marriage, Maman and the ecumenical divide were locked out, at least for the time being.

But there was another problem for them to face later on, and it was one they weren't expecting.

That night they lay in one another's arms in the luxuriance of their high double bed until the town clocks struck two.

'Time I went to my own bed, I suppose,' Charlie whispered into her hair.

'It is *really*,' she whispered back.

And four kisses later it *was* really. He tiptoed across the room in the moonlit darkness and struggled out of his trousers and into his pyjamas. 'Goodnight, my sweetheart,' he whispered and pulled back the counterpane on the single bed.

There was nothing else on the bed except the mattress and a pillow, no sheets, no blankets, not even a pillow case. 'Oh for heaven's sake!' he said.

Ginny sat up among her own tumbled bedding, large-eyed in the moonlight. 'What's up?' she whispered.

He came back to the high bed to tell her.

'Well, you'll have to sleep in here,' she said.

All night long, warm together under the blankets, flesh against flesh, and mouth to mouth, what rapturous impossible temptation! They kissed until they finally fell asleep with exhaustion, and they woke late in the morning to kiss again.

'We'll tell Madame about the bedding after breakfast,' Ginny said.

'How very remiss of me,' Madame said. 'I will attend to it.' But she was beaming at them as though they were congratulating her on a great success instead of reminding her of an oversight.

It was, as they told one another afterwards, a bit odd.

'Almost as if she'd done it deliberately,' Ginny said. 'You don't think she did, do you?'

Charlie said he didn't know. Privately, he didn't care. He was still dizzy after the temptation of their night together and secretly hoping that Madame wouldn't attend to it just yet, no matter what her motives.

The single bed was still bare that night. And the night afterwards. And by then they'd decided not to mention it to Madame again, because she was very busy. In any case they had grown too used to sleeping together to want to sleep apart.

If I can withstand *this*, Charlie thought, as they lay side by side on their fourth morning, with his arm under her neck and her head on his shoulder, I shall be a saint.

But a saint he was and remained, to Ginny's comfort and his own admiration.

Their fortnight lasted for ever and no time at all. Sunday was a perfect day, full of sunshine and the smell of the sea and herring gulls mewing. Neither of them went to church and neither of them felt guilty about it. They were on holiday and set apart from the pressures of the everyday world. They had been given time to talk and laugh and tease, to sit on the pavement and watch the world go by, to eat whatever they fancied, to spend the afternoon in one another's arms if they wanted to. And they did want to. Naturally.

The days merged one into the other. When the sun shone they went on outings, north to Wimereux or south to Le Touquet. When it rained they went to the cinema or dawdled over a leisurely meal. On the first Monday they rediscovered the Haute Ville, on the second they walked for miles along the sand dunes at Etaples. And they talked. There was so much to say, opinions and beliefs to be offered and accepted – because it was so important to have them accepted – feelings to be explored, dreams to be remembered and recounted, as love dizzied them, day after dazzled day.

At last, and too soon, it was their third Saturday and their very last night together. Now there was a bitter-sweet quality to their kisses. They lay wrapped in one another's arms, with nothing more between them than the flimsy cotton of her petticoat. The ache of his desire made him groan. 'My sweet, sweetheart.'

She had never seen him in such a state and was filled with pity for him. 'I do love you, Charlie. So much.'

277

'Oh!' he groaned. 'Let me in. I can't bear this a minute longer. I want you so much. Let me in, Jeannie.'

'Is it so bad?' she asked, kissing him.

The length and ferocity of his kiss was answer enough. I can't say no to him, she thought, as the kiss went on, lifting her to anguished pleasure. Not now, not when we've gone so far, not on our last night. It would be cruel to stop now. She knew, somewhere in the recesses of her mind, that it would be a sin, that it might lead to *that* illness, that her entire upbringing was against it, but her judgement was swollen by sensation and confused by pity. The kiss was ending, he was lifting his mouth from hers, panting, his eyes enormous.

'Yes,' she said, making up her mind quickly, before she could think any further. 'Yes.' She was frantic, determined, afraid and passionate, all at the same time.

'You mean it?'

'Yes. I do.'

'Oh my sweet, sweet, sweetheart.' He was all instinct, thrusting and thrusting, groaning into an extreme of pleasure. 'My sweet, sweetheart.'

Perversely, Ginny's desire receded the minute she'd made her decision, as if the word 'yes' had thrown her senses into reverse. Then it was all over so quickly that she had no time to think or to react. Or to enjoy it. When he fell away from her, rapturously spent, she felt nothing, until her emotions boiled over into tears she couldn't control.

He was very upset. 'Jeannie, sweetheart, what's the matter? I didn't hurt you, did I?'

'No, no,' she wept. It's just . . . Oh! I don't know what it is.'

Riven with compassion and guilt, he took her in his arms again and kissed her wet cheeks, stroking her hair out of her eyes. 'My sweetest heart,' he said. 'Don't cry. You mustn't cry.'

She was feeling even more guilty than he was. 'It was a sin,' she wept. 'We've committed a sin.'

'No, it wasn't,' he said forcefully. 'We haven't. That's old-fashioned nonsense and you're not to think it. We've just started our married life before the priest gave us permission, that's all. Lots of people do *that*. It's not a sin. It's natural.' But Ginny continued to cry. 'Look, when we're married we'll do it whenever we like and it won't be a sin then, will it? So what's the difference?'

'We're not married.'

'We will be. The minute I've passed my exams and got a position.'

Ginny's tears still flowed. She was overwhelmed by fears; that someone would find out, that she would be ill, that she'd made herself cheap, that she might have a baby, and worse than any of the others, that he wouldn't love her any more. 'You promise?'

'I don't have to promise,' he said. 'You *know* I'll marry you. Especially now. We belong together for ever.'

Such a passionate declaration made her feel marginally better. But there was still the illness and Maman's warning.

'What is it?' he said, stroking her damp hair. 'Is there something else? You must tell me, Jeannie. I can't bear to see you cry.'

So she told him about the illness. It took a long time because there was a lot to tell, about Maman's warning in the cemetery, about how frightened she was, about how awful it was not to know whether it was true or not. 'She said it would start if we fell in love,' she said. 'As long as we kept away from men we would be all right, but if we fell in love, made love . . . So you see . . .'

'I never heard such tripe in all my life,' he said.

'Tripe?'

'Rubbish, nonsense, tripe.'

'Then you don't think it's true?' Oh, how sensible he was and how reassuring.

' 'Course it's not true. It's a load of rubbish. Think about it. If there really was an illness that made people ill if they made love, nobody would ever make love. And you'd certainly hear about it. It would be in all the papers.'

'Then why did she say it?'

'To frighten you off, I should think. Mothers do funny things sometimes.'

279

'You really don't think there *is* an illness?'

'No. I don't. So you can stop worrying.'

She wasn't entirely convinced, but it was reassurance enough to stem her tears. 'Oh Charlie,' she said. 'I do love you.'

'Get some sleep,' he advised drowsily. 'Tomorrow is the first day of our married life.'

It was also the day they would have to part. Although they spun out every minute of their precious time, making love whenever they could, and with increasing skill and increasing gratification, there were only twelve hours between their waking and the departure of the Channel ferry. They walked to the quay arm in arm, and Ginny wept as they said goodbye.

'I'll come back as soon as ever I can,' Charlie promised, kissing her for the last time. 'I'll start saving the minute I get back to the office.'

'I can't bear to let you go,' she said tearfully. 'When will you come back, Charlie? It will be soon, won't it?'

'A fortnight,' he promised, knowing it would probably be impossible but too torn by parting to be truthful. 'Three weeks at the outside.'

'I shall miss you so much,' she said. She was missing him already. 'Why must you go? Couldn't you stay here and get a job in Amiens?'

'I can't get a job anywhere until I'm qualified. You know that really, don't you, my sweetheart. But it won't be long before I am. Truly. I'll soon pass my exams and then it'll all be different. Look, it's nearly time for the off. I shall have to go.'

They kissed for the last time. And for the last time. And for the truly last time with more anguish than pleasure. Then he was running into the customs shed, his long legs straight and quick as scissors. He looked back once to wave and to blow a kiss. Then he was gone.

Bleak with loss, Ginny walked back to Madame Boulanger's as slowly as she could. The weight of her situation pressed down on her shoulders. Now she would have to think about what they were going to do next, about facing Maman, about whether they would ever be allowed to marry, about whether the illness really *was* nonsense. Without Charlie's cheerful determination, the world was suddenly a very difficult place indeed. And it was raining again.

# CHAPTER TWENTY

By the time Charlie got back to Abbeville Road on Monday evening, he'd made up his mind to tell his mother about Jeannie. Grandpa already knew, of course, and it was more than likely that Dad had a vague idea something was going on. The old feller was too shrewd not to have put two and two together after all those trips to France. But you had to spell things out to Mum, whom he ought to have told weeks ago to get her used to the idea. Still not to worry, he would tell her now. Wouldn't she be bucked!

He was a bit put out when he let himself into the hall to find an empty house. The table was laid for one and there was a note in his mother's handwriting propped up against the clock.

'Gone to Fred's fiftieth,' it said. 'Shan't be late back. Your supper is in the oven.'

It was cottage pie, which was his usual Monday evening supper. Obviously it had been waiting for him rather a long time because the crust had dried out into sharp peaks of brown-edged mashed potato. After sixteen days of French cooking it was distinctly unappetising. Charlie ate as much of it as he could and still felt hungry. He toyed with the idea of going out for some chips and decided against it – just in case they came back while he was out. After all, Mum *had* said they wouldn't be late.

In fact, it was nearly midnight by the time the four revellers came tumbling into the house. Wearing paper hats and rosy with beer, they were so full of the party (what a good time they'd had and how it had done them all a power of good) that he couldn't get a word in edgeways. It wasn't until Mum had made a pot of tea and they were all settled in the kitchen with a steaming cup and a cigarette that he got a chance to say anything, and then he blurted out his news in a rush which put eyebrows up all round the room.

'I'm thinking of getting married,' he said.

His father grinned at him. 'Bit sudden innit?'

'No,' Charlie parried. 'Not really. I've known her a long time. More than a year. Since last July.'

'Who is she?' Ruby wanted to know, not quite sure how to take this news. There had been no sign of a girlfriend – she would have noticed. Perhaps he was going to turn out to be a kidder like his father and, if that was the case, it might be a joke. 'Do we know her?'

The answer was straight and serious. 'No. She's French. I met her in Amiens. Her name's Jeannie Lisieux.'

That was a shock to poor Ruby and she couldn't disguise it. 'Oh Charlie!' she said, her voice falling.

'She's lovely,' Charlie said, springing to Jeannie's defence. 'You'll love her. I'll get her to come over and you'll see.' To be rebuffed when he'd expected congratulation made him feel uncomfortable and angry.

'You don't wanna marry a Froggie,' Grace said, smugly. 'Horrible lot, the Froggies.'

Charlie rounded on her. 'Well that's where you're wrong!' he said. 'They're a darn sight more civilised than we are.'

'Hang on a minute,' Stan intervened, keenly aware of Ruby's agitation. 'Let's take this one step at a time. You was talking about getting married.'

'Yes,' Charlie said stubbornly.

'When, might I ask?'

'Soon as I can. Before Christmas.'

Stan's next question was instant and blunt. 'You ain't got 'er into trouble 'ave yer?'

'No,' Charlie said, outraged – and also alarmed. 'What a thing to say!' And what a worse thing to think! My God! It *could* be true. He must write to Jeannie and ask her. If he could find the words.

His father was talking quietly. '. . . That's all right then. So what's the rush?'

'I love her.'

'No doubt you do,' Stan agreed, 'but you got a career to think of, too, don't forget that. You ought to qualify yourself first before you start thinking a' getting married. You're still articled, don't forget. You still got those exams to pass.'

'I'll pass them this time, you'll see.'

'And then you'll need to get yourself a job.'

'That's right,' Ruby put in. 'Anyway, don't you think you're a bit young for all that sort of thing.'

'All what sort of thing?'

'Settling down, paying rent, keeping a wife. It don't come cheap, you know, Charlie.'

'Quite right,' Grace said, sniggering at him, false teeth much in evidence. 'You're too young.'

'I don't think so,' Charlie said, stubbing out his cigarette. 'And anyway what's "young"? Tom Kelly's been married a year and he's younger than me.'

'Twenty-one!' Grace said. 'That's young. Twenty-one like you are. Twenty-one an' apprenticed. Watcher gonna use fer money, you an' this Froggie o' yours?'

Charlie could feel anger stirring in his chest. This wasn't the way he'd expected his family to take his news. All carp and criticism. What was the matter with them? He stood up. 'All right then,' he said, towering above them. 'I'll show you who's too young. I'll hand in my notice. Get a proper job. Work in France somewhere. I don't have to stay tied to Mr Hedgethorn for ever.'

Ruby was so appalled she said the first thing that came into her head. 'You can't do *that*, Charlie. It'd be wicked. Don't you even think it. Not after all the money we've . . .'

Stan was sending her warning signals as strongly as he could. But the truth was out. It was too late.

'What money?' Charlie said, feeling suddenly cold.

Ruby tried to backtrack. 'Nothing. It's nothing. Don't mind me.'

'What money?'

It was Grandpa who enlightened him. 'Your fees, mate,' he said. 'It's no good, Ruby. You'll 'ave to tell him now.

284

Entrance fees fer a start, so's they'd take you on. Then exam fees. That's what she's on about.'

'I thought . . . there was a grant, wasn't there?' Charlie stammered. He felt deflated; thinking, But I should have worked that out. How did they hide it from me?

'That don't cover fees,' Grace said, sucking her teeth and ignoring Stan's scowls. 'Why d'yer think they took us as lodgers.'

Charlie sat down, miserably. 'Is it true?' he asked his father. He didn't really need confirmation. Of course, it was true.

'We was going to tell you when you qualified,' Stan explained. 'We thought it all out, yer Mum an' me.'

'You've been paying for me.'

Ruby put a commiserating hand on his arm. 'Only the fees. To get you started. An' the exams, of course. We couldn't turn up a chance like that, how could we, Charlie? Not for a few bob here an' there.'

'But it's not a few bob here and there,' Charlie said. 'It couldn't possibly be. It must be hundreds of pounds, when you tot it all up. How much did you have to pay to get them to take me on?'

'Don't you worry yer head about that,' Stan said, taking his packet of Weights out of his pocket. 'You was well worth it. 'Nother fag?'

'No thanks,' Charlie said absently. Hundreds and hundreds of pounds. He'd have to repay it. There was no hope of getting married now. Not till that was done. 'I'll pay it back,' he promised. 'Every penny.'

'No need for that son,' Stan said.

But it was a matter of pride and Charlie insisted. 'I'll pay it back,' he said. 'The minute I'm qualified and earning I'll pay back every penny. And I'll pay back my exam fees, too. I'm twenty-one, for God's sake. I can't have you paying for me all this time. I'm not a child. You should have told me. I'll get an evening job to cover November's fees for a start.'

How was he going to explain the situation to Jeannie? And just at the very moment when they ought to be getting married. He couldn't think how to begin. Life could be bloody difficult sometimes. Why, oh why, hadn't he taken a grip on what it cost to train?

As soon as he got home from work the following day he went job hunting for something he could do in the evenings or early mornings. The best that was offered was part-time barman at the Windmill pub on the Common. The hours were long and the pay poor but the landlord seemed an amiable man who said he didn't mind if his new barman were to miss the odd weekend, when his firm sent him abroad. 'Only don't make a habit of it, son, that's all. Start tonight.'

This time last week, Charlie thought as he walked home across the Common, I was with Jeannie in Boulogne and I hadn't got a care in the world. The chestnut trees that lined the Common were still heavy with summer foliage but their leaves were beginning to turn yellow. Charlie eyed them. That, he thought, is what responsibility does for you. What on earth am I going to say to Jeannie?

In the end, after much thought and several false starts, Charlie simply told her how much he loved her, and promised that he would be back in France as soon as he'd saved up the fare, '*which won't take too long because I've got myself a part-time job in a pub to supplement my grant.*' Even with exams to revise for and a debt to pay, one trip to Boulogne was permissable. He had to see her again. Just once. He'd promised.

It took him till the end of the month to save up the fare. By that time, he had grown accustomed to hard work behind the bar, had got the names of most brands of spirits off pat, could remember the preferences of his regulars and knew how to roll beer barrels without making his back ache. But he hadn't told Jeannie about his awful discovery about the fees, nor summoned up the courage to ask her if she was pregnant, although he *had* asked her if she was '*all right*' adding, '*I wouldn't want anything bad to happen to you as a result of our holiday.*'

Ginny wrote back by return of post to say that she was

quite all right, except that she was missing him dreadfully. Charlie wasn't reassured. She might not have understood what he'd really been asking. The trouble was, important things simply had to be said face to face – and they had to be said very, very carefully.

Throughout the journey across the Channel he rehearsed his story, struggling to find the best form of words, the least upsetting, the clearest, the most loving. Especially the most loving, because he couldn't bear to think he might hurt her. It kept him awake all night.

But the minute he saw her, stepping down from the train in that familiar blue coat and that daft lopsided hat of hers, he forgot every word he'd prepared and simply leapt forward to gather her in a bear hug and kiss her again and again. And her first words to him drove all his careful plans right out of his head.

'Oh Charlie,' she said, her arms twined about his neck, 'you do still love me.'

'I should just think I do!' he said. Then he stopped because he could see that she was relieved. 'Well, for heaven's sake! You didn't think I'd stop, did you?'

'I didn't know,' she confessed. 'After . . . you know . . . I wondered. Maman always told us men didn't like women once they'd made love to them.'

'Your Maman doesn't half tell you some daft things,' he said. 'Let's get to Madame Boulanger's and I'll show you how much I love you.'

Madame Boulanger welcomed them like old friends. Their double room was ready, the sun was shining, the baguettes crisp from the oven, the coffee piping hot. They were back in their own magical world.

And magic it was: a rush and tumble of warm limbs, half-discarded clothes, eager mouths and the all pleasurable, mind-stopping, undeniable urgency of desire. But, for all that, still a lopsided magic.

Afterwards, while Charlie lay sprawled across the bed, wonderfully contented and drowsy, Ginny got up and poured water into the washbasin. She'd left the house so early that morning she hadn't had time to wash and she needed the comfort of a familiar routine. She had been puzzling over their lovemaking since their holiday, not just because she was afraid they'd been committing a sin, but because she'd been so unsatisfied. Now, after yearning for him all these weeks and counting the days until they could be together again, she was still dissatisfied – restless, fidgety and unsure of herself. There has to be more to lovemaking than this, she thought, splashing soap from her face. Veronique vowed it was the greatest pleasure in life and seemed sure about it even though she had never tried it! It can't be right to feel so . . . well, peculiar afterwards. Charlie doesn't. He looks really pleased with himself. It surprised her to realise that she was envying her lover. Sighing she put the soap neatly back in the soap dish and picked up her towel from the rail.

'What's up?' Charlie asked.

She turned to smile at him, her olive skin glowing against the white cotton of her towel, her eyes very dark. 'Nothing.'

'You're all right, aren't you? I mean, you're not pregnant or anything like that?' He should have asked her that before they went to bed, but, at that point, it hadn't entered his head. He had only just remembered to use the 'johnny' he'd brought with him.

'I'm not pregnant,' she assured him. 'No.'

'You're sure.'

'Quite sure.'

'Then what is it?'

'I don't know. I feel sort of – well, restless, I suppose. Not satisfied.'

'As if you'd like us to start again.'

'Well yes,' she admitted. 'But you couldn't, could you. Not after . . .'

'Try me,' he said, daring her.

Her desire jumped to full strength. 'What now?'

'Yes. Now. Come back here. Or have I got to come and get you?'

This time he was less quick, she was more relaxed and

288

they were both rewarded. Her pleasure was so surprising and so extreme it made her catch her breath. And the little rapturous sounds tumbled Charlie into a second onrush which surpassed the first. This time they both slept afterwards.

Mutual pleasure shed sunlight over the entire weekend. They could hardly bear to be out of one another's arms. They sat side by side to eat their meals, strolled about the town with his arm round her waist, climbed the stairs to the delights of their room, hand in amorous hand.

Sunday evening came far too soon for both of them. Charlie still hadn't told Ginny his news. It wasn't until they were packing that the subject came up – and then it was in quite the wrong way.

'I can't bear for you to go,' she said, watching him as he fastened his case.

'No,' he said. 'Nor can I.'

'When will you come back?'

'Well . . .'

'Next weekend,' she suggested. 'Why not? You could borrow the fare from your grandfather, couldn't you? Oh, do say you could.'

'Well no,' he confessed. 'I couldn't.'

'Why not?'

Charlie told her the whole story. 'I'm really sorry about all this, Jeannie, but you see how it is. I can't spend any more money on fares until I've got a position and I can't get a position until I've passed these exams, and I shan't be sitting the exams until November. I shall just have to stay in London and swot hard until they're over. It's horrid, but we've got to accept it.'

'It isn't horrid,' Ginny said, anger rising. 'It's cruel. Say you don't mean it, Charlie.'

'I can't. I've got to mean it.'

'You can't leave me all alone until November.'

'It's only a few weeks,' he said, keeping calm because he was beginning to understand it was the best way to cope with these sudden rages of hers.

'November,' she yelled at him. 'That's months.'

'Only two.'

'What am I supposed to do for two months? Tell me that.'

'I'm sorry,' he said, speaking firmly and looking her straight in the eye. 'It can't be helped. Oh look, Jeannie, you must understand. I've got to pass this time or they won't take me into the firm. You don't want me to fail, do you? Not after all this time. It's only a few weeks, really it is, and then I shall be qualified and the firm will take me on and I can start to earn good money and pay off all the debts, and then we can get married. I've got to be sensible.'

'Sensible' was the wrong word to use to Ginny in her present mood. 'I don't want to be sensible,' she said. 'I want to be with you.'

'Yes. So do I. But we really *do* have to wait. I must pay them back. You *can* see that, can't you?'

'So meanwhile I just sit round twiddling my thumbs,' she said flouncing away from him. 'I spend half my life in trains coming to see you, I hope you realise, and the other half just waiting about. I'm always waiting. Always. That's all I ever do. I never get what I want, I just wait for things.'

'Don't exaggerate.'

'I'm not exaggerating.'

'All right then, what things?'

'Trains, trams, letters, someone to stop this damn war in Spain, you to make up your damn mind. It's all very well saying we'll get married. You never say when. You can't make up your mind.' She was being unfair and she knew it, but misery at their parting, and anger at his news, had upset her too much.

'That's not fair!' he said, stung to anger despite himself. 'I *have* made up my mind. How many more times have I got to tell you? We're going to get married. You know that perfectly well.'

'Do I?' Yes, of course she did, but she couldn't back down now. Not in the middle of a row.

'Yes, you do. So don't talk rubbish.'

'I'm talking rubbish now, am I?'

There was only one way to stop her, and now that he'd lived with her for a fortnight he knew what it was. He sprang at her, grabbed her by the shoulders and kissed her fiercely. 'Don't – talk – rubbish,' he said, between kisses.

She kissed him back equally fiercely. 'I hate all this waiting,' she said, 'all this being apart. I want us to be together all the time.'

'I know,' he soothed, kissing her anger away. 'So do I. It won't be for long, my sweetheart. It's only till November.'

'You promise?' she said, putting her arms round his neck.

'I promise. I'll be back here on the second weekend in November. Honest Injun.'

The odd phrase made her smile again. 'What?'

'Honest Injun,' he explained. 'It means I promise, I promise, I promise.'

'It's such a long time,' she said.

'It'll soon pass,' he reassured them both, 'if we keep busy.'

There was plenty to keep them busy. The very next morning a rush of cases arrived at Hedgethorn and Crabbit. And on Wednesday an international conference began in London that was to keep Ginny politically active for weeks.

The civil war in Spain had been going badly for the Spanish government. They still held Madrid, but General Franco's Moors and Legionnaires had captured Badajoz and slaughtered hundreds of their disarmed opponents in the local bull ring. Naturally, after such a massacre, Ginny and her friends expected their own Popular Front government to send more aid to the Spanish *Fronte Popular*. So when they read that delegates from the French and British governments were to meet in London to discuss 'the Spanish situation' they were sure that help would soon be on its way. The announcement made at the end of the conference was so dreadful that they couldn't believe their ears. The two governments had actually agreed not to send arms to either side.

'*It's wicked!*' Ginny wrote furiously to Charlie, her pen spattering ink. '*Hitler and that foul Mussolini are sending*

*Franco every damn thing he needs. There are forty thousand Italian troops in Spain now, and all helping General Franco, naturally. Nobody does anything to stop them. They're too busy having conferences about not selling arms or piracy, as if that's relevant. Who cares about piracy when the fascists have taken Santander?*

*Gérard is right in the thick of it. I had a letter from Mauricette yesterday. She is very cross and very worried about him.*

*I wish I could see you. November is a long way away. Your ever loving "Jeannie" XXX.'*

Old Joliot was the only one who had a good word to say for his government. 'Anything's better than fighting,' he growled. 'We had enough of that last time. If they can stop people sending guns out there, then so they should. That's what I say. Quite right.'

Over in Wolverhampton Claud Everdale didn't agree with him at all.

'Damn stupid lot of nonsense,' he said to Agnes. 'Just think of the business this is going to cost us. What were they thinking of? They must have been out of their minds.'

'I think the object of the exercise,' Agnes said mildly, 'was to try to stop the war.'

'Stop the war!' Claud mocked. 'This won't stop the war and they needn't think it. If we don't arm them someone else will.'

'I hope it won't prevent that young man going over to France for us,' Agnes said to Miss Babbacombe, later that day. 'It makes you wonder what will happen next, doesn't it, with all this going on.'

'Perhaps they'll have an armistice if they can't get any guns,' Miss Babbacombe said.

Agnes sighed. 'I'm beginning to think *I* ought to stop this search,' she said, gazing sadly out of the drawing room window at the dahlias shaking shaggy heads in the long border. 'After all that effort in the summer, I really did think we'd get some sort of response. It's as if they've disappeared from the face of the earth.'

'Never say die!' Miss Babbacombe said brightly, from among the teacups. 'We'll find 'em sooner or later. You'll see.'

'You're so confident,' Agnes sighed, with a mixture of envy and depression.

'There's no good looking on the black side, is there?'

'It's disheartening though,' Agnes said. 'All that effort and not a thing to show for it.' To say nothing of the money it was costing in legal fees and fares. What Claud would say when he found out about that, she quailed to think. He was in a bad enough mood without having bills to annoy him. 'And then there's all this trouble with that awful gun.'

'What awful gun was that?'

'Oh some gun of Claud's. He's been on about it for ages. A sort of rifle. Anti-tank or something like that. Mr Pennyfield's been running trials with the first ones off the line and they are all faulty. He says they're too dangerous to use. He wants me to persuade Claud to stop production.' She sighed to think how totally impossible *that* was.

'If I were you,' Miss Babbacombe advised, 'I'd go away for a nice little autumn holiday and forget all about it.'

'What would be the good?' Agnes said, more sadly than ever. 'Where would I go? More to the point, who would I go with?'

'Haven't you got any relations?' Miss Babbacombe asked, remembering her own happy trips to Margate every summer.

'Yes,' Agnes said, giving Miss Babbacombe a wry smile, 'but I can't find them.'

There was a despondency everywhere that autumn. Only Emily was unaffected by it and, despite distant wars and local squabbles, she remained her usual contemplative self, patiently enduring whatever came her way, saying her prayers, doing the housework and waiting for Ken's letters, which came with dependable regularity. They were dull letters, and sometimes Ginny found herself yawning while she was reading them and resorted to pretending she was tired so as not to hurt Em's feelings.

Even the card Ken sent to say he was coming to France at last '*on the overnight boat on Saturday*' was written in the same uninspired manner. And Emily received the news with her usual calm, simply saying, 'Yes. I see.'

That evening she felt her way down to the station to meet her sister, and they walked home together in the twilight.

'Read the whole thing,' she ordered. 'From start to finish. I want to hear every word.'

So, when they reached the crossroads, they came to a halt and the card was read out again – with some difficulty because it was getting dark. But it was listened to with total attention.

*'Dear Emily,*
*Everything has gone according to plan. Profits are rising. Completion date is Thursday. I shall travel to Boulogne on the overnight boat on Saturday, bringing everything necessary with me. Please meet me on Sunday in the basilica for second mass. All other news will keep until I see you. The goddess will be soon in her bower. Yours, Frog.'*

No, Ginny decided, it couldn't be a love letter. It was too unemotional. It didn't begin to compare with the sort of things she and Charlie were writing to one another. 'Will you go?' she asked.

'Yes,' Emily replied, as they continued up the road. 'If you'll come with me. Will you, Ginny?' It was important to have Ginny with her, just in case she and Ken . . . because it was likely that she . . .

'Do you want me to?' Ginny asked. 'I thought you were getting good at travelling on your own.'

'Yes. I *do* want you to. Very much. Will you come?'

'Of course,' Ginny said. 'If that's the way it is.' A dreadful thought struck her. 'What are we going to tell Maman?'

'Leave that to me,' Emily said. 'I'll do it. But not a word till Sunday. Promise?'

294

'Yes of course.' This was beginning to sound quite exciting. Perhaps it was going to turn out to be a proper love affair after all, despite all those boring letters. 'What do you think he'll . . .'

Emily didn't give her the chance to finish the question. 'We must hurry up,' she said. 'It's getting cold.'

As they brisked back to the house, Ginny watched her sister's face for signs of excitement and couldn't find any. Her cheeks seemed redder than usual, but that could have been the chill air, and there was an unfamiliar tension to her shoulders but that could have been because they were walking so quickly. The only thing that was quite certain was that Emily wasn't going to say anything else about the letter. The set of her mouth made that quite clear. So nothing else was said.

During the next few days the twins went to work as usual and Ken's letter was hidden away as if it had been forgotten. On Sunday morning, when Old Joliot had already left for Mass and Maman and Cousin Berthe were putting on their hats and coats and 'making themselves presentable', Emily surprised them both by announcing that she and Ginny were going to mass in Boulogne.

'And what's wrong with Boves, might I ask?' Maman said, pausing with her hatpin halfway to her head.

'Nothing's wrong with it, Maman,' Emily said coolly. 'We're going to mass with a friend in Boulogne, that's all.'

'What friend in Boulogne?' Maman said, easing the pin through the crown of her hat. 'I hope you're not turning to politics like your sister. One politician in the family is a sufficiency, let me tell you.'

'No, no, Maman,' Emily said, still admirably cool. 'This time it's a friend of mine. Someone I met in Paris. Nothing to do with politics, I assure you.'

'The clock's ticking,' Cousin Berthe said, looking at it anxiously. 'Mustn't be late!'

So, although Hortense was vaguely alarmed by this sudden change in their routine and Ginny was prickly with fear of a row, nothing more was said. The four women parted with kisses on the doorstep and went their separate ways. It had all been so calmly done that Ginny found it hard to believe.

'Weren't you afraid she might ask you who it was?' she said to Emily, when they were out of earshot.

'No,' Emily said.

'What would you have done if she had?'

'I would have told her.'

That was a great surprise, especially after all the conversations they'd had about how and when and whether. 'You wouldn't!'

'Oh, yes,' Emily said. 'I talked to Father André about it and I've been praying about it for ages. I knew what I had to do. It was quite simple really. I had to answer any question she asked me with the truth. Is that the train coming?'

'You're amazing!' Ginny said. 'After all this, you just up and say, "I'm off to Boulogne, Maman, to see a friend" as if it was nothing, and she lets you go. I don't believe it.'

Emily began to giggle. 'I don't quite believe it myself,' she said. 'Oh dear, Ginny, am I being wicked?'

'No,' Ginny said stoutly. 'You're not. You love him. Why shouldn't you see him? I'm dying to see him myself.' There must be something extra special about a man who could turn her twin into someone capable of being devious.

But it was to take a little time before they met. They arrived at Boulogne after the second mass had begun, and being late-comers, they had to creep into the back of the basilica behind a pillar where they had a very poor view of what was going on. So Ken Hopkirk wasn't able to find them until the mass was over and the congregation was filing towards the door. He approached them slowly, edging his way along the empty pew as delicately as he could for his size, calling to her, 'Emily! Emily!'

Emily turned at the sound of his voice and the rapturous smile on her face quite took her sister's breath away. 'My dear!' she said.

She *does* love him, Ginny thought. Then, as Ken came into view, surprise gave way to something more like shock.

After Charlie's blond good looks, this man was ugly, large and shambling and awkward, with a horrible lumpy face all nose and chin. And going bald, too. Oh Em! she thought, you could have done better for yourself than that.

He held Emily's outstretched hands and bent to kiss her. A chaste kiss, Ginny noticed, which simply brushed Emily's forehead. 'You got here safely,' he said.

'My sister brought me,' Emily said, reaching out for Ginny with her free hand.

'I'm very pleased to meet you,' he said, looking Ginny straight in the eye and smiling.

Perversely, far from placating her, the smile increased Ginny's initial dislike. She was cool to him, holding out her hand but saying, 'How do you do?' in a polite, distant voice.

'I can see you're twins,' he said.

What a fatuous thing to say. 'Well obviously,' she said, shrugging her shoulders and giving him a pitying look.

'I hope we shall be friends,' he said and, tucking Emily's hand in the crook of his arm, led her from the church. The gesture made Ginny feel jealous. That was her job, not his. But she tried to be diplomatic.

'Is there any reason why we shouldn't be?'

'Well,' he smiled. 'I shouldn't like you to think I was taking your sister away from you.'

As if you could, Ginny thought, a great, ugly, clumsy thing like you. 'Oh I don't think that's likely,' she said. 'Do you, Em?'

'Is there somewhere we could get something to eat?' Emily asked, cuddling against him. 'I'm hungry. We've got time for a meal, haven't we, Ken?'

Why ask him? Ginny thought crossly. Of course we've got time. 'How about Madame Boulanger's?' she said.

They set off towards the quayside and Madame Boulanger's. And got rather wet because a sharp rain was beginning to fall.

It seemed odd to Ginny to be sitting in that familiar crowded café with her sister and this ugly foreign man. But the meal was good and they ordered a bottle of *ordinaire* to

297

wash it down; although Ken spent the entire time talking about his factory and the bungalow he'd just bought, it was pleasant enough.

But, when Madame had served coffee (and told the twins how pleasant it was to see them both again), the ugly man ⁻⁻d something that stopped all pleasure at once. He took a ₃ritish passport out of his pocket and placed it in Emily's hand.

'I got it,' he said. 'All signed and sealed and legal.' He guided Emily's fingers over the wax seal and watched while she explored it in her delicate way. 'You can travel whenever you like.'

'That's not your passport,' Ginny said.

'Yes, it is,' Emily replied, still exploring it. 'I filled in all the forms in the summer when I went to stay with Mauricette. It's my passport. Emily Holborn, British citizen.'

'You're not going to England, surely?' Ginny cried. What would Maman say? If there was one thing Hortense could not contemplate, it was the thought of either of them having anything to do with England.

But Emily was smiling. 'Yes,' she said, holding her lover's hand. 'I am. I should have told you before, but I wasn't sure until now.'

Ken Hopkirk kissed her fingers. 'And you *are* sure now?' he said.

'Yes,' Emily said, and her voice sounded breathless.

'Quite sure?'

'Quite, quite sure. I shall travel back with you this afternoon.'

Ginny was so shocked she said the first thing that came into her head. She spoke in French for privacy. 'You can't do that, Em. What about poor Maman? You just can't rush off like that.'

'I've made up my mind, Ginny. I've thought and thought. It isn't sudden.'

'But you're not going this afternoon.'

'Yes. I am. It's my one great chance. Oh Ginny, you must

understand. I love him. He loves me. We're going to get married.' Her sister was silent with distress. 'If I stay here, Ginny, I shall never be anything more than a servant, living with Maman for ever and ever. I shall never get another chance, never be loved. Haven't I got a right to be loved? Like other women?'

'We love you.'

'Yes, yes, I know you do. But to be loved and married. You must see how important that is, you of all people. What if I were to say you weren't to marry Charlie? Think how you'd feel.'

That was an unanswerable argument. 'Oh Em,' Ginny said, and threw her arms around her sister's neck and burst into tears.

And naturally Emily wept with her. It was some minutes before they could recover themselves and Ken waited patiently, handkerchief at the ready.

The conversation became practical. And English.

'Will you tell Maman for me?' Emily asked. 'I thought of writing her a letter but that would be too cold, wouldn't it. As if I didn't love her.'

'Do you love her?'

'Yes, yes, of course. More than ever now. You must tell her so. I don't want to hurt her, Ginny. I wouldn't want her to think . . .'

'I'll tell her,' Ginny said, promising valiantly, although her heart sank at the very idea.

'You're the dearest sister anyone could have.'

'You didn't bring any luggage,' Ginny said, blinking the last of her tears away. 'What will you do for clothes?'

Emily turned to her lover. 'There are clothes waiting for me in the bungalow, aren't there, Ken?'

'Everything you could need,' he said, and even to Ginny's prejudiced eye his expression was most loving. 'You needn't worry, Ginny. I'll look after her, I promise you. I've had the bungalow fitted out with rails along every wall so that she can find her way about. I've got a maid coming in every day while I'm at work. There are tradesmen to deliver the shopping. We've got a telephone. She'll be well looked after. Really!'

'Yes,' Ginny said. 'I can see that.' And she could, despite her misgivings.

'I'll write to you as soon as I arrive,' Emily promised. 'Send you my address and everything.'

That sounded like a farewell. 'You're not going just yet,' Ginny said, and her voice was stricken with distress.

'In about half an hour,' Ken Hopkirk told her.

So soon, Ginny thought, and it seemed to her that her whole body was lurching into grief. 'Oh Em!'

They walked to the quayside arm in arm and kissed goodbye most lovingly. It was all a bit unreal. And exquisitely painful. As Ginny watched her sister walking away her grief was so acute, she felt as though she was watching her die. Now she wished they'd given her their address before they left. I should have insisted on it, she thought, the minute I knew Emily was going. But it was too late to call them back. Much, much too late.

She stood on the cold quay with the wind scattering rain against her face and whipping the skirt of her old blue coat like a flag, and she felt horribly alone. To make matters worse, her grief was compounded by fear of what Maman would say. Oh, poor, poor Maman, she thought. How on earth am I going to tell her? It's all very well Em saying she doesn't want to hurt her. It will break her heart.

# CHAPTER TWENTY-ONE

The rain began to fall on Boves as the first mass was coming to an end. Hortense was feeling anxious about the twins and, when she and Cousin Berthe stepped out of the church into a stinging shower and a sharp October wind, her anxiety spilled over into irritation.

'That's all we need,' she said as her scarf was pulled from her collar and her hat shifted on its anchoring pins. 'I hate being blown about. It's altogether too unsettling.'

Her neighbours were clutching their hats, too, some laughing, some grumbling, and Father André, standing on the steps in his white surplice, billowed like a ship in full sail.

Cousin Berthe allowed herself to be pushed into the square. Her round face was pink with excitement. 'Look at me, Hortense! I'm flying!'

Hortense looked. Which was how she saw the faces in Madame Gambetta's window: two brightly coloured, permed heads, one peroxided yellow, the other hennaed red and two professionally painted faces, eyebrows plucked, eyelids blue, lips two scarlet cupid's bows. She recognised at once what they were. Whores! Holy Mary, Mother of God. What were two whores doing in a nice respectable village like Boves? Trust Madame Gambetta to give them house room. Wasn't that just what you'd expect?

Then, to her horror, the blonde lifted up the window, leant right out over the sill and addressed Hortense by name, shouting against the wind.

'Hortense Lisieux,' she called. 'It *is* you, is it not? Babette look. It's Hortense. Hortense Lisieux. What are you doing here?'

Hortense was so terrified she was rooted to the spot. She knew that her neighbours were listening avidly. She could feel their eyes burning her from every direction. Oh sweet Jesus! How could this be happening? The shame of it.

'Stay there,' the blonde commanded. 'We'll be right down.'

Worse and worse. What am I going to do? Hortense thought. She was still transfixed by fear and shame, even though the wind was buffeting against her and her mind was spinning with panic, urging her to run away, disappear, die, anything.

'Look at me!' Cousin Berthe shouted, puffing back towards Hortense. 'I was flying! Did you see me fly?'

'We must get home,' Hortense said. 'Prepare the meal.' If she could just get home and shut the door everything would be all right.

Cousin Berthe wasn't listening. She had surrendered herself to the elements again. And the two whores were bearing down upon them, bent forward against the wind and gaudy under two brightly patterned umbrellas.

'You don't remember us, do you?' the blonde said. 'Jacquetta and Babette. We were in Étaples in 'fifteen.'

Memories came flooding back. *Étaples and the streets full of khaki soldiers and staff cars, endless rain, legs wrapped in puttees, muddy boots, Edouard singing with a glass of whisky at his elbow, Edouard paper-white with exhaustion, Edouard saying goodbye before he returned to the front. Endless, endless rain as if the entire world was weeping. Étaples.*

Hortense made an enormous effort to control herself and the situation, straightened her spine and stood up as tall as she could. 'You must be mistaken,' she said. 'I'm afraid I don't know you.'

Messages flashed from eye to eye under the umbrellas. Understanding, comradeship, memory.

'A thousand apologies,' Babette said. 'We thought you resembled a girl we used to know many years ago, but of course now that we are close to you it is evident that you are no such person. A trick of the light, *n'est-ce pas*, Jacquetta?'

'Without doubt,' Jacquetta smiled. 'You work here, I expect, Madame?'

'I am housekeeper to Monsieur the Advocate.'

'But, of course. That is understood. We are here for the wedding of an old friend. We work in Metz now. Near the Maginot Line.'

'Really,' Hortense said, her voice marginally warmer. Oh how well she remembered them and the fun they used to have back in the old days. 'In Metz. Yes I understand. Metz. Yes.'

'We mustn't keep you,' Babette said, smiling into her eyes. And then she spoke louder so that the listeners would hear her. 'A thousand apologies, Madame.'

Now, and at last, Hortense regained the use of her legs and although her heart was still swelling painfully at every beat she walked out of the square, aware that her hips were hurting her and that for some inexplicable reason she was waddling like Cousin Berthe. She wanted to run but that was neither practicable nor possible. And when Cousin Berthe came babbling up beside her she was grateful for her company.

Damage had been done. There could hardly be any doubt about that. Too many people had heard and seen. Word would get back to the Advocate. There would be trouble. It had been a shock to see those two again and caught her off guard. Holy Mary, Mother of God, she thought, what a life this is that you have to deny your old friends. How dreadful that friendship can harm you. But it could, it could. And what could she do about it? What could she ever do about anything except run?

The urge to escape was so strong Hortense would have packed the minute she got back inside the house and left there and then, if the girls hadn't gone off to Boulogne. But she couldn't go without her girls, could she? No, of course she couldn't. There was nothing she *could* do for the moment except to prepare their evening meal and even that was difficult because her fingers were trembling. When that was done, she threw a shawl across her head and shoulders against the rain and ran down the street to the Advocate's house to get her chores done there, too. With luck she could sneak in and out of the house without anyone noticing.

303

But luck was against her.

Five minutes after she'd set the vegetables to steam and was mixing the sauce, the Advocate's sister appeared in the kitchen, her little dog at her heels.

She came to the point at once, her face taut with displeasure. 'Madame Lisieux,' she said, 'my brother and I have been hearing some most disturbing things about you.'

Hortense was silent.

'I feel you owe us an explanation,' Mademoiselle said.

'If that is so, Mademoiselle,' Hortense said, taking refuge in meek speech and careful politeness, 'you have only to ask and it will be given. What am I to explain?'

'Hmmmm,' Mademoiselle said, looking at the kitchen table as though it were a source of her annoyance.

'I would never willingly do anything to upset you, Mademoiselle,' Hortense struggled. 'Nor Monsieur the Advocate.'

Mademoiselle gave a little gulp and plunged into the attack, her cheeks reddening.

'You were seen, Madame,' she said. 'You were seen this morning after mass talking to . . . Madame Gambetta's . . . guests, who are women of a certain . . . how should one say? . . . occupation.'

'A mistake, Mademoiselle, I do assure you,' Hortense said, panic scrabbling in her belly. 'They mistook me for someone else.'

'They addressed you by name, Madame.'

'A similar name. They are not known to me, Mademoiselle. I swear it.'

'These women,' Mademoiselle said firmly, 'are not the sort we wish our cook and housekeeper to . . . shall we say, have dealings with. Not the sort at all. There is the matter of morality, you understand, which is of the greatest importance to my brother. There is the matter of disease. Women of that kind are carriers of the most disgraceful diseases. Disgraceful. As public officials we have to be extremely careful about such matters. A breath of scandal would be sufficient to ruin us. Ruin us completely.' She was

304

warming to her task now, finding disapproval easier, justifying her annoyance, enlarging it agreeably into anger. 'We have a position in this village.'

Hortense kept silent. What could she say?

'I see the meal is prepared,' Mademoiselle went on. 'You may leave the rest to me. I will serve it.'

'Yes, Mademoiselle.'

'We will talk of this further. Not now, you understand. Tomorrow.'

'Yes, Mademoiselle.'

'You may go.'

May, Hortense thought wildly, as she threw her old shawl over her head ready to escape. Not may. Must. And soon. This minute.

When she rushed through Old Joliot's door she looked so distraught and dishevelled that he was alarmed. She'd closed the door behind her and stood with her back against the protective wood, white-faced and gasping for breath.

'What is it?' he said. 'What has happened?'

'It's all up with me,' Hortense said. 'I've lost my job at Monsieur the Advocate's.'

'Lost your job.'

'Lost my job.'

'But why?'

'I was seen talking to the two . . . to Madame Gambetta's guests.'

'To the little *poules*,' Old Joliot said easily. 'So what's wrong with that? Why shouldn't you talk to 'em, eh? Good women. Did us sterling service in the Great War, I can tell you. Last taste of life for some a' my poor boys, that's what they were. Good women. Better than a lot of wives. Bit pricey, some of 'em, you got to admit that, but they had to make a living. You talk to 'em all you want, my dear.'

But Hortense was past talking. She leant against the door, her misery too intense for speech.

'Sit yourself down,' Old Joliot said, leading her to a chair. 'Berthe! Where are you! Get the brandy, little one. Hortense is poorly.'

The brandy warmed Hortense's throat, but, taken on an empty stomach, it made her head swim alarmingly and did nothing to still her panic.

'I must dish up,' she said.

But Cousin Berthe said she'd do that. 'You go upstairs, my dear,' she explained. 'Have a little lie-down. I should. I'll call you when the girls come home. How about that?' She turned to Joliot to explain things. 'That's the ol' wind,' she said. 'Blew us about something dreadful. I was flying, wasn't I, Hortense? That's blown her brains all about, that's what. Bad ol' wind!' And she led Hortense up the stairs chattering all the way.

Hortense allowed herself to be taken in hand because she didn't have the energy to resist. She was tucked under the covers and patted and kissed and called 'a dear good girl' until Cousin Berthe finally decided she was fit to be left and went chattering off downstairs. It was a relief to be on her own. Now Hortense could weep her tears away, if not her misery, could blow her nose and wipe her eyes. She knew she ought to try to work out what to do next but that was beyond her, and presently, exhausted by misery and stunned by brandy, she fell into an uneasy sleep.

And dreamed that she was being pursued by faceless monsters threatening to tear her to pieces. People were screaming abuse at her and pulling her clothes from her back, skin and all. Claud Everdale waved a poster about and Hortense knew there was something terrible written on it about her and she couldn't see what it was, and he wouldn't stop brandishing it. 'Oh stop, stop, please,' she begged. And he laughed as the poster got bigger and bigger and the monsters leapt out of the print and ran towards her, yelling . . .

She woke with a start, sweat greasing her forehead and her heart beating painfully. How long had she been asleep? Minutes? Or hours? She had no way of knowing. The nightmare still pulsed around her, filling the room and springing monsters in every shadow. Presently she realised that there were voices in the room below her and that one of them belonged to Ginny. They're back, she thought. Oh praise be to God! They're back. She sprang out of bed at once, scrambled into her shoes and stumbled down the stairs to see them.

'Virginie!' she cried, blinking in the gaslight. 'Virginie, *chérie*, the most dreadful thing has happened. I've lost my job. What are we going to do?' But then she stopped, alerted by the atmosphere in the room.

Ginny had been talking to Cousin Berthe and Old Joliot, her voice serious and low. When she looked up Hortense was aware, even through her misery, that there was something odd about her, something different, something almost guilty. And why was she on her own? Surely she hadn't come back without her sister.

'Where is Emilie?' she said, getting to the heart of the matter at once.

'Oh Maman,' Ginny said, torn with pity for her, 'my dear Maman, my poor dear Maman, you must prepare yourself for a surprise.'

But Hortense had already sensed it was going to be a shock. Nightmare and reality had become a single terrifying pressure. 'Where is Emilie?' she repeated, her voice grim with foreboding.

'Gone off to get married,' Cousin Berthe said, her round face beaming with delight. 'That's what she done. Gone to be a bride. Gone to get married. What a lark, eh?'

'You're wrong!' Hortense screamed. 'She hasn't. She can't have done. You mustn't say such things. Say it isn't true, Virginie.'

'Maman,' Ginny tried, stepping towards her.

Her mother backed away. 'She can't! She can't! Don't you understand. She must never marry. Never. It'll be the death of her. Oh, I *did* try to warn you. Didn't I? I did. Both of you. Why didn't you listen? I thought you understood. You promised me. Up in the cemetery, you must remember. You promised me. How can she be getting married? She doesn't know anybody.'

'Maman!' Ginny begged, trying to hold her.

Hortense shook her off. 'I thought it would be you,' Hortense said wildly. 'You were always the wild one. Not Emilie. How can it be Emilie? She's such a good girl. It'll be a mistake. That's what it'll be. We must get her back. We must go there at once. Now. Tonight. Where did you say she'd gone?'

There was no way of softening the blow. 'To England, Maman.'

'No, no,' Hortense screamed. 'Not England. She can't have gone to England. Say it isn't true. Please, please, say it isn't true. She'll die. Like your father. How could she have done such a thing? And me with no job. What will become of us? We shall all die. I wish I was dead.' And she threw herself into the nearest chair so violently that she nearly toppled over and, covering her face with both hands, began to howl.

'Enough!' Old Joliot ordered, moving in upon her. 'Calm yourself! At once! I will not have hysterics in my house!'

Hortense didn't seem to hear him.

'Babette is here,' she wailed. 'Here in the village on the very day . . . I am cursed. Cursed. Nothing will ever go right for me. I said I didn't know them. Simon Peter, you see. After all these years . . . I thought we were safe and then she comes and I say . . . and she goes to England and gets married . . . to England of all places! She'll die! And it's all my fault. Simon Peter, you see . . . A traitor. *Mon dieu. Mon dieu.*'

Ginny was so upset she couldn't speak. On the way home from Boulogne she had worried about what would happen when she told Maman but, even in her worst fears, she hadn't imagined anything as extreme as this.

'Maman dear,' she begged, kneeling at her mother's feet. 'Please don't. You'll make yourself ill.'

'I don't care. I deserve to be ill.'

'Please Maman. It'll be all right. Really it will. He's a good man.'

'How can he be a good man?' Hortense cried. She'd never been able to understand all this and fear had totally muddled her grasp of the medical facts. 'He'll be the death of her. Love is what kills you with this disease. Don't you understand? Love kills you.'

What can I say? Ginny thought despairingly. She's hysterical. I don't think she can hear me. But her mother's terrible sobs had to be soothed somehow or other.

'Ken is a good man,' she repeated speaking slowly and distinctly as though her mother were a child. 'A very good man. He'll look after her, Maman, you'll see. He's built her a bungalow. She's going to have a maid to help her. He's thought of everything. He loves her.'

'It's all my fault,' her mother sobbed. 'All my fault, all my fault.'

'No, no. It isn't.'

Hortense took her hands away from her eyes and glared at her daughter. 'How do you know?' she yelled. 'You don't know. I'm the only one who knows. The only one. I've known all these years. And I can't tell you. I can't tell anybody. It's too dreadful. All these years, worrying and waiting. The pain of it. He suffered so much. So much. I can't bear it.'

Old Joliot's face was working with anger. He put both hands on Hortense's shoulders and shook her, glaring into her face. 'Stop this at once,' he said. 'You shame us all. The child is alive and with her lover. Is that any reason for weeping? There is only one reason for weeping Madame and that is death. I will not have this yowling in my kitchen.'

Hortense sprang to her feet, knocking the chair on to its back. The last traces of the old elegant Hortense, the cherished wife from England, had finally vanished. 'Then I'll go!' she said wildly, and before any of them could stop her, she'd grabbed her hat and coat from the hook on the door and barged out of the room into the street, still sobbing.

We must stop her, Ginny thought, and she steadied herself on the chair and tried to stand up. But there was a roaring in her ears and her legs wouldn't support her. They seemed to be bending sideways as if they were made of rubber. She gave a long groan and fell forward over the chair in a dead faint.

Old Joliot was at her side at once, lifting her up and easing her head between her knees. 'Go after the other one, *ma petite*,' he said to Cousin Berthe, who'd been cowering in the corner, watching wide-eyed. 'You look after her, eh?'

Although she couldn't make sense of the things she'd just seen, Cousin Berthe was obedient. If Joliot said she was to look after Hortense then that was what she would do. She put on her hat and coat, draped her shawl over her shoulders, and plodded out into the evening.

In contrast to the yellow illumination of their gaslit room, it seemed pitch black out in the village street, but at least the wind had dropped and there was no more rain. After a few seconds Berthe's eyes adjusted to the darkness and she made out a shape striding uphill towards the square. She followed, quickening her pace as best she could. The shape moved very fast through the square, and out of the village, following the dirt track through the fields where there was no light to guide them except the moon.

Now Hortense was walking more slowly, stumbling against the hedges when the moon was obscured by cloud, stopping every now and then to moan and sob. It wasn't long before Cousin Berthe was near enough to call out. 'Hortense, my dear. Wait for me. It's only Cousin Berthe.'

'Oh Berthe,' Hortense called back. 'What am I going to do?'

Cousin Berthe considered the problem as she plodded along the track towards her friend. 'Have a little rest,' she suggested.

'No, no. I can't.'

To Cousin Berthe's simplicity there was only one other alternative. '*Eh bien*,' she said, 'we walk on.'

They walked on and Cousin Berthe held on to Hortense's arm for support the way she always did, and for the second time that day, Hortense was glad of her company.

It was peculiarly peaceful walking along together in the darkness. The light from the moon was fitful but they soon learned to stop when clouds were approaching. And if light was sometimes lacking, sounds were magnified. They heard an owl hooting in the cemetery, horses snorting in the fields, the rustle of small animals in the undergrowth, the scuff of their own shoes on the rough earth. And bit by bit, as they walked in silence, Hortense began to calm.

They'd been going for about an hour when they came to a crossroads.

'Where we going, then?' Cousin Berthe said cheerfully. She was enjoying her stroll in the night air and had quite forgotten why she'd been sent out.

'I don't know,' Hortense said wearily. 'And that's the truth.'

'Home?' Cousin Berthe suggested.

'No, no, no, no. I can't go back. Never.'

'I know then,' Cousin Berthe said, looking at the signpost. 'We'll go to the convent.'

Hortense looked at Cousin Berthe's innocent face gleaming in the moonlight and, although she suspected they could walk about all night long and never find another house, let alone a convent, she was too stunned to make a decision of her own. 'Yes,' she said.

Cousin Berthe grinned with delight. 'This way,' she said.

Arm in arm, they walked into the darkness.


Back in his cottage at Boves Old Joliot revived his poor Virginie, bathed her poor sweating head and persuaded her to sit in his armchair while he made some coffee.

'You eaten anything today?' he questioned. When Ginny shook her head, too bewildered to remember whether she'd eaten or not, he lumbered off to find what he could in the larder.

'Bread and cheese,' he said, returning with a platter. 'You get that inside you my little one. No wonder you go fallin' down when you haven't eaten.'

'But Maman. I must go after Maman.'

'Cousin Berthe is looking after your mother,' Old Joliot said. 'She'll come to no harm with Cousin Berthe. You eat and rest. You're the one who needs looking after now. I seen enough men fall of a heap to know that. Don't you worry about them. They'll be back in no time.'

'Are you sure?'

'Quite sure. Now tell me about this lover of our little Emilie's.'

It was comforting to tell Old Joliot what had happened, knowing he would approve and understand and, that for the time being, they could avoid the subject of her mother's terrifying hysteria. That was too close and too frightening even to be thought about.

'Is he handsome?' Old Joliot asked, hacking a chunk from the loaf and handing it across the table to her.

'Well no. He's not. But he loves her very very much.'

'And she loves him?'

'Yes, she does. She's loved him for ages.'

'But, of course,' Old Joliot said, smiling his lopsided smile. 'Naturally. What could be better?'

Put like that, the love affair began to feel possible and normal.

'So tell me all about it,' Old Joliot encouraged. Keep her mind off things, poor little one.

They were still talking when the church clock struck midnight. Now neither of them could avoid the fact that Hortense and Cousin Berthe were still not home.

'They'll have gone in somewhere out of the cold,' Old Joliot reassured. 'Our Cousin Berthe's got plenty of common sense. She won't let them come to no harm. Not our Cousin Berthe. We'll leave the door on the latch just in case they come back later, eh? But we ought to get to bed, *n'est-ce pas?*'

It was an order and had to be obeyed. They're bound to be back soon, Ginny thought, as she crept into her empty bed in her miserably vacated room. They can't walk about in the dark for ever.

The long hours of the night passed, quarter by quarter, with impossible slowness, and there was no sound of a return. Finally, the dawn began to streak the windows with the pale blue-green of very early morning. Hortense and Berthe still weren't home.

Now there were chores to do, a stove to coax alight, fresh bread to be bought down at the bakers, coffee to brew, and Ginny was the only one left to do it all. She tried to comfort herself that they would reappear in time for breakfast. But they didn't.

'What are we to do?' she asked Old Joliot, as she poured his coffee.

'You, my little one, are to go to work as usual,' Old Joliot said. 'You have a living to earn. I will find them.'

He seemed very confident. 'Do you think you'll be able to?'

'But, of course. You go to work.'

'But we don't know where they are,' Ginny worried. The coffee cup shook in her hand. 'They could be anywhere. Out all night in the dark. Anything could have happened to them.'

'Not in the Somme Valley,' Old Joliot said. 'Not with a million men to care for them.'

A million ghosts, Ginny thought; what good are a million ghosts? He should be thinking about the living, not the dead. 'But where will you look?'

'First I shall cycle over to Monsieur the Advocate and tell him your mother isn't well. Then I shall go to work in the cemetery and see to that ol' hedge. This afternoon I shall visit the farms, one by one. I shall find 'em, never fear.'

He seemed so positive about it that Ginny went to work, despite her misgivings. But she worried about her mother all day long. *Where* could they have got to?

When that slow blue-green dawn rose above them, Hortense and Cousin Berthe were more than twenty kilometres from Boves and still walking. Like her daughter, Hortense had talked into the small hours, spilling all her troubles into Berthe's inattentive ears: about Babette and Jacquetta and how disloyal she'd been to them, about the Advocate's sister and how she'd lost her job, about Emilie's blindness and her husband's illness and the terror of being found out, the horror of being blamed, the daily, inescapable weight of the sin she couldn't confess. And Berthe

313

plodded beside Hortense making companionable grunts and murmurs and not understanding a word.

At last Hortense fell silent, but the two of them continued to walk, placing one foot in front of the other, mechanically and endlessly, despite the jabbing pain of the blisters they'd rubbed. Three o'clock. Four o'clock. Five o'clock . . .

When the sky began to grow lighter, Hortense asked Cousin Berthe if they were nearly there. And Cousin Berthe looked round her as if she knew exactly where she was and said, 'Yes, very nearly. Not far now.'

They walked on. By now the cocks were crowing, the dawn chorus was in full song and light was clearing the night sky with visible speed. Hortense watched the pattern emerging on her skirt, aware that she was hungry and thirsty as well as footsore. They rounded a bend in the track and found that they were walking towards a high brick wall. It seemed to surround a garden, for the branches of several apple trees rose above the brickwork, and beyond the branches Hortense could see the chimneys of a very large house.

'*Voilà!*' Cousin Berthe said, stopping triumphantly in front of a wooden door set in a wall.

To Hortense's weary eyes it wasn't a particularly welcoming door. Made from oak and patterned with large iron studs like the entrance to a fortress, it had a large iron bell hanging above it, and an iron grille in the middle of it, at eye level and tightly closed.

'The Convent of the Little Sisters of Divine Mercy,' Cousin Berthe said. 'We have arrived.' She pulled the bell, which clanged vigorously.

'Berthe, my dear,' Hortense said. 'Do you think you should? At this hour of the morning?'

'*Mais oui*,' Berthe said. 'Always someone to answer that ol' bell in the convent.'

She was right. Presently the grille was opened to reveal two brown eyes. A gentle voice enquired who they were.

'Cousin Berthe,' that lady said happily. 'Come to see Mother.'

And the door was opened to them.

# Chapter Twenty-Two

Hortense never forgot her first sight of the Convent of the Little Sisters of Divine Mercy. It was such a peaceful place, tranquil, orderly and lush with growing plants, herb borders and vegetable beds. Its lawns shimmered white with early morning dew, its flower beds were crammed with dahlias and chrysanthemums still closed against the night, and, down in the orchard, there were more fruit trees than she could count.

The convent itself looked like a chateau. Or, to be more precise, a picture of a chateau. There was something ethereal about the building, as if it had withdrawn behind the foliage to hide and dream. Built in stone, it was an E-shaped mansion with tall chimneys, a grey-tiled roof and long white shutters at the windows. But the west wing was partly hidden by shrubs and the ground floor was swathed by ribbons of mist, blue as cigarette smoke, lazily swirling and rising as the air gradually warmed.

It's all grey and white and blue and green, Hortense thought, as she and Cousin Berthe followed the sister along the gravel path toward the house. Peaceful colours. Even the sister was dressed in blue. Her long robes swished like leaves as she walked, and her white coif, balanced by two elaborate white wings on either side of her forehead, was stiff with starch.

'Mother is in the infirmary,' she said, as they reached the side door. 'If you will follow me.'

'The infirmary,' Cousin Berthe said happily. 'That's where I was. I was there. You'll like the infirmary.'

The room into which they were ushered turned out to be a long draughty hall filled with trestle tables, where about thirty extraordinary children were being prepared for their breakfast. They were every age, from two to fourteen, and all of them were handicapped, some severely. Several were mongols like Cousin Berthe, only younger and less controlled; a few sat patiently, some wandered the room, most of them were dribbling. Some were blind. Others were brain damaged, with awkward stick legs or perpetually clenched hands or twitching heads. Yet others gave high-pitched cries like birds, or muttered, or sang tunelessly. Two, who were already sitting at table, talking sensibly to one another, were dwarfs with adult faces and the bodies of small children. Hortense was overwhelmed with pity for them.

But Berthe went waddling off into the throng as if the sight was all perfectly normal.

'There's Mother,' she said. 'Now we shall be all right.'

All round the room there were blue-clad nuns swathed in rough aprons, struggling to fix towelling bibs round the squirming necks of their charges, or to ease kicking limbs into the restraints of a high chair. As there didn't seem to be any point in adding to the crush, Hortense stood where she was and waited. Presently Cousin Berthe returned, triumphantly leading a small, fat nun by the hand.

'This is Mother,' she said. 'Mother, this is my friend Hortense. She's got nowhere to go, so I brought her to you. That was right, wasn't it?'

'Quite right,' Mother said patting Berthe's plump hand. Small for the great authority of a Mother Superior, she was an unprepossessing woman with a dumpy figure and a face like a gnome. Untidy wisps of coarse grey hair escaped from her coif to straggle at her temples, a large mole sprouted grey hairs on the left side of her chin and she wore round iron-rimmed glasses perched on the inadequate button of her nose. But her smile was welcoming and she was plainly fond of Cousin Berthe.

'Of course,' she said. 'Quite right. But you must wait until *les enfants* are prepared. It is not possible to talk now, you understand.'

'We'll help,' Berthe offered happily. 'Won't we, Hortense?'

So they helped. And very hard work it was, for *les enfants* were heavy to lift and awkward to manoeuvre. At last they were settled, an approximate silence had been achieved, grace had been said and the food had been served – bread and coffee for those who could hold it in their hands and a milky gruel for those who couldn't and had to be fed. Then, having established that they hadn't eaten, Mother took her two unexpected guests to the convent refectory to share her own breakfast.

Cousin Berthe sat beside her old friend radiating happiness.

'You see,' she said to Hortense, clapping her hands gleefully. 'Didn't I tell you?'

Now that they were facing Mother Superior, Hortense felt uncomfortable, and the presence of other nuns at the tables added to her unease. When Mother Superior turned to her and asked, 'How can we help you, my daughter?' she was suddenly full of shame, that she, a grown woman, a woman in the prime of her life, should be here in this place asking for charity as though she were one of *les enfants*.

'I shouldn't be asking for help,' she said. 'Not when . . . I mean . . .'

'We all need help,' Mother Superior said. 'From the dear Lord, from one another. We all need to give it when it is asked of us, and we all need to receive it. That is the nature of things.'

'Yes,' Hortense said. 'I suppose so.' She managed a weak smile. 'But to come here for help, to the Church, when I . . . When I don't deserve it . . . when I haven't been a good Catholic . . . when . . .' And she sighed profoundly.

The Mother Superior might have been small in stature but she had the shrewdest brain in the entire convent, and she recognised a spiritual crisis when she saw one.

'We could give you sanctuary here for a few days,' she said. 'In return, you could help us with *les enfants*. We always need help with our little ones, as you saw just now. Would you be prepared to do that? And to join us in our prayers, of course.'

317

'Yes, Mother.' Hortense said gratefully. 'Thank you.' That was possible. That was something she could do. It would give her time to recover from the shocks of the last twenty-four hours. 'I could help with the blind ones, perhaps. My elder daughter is blind.'

Mother Superior gave out a great hoot of delight, as if that was just what she expected her guest to say. 'But of course,' she cried. 'You see how perfectly the dear Lord has our lives in His hands.'

And so it was decided. The ease and simplicity of the arrangements were quite amazing. There was a plain white cell for their new guest's temporary occupation, a blue apron 'to spare her clothes', a rosary at her bedside 'to pray for grace' and two blind waifs to be cared for during the day.

Even Cousin Berthe's return to Boves was taken care of. 'You can travel with the carter,' Mother said. 'He arrives at nine o'clock so you can be home with your soldier before midday. You are still with your soldier, *n'est-ce pas*? It wouldn't do to leave him on his own for too long.'

'Oh yes,' Berthe agreed. 'Better look after Old Joliot. I keeps him fed like you told me, Mother.'

'Good girl,' Mother said. 'Now run along and say goodbye to your friend. She is in the promenade garden giving the children their airing.'

The promenade garden was a private space behind the house where the children were taken for their daily exercise. It consisted of a series of leafy shrines linked by gravel paths and divided by meadow grass. Each little grotto contained a life-sized statue of a saint, and each was visited in turn for a soothing of prayers, and a chance for the most badly handicapped to catch their breath, and their balance, after their exertions. Cousin Berthe knew the walk by heart, so it didn't take her long to work out where Hortense would be heading next.

'I'm off with that ol' carter,' she said, ambling into the group.

Hortense kissed her fondly.

'This was the right place, wasn't it?' Cousin Berthe said,

beaming at her friend. 'I brought you to the right place, didn't I?'

Mouths moist and hats askew after their prayer to St Theresa, the procession stumbled on towards the next statue. There was little time for farewells and less to gather thoughts, but the pressure of parting made Hortense aware of how much she ought to say. Poor Ginny, she thought, she'll be worried out of her mind not knowing where I am. I've treated her badly. It wasn't her fault Emilie ran away with that man. Joliot, too. I should never have gone rushing out of his house like that. It was ill-mannered. Making amends would be difficult with Cousin Berthe as her messenger.

'Give my love to Virginie and Old Joliot,' she instructed. 'Tell them I'm sorry. Don't tell them where I am just yet. Tell them I'll write. Do you understand?'

'Yes, yes,' Cousin Berthe said, nodding. 'Virginie and Ol' Joliot. Don't tell 'em.'

'Give them my love.'

'Yes.'

'What have you got to do?'

'Give 'em your love.'

'That's right,' Hortense approved. 'Good girl.' Now what else did she have to think about? Virginie would make excuses to the Advocate and help him with the cooking at home. There was no need to say anything about that. But wait, there might be letters. Emilie would surely write to tell her how ill she was. Or somebody might write on her daughter's behalf. If there was a letter like that, she, Hortense, had to be the first one to read it. It would be disastrous if it fell into Virginie's hands by mistake, especially if Emilie wrote about her symptoms. Information like that *had* to be hidden.

'Now then, Berthe,' she said. 'If a letter comes to the house from abroad would you hide it away for me. You could put it somewhere safe, couldn't you, and keep it for me.'

This baffled poor Berthe. 'Letters?' she said, blankly

repeating the one word she'd understood. Letters she could cope with but not all those other words. She smiled just the same to show how willing she was.

'A letter from abroad,' Hortense tried to explain. 'With a foreign stamp.'

'Stamp,' Berthe said happily, without understanding that word either.

The children arrived at the next statue and settled noisily. I must hurry, Hortense thought. I can't keep everybody waiting. I must think of something to show her what I mean. But what? Surely she knows what a letter is. Letters are so important. Beyond price. Suddenly she remembered her own letter – the one Edward had sent her from England to ask her to marry him, the one she carried in the inner pocket of her old coat, her best and most treasured relic in the last bit of clothing that remained from her life in England.

She drew it from her pocket and held it tenderly in her hand. 'A letter,' she said. 'See. That's a letter. And that's a stamp.'

Berthe nodded.

'So, if a letter comes with a stamp like that on it, look at it Berthe, you're to put it somewhere safe and keep it for me.'

'Keep it,' Berthe said. 'Yes. A stamp like that.'

Cousin Berthe might give the impression she understood but you could never be sure and Hortense knew how important it was to get this quite clear. It pained her to be destroying the perfection of her perfect letter, but she tore the stamp from the envelope and tucked it into Berthe's hatband.

'You keep that,' she said. 'Understand. Keep that. And when you get home, take it out of your hat and stick it in the corner of your mirror, where you keep your picture of the Blessed Virgin. You understand? When a letter comes, with a stamp like that on it, you keep the letter.'

'With a stamp like that,' Berthe said and held it seriously. 'By the Blessed Virgin. Yes, yes. I'll do it.'

Yes, Hortense thought with relief, she has understood. When news comes, when my poor Emilie is ill . . . And she will be ill. She's bound to be ill. But don't think of that now. Not now. It's too awful. Time for that later. The great thing is that when the letter arrives I shall be the only one to see it. I can keep it hidden.

Now that she'd settled her affairs, Hortense realised that she didn't feel at all well herself. She was drained of energy, her shoulders ached, and her throat felt dry and sore. But she tried to ignore her discomfort. She couldn't be ill. Not now. It was fatigue after walking all night, that's all.

Nevertheless, as she kissed Cousin Berthe goodbye, she began to cough, and she went on coughing for some time, aware that her chest felt painfully tight and that her forehead was clammy with sweat. Berthe didn't notice that anything was amiss. She simply ambled back to the house where the carter was waiting.

'Come along,' Hortense said to the two blind children, who were still standing patiently beside her, 'we must catch up, mustn't we, or we shall miss the prayer.' She spoke carefully, partly to encourage them, because she was afraid she'd been rather selfish making them wait for such a long time, but mostly to encourage herself. Inwardly she was very far from cheerful, and feeling worse by the minute. She couldn't avoid the fear that she was going to be ill. Berthe was gone and the last link with Boves was broken. She had no idea when she would see either of her daughters again. Poor Virginie. Poor, poor Emilie. But what else could she have done? What other choice did she have? She couldn't have stayed in Boves, forced to watch as her secrets were revealed, and to know that everybody knew. That would have been too awful to endure.

The prayers were beginning again, the familiar chant both comforting and sustaining. 'Hail Mary, full of grace: the Lord is with thee: blessed art thou amongst women, and blessed is the fruit of thy womb, Jesus.' Sanctuary, Hortense thought, I'm in sanctuary. And even though she knew that the convent couldn't protect her against all the terrible things that could happen, at least she felt protected for the time being. 'Holy Mary, Mother of God, pray for us sinners, now, and at the hour of our death. Amen.'

Virginie will forgive me, she thought, as another coughing fit began, once I've written to her and explained. She's a loving girl for all her temper. But Emilie. Oh my poor daughter. My poor, dear daughter. Whatever can I do about Emilie? It hurt even to think about Emilie. She yearned to rush across the Channel and carry her away from the madness of love and marriage, to look after her again, the way she always had. But it was all too late. Emilie was gone. She would marry. The man would see to that. He would marry her and make love to her and that would make her ill. She was filled with hatred of this man. He must have bullied poor Emilie most dreadfully to make her run away like that, without a word to her Maman. Oh, my poor darling. I wonder where you are. How must you be suffering!

Emily was happier than she'd ever been in her life.

Ken Hopkirk never left her side throughout their journey across the Channel. 'Don't worry,' he said, over and over again. 'I'm here. I'll look after you.'

'I'm not worried,' she said.

And she wasn't. He was so strong and loving and completely dependable and explained everything. 'We're casting off now. That's the first rope gone. And there's the second. You'll feel us moving presently. That's the sound of the engines going full steam ahead now we're clear of the harbour.'

'Is the sea rough?' she asked. 'It was terribly rough when we came across. I was seasick.'

'No,' he assured her. 'It isn't, and, in any case, even if it was, you won't be sick this time.'

'Won't I?' How could he be so sure?

'No. You won't. I know how to stop seasickness.'

'Do you?' She was impressed.

'I do,' he said, smiling to himself as he cuddled her against his side. 'All we've got to do is keep talking to one another, all the way across. D'you think we could manage it?'

How could they fail?

They talked and talked. He told her about the factory and the bungalow and how he'd thought about her every day when things were really ghastly. She told him about her dreams and how completely he'd occupied them in all the months of waiting. They laughed and teased and said how much they loved one another, and sat hand in hand, not at all seasick, as the ship rolled from the trough of one wave to the crest of the next.

It seemed no time at all before they were walking unsteadily down the gangplank and Emily was back in England, with English voices all around her, warning, thanking, announcing. 'Mind yer backs.' 'Thank you very much, sir.' 'Victoria! This way for Victoria.' 'Carry yer bags, sir?'

'Is it far?' she asked, as they climbed into their train.

'No distance. Are you tired?'

'Not now I'm with you. I can't wait to get to the bungalow.' Ken had described it to her in such detail she knew it already.

They went home as quickly as trains could take them.

The little house was a pleasure to both of them – for Emily because she was in her own home at last; for Ken because he could show Emily all the things he'd arranged to suit her. He led her happily from room to room.

'There's the rail I was telling you about. It runs all round the house. And there's a button – do you remember I told you about them? – to show you there's a door coming.'

Yes, she remembered and knew it would be helpful. 'And this is the kitchen.' She could smell it was the kitchen. There was something cooking there.

'Mrs Quern's been in,' Ken explained. 'Left a casserole. I'll show you where the bathroom is and then I'll dish up. I'll bet you're hungry.'

'Oh, Ken, my dear, darling man,' she said. 'You've thought of everything.'

In his dogged methodical way, he had.

They ate their meal and Ken enjoyed it very much. Emily found her first taste of English cooking rather disagreeable but was too tactful and too happy to say so. Afterwards they washed the dishes and tidied the kitchen. Then, with the wireless playing companionably beside them, they sat side by side on their new settee for three delightful hours. And after that Ken wrote a letter to her dictation so that Maman and Ginny would know she'd arrived safely. It was propped against the clock on the mantelpiece waiting to be posted in the morning.

But now it was necessary to make sleeping arrangements quite clear, for both their sakes, his perhaps more than hers. There was a trusting innocence about Emily that made him wonder whether she actually knew what married life was going to be like. He couldn't ask her. Not yet, anyway. That would have to come later. In the meantime she had to be protected.

'This is your bedroom,' he said and led her into it. 'I shall sleep in the spare room across the hall, until we're married. If you want anything in the night there's this buzzer by the bed – feel it? – and all you've got to do is give it a push and it'll ring right by my ear. There's your nightie, on the pillow. It's made of lawn. The girl in the shop saw to it. I told her to find something really nice.'

'It's lovely,' she said, smiling as she fingered it.

The sight of her, standing in their bedroom, beside the double bed they would be sharing in just a few weeks, holding the nightdress he'd chosen for her and looking so warm and voluptuous and at ease, aroused such desire in him that he was afraid he wouldn't be able to control himself if he stayed in the room with her for a moment longer.

'Mrs Quern is coming in first thing tomorrow morning,' he said, struggling to be matter-of-fact. 'If there's anything you want, don't forget the buzzer.' He kissed her as gently as he could and went to bed before harm was done. It was important that they should both be virgins on their wedding day. The sacrament of matrimony was too precious to spoil, especially at the eleventh hour. He owed it to Emily to protect her from everything, even his own desire.

As he left the room he remembered the words of the

Catechism. '*We are bound to deny ourselves because our natural inclinations are evil from our very childhood.*' And was pleased to think that, despite the greatest temptation that had ever faced him, his own natural inclinations were firmly under control.

Left on her own in the bedroom, Emily knelt by the bed and held her silver cross between her fingers and said her evening prayers. She asked God to bless her dear Kenneth and her family, Berthe and Old Joliot. Then she said a special 'Our Father' for the grace to be worthy of the man who was going to be her husband. Then she tried to settle to sleep. It took a very long time. There was a journey to re-live, a parting to remember and regret (but that could all be put right when they were together again), Ken's words to savour (how dear and tender and loving he'd been, her dear, dear Ken), and all the sounds and scents of this new home of hers to absorb and locate. And then there was the woman who was coming tomorrow. She had to be thought about, too.

Mrs Quern arrived the next morning before Ken left for work. She had a friendly voice, a rough hand and smelled of cooking.

'Pleased ter meet yer, Miss Holborn,' she said. 'I'm Molly Quern. My ol' man works in the pressroom up at Mr Hopkirk's. I come here to help. I daresay Mr Hopkirk's told you. He's explained everythink to me. I'm to help you get yer bearings sort a' thing. Do all the things you can't do yet awhile. I shan't get in yer way or nothink.'

Emily liked her at once, although she couldn't understand everything she said and it was a surprise to be called Miss Holborn.

'My name is Emily,' she said. 'I'm sure we shall get on . . .' What was it Miss Babbacombe used to say? '. . . like a house afire.'

And by and large, they did, for although Molly Quern was a motherly soul, she knew how important it is for a woman to run her own home, so she deferred to her new mistress in all things, even when she already knew the answer to the question she was asking.

During those first hesitant days Emily gradually got used to her new surroundings. She learned how to make the beds, how to light the geyser to run a bath, how to use a carpet sweeper, how to make a telephone call to the factory and how to brew tea in a pot just the way her dear Ken liked it. On Friday she went down to the shops, with Mrs Quern leading the way, and tried to find the ingredients to cook a good French meal. It was very difficult because nobody seemed to have heard of aubergines or *haricots verts*, pepper was already ground, and olive oil was only to be found in a chemist's shop.

However, on Saturday, she did her best to produce an English version of *coq au vin*, astonishing Mrs Quern with her dexterity, and eliciting cheers from her fiancé. And, on Sunday, she and Ken went to mass together, she in her new clothes, he in a high state of excitement.

It brought their wedding very close indeed and reminded her that she hadn't had an answer from Maman or Ginny.

'We must write to them again,' she said, as they walked home together, 'and tell them the date of the wedding. If we know it. Do we?'

'Well, no. Not exactly. I was waiting for you to decide. It ought to be soon. We can't go on living in the same house for very much longer, not without being man and wife. It wouldn't be proper.'

She smiled at his correctness. 'Soon then,' she said. 'How soon could it be?'

'I thought today month.'

She wasn't sure what he meant. English was more complicated than she remembered. 'Today month?'

'In four weeks' time. The fourth Saturday in November. What do you think? I could hire a caterer to take care of everything.'

'Would we go on honeymoon?'

'If you want to.'

She answered him honestly. 'I'd rather stay in the bungalow, if you don't mind. I'd feel safer there.'

Her answer pleased him because it was what he wanted,

too, peace and privacy in their own home. 'Then that's what we'll do,' he said. 'We'll have our reception, say goodbye to our guests and come straight back to our own home all on our own.'

'That would be perfect,' she said. 'Who are we going to invite?'

It was a very short list, for she only had Maman and Ginny, and Ken had no one who lived near enough to be able to attend. But there was Molly Quern and her husband and Ken's foreman, Bill Murgatroyd, and 'the lads' from the factory. Emily said they would be quite enough to make a lovely wedding party, explaining that she couldn't cope with lots of people all at once. The only two people she really wanted to attend were Maman and Ginny, and providing they came it didn't matter what other guests there were.

But it worried Ken that she would have so few people to support her. 'What about your friends in Paris?' he wondered.

'Mauricette Lalange,' she said. 'Dear Mauricette. I'd love to invite her but I don't think I can. She couldn't afford the fare, you see. And the family certainly couldn't. There are ten of them. Better not. We could visit her in Paris, later, couldn't we?'

He agreed that they could, but he was still trying to think of possible wedding guests for her. 'Haven't you got relations in England?' he asked. It had been rather a surprise to him when he'd seen her passport, to find out that she'd been born in Wolverhampton and had an English surname.

'Well, yes,' she said, 'I suppose I have, but we can't invite them. There was a quarrel when Ginny and I were little, when we left England. I think that's why we left. Anyway, Maman said we were to forget all about them.'

'But you didn't, did you?'

'Well, no, not entirely. You don't, do you? But we weren't allowed to write to them. I don't know where they are. Anyway it was all a long time ago. There's no point thinking about it now.'

He could see that she was beginning to get distressed, but

he persisted. Families were important at weddings. If he knew nothing else, he knew that. They ought to be there. 'Do you know where they *were*?'

'No,' she said, and now there was no doubt about her distress. 'Addresses never meant anything to me, Ken. Addresses are things other people might see, things people write. I went where I was taken. Ginny might know. But I doubt it because I'm sure she never wrote to them. I'll ask her when she writes back. Only please, don't let's talk about it any more now.'

So a limited number of invitations were sent and then it was simply a matter of waiting for the replies. All Ken's friends at the factory answered at once and with obvious delight, for despite his temper they were fond of the gaffer and wished him well. But there was still no letter from France.

By this time Emily was beginning to worry. A few days delay had to be expected, but this was more than a week.

'I can't understand it,' she said. 'Surely they're going to come to my wedding.'

'Their letter's been held up,' Ken said, trying to reassure her. 'That's what it is. It's a long way from France. You'll hear in a day or two. Bound to.' Privately, he was beginning to wonder whether her mother was so angry at their elopement that she was prepared to ignore the wedding. Her twin had reacted quite strongly against him when they met. But, of course, he didn't say anything about that.

The next day passed like all the others and there was still no letter. Now, the reception had been arranged and there was only a wedding dress to be bought and everything would be ready.

During the day Emily had so much to do there wasn't time to worry but, alone in her quiet bedroom, her mind returned to the misery of this long inexplicable silence like a tongue to a broken tooth. Had they decided to ignore her? Was that it? Were they punishing her for coming to England? Oh, surely not. She had to admit that Maman was quite capable of doing such a thing (in one of her bad moods and on the spur of the moment) but she found it hard to believe that Ginny could be so unkind. Even if Maman was angry and wouldn't write, Ginny could at least have sent a postcard. Something must have happened. But what? If there'd been some trouble Ginny would have written to tell her about it. Ginny, of all people, knew how much she loved Kenneth. After all those months writing to him at her dictation and reading his letters back to her, she *must* do. Surely, she wouldn't just cut them both now.

In the end she dictated yet another letter to her sister.

*My dearest Ginny,*
*Please write to me. I am so worried not hearing from you. I realise that Maman might well be angry at what I've done. She probably is. But you understand why I acted as I did, don't you? Please write and say you will come to my wedding. I enclose another invitation card in case the first one went astray. Oh please do come. It won't be the same without you, I love you so much.*
*Your ever loving sister,*
*Emily.*

'If I don't get an answer now,' she said to Ken, when it was written and addressed, 'I shall know they've cast me off.'

He caught her hand and kissed it. 'They haven't cast you off,' he said. 'Nobody could cast you off. You're too precious.'

Emily enjoyed the kiss, but she didn't answer him. If there's no answer, she was thinking, I shall know I've lost them. Oh please God, let there be an answer.

That night she said fervent prayers for all her family and followed with an entire rosary to make amends for all her sins remembered and forgotten.

But the mornings passed and there was still no answer.

'Oh, Ken,' she mourned. 'Why hasn't she written to me? I don't understand it.'

329

# CHAPTER TWENTY-THREE

In Old Joliot's cottage in Boves, Ginny was saying exactly the same thing in another language.

'Why hasn't she written, Monsieur Joliot? It's over a fortnight now and she hasn't even sent a card. I don't understand it. No letter from Emilie and no letter from Maman. It's beginning to worry me.'

Charlie had written, the same as ever, via Veronique, and at great length, telling her how much he loved her and missed her, and promising to come over to Boulogne the minute his examinations were over. She'd written back at equal length to pour out her woes and worries, telling him she couldn't wait to see him again and suggesting that, since Maman had left the house, he might as well write to her at Boves. Charlie hadn't answered her letter, yet, but that was probably because he was studying so hard. Emily really *ought* to have written, and so should Maman. There was no excuse for either of *them*.

Since that awful day when Maman ran away, life in Boves had been very difficult. There'd been a lot more housework to do and the rent to find all on her own. On top of that, so many people had been angry with her – as if the situation were her fault! Even mild-mannered Monsieur the Advocate was annoyed to have lost his housekeeper, and told her so in terms that for him were really quite sharp.

'I don't understand it, Mademoiselle Lisieux,' he said, 'to leave such a good job and so precipitously.' And he turned to his sister who stood behind him looking inscrutable. 'She was well enough when you last saw her, wasn't she, Marie?'

Marie said nothing, but her face spoke volumes. It was an expression Ginny was to see on far too many faces during the next two weeks. Madame Gambetta had spread her gossip most efficiently and everyone knew that her old enemy had left the village in disgrace because she was 'an associate of women of ill-repute'.

The only woman in the village who hadn't heard the gossip was Ginny herself, so it was hard for her to understand why so many of her neighbours were glaring at her. But the lack of letters was the worst thing to endure – it didn't make *any* sort of sense at all. Neither did Cousin Berthe's peculiar behaviour.

The first evening after Maman ran away, Ginny had come home from work to find Cousin Berthe in the kitchen, cheerfully cooking their dinner as if nothing had happened.

'Where's Maman?' she demanded, running into the kitchen. 'Is she all right?'

Berthe assumed an expression that was quite new to Ginny, the hideous smirk of a teacher's pet about to drop someone into trouble. 'Mustn't say,' she said, and nodded her head importantly.

Ginny decided to ignore the expression – for the time being at least. 'Where is she?' she said quietly. 'Did you come back together?'

'No.'

'No. What do you mean, no? Hasn't she come back?'

'No. She hasn't.'

'Then where is she?'

'Mustn't say.'

'Oh, come on!' Ginny said, beginning to get cross. 'Where is she? You can tell me that, can't you? Think!'

But all she could get out of Berthe was the same parrot answer. 'Mustn't say. Mustn't say.'

'Why mustn't you say?' Ginny tried. 'Who told you not to?'

But that didn't work either. The answer was the same. 'Mustn't say.'

I'll wait till Old Joliot gets in, Ginny decided, setting to work and clearing the table. (Berthe always made such a mess when she was cooking.) Perhaps he'll know something. And, if he doesn't, perhaps he'll know how to get her to tell us.

Old Joliot was as baffled as she was. 'Won't say a word,' he said. 'I been on at her all day, off an' on. Can't get anything out of her no matter which way. We'll have to give her time, that's about the size of it. I think she's been told to keep quiet for a while.'

But it didn't seem to matter how much time they gave her; Berthe was adamant. She'd been told to say nothing and she was as obedient as a robot. 'Mustn't say,' she said, over and over again. In the meantime the gossips were talking nineteen to the dozen, all round the village. And there were no letters.

'Something is the matter,' Ginny confided to Veronique, when another week had passed and she still hadn't heard. 'It's not like Emily not to write. You don't think something's happened to her, do you?'

'Who knows?' Veronique said, feeding a fresh sheet of paper into her typewriter.

'She must have got there safely,' Ginny worried on. 'If there'd been an accident it would have been in the papers, wouldn't it?'

'She'll be busy settling into her new home,' Veronique said. 'You'll hear soon.'

'But what about Maman? She doesn't write either.'

'Now that *is* a mystery,' Veronique admitted, flicking the paper with her finger tips. 'Perhaps she's got to work so hard there isn't time for writing.'

'I don't know where she is or what she's doing,' Ginny said, irritable with anxiety. 'You really would have thought she could have managed a postcard.'

But Hortense couldn't manage anything. She was lying flat on her back in the narrow bed in her narrow cell in the convent, her lovely face blotched with fever, and so ill she couldn't sit up without fainting.

From time to time, when one of the sisters came into the cell to see how she was, she opened her eyes and tried to talk.

'No doctor,' she said thickly. 'I shall be – all right. Better in – minute. Mussen call – doctor. Tell my Virginie.'

But the doctor had been called and visited her every day, because she had congestion of the lungs. That morning he had predicted that the crisis would be coming soon.

'Her fever is very high,' he told Mother Superior. 'It can't be much longer now.'

They looked at their patient with loving pity, powerless to assist her through the trial ahead. There were no drugs to cure pneumonia and no help that either of them could offer, except daily blanket baths and constant prayer. They were well aware that by the next morning she would either be dead or on the long road to recovery.

'Tonight I will sit with her myself,' Mother Superior said.

'As I knew you would, Mother,' the doctor said. 'We will all pray for her.'

It was a long vigil and a cold one. Hortense tossed and turned, fiery-faced and coughing incessantly. Mother Superior sponged her forehead when the sweat ran into her eyes, and held her hand when she was calm enough to take comfort from it, and prayed . . .

'You are in God's hands, my dear,' she said, placing her mouth close to her patient's ear whenever she woke. 'God's good hands.'

Hortense muttered and groaned and grew more and more distressed. 'I can't be ill,' she wept. 'I daren't. It's too dreadful. It's the taint, you see. How shall we manage? Oh my poor little ones. I must get better.'

'Reserve your strength, my dear,' Mother advised. 'Don't try to talk.'

But Hortense was too distraught to hear her. 'It is all my fault,' she wept. '*Mea culpa. Mea culpa. Mea maxima culpa.*' And she went on weeping until she fell into an uneasy sleep.

Just after two in the morning she had a violent shivering fit and called out for her mother, her voice shaking like her body. 'Maman! Maman! Forgive me!'

'I am here, my child,' Mother Superior said, holding both her hands.

'Oh Maman,' Hortense babbled. 'I didn't mean to grieve you so. You must believe me. I'm so sorry. So very, very sorry. I should never have done it. I wish I hadn't. I love you so much, you and Papa. I should have stayed on the farm. You always told me . . .'

'Hush now,' Mother said, sponging her forehead.

'I've been a bad daughter to you,' Hortense wept. 'A bad daughter. I've brought you such grief. To have caught such an illness! The shame of it!' And then, on a note of rising panic, 'Maman! Maman! Where are you?'

'I'm here.'

'Yes. Yes. I can see you. Hold my hand, Maman, please. I've got something to tell you. Something you won't like. But I must say it. I haven't been to confession for years and years. I couldn't do it, you see. Not with such sins . . . such terrible sins. You understand that, don't you, Maman? Oh please, say you understand. I couldn't bear it if you didn't understand. I never meant to hurt you. Say you understand.'

'I understand,' said Mother Superior. 'Try to rest now, my child.'

'Pretty clothes,' Hortense said wildly. 'If it hadn't been for all those pretty clothes I would have stayed on the farm like a good daughter. I'm lost. Lost. I can't confess. I want to so much, and I can't do it. Oh Maman, my dear good Maman, say you love me. I'm not worth loving. How could anybody love me?'

'Jesus loves you,' Mother Superior said quietly. 'Never forget that, my child. No matter how bad the sin, Jesus loves you.'

'I've been such a terrible sinner,' Hortense wept. 'If I told you half the things I've done, you wouldn't be sitting beside me like this, looking after me. You'd be afraid of me. You'd run away. We loved one another, you see. Is love like that so very wrong? It must be, otherwise we wouldn't suffer so. He did suffer so, Maman.'

'Hush, my dear.'

'We gave one another this shameful illness, this taint. This is how he began — with sweating and fever and congestion of the lungs — after that he got worse and worse. In the end he was quite demented. Quite demented. That's

334

what it does to you, this illness. It was a terrible death. Oh Maman! Help me! I mustn't tell you this. Nobody must know. I promised. Oh! Oh! But I've told you, haven't I? I've shocked you. You'll leave me.'

'No,' Mother Superior said gently. 'You haven't shocked me and I shan't leave you. Your illness is not unknown to me, Hortense, my dear. I've seen it before.'

'Can I ever be forgiven?'

'Of course. God's mercy is infinite.'

Hortense was too far gone with fever and distress to understand her. 'Nobody would ever . . .' she said. 'And my poor Edouard gone. I loved him so much. We loved one another . . . through it all . . .' And then a fit of coughing made it impossible to say anything else, and when it eased, she lay clutching Mother's hand, too exhausted to speak. Then the fever burned her into unconsciousness.

Towards dawn she woke again and recognised the woman who was sitting beside her, rosary in hand.

'Mother,' she said.

'My child.'

'Am I very ill?'

'You have been. Very ill. Now you are getting better.'

'Have you been here all the time?'

'Me or one of the sisters.'

'You are very good. Am I really getting better?'

'Yes. Sleep now, my child. The more you sleep the sooner you will heal.'

But Hortense took a long time to recover. Although the danger had passed, she was ill for another fortnight, with night sweats and a terrible racking cough. Even when she was well enough to sit up and sip a little of Mother's watery gruel, she was thin and weak and depressed by the least little thing. Rain made her weep in sympathy, a tangle in her hair reduced her to angry sobbing. Her weakness terrified her and, after every shameful outburst, she apologised abjectly for her behaviour.

Taking it in turns to sit up with her when she was bad at night, the sisters nursed her devotedly, washing her tenderly

335

every morning, feeding her when she was too fatigued to feed herself, brushing her hair and drying her tears. They were difficult days because Hortense hated being such a nuisance. It seemed a very long time before she was able to get up, wash and dress herself, and go down to the chapel for prayers – the relief of which was so exquisite she wept all through the mass.

'Now you are truly on the mend,' Mother said to her, as they walked slowly down to the refectory for their evening meal.

'I must write to my daughter,' Hortense said. 'She will be worried.'

'Without doubt,' Mother said. 'But perhaps it would be better if you went to confession first. Your sins weigh heavily upon you.'

'Did I speak of them when I was ill?' Hortense asked.

'Only to me,' Mother said, understanding what lay behind the question. 'Now you should tell the Father Confessor.'

'I can't,' Hortense said, hanging her head. 'They are too dreadful.' And not the sort of things to confess to a man. Dear God, never to a man! Not even to a priest. Bad enough that this shrewd, patient woman should know about them. 'I can't.'

'Then you must pray for grace,' Mother Superior said, 'and we will add our prayers to yours. Sin is too great a burden for anyone to carry alone.'

'Yes Mother. I will pray. I promise you that.'

Mother smiled at her. 'I'm sure you will. Meantime, you must write your letter.'

So, at last and to Ginny's great relief, a letter arrived from Maman. It was three pages long and very involved. It explained how Berthe had taken her to the convent, and how ill she'd been, and apologised for her long silence and her '*stupid departure*'.

*'I am still quite weak and would rather nobody came to visit me, just for a week or two. I have a job here in the convent looking*

*after the children as soon as I am well enough to do it. The sisters are looking after me and I have a great debt to repay them. I pray for forgiveness. I love you dearly. Give Emilie my love and tell her my news. I do so hope she is well and that you are, too. Write back to me soon and pray for me. I am your most loving, Maman.'*

'She's in the Convent of the Little Sisters of Divine Mercy,' Ginny said to Old Joliot when she'd read the letter through. She was disappointed that her mother hadn't said anything about coming home, but at least she knew where she was and why she hadn't written. 'I shall write back at once.'

Which she did, choosing her words to be ambiguous saying, '*we are all well'*, so that Maman would think Emily was included. And she urged her mother not to worry. '*We all understand why you had to leave,'* she wrote. '*I know that there are times when you have to move away. I hope you will say I may visit you soon and that you will soon be completely recovered from your illness. My poor dear Maman. I would do anything to help you. You know that. Meantime, I send you my fondest love.'*

'Would you like to send her a message?' she asked Old Joliot, as she put her pen down.

To her surprise it was Cousin Berthe who answered. 'Yes,' she said. 'You tell her I hid all them things away like she said.'

'What things?'

'Never you mind what things. Tell her I hid 'em. Like she said. You tell her that.'

Ginny looked a question at Old Joliot.

'Humour her,' he said. 'It's all nonsense, but it pleases her.'

So the message was written, verbatim, and Berthe came up to the table to admire it.

'I was to give you her love,' she said. 'She tol' me.'

'Who did?' Ginny asked.

'Why your Maman,' Berthe beamed. 'Your Maman, that's who. When I took her to that ol' convent, that's what she said. Give 'em my love she said. So I have.'

'Oh, for heaven's sake!' Ginny said furiously. 'Do you mean to say you've known where she was all this time?'

' 'Course.'

'Then why didn't you tell us when you came back?' It would have made all the difference to have a message like that.

'You didn't ask me,' Berthe said, and this time she smiled quite brightly. 'Give my love to Ginny and Old Joliot she said. Say – um – something else. Can't remember what that was. Something else. We're to visit in a few days.'

Hot with anger at Berthe's stupidity, Ginny went out into the scullery to wash the dishes, clattering them together noisily.

'I wonder at you sometimes, Berthe,' she said. 'I really do. If you've got a message for someone you're supposed to tell them straightaway, not three weeks later.'

'That's right,' Berthe said happily. 'Straightaway.'

'No good scoldin' her,' Old Joliot said, peaceably smoking his pipe. 'She don't understand.'

'All this time,' Ginny said crossly. 'She could have said. She could have told us the minute she got back instead of all that stupid smirking and "Mustn't say" all the time.'

'She means well,' Joliot said. 'She wouldn't harm a fly.'

He was wrong. Although she didn't know it, Cousin Berthe was actually doing Ginny a lot of harm.

Hortense's foreign stamp was still stuck in the corner of Cousin Berthe's mirror in the little cupboard room where she slept and snored, away from the rest of the house. She'd taken it out of her hatband and put it there, the minute she'd returned to the house. Since then she'd been looking after the letters, just the way Hortense had told her to.

At first, she hadn't been quite sure what she had to do. The first post always arrived after everyone else had gone to work and the last one came before they got home, so there was no one to ask. She stood in her room with the foreign letter in her hand and checked the stamp on the envelope against the stamp in the mirror over and over until she was quite sure it was the right one. It was the right one. But then she'd had to think for quite a long time because she couldn't remember what she was supposed to do next.

Eventually she'd walked into the kitchen with the letter. And there was the stove, all warm and glowing, and that made her remember. She had to hide it. That was what she had to do. She had to hide the letter somewhere safe. And what better place than the stove? No one would think of looking there.

She opened the lid and looked down at the red coals glowing on their bed of ash. What a good place! Smiling with satisfaction she dropped the letter in.

She'd hidden all the other letters there, too, both of Emily's invitations, her letter to Ginny and seven letters from Charlie. Wasn't she a good girl?

# CHAPTER TWENTY-FOUR

The examination hall was three-quarters empty on that November afternoon and as clammy as a coal cellar. In the summer it had been crammed to capacity and extremely hot, but now there were only the 're-takes' to sit, and the heating appeared to have broken down.

Charlie Commoner was sitting in the second row and writing hard. After his long self-imposed absence from Jeannie (and the responsibility of the debts he had to pay), he couldn't run the risk of a second failure. Too much depended on it. He had revised more thoroughly than he'd ever done in his life, and now there were just a few more points to make in the last answer and the penultimate test would be over and done.

Outside the long windows of the hall, the trees were bare, their branches black against a colourless sky. To Charlie's over-stimulated vision, they looked moody and atmospheric, like a shot from a Russian film. Once, when he looked up, a black crow flew past the window; its serrated wings moved heavily and its fat body was shaped like one of the new Hurricane fighter planes he'd seen in the papers. How much longer have I got? Ten minutes. God! I'd better write quicker!

By the time the papers had been collected, it was already evening. Out in the street, it was darker than he expected, and the air was raw and smelled of soot. There was a newspaper-seller standing at the entrance to the Underground, shuffling his feet to keep warm and chanting his evening cry *Star-new-stannard!* over and over again. Charlie bought a copy of the *Evening News* to read on the way home.

It was such a depressing edition he'd stuffed it in his pocket before he reached Stockwell. There was nothing in it except wars and misery. The Japanese had captured Shanghai, Hitler and Mussolini had had a meeting and 'pledged to work together' (I'll bet they have!), the House of Commons had voted to build air-raid shelters in all the big cities (so *they* think there's a war coming), and there were 'several more cases of typhoid' reported in South London. The deliberate vagueness of that report annoyed Charlie and scared him, too. Typhoid was a nasty disease. A killer. And if they said there were 'more' cases that must mean there'd been several already. He didn't like the sound of that at all, especially as it was in 'South London'. But whereabouts in South London? It could be anywhere. I'll ask Mum, he decided. She'll be bound to know where it is.

She did. 'I wasn't going to tell you,' she said, prodding the potatoes with her fork to see if they were done. 'Not yet, awhile anyway. No good getting alarmed before you need to. There's been rumours going round since last Friday. I thought it'd be in the papers sooner or later. What's it say?'

He showed her the article. 'Not much.'

His mother read it, fork in hand but turning her head away from the cooker. 'Very cagey,' she said. 'It's in Croydon, so they say. In the watercress beds. That's why we never 'ad watercress Sunday.'

'You don' wanna take no notice a' that,' Aunty Grace said coming into the kitchen. 'Scare stories that is. Watercress is good for yer. It's ice cream you got ter watch out for. Some a' them Eyeties make it out a' bath water. 'Lo Charlie how d'you get on with your exams?'

'All right.'

'I got some Lysol today,' Ruby said, pointing at the bottle, ribbed and green on the windowsill. 'They say that's the best thing. If we keep everything washed down, and do the drains and everything we ought to be all right. No going to Croydon, though. That'd be asking for trouble.'

'Righto!' Charlie said. 'I'll only go to the office and the exam hall. Word of honour. They don't serve watercress there. Or ice cream.'

'Well, that's daft, if you ask me,' Grace said. 'That's

341

lettin' 'em push you around. If you wanna go to Croydon, you go.'

'He doesn't want to go to Croydon,' Ruby said wearily. Grace had been more cantankerous than ever during the last few days and she was finding it hard to cope with her.

'I'm goin' Thursday,' Grace said. 'Won't stop me.'

'Goin' where?' Grandpa said, joining them in the kitchen.

'Croydon,' Grace said, looking stubborn, 'and don't you start, neither.'

'I wouldn't if I was you,' Grandpa warned. ' 'Lo Charlie.'

Grace was bristling with annoyance. 'I don't need your permission, thank you very much,' she said, glaring at Grandpa. 'If I want to go to Croydon I shall go there, don't you worry.'

Grandpa was hungry so he changed the subject. Temporarily. 'You gonna dish up, Rube?' he said plaintively. 'My belly thinks my throat's been cut.'

'Go through,' Ruby said. 'I shan't be a tick.'

When the two adversaries had gone, Charlie made a grimace at his mother. 'Oh, lor'!' he said.

'We shall 'ave ructions all through supper,' Ruby said. 'You can't tell Grace what to do. He ought to know better'n that. Still there you are, they been in a wicked mood all day, the pair of 'em. Oh! There's a letter for you on the mantelpiece. I almost forgot.'

'From France?'

'Where else?' Now that she'd got used to the idea, this French girlfriend of his was an accepted fact, almost as if she were part of the family.

'And about time, too,' Charlie said. 'She hasn't written to me for ages.' And he went off at once to retrieve it and bring it back into the kitchen.

It was a surprising letter.


*Dear Charlie,*
*I know you're very busy revising for your exams but I do wish you'd write to me. Even a postcard would do. I haven't heard from*

*you for such a long time. Nearly two weeks. I suppose they are still sending letters across the Channel!*

*Maman is in a convent. She says she's got a job there. She's been ill but she is better now. I think she is going to stay there for quite a while so we shall have a free run for our next weekend. I shan't have to think up excuses or anything. I am looking forward to it. I haven't seen you for such a long time. Are you still coming on the morning ferry? I shall be there to meet you when you dock.*

*Please write back as soon as ever you can. I miss you.*

*Your ever loving, "Jeannie".*

'Everything all right?' Ruby asked, seeing his scowl.

'No. Not really. She says I haven't written to her for – what was it? – nearly two weeks. I don't know what she's on about. I've written her – oh – seven letters, at least.'

'P'rhaps they got lost in the post.'

'Seven letters?'

'Never mind,' Ruby said, draining the cabbage into the baking tray. 'You can write her another one, can't you? Explain sort a' thing. Is that your father? Oh good. Now I can dish up an' we can have a stop to all that argument.' For Grandpa and Aunt Grace were shouting at one another at the tops of their voices.

No matter how much food she piled on their plates, nor how tactfully Stan tried to introduce new topics of conversation, the two old enemies argued throughout the meal. After the table was cleared, they took themselves off to bed and wouldn't even stop for tea and cigarettes.

And the following afternoon Grace carried out her threat and went to Croydon.

Ruby was worried sick about her. 'It's so silly,' she said to Charlie, when he got in from work. 'Running risks like that.'

'Where is she?' Charlie asked.

'Not back yet.'

'She'll be all right,' Charlie said. He wanted to get upstairs and do a bit of revision before everybody came home and there was too much noise. 'Where's Grandpa?'

343

'Asleep, thank God. Don't wake him. He's been driving me crackers today. I've had *all* his stories, non-stop.'

'I'll go up on tiptoe,' Charlie assured her. And he did.

It was past eight o'clock before Grace came home and, by that time, Ruby was convinced that she'd been taken ill in a shop and 'carted off to hospital'. But Grace was fighting fit and full of stories about how frightened they all were in Croydon and what a state her friend had been in.

'Her place pongs a' disinfectant,' she said. 'I said to 'er, I said, you wanna get out of it. Go somewhere else for the time bein'.'

'Just so long as she don't come 'ere,' Grandpa Jones said sourly.

'Oh you're still alive, are yer?' Grace said scathingly.

'Time you was at the pub, Charlie,' Stan said, sending sympathetic signals to Ruby. 'Tell 'em I'll be down presently for a quick one.'

Charlie was glad to get out of the house. It wasn't his fault that their two artful pensioners kept quarrelling all the time but he was the reason they were in the house in the first place. Roll on, Friday, he thought. Once his last exam was over he could plan the future. Stop being a barman. Get a position. Earn a salary. Pay off his debts. Take control of his life. Go to Boulogne. Go to Boulogne – that was the thing. He couldn't wait to get there. Jeannie was right. It *had* been ages.

But there was still the weekend to get through, four long days of the week and an exam on Friday.

It wasn't an easy week. The weather was raw and damp and Jack Bond had a cold and coughed and sneezed all over the office. On Wednesday, Mr Crabbit called Charlie in to the inner office to show him a letter from Mrs Everdale. She wanted 'that nice Mr Commoner' to go to Paris, as soon as possible, to put advertisements in all the main newspapers in time for Christmas.

'Aren't you off there this weekend?' Mr Crabbit said. Charlie said he was. 'Thought so. Well then, you can kill two birds with one stone, can't you? Cut off to Paris and see to this at the same time.'

It took courage for Charlie to refuse, but really he couldn't agree to that. Not after all the fuss there'd been the last time he and Jeannie were in Paris. 'No sir,' he said, speaking politely but firmly. 'I'm afraid that wouldn't be possible. I have – things to attend to in Boulogne.'

'Won't take the whole weekend, surely?'

Charlie stuck to his guns. 'Yes sir. I'm afraid it will.'

'She's extremely anxious that we should find her nieces.'

'I appreciate that, sir. I can assure her I'm every bit as anxious as she is. But I can't act for her this weekend.'

There was a long pause while the two men looked at one another, and Mr Crabbit summed up the situation. Then he threw back his head and gave a great roar of laughter.

'Good for you, young shaver,' he said.

'I'll write to Mrs Everdale, shall I?' Charlie said, relieved and encouraged, but still polite. 'Suggest an alternative date.'

'Capital idea,' Mr Crabbit said, dismissing him with a grin.

Mr Crabbit's elderly secretary had been sitting in the corner all through the exchange, pretending to type. 'Good heavens!' she said. 'Fancy him standing up to you like that Mr C. I always thought he was such a nice, quiet, young man.'

'He's maturing, Miss Murphy,' Horace Crabbit said, lighting the first cheroot of the morning. 'He's maturing very nicely.' There was no doubt now that Mr Commoner would be taken into the firm. 'He'll go far will our Mr Commoner.'

'But not to Paris, apparently,' Miss Murphy said, pursing her lips.

The last examination was easier than Charlie had dared to hope. This time, he emerged from the exam hall feeling quite light-headed. One more night and one more day and he'd be on the boat train and heading for Boulogne. The thought made him throw his hat into the air, to the consternation of two elderly ladies in furs who happened to be passing by.

345

'I'm going to Boulogne,' he explained.

'And the sooner the better, if you ask me,' the nearest lady said. And was put out when he gave her a rapturous smile.

Charlie didn't bother buying an evening paper (he wouldn't have read it, anyway) and went straight home, cocooned in happy dreams. He ate his supper in a dream, and went off to meet his friends for a celebratory pint, still in a state of cheerful euphoria. And, naturally, when the pubs closed they all went back to their friend Jimmy's house to celebrate a little more. It was very late by the time Charlie got back to Abbeville Road, and although he wasn't exactly drunk, he was certainly a bit squiffy.

The lights were out except for a little pink one in the hall. He took off his shoes very quietly and crept up the stairs. One of the water pipes was making a peculiar gurgling sound somewhere above him and he was just thinking he'd have to tell Dad about it in the morning when he realised that there was a figure stooping and swaying at the turn of the stairs. The noise he was hearing was somebody being violently sick.

He had the lights on and was up the stairs in a second, calling for his mother as he ran. It was Aunty Grace and she'd been sick all over everything, up the wall and all over the carpet. Everywhere. It made him gag just to look at it.

'Go 'way!' she said, waving at him. 'It's the typhoid. Go 'way!'

For a few seconds his mind stopped working altogether, stuck on the horror of that word. Typhoid! My God! Typhoid! She's got the typhoid. Then Mum was flapping on to the landing in her slippers, doing up her dressing gown as she ran. 'Keep away Charlie!' she called, 'Keep right away! We don't want you catching it an' all. Oh I knew this would happen.'

'Get the Lysol, son,' Dad's voice commanded. 'There's a bottle on the windowsill in the kitchen.'

As Charlie ran off on his errand, Grace slumped to the floor and began to groan. 'I'm dyin' Rube,' she wept. 'I'm dyin'. Send fer a doctor, fer pity's sake.'

'Lysol first, then the doctor,' Stan told them. 'We'll make masks with hankies like they do in the hospital. We ain't runnin' risks. Not with this.'

Charlie passed the Lysol over Grace's groaning head and tried not to gag; presently Dad handed down a sopping wet handkerchief for him to tie round his mouth and chin and that made him feel better, giving him something else to smell. He knew what a terrible illness typhoid was and how easily you could die of it, but there was too much to do to stop and think about it.

It took three of them to haul Grace to her feet and half drag, half carry her into the bathroom. And if that was hard, removing all those foul-smelling spattered clothes to bathe her was even worse, because Grace protested all the time, and groaned and flung herself about and wept that she was dying.

'Mind my 'ead, Rube,' she begged. 'I got such an 'eadache.' And 'Look out fer me stomach. It don't 'alf hurt. Oh Gawd, Charlie, I'm dyin'.'

Charlie was very relieved when she was stripped to her combinations, and Dad told him to cut off to the telephone box down by the shops and phone the doctor.

'His number's in the book in the hall drawer. Dr Groizard.'

It was cool and quiet and wonderfully sweet-smelling out in Abbeville Road. Clean, normal smells, like pumicestone and privet hedges, and dust and crushed grass. Wonderful smells after the stench on the stairs.

The doctor was cool, too. The word typhoid didn't ruffle him at all. 'Tell me her symptoms,' he said. 'How long has she been ill?'

Charlie explained what he could. 'Not long. She was all right at supper.'

'Ate well?'

'I suppose so. I didn't notice.'

'Any fever?'

'Yes.'

347

'Headache?'

'Yes. Very bad.'

'I'll come round,' the doctor said. 'It probably isn't typhoid, but its best to be on the safe side. Keep her warm. Watch her. Don't worry. I shan't be long.'

Aunt Grace was propped up in bed when he got back. She was washed and scrubbed and looked as though she was asleep, but when he told his parents that the doctor was coming she opened her eyes and began to groan.

'I do feel bad, Charlie,' she said.

'I'd try an' get some sleep, if I was you,' Ruby advised her. 'I put yer pot right by the bed. See.'

'Sleep!' Grace said. 'With typhoid fever!'

'We don't know if it is yet,' Ruby said.

' 'Course we know,' Grace said. 'I feel too bad for it to be anything else.'

'The doctor said he didn't think it would be typhoid,' Charlie said, trying to reassure her. 'It could be anything.'

But that provoked indignation. 'Fat lot *he* knows,' she said. 'He ain't seen me yet. An' I'll bet 'e takes 'is time an' all. They're all the same these doctors. You could be dead in yer grave before they come out to see yer. Did you tell 'im how ill I was?'

' 'Course.'

'Well I wish 'e'd hurry up.'

'He'll be here soon,' Ruby comforted.

It seemed a very long time before the doctor arrived.

He sent both men out of the room and, despite his obvious fatigue, examined his patient carefully, talking quietly to her.

'Nothing too alarming, Miss Allicott,' he said, when he'd finished.

'What've I got?' Grace said, squinting at him through her headache.

'I can't be sure yet,' he said, giving her his best bedside smile. 'But I shall keep an eye on you and the minute I know what it is I shall tell you, you can depend on it. And now, if I were you I'd settle down and try to get some sleep.'

To Ruby's relief Grace didn't argue with him. 'Yes doctor,' she said, and closed her eyes obediently.

Down in the kitchen where Stan was making a pot of tea, Dr Groizard was more forthcoming.

'She's got a slight temperature,' he said. 'Nothing much, but that's no consolation, I'm afraid, in this epidemic. No rash as yet. We shan't see it for another seven days if we're to see it at all. We'll hope not. But the stomach pains and the headache are rather worrying. Particularly the headache. We must watch that very carefully. You'll let me know if it gets any worse, Mrs Commoner?'

'Of course,' Ruby promised. 'Will she have to go to the 'ospital, Doctor?'

Doctor Groizard ran his hand over his forehead, as if he were mopping it with a cloth. 'Possibly,' he said. 'And then again, possibly not. It depends how bad it is. We shall have to wait and see. I'll call in tomorrow morning. And now, if you'll allow me to advise you, I should go back to bed and try and get some sleep. If this is typhoid and you're going to nurse it at home you'll need all your energy.'

'We could all do with a bit a' kip, an' that's a fact,' Stan said ruefully. 'I doubt if we'll get it though.'

He was right.

Grace spent most of the night calling for help, groaning and weeping, and Ruby was up and down the stairs over and over again, emptying her chamber pot and re-making her bed, and sponging her down with water and Lysol. By the time Stan's alarm clock rang its unnecessary bell at six o'clock, the house smelled and felt like a hospital. The only good thing that could be said about the entire night was that Grandpa Jones had slept through it all.

Charlie and Stan struggled to cook themselves some breakfast and tried to make plans. Grandpa was still snoring and Grace was asleep at last, so they'd decided to let poor Ruby lie in.

'I don't know how we shall make out, and that's a fact,' Stan said, spearing a sausage on the frying fork. 'Your poor Mum'll have ter bear the brunt of it. I can't stay off work, not the way things are. I'm due in eight o'clock this morning. And you're off to France, ain't cher.'

'Not till ten o'clock,' Charlie said, making the tea. 'I *was* going in to the office for a couple of hours but I can give that the go-by.'

'You sure?'

'Yep. Can't leave Mum all on her own with all this.'

'You're a good lad, Charlie,' Stan said. 'See what the doctor says this morning, eh? A lot's gonna depend on that.'

Neither of them had much idea what would happen if it really *was* typhoid.

'I can always catch another boat,' Charlie hoped. 'Anyway, you're right, we shall know when the doctor's been.'

The doctor's next visit left them no wiser. Grace was worse, but he couldn't say for certain whether she had typhoid or not. 'We'll watch her over the weekend,' he said. 'I'll come in again on Monday. We shall know in a few days. Meanwhile keep everything scrubbed down with disinfectant and be very careful when you're preparing food. Scrub your hands before you touch anything. What did you do with her soiled clothes?'

'They're in the copper, steeping.'

'In disinfectant?'

'Yes.'

'Good. Good. I'll see you on Monday, then.'

And that was that. It was such an anti-climax that as soon as Ruby closed the door on him she began to cry.

'Oh, Charlie,' she wept 'I'm sorry. I shouldn't go on like this, but what are we going to do? It *is* typhoid. I know it is. I'm worried out a' me wits.'

'What's goin' on down there?' Grandpa said. He was halfway down the stairs and horribly dishevelled in that tatty dressing gown of his. 'You was makin' enough racket last night, weren't yer? What's fer breakfast?'

'Aunty Grace is ill,' Charlie said. Mum was crying worse than ever. He could sense her shoulders shaking just behind him. Poor Mum. 'Go in the kitchen and I'll get you some tea.'

'Tea?' Grandpa scoffed. 'I want a lot more'n tea, Charlie boy. I got an appetite.'

'Then you'll have to live with it,' Charlie said. 'Aunty Grace has got the typhoid.'

The old man's jaw fell open. 'Never!' he said. 'She ain't! Oh my good Gawd, Charlie, we shall all catch it.'

'Ruby!' Grace's voice called from the front room. 'Ruby! Where are you? Oh Gawd, Rube, I do feel bad.'

Ruby dried her eyes and tried to control herself but it was almost beyond her. 'Oh Charlie,' she said. 'What are we going to do?'

In the kitchen a flicker of pale sunlight edged the toasting fork with gold and the glimmer of it caught Charlie's eye. He turned and there it was, the essence that was his home, fixed like a photograph in all its mundane, much loved detail; the red fringe of the mantle cover, Mum's two horse brasses, patient clock, battered fire irons, coal scuttle at the ready with coal and kindling, matches in the grate, ciggies on the mantelpiece. His home where he'd always been loved and cared for, no matter what. And in that moment he knew what he had to do and decided to do it.

'You go in the kitchen,' he said to his grandfather, 'and I'll see to your breakfast.' Then he turned to his mother. 'And you go and see to Aunty Grace, and don't worry.'

'You'll miss your train,' Ruby said.

'I'm not going.'

'Not going?'

'No,' Charlie said, putting his arm round her shoulders. 'I'm going to stay here and look after you.'

'But weren't you going to. . . ? What about. . . ?' Ruby was worried. 'Your girl'll be waiting for you. How're you going to let her know you won't be there?'

'I'll write,' Charlie said. 'She'll understand.' She would, wouldn't she? 'There'll always be another time. Come on, Grandpa, shift your shanks.'

# Chapter Twenty-Five

Ginny was awake at six o'clock that morning, too, taut with excitement and happiness. She'd been too restless to sleep much that night, and at six o'clock she gave up the struggle, lit a candle, got up and dressed. She was too het up to eat breakfast either, so she was out of the house much earlier than usual, on the grounds that she might as well wait on the platform as in Old Joliot's kitchen, especially as Berthe was being hideously slow and talkative. At least she'd be alone on her way to the station and free to give herself up to her thoughts.

But as she stepped into the street, there was Madame Gambetta, resplendent in new red hat, a new navy-blue coat and very high heels, trotting down the hill to join her. Madame Gambetta was on her way to the station, too.

'You are off to work, I daresay, Mademoiselle Lisieux,' she said brightly. 'What a bit of luck. I am going to Amiens, too. We shall be company for one another. How is your dear Maman?'

Horrible woman, Ginny thought. I don't want to talk to her. She doesn't care how Maman is. She only wants to make mischief. But she answered politely, 'She's very well, Madame.'

'And happy in her new job, doubtless,' Madame Gambetta persisted.

'Very happy. Yes.'

'And where was it, did you say? This new job.'

'Oh, a long way away,' Ginny said vaguely. 'In a convent.'

'A convent! Well, well!'

Ginny didn't quite know how to respond to that. It sounded almost like a taunt, as if Madame Gambetta thought a convent was the last place Maman should be. Best to ignore it.

The two women proceeded along the dark street in silence, past cottage windows, yellow with gaslight and the baker's shop with its appetising smell of newly baked bread. Madame Gambetta resumed her interrogation.

'And your sister,' she said. 'That was a great surprise to us too, my dear. How is your dear sister?'

'Very well, Madame.' (And you needn't think you're going to catch me out on that either.)

'And happy? She left to get married, I believe.'

'Yes. An Englishman. An industrialist.'

That *did* surprise the lady. 'You don't say so!' she said. 'An industrialist. She *has* gone up in the world. Are they to marry in our church here in Boves?'

'Oh no,' Ginny covered. 'It will be in England, naturally, since it is at his expense. He is a very generous man.'

'And an industrialist, you say?'

'Oh yes,' Ginny said. She was quite enjoying the conversation now that she'd got the upper hand. 'He owns a big factory in London. He's quite a rich man. And passionately in love with our Emilie. Naturally.'

'You don't say so!' Madame Gambetta said again. 'A love match, eh? Well, I'm blessed. And never a word about it from any of you. We should never have guessed.'

'Some things are private, are they not, Madame?'

Madame Gambetta had to agree. '*Mais oui*. But, of course.' But then she returned to the attack. 'And so you are the only one still at home. How sad. We must see that you are not left an old maid, must we not.'

'No fear of that, Madame,' Ginny said, stung again. It was extraordinary how easily this woman could root out a weakness and tug at it. 'I shall soon be married myself.' What a marvellous thing to be able to say, she thought. The waiting is over. In a few hours I shall see him again.

'You don't tell me,' Madame Gambetta was saying.

Ginny pulled her mind back to the conversation. 'I do.'

'What a dark horse you are, my dear,' Madame Gambetta said. 'And who is he, this young man of yours? Do we know him?'

The temptation to talk about her Charlie was too strong. There was no harm in it now. Maman had gone away and couldn't be upset by anything she said; Emily was in England and out of reach.

'No, Madame,' she said. 'Actually you don't know him. He is a solicitor from London.'

'A solicitor, eh?' Madame Gambetta said, somewhat discomfited. Then she recovered. 'An older man, doubtless.'

'No,' Ginny told her. 'A young man. The same age as me. And very handsome. Tall and fair with lovely grey eyes.' Just to think of those eyes made her feel quite weak.

'What good fortune!' Madame Gambetta said. 'And are *you* to marry in Boves, my dear?'

Fortunately they had reached the station and Ginny was spared having to give an answer, because they were both fully occupied with exchanging greetings with their travelling companions, who were standing along the platform huddled into scarves and shawls.

It was very cold indeed on the station, with an early-morning dankness that reduced the gaslight to a fuzzy halo and seeped chill into their bones. The train was late. But, in one way, that was fortunate, for as soon as it arrived there was a scramble to get aboard, and Ginny managed to shake off Madame Gambetta and her inquisition.

Once she was on her own, Ginny began to fear she'd told her neighbour far too much. She'll spread it all round the village, she thought. But then happiness welled up in her and she knew it didn't matter. She was going to see her dear Charlie again. *That* was what mattered. In eight hours – no less than eight hours – she would be in his arms, kissing him and telling him how much she loved him. That was what mattered.

Happiness bubbled her along for the rest of the morning, even though Monsieur Guerin was in one of his moods. When he rushed from the factory tearing at his hair and shrieking that he hadn't got time to *breathe*, she burst into a fit of giggles.

354

'So today's the day,' Veronique said. 'When do you meet him?'

'This afternoon. This afternoon, Vron! Imagine that!'

'*Vive l'après-midi*!' Veronique said.

The morning passed with dramas and giggles and aggravating slowness. It seemed ages before Monsieur Guerin closed his premises for the weekend when Ginny could squash her hat on to her head, swathe herself in her scarf and rush for the train.

At last she was in Boulogne, with a watery sun shining on her as the cross-Channel ferry inched into harbour. She was so tense with anticipation that she couldn't keep still. She danced and dodged, stood on tiptoe in a vain attempt to see over the heads of the crowds in front of her, and jumped up and down for her first glimpse of him.

'Oh, come on, Charlie!' she said, speaking out loud because no one could hear her in the noise. 'Come on. Where are you?' If only people wouldn't disembark in such a swarm. 'Come on! Come on!' But although she watched until the very last person had ambled down the gangplank, she didn't see him.

After waiting so long and hoping so much, it was a crushing disappointment, but she tried to be sensible about it. I must have missed him, she told herself. I'll go to Madame Boulanger's. That's where he'll have gone.

He wasn't there, either.

'Missed the boat, my dear,' Madame Boulanger commiserated. 'That's what he's done. These young men are all the same. No sense of time, that's the trouble. He'll be on the next one, you'll see.' And she patted her cat with her nice plump hand.

He wasn't on the next boat, either. This time, Ginny was quite sure about it, having found an excellent vantage point where she could watch the descent of every single passenger.

'Oh dear,' Madame Boulanger said, as her guest came drooping back to the café. 'So he's missed that one, too. Never mind, my dear, it will be all the better when you see him in the morning.'

'But we've lost our first day together,' Ginny said. And our first night, too, which was worse. It depressed her to think of a night all on her own, especially in Madame Boulanger's front bedroom. 'If only I knew what was keeping him.'

'It'll be something important,' Madame Boulanger said. 'You mark my words. I can't quite imagine our young man staying away from you without very good reason, my dear.'

But when Ginny had met the morning ferry and been disappointed for the third, and most miserable time, she began to fear that she knew what the reason was.

She walked slowly back to Madame Boulanger's, deep in the most troubling thoughts. It was no use hoping and pretending any longer. She had to face the fact that there was something the matter. It was more than a month since Charlie had written to her. More than a month, even though she'd sent him two letters to tell him how unhappy she was, how much she missed him, and how much she wanted him to write. A month was a very long time without a letter. There had to be a reason for *that*. Perhaps he'd grown tired of her, or found someone else, and he didn't know how to tell her so he was just letting things slide. If that was the case, she'd been making herself cheap again, throwing herself at him, writing to him when he didn't want her to. He should have been honest with her. He should have written to tell her what he was feeling. It wasn't fair just to keep quiet and say nothing and hope she'd go away.

Well, if this is how he's going to behave, she thought angrily, see if I care. I'll write him such a letter it'll make his eyes ache to read it. I'll tell him just what I think of him, standing me up like this.

She'd found a quiet corner in a café she hadn't visited before and wrote a long, sarcastic letter to him (in French because she was too angry to write in English). She mocked him for being such a *faithful* lover, and said she was glad he'd turned up so *promptly* to meet her. 'I *like* waiting in the cold for someone who doesn't even have the *courtesy* to tell me he's not coming,' she wrote.

But when her anger was spent and the letter posted, she felt bleak with loss, remembering his beautiful eyes, and how wonderful it was when they made love. And that made her miss him more sharply than ever.

'Something must have happened,' she told Madame Boulanger as calmly as she could, when she got back to the café. 'He won't come now. Not just to be with me for an hour or two. It wouldn't be worth it.' Yet she couldn't help hoping that he would.

It was the final, and most bitter disappointment, that he wasn't on the afternoon ferry. As she travelled back to Boves through the dispiriting darkness of a late, cold afternoon, she wept with despair. She couldn't help it, for it seemed that all the people she loved most in the world had turned away from her and rejected her; Maman going to the convent, Em not writing and now this. It was more than she could bear. Nevertheless, she had to bear it. She knew that. And on her own because there was no one else to help her.

'You got back, then,' Cousin Berthe said, as Ginny came wearily through the cottage door that evening. 'When's that ol' wedding?' She was sitting by the stove, sewing up a hole in one of her stockings, cobbling the wool together in the clumsiest way. There was no sign of Old Joliot, so presumably he was still out with his cronies. 'When's that ol' wedding, eh?'

'We haven't had a letter, have we?' Ginny said. 'We don't know.'

'What ol' letter?' Berthe said, looking very puzzled.

'The letter from Emilie,' Ginny said, holding on to her patience.

'No! Not Emilie,' Berthe said. 'Not the wedding of Emilie. The wedding of Virginie. When's *that* ol' wedding?'

In the misery of the weekend Ginny had forgotten all about her conversation with Madame Gambetta. Now it returned to plague her, sharp and mocking like some spiteful hobgoblin.

'Oh *that* wedding,' she said, trying to speak lightly. 'I don't know when that's going to be. Not yet anyway. I shall have to wait and see.'

'You'll tell Berthe.'

'Yes. Of course.'

'Soon as you know. You promise?'

'Yes. I promise. Where's Old Joliot?'

To her relief, Cousin Berthe began a long stammering account of where Joliot was, or where he might be, or where she thought he was, and for the moment the wedding was forgotten.

But the misery wouldn't go away and nor would her aching sense of isolation. She was so completely on her own. There was no one to confide in, no one to protect her from gossip. No one at all. Oh Em! she grieved, if only you hadn't gone to England. I could have shared all this with you and then it wouldn't have been so bad. I miss you so much. And the thought that she would never see her sister again dragged her heart down and down, as if it were being tugged by pincers. Then there was Maman. If she'd still been in the house there would at least have been someone to care for. The one good thing about looking after Maman was that she kept you fully occupied. But I've got no one. I haven't even got Charlie. Oh Charlie, Charlie, why didn't you come to Boulogne?

It took every ounce of self-control to remain calm during the next few days. She was so withdrawn at work, and so obviously unhappy, that even Monsieur Guerin noticed it, and Veronique had to pluck up courage to ask how the weekend had gone.

'Not very good,' Ginny admitted. 'I'll tell you about it later. Just at the minute I'm waiting for a letter.'

'He didn't turn up,' Veronique guessed. 'What a brute.'

'There's a reason for it,' Ginny defended. 'I shall know when he writes. If the letter comes to your house you'll bring it in, won't you?'

'He hasn't written to our house for ages,' Veronique said.

'No. I know he hasn't. But I suppose he might. You never know, do you?'

This is all as wrong as it can be, Veronique thought, reading the signs, but she promised to keep a look out for any letter and to bring it in if it arrived. But no letters arrived from England at either address.

In Boves, in the meantime, Ginny was being given meaningful looks, long, searching, knowledgeable stares that she couldn't help noticing. At first she tried to persuade herself that her neighbours were simply being friendly, but she knew it was more than that. Eventually, the smile on Madame Garnier's face was followed up by an enquiry that made everything too painfully clear.

'I hear you are to be married, Mademoiselle Lisieux,' the lady said. 'What good fortune, my dear. When is it to be?'

Ginny could feel her heart sinking. How could she answer? Now of all moments when she didn't know if she would ever see him again.

'I – um – I don't know the date yet, Madame,' she stammered. 'We – um – there are all sorts of things . . .' To her horror and confusion she felt herself blushing.

'There, my dear,' Madame Garnier said, delighted by the blush. 'I mustn't press you. As you say, there are many things to be considered at a time like this.' She bustled off to spread the news.

Oh please, God, Ginny prayed as she walked on, let there be a letter for me. This is too awful.

But there was no letter from anybody. And although she knew she shouldn't have expected to hear from him so soon, she was miserably disappointed just the same. Her letter should have provoked *some* response. Tuesday brought more meaningful looks and no letter and so did Wednesday, but she still tried to be sensible, hoping against hope that she would hear the next day and trying to think of some reasonable excuse for the delay.

Thursday's disappointment was too crushing to be deflected by hopes or excuses. Charlie was not going to write. There was no doubt about that now. He wasn't going to write and he'd never intended to come to Boulogne. Somehow or other she'd lost him. In her confusion and misery she couldn't think what she could have done, but she must have done something. She had to admit in her private and pessimistic heart that she would never hear from him or see him again. It was all over.

That night she put her face in the pillow and wept for her lost love, and the sister she would never see again, and Maman, crying until all her hopes and dreams were sunk in despair.

And the next morning she got up and bathed her eyes and began to re-shape her life. One thing was certain, now. She couldn't stay in Boves to be mocked and pitied. She would have to find somewhere else to live, and as quickly as possible. Somewhere nearer work that wouldn't cost so much in rent and train fares. Since Maman left she'd been paying the rent entirely on her own and it took a sizeable chunk out of her wages.

'I am going to get a room for myself in Amiens,' she said to Old Joliot, as she poured him his breakfast coffee. 'It's time I struck out on my own, don't you think?'

'You must come or go as you please, my little one,' Old Joliot said mildly. It came as no surprise to him. She was on her own now without her mother and little Emilie and he knew there'd been gossip. Not that he'd paid any attention to it, but he'd seen the heads nodding together. That wretched Gambetta woman again, she had too much of a mouth on her, that one.

So that Saturday afternoon Ginny stayed in Amiens and went househunting. By four o'clock she'd found herself a small room, overlooking the river in the old town, and a mere three minutes' walk away from the factory. It was sparsely furnished, rather dark and very impersonal, but it was cheap and it would do because she wouldn't be spending much time in it except for sleeping. By day she would be in the factory and her evenings would be devoted to working for the socialist party. She'd lost Charlie, and there was no hope of love in her life any more. Maman was in the convent and she'd lost Emily too. But *that* was a loss she could do something about. First she'd apply for a passport, then she'd save up enough money for the fare and then she'd go to England and find her. There must be some way of finding her. It might take ages but she would do it.

By seven o'clock that evening she had gathered her few belongings from that awful empty room in Boves, said goodbye to Cousin Berthe and Old Joliot and moved into her new lodging house.

Cousin Berthe was most upset to see her go.

'She'll come back, won't she?' she said to Old Joliot, as she stood behind his chair waiting on him at supper time.

'Yes, yes.' Old Joliot said. 'She'll visit. She promised.'

'I been ever such a good girl,' Berthe said. It didn't seem fair to send Ginny away when she'd been such a good girl. Why only that morning she'd hidden two more letters with the funny stamps. They'd burned ever so prettily, too. She could see all the funny foreign words on the bits of paper as they curled over in the heat.

*Ginny, my darling sister.*
*It is my wedding day on Saturday. Do write to me, my darling. I miss you more than I can say. Please don't be cross with me. I would give anything to see you at my wedding. Ginny, my darling*
*. . .*

*. . . I had to stay here. I couldn't leave Mum on her own. I thought you'd have understood. Please don't ignore me like this. I love you so much. You know that, don't you? I shall always love you. Always and always. You're the only girl in the world for me. I know you didn't mean half the things you said in your letter. You were cross with me for not turning up. That was it, wasn't it? Please write to me again, Jeannie, and tell me you still love me . . .*

# Chapter Twenty-Six

Emily Holborn was sitting in state in one of the new armchairs, in the corner of her new parlour, next to the fire. It was her wedding morning and she was already wearing her wedding dress, so she was thankful to be somewhere warm.

She'd chosen the most sensuous gown from the selection that had been put into her hands. It had a bloused bodice and long sleeves covered in embroidery that was quite delightful to the touch, a flared skirt and a simple V-shaped neckline to set off her silver cross. But it was made of cream-coloured silk, which is not the warmest of materials to wear on a November morning. Nevertheless, despite the cold, and the solemnity of the occasion, and the worry and disappointment of the last few weeks, she looked serene sitting there, with her dark hair clustering thickly around her face and her hands folded peacefully in her lap.

Whatever else was to happen in her life, this day would mark the start of happiness. From now on she would never be alone, and she would always be loved. Ken would be her eyes, her guide and her support in every way, she was quite sure about it. Dear dependable Ken. Why even this morning he had tried to smooth over her worries.

Right up to the last moment, she'd gone on hoping to receive a letter from Ginny. This morning (when it was really too late for hope) she'd got out of bed as soon as she heard the postman walking up the path and felt her way to the front door to pick up the mail.

'Is it there?' she asked, as Ken took the letters out of her hand.

It wasn't.

'Never mind,' he'd said. 'Once we're married and the

weather's picked up a bit, we'll take a trip back to Boves and you can find her. I promise. It'll turn out to be something quite simple. You'll see. Something we can put right in a moment. Meantime we've got one or two other things to think about today, if you remember. And the first is your breakfast, which you're going to have in bed because you're a bride.'

He was wonderfully kind to her and very attentive. He sat on the edge of the bed and fed her what he called 'choice bits', and even though the breakfast was more than she wanted, she did her best with it because she couldn't have borne to disappoint him.

Afterwards, Mrs Quern came in to help her bathe and to dress her in her finery. Since then she'd been sitting in her chair breathing in the scent of her bouquet, waiting and thinking, deliberately counting her blessings. She was very, very lucky to have found such a partner, and she knew it. Of course, it would have been wonderful to have had Ginny and Maman at her wedding, but if they'd decided not to come there was nothing she could do about it. Not now. Now was the time to prepare herself for the sacrament, to be still and quiet and suppress all bad thoughts.

A car was drawing up in the road outside. Ken's footsteps were approaching through the hall. It was time. Now all the good things could begin.

It was lovely to be sitting beside him in the car, smelling the polished leather of the seats and listening to the purr of the engine. Even better to be walking into the church on his arm.

It is always the same, she thought happily, the lovely peace of the church. What a blessing it is. It never varies and it never fails, no matter where you are in the world, the scent of incense and flowers, the rustle of vestments, the organ playing in that lovely resonant way. With Ken's hand to guide her, she dipped her fingers reverently in the stoup and made the sign of the cross that always comforted her so much. And, as the mass began, she was blessedly, totally happy.

363

Observing her all through the long ceremony, Ken Hopkirk was amazed at how beautiful his Emily was. In the soft light at the altar rail, her face glowed and, if he hadn't known better, he could have sworn that those pale eyes of hers could see, for she fixed them unwaveringly on the priest and appeared to be following his movements as well as his words. Now, Ken thought, caught up in the magic and wonder of it all, I know what they mean by the mystery of the sacrament.

But supreme moments are ephemeral and magic must fade by its very nature. Wondrous though the ceremony was, it finally came to an end and the new Mr and Mrs Hopkirk found themselves in a draughty hall, standing side by side to welcome their guests to the reception, in a confusion of noise and movement. It was such a sudden transition that Emily actually found it rather upsetting although, true to her nature, she did her best to find the good things in it.

There were obviously lots of flowers; she could smell them, mostly chrysanthemums. Their peppery scent competed with the smell of a cold roast, the sulphur of hard-boiled eggs and a rather sickly, creamy smell that she assumed was a trifle of some kind. People laughed and giggled round her. Feet approached, padding across linoleum. Strange voices wished her luck and strange hands patted her face and her shoulders, as though she was some kind of pet.

Then they were at table and the wedding breakfast was being served, and it was every bit as unappetising as it smelled, although the guests seemed to be enjoying it. They were talking to Ken in a quick slurred English that she couldn't understand, and he was talking back in a hearty voice she hadn't heard before. His work voice, she thought, listening to it. She wished Ginny could have been sitting beside her to tell her what they looked like. They could have talked to one another in French in their old private way. Oh Ginny! If only you . . . But what was the good of thinking like that?

There was a woman at her elbow asking, 'Have you finished, love?'

'Yes, thank you,' she said, adding politely, 'It was a lovely meal. It's just that I'm not very hungry.'

'Saving your strength for tonight, eh?' the woman said. And laughed in rather a horrid way as she moved back from the table.

There'd been rather a lot of jokes about 'the wedding night' during that meal and although Emily pretended she hadn't heard them, they all gave her the same unpleasant feeling. It was as if she was going to be hurt in some way, or humiliated, and they all knew it. Even though it was only an undercurrent to the general tone of jollity, it was in horrible contrast to the beauty of the service she'd just enjoyed – and the more jokes there were, the more vulnerable they made her feel.

Fortunately, vulgarity is subject to the same rules of diminishing effect as sublimity. Eventually the last beer had been noisily drunk, the last good wishes heartily bestowed, and Ken led her out to his car in a shower of confetti and drove her back to the lovely privacy of the bungalow.

'Oh Ken,' she said, as she shivered on the doorstep waiting for him to open the door, 'it *is* good to be home.'

'Stand still,' he ordered, as she heard the key click and started to move forward. 'I've got to carry you over the threshold.'

'What for?'

'I don't know,' he said cheerfully, picking her up in his arms and carrying her like a child. 'Good luck, I think.'

They were in the hall and he was closing the door with his back. She was still lying in his arms, with her head against his shoulder, breathing in the scent of his skin and disentangling it from the overlying smell of cigarettes and beer.

'Kiss me,' he urged. 'Turn your Frog into a prince, my lovely darling girl.'

She turned her mouth to his at once. This was better. This was much, much better.

He lowered her feet to the ground as they kissed and they stood locked together as the kissing went on and on. For the first rewarding time he was free to explore the luscious curves of her body. Oh the enticement of running his fingers down her belly! 'You're gorgeous,' he said, pausing to catch his breath.

His ardour was so overwhelming it made her tremble. And her trembling was so exquisite it roused his desire to painful intensity.

'Come to bed,' he said.

'Is it bedtime?' she asked between kisses. Everything was so muddled. In the surge of strong feelings he was rousing, she couldn't be sure of anything.

'Yes. Yes,' he said, leading her to the bedroom. His arm was wrapped so tightly round her waist, he was turning her body towards him as she walked. They were inside the room before she realised it and he was undressing her, unbuttoning her long sleeves and kissing her wrists, picking open the fastenings all down the back of her bodice and nuzzling her neck. 'My darling, darling girl.'

'You're making me dizzy,' she said, putting a hand on his chest to steady herself.

'You're all gooseflesh,' he said, running his hands up and down her bare arms. 'Get those clothes off and come in under the covers quick and let me warm you.'

She stood before him in her petticoat, with her beautiful wedding dress tumbled about her ankles, like an olive-skinned mermaid with a creamy tail. 'I must hang up my dress,' she said.

It was time to be masterful. He knew from jokes and hints and the few things his friends had told him over the years that bridegrooms had to be masterful.

'Leave it,' he said. 'You can do that later.' And he scooped her up in his arms and carried her to the bed.

'I've still got my shoes on,' she said weakly. But they were taken from her feet as she spoke and she could hear his shoes falling to the floor after them, clunk, clunk. She sensed that he was throwing his clothes on to the chair because the breeze from their movement lifted her hair. Then they were both under the bed covers and she was engulfed in the warmth of his body. He was kissing her again and holding her so tightly she could hardly breathe. And there was something hard and hot, pressing against her leg and she moved her hands down his body to see what it was. She was startled to find that it was flesh.

'What's that?' she asked him, amazed and curious.

He couldn't find a suitable word. Not one. The pleasure of being touched by those exploring fingers of hers was making him groan. 'It's what I'm going to love you with,' he said. And fitted the action to the words.

The shock of his entry was so sharp and so unexpected that Emily cried out in alarm and pain, but he was too far gone to hear or understand her. His pleasure was so intense that he assumed it was the same for her. Certainly it never entered his head that he might be hurting her. There was only this superlative sensation roaring towards release, this pure, magnificent, God-given pleasure.

'My darling, *darling* girl,' he said as he rolled away from her at last, spent and satisfied and successful.

She lay beside him in the tumbled bed, trying to make sense of what had happened to her. She felt very sore down in her private parts, as if she'd been kicked, and that seemed – well – a bit peculiar when kissing had been so pleasurable.

'Wasn't that wonderful!' he said in her ear.

No, she thought honestly, it wasn't. It was puzzling, painful and disappointing. But she didn't tell him what she was thinking. She asked him a question instead, careful to keep her voice affectionate, even if it *was* full of curiosity.

'Was that love?' she said.

'That's love,' he told her happily. 'That's love, my darling girl.' He sounded as though he was half asleep.

'Is that what all married people do?'

'Yes. Didn't you know?'

'No,' she said. 'I didn't.'

'Then you've had a nice surprise, haven't you?' he said, well pleased with himself. Seconds later he was fast asleep, leaving his wife alone with her thoughts.

Years ago, when she'd first gone to live in Boves, Emily

had heard a group of women taking in a half grumbling, half congratulatory way about the joys and problems of the married state. 'Ah well,' one of them had said, 'that's the price we women have to pay for being married.'

The conversation had intrigued the young Emily and had stuck with her over the years. She hadn't understood it but she knew, instinctively, that she would be forbidden to ask anyone to explain it to her. Now she remembered and wondered. Was this what they'd been talking about? Was this the price women had to pay? It was an unpleasant price, to say the least. Surely someone should have warned her? And if that was what married women had to endure, were they all hurt by it, like she'd been? Or was she different from other women? That's what Maman had said, that awful time in the cemetery. Perhaps it was because of their mystery illness.

But her mind shied away from that because it was too awful. Our Father, she prayed, Thy will be done, but please don't let it be that. Not that awful illness. I couldn't bear it. Not after being warned. For Maman *had* warned her. 'You will be perfectly all right providing you don't marry, providing you don't love a man. If you love a man you will be ill.' She had been quite clear. Supposing she was right after all. That could be the reason why I'm feeling so sore and uncomfortable. It's a punishment for my sins. I should have told Maman I was going to get married. I should have told her when I met Kenneth in Versailles. I've been secretive, dishonest, untruthful and Maman always told me the truth; now I'm being punished for it. I knew I was doing wrong. There's no excuse for me. Holy Mary, Mother of God, pray for us sinners now and at the hour of our death. Amen.

Kenneth stirred in his sleep and flung out an arm across her body. She removed the weight of it, careful not to wake him, and tried to settle to sleep herself. Perhaps by morning she'd feel better. Sleep was a great healer.

But although she didn't know it, it was actually early evening, and the morning was a very long way away. There was a supper to prepare and eat and more 'love' to endure before she could settle to sleep. By then, she was so tired and sore she forgot to say her prayers.

The next morning she woke up disorientated, with such an overpowering urge to spend a penny that she was afraid she wouldn't be able to get to the lavatory in time. It was really quite frightening and unlike anything she'd ever experienced before. She struggled out of bed and felt her way along the handrail to the toilet seat. And then, despite the urgency, she hardly did anything at all and what she did was searing hot and hurt as though she was being stuck with pins.

Now, there's no doubt, she thought. I *am* ill. Something's terribly wrong. It shouldn't be like this. She sat on the toilet waiting for the dragging urge to fade; but, if anything, it got worse. She was so frightened she didn't know what to do.

Ken was calling to her, from the other side of the door. 'Em! Are you all right?'

'No,' she called back. 'I'm ill.'

In an instant, he was inside the bathroom and kneeling beside her, his voice full of concern. 'What is it, my little darling? What's the matter?'

She told him as well as she could without being immodest. 'I want to spend a penny and nothing – comes.'

'You've caught a cold on your kidneys,' he said. 'That's what that is. And here you are sitting about in your nightie. I'll get your dressing gown. We shall have to keep you warm.'

'Yes,' she said, eased by his good sense. 'A cold on the kidneys. Of course, I didn't think of that. I was ever so cold yesterday.'

'Nice warm bath,' he said. 'Warm clothes. I'll soon have you right.'

But although the warm bath eased the stinging, and the warm clothes were comforting, the dragging urge to pass water went on all day and woke her three times in the night. And 'love' was more uncomfortable than ever.

'I *am* ill, Ken,' she said on the second day. She was beginning to feel weepy now, low and vulnerable and guilty.

'I knew this would happen. I should have told you. It's all my fault.'

'Don't be daft,' he said jollying her. 'You can't help being ill. Nobody can.'

'Yes, yes,' she insisted tearfully. 'I could have done. I knew I was going to be ill. I've been ill all along. Maman told me.'

He was torn between wanting to change the subject to divert her from her misery and the need to know what she meant. Curiosity won out, and a sixth sense that this was more important than it appeared. 'What are you talking about?' he said.

'I've got a disease,' she said. 'Maman told me. I've had it all the time but it only comes out when you get married.'

He reacted strongly because it alarmed him. 'What tosh!' he said.

'If only it was,' she said. 'Oh Ken, if only it was. But it isn't, is it? She said I'd be ill if I got married. And I am ill. It isn't a cold on the kidneys. I wish it was. It's an illness and she knew I was going to get it.'

'If you're no better by tomorrow,' he said, 'we'll go to the doctor and see what he says. Now, dry your eyes and we'll go out for a nice walk. There's a park round the corner. You'll like that.'

The walk was a nightmare because she kept wanting to go to the toilet all the time and, in the end, they had to admit defeat and come home. While she was making the tea, Ken phoned the doctor.

Doctor Griffith Jones was an avuncular man who didn't like women, and a perfunctory examination of this one soon told him all he needed to know.

'You've got cystitis, my dear,' he said. 'Honeymoon cystitis, we call it. Nothing to worry about. It'll soon clear up. Have a nice hot bath, keep warm, drink plenty of fluids, and we shall have you as right as rain in no time.'

Emily wanted to believe him, but the facts and her feelings militated against his diagnosis. She was convinced the situation was much worse than he was telling her, but the tone of his voice precluded argument.

'Yes, doctor,' she said. What else could she say?

'That's a good girl,' the doctor approved. 'Now you run along with nurse while I have a word with your husband.'

'Then it's not serious,' Ken said, when she'd been led from the room.

'Good lord, no,' the doctor said, and laughed. 'Common to womankind. Oh, dear me, yes, very common. Very, very common. Of course it's worse with the nervy types. Does she suffer with her nerves at all?'

'Not that I've noticed. Well, not till now.'

'Thought as much,' the doctor said, as if his point had been proved. 'I'll give her a tonic. That'll pick her up. And if you'll take my advice, Mr Hopkirk, you'll keep her busy. Doesn't do to give 'em too much time to sit around. They only start pitying themselves. Brisk walk every day. Plenty of housework. That's the ticket.'

'Yes,' Ken said. 'Thank you, Doctor. I will.'

The doctor gave his avuncular smile. 'You tell her she ought to think herself lucky she hasn't got typhoid fever,' he said. 'It's terrible in Croydon, so I'm told.'

'There,' Ken said, as he drove his darling home again. 'Nothing serious, you see. You'll be as fit as a flea in no time at all.'

But her face was withdrawn, as though she was hiding in her blindness. 'I'm ill,' she said.

'And you'll soon be well,' he told her, negotiating a corner. 'You heard what the doctor said.'

'He didn't like me,' she said, and there was a stubborn expression on her face that he'd never seen before.

'That was just his way,' Ken said, feeling he had to make excuses for the man. 'He's like that with everybody.' But he was wondering. Is she nervy? Is that what's the matter with her? And it occurred to him that he really didn't know her at all. 'Cheer up,' he said. 'We'll soon have you well.'

She tried to agree with him. 'Yes, I suppose so.'

But it was nearly a week before she would stir out of the house.

'I daren't be far away from a toilet,' she said, whenever

he suggested an outing. 'I never know when I'm going to need it.'

Making love became more and more difficult. The first time she refused him he was so angry he took himself off without a word to sleep in the spare room. The second time provoked a long miserable argument which only ended when she agreed that she was being selfish. The lovemaking that followed was almost as miserable as the argument because, although she allowed him to do whatever he wanted, she didn't respond. She just lay in his arms and endured. Afterwards, when she thought he was asleep, she crept out of the bed and felt her way to the bathroom, where she stayed for a very long time and where he was sure she was crying.

If this is a honeymoon, he thought resentfully, I don't think much of it. It seemed horribly unfair that they should be so unhappy in their love when they'd obeyed the rules and stayed virgins, coming to their wedding pure in every sense of the word. We should be enjoying this, he thought. We've got a right to enjoy it, whenever we feel like it. It should be wonderful.

Poor Emily, weeping in the bathroom, was a long way from resentment. She was simply and terribly afraid. If Maman was right – and it looked as though she was, despite what that callous doctor had said – she would get worse and worse with this illness and in the end she would die of it, like Daddy had, losing control of her legs, stumbling and falling, being carried away to a clinic. And heaven knows what would happen to her there except that she would die. She was cold with fear, palms clammy, throat full, stomach dragged down, because whatever she did she knew she couldn't escape. Her mind was stuck fast in the horror of it, like a fly in resin. I am ill. I shall die. Maman was right.

'Our Father,' she prayed, 'who art in heaven, hallowed be Thy name; Thy Kingdom come; Thy will be done on earth as it is in heaven . . .' The words offered a grain of comfort. Her future would happen, whatever she said or did. There was no good kicking against the pricks. Somehow or other, she had to accept it and get on with her life as well as she could '. . . deliver us from evil. Amen.'

In the weeks that followed she *did* try to accept her fate. At first it was terribly difficult because the fear was always there, just under the surface, but gradually the cystitis eased and cleared, and although she was worried in case it returned, she found a pattern of living and praying that managed to contain her fear. But there was a distance between her and her dear Kenneth, and she was never more miserably aware of it than when they were in bed and he was urging her to love him. It was at this time that the fear returned with sense-numbing force.

For his part, Ken Hopkirk was glad to get back to the factory where he was succesful and knew it. He told his friends he'd had a first-rate honeymoon, then closed the subject and got on with his work. If he wasn't as rapturously happy as he'd expected to be, he had the sense to enjoy the good things in their life together and not to worry unduly about the bad ones. When Emily wept for no apparent reason, he put his arms round her and tried to comfort her. When she muttered in her sleep (always in French) he listened with sympathy, even though he couldn't understand her. When she said she would like to try another letter to France, he wrote it at her dictation and tried to convince them both that this time they would get an answer.

But her sadness disturbed him, no matter how hard he tried to be sensible. Sometimes it roused him to pity and then he would pet her and spoil her and feed her titbits, as if she were a child. At other times, he was aware that there were things she was keeping hidden from him and that provoked such bad temper that the least little thing would trigger a fury. He roared that he couldn't find the shirt he wanted, that he'd lost his toothbrush, that he'd be late for work. At that, Emily rushed to attend to him, and her activity shielded them both from her sadness until he'd left the house.

But it wasn't what either of them had hoped for. And when the first fog of the winter seeped into the bungalow one dank December afternoon, as Emily was preparing the dinner, it felt like a judgement.

# CHAPTER TWENTY-SEVEN

It wasn't a particularly bad fog, but the newspapers made the most of it.

'Chaos at Channel ports,' the *Star* said dramatically. 'Fog and confusion. London at a standstill.'

'Only wish it was,' Jack Bond said, looking up from the paper to peer gloomily out of the office window. A sulphur-yellow mist had been choking the Strand since early morning, but they'd all got in to work more or less on time. 'It wouldn't hurt the old man to let us off till it's over. D'you think he will? I could do with a couple of days at home.'

'Speak for yourself,' Charlie said with some feeling. The less he saw of home at the moment the better. 'I'd rather be at work.'

'It's the way it closes in on you that I don't like,' Mr Grossman confessed, 'as if everything's stopped and you'll never get going again. It's like being suspended in limbo.'

That was something Charlie could understand just a little too well. Hadn't his own life stopped in the last two weeks, with Aunty Grace being so ill, and his mother so harrassed, and no letter from Jeannie in all that time?

Mr Crabbit's secretary appeared in the doorway to the inner office. 'Mr Commoner,' she said. 'You're wanted on the telephone.'

For a lurching second Charlie was afraid it would be his mother with bad news of Aunty Grace. But it wasn't. It was Mrs Everdale, faint and rather apologetic on the other end of a crackling line.

'I've just called to enquire about our advertisements,' she said. 'I've been listening to the wireless. They say the Channel ports are closed. Is that right?'

'So I believe, Mrs Everdale,' Charlie said. 'But you needn't worry about the advertisements. I phoned them in last week. They're to run for a month, according to your instructions. It's all settled.'

'Oh. You're not going across then?'

'No. There isn't any need.'

'But if anyone turns up . . . You'll be able to go then? To see them.'

'Of course. You have my word.'

'Forgive me for saying this,' Agnes said delicately, 'but I was under the impression that you went to France quite frequently.'

'I did. Yes,' Charlie said, and the tone of his voice gave away more than he intended.

'But not now,' Agnes said, understanding him. 'How sad.'

'These things happen,' Charlie said, trying to sound worldly wise. 'But I'll go straight across if we hear anything, I promise you.'

'Did you include the newspapers in Amiens?'

'Yes. Of course.' They were the most important of all and he'd phoned them in first, feeling that he was dicing with fate. If one of the heiresses turned up in Amiens, he would *have* to go there, wouldn't he? He couldn't avoid it. And that would give him the chance to go and visit Jeannie. After being spurned for so long he couldn't just turn up on her doorstep without some other reason for being in the district. If she'd decided not to see him again – and after all the letters she'd ignored it was pretty obvious that was what she *had* decided – it would be demoralising to chase after her. But a chance meeting would be different.

'You'll keep me informed,' Mrs Everdale was saying.

'Of course.'

'I hope this fog doesn't go on too long.'

'So do I,' Charlie said with feeling. And it wasn't just the London fog he had in mind.

'How is your aunt?' Mrs Everdale asked. 'Mr Crabbit tells me she's been very ill.'

'No better, I'm afraid.'

'I *am* sorry.'

'Yes,' Charlie said. 'So am I.'

Grace Allicott had been ill for ten days and although the telltale rash of typhoid fever hadn't appeared, she'd made such a fuss that Ruby had called the doctor in to her three times, despite the cost. She complained endlessly. Her headache was so bad it was all she could do to lift her head from the pillow, her stomach was too tender to touch, she was sure she was going to get diarrhoea.

'I'm at death's door,' she said to Ruby. 'That's the truth of it. They'll 'ave ter send me to 'ospital come the finish.'

However, on that foggy Monday morning (at the very moment when Charlie was on the telephone to Wolverhampton), Dr Groizard told her there was nothing the matter with her.

'Simple food poisoning,' he said, when he'd sounded her chest, 'that's all. For a woman of your age, you're fighting fit. You can get up, if you like.'

Grace was furious.

'Fat lot he knows!' she said, when the doctor had gone. 'I'm terribly ill. Any fool can see that.'

'Be nice to get up, though, won't it,' Ruby said placatingly. 'I've got a good fire going in the kitchen.'

'If I get up, it'll be the death of me,' Grace said, pulling the covers over her chest. 'In this fog! The very idea!'

'You can't go on staying in bed,' Ruby pointed out, keeping her temper with difficulty. 'Not now there's nothing the matter with you.'

'I'm ill,' Grace said stubbornly. 'These pillows are sticking in the back a' me neck, sommink chronic. Plump 'em up fer me, there's a dear.'

Ruby was glad to escape from her and get to work.

You try so hard to do the best for your family, she thought, covering her nose and mouth with her scarf, and you end up doing the worst. She's a horrid old thing. She's been putting it on all this time and my poor Charlie's been stuck here looking after her when there wasn't any need. Poor boy. And that girl of his not writing. I do hope they haven't quarrelled. Not that she'd said a word about there being no letters. Bad enough that there wasn't, without rubbing his nose in it. Well, she reflected, as she walked out into the fog, there's nothing to keep him in London now. At least that's one consolation.

It was puzzling that the poor boy didn't seem to realise that he'd been released.

'No,' he said flatly, when she suggested he could go to France now. 'I shan't go. There's no point.'

'But I thought . . .'

'We've done all the work over the phone.'

'What, all the way to France?'

'Yes. Weeks ago. Just after Aunty Grace was taken bad.'

'Best thing,' Grandpa Jones said, trying to find something to say to comfort his grandson, because he'd noticed the lack of letters, too, and could see how miserable the poor little beggar was. 'I wouldn't go crossing the Channel in this weather, not fer all the tea in China. Not with all this fog. Reg'lar pea-souper this is. An' you imagine what it'll be like in France.'

In fact, it was cold and clear in Amiens that afternoon, and Ginny was in a blazing temper.

It had been a dreadful day, the sort when everything goes wrong, and Monsieur Guerin had been in the foulest mood she'd ever seen. First two looms had broken down and he'd screeched and screamed until they were mended, then his second van driver hadn't turned up and he'd screeched and screamed down the phone until the agency sent him a replacement, and then, horror of horrors, he received a call from one of his Paris fashion houses to say that their last consignment of velvet had arrived but it wasn't what they'd ordered.

He was conciliation itself on the phone, profuse with apologies and promising instant redress, but the minute he put the receiver back in its cradle, he turned on Ginny and Veronique and roared that it was all their fault.

'Incompetence!' he yelled. 'That's what it is. Incompetence. You must have sent down the wrong invoice.'

The unfairness of it stung Ginny to defend herself. 'Oh no!' she said. 'The invoices are all double-checked. I would never make such a mistake.'

'Then how did it happen?' Monsieur Guerin roared. 'Explain that to me.'

'I expect your packers used the wrong invoice,' Ginny said. 'It wouldn't surprise me. They're usually rushed off their feet. It's a wonder they get anything right.'

Monsieur Guerin was *not* pleased at being stood up to like that. 'My packers do as they're told,' he shouted. 'It's got nothing to do with my packers. My packers are under my personal supervision. And I hope you're not suggesting *I* make mistakes. Oh no, I'll tell you how this happened, Mam'selle. There's no organisation. That's the trouble. And where is there no organisation? In this office. That's where. How can I send out correct orders from a disorganised office? You must mend your ways, Mam'selle Lisieux. You're costing me money.'

Ginny's miseries gathered into a towering anger, the bleakness of her room, lack of sleep, homesickness, loneliness, and the awful triple grief of being abandoned. 'No,' she said coldly. 'That's not true, Monsieur. My invoices are always correct. It is a point of honour with me.'

'You grow conceited, Mam'selle.'

'Not at all, Monsieur. I know my own worth.'

'Worth! Worth!' her employer shrieked, jumping up and down in fury. 'You lose an order and you talk to me of worth! How dare you do such a thing. The presumption of it. You ought to be . . .'

Ginny interrupted him in mid bounce. 'That's it!' she said. 'I quit. I'm not staying here to be insulted.' She was gathering her belongings as she spoke, taking her hat, coat and scarf down from the peg, checking her handbag. 'Find someone else to be abused, Monsieur. I've had enough.' And with a wonderful sense that she was striking a blow for freedom, she walked out of the office, down the spiral staircase, through an admiring chirrup of catcalls and whistles in the workshop and out into the December air.

She was walking quickly, her heels clicking on the cobbles and there was such a noise in her head that, at first, it didn't register that someone was running after her, calling her name. 'Ginny! Ginny! Wait for me. Oh please, wait for me.'

It was Veronique, flushed and hatless and in tears.

'Vron! What are you doing?'

'I've given in my notice, too,' Veronique said, breathlessly. 'I can't stay there without you. It isn't possible.'

'Well, serve him right!' Ginny said, with great satisfaction. 'He doesn't deserve us. He's never deserved us. Bad-tempered thing. He's pushed us around just a bit too long, so serve him right.'

'What are we going to do now?' Veronique said, blinking away her tears.

Ginny was warm with righteous anger. 'We're going to celebrate, that's what,' she said. 'We're going to a posh restaurant and we're going to treat ourselves to the best dinner we've ever had. Defeat to all capitalists, that's what I say!'

And that was what they did. They strode into the finest restaurant in the town with splendid aplomb, as though they belonged there, and then ordered recklessly. Actually, when the main course was served they both began to feel a bit anxious in case they couldn't rustle up enough cash to pay the bill. But despite their anxieties, or maybe because of them, they were raucously jolly and drank toasts to 'freedom' and 'fraternity' and 'success to socialism' while they did complicated arithmetic in their heads. By dint of pretending that they were too full for coffee, they managed to pay the bill and even to leave a modest tip.

'Now what?' Veronique said, when they were out on the pavements again and walking among the evening throng.

Their money was gone, it was cold and getting late. Now and too late, Ginny realised that she would have to live off her precious savings until she found herself another job.

There would be no hope of going to England and finding Em. Oh Em! she thought, feeling angry with herself, shall we ever see one another again?

'Now what?' Veronique repeated.

'Home, I suppose,' Ginny said.

Veronique's plump face dropped perceptibly, as Ginny was quick to notice. 'Oh not yet, Ginny,' she begged. 'It's early yet.'

She's afraid, Ginny thought. She's afraid of telling them at home. 'I'll come back with you, if you like,' she offered.

'Would you?' Veronique said gratefully. 'It's not that I'm worried, it's just – well – it's a bit hard sometimes to get Maman to – well – understand things. You'd be able to explain it to her, wouldn't you? You could get her to see sense.'

But nobody could get Madame Tilliette to see sense that evening.

She was white with fury. 'I never heard such foolishness in all my life,' she said, rounding on her daughter. 'To give up a perfectly decent job, just like that, with no thought to the consequences. And at a time like this, too. Do you know how many people are unemployed in this country? Have you any idea? I despair of your sanity.'

'She'll get another job, Madame,' Ginny tried to point out. 'She's a good worker.'

'Never mind another job,' Madame Tilliette said. 'She should have stuck with the one she had.'

'If the worst comes to the worst I can always go and work with Uncle Jules,' Veronique said.

'On the farm?' her mother said, stopping in mid breath because she was so surprised. 'But you said you would *never* work on the farm.'

'Well, I've changed my mind,' Veronique said defiantly. 'I'll go tomorrow morning. First thing.'

Madame Tilliette turned her anger on Ginny. 'This is all your fault, I hope you understand,' she said. 'You should have shown more self-control.'

'We are all free agents, Madame,' Ginny said, fighting her corner. 'We make our own decisions.'

But when she'd extracted herself from the row and said goodbye to Vron, promising to write to the farm as soon as she'd got herself another job, she had to face the fact that Madame Tilliette was right. We're like shunting trains, she thought, as she stood waiting for the tram that would take her back into the centre of town. A movement from one of us and the rest are shunted in every direction. I never meant to throw in my job and yet I did, and I've lost a week's wages on top of everything else. I never meant to get Vron involved and now look how everything's turned out. Oh, if only life wasn't so horribly complicated! Or so horribly lonely.

But it was. That night her bleak room seemed lonelier than ever.

'Why do we make so many mistakes?' she asked her reflection in the triple mirror on the dressing table. But none of her images could tell her.

In Clapham, Charlie was smoking his last cigarette of the day, lying on his bed in the crush and muddle of his over-crowded room. He'd taken Jeannie's letters out of the top drawer of his chest of drawers, where he kept them hidden, and was reading them through, tormenting himself with memories and trying to make sense of the inexplicable rejection he was suffering. Her handwriting was as dark and passionate as she was herself. It was anguish to look at it. And worse to read.

I loved you so much, he thought, folding up her last sarcastic letter and replacing it in the envelope, and you wrote to me like that. He thought of all the loving letters he'd written to her since Aunty Grace took ill, explaining things over and over again, pleading with her to write, begging her not to be angry with him, not to reject him. And she'd ignored them all. Every single one. It was all over. He knew it. And yet he yearned to see her again, to hold her in his arms and to kiss her and love her and put everything right.

If only the heiresses would turn up, he thought. In Amiens, Paris, anywhere, it wouldn't matter. All I need is an excuse and I'll go back to France like a shot, fog or no fog.

Goddamn Aunt Grace. This is all her fault. I might have known she was putting on an act. I'll never make a mistake like that again.

The weeks passed. Aunt Grace stayed in bed until midday every day. There was no response from any of the advertisements and no letters from Jeannie. The examination results were published and Charlie discovered that he'd passed with distinction. He had his shoulders thumped by all his colleagues and went off to the pub for a celebration, but it meant very little. Two days later Mr Hedgethorn called him into the office to congratulate him on his success and to offer him a place with the firm, now that he was 'so satisfactorily qualified'. That didn't mean much, either, apart from the fact that he could earn a salary, give up his part-time job and pay off his debts to his parents.

The irony of it was too sharp. When his love affair had been going well, he'd failed his examinations; now, when the affair was over, the whole thing broken to bits, without hope or explanation, he'd passed with distinction. It was cruel.

Meantime, Aunt Grace had made up her mind to be an invalid.

'I can't get up to a cold house,' she said. 'Not with my chest. You don't mind me having a lie-in, do you, Rube?'

Ruby said she was worn out with all the fuss Grace was making.

'It'll have to be a quiet Christmas this year,' she told the others. 'I haven't got the energy for anything else.'

'Quite right,' Stan agreed. 'Nice an' restful. Won't hurt any of us.'

'We'll 'ave brandy on the pud, though,' Grandpa insisted. 'Won't we? Wouldn't be much of a Christmas without brandy on the pud. I'll buy it. Be my treat. It'll buck you up, Rube.'

But Charlie didn't care what sort of Christmas it was. He spent most of it out in the pub with his friends being deliberately cheerful and for the few hours he was at home he helped with the housework, washed endless dishes and glasses, peeled endless vegetables, ate very little and said even less.

On Boxing Day he and his friends went to the West End to see Ronald Colman in *The Prisoner of Zenda*. But he'd lost his taste for the pictures and didn't enjoy it at all. It was Jeannie he wanted to see, not Ronald Colman. And Jeannie he dreamed of night after difficult night, wondering where she was, and how she was, and if she ever felt sorry for the awful way she'd treated him.

Ginny was in Paris that Christmas staying with Mauricette Lalange, and she thought of him every day, usually angrily, and dreamed erotic dreams about him every night.

It was lovely to be part of a family again. Although she'd found herself another job easily enough – in a factory making velour hats – and even saved a little money, she'd been more lonely than she dared to admit, in her cold single room. To be sitting at table with Monsieur and Madame Lalange, squashed elbow to elbow among their eight voluble children, surrounded by talk and jokes and arguments and laughter was nothing less than sheer pleasure.

Madame Lalange was most surprised to hear that Charlie had thrown her over.

'It just shows you can never be sure of anything in this world,' she said. 'I thought he was going to marry you. Well, we all did, didn't we, Mauricette? Now you tell me this. Dear, dear, dear.' And she clicked her teeth with disapproval.

'Men are all the same,' Mauricette said disparagingly. 'Look at Gérard. He can barely bring himself to write to me. After all the work I've done for the group and the letters I've written to him out in Spain. Do you know, when he came home on leave he wouldn't even sit next to me at the meeting. He's callous, that's what he is.'

Ginny didn't remind her friend that Gérard had never loved her. That would have been cruel. 'You love them and they break your hearts,' she said. It was comforting to complain. It reduced the awful feeling that she'd been

384

responsible in some way. 'He knew how much I was looking forward to our holiday and he couldn't be bothered to turn up.'

'Heartless,' Mauricette agreed, helping herself to more beans.

'I could have understood it if he'd written. But not one word. Not one single word.'

'I told you,' Mauricette said. 'He's heartless.'

'Are you going to eat all those beans?' Zabette said to her brother. 'Or can I have the rest?'

'You had all the chestnut stuffing,' Jean Paul said.

'I didn't.'

'You did.'

'Manners!' Monsieur Lalange said, rebuking them, but mildly because it was Christmas.

'We've got a Yule log,' Zabette said to Ginny. 'I like Yule logs, don't you?'

'I like everything about Christmas,' Ginny told her. But, she was thinking, I like everything except missing my family and knowing I shall never see Charlie again. Even now, when she was putting the blame on his shoulders and feeling furious about the way he'd treated her, she still missed him. That was the worst thing of all.

'And how is our dear Emilie?' Monsieur Lalange asked.

'I don't know,' Ginny confessed. 'She hasn't written to me, either.'

'Not written?' Madame Lalange said, raising her eyebrows in astonishment. 'After all this time? That's not like our Emilie. Have you written to her? But of course you have. Naturally.'

'Well no, actually, I haven't. I don't know her address.'

'But you were always so close,' Madame Lalange said. 'I hope she's not ill.'

It was exactly what Ginny had been worrying about herself through all these awful weeks without letters. 'Oh no,' she said at once. 'She's not ill. I'm sure she's not ill. She's always been very healthy. We both have. She'll probably write over Christmas. I shall find a letter waiting for me at Old Joliot's. I'll call in for it when I get back.'

'Am I allowed to have those beans or not?' Zabette said impatiently.

In their bungalow in Seddon Road, Ken and Emily were spending their first Christmas in a subdued mood. Ken had given a rowdy party at the works, but at home they were extremely quiet. They went to midnight mass together, and ate a capon, and listened to the wireless – and even pulled crackers – but their hearts weren't in it. There were too many things they couldn't talk about.

Emily knew she ought to be rejoicing in the birth of Christ the way she'd always done, but all she could think about was the possibility that Maman had been right about this illness. And the more she thought about it the more terrible it became. Lovemaking was a private torment to her now, something she dreaded because she knew it would make her ill again. She had to allow it now and then, because her poor Ken was always so upset when she refused him, but it was a sacrifice.

On his side, Ken became more and more miserable. It made no sense to him to be denied, not when they loved one another so much and he was doing everything he could to please her. Sometimes her refusal made him angry and sometimes it depressed him and, worst of all, sometimes it made him feel worthless. But he couldn't talk about it, any more than she could. Nor could he accept it. The only thing he felt he could do was to escape into work, where he was admired and successful.

That Christmas he spent most of the holiday writing letters. The most important one was to Hawkers of Kingston, a firm which had plans to manufacture a new fighter plane called the 'Hurricane'. He'd been in close touch with Hawkers ever since the plane had first been mooted, and after considerable badgering and persuasion on his part they'd asked him to submit a design for the flight panel. He'd worked long, comforting hours over the design –no matter how bad he might be as a lover he was a good engineer –and was confident that he'd produced a blueprint

386

that was superior to anything his competitors could manage. Now he was after the contract and, as it was a government contract, he took great pains over the application. A commission like that could double the size of his company overnight.

But although he kept himself as busy as he could, there was a bleakness about the holiday and he couldn't always avoid noticing it. If only Emily would love him the way he wanted.

In the convent of the Little Sisters of Divine Mercy, Hortense was keeping herself busy, too. She'd found herself a room in the hamlet of Villefleurs, which was the nearest habitation to the convent, and she had been working fulltime with *les enfants* ever since.

She had returned back to Boves at the end of November to see Old Joliot and Cousin Berthe and to collect her letters. She was surprised when Berthe told her there weren't any.

'The letters with the stamp,' she prompted. 'You said you'd hide them for me.'

'Yes,' Berthe said. 'I did, didn't I?'

'Where did you put them?'

Berthe was in one of her vague moods and couldn't remember any further back than that morning. 'No letters,' she said. 'That ol' postman walked right past.'

In one sense, Hortense was relieved to think that Emilie hadn't written. It must signify that she hadn't fallen ill – yet. She'd have been certain to have written to Virginie, and if there'd been anything important in any of her letters Virginie would have passed the news on.

I must be thankful for small mercies, she told herself, as she set out on her cold journey back to the convent.

But Christmas, the great celebration of birth and hope and family life, brought her such pain she could hardly bear it. She took her two blind charges to midnight mass and prayed earnestly for them – and for her poor dear Emilie who hadn't written to her, and her dear, hard-working

Virginie who wrote every week without fail, but she was anguished with loss.

Although she'd tried several times, she still hadn't summoned up the courage to confess her sins. She knew that confession would have to be the first step if she was to return to the world again, the first step if she was to feel whole enough to let anyone visit her. But when it came to it, she couldn't say the words. Not yet. Not just yet. Even knowing how much depended on them. They were too ugly, too fearsome, too shameful. Like her sins. She could only follow Mother's advice and pray for grace, miss her daughters, wonder where they were and whether they were well, and grieve because she'd treated them so badly.

I've been a wicked sinner, she thought, watching the snow flakes as they tumbled past her attic window, and I *do* repent. Would she ever find the courage to confess?

# CHAPTER TWENTY-EIGHT

The March winds had dropped to a breeze, the sky over Morden was springtime blue and the daffodils were in bud in the front garden of Emily's bungalow. The sight made Ken Hopkirk feel more optimistic than he'd done in months.

'The first flowers of Spring,' he said, leading Emily's hand to the nearest bud. 'Grand, eh?' They'd just returned from church and he could smell the Sunday joint cooking. It was a grand old world, if you didn't let yourself get down in the dumps.

Emily took her time to explore the bud, enjoying the sculpted curves of it as it lay cool and contained in her hand. She was remembering other daffodils in other Springs and her face was rosy with pleasure. 'There was a bank full of daffodils at High Holborn,' she said. 'When I was little. Miss Babbacombe used to take us out to pick them.'

Ken found that hard to believe. 'At High Holborn?' he said. 'In the City?'

'Which city?'

'London. That's where High Holborn is. It's a place in the City.'

'Oh,' she said, still tracing the line of buds and smiling with pleasure. 'That must be another one. *My* High Holborn was a house. I was born there.'

'You said you were born in Wolverhampton,' Ken said, remembering the entry on her passport form.

'Yes. That's right. High Holborn in Wolverhampton.'

He watched her as she ran her fingers delicately over the buds. She was sniffing the air, lifting her head into the breeze. The sight of her gentle, vulnerable face filled him with tenderness. He forgot how angry she'd made him during the last four months and how much she'd disappointed him. All he wanted to do now was to protect her and spoil her and take her away from the miseries and worries she'd been hiding and enduring since they married. In that instant he knew how he could do it.

'Would you like to go back there?' he asked.

'Oh yes,' she said. 'I'd love to.' She released the flowers and stood up to consider what she'd just said. 'But I can't.'

He took her arm to lead her into the bungalow. 'Why not?' he asked. He knew instinctively that this was important and that he had to handle it very carefully. 'If it's a house with a name it'll be on a list somewhere.'

'No, it's not that,' she said. 'I'm sure we could find it. It's just that's it's not allowed.' She seemed nervous even to be talking about it and that made him remember how agitated she'd become when he'd suggested inviting these distant relations to their wedding.

'Who doesn't allow it?' he asked, leading her very gently.

'Maman,' she told him. 'She said we were to forget all about them. We weren't to write. We weren't to let people know we were English. Nothing. It's all to do with this illness, you see.' But then she shut her mouth tight. She couldn't talk about that. He'd be cross and she might say too much. She wanted to tell him everything, to pour out her fears and to weep on his shoulder . . . to be comforted and told it hadn't happened, that she wasn't going to die, that . . . But she couldn't, and anyway he was talking again.

'You're married now,' he was saying. 'So you don't owe your obedience to your mother any more, do you? You owe it to me.'

'Yes. I suppose so.'

'So, if I say you can go to Wolverhampton and find this High Holborn place, you can. If you want to.'

He led her into the kitchen and lit the gas under the vegetables, as she thought over his words.

'Yes,' she said, dropping salt into each of the saucepans in turn. 'I suppose that's true. I suppose I could.' But she didn't sound convinced.

Ken decided to take another tack. 'Who's Miss Babbacombe?' he said.

'Our governess,' she said. 'We were taught at home, you see, because of me being blind.'

'Did she live at High Holborn, too?'

'No. She had a flat over the post office in the village.'

'What village?'

'Wittick,' she said, surprised by how much she was remembering. High Holborn and the wisteria on the terrace and the pond where the fish plopped out of the water on hot days and the roses scented the air. What a long time ago it was.

The wistful yearning on her face made up his mind for him.

That night he wrote a letter addressed to '*Miss Babbacombe, c/o The Post Office, Wittick, Nr. Wolverhampton.*'

> '*Dear Miss Babbacombe,*
> *I trust you will forgive me for writing to you, but my wife tells me that you were her teacher. She would very much like to meet you again. In the eventuality that such a meeting would be possible would you be so kind as to write back to me at the above address. I enclose a stamped addressed envelope.*
> *Yours very sincerely,*
> *K. P. Hopkirk.*'

Two Saturdays later he told Emily they were going for a spin.

'Where to?' she asked.

'Quite a long way,' he told her. 'You'll see.'

It was the furthest Ken had ever driven and quite an adventure. He wasn't sure how his Morris Minor would withstand such a trek, although of course he didn't tell Emily that. They took the great north road out of London and travelled by easy stages, stopping for breakfast at St Albans and elevenses at Rugby. Just after midday, they pulled up outside the Post Office in Wittick village.

It was a sleepy place, a higgledy-piggledy collection of

cottages set among winter trees, a church, the Post Office, three very small shops.

'Are we there?' Emily asked.

'Nearly,' Ken told her. 'I'm just going to pop across the road for some ciggies. You'll be all right here, won't you?'

'Are you going to tell me where we are?' Emily said. She wasn't anxious, just curious. His suppressed excitement was a sure sign it would be somewhere pleasant.

'When we're there,' he said, kissing her quickly. And was gone.

There were two women in the Post Office, one plump and cosy, the other awkward and angular. Ken took his question to the counter.

'I've got an appointment to see a lady who lives in the upstairs flat,' he said. 'Miss Babbacombe. Could you tell her I've arrived.'

The angular lady was at his elbow. 'That's me,' she said. 'Felicity Babbacombe. You must be Mr Hopkirk.'

He turned to greet her. She was a most peculiar looking woman, tall and skinny, with a pageboy bob of grey hair sticking out from under a masculine tweed hat, and a regular beak of a nose. She had a bossy voice, too, the kind you instinctively obey. Ken held out his hand to her.

'I'm very pleased to meet you,' he said.

'Your wife was a pupil of mine, I believe,' Miss Babbacombe said. 'You wanted us to meet again. Isn't that right? Is she with you?'

'She's in the car. Just outside.'

'Ah, well, if that's the case, you'd better introduce us,' Miss Babbacombe said, but as they walked to the door she felt she ought to warn him. 'I've taught a great many pupils, you know, Mr Hopkirk. It is possible I might not recognise her.'

Emily had been sitting in the car patiently waiting. First she'd wriggled about until she was in a more comfortable position, because she'd grown stiff during their long drive. Then she sat very still and tried to work out where she was from the sounds. She'd recognised a horse and cart, a wireless playing in a house some distance away, and the sound of a group of children passing by in hobnailed boots, when she suddenly heard a voice she knew. It couldn't be, could it? And yet it did sound like her. She reached out her hand towards the voice, instinctively.

'Miss Babbacombe?' she said.

'Yes,' the voice said. 'That is my name.'

Emily felt the tears pricking under her eyelids. 'You used to be governess to the Holborn twins,' she said.

That was admitted on a fluctuating note of growing surprise. 'Yes. I was.'

'I'm Emily.'

'Why bless my heart and soul!' Miss Babbacombe exclaimed. 'So you are! Emily Holborn. After all this time. My dear girl! My dear, dear, dearest girl!' And then Emily was out of the car and in her arms and the two of them were in tears and both talking at once.

'I can't believe this! Let me look at you!'

'It really is you, isn't it, dear Miss Babbacombe?'

'My dear child! What a beauty you've grown.'

'I sent you a card once, from Paris. Did you ever get it?'

'I suppose you saw the advertisement. What a splendid thing!'

'Oh Miss Babbacombe, you sound just the same and I thought I'd never hear your voice again.'

'What advertisement?' Ken said, when the babble had subsided. 'If you don't mind me asking.'

'You mean you haven't seen it?' Miss Babbacombe said. 'That's not why you're here? Well, bless my soul. You'd better come up to the house, my dear, and I'll tell you as we go.'

'Are they still there?' Emily asked. 'Aunt Agnes and the boys and everybody?'

'Of course. Won't they be bucked when they see you.'

They bundled into the car and, in between telling her dear Emily about her grandfather's death and the will and how they'd all been trying to find her ever since, Miss Babbacombe gave directions. 'We've had advertisements in

393

all the papers, English and French. No stone unturned. And you never saw one of them? Take this turning up here, Mr Hopkirk, by The Mermaid.'

'No,' Emily admitted. 'I'm afraid we didn't.'

They were driving uphill towards a large house obscured by trees. On Miss Babbacombe's instructions, they stopped outside a pair of iron gates.

'Your aunt'll have fits!' Miss Babbacombe said. And she sprang from the car with a dashing glimpse of lisle stocking and rang the bell like a fire alarm.

'Benson!' she said, when that gentleman arrived to admit them. 'You'll never guess who I've found.'

The gardener looked patient and baffled.

'Well look, man! Look at her!' Miss Babbacombe insisted. 'Who have we been searching for all this time?'

'It's never Miss Emily.'

'Isn't it just!' the governess said with delight.

'Miss Emily, as I live an' breathe,' the gardener said. 'Well welcome hoam, miss. And you too, sir, I'm sure. I'll get these gates open for you, sir, in just a jiffy.'

Ken Hopkirk was so overwhelmed by the size and style of the house that he found it difficult to take anything in. Words were spoken but their meaning was a long way behind their sound. He was aware that Emily was hanging on to his arm and that her face was glowing with happiness. He noticed that the door was opened to them by a butler in a black suit, and that the hall was so big that it had a fireplace along one wall where a log fire was crackling and smoking. Apart from that, it was just a confusion.

The butler knocked on a door and Miss Babbacombe rushed in. Then there was a scamper of feet as she rushed out again. She was followed by a dumpy woman in a plain skirt and a rather splendid embroidered blouse, who ran across the carpet to scoop Emily into her arms and kiss her over and over again.

'Oh, where are my manners?' she said to Ken, when Emily finally caught her breath and introduced him. 'But to see this dear girl again. You've no idea, Mr Hopkirk.'

'I can see how pleased you are,' he laughed at her, as they shook hands.

'I can't thank you enough,' she said. 'But what are we all doing standing out here in the hall? You must come into the parlour.'

They followed her, and Ken found himself in a very grand room, full of paintings. Not prints, but real bona fide paintings. There was a grand piano there, made of inlaid woods, three sofas drawn up around yet another blazing fire and five windows made of stained glass. Five. He counted them in a vain attempt to steady his wits. Five windows giving out on to a garden as big as a park. The three women talked and talked about a will, and the advertisements that had been put into the papers, and how Hedgethorn and Crabbit had been trying to help, and what a miracle it was to have their dear Emily turn up on the doorstep just when they were beginning to give up hope.

A cook was sent for, lunch was ordered and presently they all trooped across the hall and down a long corridor into a dining room that was even more sumptuous than the parlour. The table was set with green glass, the walls were panelled and there was a thick blue and red carpet on the floor. Ken ate his meal in a daze, answering when he was spoken to, but too amazed to contribute to the conversation. Not that any of them noticed, for the lady (who turned out to be Emily's Aunt Agnes) asked Emily one question after another, and when she wasn't talking, Miss Babbacombe took over.

Halfway through the meal Emily suddenly remembered that there was a portrait of her mother and father in the room. They all got up at once to take her to it so that she could run her fingers over the frame. Then she felt her way along the panelling to the window.

'I remember you doing that when you were just a little thing,' Agnes said, watching her. 'You'd say, "This is Daddy and this is Maman and this is the way to the window."'

Ken looked at the picture with as much attention as he could muster. Her mother was a striking-looking woman, with thick dark hair and enormous brown eyes. She was beautifully dressed in a long Twenties' gown with beading on the bodice. And there was no doubt that the man in the picture was Emily's father. He had the same long nose and the same tender mouth. But they were not the sort of people he had imagined as Emily's parents. They were rich. Very rich, indeed. It was all too amazing to understand. His dear, quiet Emily – the girl he'd always thought of as poor and needing protection – was the daughter of a very rich man and had grown up in a house like a palace. It would take some getting used to.

'Now,' Aunt Agnes said, when they were all settled at the table again, 'we must find your sister, mustn't we? Is she in England, too?'

At that, Emily burst into tears. The overwhelming emotion of meeting Babbers and finding her aunt again finally caught up with her, dissolving both discretion and self-control. The story came tumbling out, how Maman had told her she was never to marry, how Ken had met her in Paris and courted her in secret, how she'd run away with him to England to get married and how nobody had written to her since. 'I can't understand it,' she wept. 'I've written over and over again, haven't I, Ken, and they won't answer.'

'My dear girl,' Miss Babbacombe said. 'What a romantic story.'

Her practical aunt said, 'You know their address, though, don't you, my dear? You know where they are?'

'Yes,' Emily said, wiping her blind eyes, 'but what's the good of that when they won't write to me?'

'All the good in the world. We'll go straight over to France and find them. That's what we'll do. An address is all we've ever needed, isn't it, Miss Babbacombe, and now here you are out of the blue to give it to us. We shall find them in no time at all now. Then you'll know why they haven't written and we shall put everything right. I shall get on to Mr Crabbit, first thing Monday morning. How long are you staying?'

Ken gathered his wits to answer her. Things were

396

happening so quickly he felt he had to make a stand or his life would be totally rearranged before he could prevent it.

'We've got to be back in Morden by evening,' he said.

'This evening?'

'I'm afraid so. I have to be at work at half-past eight on Monday morning, and there's a lot to do before then.'

'But of course,' Agnes said, smiling at him. 'How very remiss I'm being. Here I've been chattering to Emily and quite forgetting you have lives of your own to lead. What line of business are you in?'

He told her, but added, with a sense that he was retrieving his importance, 'I'm extending my factory, you see. Branching out. We've just got a government contract to make the flight panels for the new Hurricane fighters.'

'Well, that all sounds rather splendid,' Agnes said. 'You're in the same line of country as Holborn's. We're in armaments. Rifles and machine guns, that sort of thing.'

Which accounts for the wealth, Ken thought, and, for the second time that afternoon, wondered what effect this was all going to have on his life with Emily.

But he couldn't allow his apprehension to disturb the happiness of the first meeting. By the time they left, late in the afternoon, he'd agreed to take Emily to Hedgethorn and Crabbit as soon as Agnes could arrange an interview.

'I'll try for Wednesday afternoon,' Agnes said, as they parted in the drive. 'I'll phone you as soon as I know anything. Oh my dear, this has been the happiest afternoon of my life.'

'I still can't believe it,' Emily said, kissing her.

'You'll come again very soon.'

'Oh yes. Very, very soon. Won't we, Ken? Goodbye, Miss Babbacombe.'

'Goodbye,' Miss Babbacombe said, kissing her, too. 'My darling girl!'

'I can't believe it,' Emily said, as they drove away. 'I simply can't believe it. They've been looking for us all this time and we never knew. Oh Ken, you are the dearest man to do all this for me.'

'I love you,' he said simply.

'And I love you. So much.'

Being praised gave him the courage to broach the subject that had been worrying him all afternoon. 'You're an heiress,' he said, watching her face to see how she would react.

She was calm about that. 'Yes. So they say.'

'You'll be rich.'

'I suppose so,' she said, hearing the discomfort in his voice. 'Will you mind?'

He gave her an honest answer. 'I don't know. It's too soon to tell.' But, he was thinking, whether I mind or not, at least it's taken her mind off all this silly nonsense about being ill.

'I wonder what the boys are like.'

'The boys?'

'My cousins. Aunt Agnes's children. They must be quite grown up by now. George is sixteen, so Miss Babbacombe said. Sixteen and in the sixth form. I can't believe it. Oh Ken, fancy having a family all this time and not knowing. I wonder what Uncle Claud will say?'

Uncle Claud had spent his afternoon playing golf. He'd had rather a good round, four over par, with five birdies and an excellent drive on the eighteenth, with a good iron to the green and a peach of a put. He'd come home well pleased with himself, buoyed up by the congratulations of his golfing friends and looking forward to the Millichip's party that evening. Agnes's news was a hideous shock.

'Isn't it wonderful!' she said, smiling at him through the triple mirror on her dressing table. 'Out of the blue and just when I'd given up hope. It's like a miracle.'

Her happiness annoyed him so much he almost lost control of himself. 'Hardly the way I'd describe it,' he said.

'Whyever not?' she asked, returning to her make-up.

'Well, for a start,' he said, 'it might have entered your head to consider how much it will complicate our lives.'

'Yes,' she said comfortably. 'It will, won't it? Another branch of the family. And babies, too, I daresay. In time. I think it's marvellous.'

'You have forgotten the will,' he said, and his voice was cold with anger. 'If *both* these wretched twins are found, control of half the company will pass to them. Or, to put it another way, your sons will only be entitled to half their rightful inheritance. Doesn't that worry you?'

'Not particularly,' she said powdering her nose. 'It's a very big company, isn't it? I should have thought there'd be plenty of room for everyone.'

'That just shows how little you know about business. Good God, you can't have a great armaments company run by women.'

'I don't see why not.'

'They wouldn't know the first or last thing about it. They'd run it into the ground in six months. Or worse. They could be pacifists. Have you thought of that? We could have our swords beaten into ploughshares before we could turn round. Where would our profits be then? The French are a peculiar race. And they're half French.'

'And half English.'

'They're women, whatever else they are. Women. Oh, for crying out loud. We can't have women running the firm. It isn't on.'

She was in the most aggravating mood. 'I'm a woman,' she said, 'and *I* found the twins, didn't I?' She smiled at him again.

'Only one twin, if I've understood you.'

'But we'll soon find our little Ginny. We've got an address.'

Claud's annoyance erupted into anger. 'Goddamn it all, you stupid woman,' he shouted. 'Can't you understand anything? We don't want to find her.'

She was perfectly calm. 'You must speak for yourself,' she said. '*You* might not want to find her. *I* do.'

'There are times when your stupidity is quite intolerable,' he said. 'We *don't* want to find her. If we do she will inherit. Don't you understand? While it's only one twin who's turned up the will isn't valid. If both are found everything will change.'

'Then everything will change.'

'But it needn't. Let's face it, if what you say is true, Virginia doesn't want to be found. She won't write to her sister. She hasn't written to you. Very well then, let sleeping dogs lie. If she doesn't want to be found, she doesn't want to be found. There's probably a very good reason for it.' He wondered whether he should mention the illness but decided against it. It was that weapon in his armoury he would keep. 'Anyway, what I'm saying is, there's no need to go looking for her. You've wasted enough money on all those advertisements they never read. So now stop. Leave well alone.'

'And that's your advice, is it?' she said, giving him the oddest look, both quizzical and mocking.

'Well, of course,' he said, pleased that she wasn't arguing. 'It's the only sensible thing to do.'

She seemed to have given in. 'The car will be here presently,' she said patting her hair. 'Are you ready?'

'Then you'll do as I say?' he persisted.

'When have I ever disobeyed you?' she replied, remembering various recent occasions.

'Well, I'm glad that's understood,' he said. And because she'd given him the right answer he changed his tone and began to charm her. 'I knew you'd see it my way. It *is* for the best, you know, my dear.'

But he had misjudged his wife's mood and her intentions. With a great sense of mischief and satisfaction, Agnes had made up her mind to disobey him completely.

On Monday morning she telephoned Mr Crabbit, told him the news and arranged a meeting at his office on Wednesday afternoon. Then she telephoned her niece. It was a very long phone call and probably cost a great deal of money, but she didn't care. She had found the missing girls. Or as good as found them. She, Agnes Everdale. If there *was* a heaven and her father was in it and looking down on her now, he would be very proud of her. 'I'm not so useless after all, am I, Father?' she said to him. And just to ask the question was the most rewarding pleasure.

Mr Crabbit called Charlie Commoner into the inner office as soon as he'd put down the phone.

'Got some news for you, young Commoner,' he said. 'One of your heiresses has turned up.'

'Good lord! Where?'

'Walked into the family home apparently. Saturday afternoon. They're coming to see you on Wednesday. I've just fixed the appointment.'

The news gave Charlie such a surprise it stuck his mind in a groove. 'Good lord!' he said again. After all this time and all those advertisements. What an amazing thing!

'You can use this office,' Mr Crabbit said. 'There's quite a crowd coming, but you can handle it, can't you?'

My first big case, Charlie thought, agreeing that he could. He was pleased with himself despite his misery over Jeannie. The Holborn twins found at last. Imagine that!

It was quite a disappointment when Wednesday afternoon arrived and only three people were ushered into the office, Mrs Everdale, who beamed at him as she settled herself into the armchair, an ugly man, who seemed vaguely familiar and, hanging on to his arm, a short, dark-haired buxom girl, who looked so much like Jeannie that for a few seconds his heart contracted with misery at the sight of her. But then he realised that her eyes were flickering in that odd way because she was blind, and sympathy for her pushed out all other emotions.

Introductions were made and the story pieced together. Charlie made careful notes. At first, he felt annoyed that no one had informed him that one of the twins was blind. It could have made all the difference in the advertisements. However, as the story unfolded he realised that it wouldn't have made any difference at all. It was rather demoralising to think that, after all the effort and all those advertisements not one had actually been seen by the twins. But, at least, one of them had been found. That was what really mattered.

'And you say you haven't received an answer to any of your letters,' he prompted Mrs Hopkirk.

401

'No,' she said sadly. 'Not one.'

'Would it help if I were to write?'

'It might,' she said. But she sounded doubtful.

'If I could have the address,' he prompted again.

'It's in Boves,' she said. 'Near Amiens. *26, Rue Jeanne D'Arc.*'

The shock of hearing that address was so extraordinary that he forgot to be professional. 'Good lord!' he said. '26, Rue Jeanne D'Arc. What a coincidence!' Pieces of evidence jostled in his mind like the coloured fragments in a kaleidoscope, touching, almost making a pattern, spinning away again. Letters unanswered, the similarity to Jeannie, 26, Rue Jeanne d'Arc.

'What is it?' Mrs Hopkirk was asking. 'What is it?'

'I'm sorry,' he apologised. 'That's very unprofessional. I shouldn't have . . . It's only . . . I know someone who lives at that address. Or perhaps I should say I knew someone.'

'Who?' Oh, the eagerness in that question.

'Jeannie Lisieux. Do you know her?' But he could see she did. Her face was expanding into smiles of delight.

'She is my sister. Virginie Lisieux, Ginny Holborn. We used Maman's name when we were in France. Oh Mr Commoner, you must be Charlie. I never knew your other name. I must have heard it once but we always spoke to one another about Charlie and Ken. Oh, I *am* glad to meet you.' And she held out both hands towards him across the desk.

The room erupted into such a babble of questioning and amazement and laughing delight that heads bobbed up on the other side of the frosted glass, curious to see what was going on.

'And the odd thing is,' Charlie confessed to Ken Hopkirk, when Emily had kissed him and felt his face to see what he looked like, 'that it was *you* I felt I recognised when you all came in. I was sure I'd seen you somewhere before.'

'Not to my recollection,' Ken said. 'I think I'd have remembered meeting a solicitor.'

'I think we ought to go somewhere more private,' Agnes said. 'This calls for champagne.'

So, still giggling and laughing, they went to the Savoy Hotel.

It took them hours to say even half the things they wanted to, but at the end of it all they had decided to go to Boves together. They would take passport forms ready for Ginny to sign and they would begin their search for her at 26, Rue Jeanne D'Arc. Where else?

# CHAPTER TWENTY-NINE

It was quite an expedition that set off through the clouds of steam in Victoria Station on that April evening. Agnes Everdale led the way, bulky in her waterproof travelling cape and a green pork pie hat, accompanied by a suitcase so big that it took up half the porter's trolley. She was followed by Ken and Emily; he, in his Norfolk suit, an overcoat and a fedora, she, swathed in a long pink scarf mounded over her greatcoat and with a green and pink knitted hat pulled down over her ears. And, bringing up the rear in his rather humbler capacity as family solicitor, Charlie Commoner, travelling light with his knapsack over his shoulders and his winter trilby brushed and steamed for the occasion.

He was still stunned by the events of the last few days and couldn't rid himself of the feeling that it wasn't really happening. Even telling his parents (and enjoying their amazement) hadn't convinced him it was true. Nevertheless, here he was, on his way to France again and with three determined people to help him in his search. So it *must* be true and this time they *must* find her. Somehow or other. Their campaign was planned. They knew where they were going and what they were going to do. A car had been hired for Ken to drive them round Amiens and out to Boves. They were travelling first class, too. Doing things in style. And although it was probably snobbish to think it, he couldn't help feeling that *that* would make a difference, too.

In the station, newspaper sellers were still hawking the evening papers. All three headlines were about the Spanish Civil War. 'INSURGENTS CLAIM VICTORY', 'GENERAL FRANCO REACHES COAST' and 'FRANCO CUTS REPUBLICANS IN TWO'. Ken Hopkirk bought a copy of the *Standard* to read on the train.

'Looks as if it'll soon be over,' he said.

'Well, let's hope so,' Agnes said, settling herself into the seat that had been reserved for her. 'All this fighting! It's horrible.'

'Don't let's talk about war,' Emily said, shuddering. 'Not when we're going to find Ginny.' It made her worry that their search might go wrong, that they might find out that there'd been some awful quarrel or that something dreadful had happened. More than anything, she wanted to find her sister. If only they could be together again, sending pinching messages to one another and talking things over in their old easy way. Oh Ginny, she yearned, you're the only one I could ever really talk to. She did so need to talk, about the illness and how frightened she was.

'You are quite right, of course, my dear,' Agnes said. 'Finding Ginny is the important thing. Oh, this is such an adventure! Don't you think so? I can't wait to see where you used to live. It still doesn't seem possible you were there all those years and we never knew.'

'I think Maman wanted to keep us hidden,' Emily said, focusing on what her aunt was saying. Now that they were on their way, she was worried about how her mother would take their sudden appearance in the village. They'd sent a letter ahead of them to warn her, but even so . . . 'We shall have to be – well – rather tactful,' she warned.

'Don't worry, my dear,' Agnes said, patting her hand. 'Your Maman and I are old friends. In any case, once she sees you . . . Well, you just imagine how happy she'll be. It'll be wonderful! I can see her now, standing at the door welcoming you back with open arms.'

When they reached Old Joliot's cottage, there was no one at home.

'They'll all be at work,' Emily said, when they'd knocked three times without reply and Charlie had peered through the window into the empty parlour. 'I should have thought of that. We shall have to go and find them there.'

'Is it far?' Ken asked her.

'Ginny works in Amiens,' Emily said, 'but Maman and Cousin Berthe keep house for the Advocate, in the big house just across the road.'

Excitement growing, they trooped across the road.

Cousin Berthe was most put out to be confronted on Monsieur the Advocate's doorstep by four total strangers, especially as they'd obviously come in a great, big, foreign-looking car that was blocking the road outside her cottage.

'You go 'way,' she said, shaking her head at them. 'I don't talk to foreigners. No, no, no. You go 'way.'

But then one of the ladies stepped towards her and she saw that despite the fine new clothes it was her dear Emilie. And that changed things.

'Emilie!' she said, leaping to kiss her. 'Where have you been? You naughty girl!'

'Where is Maman?'

'In the convent,' Berthe said happily.

'The convent?' Emily said, her heart sinking. Why would Maman be in a convent? 'What convent?'

Berthe gave her old answer, smiling and nodding. 'Mustn't say.'

'When did she go there?'

'A long time ago. I mustn't say.'

'Let's go and ask Monsieur the Advocate if you can come home for an hour or two,' Emily said, taking her arm, 'and then you can tell me all about it.' There was a mystery here. She knew it. And it would take patience to get to the bottom of it.

Monsieur the Advocate gave his permission easily enough, but it was almost impossible to get any information out of Berthe. She led them into her house and fussed until they were all seated, but she answered every question with a negative. She didn't know where Ginny was. 'She don't live here now. No. Came here at Christmas time. We haven't seen her since.' She hadn't seen Hortense since Christmas either. 'She's in that ol' convent.' And she parried every question with her old parrot cry. 'Mustn't say. Mustn't say.'

'We're wasting our time,' Agnes said, when Emily's patient questioning had gone on for nearly half an hour and they were still none the wiser. The chair she was sitting in was horribly uncomfortable and the smell drifting into the room from an awful scullery she could just glimpse through an equally awful cracked door was really most unpleasant. My poor girls, she thought, having to live in a slum all these years. The sooner we are out of here the better.

But Charlie had a question he wanted to ask.

'What happened to the letters, Cousin Berthe?' he said. 'The letters from England.' They must have come and somebody must have seen them.

'With the stamp on,' Berthe said, smiling at him.

'Yes,' Charlie encouraged her. 'Have you seen them?'

'I show you the stamp,' Berthe said, and she got up and taking him by the hand, led him through the scullery and into her little cupboard bedroom. 'There!' she said, waving a fat hand at the mirror.

'Yes,' he said. 'That's the sort of stamp. Did you see the letters?'

That got her quite excited. 'With the stamp,' she said. 'Yes, yes. I been a good girl, Monsieur.'

'I'm sure you have,' he said, still encouraging. 'What did you do with the letters, Cousin Berthe?'

'I hid them. Like she said. I been a good girl.'

Emily and Ken and Agnes were listening at the door to the scullery, all three heads alert and very still. 'Where did you hide them?' Charlie said. 'Can you remember?'

She led them all to the stove. 'In there,' she said, beaming at them. 'In the stove. Wasn't I a good girl? Look Emilie, wasn't I good?'

Emily felt so angry she wanted to scream. 'All those letters!' she said, hanging on to Ken's arm as they walked out of the cottage. 'We've all suffered so much and she's been *burning* our letters.'

'Well, at least we know why nobody answered,' Charlie said. The discovery had filled him with hope. Ginny hadn't been ignoring his letters after all. She simply hadn't seen them. And if she hadn't seen them, he could explain once he'd found her.

'Where to now?' Agnes said.

'To find Old Joliot,' Emily said. 'We shall get more sense out of him.' And she led them up to the village square, found the entrance to the Chemin de la Montagne and climbed to the cemetery, proud that she knew exactly where she was going, blind though she was.

Old Joliot was cutting the grass verges between his row of war graves. He didn't seem at all surprised to see Emily again. 'Knew you'd come back, my little one,' he said straightening his back. 'Did you marry your young man?'

So he hasn't seen the letters, either, Emily thought, as she made her introductions, 'My husband Kenneth Hopkirk, my Aunt Agnes, Virginie's fiancé, Charlie Commoner.'

Old Joliot grunted greetings to each of them in turn, but his eyes were on the graves. 'All over weeds,' he said. 'Worse than ever this year. Too much rain. That's what done it.'

'Do you know where my sister is?' Emily said.

'No, my little one. Got herself a room in Amiens, just after your Maman went away to the convent. That's all I know.'

'Do you know where it is, this room?'

'No. That's her affair, *n'est-ce pas*?'

Emily was crestfallen and showed it.

'I know where your Maman is though,' Old Joliot said. 'Convent of the Little Sisters of the Divine Mercy, over by Villefleurs. Happy there, so she says, working with the little crippled children. She writes to us now an' then. Come to visit her, have you?'

'Well, no,' Emily admitted. 'Not yet. Later perhaps. We've come to find Virginie.'

'Can't help you there,' Old Joliot said, returning to his grass cutting. 'You've seen Cousin Berthe, have you?'

'He knows where Maman is,' Emily translated for the others as they climbed down the hillside path. 'She's working with crippled children in a convent near Villefleurs.'

'But he doesn't know where Ginny is,' Charlie said.

'No.'

'Perhaps we should go to this convent, then,' Agnes said, 'and ask your mother. She'd be bound to know. Is it far?'

'I don't know,' Emily told her. 'He says it's near a place called Villefleurs. We could find it on the map, I suppose, but . . .' She really didn't want to have to face Maman. Not yet. Not without Ginny.

'You'd rather go to Amiens first and look for Ginny,' Ken said.

They'd reached the square again. 'Well, yes,' Emily admitted.

'Then that's what we'll do,' Ken decided, looking round at the others for support. 'Won't we?'

'But where would we start?' Emily worried.

Charlie knew the answer to that. 'Monsieur Guerin's quality velvets.' he said.

They were due for yet another disappointment. The young woman who teetered down the spiral staircase to attend to their enquiry hadn't even heard of Mademoiselle Lisieux and could only imagine that she must have left the company a long time ago. There was no record of her, she said, and no forwarding address, nothing.

'She can't just have disappeared,' Agnes said, as Ken drove them all back to the centre of the city.

'I think she's done a bolt,' Charlie said. 'That's what I think. She did it once before, in Paris, when we had a row. She isn't living in Boves – that much *is* clear, because that gardener chap said she'd got a room here. No, if you ask me, she's left her home and her work and done a bolt.'

'Could that be right, Emily?' Agnes said.

Emily considered it. 'Yes,' she said, at last. 'It could be. She's very like Maman and Maman was always running away. We'd get settled into a job and everything would be going well and then she'd see someone or someone would say something and we'd be off as soon as we could pack.'

'Where would she have gone?' Ken asked her.

Emily didn't know. But Charlie did.

'To Veronique's,' he said. 'Where I used to send my letters. I'll bet we'll find her there.'

'No, she is *not*!' Madame Tilliette said furiously. 'As if I'd give house room to such foolishness. Walked out of her job, she did, and all for no good reason – and my foolish girl after her. We haven't seen her since and we don't want to. No, thank you!'

'Did she leave an address?' Charlie asked. It was a shock to be given such a hostile reception, but he was doing his best to be polite.

'No. She did not.'

'With Veronique, perhaps?'

'Veronique went to work on a farm, poor fool. Just the one thing she never wanted to do, I hope you understand, and none of it would have happened if it hadn't been for your precious Virginie.'

'Could you tell us Virginie's address?'

But the door was firmly closed.

Charlie and Emily were both looking so downcast that Agnes felt she had to take charge and say something to cheer them up.

'We will go to our hotel,' she told them. 'We've done enough for one day, don't you think so, Kenneth? It *is* only our first day, don't forget. We can't expect to get everything done in twenty-four hours. That wouldn't be humanly possible. We've got plenty of time. A long weekend is four days, don't forget, and we can take longer if we need to. I know you'll have to go back to London on Tuesday, Kenneth, but the rest of us could stay.'

'Back to the hotel then,' Ken said, driving off. Emily was looking pinched with fatigue and he didn't want her to be ill again.

'We'll get into fresh clothes,' Agnes said, 'and have a nice meal. Then we'll all relax for an hour or two and *then* we'll think about what we should do next and where we should go tomorrow.'

Discounting the convent, there was only one place they could go to, and that was Mauricette's apartment in Paris. The trouble was that none of them actually had the address.

Emily didn't know it because she'd always been escorted there, and although Ken had used it when he wrote his first letter to Emily, he'd thrown it away when she gave him Veronique's address.

'I know where it is, though,' he said. 'I've taken you there enough times, haven't I, Em? And called for you. I'll soon find it.'

'And I've been there once,' Charlie said. 'We'll find it between us.'

'Oh Ken!' Emily sighed. 'I never thought this would all be so difficult. I was sure we'd find her in Boves.' During the disappointments of that long day, the euphoria of their meeting in Hedgethorn and Crabbit had been seeping away. Now, she felt tired and dispirited.

'We shall find her, never fear,' Agnes comforted. 'Have some more wine, my dear. I have very high hopes of Paris.'

Both young men grinned at that, and even Emily managed a smile.

'It sounds silly, doesn't it?' she said to them. 'But it's the city. I've always wanted to see Paris, you see, especially in the Springtime. Your father told me so much about it, Emily. He said it was the most beautiful city in the world. Just to walk along the boulevards made you feel a better person. The happiest place he said. The happiest and most beautiful.'

'Paris is full of traffic,' Emily warned, remembering how bewildering she'd found it that first time. 'And very noisy.'

'I can take you for a walk in the Tuileries Gardens,' Ken reminded her. 'And the Bois de Boulogne. Remember that? You're right, of course, Aunt Agnes. It's a wonderful place.'

And never more beautiful than on that Saturday morning, for the sun was shining, the flags were flying, the streets were newly washed and the chestnut trees were already blossoming.

'It smells like a garden,' Emily said. They'd booked in at an expensive hotel and now she was leaning out of her bedroom window.

'It looks like a garden,' her aunt agreed, for the hotel was

411

alongside the Champs Elysées. 'So green. And the women are all wearing such beautiful clothes.' They reminded her of Hortense, although, of course, she was too tactful to say that. Poor Hortense! What was she doing in a convent?

'Stay here with Aunt Agnes,' Ken said to Emily, 'and Charlie and I will go and see what we can find out at Mauricette's.' There was no need to drag her across Paris through all the noise and the traffic, especially if they were just going to be disappointed again.

This time they were given a most affectionate greeting.

'But how delightful!' Madame Lalange said, reaching up to kiss Ken on the cheeks, once, twice, three times. 'How is your little Emilie? Is she here with you?' And on being told that she was, 'Oh what happiness! Then we shall see her, without doubt. Are you married? How well you look! Come in, come in.'

She was delighted to see Virginie's fiancé again. 'What happiness!' And she was thrilled to think that they'd come to Paris specially to find little Virginie. But she didn't know where she was. Mauricette would know, she said. Naturally. But Mauricette was at work and wouldn't be back until late. 'Very late, if I know that young lady. There's a demonstration on this afternoon, you see. The veterans are returned from Spain or something of the sort. It is always something to do with this Spanish war. As if General Franco takes any notice!'

'Where is it, this demonstration?' Charlie asked. 'Will Ginny be there, do you think?'

'I don't know,' Madame Lalange said. 'It is possible, I suppose. She comes here for these demonstrations from time to time. But as to this one . . .' And she shrugged her shoulders.

'We will look there,' Charlie said. 'Where does it begin?'

'I don't know,' Madame Lalange said again. 'It's to be very big, so Mauricette says. Thousands and thousands. And the *cagoulards* will be there. I wouldn't go if I were you. Come back here tonight when it's all over. Meet the family, eh? They'll be thrilled to see you.'

But, although Charlie promised to return in the evening, he'd made up his mind about the demonstration. 'There'll be posters about it,' he said to Ken, when they'd left the apartment and were walking down the cobbled alley towards the Seine. 'There are always posters. I shall find it.'

'What are these *cagoulards* she was talking about?' Ken said.

'Fascists in hoods,' Charlie said.

'Sounds rough.'

'Yes.' But what of it? He was so near to finding Ginny now a few hooded louts weren't going to stop him.

'Shall we go back and tell the others what we've found out?'

'No. Not yet. Not all of it anyway. I'll tell you what we'll do. You keep them occupied this afternoon. Tell them we've found the apartment and that Mauricette was at work and we're going back this evening to see her. I'll see if I can find the demonstration.'

'OK. But where shall I say you are?'

'Tell them I've gone to a newspaper office to cancel an advertisement.'

'I thought that was all seen to.'

'It is, but they're not to know that. Tell 'em this one slipped through the net.'

'OK,' Ken said. 'Wouldn't it be better to wait until this evening, though?'

'No,' Charlie said, his face stubborn. 'All this hanging about not knowing is driving me crazy. I've got to *do* something. I'll see you back at the hotel at dinner time.'

'Watch out for the *cagoulards*, then,' Ken warned, and headed off towards the Pont de la Concorde.

It didn't take Charlie long to find a poster and to learn that the demonstration was to begin in the Place de la Bastille at two-thirty. He made rapid calculations. If it was all going to start at half past he ought to be there sometime after two. He could find a good vantage point and watch the demon-strators as they arrived. Time for a bite to eat and then he'd be off.

413

But it was a serious miscalculation. For a start, the area around the Place de la Bastille was a part of Paris he did not know, and, after the spacious parks along the Champs Elysées and the splendour of the Louvre and the Madeleine and the Arc de Triomphe, the contrast came as quite a shock.

Here the streets were so narrow and the tenements so high that the Spring sun couldn't penetrate the darkness. The alleys leading out of them were more evil-smelling, dirty and down-at-heel than anything he had ever seen in London. Many of the buildings were black with soot, and although there were cafés at the street corners, they were rough-looking places, small and greasy and full of dockers eating and drinking as they stood at the bar. The sooner I find my Jeannie and get her out of this, he told himself, the better.

By the time he reached the Place de la Bastille it was already so crowded that there wasn't a vacant vantage point anywhere, and it was impossible to see from one side of the square to the other because the monument blocked every view. There were no less than ten side streets leading into the square, and he didn't know where Mauricette worked, so he had no idea which street she would come through. To make matters worse, more people were arriving by the minute. They poured into the square from every side and at such a rate that he couldn't keep track of them.

Oh hell! he thought. This is worse than looking for a needle in a haystack. (At least haystacks are quiet places and the straw doesn't shift around all the time!) But he wouldn't give up and he certainly wasn't going to leave. It was a matter of being logical, that was all. He stood as still as possible in the crowd and tried to think.

It was obvious there was no hope of finding anyone in the square, but when the demonstration began, the marchers would have to file out of it in some sort of order. The veterans were lined up opposite the Rue St Antoine, all very young, deeply tanned and wearing their army uniforms. Obviously that was the point where the march would begin.

414

I'll walk down the Rue St Antoine, he decided, and I'll watch from there. Perhaps I can find something to climb on.

Unfortunately, there were rather too many other people in the Rue St Antoine with the same idea. The best Charlie could manage was a perch on the top of a short flight of steps beside a warehouse. Thank God I'm tall, he thought, as drums began to beat in the square and the waiting crowds turned towards the sound.

Preceeded by banners and accompanied by a band, it was an orderly procession, but it occupied the entire width of the road, and from where he stood Charlie could only see half the advancing column. Let her be on this side of the road, he prayed, as the veterans passed.

And suddenly, miraculously, there she was. Striding purposefully along, carrying one end of a long banner which proclaimed, 'AID THE SPANISH GOVERNMENT'.

'Jeannie!' he yelled, waving his arms. 'Ginny!' Oh God what was he supposed to call her now? Try her French name. 'Virginie Lisieux!' Sure she'd hear *that*.

She looked round but she didn't see him. The march was picking up speed.

He was propelled after her by panic and instinct, leaping from the steps and pushing his way through the crowds. 'Excuse me! *Please*!' 'Excuse me, *s'il vous plaît*!' He could still see the arm of her blue coat and that cock-eyed hat of hers. 'Let me through, Monsieur. I *must* pass.' If they didn't get out of the way in a minute he'd lose her.

There was only one thing for it. He stepped off the pavement and joined the demonstrators in the road, running and dodging through the ranks until he'd caught up with her.

'Jeannie!' he said. 'I've been looking for you everywhere.'

She turned her head and for one brief, wonderful second they stood eye to eye, held motionless by surprise and the joy of seeing one another again. Then the marchers jostled them both forwards and that gave Ginny time to remember her outrage at his long silence.

'Oh, *have* you?' she said, coolly.

'Everywhere,' he told her. 'You've no idea.'

'You should have tried writing.'

'I did. Every other day. Cousin Berthe's been burning the letters.'

'What?'

'She told me yesterday.'

'What for?'

'Your mother told her to hide them and she hid them in the stove.'

That provoked exasperation and the first smile. 'Oh, for heaven's sake! Then you *did* write.'

'Of course, I wrote.'

'I thought you'd stopped loving me.'

'Never,' he said passionately. 'Never for a moment. Berthe burnt the letters. Oh Jeannie! I've got so much to tell you I don't know where to begin.' He wanted to fling his arms round her and kiss her. 'Sweet, sweetheart.'

She smiled at him, but for the moment neither of them could say anything more because the marchers had sent up a chant and the noise was so loud it blotted out every other sound. To Charlie's pent-up excitement it was frustrating in the extreme, and when the last slogan petered away, he said the first thing that came into his head before the racket could start up again.

'You're my heiress.'

That *did* surprise her. 'What?'

'You know I've been looking for two heiresses all this time. Well, you're them. What I mean is, they were you all the time.'

It was such a surprise Ginny couldn't absorb what he said. 'What are you talking about?' she said.

'You're Virginia Holborn,' he explained, face blazing. 'You and Emily are the heiresses. Your grandfather's left you his estate.'

The anger against him that she'd been carrying (and trying to ignore) ever since that miserable weekend in Boulogne suddenly gathered to shouting point, drowning out her joy. 'So that's it, is it?' she yelled. 'I'm rich now so you think you can start again.'

He was appalled to have such an accusation flung at him. 'No, no,' he said, grabbing her arm to restrain her. 'It's not like that. Jeannie, please. You mustn't . . .'

'All these months you've been ignoring me,' she stormed, 'no letters, no visits, nothing, and you think you can just walk back into my life and start again as if nothing's happened. Well, you can't. Why didn't you come to Boulogne, eh? Tell me that. I waited all weekend. Every single boat I met. You didn't care about that did you?'

'My aunt . . .' he tried to explain.

'Damn your aunt,' she yelled. 'I don't care about your aunt. And I don't care about you. It's over. Do you understand. Over. I never want to see you again.'

'Jeannie!' he begged.

But she only yelled at him. 'Go away!'

There was only one thing to do now she was in a temper like this. He seized her by the arm to pull her to him and kiss her. They were still keeping pace with the marchers and the banner was in the way. The pole struck Charlie against the shoulder, and Ginny was struggling to get out of his grip. Out of the corner of his eye he saw a large young man with a scar on his forehead looming down upon them from the other side of the road. There were angry faces all round them and voices shouting. 'Leave her alone, you bully. Shove off.' And he couldn't think of the French to explain what he was doing and why it was necessary.

Then the young man with the scar was in between them, fending Charlie off with both arms and shouting.

Charlie shouted, too. 'Jeannie! For God's sake!'

But her voice was still the same, angry and rejecting. 'Go away! Do you hear me? Go away!'

'You heard what the lady said,' a voice roared in his ear. Then he felt a hard blow on the side of his head and the street tipped over sideways and seemed to be shaking. He fell into a rush of skirts and trousers and trampling feet and put out his hands to steady himself as he hit the pavement.

For a few seconds he lay where he'd fallen, feeling confused, as if he'd just woken up. Then he tried to get to

417

his feet and was furious because he couldn't do it. He seemed to have lost all his strength. The marchers were trampling round him, and over him, yelling to him to get up and he couldn't do it. What was worse, he couldn't see Jeannie any more and, even in his confused state, he knew it was important to keep sight of her. Then a hand seized him by the collar and he was hauled to his feet. He realised that two gendarmes were supporting him on either side.

'No, no,' he said as they hauled him out of the road. 'You don't understand.'

'*Ta gueule!*' the taller of the two commanded.

'*Je suis Anglais.*'

They didn't seem to care.

'*Merde alors,*' the taller one shrugged.

Charlie saw that there was a prison van waiting in a side street and realised with yet another shock that they were hauling him towards it.

The doors of the van were being opened, to a sour stink of sweat and unwashed clothes, garlic and Gauloises. The men in the van were making room for him, growling greetings and swearing about *les flics*.

Oh God! he thought, as his head began to throb. Now what?

# CHAPTER THIRTY

Emily and Agnes spent their Saturday afternoon in the Faubourg St Honoré buying fashionable clothes. It wasn't what Emily wanted to do at all. She would much rather have looked for her sister with Ken and Charlie. But that wasn't possible and she had to accept it. Something in the tone of their voices had made it clear that they didn't expect to take Emily with them.

'You mustn't worry, my dear,' Agnes comforted, after the two men had left the hotel and they were on their own. 'They'll find our Ginny, you'll see. Your friend will know where she is.'

'Paris is a very big place,' Emily said. Even here, in Agnes' comfortable bedroom suite, the old terror of crowds and traffic was making her flinch. 'I wish she'd been in Boves. We could have found her there. Oh, Aunt Agnes, she's been on her own, all this time, without any letters. It must have been awful for her. Just imagine it. All on her own without me or Maman or Charlie, thinking we didn't love her any more. My poor Ginny.'

'We'll have a little light lunch,' Agnes decided, briskly, 'and then we'll go shopping. That'll pass the time and it could be quite fun. There's no sense in sitting about and worrying, is there?'

So that was what they did and although her heart wasn't in it, Emily tried her hardest to enjoy herself. They bought two new, Spring costumes for Emily that Agnes had been admiring. One was apple-green and the other charcoal-grey and both were made of a wool-and-silk mixture that was beautifully soft to touch, and which Aunt Agnes said hung superbly. Then they purchased two little hats to match, crocodile-skin court shoes, two handbags, dozens of silk stockings and more lingerie than Emily had ever possessed.

'Your trousseau, my dear,' Aunt Agnes said, when the last purchase had been made. 'A little late, but better late than never. New outfits for the new season and your new life with Kenneth.'

Emily kissed her and tried to thank her properly, but it was difficult because she was still preoccupied, thinking about Ginny.

By the time they struggled back to the hotel, they had so many bulky parcels they could hardly negotiate the revolving doors. It was just as well that Ken was waiting for them in the foyer. 'I promised we'd all be at Mauricette's at six o'clock,' he said, relieving them of all the biggest boxes. 'We shall have to hurry.'

This time Emily needed no urging. Within a quarter of an hour, they were in a taxi hurtling towards the Left Bank. Now, oh now, she thought, now we *must* find her, Mauricette *must* know where she is. By the time they reached the apartment, she was trembling with tension and hanging on to Ken's arm for support.

'Someone's coming,' Ken said, patting her hand.

The door opened to a howl of anguish.

'*Emilie, cherie,*' Mauricette said, grabbing Emily's hands. 'The most terrible thing! Charlie has been arrested!'

'He can't have been,' Agnes said, when Emily had translated for her. 'He's a solicitor.'

'The *cagoulards* were there,' Mauricette said, dragging Emily into the flat. 'You never saw such fighting. The police took him away before we could say anything and after that there was such a fight and so many arrests ... It was terrible.'

The rest of the family rushed at them to take up the story, all speaking at once and with enormous excitement so that nobody could hear or understand what was being said.

Mauricette was at Emily's elbow. 'Ginny was carrying the banner,' she shouted, 'weren't you, Ginny?'

'Ginny?' Emily said into the babble.

420

There was a rush and rustle towards her and then, at last, her sister's arms were round her neck. Emily caught her breath in a long shuddering sigh and began to weep. 'Ginny, Ginny, Ginny!' And Ginny wept, too, as Emily explored her face with loving fingers and, in a moment of pure joy and ineffable relief, brushed away her sister's tears. The sight of their happiness was so touching that the room grew quiet around them, as they kissed one another over and over again, and stammered into a fragmented conversation, Ginny in French and Emily in English.

'Emilie, *chérie*, I thought I'd never see you again.'

'Oh Ginny. Are you all right?'

'That stupid Berthe burning the letters,' Ginny said. 'I thought you hadn't written to me.'

'As if I wouldn't,' Emily said, 'I wrote over and over again, didn't I, Ken?'

Ginny turned to look at Ken and saw her aunt, who was standing awkwardly, just inside the room, blinking back tears. 'Aunt Agnes?' she asked in English.

'Ginny, my dear, dear girl!' Agnes said, as it was her turn to be swept into her niece's arms. 'To find you again, in such circumstances. Has your Charlie really been arrested?'

'No,' Charlie's voice came from behind the crush of bodies. 'He hasn't.'

And there he was, sitting on the sofa. He looked even paler than usual and was clutching a pad of bloodstained towelling to the side of his head, but he was grinning and obviously a free man. Naturally they all rushed to give *him* their attention.

'My God, you have been in the wars,' Ken said. 'What happened?'

The story was pieced together with Monsieur Lalange calming his children, Madame Lalange loud with sympathy and Ginny and Emily squashed into an armchair with their arms round each other's waists.

'They marched him to the door of the van,' Ginny explained in her lilting English. 'The *gendarmes*, you understand. There was such a crowd, so many people. We had to push through.'

'Who hit you?' Ken wanted to know. 'Was it the *cagoulards*?'

'No,' Charlie said wryly. 'It was one of her friends.'

'It was all a mistake,' Ginny said quickly, warning him with her eyes that there was no need to go into details. 'When we told the *gendarmes* what had really happened, they let him go.'

'They let me go,' Charlie grimaced, 'when your friend said he didn't want to press charges. That's when they let me go. Although, in point of fact, I should have been the one pressing charges against him, cracking me over the skull like that.'

'You should have seen the way Ginny ran,' Mauricette told them. 'She was so fierce. I thought she was going to hit one of the *gendarmes*.'

'I couldn't allow them to arrest him for something he hadn't done,' Ginny said, her face glowing with love. (It seemed impossible now that she could ever have shouted at him to go away.)

What passion! Agnes thought. They're so young and splendid and they love one another so much. She remembered Edward and Hortense looking at each other in exactly the same way, as the old, affectionate envy stirred in her again. To love and be loved like that, she thought. But wasn't it to be expected? Like mother, like daughter. What a wonderful thing it is that they've found one another again.

'Well, now,' she said to Charlie, deliberately practical. 'You're here now. That's all that really matters, isn't it? We must get that head attended to. There'll be a doctor attached to the hôtel, wouldn't you think?' And she took command of her family and sent Ken out to find 'a couple of taxis'.

Twenty minutes later, they left the Lalange apartment in an uproar of vociferous kisses, and were driven back to the hotel. There the doctor was called and Charlie had two stitches put into the hairline, just above his temples.

Emily was exhausted by so much emotion. 'To find her again,' she repeated to Ken, over and over again. 'To find my dear Ginny again.' It was the answer to all her prayers, to have her sister to confide in, at last. The one person who would understand about her illness, know what she felt, tell her what to do. 'My dear, dear Ginny!'

There was so much catching up to do over their late dinner, so much to tell. The demonstration and Charlie's arrest, Grandfather's will and Agnes' long frustrating search, Emily's wedding and the bungalow in Seddon Road, Maman's flight to the convent, Cousin Berthe's letter burning, Ginny's life in Amiens and why she'd quit her job, gone to live on her own and flung herself into politics.

'I kept saving up the fare to come to England to find you,' she said to Emily, 'and then something would happen and I'd have to spend the money. I always started saving up again immediately, and I got a passport and everything.'

'Oh Ginny!' Emily said.

'Have you still got it?' Charlie asked.

'What?'

'The passport!'

'Ah, I see. Yes. It's in Amiens.'

'Good,' Charlie said. 'That's excellent. We thought we'd have to wait here until we could get you a British passport. That means we can get back very quickly.'

'But not tonight,' Agnes intervened, laughing at him. 'If we don't get to bed soon it'll be morning and there'll be no sleep for any of us.'

There was still so much to say, although Emily knew, with a private aching sadness, that the most important thing of all hadn't even been mentioned. That would have to wait until she and Ginny were on their own together. In the meantime, Aunt Agnes was right, they really ought to try and get some sleep.

'We can talk again in the morning,' Ken promised. Emily's glowing face as she listened to her sister had roused him to a pitch of such desire it was painful. Bed was what he wanted. Bed, and now, and not for sleep. She couldn't push him away tonight. Not after all this.

'Will you be all right?' Ginny asked Charlie, as they went

up in the lift together. It was the first time they'd been alone since he'd found her.

'I'd be better if I could sleep with you,' he said, grimacing slightly at the fact that Agnes had arranged for Ginny to sleep in her suite.

She kissed him very gently so as not to hurt his head. 'I shall see you in the morning,' she said, lovingly. 'I'm so sorry I shouted at you.'

'It's forgotten.'

'I do love you, Charlie.'

'I know. I love you.' The lift jolted to a halt.

'Sleep well,' Ginny said, kissing him again.

'I'll try,' he promised.

But sleep was impossible. His head throbbed painfully and, besides, there was too much to think about. In the rush of preparation for this trip, the confusion of travel and the non-stop effort of their search, all sorts of things that should have concerned him had been pushed to the back of his mind. Now, they returned to plague him.

When he'd first found out that Jeannie Lisieux and Virginia Holborn were one and the same, it had been too much of a surprise to think beyond it. Now, lying in an expensive bed he wasn't paying for, he realised that it was going to cause a problem.

Until that amazing afternoon at Hedgethorn and Crabbit, he'd geared all his hopes and plans towards the day when he could pay off his debt to his parents and put down the deposit on a modest home in the outer suburbs of South London, where he and Jeannie could live. He had assumed that he would be the provider in their marriage – as a junior partner in a local firm of solicitors perhaps, or with Hedgethorn and Crabbit – but certainly the mainstay of the family. Now he could see that if he wasn't careful he could be the junior partner in his marriage, too; the poor husband of a very rich woman. That seemed a shameful position for any young man to be in, only one step up from a gigolo, and worse for someone who'd made his own way and had struggled to succeed.

Even so, he knew he couldn't live without his Jeannie. He wanted to marry her more than he'd ever wanted anything in the whole of his life and he'd known it with total certainty the minute he saw her again, striding along in her blue coat with that great heavy banner in her hands. It was a difficult situation and the throbbing pain in his skull didn't make it any easier to resolve.

Finally, he gave up all hope of sleep, got up, slung his coat round his shoulders and sat by the window. The dawn rose with an opalescent shimmer across the eastern horizon and a glitter of dew in the gardens below him. Whatever else, Charlie reflected, he'd found his Jeannie again. Or his Ginny. He would have to get used to *that* first. Ginny Holborn. The future Mrs Virginia Commoner.

The future Mrs Virginia Commoner slept late that Sunday morning. It was past ten o'clock before she finally stirred. The rooms were empty and there was a note from Charlie propped up on the dressing table.

> *'We have gone down to breakfast. 9.15. Ken says, will you look in on Emily? Love, C.'*

Ginny went along the corridor to her sister's room. The bedroom door was ajar and Emily was awake and sitting up in bed. She looked very pale and restless. *'Bonjour,'* she called, when she sensed her sister's approach.

'It's me,' Ginny said.

'I'm *so* glad,' Emily said. 'I want to go to the bathroom.'

'Are you all right?' Ginny asked, as she led her sister down the corridor.

'No,' Emily said, biting her lip, 'not really. I'll tell you in a minute.'

But she didn't elaborate until they were back in the bedroom. Even then she hesitated.

Ginny found a hairbrush on the dressing table, and sitting on the side of the bed beside her sister, began to tease the tangles out of Emily's long, thick hair, exactly as she'd done on so many mornings, when they were young. 'Now tell me what this is all about,' she said.

Eased by the familiarity of their morning routine, Emily poured out her troubles, at last. 'It's the illness. I think I've got the illness. I keep having to – *faire pipi*. And it hurts me. I had to get up twice in the night. Oh, Ginny, I'm so frightened.'

'Have you been to a doctor?' Ginny asked, and listened carefully as the full story was told.

'I'm so frightened,' Emily confessed. 'If this *is* the illness, Ginny, what shall I do?'

Ginny tried to sound sensible. 'I'm sure it's not, Em,' she said. 'It's not what Daddy had anyway.'

'I'm afraid it is.'

'Have you told Kenneth?'

'Not really. He won't talk about it. He edges the conversation aside. He says it isn't serious.'

'Perhaps it isn't.'

'It feels serious, Ginny. And she *did* say it would start if we got married.'

'I talked to Charlie about it once,' Ginny remembered, 'before all this ... muddle. He said there was no such illness.'

'But I *am* ill, Ginny. I get better for a few weeks and then it comes back again, like it did last night. And it's always when we've been . . .' But then she stopped, embarrassed by the things she'd almost said.

'It'll be all right, you'll see,' Ginny told her, putting the hairbrush down. In one way, she felt a sneaking sympathy for Ken. *She* didn't want to talk about this illness, either, because it frightened her too much. Nevertheless, she could hardly let poor Em go on worrying and not try to comfort her. 'If you ask me it's just an ordinary illness, like the doctor said. He ought to know and he didn't think it was bad, did he?'

'He didn't. No. But I . . .'

'We'll go to the convent and see Maman,' Ginny decided. 'She'll have to tell us the truth about it now. And then you'll know. We'll both know.'

'I should have gone to see her yesterday,' Emily

confessed, rather shamefacedly, 'when I was in Boves. But I couldn't face her, not without you, Ginny, not on my own. Not after . . . Well, you know.'

'We'll go together,' Ginny promised.

'Oh, Ginny,' Emily said, turning to throw her arms round her sister's neck. 'I *am* so glad we've found one another again. I feel better already. Perhaps this illness isn't . . . Perhaps it's just . . .'

'Time we went down to breakfast,' Ginny said. 'They'll be wondering where we are.'

The others weren't wondering about anything. They were making decisions.

'Your aunt and I have got everything planned,' Ken informed the two girls as they settled at the table. 'We're all going back to London tonight. Emily's a bit under the weather, so the sooner we're home the better. You and Charlie can go on ahead to Amiens, and pick up your passport and that sort of thing, and then we can all meet up on the boat. How's that?'

'What about Maman?' Emily asked, her face falling. 'We want to visit her, don't we, Ginny?'

'Yes,' Ginny said. 'We've got something to ask her. Something particular. Anyway we *can't* possibly leave without seeing her.' She glared at her brother-in-law to show him she disapproved of being organised like this.

'Do you know where this convent is?' Charlie asked.

'Not far from Boves,' Ginny said. 'It would be on a map.'

'We could go there on the way to Amiens. Do you want to come with us, Emily?'

'No,' Ken said firmly. 'It wouldn't be wise.' In his view, Hortense had done enough damage, filling his Emily's head with all this stupid nonsense about a mystery illness, and she could wait for attention. Emily tried to argue but he cut her off. 'Besides, we've got to pack and send telegrams to Hedgethorn and Crabbit and High Holborn, *and* get tickets for your sister. There's a lot to do. We can't risk missing the boat. I know you'd like to see your mother, Emily, but there's always another time.'

'You could wait for another day, surely?' Ginny said.

'No,' Ken said. 'All Em's medicines are at home. Aren't they, Emily?'

To Ginny's annoyance Emily agreed with him.

'You two can stay on in the hotel, if you like,' Agnes offered, trying to smooth things over. 'Get the bill sent to Holborn's.'

Ginny had another idea. 'I'll buy my ticket,' she said, 'and then Charlie and I will travel to Boulogne with you tonight, and stay there. We've got a good friend in Boulogne, haven't we, Charlie? And it's nearer to Maman's convent. Don't worry, Em. I will visit Maman first thing tomorrow morning, I promise. *I* won't let you down.'

In fact, their friend in Boulogne had got the decorators in, and when Charlie and Ginny arrived on the doorstep, the café was closed. There were chairs and tables stacked in the middle of the room, ladders against all the walls and paint pots all over the bar. But Madame Boulanger came down to answer the bell, with her cat tucked underneath her arm, and, despite the muddle, she made them very welcome.

'*M'sieur, Mad'moiselle!*' she said. 'What happiness to see you together again. Are you well? Yes, yes. I see that you are. Didn't I say he would turn up, Mad'moiselle? Didn't I say there would be a reason? I knew it. It is always the same, you see, my dear, simply a matter of waiting for the right tide.'

'We're going to England,' Ginny told her, 'as soon as I've collected my passport. May we stay here until Monday evening?'

'But, of course. I'm not open officially, you understand, except to my regulars. Your room isn't decorated, but you won't mind that, will you?'

'Not at all,' Ginny said. 'We prefer it as it is.'

'Ah!' Madame Boulanger sighed. 'But, of course. So romantic. I shan't need to show you up, shall I?'

With its old pink washbowl, the cracked jug and the soap dish that didn't match, the crucifix over the bed and the wallpaper with its faded pink roses and those odd blue leaves, it was like coming home to be back in 'their' room again.

Ginny was growling with ill humour. 'I do think Ken's unreasonable,' she said, taking off her hat and coat. 'It wouldn't have hurt him to let Emily stay on for another day. She *did* want to see Maman.'

'Never mind Ken,' Charlie said, flinging their cases on the bed. 'It's *us* we should be talking about. We've got to get one thing clear. Now. Right at the start. We're going to get married.'

She laughed at him. 'Of course we are.'

He wasn't sure she'd understood the importance of what he'd said. 'Not later,' he insisted. 'Not when we've thought about it. Not when your mother gives permission. Now. The minute we get back to England.'

'Yes,' she said.

'I mean it, Ginny. We'll call the banns as soon as we're back in London. I can't have you running off and getting lost again. Enough is enough.'

He looked so determined and so brave, with his blood-stained hair and those two ugly stitches sticking out of his forehead like bits of black wire. How could she resist him? 'Oh, I *do* love you,' she said. 'Can I kiss you, or would it hurt your head?'

'My head's all right,' he said, dismissing it. But much though he wanted to he didn't kiss her. There were things that had to be made crystal clear first. 'I don't like the idea of marrying a rich woman,' he said. 'You understand that, don't you? I ought to be supporting you. That's the natural way. So I'm not going to live off your money. You've got understand that right from the start. I'm not going to be a kept man.'

She laughed up at him. 'I can't imagine anybody keeping you,' she said. 'You're too proud.'

'And a good thing, too.'

She held his face between her hands and stretched up to kiss him. Gently. 'We shall work it out,' she promised. 'Money's only important if you let it be.'

'I love you,' he said earnestly. 'That's what's important, but I've got to pay my way. I can't live off your money.'

It seemed so simple to Ginny. Everything in life seemed simple to her now. 'We will – I don't know what it is in English – *nous mettrions nos ressources en commun . . .*'

'Pool our resources.'

'That's right. Pool our resources and live off *our* money. How would that be?'

'Possible,' he had to admit.

'And I'll marry you whenever you like. I'm free, white and twenty-one. There's nothing to stop us.'

Only the niggling fear of that illness and the fact that Maman would object, but she would face that later, if she had to.

'We'll find your mother's convent first thing tomorrow morning,' he decided, as if he'd read her thoughts. 'Get that over with.'

But meantime, they were together again, back in their room, with plenty of time and plenty of money and no one to interrupt them.

'What are those cases doing all over the bed?' he asked.

The next morning the sky was overcast. Ginny borrowed an umbrella from Madame Boulanger, Charlie bought a map at the local tobacconist, and they went to Villefleurs.

'I haven't seen Maman since she walked out,' Ginny said, as the convent wall came into view. 'I've written to her at the convent every week and she's written back now and then, but she's never *said* anything, except that she sends her love and I wasn't to visit her. I hope I'm doing the right thing.'

'I'm sure you are,' Charlie said, trying to be positive.

Ginny was still anxious and her anxiety grew visibly when a nun opened the convent gate and asked them to follow her into the gardens.

Hortense was working with a group of nuns and lay workers who were forking over the vegetable patch. From a distance she didn't appear to have changed. She was working steadily in her old methodical way and, apart from a long blue apron that Ginny didn't recognise, she was dressed in the same clothes she'd worn in the garden at Boves – an ancient straw hat, her black skirt and blouse, a piece of sacking tied round her waist, even the same battered clogs.

When she straightened up to welcome them, Ginny saw that her face had changed. Her harassed expression was gone, replaced by a soft-eyed gentleness that, in any other woman, Ginny would have recognised as serenity, and her lovely brown hair was hidden under a nun's coif. It was such a surprise that Ginny stopped, uncertain how to go on.

'Maman, *cherie*, how are . . .'

'Well, Virginie, as you see,' Hortense said, but her voice wasn't as calm as her face. 'Very well.' Then she held out her arms and Ginny ran into her embrace. 'Oh, my dear child, how good it is to see you. Are you well?'

'Yes,' Ginny said, kissing her mother's cheek. 'I am.' Now that they were so close, she could see that her mother wasn't well at all. Her skin felt rough, her cheeks were lined and she'd obviously lost weight.

'Let me look at you,' Hortense said, and she caught her daughter's hands, noticing the absence of rings. 'You are not married?'

The question made Ginny feel ill-at-ease, aware of Charlie standing patiently behind her. And in her awkwardness, she became formal. 'Allow me to introduce my fiancé, Charlie Commoner,' she said. 'Charlie, my mother.'

'Ah!' Hortense sighed, looking from one to the other. 'You mean to marry then, my little one.'

'Yes, Maman. I do. With your blessing, I hope.'

'You have considered what you are doing?'

'Yes.'

'I *did* warn you.'

'Yes. I know.'

Hortense sighed, rested both hands on her fork and lifted her head to gaze at the distant trees in a vague, dreamy way. 'I can't stop you,' she said. 'Not now. Now, I have to make my peace, you understand.'

'Emily is married,' Ginny said. 'She sends you her love.'

'Yes,' Hortense said. 'I daresay she is. She went away to marry, *n'est-ce pas*? I *did* warn her.'

'You told us we would be ill if we married,' Ginny prompted.

'Yes,' Hortense said. Then she seemed to be waiting, standing quite still with her clogs on the damp earth and her earth-stained hands on the wood of the fork handle, the young leaves of the distant trees tremulous behind her.

It took courage for Ginny to continue. 'Was it true?' she dared. 'Did you mean it, Maman, or were you just trying to frighten us?'

'No,' Hortense said calmly. 'It is all true, I fear. You will be ill. I cannot prevent it. I did what I could. Now it is in the hands of the *Bon Dieu*.'

To be told such a thing, with such calm and after Emily's confession, was more terrible than any row could have been.

'You don't mean it, Maman,' Ginny begged. 'Say you don't mean it.'

Hortense had returned to her gardening. 'What is to be, will be,' she said.

'Then at least tell me what it is.'

But Hortense continued to fork over the earth without a word.

'If it's an illness it must have a name.'

Silence.

'Maman, please! I beg you. Tell me what it is.'

Hortense worked to the end of the border, placidly, as if there were no questions to answer. A blackbird began to sing his high, sweet song from the may tree on the convent lawn.

'When you are ill, *chérie*,' Hortense said at last, still working and still keeping her eyes to the ground, 'you must go to a doctor and he will tell you what it is. I cannot do it. Truly, I cannot do it.'

'Maman!' Ginny implored. Instinctively she put out a hand to pull at her mother's sleeve, the way she'd done when she was a child.

Hortense gazed at her daughter. Her brown eyes

432

brimmed with tears and her face was drawn into an expression of such pitiful appeal that Ginny felt the tears springing into her own eyes at the sight of it.

'Virginie, my dearest child,' Hortense begged, and now her voice trembled with emotion, 'please don't ask me any more. I *can't* tell you. Truly I can't. I love you dearly, you've no idea how dearly, but I can't do it. It's hard enough to make my peace without the pain of hurting you and Emilie more than I have done already.'

'What shall I do?' Ginny asked Charlie in English, forgetting her mother could understand.

He took her arm to lead her away. 'Say goodbye,' he advised. 'Tell her you'll come back and see her again soon. It's no good pressing her. You can see that.'

'But I want to know . . .'

'Leave her be,' he said firmly. 'You're making her suffer. She won't tell you.' From his observer's viewpoint that much was quite clear.

To their surprise, Hortense spoke straight at Charlie and in English. 'You are a good man,' she said. 'You understand my Virginie, I think.'

'Yes,' he said to her. 'I think I do.'

'Look after her.'

'I will. I promise.'

'I will write to you, Maman,' Ginny said, stepping forward to kiss her. 'And I'll come back.'

'Yes.'

'Very soon.'

'Oh, my dear,' Hortense said. 'I do hope you will not be ill. I love you so much.'

It wasn't until she was halfway to Villefleurs that Ginny remembered all the things she had meant to say to her mother.

'We shall have to go back,' she said, halting in the middle of the track. 'I've done this all wrong, Charlie. I should have told her about Em and this illness of hers, and Grandfather's will and everything. But I was so upset I never said a word about any of it.'

433

'You can do it next time.'

'No. It will be too late. Anyway I was going to ask her to come back to England with us, and I didn't. Oh God, Charlie this is awful! What was I thinking of?'

She looked so wild that, for a moment, Charlie was afraid she was going to run back to the convent then and there. 'She wouldn't have come,' he said, grabbing her arms. 'You'd have been wasting your breath.'

'But how can I look after her if I'm in England and she's stuck out here?'

'She's your mother,' he said reasonably. 'You don't have to look after her.'

'I do!' she said. 'You don't understand. I've always looked after her.'

'That's cock-eyed,' Charlie said. '*She's* supposed to look after you. Parents look after their children. Not the other way round.'

She wasn't persuaded. '*I* look after *her*,' she repeated stubbornly.

'Then it's time you stopped.'

'How can you say such a thing? I can't stop. Somebody's got to look after her.'

'I think you should leave her alone and let her live her own life.'

'Oh, Charlie, how can I do that?'

'Easily. You come to England with me and you leave your mother here to get on with her life. That's what she wants, isn't it? You don't need me to tell you that.'

They stood together in the dust of the country lane with rain clouds massing over their heads and Ginny thought about what Charlie had said. Was it true? Had she reached the moment when she couldn't look after Maman any more? Or when she shouldn't? That was an even harsher idea to come to terms with.

'I wish Em had been with us,' she said. 'She'd have known what Maman was thinking.'

'Would she?' Charlie asked, with some surprise. They were an extraordinary family. 'How?'

'She can hear people's thoughts. I wish I could.'

'Are we going on then?' Charlie asked.

Ginny held on to his arm and they resumed walking. 'I've made such a mess of this,' she said. 'I never got her to tell me anything. Do you think there really is an illness you can catch by making love?'

'No,' Charlie said stoutly. 'I don't. I told you that before. If there was we'd all have it.'

'It frightens me, not knowing.'

'It's in her mind, if you ask me. Something she's afraid of. Something psychological.'

That sounded feasible and faintly comforting. 'But what about Em? She says she's been ill ever since she got married.'

'She didn't look ill. She was a bit pale this morning, but not ill.'

'It frightens me, Charlie.' Even out in the peaceful countryside among grazing herds, newly ploughed fields, and the familiar reassuring smells of chickens and pigs and horses and manure, her heart was contracting with fear.

'Then don't think about it,' Charlie said. 'We've got enough on our plates without worrying about an illness that might not even exist. Think about the things we've really got to deal with. You'll have to decide what you're going to do when you get to Wolverhampton.'

But that was too complicated and too distant to think about yet. 'I don't know,' she said.

'We'll go back to England tonight,' Charlie told her. 'Your sister will put you up, won't she?'

'Put me up?'

'Let you stay with her,' he explained. 'Until you go to Wolverhampton. I tell you what, while you're waiting you can come and meet my parents.'

'Yes,' she said. She could do *that*. 'What are they like, Charlie?'

'Nice,' he said. 'You'll like them.'

Suddenly Ginny wanted to be in England, looking after Em and beginning her new life. There'd been too many difficulties for her and too much loneliness during the last few months in France. 'Yes,' she decided. 'That's what we will do.'

'I'll send them a telegram,' Charlie said, glad that he'd managed to cheer her up. It was an extravagance, but so what! He was earning a salary now. He could afford it.

# CHAPTER THIRTY-ONE

Sending the telegram was a mistake. Telegrams usually meant bad news. So it gave Ruby Commoner a shock, and Grace Allicott was scathing about it.

'A telegram!' she said, rolling her eyes at such extravagance. 'Whatever next? They cost the earth, them things. What's 'e wanna go sendin' you telegrams for?'

Ruby sat down at the breakfast table and poured herself another cup of tea to help herself recover. 'He's coming home,' she said.

'When?'

'Today. On the first boat, so he says. With his girlfriend.'

'Not the heiress?'

'That's the one.'

'Well, if that ain't just typical!' Grace said, scowling horribly. 'An' me with me barnet all over rats' tails. I knew I should've had that perm. I'd ha' gone last week if I hadn't been so poorly. Now what am I supposed to do?'

'Eat yer egg an' stop making such a fuss,' Grandpa Jones advised, emerging from the scullery with a plateful of sausages and bacon. 'No one's gonna pay any attention to *you*.'

'Well, that's where you're wrong,' Grace said. ' 'Course they are. Watcher think they're coming for?'

'Not to look at you,' Grandpa said, pouring brown sauce over his sausages. 'Silly old bat!'

'You can be vile when you like,' Grace said. 'D'you know that? I really would ha' thought after all I been through you'd've had a bit a' sympathy. Damn nearly dead I was with that typhoid.'

'So you keep sayin'.'

'Don't let's have ructions,' Ruby pleaded, setting down

437

her cup to intervene. 'I tell you what, Grace, you look sharp and eat up your breakfast and I'll set your hair for you before I go to work.'

'She's all heart, your daughter,' Grace said to Grandpa Jones. 'I don't know where she gets it from, I'm sure. Must be her mother's side a' the family.'

A bottle of bay rum was brought down from the bathroom cabinet and Grace's straggly hair was soused in it until they could see so much of her scalp that it looked as though she was suffering from the mange. Then Ruby did what she could to arrange the hair into the three rows of corrugated waves that Grace considered necessary for beauty, holding them rigid with a battery of huge steel hair grips, each with a double set of shark's teeth and a hinge like a man trap.

'Now I suppose you're gonna sit there all day like Lady Muck with a head full of ironmongery,' Grandpa said.

'Leave her be,' Ruby said, checking her handbag. 'I shall have to rush or I'll be late for work. Where's me purse? I'm all at sixes and sevens!'

She was in such a state when she got to the newsagents that she spent most of the morning making clumsy mistakes and was rebuked for carelessness.

'This ain't like you, Ruby,' her employer said, when she dropped a pile of papers. 'An' that's a fact.'

Ruby apologised for every error, shamefacedly, saying, 'I'm ever so sorry. Really.' After the fifth mistake, she explained, 'I'm not quite meself today.' Which was perfectly true. Apprehension about this visit was making her feel as though she'd been turned inside out.

Since Charlie dropped his bombshell about his girl and the heiress being one and the same, she and Stan had talked it all over several times. They'd both agreed that, heiress or not, they weren't going to let it make any difference to *them*. But agreeing on an opinion was one thing. Actually welcoming an heiress into her house was quite another, especially when she was going to marry her son. Ruby now realised with some shame that her comfortable home was rather shabby. There were threadbare patches on the easy

438

chairs, the curtains were faded and there were too many chips in the china.

I'll nip back home nice and quick as soon as I've finished here, she promised herself, and give it all a good polish before she comes. Dust round, make up the fire, set the tea things all nice. We don't want to look like scruffs.

She was none too pleased when she got home to find the table still covered with dirty dishes from breakfast time, Grace fast asleep by the fire (still in her curlers) and Grandpa soaking his feet in the washing-up bowl.

'Well, if you two don't take the biscuit,' she said in exasperation. 'Today of all days!'

'I'll just get this corn out,' Grandpa said, 'an' then I'll give you a hand.'

'Look at the state a' this room,' Ruby protested, putting on her apron. 'It's a pig 'eap. An' I've told you before about using that bowl, Dad. I don't like your feet in with my washing-up. It ain't hygienic. You know that.'

'Yes, well . . .' Grandpa said, digging at the corns with his penknife.

There was a key in the door.

'Stan?' Ruby said, rushing into the hall.

It was Charlie. And standing behind him, a short, slim girl with a shock of dark hair. A short, slim, foreign-looking girl. Oh, my goodness! They're here!

For a few seconds nobody spoke, as Charlie waited, feeling suddenly nervous, and the two women took stock of one another.

She's only a little thing, Ruby thought, but a fighter, you can see that. Hope she don't fight me. She was impressed by the style of that jaunty winged hat and took comfort from the shabbiness of the blue coat. That's seen better days and no mistake. She might be rich now but she ain't always been. Even so . . . Oh God! If only the kitchen wasn't such a tip!

Will she like me? Ginny was worrying. She's very fond of Charlie – I can see that – but will she like *me*? I do hope she does. She looks a bit cross. What shall I say to her?

439

Then Charlie made the introductions and Ruby recovered sufficiently to welcome them.

'You mustn't mind us,' she said to Ginny. 'I'm afraid we're in ever such a pickle. I've only just this minute got in from work, you see. Would you like a cup of tea?' And as there was nothing else she could do, she led them into the kitchen.

Their arrival in the room produced several seconds of what could only be described as howling dismay. Aunt Grace rose to her feet clutching at her head, with her glasses on the end of her nose and her eyes round with horror. 'Don't mind me!' she cried, pulling the curlers from her hair. 'You mustn't mind me!' Then she bolted from the room, scattering curlers as she ran and moving so clumsily that she stepped on the edge of Grandpa's bowl and turned it completely over, leaving the old man standing barefoot and abashed in a pool of soapy water.

'Ah!' he said, blinking at them. 'You'll be the French gel.'

Ginny took it as calmly as she could. 'I'm Ginny,' she said. 'Yes. That's right. And you must be Grandpa Jones.'

'Blimey!' Grandpa said. 'You speak English. I thought you was French.'

'Get that cleared up,' Ruby said to her father. 'Look at the mess!' When he'd picked up the bowl and carried it out of the room, she turned to Ginny to apologise. And saw Charlie's stitches. 'Good God alive!' she said. 'What you been doing with your head?'

'It's nothing,' Charlie said, looking uncomfortable. 'Don't fuss.'

'You've had stitches! What've you been *doing*?'

'I lost my footing – got pushed over – in a crowd. It's nothing.'

'Never mind nothing, it's all over blood.'

Charlie was hot with embarrassment. She was treating him like a child. 'Fine sort of homecoming this is,' he protested. 'Room full a' rubbish, cups and saucers all over the table . . .'

'We ain't always in such a mess,' Ruby said crossly, looking at Ginny. 'I was late getting out this morning.'

There was a sudden rush of cold air from the hall, a smell of wood shavings and brick dust, and there was Stan in his grubby workclothes, beaming at them all.

Ruby hardly gave him time to draw breath. 'Look at his head,' she cried, pointing at her son. 'Look at the state of him.'

Stan's good sense was like a breeze in a stale room. 'Looks all right to me,' he said, putting his tool bag away in the cupboard. 'Been in the wars, ain't yer, son. You got to expect that, Rube. Worse things 'appen at sea. Well, come on then, Charlie, introduce me to your young lady.'

The introduction was made. Order was restored. Grandpa crept into the kitchen with an old towel and mopped the damp patch on the hearthrug. Grace emerged from her room with her hair neatly brushed. Ruby put the meat pie in the oven and began to clear the table.

'We ain't always in such a pickle,' she repeated to Ginny.

Ginny moved forward at once to reassure her. 'I've seen a lot worse than a few cups and saucers,' she said. 'I used to work as a housemaid when I was in Le Touquet. You'd be horrified if I told you some of the things I've seen. I'll help you, shall I?'

'No, no,' Ruby said, more flustered than ever. Then, feeling she was being ungracious. 'I mean . . . well, it's ever so good of you. Oh dear, I was going to have everything ready for when you came and now look at me.'

Charlie had got a tray from the scullery. 'Many hands make light work,' he said cheerfully, stacking the plates. 'We'll have this clear in no time. Cheer up, Mum. It's not the end of the world.'

'Tell you what,' Stan said, taking off his boots. 'Why don't we go down The Windmill for a quick one while the pie's cooking? Grandpa'll set the table, won't you?'

'Pleased to,' Grandpa said, relieved to be able to make amends.

So Ginny and Charlie and his parents went down to the pub.

'When d'you get back?' Stan asked, when they were settled into their favourite corner.

'This morning,' Charlie told him.

'You went in to Hedgethorn and Crabbit, then?'

'No,' Charlie said. 'I phoned in from Folkestone but they said not to rush. Mr Crabbit's been on to Holborn's. He's arranged the first meeting of the new management board for Wednesday next week.'

' 'E don't waste much time, your Mr Crabbit.'

'No.'

'So you'll be working in your company straightaway,' Stan said to Ginny.

'Yes,' Ginny said. 'I suppose so.' But the expression on her face was sombre.

'What's the matter?' Charlie asked. 'Is that too soon?'

'No,' Ginny said. 'It's just . . . Oh, I don't know. I'm really not sure about all this, you know.'

Stan took a thoughtful puff of his cigarette, smiling at her through the wisp of blue smoke. 'What ain't you sure about?' he asked.

'It's all so complicated,' Ginny told him. 'Everything's happened so quickly. I hardly have time to get used to one thing before something else happens. It's as if my life has been speeded up.'

'It's a big change,' Ruby said sympathetically. 'Change takes a bit a' getting used to.'

'Don'tcher want to be an heiress?' Stan asked in his thoughtful way. 'Is that it?'

'No,' Ginny said. 'It's not that. To have enough money will be nice. We've been very poor sometimes.'

'What, then?' Stan asked, smiling at her again.

She was surprised at how easy it was to confide in this man. 'I don't want to run the company,' she said. 'I don't like the idea of making money out of munitions, that's what it is.'

Stan waited.

After a pause, Ginny continued, struggling to find the right English words. 'Leon Blum said it was – immoral for one man to grow rich out of another man's pain. That makes sense to me. I've always believed it. Now, here I am – inheriting a quarter of G. S. Holborn's, and everything that

442

company makes is – designed to bring pain to someone or other.'

'But you don't want the fascists to take over, do you?' Charlie said, explaining to his father, 'She's been fighting fascists for years.'

'No, of course not.'

'And you don't approve of what's going on in Spain.'

'No. It's dreadful. You know that.'

'Then somebody's got to fight them.'

'Yes. I suppose so.' It was true and she had to admit it. She'd always admired Mauricette's Gérard for what he was doing in the International Brigade and she'd spent more hours than she could count campaigning to persuade the French government to send aid to the *Fronte Popular*. 'I'm being illogical. But I still think anything is preferable to war.'

'So do I,' Stan said. 'Trouble is, once the fighting starts you can't just walk away from it, can you?'

'And if there are people prepared to fight the fascists,' Charlie said, 'somebody's got to provide the weapons.'

'Yes, I know that, too,' Ginny said, 'but . . .'

There's more to this than guns, Stan thought. But he didn't say anything. He simply waited again.

'I think,' Ginny said. 'I think I'm worried about Uncle Claud, too.'

That *was* a new direction. 'Why?' Charlie asked.

'He was always a bit of a bully,' Ginny explained. 'At least that's the way I remember him. He used to make Aunt Agnes cry. I remember that. Maman spoke about him as if she was – well, frightened of him. She never said why. The other thing is, he's been running the company all the time we've been in France, so I can't – think – imagine him welcoming us with open arms. I think we might have a quite a lot of trouble with Uncle Claud.'

'Then if you'll take my advice, you'll stand up to him right from the start,' Stan told her. 'Bullies are all the same. Give in to 'em, an' they'll push you around till Kingdom come. Stand up to 'em, an' they back down.'

It sounded such sensible advice. 'Yes,' Ginny said, smiling at him. 'You're right. That's what we ought to do.'

'Time for that meat pie a' yours, Ruby,' Stan said, finishing his pint.

So the future Mrs Commoner weathered her first visit to her in-laws, and even if it wasn't exactly an unqualified success it went well enough for Charlie to feel at ease about it. Dad and Ginny had hit it off at once, and Mum had approved by the end of the visit. That was what mattered.

'Ginny was wonderful,' he told Emily later that evening when he delivered her 'home' to Merton. 'I don't know how she stayed calm when we first walked in.'

'That was easy,' Ginny said. 'We've been used to Cousin Berthe, haven't we, Em?'

Em was more concerned with their visit to Hortense. She'd hardly been able to think about anything else since she got back to England. She waited patiently until Charlie had gone and Ginny had settled into her bedroom. Then she left Ken splashing in the bathroom and felt her way along the guide rails to the spare room to talk to her sister.

'Are you all right?' Ginny asked anxiously, as she opened the door. 'I didn't like to say anything in front of Charlie.'

'Yes,' Emily said. 'I'm a lot better.'

'Really?'

'Really. It cleared up quickly this time, once I started drinking my barley water. Did you get to Villefleurs?'

'Yes,' Ginny admitted.

'And?'

'She wouldn't tell me anything.'

'There *is* an illness.'

'Yes. So she says. She wouldn't even tell me what it's called.'

'I knew it,' Emily said. She was surprised at how calmly she was taking the news. I must be resigned to it, she thought. Or perhaps it's because I'm not feeling ill any more.

'Do you think we ought to see a doctor about it?' Ginny said. 'We could go together, couldn't we, and tell him everything.'

That made Emily shudder. 'Not yet, Ginny, I couldn't. What if . . . No, I couldn't. When I'm ill, I think perhaps I ought to, but I don't. Not when it comes to it. And when I get better, I can't face it at all.'

'Well, it's up to you,' Ginny said.

'Then not yet. It doesn't have to be yet, does it?'

'We'll get this meeting over with first,' Ginny decided. 'Charlie's Dad gave me some very good advice about that. I'll tell you in a minute. I'm not looking forward to it, are you?'

'No. I'm not,' Emily said, relieved that they had deferred their worst decision. 'I wonder how Uncle Claud is taking it.'


Uncle Claud was roaring.

'No, no, no! It's intolerable! I won't have it. Do you hear, Agnes?'

'I should think the whole house could hear,' Agnes said mildly. She was arranging her hair, ready for her trip to the shops in Wolverhampton.

'Wednesday!' Claud yelled. 'Wednesday, for crying out loud. What's the matter with that damn fool Hedgethorn? Doesn't he realise we've got work to do? I can't manage Wednesday. It's much too soon.'

'Then write and suggest another date,' Agnes said, smoothing powder on to her nose with delicate strokes of the powder puff. 'I'm sure he'd be agreeable.'

'What's all this nonsense about holding it here?'

'That was my idea,' Agnes said coolly. 'I suggested it.'

'We never have board meetings here.'

'*You* don't. No, that's right. But Father always did. We used the great hall. It was lovely.'

'Board meetings aren't supposed to be lovely,' Claud said disparagingly. 'We've got a perfectly adequate boardroom at the works. What's wrong with that?'

'It's cramped at the best of times and now we've got an enlarged board . . .'

445

'We haven't got an enlarged board,' Claud said, hunting through his pockets. He was suffering from violent indigestion, and she was making it worse, arguing all the time. And he couldn't find his tablets. 'It's a damn load of nonsense. That's all it is. I can't see why we've got to have a meeting at all. There's no need for it. Oh Goddamn and blast it! That bloody Hedgethorn's undermining my constitution. Where're the Rennies?'

'Where you left them last time, I expect,' Agnes said.

'How am I supposed to know where that is? Come on, Agnes. I'm in agony. And he thinks he can arrange bloody meetings whenever he feels like it. And in my house, too!'

Agnes swivelled on the dressing stool to face him. 'It's no good, Claud,' she said. 'You'll have to accept this sooner or later. It won't go away.'

'Well that's where you're wrong,' he said brutally. 'That's where you're quite wrong. I don't have to accept anything and certainly not this. Not knowing what I know. Oh no! I shall fight your wretched girls, Agnes. Make no mistake about that. I shall fight them tooth and nail, and if either of them lays claim to this firm, I shall tell the entire meeting exactly what sort of bad blood they've inherited. The whole rotten stinking story. I shall shame them. Publicly. So let that be clearly understood.' His face was dark with fury, his eyes bloodshot and that clipped moustache sharp and bristling. 'I shall shame them.'

Agnes turned back to the mirror and said nothing. His anger was too frightening. In any case, what could she say? The girls were found, the meeting was arranged, it was all pre-ordained by her father's will, no matter what Claud said or might say.


So the various members of the new management board of G. S. Holborn's munitions prepared themselves for their very first meeting.

George and Johnny Everdale had been given a day off school in order to attend and told their friends it was 'a bit of a lark'. Jack Pennyfield told Fred Manners all about the

446

board meetings up at the house in old Mr Holborn's days and hoped that the twins would be a chip off the old block. Mr Reinhart, the company secretary, gathered together three huge folders of information about the company, should the new owners wish to see it, and confided to his wife that he thought it was going to be a regular power struggle.

Ken and Charlie spent an evening in a pub planning their strategy for, as Ken said, 'We're the odd ones out in all this, the outsiders, and if we don't do something to keep our ends up we shall be squashed flat.'

'We shall have to make it quite clear that we've got jobs of our own,' Charlie said.

'You can say that again.'

'That we're not part of their empire.'

'Quite right. Have you met this uncle of theirs?'

'Yes.'

'What's he like?'

'Used to getting his own way.'

Ken grimaced. 'Will he be chairing the meeting?'

'No. Our Mr Crabbit's doing that.'

'That's one good thing,' Ken said. 'He'd better be tough.'

# CHAPTER THIRTY-TWO

There was nothing Horace Crabbit enjoyed so much as chairing a difficult meeting. On that Wednesday afternoon at High Holborn he was in his element. There were so many conflicting interests in this affair and, to give an added piquancy to the proceedings, he knew that Mr Everdale would be annoyed to see him because he had issued special instructions that the meeting should be chaired 'by Mr Hedgethorn only'.

Nobody in the office had been surprised when Mr Hedgethorn discovered he was far too busy to travel to Wolverhampton.

'You see how it is, Horace,' he said, waving his hands at the pile of papers on his desk. 'If only I weren't so heavily committed. You must make my excuses to Mr Everdale. Explain the situation and so on and so forth.'

'Of course,' Mr Crabbit reassured him. 'Leave it to me. I'll take care of everything.'

And, with his customary foresight, he had.

First he had arranged the seating to suit his purposes – knowing, as he did, how important it is on such occasions to put everyone precisely, and literally, in their place. He had already asked Mr Commoner to sit at the top of the table on his left hand, and had written to the company secretary to ask if he would be so good as to bring all necessary documentation to the meeting and be prepared to take notes if and when required. He also suggested, as an apparent afterthought, that he should arrange to sit at the chairman's right hand, with his colleagues ranged beside him.

Now, all five gentlemen were in their places and everybody else had fallen into line – except Mr Everdale.

On principle, Claud Everdale arrived late. (He saw no

reason why he should allow Mr Hedgethorn to dictate to *him*.) He was furious when Mr Crabbit introduced himself.

'I understood Mr Hedgethorn was to chair this meeting,' he said coldly.

Mr Crabbit explained Mr Hedgethorn's position, while Charlie kept a straight face by looking out of the window.

'If that's the case,' Claud Everdale said, 'I'm not sure we should proceed.'

'That is entirely your decision,' Mr Crabbit replied agreeably. 'My function is simply to assist you in any way possible.' And he looked at Agnes to engage her opinion.

'I think it would be rather a pity not to go on,' Agnes said. 'Now that we're all here.'

'We'll not want to lose too many man hours, eh, Mr Everdale sir,' Jack Pennyfield said, turning from the table to look at his boss.

'Very well, then,' Mr Everdale said. 'I'll agree to it. But under protest, you understand, and simply to suit your convenience.' He bestowed a tight smile on Mr Manners, who smiled back sycophantically.

Ah! Mr Crabbit thought. I see how it is there. He indicated the chair between Mr Manners and Mr Pennyfield – which was the one he had had in mind for Mr Everdale.

'There's a drink list going the rounds,' Agnes said from the far end of the table. She'd been tucked neatly and safely between Ken Hopkirk and young Johnny. Sitting in her elegant panelled room in her own comfortable home, with the light streaming in upon her through the long windows, she was feeling quite skittish now that the meeting was about to begin. 'If you'll just sign your initials alongside the name of the drink you'd like, it will be served to you when the meeting is over. I've ordered a shandy for my sons, as it's a special afternoon.'

'Very handsome, I'm sure,' Jack Pennyfield said. 'Thank you ma'am. Quite like the old days.'

'That's what I intended,' Agnes said. 'I remember my father always used to . . .'

'If we've finished with the preliminaries,' Claud interrupted her, 'I think we ought to get on. Time being money, as the saying goes.' He looked across the table at his nieces sitting opposite him, small and quiet between their two young men. Don't imagine you're going to take this firm from me and my sons, he thought. Oh no! Not without a struggle. I hold all the big guns.

'Quite!' Mr Crabbit said. 'I've jotted down a short agenda, if you'll just pass it round, Mr Commoner.'

The papers were passed as Agnes retrieved the drinks list and left the room. The agenda was read. It listed three topics, neatly and succinctly. Ginny read them in an undertone to her sister.

'*1) G. S. Holborn's will.*
*2) Composition of new management committee.*
*3) Future of firm.*'

Claud Everdale opened his attack at once, while his passion ran high and before Agnes could return. 'I feel I should warn you,' he said to Mr Crabbit, 'that I intend to contest this will. I had very grave doubts about it, as I told you at the time, Mr Commoner.' Charlie nodded to show that he remembered. 'I have my reasons for opposing it now, and very good reasons, compelling reasons, which I'm quite prepared to lay before this meeting, painful though that might be.'

The words tore into the quiet of the room like bullets, stopping conversation in his workmates and breath in his relations.

Ginny and Emily were instantly and painfully alert. Claud sounded frightening and, to Ginny's startled eyes, he looked as aggressive as a *cagoulard*, his dark hair shining with brilliantine and fitting over his skull like a black cap. It will be the illness, they both thought. He knows.

'For a start,' Claud ploughed on, 'I shall require medical evidence to prove that Mr Holborn was of sound mind when he made that will. I find it very hard to believe that he would knowingly hand over the running of this firm to a foreigner . . .'

450

'Now, just a minute,' Ginny interposed, anger rising. 'We may be half French but we're half English, too, and just as much part of this firm as your sons.'

'. . . To a foreigner with a highly dubious character, by which I mean your mother. I'm sure you wouldn't wish me to elaborate on *that*.'

Emily drew in her breath and pinched Ginny's hand in warning. But her sister was too enraged to stop.

'If you've got something to say about Maman,' she challenged, 'you'd better say it now and be done with it, instead of hinting.' She could see the secretary and old Mr Pennyfield were embarrassed, but it was such a calculated insult she had to fight it. Charlie's father was right. You had to stand up to bullies.

'Very well, then,' Claud said, delighted to see her so rattled, 'I will say what I mean. I have no intention of opening this house or this company to the influence of your mother. She is not a fit person, as I know and can prove. If she turns up on my doorstep I shall refuse her entrance. Is that clear enough for you?'

'You needn't worry,' Ginny fought back. 'She won't "turn up", as you put it. She's in a convent.'

That was a surprise, but Claud recovered quickly. 'The best place for her – in the circumstances.' How menacing he made those three words sound. 'Now, as to the will, which concerns you and your sister, I intend to fight it every inch of the way. Through the courts, if necessary.'

The unease in the room was palpable. Even Mr Manners was shifting in his seat and glaring at the table. Mr Reinhart coughed. Ginny pinched Emily's hand. Oh God, what now? And Emily pinched back. Be calm, please be calm.

Rescue was at hand.

'That is your prerogative, of course,' Mr Crabbit said, intervening smoothly. 'From a professional point of view it might be a trifle, shall we say, precipitate, given that the terms of the will are not . . . How shall I put this? Not as straightforward as we might wish.'

'Dear me!' Claud reproved. 'Am I mistaken in thinking that your company drew up the will in the first place?'

'No. You are quite correct. We did. In fact, to my shame, I was the person most responsible.'

Claud controlled the movement of his lips before they could smile. Now this *was* a turn up for the books. 'You do surprise me, Mr Crabbit,' he said.

'These things happen, I fear,' Mr Crabbit said, courteously apologetic. 'However, as matters stand at the moment I must confess I am a little unclear as to how we should proceed.'

'What's the problem?' Claud asked. 'Isn't the will valid? Is that what you're trying to say?' How ironic after all the effort they'd made to find those girls.

'Not exactly not valid,' Mr Crabbit said. 'More . . . How shall I put it? Complicated. Ah, Mrs Everdale, I'm glad you're back again. I was just about to explain a little difficulty we're having with your father's will.'

'Oh yes,' Agnes said mildly, settling back into her seat. 'What was that, Mr Crabbit?'

'As you know,' Mr Crabbit said, 'the estate was to pass, in toto, to Mr Holborn's four grandchildren, George Norman Everdale, John Arthur Everdale, Virginia Holborn and Emily Holborn, as she then was, Mrs Kenneth Hopkirk as she now is. However, it stipulated that this was to occur when the two young women were found, as we are all glad to see they have been, *and* when the two boys had achieved their majority, which, tall and mature though they undoubtedly are, has not yet occurred.'

'I'm sixteen-and-a-half, sir,' George said, 'and he's fourteen.'

'Nearly fifteen,' Johnny corrected.

'Exactly,' Mr Crabbit said.

'So what is the problem?' Agnes ventured.

'An hiatus of seven years or thereabouts.'

Claud was doing rapid mental arithmetic. 'You mean the will can't be validated until 1945.'

That wasn't the true fact of the matter but Mr Crabbit wasn't going to admit it.

'Let's put it this way,' he said. 'Some other formula will have to be found that will satisfy both your father-in-law's intentions and the company's needs in the meantime.' He glanced around the table until his eye caught Charlie Commoner's.

It was the moment Charlie had been waiting for.

'As this is an *ad hoc* meeting, Mr Crabbit,' he said, 'are we required to take the items on the agenda in numerical order?'

'No, not necessarily,' Mr Crabbit said. 'Is there any other order you would prefer?'

'Well,' Charlie said, 'given today's news from Czechoslovakia, perhaps the third item would be more appropriate.'

'What news?' Jack Pennyfield asked, looking up with interest (and relief). 'What's happened now?'

'German troops are being moved towards the Bohemian border,' Ken informed them, seizing the moment, because he'd had quite enough of Claud's aggression. 'It was on the wireless.'

Claud Everdale was still too busy working out the implications of Mr Crabbit's confession to respond. Mr Pennyfield spoke up. 'Invasion, d'you think?' he asked.

'Looks like it,' Ken said.

'Well, I'm not surprised,' Mr Reinhart said, glad to be on to a safe topic. 'It's been on the cards.'

'It's the same trick they played in Austria,' Ginny explained to her aunt, 'and it'll work the same way. First, you get the local Germans out on the streets demanding a referendum or a plebiscite or something like that and then you see to it that they get reported in the papers and put in the newsreels at the pictures. Then, when they're making enough noise and people are beginning to say they ought to get what they want, Hitler walks in and occupies the whole country.'

'Good heavens!' Agnes said, impressed by Ginny's grasp of current affairs. 'Then *you* think Herr Hitler's going to invade Czechoslovakia.'

'It looks very much like it,' Ken said. 'If that *is* the case, and given the state of our alliances, we shall be at war with Germany. I've already taken orders for my company to increase output.'

For the second time that afternoon a chill descended on the meeting. They knew war was coming and there was nothing any of them could do to prevent it. They didn't want it and they weren't ready for it, but it was coming just the same. For a few seconds, and with the exception of Claud Everdale, they reflected on it in their different ways. Jack Pennyfield, Horace Crabbit and Agnes remembering the horror of the Great War; Emily thinking of the Somme and of Old Joliot's graves; Ginny caught between her passionate conviction that fascism was evil and should be stopped and the anguish of knowing that war kills the innocent along with the guilty; Mr Reinhart recalling the Zeppelin raid he'd seen as a young man and shuddering at the memory; George imagining what it would be like to be in a dog fight; Johnny recoiling from the idea of being in any sort of fight at all; and Charlie, Ken and Mr Manners facing the fact that, whatever sort of fight it was and whenever it actually began, they would be in the thick of it.

'Is Holborn's increasing output, too?' Agnes asked. If this war was coming, they'd better be ready for it.

'Of course,' Claud said, recovering himself. It was the first he'd heard of German troop movements but he certainly wasn't going to lose face by admitting *that*. He'd been watching the events in Czechoslovakia very closely and knew, like everyone else in the armaments industry, that war was likely.

'Actually,' Ken Hopkirk said, scoring a point (and serve him bloody well right), 'Mrs Everdale and I have been discussing the possibility of a joint venture between our two companies. It's probably not the right time to mention it but . . .'

'Ah yes!' Agnes said. 'The Bren gun.'

'Should I tell the meeting about it?' Ken asked, looking round the table for assent, but particularly at Mr Crabbit.

'Fire away!' Mr Crabbit said. 'If you'll pardon the pun.'

Ken told them all he knew about the new light machine gun. 'It's been developed at Enfield,' he said. 'Looks like a pretty good gun to me, very versatile, but you'd know more about that than I would. It's a lot lighter than the old machine gun, two-thirds the weight, so it can be fired from a variety of positions, lying prone, from armoured cars, free-standing. If it were mounted on a revolving stand it could be used for anti-aircraft purposes. Which is where Hopkirk's comes in. I've been designing the stand.'

'We're talking of large orders then,' Claud said, torn between the need to root these two usurping girls right out of the firm and the temptation of a deal that was plainly going to make a lot of money. Even in his present angry state, he could see that this young man was inventive and resourceful.

'Very large,' Ken told him. 'According to Bentley's there are plans to issue it on quite a scale. Fifty to a battalion so they say. Enfield's are sub-contracting.'

'I was thinking,' Agnes said, 'if we could get the contract we could make the guns, and Ken here could provide the stands.'

'Would this be in your factory in London?' Mr Reinhart wanted to know.

'It could be. I've got the space. Or it could be somewhere else, given I've enough capital.'

'You have some plan in mind,' Mr Crabbit prompted the secretary.

'We've had our eyes on a possible new site,' Mr Reinhart said, 'with a view to the expansion that would be necessary in the event of a war, you understand. I was wondering whether the two firms might not join forces and build two new factories side by side. It would save transport costs. And time, of course.'

'Now that's a first-rate idea,' Mr Pennyfield said. He looked at Claud.

'Would the site take two factories?' Claud asked, business acumen taking over.

'It would take four,' Mr Pennyfield told him. 'If it's the one I'm thinking about.'

'We'll inspect it first thing tomorrow morning,' Claud said to Ken Hopkirk. 'Take a team down. You're right. This has distinct possibilities.'

'If I might make a suggestion?' Mr Crabbit said.

'Yes?' Claud asked. The man was a muddling old fool but he *was* in the chair.

'If this goes through, as I have no doubt it will, then you will need the services of Hedgethorn and Crabbit in a little matter of conveyancing, I daresay. That being so, perhaps you would care to retain the services of our Mr Commoner here.'

'What a sensible idea!' Agnes said. 'Don't you think so, Claud?' And seeing that he didn't, she went on very quickly. 'It's high time Holborn's had a company solicitor. And here's the very one. Would you be agreeable, Mr Commoner?'

Mr Commoner said he would be very agreeable. 'Although I still have a contract with Mr Hedgethorn and Mr Crabbit.'

'I'm sure we could come to some arrangement about that,' Mr Crabbit said. 'My own personal opinion, for what it's worth, is that it would be an extremely apposite arrangement. However, it is not a decision to make in a hurry. That is so, is it not, Mr Everdale?'

Mr Everdale agreed that it was, scowling despite his efforts to smile.

'Well, now,' Mr Crabbit said, rubbing his hands together with satisfaction. 'We seem to have made extraordinary progress for an *ad hoc* meeting. We've certainly discussed the future of the firm.'

That was agreed all round the table and with considerable self-congratulation.

'Mr Crabbit,' Emily's clear voice sounded above the hubbub. 'May I say something?'

'Of course.'

'I've been sitting here listening,' Emily said, 'and it seems to me that we've actually been dealing with all three of the items on our agenda.'

'No, no,' Claud said condescendingly. 'We've been talking about the future plans of the firm, my dear. We haven't dealt with the will at all. Nor shall we, if I have anything to do with it.'

'I think,' Emily persisted, 'we've dealt with the future of the two firms so well that we've actually solved some of our other problems, too. Can I explain, Mr Crabbit?'

'Please do,' Mr Crabbit was intrigued. By now the other members round the table were listening closely.

'Well, then,' Emily said, eyes flickering. 'We've made plans, we've taken decisions. But what's really important, it seems to me, is that we haven't had to fight about them. They've been – almost natural. We've done it as a committee or a board or whatever I ought to call it. So I think what I'm saying is we don't have to discuss the . . . what were the words of the second item, Ginny?'

' "The composition of the new management committee",' Ginny said.

'That's it,' Emily said. 'We don't have to discuss it. We've done better than that. We've brought it into being this afternoon, haven't we? We are it.'

'Damn me!' Mr Pennyfield said, giving his great head a shake. 'You're right. We have, too.'

Despite himself, Claud Everdale was impressed. She'd got a good head on her shoulders, blind though she was. She could see what was what. She'd chosen a good husband, too, a businessman.

'Well, it might work,' he said. 'We could give it a try, I suppose.'

'For the next three months?' Mr Crabbit queried. 'Or would six be better?'

'We'll try three and then see what six would do,' Claud said, thinking, after three months everyone would know how foolish it was to have a whole lot of women on the board.

But there was still the will. And everyone in the family knew *that* hadn't been solved. But she wouldn't talk about that. Would she?

She didn't. But Charlie Commoner did. 'Now as to Mr

Holborn's will,' he said. 'It seems to me that we've made progress with that, too.'

Claud bristled, ready to protest again, but Mr Crabbit made a sign that they should all remain quiet.

'As I understood it, nothing can be done about the will until George and Johnny are both twenty-one,' Charlie continued. 'Very well, then, I suggest you leave things as they are, *pro tem*, and run the firm with this committee, or a modification of it, if that is what you wish after three months. Mr Hopkirk and I would not become members of the board at this stage, as I'm sure you will understand. We have too much to do, at present, in our own particular fields. You would need to review the pay of the non-family members of the board, and come to some arrangement about the shares that will keep all the family members of the committee on equal terms with one another. After that, you can bide your time.'

'With the possibility of regular reviews at – shall we say six-monthly intervals – to see how the arrangement is working out and the concommitant possibility of emendation, if necessary,' Mr Crabbit suggested. 'That seems an eminently sensible arrangement, Mr Commoner. Would it suit the board?'

Hands were raised all round the table. And raised high.

It'll do for the time being, Claud calculated. Once these solicitors are out of the way, I shall be in virtual control of the firm. The two girls will have votes but they won't signify and, anyway, we can get rid of them in three months' time. There was hope in all this *and* the certainty of profit besides. All in all, quite a victory for me, if I play my cards right.

'Time those drinks were served,' Agnes said. 'We've got something to celebrate.'

The board meeting rapidly turned into a party.

'I say!' Johnny said to his newly discovered cousin Emily. 'I thought for a minute that the Pater was going to blow you out of the water.'

'So did I,' Emily confessed. 'I'm glad he didn't.'

'Shall you live here now?' George asked Ginny.

'I don't know. Would you like us to?'

'Rather! We could make up fours for tennis.'

'Don't bully them,' Agnes laughed, coming up beside them. 'You must let them make up their own minds.'

'I can't imagine anyone being able to bully Emily,' Johnny said with admiration.

'Nor me, Johnny,' Ken said, giving his wife a hug. 'She's not as quiet as she looks, is she?'

'It would be nice to have you living here,' Agnes said. 'It's a company house, you know. The upkeep is paid for by the firm, so you'd have every right to it, even if we haven't quite settled the will. It doesn't belong to Claud for all his talk. We hold it in trust for the four of you. There's plenty of room. Well, you remember that. But you must decide.'

'What do you think?' Emily said to Kenneth that night, in the room allotted to them in the west wing. 'Ought we to live here?'

'Would you like to?'

'It's up to you, really,' she said, trying to give him a diplomatic answer. But her true feelings shone on her upturned face.

'We'll keep the bungalow so that we can go there from time to time and I can keep an eye on the meters.'

She agreed to that very readily. 'Yes. Of course. We couldn't get rid of our first home. Not when you've made it so perfect. But we could live here as well. Sort of turn and turn about.'

'Yes. We could. As it seems, I could end up being a Wolverhampton factory owner. D'you think Ginny will live here, too?'

'When she's married. Yes, I'm sure she will. Especially if Charlie takes this job with the firm. After all, we're the new owners.'

'Well, not quite,' he felt obliged to point out. 'The will was put to one side, wasn't it?'

'There was nothing wrong with the will,' she told him with a wicked expression on her face. 'It could have been read and accepted there and then if Uncle Claud hadn't been so opposed to it. Oh no! The whole thing was an act, wasn't it, and very neat, too. I think Mr Crabbit is one of the cleverest men I've ever met.'

'You've lost me,' Ken said. 'You'll have to explain.'

'The wording of the will was very clear,' she said. 'Charlie read it to me this morning.' And she quoted it. 'He said, "*I leave and bequeath my estate in toto to my four grandchildren*." Just that. There wasn't a word about having to wait for the boys to grow up. If we hadn't been found, then the whole estate would have gone to George and Johnny when they were both twenty-one, but that was the only mention of their age. Oh no, it was all an act they were putting on, and Charlie was part of it.'

'How on earth did you know all that? Did Mr Crabbit tell you beforehand?'

'No,' she laughed. 'I heard it. When Charlie asked if he could make an observation, he was much too meek. And when Mr Crabbit said he was ashamed to be the man responsible for drawing up the will, do you remember? I heard it then.'

'You're a witch,' Ken said, pulling her towards him to kiss her.

In the happiness of the moment, his kiss was lovingly returned.

In the suite of rooms in the east wing Charlie was kissing his lovely, loving Ginny. 'Can't I stay?' he begged. 'They'd never know.'

'They would,' Ginny whispered. 'This is England. People don't sleep together before they're married in this country. You ought to know that. If you're still here in the morning there'll be a scandal. In fact, if anyone came in and saw you like this there'd be a scandal.'

'What d'you mean, like this?' Charlie protested. 'I'm not doing anything.'

'Not now, you're not, but you think if someone had come in a few minutes ago.'

'But they didn't, did they?'

'It's no good, Charlie. You'll have to go. Come on, get dressed.'

'That wasn't what you were saying a few minutes ago, either.'

She kissed him in answer to that and he groaned with mock frustration. 'We'd better call the banns straightaway,' he said. 'That's all I've got to say. We can't live like this.' They'd hardly had any time on their own since they got back to England, and always slept apart.

'Where are we going to get married?' she asked.

'Here, Clapham, the City of London. I don't care where. When's all that interests me.'

'Are you going to take this job?'

'Probably. If only to annoy your uncle.'

'Not to please me?' she teased.

'I've got better ways to please you.'

'Bragging again,' she said, kissing him.

'And why not?' Answering the kiss with passion.

She disentangled herself, laughing at him. 'Is it going to be a Catholic wedding?' she asked.

'No. It's not,' he said, rolling over on to his back. There was no need to argue about *that*. 'It'll be Church of England. There's more of them.'

She was impressed by his decisiveness. I ought to argue, she thought. Maman and Emily would have put up all sorts of objections if they'd been in her place. But it didn't seem worth the effort. The great thing was that they were getting married – even though Charlie didn't want to be a rich woman's husband.

'That's all right,' he said, 'isn't it?'

'Yes,' she said. 'That's all right.'

'Thank God for that. I should never have made a Catholic.'

'But if we have children they'll have to be brought up Catholic. You understand that, don't you?'

'We'll cross that bridge when we come to it.'

'So when will it be?' she said. 'Have you decided that, too?'

'I'd marry you tonight,' he said, 'if you could find a priest. As soon as possible.'

Ginny became serious. 'I'm going to stay here for a day or two and have a good look round the factory,' she said. 'Now that I'm part owner.'

'You're going to run it after all, then,' he teased her.

'I'm not going to let Uncle Claud run it. I can tell you that. Not after the way he behaved at the meeting.'

'I love you when you're fierce,' he said.

# CHAPTER THIRTY-THREE

Ginny's first visit to G. S. Holborn's munitions factory lasted over three hours. She came back to tea at High Holborn dirty and exhausted, and full of furious sympathy for the workers.

'It's an enormous place,' she said to Aunt Agnes, as they sat in the morning room with the teapot on the table between them. 'I never realised it was so big. And the noise!'

'All factories are noisy,' Agnes said mildly. 'You can't do much about that, I'm afraid.'

'Maybe not,' Ginny said. 'But I can do something about the way they treat injuries. That's a disgrace. Have you seen what they do? Apparently, the men are always getting cuts and gashes and there's no one to attend to them. They just tie up the wound with a piece of rag. They could get – what is it called? *L'empoisonnement du sang* – blood poisoning. We should have a proper medical room, with a nurse in attendance. I shall propose it at the next management meeting.'

Which she did, to sympathy, interest and considerable enthusiasm. Claud Everdale was none too pleased, especially as it took him twenty minutes, even from his commanding position as chairman, to persuade the new board that 'admirable though it was' the firm 'simply couldn't afford it'.

'What did I tell you?' he said to Agnes, that evening. 'I knew those girls would be trouble. Medical rooms! I ask you! Namby-pamby nonsense.'

'It's very popular with the workers,' Agnes said. 'Sarah was telling me this morning when she brought up the tea . . .'

'Virginia is the worst,' Claud said. 'If I don't put a stop to her, she'll be the ruin of us. However, I managed to bring them round in the end, and that's what counts. Talk money, and people soon see sense.'

He would have been very annoyed to know that, at that very moment, Ginny was deciding to talk money, too.

'I'm not going to let him pull a trick like that and get away with it,' she said to Charlie, Emily and Ken. 'If money really is short, we must find some way to make economies.'

'I think it was a mistake to let him take the chair,' Charlie said. 'He's manipulative enough without that. There must be a constitution somewhere that we could use to unseat him. I'll phone Mr Crabbit.'

'I suppose you're going to stay here till you've got it settled,' Emily said.

'Of course,' her sister told her. 'Why don't you stay as well, for a day or two. We could achieve a lot more if there were two of us.'

To her surprise, Ken agreed. 'Good idea,' he said. 'I shall be up to my ears in work this week.'

So the campaign doubled in intensity and, what was even better, the constitution was found and proved to be extremely useful, although Charlie saw it as a mixed blessing. It gave Ginny and Emily the undeniable right to chair all board meetings – but it also encouraged Ginny to give far too much of her attention to G. S. Holborn's. The date they'd chosen for their wedding was now only eight weeks away but she rarely talked about getting married. In fact, as far as Charlie could make out, Ginny hadn't made any preparations at all, beyond sending out the invitations. After the passion of their reunion, it was rather discouraging.

Although she didn't tell Charlie, Ginny was hoping that her mother would come to England to see her married, so she was waiting for Hortense to answer the invitation. Either way, she needed to know what the answer would be before she could give her mind to the wedding.

It was a bitter disappointment when Hortense finally wrote back. It was a long letter and, at first, it said all the right and loving things. '*You are my own dearest daughter and I love you with all my heart. I wish you happiness and health in your marriage.'* But then it continued in a flat, dispirited way, *'But I cannot come to your wedding.'* What more could she say? Her dearest Virginie knew that this would have to be her decision. She promised to pray for both her daughters night and day, but she couldn't leave the convent. She was sure they would understand: *'Not now, when there is so much to pray for in our unhappy world.'*

'Oh Ginny!' Emily said. 'I'm so sorry. Is it because it isn't a Catholic wedding, do you think?'

'No. I didn't tell her.'

'Are you very disappointed?'

'Yes,' Ginny admitted. 'But it's not a surprise. I hoped, but I never really thought she'd come.'

'What shall we do about her, Ginny? We can't leave her in France for ever.'

'No, we can't,' Ginny said. 'But it's obviously no good writing letters to her. And it's no good expecting her to come here either, not on her own and not without a lot of persuasion. We shall have to leave her where she is for the time being. Charlie was right. Still,' she shrugged, 'that's how it is. It can't be helped. Meantime we've got the board meeting. You'll be here for that, won't you?'

'I wouldn't miss it for the world.'

'If everything goes according to plan,' Ginny said, 'our Uncle Claud could be in for a bit of a surprise.'

In fact, what Uncle Claud was in for was the shock of his life. To be told he wasn't going to take the chair was insult enough, even if it *was* done in the privacy of the library before the meeting began, but the agenda his wretched niece had drawn up for the occasion was a real kick in the teeth.

*'Item 1 – Finances*
*(a) Economies*
*(b) Expenditure on medical room.'*

Whatever next?

'If I may be allowed to point this out,' he said, from his

465

vantage point at the foot of the table, 'Item 1(b) was dealt with at our last meeting.'

'No,' Ginny said from the chair. 'I think not. Charlie has the minute book. He could tell you. Charlie?'

'It was deferred, I believe,' Charlie said. 'Mr Everdale was concerned that the firm would not be able to afford a medical room. Miss Holborn said she would look into it.'

'Which I have done,' Ginny said. 'Item 1(a), Economies. I've taken a close look at the various guns we are producing and I've discussed them with the people most concerned and I think I have found a way to save enough money to pay for the medical room, if the board is in agreement.'

'Holborn's guns make good profits,' Claud said, thinking what a fool she was. 'There's no way we could make economies there.'

'All bar one,' Ginny said coolly. 'I find we've been running very expensive trials on an anti-tank gun, which isn't in production. Isn't that right?'

'There have been one or two problems with that gun, yes,' he had to admit. 'It'll be a money-spinner when we've got it right.'

'That might not be the opinion of the board,' Ginny said. 'Personally I feel we've wasted far too much money on it already. I think it would be unwise to proceed with it. However, I will take the opinion of the board. Mr Pennyfield?'

One by one, the members of the board told her what they really thought of Claud's gun. Even Mr Manners said he wasn't entirely happy with it. Claud spoke for fifteen minutes in its defence but he was fighting a losing battle.

'Any further comment?' Ginny asked, when he'd finished. 'Good. I put it to the vote that the anti-tank gun be scrapped.'

Claud was so shocked he could hardly believe his ears. 'You can't do that,' he protested.

Nevertheless, according to the company secretary and

that wretched Commoner, she could. The vote was taken and carried by an overwhelming majority. And the next vote, for the proposed medical room, was unanimous, except for his own, lone, dissenting voice.

That evening Claud Everdale returned to High Holborn flushed with rage.

'I can't believe it!' he said to Agnes. 'For sheer, unadulterated, black-hearted treachery, I simply can't believe it. She must have been round the factory canvassing support. She'd *really* put the pressure on them. They were all for her, the stupid fools. Eating out of her hand.'

'Fancy,' Agnes said quietly. She was paying more attention to a book of wallpaper samples.

'You should have been there,' Claud said. 'I could have done with your support.'

'Um,' Agnes said, matching a swatch of brocade against one of the patterns. Knowing that a fight was brewing, she had deliberately stayed at home that afternoon out of harm's way. Now she felt ashamed of her cowardice and wished she'd been there to see the fun.

'What am I going to do, Aggie?' her husband asked, helping himself to his second sustaining whisky. 'That's *my* gun they're scrapping. You realise that, don't you? I've put years of my life into that gun. I can't let her get away with this.'

'I don't see how you can stop her,' Agnes said, without looking up from the samples. 'After all, she *does* own the company.'

'What nonsense you talk!' Claud bristled. 'She doesn't own the company. The will wasn't proved.'

'I think you'll find that she and Emily are the two co-owners, nevertheless,' Agnes said implacably. 'They chair the meetings, don't they? It's all in the constitution. You and I have no power now, Claud. We're just keeping the seats warm for the boys.' She turned over to the next page.

Her calm infuriated Claud. 'Put that bloody book down!' he ordered. 'I'm talking to you.'

Agnes marked her place with a swatch of cloth and set the book aside.

'What is that?' he said, squinting at it across the rim of his glass.

'Wallpaper.'

'What on earth for?'

'Redecorating.'

'Redecorating!' he roared. 'What do you mean, redecorating? We've only just had everything done. We don't need redecorating.'

'Actually, that was three years ago,' Agnes said. 'But you're right. *We* don't need it. This is for the west wing. For Emily and Kenneth.'

'What? What?'

'Oh dear,' Agnes said, sighing. 'Must I repeat every single thing I say? I'm having the west wing decorated for Emily and Kenneth.'

'What for?'

'For when they come to stay and . . .'

'Ah! Well, I suppose that's all right,' Claud said, tipping back a third whisky. 'Just so long as they're not going to live here. For a minute there, I thought that was what you meant. I don't mind putting up with them now and then, for board meetings – I'm a reasonable man – but they needn't think they're going to muscle in on my home. I draw the line at that. A man's home *ish hish* castle.'

'Of course they're going to come and live here,' Agnes said, implacably. 'Where else would they live?'

'Not in my house.'

'It's not your house.'

'Goddamn it, of course it's my house. I live here.'

'So you do, but it's not your house. It belongs to the company, or, if I'm really accurate, I suppose I should say to the people who own the company. That's Ginny and Emily. And the boys, when they're twenty-one. Me for the time being.'

'Legal mumbo-jumbo,' Claud said, pouring another whisky. 'We don't need to pay any 'tention to *that*.'

Agnes didn't answer and her silence was potent.

'Now, look here!' Claud said, fired by rising anger and descending whisky. '*Thish* has gone far enough. I will not have those girls in my *housh*. Do I make *myshelf* clear. I *shimply* won't allow it. They are not allowed.'

She returned to the book of samples, still silent.

'I forbid it,' he roared. 'I mean it, Agnes. If they come into *thish* house, I leave it. You *unnershtand* me?'

'It's no good going on like that,' Agnes said calmly. 'They're moving in on Thursday fortnight. In nice time for Ginny's wedding.'

He was so enraged he seized the book from her hands and, heavy though it was, hurled it into the corner of the room.

'You're not listening to me,' he shouted. 'I told you. It's either them or me. If they move in, I leave.'

She looked him straight in the bloodshot eye. 'Then you must leave,' she said.

The shock of such treachery sobered him. 'But I'm your husband,' he said. 'You love me.'

'No,' she said. 'I don't think I do.' And she got up and walked across the room to retrieve the book.

For a few seconds he was rooted to the spot, whisky glass in hand. 'How can you say such a thing?'

'Because it's true,' Agnes said. 'I haven't loved you for years.'

'I don't *unnershtand* you,' he said. 'I don't *unnershtand* anybody. The world's gone raving bloody mad.' Having made that perfectly clear, he picked up the decanter from the sideboard and walked with drunken deliberation out of the room, down the stairs and into the library.

He was still there at midnight when Charlie, Ken and the twins returned from the theatre and a late supper. They could see him, slumped in the leather armchair with a glass and an empty decanter on the table beside him.

'Oh dear,' Ginny said. 'He *has* taken it badly. Do you think he's all right?'

'You go up,' Ken said. 'I'll just pop in and see. He's probably too drunk to get up to bed.'

In fact, by this time, Claud was maudlin. 'Bloody women,' he growled, as Ken walked in. 'They skin you alive.'

'D'you need a hand?'

'Don't unnerstand 'em. Bloody women. All the same. Can't go upstairs, ol' son. Wife won't have it. Bloody woman. Got to leave the house. Marchin' orders, I've had. Well, let me tell you, I'd leave the house tomorrow if I knew where to go. This very minute. Between you an' me I've got a bit put by, for emergencies. I'm not a pauper. An' she needn't think it.'

It took a little while and patient questioning to prise the story out of him, but Ken persisted, an idea growing with splendid clarity inside his business brain.

'Don't you think that's diabo-*lo*-lical?' Claud asked. 'Absolutely diabo-*lo*-lical. An' someone's drunk all the bloody Scotch.'

'You need a factory of your own,' Ken said. 'That's my opinion.'

'Qui' right. So I do. If I could find one.'

'You could buy mine if you'd like to. It's on the market.'

'Is it?'

'It is.'

'Since when?'

'Since now. You could make your anti-tank gun there with no one to stop you.'

Drunk as he was, Claud sensed a bargain and recognised a solution. 'I shall go an' inspect it,' he decided, struggling out of the chair. 'Right away.'

'Are you sure that's wise?' Ken asked, watching the struggle. 'It would wait until morning.'

'No, no. Go now. That's the ticket. Time an' tide wait for . . . an' all that sort of thing. Anyway, I can't stay here. Wife won't let me. I shall take my briefcase. That's what I'll do.' Claud spotted it, propped up against one of the bookcases. 'I shall go to the station. Catch a train. What's the address?'

Ken wrote it down for him and tucked it into the top pocket of his jacket. 'How will you get to the station?' he asked.

'I shall walk,' Claud said grandly, and he staggered out into the hall. He took down Ken's trilby from the hatstand, put it on and left the house.

His departure was the one topic of conversation at the breakfast table next morning.

'You don't think he really went to London, do you?' Ginny asked her brother-in-law.

'He'll have had to sit on the platform till six o'clock, if he did,' Charlie said.

'What do you think, Aunt Agnes?' Emily wanted to know.

'He'll do whatever he wants to,' Agnes said. 'He always has. But he's not coming back here, I can tell you that.'

'Do you mean he's left you?' Emily asked.

'I *do* hope so,' Agnes said.

Two days later Ken and Emily went back to London and the following morning Claud turned up at the factory in Streatham. He was completely sober and meant business. By the end of that afternoon the factory had changed hands. Four days after that, Ken made an offer for the second factory site at Wolverhampton.

'First rate,' Agnes said, when she was told the news. 'Just in good time for Ginny's wedding.'

'Just in time to make all the flight panels we shall need if Hitler invades the Sudetenland,' Ken said. The situation in Czechoslovakia grew more serious by the day. There were rumours that Hitler was mobilising his army, and street fighting in the Sudetenland was so violent that the area had been put under martial law. On the day the trestle tables were set up on the terrace at High Holborn, ready for the wedding breakfast, Mr Chamberlain announced to the House of Commons that he was sending Lord Runciman to Prague in an attempt to find a solution to the Czechoslovakian problem.

There was so much excitement in the house of Holborn that nobody there took much notice – although Ken and Charlie followed the news on the radio at regular intervals throughout the day.

Guests arrived throughout the afternoon. Mauricette,

Monsieur and Madame Lalange and their entire family (their journey made possible by the tickets that Ginny had very tactfully sent across for them), Veronique, determined to look stylish in a splendid Parisian hat, and distant aunts and uncles on the Holborn side that only Agnes could remember. Miss Babbacombe arrived, resplendent in a brand new outfit, hat, shoes, handbag and all, as well as Mr and Mrs Commoner, trying hard not to look ill-at-ease among such wealthy people, with Grandpa Jones in his best suit, even though it didn't fit, and Aunt Grace in a fox fur that was horribly moth-eaten and had to be rearranged every few seconds to hide the bald patches.

It was a glorious summer day, and there were roses in such profusion that they scented the house as well as the garden. Up in the east wing in the bride's bedroom Ginny and Emily leant out of the window to enjoy the scent and sunshine.

They were both dressed and ready for the ceremony, and very pretty they looked; Emily in her apple-green costume and a blue and white deep-crowned hat; Ginny in a dress made of pale blue georgette and a picture hat covered very appropriately in pink and white roses and blue forget-me-nots. There was a coat to match her dress, but that still lay on the bed because she didn't want to crush it. Like the dress, it was pale blue, but embroidered with roses in pink, white, apple-green and grey-blue, and it was too grand to be put on until the last moment. She and Emily had taken a long time over their appearance that day because they wanted to be sure they would look their best, and match and complement each other.

'How odd it is that we're back here in this house, leaning out of the windows again,' Emily said.

'We were always leaning out of windows,' Ginny remembered.

'Weren't we? And planning how we'd run the firm. Do you remember that?'

'And now here we are running the firm.'

'And leaning out of the window.'

'Do you mind me not marrying in a Catholic church?' Ginny asked. Marrying outside her faith *was* a major step, however lightly she was trying to take it.

Emily wasn't perturbed about that. 'No,' she said, breathing in the scent of the roses. 'I was a bit disappointed at first, naturally, but with this war coming I'm beginning to see all sorts of things in a different way. I don't think it matters so much now. You'll worship in the same church as Charlie, and we all worship the same God. Perhaps these things aren't as important as we used to think.'

Ginny gave her a hug. 'Charlie was so sure about it,' she said. 'He just said, "Church of England and that's all there is to it", so what could I do?'

'What you're doing,' Emily said, smiling at her. 'Are you happy? That's the main thing.'

'Do you need to ask?'

'No, not really. I can hear you are. It's just . . . Well, I've been wondering . . .'

Down by the fish pond a robin was singing and the voices of the assembled guests echoed across the garden.

'What have you been wondering?' Ginny asked.

'I don't know,' Emily said. 'Perhaps I'd better not . . . What I mean is . . . Perhaps it isn't the right time.'

Ginny was intrigued. 'The right time for what?'

'Well, what I mean is . . . the right time to . . . well, warn you.'

'What about?'

'Look,' Emily said, rather breathlessly. 'Do you know what's going to happen tonight, when you and Charlie get to bed? Has anyone told you?'

Ah, Ginny thought, *that's* what we're talking about. 'It's all right, Em,' she said. 'I do know.'

'The thing is . . .' Emily said, hanging her head and looking horribly embarrassed. 'The thing is . . .'

'The thing is,' Ginny said. 'Charlie and I are as good as married.'

'Yes, but you're not, are you?'

'Yes,' Ginny said. 'We are.' And then with sudden and

necessary candour. 'Oh, look, Em, I think I'd better tell you, we've been lovers for ages.'

Emily was shocked and her face showed it. Imagine her sister doing such a thing! Why it was awful, against the teachings of the church, against everything Maman had hinted, awful. She could hardly believe it. 'Ginny!' she said. 'You don't really mean lovers, do you? You don't really mean you've . . . You haven't been . . . ?'

'Yes,' Ginny told her, speaking firmly to defend herself from Em's implied criticism. 'We have. And there's nothing wrong in it. It's natural.'

'Oh, Ginny! I wasn't saying it was wrong. It's just . . . Well, are you all right?'

'Perfectly all right.'

'You've not been ill or anything?'

'No. I'm not ill. I never have been. That's why I never really thought your cystitis was the illness. Only I couldn't tell you.'

'But doesn't it hurt you?'

'Hurt me?'

'Well, not now, perhaps, but the first time. Didn't it make you sore?'

What an idea! Ginny thought. 'No,' she said. ''Course not.'

'Never?'

'No,' Ginny said. 'I wouldn't do it if it hurt.' And then as she understood what Emily was really saying, 'Oh, Em, does it hurt you?'

'Well, not so much now. It did at first.'

'Em, my dear! It's not supposed to hurt. It's supposed to be lovely. You're supposed to enjoy it.'

That was another surprise. 'Do you enjoy it?'

'Yes. Very much.'

'Really?'

'Really.'

Emily sighed and the little sound told her sister more than she intended.

'What does Ken say?'

'I haven't told him.'

It was time to hand out some sisterly advice. 'Well, you ought to,' Ginny said. 'If he does something and you don't enjoy it, he ought to know.'

'What talk about it, do you mean?'

'Yes. Of course. All the time.'

'What, when we're . . . ?'

'Yes. When he does something you really enjoy tell him to do it again.'

That was a very novel idea and rather shocking. 'Do you talk about it? When you're . . .'

'Yes. Of course. How can he know what's really good if you don't tell him?'

It really was a *very* novel idea.

'Take my tip,' Ginny advised. 'Start tonight.' And because Emily was still looking puzzled and embarrassed, she gave her a hug.

'My, you do look lovely, the pair of you!' Agnes said, coming into the room. 'The guests have started leaving for church, Ginny, my dear. Your car's here, but there's no rush. Have you got everything you need?'

So the congregation gathered in Wittick church to witness the marriage of Virginia Holborn of this parish to Charles Stanley Commoner. They stood side by side under the dappled light, he so tall and fair in his dark suit, she so slight and dark in her embroidered coat, and smiled into one another's eyes as the opening words of welcome were spoken.

'Dearly beloved, we are gathered together here in the sight of God and in the face of this congregation to join together this man and this woman in Holy Matrimony.'

No one listened to the words of the service more carefully than the matron-of-honour. Was Ginny right? she wondered. Was it really a holy estate? All of it? That, as well as the mutual help and comfort? Were you really meant to enjoy it? If it *was* holy, then perhaps you were.

She could hear the shuffle of the exchange as Charlie took the ring from his best man. Then he made his second vow, speaking clearly and with passion.

'With this ring I thee wed, with my body I thee worship . . .'

And he does, Emily thought. I can hear it in his voice. Oh, Ginny, could it really be like that for me, too?

It was a seductive thought and it returned to her at regular intervals all through the wedding breakfast and long after bride and groom had driven away through a shower of rose petals and well wishes to their secret honeymoon. 'With my body I thee worship.' The more she thought about it the more enticing it became.

That night, when she and Ken were finally in bed together, she decided to put it to the test. 'Yes,' she said. 'I like that.'

He wasn't shocked or annoyed as she'd half feared he might be. He was thrilled. 'Shall I do it some more?'

Her face answered him before she spoke. 'Yes. Yes do. Did you enjoy it, too?'

It was a new experience for both of them to describe what they were feeling and it prolonged his lovemaking into a swooning languour she'd never felt before. The sudden rush of uncontrollable pleasure that finished it was such a wondrous surprise that she cried out in amazement.

'Oh!' he groaned, following her. 'My dear, darling love!'

When they'd got their breath back she had a question to ask. 'Is it like that for you when we . . .'

'Yes, my lovely, lovely one.'

'Every time?'

He understood what she was telling him. 'Was that the first time you felt it?'

She admitted it easily. 'Yes.'

He was overcome with remorse because he hadn't known it. 'Oh, Em, I'm so sorry. I always thought you were feeling it, too. I mean . . .'

'Never mind,' she said, responding to the regret in his voice. 'I've felt it now, so perhaps it'll happen again.'

'Every time,' he said. 'I promise.'

'Oh!' she said, rubbing her cheek against his hand. 'I'm so

happy. It doesn't seem right to be so happy when there are so many dreadful things going on in the world, Hitler and Mussolini and all this business in Czechoslovakia.'

'That'll go on whether you're happy or not,' Ken said reasonably. 'Anyway, why shouldn't you be happy? You've earned it.'

'You're right,' she said. 'My darling Ken.'

He was right about the crisis in Czechoslovakia, too. That continued all through the summer and grew steadily more murky. On the day the purchase of the Wolverhampton factory site was completed, Monsieur Daladier, the French Premier, came to London for a conference with the British Government to decide what should be done. Little came of it. Pro-German riots continued in the Sudetenland and the Czech Government called up its reservists. Public statements were made and contradicted. Treaties were signed and then repudiated. And the fear of war grew like a universal migraine.

# CHAPTER THIRTY-FOUR

There was a bad storm brewing. It had been gathering all day and now that evening was drawing in, the air was close, sticky and unbearably hot. Since their marriage, Ginny and Charlie had been living in the east wing at High Holborn and the sitting-room there was the coolest room in the house, but even that felt like an oven. Ginny and Emily drew back the curtains and opened the windows as wide as they would go, but there wasn't a breath of air to refresh them, in or out of the house, just an ominous heaviness brooding down upon them and making them sweat.

'Will it be war tomorrow, do you think?' Emily asked. As she spoke, the first crack of thunder exploded to the north.

'Yes,' Ginny said. 'I'm afraid it will. I don't see how we can avoid it this time.' The events of the last thirty-six hours had ensured there wasn't much doubt about it. At dawn on the previous day Hitler had invaded Poland, and that afternoon the British Government had sent an ultimatum to Germany, threatening war unless all German troops were withdrawn from Polish territory.

'So this is the last night of peace.'

'Yes,' Ginny said sadly. 'Still, at least we're better prepared than we were at the Munich crisis.' G. S. Holborn's had been working overtime for the last fifteen months and so had Ken's new factory.

'Do you think we'll be bombed?' Emily asked. She sounded quite calm, as if she was simply asking for information.

'Yes,' Ginny said, equally calmly.

'Us? Here?'

'Well, not this house, perhaps, but the factory. Being armaments. They're bound to aim at armaments.'

A flash of sheet lightning exposed the garden, in a lurid, blue glare. It held for several seconds and then it was gone in an instant, leaving a total and terrifying blackness. Thunder cracked like cannon fire, echoing and roaring in the malevolent space above their heads. This is what it must be like to be blind, Ginny thought, blind and afraid and in the middle of an air raid. She reached out in the darkness for Emily's hand, needing the comfort of contact. It seemed all too horribly appropriate that this war was beginning with a storm.

'Do you think Maman was right about the illness?' Emily said.

The total blackness was thinning and Ginny was beginning to see the garden again, eerie and black shadowed. It was time for honesty. 'Yes,' she admitted, recalling what Hortense had told her in the convent garden. That was two years ago, but she remembered it as clearly as if it had been yesterday. 'I don't know for certain, well neither of us can, but I think it's likely.'

'What are we going to do?'

'There's nothing we *can* do,' Ginny said. 'It's like the war. If it's coming it'll come. There's nothing we can do to stop it.'

'You mean we'll just have to endure it.'

'No,' Ginny said, lifting her head defiantly against the threats that were crowding down; storm, darkness, illness, coming war and all. 'That's not what I mean. That's not the way at all. We should never endure anything. We should fight it. All of it. Any way we can.'

'Oh, Ginny!' her sister said. 'How can you fight against an illness?'

'I don't know yet. But I'm sure you can.'

Charlie walked into the room. 'What are you two doing, standing there in the dark?' he said, putting his arms round their shoulders.

'We're watching the storm,' Ginny said. 'Come and join us. It'll be cooler when it breaks. There! There's the rain!' A large raindrop had splattered down on her outstretched hand.

'It's going to be a downpour,' Charlie said. 'You'll get wet.'

'Good,' Ginny said. 'It'll be a relief after all this pressure. It's just what we need. Is there any more news?'

Charlie had been downstairs with Ken and Agnes listening to the news bulletin. 'Nothing we don't know already,' he said. 'There's no reply from Berlin yet, so they say. The French have asked for a forty-eight-hour delay. Polish troops are putting up a stiff resistance to the German invasion. That sort of thing.'

'This is going to sound a silly thing to say,' Ginny observed, 'but I shall be glad when it starts. If we've got to fight, the sooner we get on with it the better.'

'I never thought I'd hear you sound so bloodthirsty,' Charlie said.

'I'm not being bloodthirsty,' Ginny said. 'I'm being realistic.'

It was a common sentiment on the second day of September in 1939.


The next day the storm had cleared and it was a lovely, peaceful summer morning. The skies above Clapham were clear blue and a blackbird was singing from the may tree in the Commoners' garden in Abbeville Road.

'Are we going to church, or not?' Ruby asked, as she washed up the breakfast things. 'What you think?'

'We'll give it the go-by this morning,' Stan said, rubbing the stubble on his chin. 'Stay here an' listen to the news.'

So Ruby prepared the Sunday dinner (and Stan had a leisurely shave before Grace and Grandpa could get up and hog the bathroom) and like most of the population of the British Isles on that awesome morning, at eleven o'clock the four of them gathered round the wireless.

The reed-thin voice of Prime Minister Chamberlain spoke wearily to them over the ether.

'This morning the British Ambassador in Berlin handed the German Government a final note stating that unless we heard from them by eleven o'clock that they were prepared at once to withdraw their troops from Poland, a state of war would exist between us. I have to tell you now that no such undertaking has been received and that consequently this country is at war with Germany.'

'What's the matter with the man?' Grace said. 'We don't want to go to war.'

'Well, we're *at* war,' Grandpa said, 'whether you like it or not.'

'Hush!' Ruby said, for Chamberlain was still speaking. 'Hear him out, poor man.'

'Never mind, poor man,' Grace said. 'We're the poor buggers what'll be bombed. I *said* you should ha' made a shelter.'

'Listen!' Stan ordered.

So they listened.

'. . . may God bless you all,' the weary voice continued. 'May He defend the right. It is the evil things that we shall be fighting against – brute force, bad faith, injustice, oppression and persecution – and against them I am certain that the right will prevail.'

'Now what?' Ruby said.

Someone was rustling papers in the studio and another voice said that he would be reading some public announcements. No one was to blow a whistle or sound a horn for fear of being confused with air-raid warnings. All theatres and cinemas were to close forthwith. It would be an offence to show a light during the black-out. All banks would be closed on Monday although it would not be a public holiday.

Then, the National Anthem was played and in the middle of the first line the horrible noise of the air-raid sirens began in the streets outside, howling up and up through a long stomach-churning scale and then growling down again, up and down, up and down, increasing panic with every howl.

'Oh, my giddy godfathers!' Aunt Grace said. 'They're 'ere!' She made a bolt for the cupboard under the stairs and started throwing the brooms and buckets out into the hall.

'Grace!' Ruby yelled, running after her. 'Stop it, do! Look at the mess you're making.'

'Never mind mess,' Grace shouted back. 'We're gonna be bombed.' She was already inside the cupboard, peering out from the doorway with a mop in her hand and her glasses slipping off the end of her nose. 'Whatcher wanna keep such a load of ol' junk in 'ere for?'

'Go out an' see what's what,' Ruby said to Stan. 'It's ever so clear. If they're coming you'll be able to see 'em for miles.'

Stan and Grandpa walked out into Abbeville Road and stared up at the sky. The barrage balloons were already up, bobbing gently against the blue; fat, friendly and shining silver. There was no sign of any bombers.

Presently, one or two of the neighbours put their heads out of doors, too.

'See anythink?' one asked.

'No,' Stan said, peering at the sky. 'Nothing yet.'

He and Grandpa remained in the hall among the brooms and buckets, dodging in and out of the house from time to time to see if there were any planes, but nothing happened. Twenty minutes later the all-clear sounded.

'That's it!' Grace said, as she crawled out of the cupboard. 'I'm off! I ain't stayin' 'ere to be bombed.'

'Off where?' Ruby asked, looking at the muddle in her nice neat hall.

'Bournemouth,' Grace said, picking cobwebs from her hair. 'To Maud's.'

'But you quarrel with Maud. You don't like her.'

'I'd rather be with Maud than bombed to smithereens.'

'But how will you get there? They're using all the trains for evacuees.'

'I'll go on a coach, then.'

'But what about your things?'

'Things!' Grace said distractedly. 'Who cares about things? You can send 'em on after.'

Six hours later she was gone.

'Good riddance to bad rubbish,' Grandpa said. 'I couldn't ha' put up with her *an'* Adolf Hitler.'

'I can't get over her just rushing off like that,' Ruby said, 'not after all this time. It isn't as if there was any bombs.'

'There will be, though,' Grandpa said dourly. 'You got to face that, gel.'

At five o'clock that afternoon, France followed Great Britain into the war.

'We'd better go and get Maman,' Ginny declared at dinner.

'If she'll come,' Charlie said.

'If it's wise,' Ken warned. 'I don't think you should be travelling abroad at all.'

Ginny ignored Ken's warning and addressed herself to Charlie and Emily. 'We must *make* her come,' she argued. 'We can't leave her at Villefleurs. Not now. It was different when there was a hope there wouldn't be a war, but now it's started she'll have to move. Em will come with me, won't you, Em? I'll book a passage.'

But, travel was extremely difficult now that the war had begun, and making a trip abroad almost impossible, as Ginny was to discover. It wasn't simply a matter of phoning a booking office.

'First,' she was told, 'you will have to get a permit and you'll need your National Identification Number for that. Have you got your identity card yet?'

'No,' Ginny admitted. 'I haven't even heard of it.'

'You will,' the voice promised. 'Come back to us when you've got one.'

Ginny was furious to be held back by bureaucracy. 'What nonsense!' she said to Charlie. 'Identity cards! Did you ever hear such nonsense.'

'Well, actually, yes,' Charlie admitted. 'I have heard. We've all got to register. It's the new rules and regulations.'

'So we've got to wait. Is that it?'

''fraid so,' Charlie said. 'Never mind. I shall be waiting with you. I'm going to apply for a permit, too.'

'What for?'

'To travel with you. Look after you. Love and cherish, all that sort of stuff.'

Ginny wasn't interested in being looked after. She was

still fuming about the permits. 'I can't see the point of rules and regulations,' she complained, 'if they make life more difficult. I'm blowed if I can.'

Whether or not they saw the point of the new rules, everybody had to endure changes in the weeks that followed.

Petrol was rationed and the streets gradually cleared of cars. By day, rural villages teemed with evacuees. By night, town centres were eerily empty and as dark as coal cellars. People carried their gas marks wherever they went. Windows were criss-crossed with sticky paper as a protection against blast, and sandbags were heaped against thicker plate glass. But, like everyone else in the country, Ginny and Emily were issued with the identity cards at last, and Ginny and Charlie filled in three forms to apply for their travel permits. Then it was a matter of waiting for the reply.

New regulations kept coming but the three permits didn't arrive. It was announced that all men between the ages of eighteen and forty-one were eligible for military service. That included Charlie and Ken. Ken was informed that he was in a reserved occupation and unlikely to be called up for the foreseeable future, and Charlie discovered that it would be some months before *his* number came up, but it was sobering to see how quickly the machinery of war had begun to grind.

Yet, despite all the annoyances of this new, bureaucratic style of government it was still peaceful in England. The bombers didn't arrive. The weather was superb and the harvest excellent.

In fact, if it hadn't been for the news from Poland, it would have been possible to think that there wasn't a war going on at all. But the pictures from Warsaw were too horrifying to be ignored: streets in ruins, homes blazing, the dead lying bloodily on the pavements and hordes of jack-booted, German troops pouring across the borders, well-fed, well-equipped and unstoppable.

The pounding went on all through September as France and England watched and were powerless to prevent it. On the day the travel permits finally arrived at High Holborn, the last units of the Polish army surrendered at a place called Luck – and, for Poland, it was all over.

'Right,' Ginny said. 'This is the time to travel. We've got our permits. Let's go now while there's a lull.'

Ken thought not, and Charlie agreed with him.

'There's all sorts of rumours going round London,' he said. He'd just been up to complete some work at Hedgethorn and Crabbit and Jack Bond had given him the gossip. 'They say Queen Wilhelmina's got a peace plan. It might all be over by Christmas. It's worth waiting a few more weeks, Ginny. Really.'

So although Ginny chaffed at the delay, they waited. For a week, a fortnight, nearly a month. German submarines took their pick of the merchant ships bringing supplies to Great Britain. The weather grew steadily more wintry. The Russians invaded Finland and the two armies fought in the snow, but there was no action on the old Western front at all and no peace plan, either.

'I'm sick of all this hanging about,' Ginny said to her sister. 'I think we ought to go over before the weather gets any worse.'

Now it was Emily who hung back. 'Could we wait another day or two?' she asked rather anxiously. She'd been feeling sick off and on for the last two days, and the thought of a sea voyage was rather worrying. 'I wouldn't want to be ill on the way over.'

'You won't be,' Ginny said. 'This is something you've eaten. It'll clear up in a day or two.'

'Can we wait till it does?' Emily asked. 'I really don't feel well enough.'

It didn't clear up. It got worse. Soon, instead of simply feeling squeamish when she got up in the morning, Emily was vomiting. And not just once and in the morning, but several times and all through the day.

'It's the illness,' she confided fearfully to Ginny. 'That's what it is. It's come back. I knew it would. What am I going to do?'

'Go to the doctor,' Ginny said. 'There's a new one in the village, so they say, a lady doctor.'

485

'No,' Emily said. 'I couldn't. What would I say?'

'Tell her what's wrong with you.'

'No. I couldn't. What if she told me something dreadful? I couldn't face it. Not now. Not yet. Let's wait a bit longer. It might go away.'

She was still pale with sickness that Friday afternoon when Miss Babbacombe came to tea.

'Poor you,' that lady said, when Emily refused everything except a dry biscuit.

'She's been like this for weeks,' Agnes said. 'We're quite worried about her, aren't we, Emily?'

'Usually stops at three months,' Miss Babbacombe said. 'Nasty while it lasts though.'

'Three months?' Emily asked.

'Three months or thereabouts. You look as if you're about that now, if I'm any judge.'

'But, of course,' Agnes said, her voice fluting with relief and self-reproach. 'How silly of us. A baby. Of course. Oh, Emily, my dear, here we've been treating you for indigestion and food poisoning and missing the obvious all the time. Why didn't we think of it?'

A baby, Emily thought, caught in such a rush of pleasure and terror she didn't know what to say. It could be a baby. She had imagined that it was because she was ill that she had not 'seen' anything for three months. That was one of the signs, wasn't it? Her thoughts shifted. But if it *is* a baby, what if it's ill? What if this illness can be passed down the generations? If it can pass from Daddy to me, it can pass from me to this baby. Holy Mary, Mother of God, pray for us! What if it's deformed or mental or blind like me?

'Seen a doctor, have you?' Miss Babbacombe was asking. 'There's a new one in the village. Very good, so they say. Lady doctor.'

'We'll make an appointment on Monday,' Agnes said. 'Oh, my dear child! A baby! Isn't that exciting?'

Waves of sickness rose into Emily's throat. 'I'm sorry, Aunt,' she said, 'but I shall have to go to the toilet.'

\*

'Wonderful! Wonderful! Wonderful!' Ginny said, when she heard the news.

'Is it?' Emily said.

'I'll bet Ken thinks so.'

'Yes, he does.'

'We must write to Maman tonight. Won't she be thrilled?'

'Not yet,' Emily begged. 'Not till I'm sure. What if it's ill, Ginny. What if . . .'

'It won't be,' Ginny said positively, 'so don't make that face. It'll be a lovely little baby. You'll see. Oh, Em! I'm so happy for you.'

'I'm ever so sorry to be holding us up like this, Ginny. We ought to have been in France weeks ago.'

'What a daft thing to say. You're not holding us up. You can't help it. Anyway you won't be holding us up for ever. We'll get there. Have you made an appointment with the doctor?'

'Aunt Agnes made it.'

'Good for her. They say this new lady doctor's ever so nice.'


Dr Claire Renshawe was a personable young woman with a brisk no-nonsense approach to her job. She'd run a practice in the East End of London for four years before she came to Wittick. She had witnessed so many cases of chronic illness caused by undernourishment that it was a pleasure to welcome such a healthy woman into her surgery, a healthy woman in the full-bosomed stage of early pregnancy.

'And what can I do for you, Mrs Hopkirk?' she asked.

Emily had spent the last hour trying to gather the right words for this consultation but now that it had begun she couldn't get her tongue to any of them. 'Well . . .' she said, and hesitated, her eyes flickering wildly.

'You've come to see about your pregnancy,' the doctor prompted. 'Your aunt told me on the telephone.'

'Yes. I'm not sure whether I *am* expecting. You see . . .'

'Well, let's find out, shall we?' the doctor said.

And did.

'Due in May,' she said. 'And a fine, fit pregnancy. No problems at all.'

'Really?'

'Oh yes,' Doctor Renshawe told her. 'I've seen rather a lot of expectant mothers in the last four years and very few of them were as healthy as you. Have you booked the midwife?'

It was the wrong moment to ask about the illness. Emily could hear that. Things would have to take their inevitable course. So, she was weighed and measured, and a midwife was recommended and accepted. The doctor entered her name and the approximate date of her confinement into a huge desk diary and closed it with a slap to show that the consultation was over.

'I'll come up to the house and visit you once a month,' she said. 'You won't want to come dragging down here, not with the winter coming on. Don't worry about the sickness. It will pass.'

Unfortunately for their travel plans, it didn't pass until after Christmas and the weather was so bad by then that no one seriously thought a sea trip advisable. Not even Ginny.

Snow fell with monotonous regularity. The roofs and gardens were perpetually white and the village looked like a picture postcard. Icicles hung from the eaves of the low cottages, water from the pump froze as it fell and the trees and hedges were lacy with hoarfrost. There were snow drifts heaped six feet thick in the lanes leading out of the village, rivers and lakes were frozen solid and, according to the papers, there were ice floes in the sea off the sunny south coast and many roads were completely blocked. The extreme cold seemed to freeze the war to a halt as well. The Russian campaign in Finland was over – the Finns defeated – and the Germans had conquered Norway with their now familiar *blitzkreig*. Jews were being persecuted everywhere (if few people knew it) but there was no other sign of military activity anywhere in western Europe.

Despite the cold, Ginny and Emily went out for a walk every day. They crunched over the impacted snow in their sturdy boots, wrapped up against the weather in layers of coats and scarves and shawls.

'We look like Tweedle-Dum and Tweedle-Dee,' Ginny said, tucking her mittened hand into her sister's elbow. 'Round as eggs, the pair of us. No one would know which of us was the pregnant one.'

'They would if they could feel this baby wriggling about,' Emily said. 'It's been kicking my ribs all the way down the hill.'

A blackbird took off abruptly from the branch of the elm, dislodging a miniature shower of snow. It fell on to Emily's upturned face, dusting her eyelashes with whiteness, and dropping a white fringe on to the edge of her hood.

'I don't think I've ever seen you look so well,' Ginny said. 'You're absolutely blooming, do you know that?'

'I feel well,' Emily had to admit, brushing the snow from her eyelashes. 'Ever so well.'

'Then don't you think you ought to write and tell Maman.'

'Yes. I suppose I should.'

'Of course, you should. Nothing's going to go wrong now. You're well, the baby's well. She ought to know. I can't bear to think of her all on her own over there, almost a grandmother, and not knowing. Let's write her a nice long letter when we get back in. We can sit by the fire and toast our toes and tell her the good news. What do you say?'

Emily squeezed her sister's supporting arm. 'Yes,' she said. 'We will.'

# CHAPTER THIRTY-FIVE

Even though she tried to persuade herself that she had moved so far away from the world that she could take any news from either of her daughters with composure, Hortense Lisieux wept happy tears when she heard that Emily was expecting a baby.

For once she wrote back immediately. *'My dearest child,'* she said. *'I read your news with such happiness. It seems only the other day that you were a newborn baby yourself. How I shall pray for you and for the little one? A new life. A new start. I can't tell you what joy your news has given me. Write to me whenever you can, my dearest, and let me know how you are.'*

She didn't mention the illness. There was no need to worry her poor Emilie at this stage. For the moment it was enough to rejoice in this new, God-given life. The mere thought of it warmed the routine of her daily work.

Days in the Convent passed like beads on a rosary, in a rhythmical, predictable order and all exactly the same – six days labour among the growing plants and the broken children, and a Sabbath for the enriching glory of the mass. More than three years had passed since Hortense had first come to the Little Sisters and nearly two since she had seen Virginie and that young man of hers in the convent garden, but it could have been a week or a lifetime.

Mother Superior was fond of saying, 'We live here in God's good time.'

That was how Hortense was living now, not in her own time but in God's. Little by little, almost without noticing it, she was drifting towards the confession she craved: praying in the peace of the chapel, thinking quietly and without panic in the hidden loneliness of her attic room and, most healing of all, talking to Mother every day.

Like everything else in the convent, there was a regular time set aside for conversation. Each evening when their charges were safely in bed and prayers had been said, the sisters – except for those who were taking their turn to prepare the evening meal – gathered in the big parlour, mending-baskets in hand, and settled in a circle to talk to one another.

Usually they discussed the children, the state of the crops and the progress of villagers who needed their prayers. Now and then, they would talk of the war and debate the great questions of good and evil and sin and redemption. Sometimes the Mother Superior revealed surprisingly unorthodox views, as Hortense discovered on the evening after she had received Emily's letter.

While the sisters were getting out their mending, Hortense took the letter out of her bag and read it through yet again.

The pleasure it gave her was combined with a pain that was so exquisite it was almost more than she could bear. She sat for several seconds simply clutching the letter to her breast with her eyes shut tight. Another life, she thought, but what sort of life would it be? If only she could be sure that this child wouldn't inherit the taint. What if it were born blind like poor Emilie? If only she could know, without doubt, that it was strong and healthy, that she hadn't harmed it. Her first grandchild.

'It is important news, is it not, my daughter?' Mother said, when Hortense finally opened her eyes.

'My daughter is pregnant,' Hortense said tremulously.

'A new life,' Mother said. 'The dear Lord provides us with so many opportunities for good. Is she well?'

'She says she is very well.'

'So you see, my dear, God is merciful.'

Can she read my heart? Hortense thought, looking at the Mother Superior's ugly, compassionate face. Does she know what I am feeling? 'That is true,' she said. 'My daughter could easily have been ill. As you know, Mother.'

'As I know,' Mother said gently.

'I wish I were not such a wicked sinner,' Hortense said.

'We are all sinners,' Mother said, squinting as she threaded another needle. 'Surrounded by temptation, how could it be otherwise? But we are all redeemed by the blood of our dear Lord Jesus. We only have to confess to receive absolution.'

'I'm a *wicked* sinner,' Hortense said sadly.

'All sin is wicked,' Mother said, returning to her cobbled stocking. Try as she might she possessed no skill as a needle woman – and she wasn't even trying because she was concentrating on the conversation. 'Even the slightest, which is why we should confess our sins at the very first opportunity.'

'May I ask you something, Mother?' Hortense said.

'Of course.'

'We're taught that actual sin is divided into mortal sin and venial sin and that venial sin displeases God but doesn't kill the soul. Surely that means some sins are worse than others, isn't that so? Or no . . . what I mean to say is . . . that some sins are lesser, not so bad?'

'Years ago,' Mother said, 'I should have agreed with that entirely. As far as doctrine goes, I agree with it. But I truly believe that all sin is equally wicked.'

That was an extraordinary thing to say – especially for a Mother Superior. Hortense had to think about it for quite a long time. She wasn't sure it was in line with the teaching of the Church but it spoke to her confusion, just the same.

Fortunately silences were quite acceptable in the convent parlour. Presently Mother spoke again, pursuing her thoughts. 'If our sins were over and done with once we had committed them then we could say; this is the greater sin and this the lesser, grading them in order like peas in a pod, as many do. But, as we know, no sin is ever over and done with until it is confessed and redeemed by the grace of our Blessed Lord. Each one grows according to its nature, and spreads – as weeds would spread in our garden if we were not vigilant in rooting them out. When we commit our first venial sin we cannot know where it will end or how many people will be hurt by it. A venial sin may lead us into mortal sin. Worse, the longer we persist in our sin the more damaging it becomes.'

It is true, Hortense thought, receiving the words into her heart and her memory. If I hadn't been greedy for rich food and pretty clothes, I would never have run away from home and none of these bad things would ever have happened. I shouldn't have committed mortal sin; I wouldn't have known anything about the illness, my life would have been entirely different, my little Emilie wouldn't have been born blind. This new child would not have been at risk.

'We must remember,' Mother went on, 'that however long we persist in our sin, redemption still awaits us. God's mercy is infinite.'

'It is the first step to redemption that is so difficult,' Sister Sebastian put in, addressing the group who had been listening in silence.

'Often,' Mother observed, 'when we make confession, it is necessary to go right back to that first venial sin in order to unravel the complications that sin invariably sets about us.'

Hortense was deep in thought. Fragments of her life were fitting together; sliding into place like pieces of a jigsaw puzzle to make sense – at last – after baffling her for so long.

'You remember the three powers of your soul?' Mother asked.

'The three powers of my soul,' Hortense said, automatically quoting the catechism, 'are my memory, my understanding and my will.'

'Given to us for a purpose, *n'est-ce pas*?'

'Yes, Mother,' Hortense said, 'for a good purpose.'

'Little Caesar has had a bad day today,' Sister Therese said, after a moment, biting off her thread between her teeth. 'We couldn't get him to eat any of his breakfast.'

'He is afraid the Germans will come here and kill him,' Sister Genevieve said. 'His father came to visit him yesterday and talked of nothing but war.'

'Tell him he is safe behind the Maginot Line, as we all

are,' Mother advised. 'Keep him busy, Sister. Give him more to do. The Devil makes work for idle hands.'

I *will* go to confession tomorrow, Hortense promised herself as the conversation flowed away from her. It is time. I will do it. I owe it to Emily and the baby to be cleansed of sin. To make a new start for this new life. A new start. If I don't do it now, I shall never do it, and I shall be lost for ever. I will take the first step tomorrow.

And so after half a lifetime without the forgiveness she needed so much, Hortense took her sins to the priest. Walking out of the world into the musty privacy of the confessional.

'Father forgive me for I have sinned.'

Her confessor was a gentle man and very patient. Using his ritual prompt, 'Is there anything else?' he eased her from the trivial sins of the present to the enormity of the past.

'I have broken the eighth commandment, Father,' Hortense said. 'I caught a bad illness when I was young and I never told anybody and I should have done. I didn't know how dreadful it was until my daughter was born. It affected her eyes. It blinded her. It was all my fault. All my fault. My most grievous fault. I was never honest about it. Never. I should have told my girls. But I didn't. It was too shameful. A bad illness. When my husband fell ill I knew what his illness was and I told lies about that. I said he'd been wounded. He *had* been wounded, Father. That was true. But the illness . . . I lied about that. Not once, but many, many times.'

'Do you repent your sin, my daughter?'

'Oh yes. Yes. With all my heart.'

'Is there anything else?'

'I ran away from home, Father. I was proud and headstrong. I wanted pretty clothes and rich foods. I didn't want to work on the farm. I wouldn't obey my parents and finally I ran away from home.'

'How old were you, my daughter?'

'Seventeen, Father.'

'Anything else?'

'I didn't write to them. I cut them out of my heart. I thought I could earn my own living and do as I pleased. I was selfish. It was wartime, you see, Father. Lots of girls were at work. There were jobs to be done. I thought . . .'

'You have been obstinate in your sin, my daughter, and that is a sin against the Holy Spirit.'

'Yes, Father. I have sinned against the Holy Spirit. I have resisted the known truth. I have been obstinate in sin. I have despaired.'

'Do you truly repent these sins?'

'Yes. Truly and with a contrite heart.'

'Is there anything else?'

'Yes.'

The confessor waited. Hortense gathered her will, remembering the three powers of her soul.

'I have broken the sixth commandment, Father. I have committed adultery.'

'Recently, my daughter?'

'No. Not recently. Not since I was married. Not for twenty-five years.' It was good to be able to say that. Even so, the sin remained.

'How many times?' the confessor prompted.

'Many, many times.'

'Is that all, my daughter?'

Hortense began to cry. Tears spilled from her eyes and rolled down her nose on to the hands clenched underneath her chin.

'No, Father. There is more.'

The confessor waited again.

It was the worst, but it had to be said. This must be a full confession or there would be no health in her.

'Father,' she said, and her voice was full of shame. 'I was a bad woman.'

'Yes?'

'A very bad woman.'

'Yes?'

'I was a whore.'

# CHAPTER THIRTY-SIX

The freezing weather continued into the first New Year of the war, grounding the fighter planes and making any kind of extended travel a misery. But Emily Hopkirk thrived on it, warm in her pregnancy, rounded and content.

'As soon as it thaws,' Ginny promised, 'we'll go to France and collect Maman.'

When the thaw finally began they were forced to postpone the journey for a second time, because Emily's pregnancy began to cause problems.

'I think the illness is coming back,' she confided to her sister. 'I had to get up twice in the night to go to the bathroom.'

'Does it hurt you?'

'No. But I had to get there pretty quickly. Oh Ginny, do you think it *is* the illness?'

'Tell Dr Renshawe,' Ginny advised. 'She'll know if it is. Or your nice midwife.'

As neither of her medical advisors were told anything about Maman's 'illness', neither were in the least worried. 'It's the baby's head pressing on your bladder,' the midwife explained. 'Happens to everyone. Don't worry. You're very fit.'

Emily wasn't convinced. 'I've felt so well in the last few months,' she said to Ginny, 'and now I feel rotten.'

'You should have told them what you were really worried about,' Ginny said.

'I can't, Ginny. I daren't. I can't face it – not when I feel so ill. You know that.'

'I should have made you tell them when you were blooming,' Ginny said, with exasperated hindsight. But one look at her sister's pale face made her relent.

'All right then,' she said. 'I won't say anything else. Only you *must* try not to worry. It's not doing you any good.'

But Emily *did* worry, no matter what her family said or did to reassure her. By day, it was easy enough for her to keep herself fully occupied so that she didn't have time to brood. Charlie and Ken both drove their own cars now, so there were trips out – when the roads were passable and petrol available – and Ginny and Agnes made it their business to be at home most afternoons and were cheerful company. The nights were more difficult. Then, Emily lay sleepless and anxious and, as the worrying days passed into weeks, began to have nightmares, often waking terrified and bewildered to weep into the darkness that her baby was deformed. After a fortnight of this, there was a perpetual lump in her throat that drove her appetite away, and she burst into tears at the least little thing.

'This can't go on,' Ken said to Ginny and Charlie. 'I've never known her like this. What are we to do with her?'

'She'll be all right when the baby's born,' Charlie hoped.

'That's five weeks away,' Ken sighed. 'We've got all April to get through. And she's getting worse.'

'I'll see what I can do,' Ginny promised.

'I don't know what anyone can do,' Ken said despondently.

Ginny knew exactly what had to be done. She'd known it ever since Emily's first confession. Now it simply couldn't be avoided. If she wanted to set her sister's mind at rest, she would have to go to the doctor herself and confess to everything. After so many years suppressing her fear, convincing herself that there were no grounds for alarm, that they were both healthy, that Maman must be neurotic, that there was no such illness, the moment of truth had arrived and was inescapable. Even so, it took her nearly a week to pluck up the courage for it.

Doctor Renshawe was rather surprised when Mrs Commoner turned up in her surgery on that bright April morning.

'I was coming up to see your sister tomorrow,' she said. 'What can I do for you?'

Now that she was in the surgery sitting opposite the doctor, Ginny was so afraid she could hardly speak. Her mouth was dry, her heart throbbed painfully and her head echoed with her mother's ominous warning, *If you love a man, you will die. You will die. You will die.*

'I don't know,' she stammered. 'What I mean is, I don't know how to begin.' Then to her shame and horror, she burst into tears.

'Now come,' Dr Renshawe spoke briskly because tears embarrassed her. 'I'm sure it's not as bad as all that.'

'It is,' Ginny said, struggling to regain control of herself, and the story came tumbling out in a muddled, stammering rush. 'I've got a dreadful disease. My mother says so. A bad disease. It's in my blood. She says it will kill me. And now Emily's expecting, we're afraid the baby . . .'

Doctor Renshawe listened. Then she asked, very calmly, 'What sort of a disease do you think this is?'

'I don't know,' Ginny said. 'She wouldn't tell us.'

The doctor opened her notebook and began to gather the facts. She started with the most obvious one. 'How long has Mrs Hopkirk been blind?' she asked.

'Since she was born,' Ginny said, wiping away the tears on the back of her hand. 'Is that something to do with it?'

The doctor's answer was splendidly calm. 'Possibly,' she said. 'I don't know yet. Have you had any symptoms of this illness?'

'No. But Emily has. She's had cystitis off and on since she was married.'

'Honeymoon cystitis,' the doctor said, noting it. 'That's very common and nothing to worry about.'

'It worries my sister.'

Dr Renshawe tried another tack. 'Tell me about your parents,' she said. 'Are they in good health?'

'My father's dead.'

'When was that?'

'In 1926.'

'What did he die of? Do you know?'

'Yes. Locomotor ataxia.'

The doctor wrote in her notebook and went on with her questioning in her professional way, checking on mother's health, sibling's health, father's occupation, medical history of the patient. Gradually Ginny began to feel more at ease.

At last, Dr Renshawe set her notebook aside and directed a long thoughtful stare at Ginny. 'I think you've probably guessed,' she said, 'that the disease your mother was talking about was very serious.'

'Yes,' Ginny said, her fears resurfacing and twice as terrible. Now she was going to be told. Now she would know. Quick, quick. Say it and get it over with.

'There's no way to wrap this up, I'm afraid,' Doctor Renshawe said. 'We are talking about a venereal disease. Do you know what that is?'

'No.'

'There are two of them, gonorrhoea, which is the least serious, and probably caused your sister's blindness, and syphilis, which is probably what your mother was referring to. Have you heard of them?'

'No.' But even the sound of their names was terrible.

The doctor was explaining in terms too medical to be entirely understood. 'The one we are concerned with is syphilis . . . transmitted through sexual intercourse . . . three stages . . . sores and discharge from the genital organs . . . a rash with fever . . .'

'Maman had a rash,' Ginny remembered. 'When we were in Le Touquet. The pharmacist gave her notice because of it. He said he didn't want her dirty disease in the house. Is this a dirty disease, Doctor?'

'There's dirt attached to most diseases,' Doctor Renshawe said, matter-of-factly, 'if we accept the popular definition of dirt. But this one is considered "dirty" because it's sexually transmitted. To a doctor disease is simply disease. Now tell me, how has your mother's health been since the rash?'

'She had inflammation of the lungs once. Lots of colds. The usual sort of thing. Are we going to get it then, Doctor Renshawe? Was she right?'

'It could have been passed to you and your sister at birth,' the doctor said honestly. 'Personally, from what I know of your medical history I should say that was highly unlikely. But there is one certain way to find out.'

'Yes?'

'What I recommend is that you allow me to take a small sample of your blood and send it away for testing. With a physical examination I can't tell you positively whether you've got this illness or not, but a blood analysis would give us the answer.'

'What about my sister?'

'If your sister is at all worried she can have the same blood test. If this test clears you I can virtually guarantee that it will clear her as well, as you're identical twins. Everything I've said to you would apply to her, you see.'

'And the baby?'

'If your sister is healthy, the baby will be, too.'

'How long would I have to wait for the results?' Ginny said. After gearing herself up to hear the worst there and then, this was an anti-climax.

'Ten days.'

'And if it *is* this illness?'

'Then we'll decide what is to be done.'

So Ginny submitted to the blood test. She'd come so far in this business it would have been foolish not to. But the anxiety she carried out of the surgery was ten times worse than any she'd felt before. She'd taken the first steps to finding out, she couldn't hide or pretend any longer.

'I'll write and tell you the result as soon as it comes in,' Dr Renshawe promised, as she saw her patient to the surgery door. 'Look out for my handwriting. It's such a scrawl you can hardly miss it.'

Ten days was an appallingly long time to have to wait. Even confiding in Charlie did not ease Ginny's ordeal.

'Shall you tell Emily?' he asked.

'No,' she decided. 'Not till I know the results. There's no point in both of us worrying, is there?'

The first week of waiting was the longest Ginny had ever

500

spent. She kept herself busy and didn't start watching out for the postman until the seventh day. Then she made an enormous effort to contain her soul in patience until ten days had come and gone. But Friday, the tenth of May was the eleventh day and still there was no letter.

'I should have heard by now,' she said to Charlie as he set out for Wolverhampton that morning. 'If there's nothing in the post by mid-afternoon I shall phone up.'

But, by mid-afternoon, there were screaming headlines in the evening papers that drove all thought of the blood test right out of Ginny's head.

Miss Babbacombe was the first person in Wittick to see the news. She whisked her copy of the evening paper straight up to High Holborn, half trotting, half running on her heron-thin legs.

'Have you seen this, Agnes?' she said, puffing into the day room brandishing the paper. 'Those damn Nazis have invaded Holland.'

Agnes jumped to her feet and ran across the room to her friend. 'Oh, my God,' she said.

Ginny and Emily both asked, 'When?'

Spreading the paper across the piano, they read it together.

'*The phoney war is over,*' it said. '*Early this morning German Panzer divisions invaded Poland, Belgium and Luxembourg. The assault was preceded by heavy bombing raids at three o'clock this morning on all major airfields, including Welschap and Schipol. Reports from Brussels say that the river Maas has been crossed and parachute troops have landed in areas around Rotterdam, Amsterdam and the Hague. Brussels has suffered heavy bombing throughout the day with heavy casualties. The Belgian and Dutch governments have broadcast appeals for assistance. Troops are on their way to the front line.*'

The twins spoke with one mind and voice. 'Maman!' they said.

'What are we going to do?' Emily asked her sister.

'I shall go straight over to France and bring her back,' Ginny decided. She was charged with new energy – as if this was the news she'd been waiting for, not the results of the blood test. She knew exactly what she was going to do. Nothing would stop her.

Agnes was horrified. 'The very idea!' she said. 'You can't possibly. What will Charlie say?'

Ginny was already on her way out of the room. 'He'll come with me,' she said. 'Don't worry, Aunt Agnes. We shall be there and back in a couple of days.'

'She can't do this,' Agnes said. 'It's ridiculous.'

'The authorities won't let her travel,' Miss Babbacombe comforted. 'She won't be able to get tickets.'

They were reckoning without Ginny's determination. A phone call revealed that there were no tickets for sale in Wolverhampton, but that didn't stop her. As soon as Charlie got in from work, she bullied him into planning their journey.

'I'll get there,' she promised her sister, 'come hell or high water. There are bound to be tickets at Victoria station, and if we can't buy them there, we'll try at Dover. We'll catch the next train to London, won't we, Charlie?'

He was as methodical about it as she was. 'The next train to London is tomorrow morning,' he said. 'So we'd better pack an overnight bag now. Have you still got the permits? Don't worry, Aunt Agnes, I'll look after her.'

'She's so impulsive,' Agnes worried, when Ginny had gone hurtling upstairs. 'She doesn't think.'

'She's going to rescue Maman,' Emily defended her sister. 'I think she's brave.'

'So she is, Emily,' Agnes agreed. 'Brave, but foolhardy.'

Early the next morning Charlie and Ginny left for Dover. The postman arrived with the first post of the morning as they drove out of the gate.

'Anything for us?' Charlie asked.

There were four letters, all typewritten.

'Bills,' Ginny said, after a perfunctory glance. 'They can wait.' She put them in her handbag. 'We've got other things to attend to.'

The first being to wangle a passage across the Channel.

502

There were tickets on sale at Victoria but the clerk warned them that there might not be a sailing, and when they reached Dover, they found the harbour crowded with troop carriers, most of which were bound for Le Havre. The ferry was destined for Le Havre, too, and was being loaded up with armoured cars and army lorries and crates of military equipment. It took a long argument and considerable waving of permits and passports, before Ginny and Charlie were allowed aboard.

'I never thought we'd get away with it,' Charlie admitted, as the ship inched out of harbour.

They were the only civilians on board. The rest were in khaki and there were notices everywhere telling passengers what to do in the event of a U-boat attack. But it was an easy crossing and the sun was shining.

'Let's read our letters,' Ginny said. 'They'll pass the time.'

The third one she opened was from Dr Renshawe.

'*Dear Mrs Commoner*,' it said. '*You will be pleased to know that the results of your blood test have come through and that there is no sign of any illness whatever. You are, and therefore always have been, completely free of the disease you feared.*

*I am so pleased to be able to send you this good news.*'

The relief Ginny felt was so sudden and so strong it made her shake. 'Oh, for heaven's sake!' she said.

'What is it?' Charlie asked.

'Just look at that,' she said, trying to hand him the letter.

He read it slowly, while she cried and shook her head and put her face in her hands. 'What did I always tell you?' he said, smiling at her. 'It's no surprise to me.'

'To hear it now, like this,' she said, 'after worrying all this time! Halfway across the channel. When I wasn't expecting it.' Then she threw her arms round his neck and kissed him. 'Oh Charlie. I'm not ill. I never was. Isn't it wonderful!'

He returned her kiss, despite the amused interest of their fellow passengers.

'I shall have to phone Em,' Ginny said. 'This is her news as much as mine. She'll be so relieved.'

'It'll be the first thing we do when we get there,' he promised.

But it wasn't possible. Le Havre had become a British garrison town, full of British soldiers and choked with army lorries. They were lined up on the quay and in the squares, ready to progress in convoy eastward along the main roads. And there were no telephone lines out of the town at all.

'We'll find one in the next stop along the line,' Charlie said confidently, and regretted it. Although there were plenty of trains in the station, they were all troop trains and nobody seemed to know if ordinary services would be running that day. 'If at all!' as one porter said, shrugging his shoulders. 'You see how it is, *M'dame, M'sieur.*'

'We'll hire a car,' Charlie said.

There were no cars for hire, either. At the first garage, they were refused point blank.

'All hirings are cancelled,' the garage hand told them. He was very young, very pimply and his overalls were covered in oil.

'Since when?' Ginny asked.

'Since this morning, Madame.'

'And what are *we* supposed to do? Tell me that.'

'I don't know, Madame. You could try along the road.'

They tried along several roads and without success. Eventually they found a ramshackle garage where the owner allowed them the two-day hire of a battered Ford with a full tank of petrol – providing they paid him an exhorbitant hiring fee on the spot.

'What times we live in, Madame!' he said, as he took their money. 'The sooner they get this fool war settled and make an armistice the better. We never wanted to fight it in the first place. Why should we fight for the Poles? Tell me that . . .'

They inched their way out of the town behind a convoy.

'Can't you go any faster?' Ginny said. 'We're hardly moving.'

'It won't go any faster,' Charlie told her. 'It's a wonder it's moving at all.'

504

Three kilometres up the road, they were stopped by a noisily important French corporal on a motorcycle. He drew up alongside, wiped his forehead on his glove and demanded to see their identity cards.

They showed their cards and their travel permits.

'English?' the soldier said. 'At a time like this?'

'Here to visit my mother,' Ginny explained, 'in the convent of the Little Sisters of Divine Mercy at Villefleurs. What's going on?'

'Who knows, Madame?' the soldier said. '*Merde alors!*' And he spat out of the corner of his mouth and roared off.

'I don't like the sound of that,' Ginny said, as they drove on again. 'You don't think they could have invaded France, do you?'

'Let's get off this road,' Charlie said, concentrating on his driving. 'It'll take us forever to get there if we have to follow a convoy all the way. Have you got the Michelin guide?'

They made three detours that afternoon and were asked to show their papers everywhere they went. Each time they returned to the main roads they found them jammed with khaki vehicles.

'Let's stop off at the next place and see if we can find out what's going on,' Ginny said.

The next place they came to was a very small village, but it had a café. The café had a wireless and half the village was crowded round the bar waiting for the next news to be broadcast. Alarm growing, Ginny and Charlie joined them. What they heard made the hair on the nape of their necks stand up.

German Panzer divisions had broken through the Ardennes and captured Sedan.

'It's not possible,' Ginny said, appalled. 'You can't drive tanks through the Ardennes. Everybody says you can't.'

But the Germans had done it and, if they crossed the River Meuse, they would be in France.

'That's it!' Charlie said, grim-faced. 'We're going straight back home.'

'We are not!' Ginny said.

505

'We're not staying here.'

'If you think I've waited all this time and come all this way just to turn back at the first obstacle, you're very much mistaken.'

'First obstacle? It's a German invasion. A *blitzkrieg*. And it's heading straight at us. Have some sense, woman.'

'I'm going to Villefleurs to get Maman,' she repeated obstinately.

'You're not.'

'I am.'

They were shouting at one another. Not understanding a word of their argument but thrilled by its vehemence and their blazing eyes, the crowd in the café watched them.

'It's too bloody dangerous,' Charlie shouted. 'We're going home.'

'You can go home if you like. I'm staying.'

'Goddamn it all, Ginny, this is war! Do as you're told.'

The crowd began to applaud. '*Bravo mon vieux!*'

'Em does as she's told,' Ginny said. 'I don't.'

'Well then, it's time you started.'

'I'm not going back. I don't care what *you* do. *I*'m not going back. I'm going to get Maman.'

They were standing face to face, hot with anger.

'If we continue,' he said, 'we shall be driving straight into an invasion, I hope you realise that. We shan't get to Villefleurs before dark.'

'We'll get as far as we can,' Ginny said determinedly.

'We could be shot on the road. Dive-bombed. Anything. Have you thought of that?'

'Don't even talk about it,' Ginny said, beating his chest with her fists. 'I can't bear it. I'm going to get Maman.'

Charlie knew her well enough to know that her extreme anger masked fear. She's as frightened as I am, he realised. And he was weakened by her resolution.

'Bloody infuriating woman!' he said.

'Yes, I am. You're right. And I'm not going back.'

Ginny was more beautiful at that moment than he'd ever seen her. Her brown eyes were so dark they seemed black.

Fury had brought a richer colour to her skin and appeared to make her thick hair crackle around her face. Charlie knew he was defeated. She would do what she threatened. How could he oppose such stubbornness? Or such courage? In a passion of fury and admiration and desire, he seized her by the shoulders and kissed her roughly.

Their audience burst into rapturous applause, and when she put her hand meekly into the crook of his arm and walked lovingly back to the car with him they were applauded all the way.

'That's the way to treat a woman,' the old men said to one another. 'Make 'em mind.'

'This is idiocy,' Charlie grumbled, as they left the village. Clouds of dust swirled around them as they drove, reminding him of dust after a bomb explosion. 'I need my head examined.'

'I shall love you for ever for this,' Ginny said.

'If we live so long. Where to next?'

'Beauvais, if we can make it.'

By the time they reached Beauvais, it was too dark to drive without lights. There was an ominous rumbling in the distant east which neither of them referred to – because neither was sure if it was thunder or gunfire.

Their hotelier had no doubts. 'Bombs,' he told them. 'They've been bombing Brussels all day. It's a bad business. Where are you headed?'

They told him and he shook his head.

'You wouldn't catch me going any further east than the end of the road,' he said. 'South and west, that's the direction for us and the further and faster the better.' He held up his hand. '*Attention!* It's the latest bulletin on the radio.'

The news was as bad as they expected. The *blitzkrieg* in Holland had continued all day. Rotterdam airport had been bombed and the city was besieged. On the west bank of the River Meuse the French army had taken up defensive positions.

'We'll stay here for the night,' Charlie decided, 'and start at dawn. I suppose there's no chance of making a phone call.'

'That depends where to, Monsieur.'

'England?'

That was greeted with snorts of derision. 'Paris would be job enough, Monsieur. We've hardly been able to get a line out of here since this began.'

'No,' Charlie said. 'I didn't think it would be possible. It was worth a try. Is the post being delivered?'

'Not today, Monsieur. You see how things are.'

'We've been seeing all day,' Ginny said. 'It took us an hour to get out of Le Havre.'

'Tomorrow morning fill your tank with petrol and take the route to Montdidier,' the hotelier advised. 'That should be clear of military traffic – although, given the situation . . .'

They took his advice and drove on at the start of another warm peaceful day. Fields of young corn whispered in the morning breeze. Larks spiralled up from dappled meadows where black and white cattle grazed and plodded. Butterflies fluttered in the hedges. All was as it should be.

The traffic began after they turned off to Amiens – and it was all heading in the opposite direction. First one expensive car, then three, one after the other, then a steady column, full of well-dressed burghers and their wives in dark coats and fashionable hats, with their dogs and their children beside them and picnic baskets and blankets piled on back seats.

Among them, driving a gleaming Austin 8, was Monsieur Guerin of quality velvet fame.

'Mam'selle Lisieux!' he exclaimed, when Charlie drew up alongside and Ginny accosted him. 'You are going the wrong way. Get out while you can – that's my advice. They've been bombing us since daybreak.'

'Where?'

'All the towns on the old Western front,' Monsieur Guerin said, grinding to a halt. 'Ypres. Bapaume. Lille. Mons. Arras. That we should live to see this happening all over again! The terror of it! They say Boulogne is ablaze. A heap of rubble. Get out while you can, my dear Mam'selle. That's my advice to you. We're going to the wife's mother in Avignon.' He crunched the car into gear and drove off, kangaroo-hopping down the road in his agitation.

Charlie had been studying the map. 'We'll cut across country,' he said. 'Go through Boves. It'll take a bit longer but it'll be quieter, because the Germans will only attack the main roads where the troops are. Don't worry. I'll get you there.'

They pressed on to Boves. Now there was no doubt about what they were hearing, clear and distinct in the summer air: heavy guns booming, bombers droning, explosions following one after another.

Yet, when they drove up the Rue Jeanne D'Arc in Boves, the village was exactly the same; shutters were grey with the same dust, horses toiled up the hill with the same farm carts, the Advocate's sister was in the process of taking her dog for the same well-watered walk. The sight made Ginny weep. She couldn't help it.

'It's too awful!' she said. 'To think of this place right in the path of a German army. What did any of them do to deserve that?'

And there was Cousin Berthe, sitting on the wall in front of the Advocate's fine house, sunning her bare legs, sandals in her hand and her skirt pulled up above her knees.

She greeted Ginny as if they'd never been apart. '*Ça va, Virginie?*'

'We must stop,' Ginny said. 'Just for a minute. I can't drive past Cousin Berthe.'

'OK,' Charlie said. 'But be quick.'

'How is Old Joliot?' Ginny called, leaning out of the car window.

'He's guarding that ol' cemetery. That's what Ol' Joliot's doing.'

'Guarding the cemetery?'

'Those ol' Boches are coming,' Cousin Berthe said cheerfully. 'He's up there guarding. He's been there all night. Didn't have no breakfast nor nothing.'

509

That didn't sound like Old Joliot. 'Why not, Cousin Berthe? Why didn't he have breakfast?'

'Nor dinner,' Berthe said, beaming. 'He's asleep.'

'Well, go and wake him up.'

'He don't wake up,' Berthe said. 'I tried. He's sound asleep that one. He's been asleep ages and ages.'

'There's something wrong,' Ginny said to Charlie. 'We'll have to go and see.' When Charlie opened his mouth to protest, she carried on, 'It won't take a minute. It's on our way. Hop in, Berthe.'

So Berthe hopped in, sandals in hand, and they drove uphill to the village square, parked the car beside the entrance to the Chemin de la Montagne and climbed up to the cemetery.

It was totally peaceful up there among the tombstones. The sun poured down out of a strong blue sky and a slight breeze rustled the trees. At first, it looked as though the cemetery was empty. Then they saw Old Joliot on the far side. He had his back to them, crouched over an old machine gun trained on to the open plain below.

Ginny called to him, but he didn't answer. They picked their way through the basalt slabs and the brooding angels until they were standing beside him. He looked very uncomfortable huddled over his gun.

'There you are, you see,' Berthe said. 'Fast asleep. What did I tell you?'

'Good morning, Monsieur Joliot,' Ginny said, putting a hand on his shoulder.

To her horror he slipped slowly sideways from the supporting tripod of the machine gun – not sleeping, not even deeply unconscious, but inescapably, horribly dead.

'Oh, Charlie!' she said.

Shocked as he was, he flung his arm round her shoulders protectively.

'Poor old Joliot,' she whispered. 'He must have been sitting up here ever since the invasion, defending his dead boys. He was always defending his dead boys. They were his life. He looked after them all the time. And now he's as dead as they are. Oh Charlie, he must have died up here all on his own. I can't bear it for him.'

'Come away,' Charlie said. 'There's nothing you can do for him now.'

'We must go and tell the priest,' Ginny said. 'He'll have to deal with this. See him buried and everything. Berthe can't do it, and we can't, can we?'

'No, we can't.'

'He's the first dead person I've ever seen, Charlie.'

'Me, too,' he said, leading her away from the body. Cousin Berthe was sitting on a tombstone, sunning her legs and completely unconcerned. Below the hill, the valley of the Somme spread before them, lush and green and peaceful. Except that . . .

'What's that?' Ginny asked, swinging round. 'Oh God, Charlie, somewhere is being bombed.'

The German planes looked like black midges in the sky, but the pattern of their flight was too obvious to require interpretation. Hurtling down and down through the blue sky and then rising abruptly, they were making a bomb run. The bombs exploded beneath them in a spurt of red flame and a high plume of dust and smoke, debris scattering in every direction.

Neither of them said anything. People out there are being killed, Ginny thought. It's Spain all over again. Undefended cities and civilians are being blown to bits. If they can bomb these places, what's to stop them bombing Amiens and Boves. At any minute one of those planes could turn round and bomb us. She could imagine it all quite clearly.

We shall be driving straight towards that lot, Charlie thought. We could be under those bombs ourselves. He tried to work out how far away they were and, noted, mechanically, that the sound of an explosion was reaching them later than the sight.

'You don't have to go on,' he said, 'not if you don't want to.'

'I don't want to,' she said. 'Only a fool would *want* to walk into that. But I've got to, haven't I, Charlie? I can't leave

511

Maman here with all this going on. We've got to take her back to England.'

Her courage was so touching Charlie was afraid he was going to cry.

'I'll go and tell the priest about Old Joliot,' he said.

'What shall we do with Cousin Berthe?' she said, turning away.

'Why do you have to do anything with her?' Charlie asked. 'She's not your responsibility.'

She ignored that. 'You can come to the convent with us,' she said, walking over to Cousin Berthe. 'You'd like that, wouldn't you? *Alors*, put your shoes on. Charlie's going to find the priest.'

'Is he dead, that Ol' Joliot?' Cousin Berthe asked, when Charlie had walked away from them out of the cemetery.

'Yes. I'm afraid so.'

Berthe accepted the news quite cheerfully. 'Have I time to say goodbye to him?'

'Yes. But be quick.'

Cousin Berthe walked round the side of the machine gun until she was looking down at the old man where he lay on his side on the ground. 'He's got a gun in his hand,' she said.

It was a long-muzzled pistol and it was still clutched in his fingers, a long-muzzled pistol with the Holborn mark clearly stamped on the handle.

This is the first dead body I've ever seen, Ginny thought, and he's holding one of our pistols. It seemed to her that it was both dreadful and fitting. She bent down and eased the pistol from his cold hands, surprised by its weight.

'You takin' that with you?' Berthe said. 'You could fight those ol' Boches with that, couldn't you?'

'Yes,' Ginny said, putting the gun into her shoulder bag. 'I could. If I had to.' There was a lot of sense in Cousin Berthe.

Ten minutes later they were on their way to Villefleurs.

In High Holborn the telephone rang, filling the library with its insistent bell.

512

'Quick!' Emily urged her aunt. 'It could be them.'

But it was Ruby Commoner.

'I'm ever so sorry to trouble you, Mrs Everdale,' she said. 'But you ain't had any news of Charlie, have you?'

'No,' Agnes said. 'I'm sorry. We haven't.'

'Oh dear!'

'It's early days yet,' Agnes said, trying to comfort. 'They only went yesterday morning.'

'Yes. I know. He sent us a letter before they went. It's only . . . what I mean to say is . . . with all this going on out there it makes you wonder. Everything's happening so quickly. You hear something worse every bulletin, and you bein' on the phone and everything we thought you might have heard.'

'If we hear anything,' Agnes promised, 'anything at all, I'll let you know straightaway.'

'Thanks. It's ever so good of you. How's Emily? Keeping well?'

'Very well.'

'That's one good thing, eh? Give her our love. I'll call again tomorrow, if that's all right. In the afternoon.'

It had taken quite an effort to ring High Holborn and Ruby was disappointed to have heard so little. She'd been worried sick ever since she'd got Charlie's letter, and Stan had been on at her all the time to phone. 'Go on. Give 'em a buzz. Set your mind at rest. They'll know if anyone does.'

She edged herself out of the telephone box, careful not to get her coat caught in the door, and walked sadly home up Abbeville Road. Such a nice, neat, solid-looking road with lace curtains at all the bow windows and the doorsteps pumice white. There were birds singing everywhere and the may trees all in bloom, too. She'd always thought may blossom was such a cheerful colour, all that bright pink. And my poor Charlie out in France. Just like his father and his grandfather before him. There was never any end to it.

Stan's bicycle was propped in the hall. 'Any luck?' he called from the kitchen as she came in.

'No,' she said. 'Not yet. What's brought you back this time a' day? You ain't been laid off, have you?'

'No,' Stan said, as she walked into the kitchen. 'Just thought I'd nip back an' see how he was.' Then, seeing the anxiety on her face, he said more gently, 'Not to fret, gel. He'll be in touch. He's a good lad.'

'You work so hard to bring 'em up right,' Ruby grieved, 'give 'em a good education, feed 'em proper, an' then just when they're settled an' you ought to be able to relax a bit, they go off to France to get 'emselves killed. It ain't right, Stan.'

He put his arms round her and held her close and comfortable. 'I know, Rube,' he said. 'It's a bad ol' world.'

'It's the not knowing that's so awful,' Ruby wept. 'If I knew where they was, it wouldn't be so bad.'

# CHAPTER THIRTY-SEVEN

The gravel drive that usually curved, well-swept and empty, up to the grey front door of the Convent of the Little Sisters of Divine Mercy was a muddle of farm carts, sweating horses and dusty lorries. There were bundles of clothes and blankets heaped on the steps, and blue-clad sisters ran in and out of the building, shepherding *les enfants* into whatever vehicle would take them.

'Ye Gods!' Charlie said. 'And you think you're going to find your mother in that?'

'Yes, I do,' Ginny said, climbing out of the car. 'I shall ask for the Mother Superior. She's bound to be here somewhere and she'll know where Maman is. Come on, Cousin Berthe.'

Mother Superior was busy in the confusion, wiping noses and eyes with the edge of her sleeve.

'Say your prayers, my little one,' she comforted. 'Our blessed Jesus will look after you. You needn't be afraid. Sister Genevieve, where is Marie Claire's little doll?'

'In her bundle, Mother. Come with me, Marie Claire, and you can sit with your very best friend.'

'Is this my very best friend?' Marie Claire asked, touching the sleeve of Ginny's coat and looking up into her face.

'No, little one,' Ginny said speaking to the child, but aiming the information at Mother Superior. 'I've come to see Madame Lisieux. Madame Hortense Lisieux.'

'She's in the dormitory helping with the packing,' Mother Superior said. 'Why, it's Cousin Berthe. What a blessing you've come to join us, my dear. We need every pair of hands we can get. Will you take these two little ones over to Sister Sebastian. There's a good girl.'

Cousin Berthe went off on her errand, beaming with

pleasure. That's a mercy, Ginny thought. At least she's being taken care of. Now I can find Maman and I'd better do it quickly before Mother Superior finds a job for me, too. It's no good expecting anyone to direct me to the dormitory. Not in this chaos. I shall have to fend for myself.

She looked over her shoulder to send a signal to Charlie, and saw that he was besieged by two determined nuns, each with a stumbling child in tow. They must think he's part of the evacuation fleet, she realised, but there wasn't time to rescue him. Maman was inside the building, seconds away from release. Dear, dear Maman. Seconds away.

Stumbling through the muddle of jerking limbs and bulky parcels, Ginny pushed her way to the open front door. Inside, there were nuns everywhere, carrying bundles and urging children to hurry – and far too many rooms, school rooms and day nurseries. Where was the dormitory? Up the stairs, into a long corridor with doors on either side, offices, a bathroom, a dormitory void of everything except two rows of beds stripped to the springs, another the same. At last there was a dormitory full of half-made beds and, stripping off the blankets from one of them was a figure that *had* to be Maman. Her head was covered by a white coif and her face was hidden by the lifted edge of the blanket, but it was Maman. The movement of her hands was too familiar for it to be anyone else. Ginny had seen her strip beds like that so many times.

'Maman!' she cried, running into the room. 'Maman!'

Hortense put down the blanket and held out her arms to her daughter. 'Virginie, my dearest child! How wonderful to see you.'

They held and kissed one another over and over again, tearfully happy.

'For you to come here now!' Hortense said. 'All this way and with a war going on! You are the dearest, dearest daughter anyone could ever wish for. Oh my dear, I *am* so glad to see you again. How is my Emily?'

'Blooming.'

'And the baby?'

'Due at the end of the week.'

'What happiness! And you are both well?'

'Yes. Better than well, Maman. We haven't got the illness.'

The news was such a happy shock that for a few seconds Hortense couldn't take it in. 'Truly?' she asked. 'Are you sure, *chérie*? How do you know?'

'Truly. I had a blood test and there's no sign of it. I haven't got it, Maman. I've never had it.'

'Oh, *chérie*, I'm so glad. So very glad. And your sister?'

'If I haven't got it, neither has she. The doctor said it was most unlikely for one of us to have inherited it without the other. We've been worrying for nothing all this time.'

Hortense was overwhelmed with relief. She got down on her knees at once and said three Hail Marys for pure joy.

And as the first prayer ended, Ginny knelt quietly beside her and they prayed together. Then they sat on the bedsprings with their arms round each other, holding one another close while they recovered. It was a moment of extraordinary relief and happiness.

'*Les enfants* have got to be evacuated,' Hortense said at last, picking up the blanket again. 'The Germans have reached the River Meuse.' She was so calm that it took a moment for Ginny to understand the import of what she was saying. If the German army crossed the Meuse they would be in France.

'Then it's just as well I'm here,' she said.

'Yes, my dear,' Hortense said mildly, handing one end of the blanket to her daughter. 'You can help us.'

Ginny took the blanket and folded it automatically, working in synchronisation with her mother, as if she were back in Le Touquet clearing the beds after a summer let. But she was listening out for the distant thud, thud, thud of gunfire and far more alert than she looked.

'I've come to take you back to England,' she said.

'My dear,' her mother said lovingly.

'Charlie's with me. We've got a car.'

'Yes,' Hortense said.

Little more than a sigh, the word was too vague to be an agreement. In fact, to Ginny's loving eyes there was something altogether too vague about Maman herself, swathed as she was in that great blue overall and with her coif covering her lovely hair. As if she was inhabiting a dream, somewhere apart from the real world. Or as if she was one of the sisters. 'So you'll come home with us?' she said.

Hortense picked up the last blanket and handed one end to her daughter in the same way as before. 'I *am* home,' she said.

'I meant to England,' Ginny said, regarding her steadily across the width of grey cloth. 'To High Holborn where you used to live.'

'England isn't my home, *chérie*. I only lived there for ten years. What are ten years in a lifetime? Ten years out of forty-two. No, no, this is my home. This is where I belong.'

'But the Germans are in Belgium.'

'Yes. And soon they will be here, which is all the more reason to stay.'

She can't be talking like this, Ginny thought. It doesn't make sense. 'We've come to take you back to England,' she said, speaking with intense determination because she had to make Maman understand. 'I'll help you with this and then we must get going. There isn't much time.'

'Oh, my dear Virginie!' Hortense said sadly. 'You were always so sure of yourself, even as a little girl, always so determined.'

'Then you'll come.'

Hortense put the blanket down and drew her daughter close so that they sat side by side on the bare mattress. The bombardment was so loud it made the windows rattle.

'You must understand, my Virginie,' she said. 'I cannot come with you, even if I wanted to. I have given my word to stay here.'

'Then break it. They'll understand. No one will expect you to stay here now. Not when the Germans are coming.'

'No, my dear. I can't do that.'

'Why not?'

'I've given my word to God, *chérie*, and that is not a promise that may ever be broken. I have taken confession. After all this time I have taken confession. This is my penance.'

'To stay here? With the Germans coming?'

'The convent is to be a military hospital,' Hortense explained, 'the same as it was for the Great War. I am to stay here and nurse the wounded.'

'You can't,' Ginny said, with an anguished face. 'What if you're bombed? Maman! Please! Anything could happen to you.'

'We are in God's good hands.'

'Maman!'

'It's no good, Virginie, *chérie*. I've given my word. It's a great consolation to me. I shall be here doing God's work among the injured.' And, she was thinking, soldiers were the cause of my sin and soldiers will be my redemption. 'And besides . . .' she said, but then she checked herself.

'Besides?'

Hortense looked at Ginny's loving face and thought of her own illness, the thinning hair under the coif, the growing clumsiness, the loss of memory. Now she could see that part of her penance was to keep this awful secret from her daughters. My Virginie is so trusting, she thought, and so entirely without guile. I can't tell her. It would be cruel to make her share it, especially now. This must be my burden. 'No. No matter.'

Ginny made her last appeal. 'If you won't come home for me,' she said, 'then come for Emily. She's afraid the baby won't be normal. She said if you could be there it would make all the difference.'

'All mothers think things like that,' Hortense said gently. 'But the truth is, it won't make any difference whether I'm there or not. We are all in God's hands. What is to be, will be.'

'You won't come back.'

'No, my dear, much though I love you both. You must lead your own lives now and leave me to lead mine.'

Ginny tried not to cry but, despite her efforts, tears oozed out of her eyes and stung her nose. To have waited so long and come so far, and all for this – the cruellest disappointment. But even as she struggled, she knew she had to accept it. 'Oh, Maman,' she said. 'I love you so much. How can I leave you here with the Germans coming?'

'With prayer,' Hortense said, earnestly. 'That is how it can be done, my *chérie*. With prayer. Now, you will need something for your journey. Stay here for a while and I will get you a food basket.'

Alone in the dishevelled dormitory, Ginny put her face in her hands and wept with disappointment and the aching misery of loss. Then, clutching her silver cross in her hand, she said a prayer, wiped her face on her handkerchief and set to work to fold the remaining blankets. What else could she do?

Charlie was perched on the running board of a lorry when Ginny emerged. He'd been talking to the lorry driver while he waited for her and had been given the latest news in lurid detail. One glance at her tear-streaked face told him all he needed to know.

'She's not coming,' he said, striding across the drive towards her.

'No.'

'Not now, or never?'

'Never.' She was close to tears again, but she stayed in control. 'Where's the car?'

'I had to hide it,' he said, and tried a joke. 'If I hadn't the nuns would have knocked me over the head and taken it by force. I never knew nuns were so fierce.'

But the joke fell flat. 'Where is it?' she said. 'The sooner we get out of here the better.'

He led her out of the grounds to the car. 'Quite right,' he said, as they climbed in. 'It's none too healthy round here. They've taken Brussels. They're across the Meuse.'

'Yes, I know. Maman told me.'

'And bombed Boulogne,' he said as he started the car. 'Did she tell you that, too? The port's closed. So we can't go there.'

'What about Calais?'

'Risky. If they've bombed Boulogne, they'll have bombed Calais, too.'

'Dieppe?'

'That's risky, too. I think our best bet would be to go back to Le Havre.'

'All that way!' she sighed.

'We'll take the south road.'

'What about the convoys?'

'They'll be going in the opposite direction now. We ought to have a clear road. What's in the basket?'

'Food for the journey,' Ginny said, lip quivering. 'Oh Charlie! In all this, she thought of giving us food for the journey.'

'Get the map,' he said. *Something to do. Something to keep her mind off it*. 'You'll have to navigate. Avoid Amiens.'

They drove south-west, following farm tracks and minor roads, planning to join the main route at Poix or Aumale. Towards midday they came to a railway line and the road curved to follow it. The road was deserted and the track empty, and that was how it remained for several kilometres. From time to time, there was a sound of distant gunfire and, twice, they heard the roar of planes but they were driving through woodland and couldn't see them. Apart from that, it was incredibly peaceful. They ate their picnic as they drove, and told one another they couldn't believe their luck.

'Perhaps we're going to get through without any trouble,' Ginny said, as they negotiated a sharp bend. 'I'm surprised we haven't seen any trains.'

'There's one ahead of us,' Charlie replied.

It was a troop train and appeared to have come to a halt on the ridge just ahead. There was no smoke issuing from the engine and no sign of life in any of the grey-green wagons.

'We'll leave the car here,' Charlie said, 'under these trees, just in case we need cover. You stay here and I'll go up and see what's going on. I don't like the look of it.'

'I'll come with you,' Ginny said. 'If we're going to be shot I'd rather we were shot together.'

They abandoned the car, squeezed through a gap in the hedge and, ready to dash for cover at any time, made their way around the edge of the field until they reached the train.

Like something from a ghost town, abandoned years since, it was completely empty.

'Where have they all gone?' Ginny whispered. She felt too exposed to speak aloud.

Charlie was more concerned with why they'd all gone.

They walked along the foot of the embankment, gazing up at the silent wagons. And there, suddenly and horrifically, was their answer. The end wagon had been riddled with machine-gun fire and what was worse, oh much, much worse, its sides were streaked red with blood.

For a few seconds Ginny was so shocked that she couldn't speak. She stood beside Charlie holding on to her cross for protection and comfort. 'My Jesus, mercy! Mary, help!'

'Let's get out of here,' Charlie said, seizing her by the hand.

'There might be somebody still in there.'

'If they are, they'll be dead,' Charlie replied brusquely. This was no time for delicacy and he was too horrified to be gentle. 'It's a troop train, Gin. The survivors will have taken their wounded and gone. Come on. There's nothing we can do here.' Except get caught in the next attack and killed ourselves.

'We ought to check,' she said, allowing him to lead her away. 'Oh, Charlie, this is awful! I thought Old Joliot's death was bad but this is ten times worse. Twenty times worse. Oh, I can't bear it. Why do they do such things?'

There was a plane approaching. 'Run!' he said frantically. 'Keep your head down! Run like hell.'

Ginny obeyed, and they ran, dodging under branches and hurtling past brambles. By the time they reached the car, the plane and the danger had passed.

'What are we going to do now?' Ginny asked, when they had recovered their breath.

'Get back on to the main road and drive like lunatics. Where's that map?'

The next turn-off took them to a minor road which led directly to the junction of two major roads, one from Abbeville and the other from Amiens.

'That'll do,' he said, jabbing his finger on the map and starting up the engine. 'Even if there's more traffic, it'll be better than being a sitting target here.'

Neither of them was prepared for what they found when they got to the junction.

Both roads were entirely blocked, and this was no ordinary road traffic. This was a population on the move, and with any kind of vehicle that could be begged, borrowed, bought or thrown together – farm carts pulled by huge chestnut horses, and battered wagons packed to bursting with bedding and children; small children hauling prams on lengths of rope; dogs pulling orange crates on wheels, even a goat cart with three small children packed into it as tightly as peas in a pod. There were hundreds and hundreds of people on foot; old men in cloth caps and patched coats bent double under the bundles on their backs; old women in black, laden like beasts of burden; young women carrying their babies in shawls slung across their backs; families hand in hand; solitary individuals with walking sticks, peasant farmers with ruddy cheeks and town dwellers with pallid faces. Many were poor and humble. All of them were dirty, weary and afraid and on the run.

For a few minutes, Charlie and Ginny sat in the car and simply watched in amazement.

'They're getting out of the way,' Charlie said at last. 'You've got to admire them. Just to up sticks and go.'

'Where are they all going?' Ginny wondered.

'God knows. Le Havre probably.'

'But then where?'

'I'm going to inch forward,' Charlie said, suiting the action to the word. 'See if we can get into the mainstream. We're all going the same way so it shouldn't be impossible.'

It wasn't impossible but it was extremely difficult, and the arrival of a car among so many weary pedestrians provoked a lot of abuse. It upset Ginny so much that she got out and walked along with everyone else. Soon she was talking to the family who were trudging beside her.

They'd come from Belgium, one man told her. The Germans were everywhere. 'They come in great tanks, Madame, Panzers they're called, terrible things and they blow everything up first. They bombed all the towns. I've never seen so many planes. The sky was black with them.'

'The Stukas are the worst,' the man's wife said.

At that there was a growl of agreement from those nearest in the line. 'They dive out of the sky. Terrible. They dive out of the sky and shoot us all to pieces. They attacked us when we were crossing the border. So many killed. It was terrible. Terrible.'

'They won't come here,' the woman said. 'We are too far away now. Right into France, *n'est-ce pas?*'

After ten minutes or so, one of the children stumbled and fell. 'She could ride in the car,' Ginny suggested. 'She and her brothers. There's room for four or five.'

In the end, the car was packed with nine exhausted children, and after they'd had an hour's rest, another weary group was gathered and given a chance to ride and sleep, too.

'You have our eternal gratitude, Monsieur,' their father said to Charlie.

'We shall run out of petrol before we get to Le Havre,' Charlie said to Ginny in English.

'What does it matter?' Ginny answered. 'We *must* help them.'

'I know,' he said, smiling at her. 'I thought I ought to warn you, that's all.'

'Just so long as we're out of range of the dive-bombers,' Ginny said. 'They've been making my blood run cold with some of the things they've been telling me about *them*.'

It was a vain hope.

Presently the column came to a halt in order to give horses and walkers a much-needed rest, and Charlie and the children got out of the car to stretch their legs. Suddenly the air filled with an excruciating sound. Ginny looked up and saw a plane diving out of the sky straight towards them – a squat, dark plane with its undercarriage down and the Nazi swastika clear on its tail fin. Her heart jumped in terror at the sight, but the noise it was making screwed her terror into agony. The nearer it got the louder it screamed in a constantly rising pitch that froze her blood.

*Stop it, stop it!* she screamed inside her head. *Make it stop!* People were screaming and scrabbled to get off the road and into the ditch. Charlie grabbed Ginny by the waist and pulled her down. The plane screamed over their heads and spat red fire. Bullets hissed through the air and pinged and thudded on to the road. Then the plane was gone, leaving screaming and sobbing in its wake.

'How dare they do that!' she shouted to the sky. 'How dare they!'

The colour had drained from Charlie's face, leaving him grey and haggard. Ginny felt so sorry for him that she stopped shouting and stood up, horrified to find that her legs were shaking and that she couldn't control them.

Minutes passed. Charlie was being sick. Somebody was groaning. Time seemed to have stopped altogether.

Then voices were warning. 'Down! Down! Take cover! He's coming back!' Sure enough the Stuka had turned and that terrible engine was screaming towards Ginny all over again.

Her rage was so intense that she lost control, and acted blindly, without thought or caution. She pulled Old Joliot's pistol from her bag and ran into the road cocking it as she ran, and began firing wildly into the air, screaming abuse, tears running down her cheeks. *'Assassin! Boche! Espèce de salaud! Foutez-nous la paix!'*

And then the plane was gone for a second time and her legs gave way under her and she sat down in the middle of the road and burst into tears.

She cried for a very long time, too exhausted by terror to do anything else. It wasn't until Charlie appeared beside her with a lit cigarette in his hand that she was aware of anything except her own anger and fear. She took the cigarette and smoked it gratefully, drawing the smoke down into her lungs, glad of its harshness. The two of them sat silently, side by side in the road, smoking. When they finally hauled themselves upright she had recovered enough to notice that some of the people in the ditch were injured, and that there was a horse on its side in the road, still alive, but with foam flecking its mouth and blood pumping from its neck. Then, the horror of what had happened began to seep into her senses.

Charlie was talking nonsense. 'You're injured, Gin.'

'No, I'm not,' she said crossly.

He was insisting. 'Let me see.' She looked down at her skirt and saw that he was right. There was a long gash in the skirt and blood was seeping through the edges of the cloth. But she felt no pain and no emotion. 'Oh yes,' she said. 'So I am.'

It was a short deep graze on her outer thigh, nothing more serious. But she didn't feel any emotion about that, either. There was the horse frothing on the road and an old lady straddled half in and half out of the ditch with two children beside her weeping. 'We must see to them,' she said. She walked across to the horse and, surprised by her own calm, fired her last bullet into his head to put him out of his misery. Then, because the gun was useless and tainted, she hurled it into the ditch.

Charlie took her hand, led her to the roadside, made her sit down, and began to attend to her wound, stolidly practical. 'I'll make a pad with my other shirt,' he said. 'If I can tear a strip from your petticoat I could bandage it. Stay there.'

She didn't have the energy to move. It was as if her life had been reduced to slow motion, by brutality and death and her own necessary violence. She watched listlessly as he climbed into the car to retrieve his shirt. She sat listlessly as he padded the wound and tied the pad in place with a strip of petticoat, knotting the ends clumsily. Then they sat and shared their last cigarette, drenched in the most evil-smelling sweat.

The car was peppered with bullet holes, a long line of them from the bonnet end to the boot. People were crawling out of the ditch, groaning and weeping. The injured were calling for water. Was there any water? There were two children standing in front of them saying something they couldn't understand.

'*Gran'mère. Gran'mère.*'

Then a man appeared, grey with shock. 'It's my mother,' he said. 'Could you come?'

It was the old lady in the ditch.

'We must help,' Charlie said, getting stiffly to his feet, and they went across to see what they could do for her.

They could see at a glance that she was very badly injured. She lay in a pool of blood, deathly pale. But she was alive, conscious and trying to speak.

'What are we to do, Monsieur?' the man asked Charlie. 'We can't leave her here and we have no transport.'

'Can you get a blanket?' Charlie said. 'She needs warmth. We'll carry her into the car. She can lie on the back seat. It's all right. We won't leave her.'

Trying hard not to hurt her, they carried her to the car, dripping blood all the way, and laid her on the back seat, while the other refugees attended to their wounded and grieved over their dead. Gradually, the convoy got under way again. They left their dead by the roadside and their blood on the road.

'I shall hate the Germans for this for as long as I live,' Ginny said.

They journeyed on, too shocked to say much. They passed through hamlets and villages, and people offered them water, but there was no food – not that they could have eaten, if there had been. It was a long hot afternoon and full of suffering. After an hour the old lady lost consciousness, but she was still bleeding and groaned at every bump in the road.

'She ought to be in hospital,' Charlie said. 'Is there a hospital in Le Havre?'

'A hospital couldn't help her,' Ginny said sadly. 'She's dying.'

At the next stop, the family came to the car and took it in turns to crouch on the floor and hold their grandmother's hand. But she was too deeply unconscious to know they were there, and her breathing was laboured and noisy. Frighteningly noisy.

'She's going,' her son said.

'Yes,' Ginny told him. 'I'm afraid she is.'

She stopped breathing as the sun was going down, just before most of the convoy stopped for the night. Her family carried her body into the woods and covered it with fallen leaves. Nobody wept. There were all too far gone for tears.

'We'll sleep in the open,' Charlie decided. 'That car's too much of a target.'

Sleep was impossible. It was bitterly cold in the woods and very dark, and they were still in a state of shock. Earlier on the road, Ginny's wound had begun to hurt her; now it stung and throbbed most painfully.

'We'll get going first thing in the morning,' Charlie said. 'As soon as it's light.'

But the morning was a long way away.

# CHAPTER THIRTY-EIGHT

Emily Hopkirk was awake very early on that Sunday morning, too, and she'd been woken by a pain. She lay quietly experiencing it – a long gathering pain like a fist slowly clenching itself low down in her belly. Clenching, clenching, holding tight and then gradually unclenching until it had finally faded away.

So it's begun, she thought to herself, and that's what it's like. She felt she was well prepared for the pains of childbirth and could cope with them, no matter how bad they might be. Her fears were another matter. During the last seven weeks they'd been growing with every nightmare, and now that the birth had begun they were sharper than any pain. Her baby could be born ill or blind or deformed, and there was nothing she could do to help it or cure it. What were pains compared to a terror like that?

Ken was still asleep beside her, his regular breathing familiar and reassuring. Emily would have liked to wake him and tell him all about it, but she couldn't. He wouldn't understand. With Ginny in France, there was no one she could confide in. 'Oh, Jesus,' she prayed, 'through the most pure Heart of Mary, I offer you the prayers, works and sufferings of this day . . .'

The next pain began as Ken was getting out of bed. The indentation of the mattress as he sat scratching his hair and yawning seemed to pull at the pain, and Emily caught her breath before she could stop herself.

'Are you all right?' Ken bent over her.

'Yes,' she said. 'Quite all right. Is it morning?'

'Seven o'clock.'

'Then I'll get up presently. You'll help me dress, won't you?'

'Don't I always?'

'Yes, my darling. You do.'

I'll sit in the morning room, she thought, until it's time to go to mass. Then I can hear the hall clock chiming the quarters and I can time the pains the way Dr Renshawe told me. However quickly they were coming she would go to church. She had to pray for Ginny and Charlie and Maman out there in France where the Germans were invading. 'I suppose there hasn't been a phone call, has there?'

'Not yet,' Ken said from the window, where he was drawing back the curtains. 'It's another lovely day.'

At breakfast the sun shone on Emily, warming her bare arms and the nape of her neck. She sat in the sunshine in the morning room, too, listening to the passing of time as, every half an hour, the pains came and went in a regular, untroubling way.

But there was no phone call.

'Are you going to church this morning?' Agnes asked, when Ken went off to get the car. 'I mean . . .'

The hesitation told Emily's sharp ears that her aunt had summed up the situation. 'Yes,' she said. 'I must. I owe it to Ginny. But you're right. It *has* started. Don't tell Ken or he won't let me go.'

'I'll get your bed made up, shall I? And phone the midwife.'

'The number's on the hallstand,' Emily said. 'Now let's talk about something else.'

'I wonder how they are,' Agnes said.

'So do I. I've been wondering ever since I woke up.'

The refugees were on the move again; dirtier, wearier, running out of water, haggard with worry but trailing on. The column broke up into small straggling groups as more and more families turned off towards towns and villages where they had friends or relations and hoped to find refuge. The sun had just risen above the horizon and the sky was pink with diffused light.

A new day brought renewed optimism to Ginny and

Charlie but it was short-lived. They'd only gone five or six kilometres when the car ran out of petrol.

'Damn thing!' Charlie said, climbing out of the driving seat. 'Are you going to be all right to walk?'

'It's only a graze,' Ginny said, determined to make light of it. Actually the wound had oozed blood all night and was now very sore indeed, and the flesh on either side of it was yellow and red with bruises. 'I'm fine.'

They set off on foot, walking at a steady pace and gradually overtaking their slower companions. After an hour, they reached the head of the column – a Belgian farmer with his wife and eldest son trudging beside him, and a cart full of children and chickens being pulled by two sturdy chestnut mares.

The road to Le Havre lay empty before them.

'Now we're really on our way,' Ginny said. 'I wonder if any of Maman's bread is still edible.'

'Say your prayers,' Charlie advised. 'I can hear engines.'

It was an army convoy – but a British army convoy, trundling steadily towards them.

'So there must still be ships coming in,' Ginny said. 'And if we can get there in time . . .'

It was peaceful in the Catholic church and, although her pains were much stronger, Emily was glad to be there. She had so many people to pray for; Ginny and Charlie and Maman, her dear Kenneth, Aunt Agnes. Most of all she prayed for the baby who would soon be in the world. Her poor, dear, precious, threatened baby. *Holy Mary, pray for my baby and for me, too. I did so want Maman and Ginny to be with me. It would have been easier if they'd been here.* Yet God's will be done 'on earth as it is in heaven'. *I'll put up with anything if only the baby isn't ill.*

Ken had been watching his wife very carefully all through the service. There was an odd flush to her face that he'd never seen before, two round patches of colour on her cheeks, like the patches on a rag doll. Now and then she drew in her breath sharply and then breathed out as though she were smoking a cigarette.

When they knelt to pray he put one arm gently round her to help ease her to her knees and took advantage of the general noise to ask, 'Has it started?'

'Yes,' she whispered, holding on to his hand. 'But you're not to worry. It is nothing yet.'

He worried for the rest of the service, quite unable to pay attention to any of it and, as soon as the final blessing had been given, he was on his feet.

'Stay here,' he ordered, 'and I'll bring the car right up to the gate. I'll be as quick as I can.'

She was perfectly calm. 'There's no rush,' she said. 'These things take hours. Sit me by the candles. I should like to feel them shining.'

With the nest of candles glowing beside her she looked like a gilded madonna and as steadfast as the flames. Such comforting flames, Ken thought, looking back at them, each centre as blue as sapphires, each corona a gleam of molten gold, holy candles with their cotton wisps of smoke ascending like prayers.

'I can see flames,' Ginny said. 'Oh God, Charlie. There's something on fire.' They were walking along a narrow gulley with wooden slopes on either side of them and the curve of the road obscured their vision ahead.

'It doesn't look as if it's on the road,' Charlie said. 'It's too far over.'

The space ahead of them was suddenly filled with smoke, acrid and black, which increased by the second, billowing in rapidly growing clouds. Now, they could see the flames, leaping behind the bushes at the turn of the road. Hot red flames, evil flames, hell fire flames.

'Something's been bombed,' Ginny said, beginning to panic. 'The Stukas have been here. They're probably still here. We can't go down there, Charlie. We can't walk past that. I couldn't bear it.'

No, Charlie thought, she couldn't. And I don't think I could, either. We've seen enough horrors. He made a rapid decision. 'Then we'll have to go round it,' he said. 'Through

the trees. You'll be able to manage, won't you?' His face was
full of anxiety and grimed with dirt, his forehead dust-grey
and every line etched in oily black.

'Yes,' Ginny said. 'Come on.'

It was a most unpleasant climb. Halfway up, Ginny's
wound started to bleed again. She could feel warm blood
trickling down her leg. But she didn't say anything to
Charlie. What was the point? There was nothing he could
do to stop it and it would only upset him.

From the top of the ridge they could see the fire quite
clearly. It was a barn, well ablaze, and beside it was an army
truck burnt to a skeleton. Further up the village street there
were three other fires spurting flames and belching grey and
white smoke, and toiling among the debris were tiny
blackened figures pointing hoses at the flames. The road
was completely blocked.

'Just as well we're on our feet,' Charlie said, wiping his
forehead on the back of his hand. 'We'll stay up here on the
ridge and keep the road in our sights. It can't be far now.'

But it was a very long way. A very long, painful way, with
no water, no news and no way of knowing exactly where they
were.

'Are we nearly there?' Ginny asked wearily, as they
trudged along. Sweat ran into her eyes and her hair was
damp. Two more army convoys had passed them by and the
sun was virtually overhead, so it must be midday.

'We're heading west.' Charlie said, squinting up at it.
'That's the main thing. We'll soon be there. You'll see.
Hang on to my arm. Next place we come to we'll buy a drink
and a packet of ciggies. We'll feel much better once we can
have a smoke.'

'I'm sorry I'm being so slow,' Ginny said. 'I wish I could
walk faster.' Her feet were sore, her wound stung and
ached, and Le Havre could be a million miles away. 'This is
all my fault, Charlie. If it hadn't been for me making such a
fuss, we wouldn't be here.'

'Don't talk rubbish,' he said, crossly. 'We *both* decided. It
was a mutual decision, mine just as much as yours.'

533

Remembering the pressure she'd put on him, Ginny smiled. She didn't argue because at that point he looked down at her, his face full of tender concern, and she felt her love for him almost choke her. She braced herself and tried to quicken her step. 'It's all right,' she said. 'I'm not giving in.'

Emily's labour was progressing far too slowly, and far too painfully, for her diminishing energies and the midwife's peace of mind.

'Don't fight it, Mrs Hopkirk,' the midwife urged. 'You're bracing yourself against it. Just let it happen.'

Her advice was wasted. 'What's the time?' Emily asked wearily.

'Nearly four o'clock. If you just go with it, it'll soon be over.'

It's been going on for nearly ten hours, Emily thought. 'There's something wrong, isn't there?' she worried. 'Something's wrong with the baby and you're not telling me.' Even with the blinds drawn, it was hot and sticky in the bedroom, and the pains were making her sweat. They were so strong now that they seemed to fill her darkness.

'No,' the midwife said. 'Your baby's fine. You're fine. It's just a long labour, that's all. Turn your face this way, my dear, and I'll sponge your forehead.'

Another pain was gripping.

I shall never have this baby, Emily thought to herself, groaning as the pain bit into her. I shall die before it's born.

'I'm going to get your aunt to sit with you for a little while,' the midwife decided, when the contraction was over. 'I'll only be a few minutes.'

A few minutes, an hour, a lifetime, Emily thought. What did it matter? Time was irrelevant.

She welcomed Aunt Agnes' arrival, just the same, and was glad to hear the familiar voice.

'Oh, Aunt Agnes,' she said, 'I'm so thirsty. Could you get me something to drink?'

'Anything, my dear,' Agnes said, and went off to get some water at once.

Down in the hall the midwife was on the phone to Dr Renshawe. 'She's fighting it,' she was reporting. 'It's almost as if she doesn't want it to be born.'

'I can't come up just at the moment,' Dr Renshawe told her. 'I'm attending to a young lad with a gash in his head. But I could send Mrs Bonney, if you're anxious.'

'I'd be ever so obliged.'

Mrs Bonney was the senior midwife in the team and she'd been up all night with a breech birth. But when she got Dr Renshawe's call and knew it was the young blind girl up at High Holborn who needed her services, she changed into a clean uniform and cycled up to the house at once.

'Well, now,' she said, sitting on the edge of Emily's tousled bed and taking both her hands when there was a lull between pains. 'You don't remember me, my dear, but I remember you.'

'Do you?' Emily said. She didn't have the energy to be surprised, but she was intrigued. 'I don't recognise your voice.'

'I delivered you, my dear,' Mrs Bonney said. 'You and your sister both. I attended your mother. She had a long labour, too, I remember.'

'Oh!' Emily groaned. 'Here comes another one.'

Mrs Bonney put her palm on Emily's hardening belly and felt the contraction from start to finish. 'You're doing very well,' she said encouragingly.

Her praise was Emily's undoing. She turned her head into the pillow and began to cry. 'No, I'm not,' she said. 'I've never done well. I've got a dreadful illness and this baby has, too. It'll be born blind like me, or worse. Maman said so.'

'Do you know why you were born blind, my dear?' Mrs Bonney said.

'Because of an illness,' Emily wept. 'An awful illness.'

'That's right,' Mrs Bonney comforted. 'Your mother had an illness and it passed into your eyes as you were born, but you didn't catch it. You were a lovely healthy baby. I remember you very well.'

Another pain was starting. 'What about my baby?' Emily said as it took hold. 'Will my baby be. . . ?'

'It'll be a beautiful baby once we can get it born,' Mrs Bonney said. 'Now let go! Let go! Take a nice deep breath and let go.'

The next pain followed on so quickly Emily only had time to gasp one question. 'Not ill?'

'Not ill. I promise.'

'Want to – push,' Emily panted.

'Then push, my dear. That's it! Well done. Good girl. That's lovely.'

Even so, it was a long second stage. Emily struggled, panted and pushed and was encouraged by both her midwives, but she was pushing against a resurgence of fear which, despite what Mrs Bonney had said, she couldn't defeat. Was the baby well? *Aaagh*! Here comes another one.

Then Doctor Renshawe was in the room, and she spoke in her ear. 'One more push. You're nearly there.'

'Really?'

'Yes. I can see your baby's head.'

Emily pushed and pushed again, straining with the enormous effort she was making, her face screwed up so hard that her eyes completely disappeared. There was no space for fear now, only this overpowering urge to push – as if her body was being taken over by a force she couldn't control, as though her darkness was exploding.

'Push again! Once more,' Mrs Bonney's voice urged. 'That's it. That's it. Well *done*!'

Suddenly, miraculously, Emily felt the child slithering from her body, little fingers scrabbling against her thighs, a rush of water damp under her buttocks. 'Is it here?'

'Yes,' Doctor Renshawe said from the foot of the bed. 'You've got a lovely baby boy. A sweetie.'

'Is he all right?'

'He's perfect.'

But Emily wouldn't believe it until she could feel the child for herself.

She waited patiently, breathing deeply to hold on to her control. And the baby was lowered into her arms.

Overwhelmed with love, she felt him all over; his tiny, tiny

536

fingers, his soft damp hair, big eyes, the dearest little nose, round cheeks, a little puckered mouth, lovely fat limbs, tiny curling fingers, even a dear little miniature 'thing'. Oh, the rounded curves and the silky skin of him and the lovely new smell. A perfect baby. Now it seemed stupid that she could ever have worried about him. The relief was so exquisite she wanted to yell and scream, but she didn't.

'My dearest, dearest darling,' she said, and her voice was a purr. 'I love you so much.'

Ken was at her elbow, holding her free hand and kissing her fingers. 'My clever darling. He's gorgeous.'

She knew that. 'Yes. Isn't he?' There was only one thing he needed to tell her. 'What are his eyes like, Kenneth?'

'Very big. Very dark blue. He's looking at me.'

'Looking? Really looking?'

'Oh yes. He can see. He's got perfect eyes.'

Then she wept. And Ken, overcome by the emotion of the moment, wept with her, and their new son looked at them with his huge untroubled blue eyes.

Later, when she'd been washed and tidied up and the baby had been eased into his first baby clothes, Agnes arrived bearing gifts and asking what he was going to be called.

'Edward Henry,' Ken told her. 'After both his grand-fathers.'

'Miss Babbacombe's here,' Agnes said to the midwife. 'Could she come and see him, do you think? She wouldn't be any trouble.'

So Miss Babbacombe was allowed in to worship the infant, too.

'Dear little chap,' she admired. 'Always knew he'd be a beauty.' Then she had to retire to the window to blow her nose and pretend to be looking at the view.

'All we need now is for Ginny and Charlie to come home,' Emily said. In the lovely aftermath of this miraculous birth, she had no fears for their safety and no doubt about their return. All things were possible now.

*

They were at the top of a low hill within sight of the Channel, which was calm, sky blue and hardly any distance away. And the town over in the west, with its great church spire pointing to heaven, just had to be Le Havre.

'Thank God!' Charlie said. 'We've made it, Ginny. Didn't I say we would? We'll rest for five minutes and then we'll go straight on down.'

Please God, let there be a ship still in the harbour, Ginny prayed. That's all I want, a ship in the harbour.

Walking in to the town on that lovely sunny afternoon was like waking into the world again after a long nightmare. It was full of refugees, thousands of them herding towards the harbour gates, and yet Le Havre looked like a holiday town. A nice normal holiday town with a beach and a blue sea, sparkling with sunlight, and shops full of holiday luxuries, crabs and oysters, iced cakes and fancy loaves, whipped cream and chocolates. All the hotels around the main square were crowded with English and French army officers in polished leather leggings, as though they were on leave from the old war. It was all a little unreal and yet reassuring, too, in a peculiar sort of way.

Once they got near the harbour they were back in the real world. There were so many people struggling to reach it that it was almost impossible to move. Here there was no good will at all, no kindness, no taking turns, only a heaving, shoving mass of determined bodies.

Ginny grew pale under their pressure.

'I can see the gates,' Charlie shouted over the noise to encourage her.

'It's more than I can.'

'One of the blessings of being tall,' he said. And immediately thought of another. I'm big enough to push my way through this scrimmage and to carry her with me. 'If we want to get anywhere we shall have to shove,' he said. 'Get behind me and hang on to my coat.'

She scrambled and pushed until she was tucked behind his back, holding on to the familiar cloth of his coat with both hands. Bulky torsos and jabbing elbows impeded her on every side, boots trampled over her feet, and the rank pervasive stink of yesterday's fear rose from her clothes and clogged her nostrils – but they were moving. She shuffled forward, stumbled, clutched his coat and shuffled forward again. It will go on forever, she thought. We shall never get out. If the Germans strafe us now we shall all be killed where we stand.

Suddenly they were squashed up against the harbour gates at the head of the queue and within shouting distance of a troop carrier. Nearly, nearly there. But the harbour gates were being closed and a Royal Navy officer barred the way.

'One more,' Charlie said, pushing Ginny towards the closing gate. 'You've got room for one more.'

'One then,' the lieutenant said, letting her through. 'That's the lot.'

Ginny turned back and stared at Charlie through the bars of the gate. 'I can't go without him,' she pleaded with the officer. 'Let him through as well. Please.'

'I'm sorry, miss,' the lieutenant said. 'There's no more room. We're overcrowded as it is. He'll have to wait till tomorrow.'

She stood her ground. 'Will there be a ship tomorrow?' *There might not even be a tomorrow.*

'I couldn't say.'

'That's it!' Ginny said. 'Open this gate. I want to get out. If he can't come with me I'm not going.'

'Don't be a fool,' Charlie shouted at her. 'Stay where you are. I'll come on after.' She struggled back to the gate as he told the lieutenant. 'Keep her there, for God's sake. You can't have her back in this. She's wounded.'

'Let me out!' Ginny demanded, pulling so frantically at the gate that her wound broke open again and wept blood down her leg. 'I'm staying with my husband.'

The lieutenant hesitated and was lost. She was a plucky-looking woman, even if she was filthy dirty, and he could see they loved each other. 'Oh, all right,' he said. 'Just you then, sir. Nip in quick before the hordes follow you.' He opened the gate just wide enough to let Charlie slip through.

The gangplank was being pulled up as Ginny and Charlie ran towards it, and they had to jump to get aboard. The ship had cast off before they could reach the deck. But they'd made it! They were going home.

They stood and watched the coastline recede. From this distance they could see the full extent of the damage that was being done. To the east, an oil refinery belched out black oily smoke that drifted for miles obscuring the coastline. There was smoke inland, too, and a cluster of fires burning on the horizon.

'My poor France,' Ginny mourned. 'I feel a traitor to be leaving her like this, invaded and bombed.' She put her hand to her throat, for the comfort of her silver cross. And the cross was gone. 'Oh no!'

'What is it?' Charlie asked.

'My silver cross. It's gone.'

'Oh, Ginny, it can't have.'

But it had. Although she searched in her clothes for it, she knew it was gone. 'It must have fallen off on the road somewhere,' she said.

'I'll buy you another one,' he said, trying to comfort her because he knew how much it meant to her. 'We're on our way home. That's what matters.'

He was right. 'I don't want another one,' she said, and meant it. 'That was my lucky charm and it brought me through, didn't it? It brought us both through.' In an odd sort of way it seemed appropriate that it was lost in France. 'There's still one left. Emily's still got hers.'

Thoughts of Emily reminded them both of the letter.

'Home,' he said. 'You'll be able to tell Emily your good news.'

She had almost forgotten about it. But now she remembered and was elated. They were going home, to see Emily, to see her new baby, to fight back.

'We'll start nightshifts at Holborn's the minute we can,' she said. 'If they're going to fight like this, we've got to fight back with everything we've got.'

'We will,' he said. 'Don't you worry. We'll be back.'

# BESTSELLING NOVELIST BERYL KINGSTON

## MAGGIE'S BOY
Beryl Kingston

Mother of two, Alison Toan, is happily settled on the south coast – until, that is, Morgan Griffiths, a debt collector, appears on the doorstep to inform her that her husband, Rigby, is deeply in debt. Thus begins a nightmare that threatens to leave Alison homeless and penniless . . .

Highly topical, this is a warm-hearted saga which touches on issues of debt and how it affects the family. Set in a south coast mining community in Wales, it bears all the hallmarks of this bestselling author's incomparable story-telling.

A Century hardback

## PLAYERS
Nina Lambert

They looked back . . . in anger . . . in despair . . . in delight.

Two aspiring actresses meet in London in 1958 – the era of the Angry Young Man and the sexual revolution – Paula, a runaway from council care and Isabel, daughter of a theatrical knight and a Hollywood film star.

So begins an unlikely but enduring friendship that binds their lives together for the next eighteen years as they struggle with the successes, heartbreaks and illusions behind the reality of an actress's life.

'A book to get lost in' *Anita Burgh*


## TRINIDAD STREET
Patricia Burns

The Isle of Dogs at the turn of the century was a close-knit community. Here in Trinidad Street, the lives and loves of the four families tangle and interweave . . .

When Tom Johnson, a union leader at the docks is sacked and set upon, his daughter Ellen has to leave school and her dreams of an office job. But she can still dream of Harry Turner . . .

But Harry, a young lighterman struggling to keep his battered family together, is bewitched by silver-tongued beauty Siobhan O'Donoghue. And Siobhan, ambitious for greater things, will use any weapon to repay the people of Trinidad Street for her disappointments.

And Gerry Billingham, if he doesn't go a deal too far in pursuit of a retail empire, will be there to pick up the pieces . . .

Through good times and bad, from the coronation of Edward VII to the dock strike, some will find what they are looking for – and Ellen and Harry realise too late what they have lost.

## DRAGONFLY IN AMBER
Diana Gabaldon

The second in a remarkable and haunting time-travel trilogy, set in Scotland in 1960 and Scotland and France during the second Jacobite Rebellion.

Claire Randall, successful physician, recent widow, mother, has returned to the Scottish Highlands to look up a Scottish historian she met twenty years earlier. Why has she come back? Who is really the father of her beautiful copper-haired daughter? The questions asked by Claire lead her back towards a far, far distant past – back to the dangers and hardships of 1745 and to Jamie Fraser, the love of her life.

## CROSS STITCH
Diana Gabaldon

From 1946 and a secure marriage, Claire Randall walks through an ancient circle of stones and finds herself in Jacobite Scotland in 1743 . . . here she is swept up into the passion and violence of life on the run with a gallant young renegade. Torn and fuelled by love, Claire pursues her destiny, haunted by the future she has left behind and the past she now inhabits.

# OTHER ARROW TITLES

| | | |
|---|---|---|
| ☐ The Inferno Corridor | Emma Cave | £4.99 |
| ☐ My Life As A Whale | Dyan Sheldon | £4.99 |
| ☐ Domestic Pleasures | Beth Gutcheon | £5.99 |
| ☐ Telling Only Lies | Jessica Mann | £4.99 |
| ☐ Queen of the Witches | Jessica Berens | £4.99 |
| ☐ Dangerous Dancing | Julie Welch | £4.99 |
| ☐ A Many-Splendoured Thing | Han Suyin | £4.99 |
| ☐ The Mountain is Young | Han Suyin | £5.99 |
| ☐ Dora | Polly Devlin | £5.99 |
| ☐ When Love Was Like That | Marie Joseph | £3.99 |
| ☐ A Better World Than This | Marie Joseph | £4.99 |
| ☐ Since He Went Away | Marie Joseph | £3.99 |
| ☐ Lovers and Sinners | Linda Sole | £4.99 |
| ☐ The Last Summer of Innocence | Linda Sole | £4.99 |
| ☐ Cross Stitch | Diana Gabaldon | £5.99 |
| ☐ The Diplomat's Wife | Louise Pennington | £3.99 |

ARROW BOOKS, BOOKSERVICE BY POST, PO BOX 29, DOUGLAS, ISLE OF MAN, BRITISH ISLES

NAME _____

ADDRESS _____

_____

_____

Please enclose a cheque or postal order made out to Arrow Books Ltd, for the amount due and allow for the following for postage and packing.

U.K. CUSTOMERS: Please allow 75p per book to a maximum of £7.50

B.F.P.O. & EIRE: Please allow 75p per book to a maximum of £7.50

OVERSEAS CUSTOMERS: Please allow £1.00 per book.

Whilst every effort is made to keep prices low it is sometimes necessary to increase cover prices at short notice. Arrow Books reserve the right to show new retail prices on covers which may differ from those previously advertised in the text or elsewhere.